Talking at Night

Claire Daverley was born in 1991 and has been writing stories ever since she was six years old, inspired by art and film and her many trips to the library. After graduating with a degree in Fine Art from The University of Oxford, she began a career in publishing, writing about books by day but penning her own by night, on trains, and in the light of the early mornings. She has spent most of her life in Hertfordshire, but now lives in Scotland with her husband and spaniel.

Her debut novel, *Talking at Night*, has sold in twenty-two languages to date.

Talking at Night

CLAIRE DAVERLEY

MICHAEL  JOSEPH

PENGUIN MICHAEL JOSEPH

UK | USA | Canada | Ireland | Australia
India | New Zealand | South Africa

Penguin Michael Joseph is part of the Penguin Random House group of companies
whose addresses can be found at global.penguinrandomhouse.com

First published 2023

005

Copyright © Claire Daverley, 2023

The moral right of the author has been asserted

Set in 12.5/14.75pt Bembo Book MT Pro
Typeset by Jouve (UK), Milton Keynes
Printed and bound in Great Britain by Clays Ltd, Elcograf S.p.A.

The authorized representative in the EEA is Penguin Random House Ireland,
Morrison Chambers, 32 Nassau Street, Dublin D02 YH68

A CIP catalogue record for this book is available from the British Library

HARDBACK ISBN: 978–0–241–60483–0
TRADE PAPERBACK ISBN: 978–0–241–60484–7

For Clive, of course

I wish I'd done everything on earth with you.

Baz Luhrmann's *The Great Gatsby*, 2013

Their lives cleave apart on a Tuesday night.

This is something her mother fixates on, in her breathless, not-yet-grieving denial, under the stark lights of the hospital hallway. The tiles are scuffed grey and the sky fringes scarlet through the blinds. It is almost dawn and Rosie stands by the glass and feels half of herself retreat to a place that she didn't know existed.

But it's a Tuesday, her mother is saying to the doctor. He doesn't go out on Tuesdays.

And the doctor is kind and well practised and reaches out a hand to touch her mother's elbow, and Rosie notices how well kept his nails are, so smooth and round and clean. She wants fingernails like that. She wants to be as kind and good and gentle as this doctor; she wants to be able to touch her mother's elbow, to steer her home once this news, this unbearable, unendurable news, has settled, somehow, absorbed.

But it will be years, of course, before anything feels like home again, and Rosie knows this, right then she knows this, as she looks at the doctor's hands, at his shirt cuff buttoned in place. Nothing will ever be right in the way that it had been before. Nothing can be ordinary or blithe or routine again, even though it was just Tuesday, even though she has a music lesson in three hours, even though his keys are still in her jacket pocket.

She thinks about his fingerprints, all over them.

How she hopes he hadn't felt a thing, when he fell.

before

one

Will realises there is something about Rosie Winters the night he meets her at the bonfire.

When he tells her that his mother left.

They are sitting beside each other with the blaze lifting into the November darkness, part of a broken circle of sixth formers. Fingerless gloves, beer cans. Distant waves beyond the pines. He doesn't know Rosie, really, despite sharing a school and some friends, but tonight, they are talking. A little.

Small talk, at first. Insignificant. Until his friend Josh – her twin brother – makes a comment about their parents, and Rosie laughs, barely audible above the bonfire, and before he can think what he's doing he's told her he doesn't know his own mother. It is something he's never said out loud before. Navigated, usually, with a dip of the head, a passing of the moment. But he finds himself telling her, this girl, with her split ends and untamed eyebrows, and her pale, slender hands. That his mother walked out, years back, while he was watching cartoons before school.

She looks at him when he says it, the flames held in her eyes. There isn't sympathy or curiosity in her face; no frown or twitching mouth, reactions he might have expected, if he'd had time to think about it.

Where do you think she is, she asks him, after a moment.

He pauses. Looks at the sky, patched through the gaps in the trees. The smoke from the fire curls upwards, and there are stars, with one larger, whiter, than the others. A planet perhaps, or a moon.

I don't know, he says to her. Anywhere.

And Rosie Winters repeats the word back at him, like she's really thinking about it. Like she's wondering what anywhere might look like.

It is early winter and the wind slices through the forest, but still they remain outside. It is better than being at home, warm yet uninterested in the television.

This, their skin turned blood orange in the firelight, is new.

It sets something burning.

They spend the night talking, their knees almost touching. Saying very little, though he has never known himself to be so attentive, so desperate for another sentence, so surprised by the words she chooses. People drift away in pairs, to touch one another behind the trees and fumble in the sand, or to seek out late-night noodles, chips in oil-stained paper. Only he, Rosie, Josh and two others remain. One of them gets out a guitar and strums, alongside the dying fire. Will watches the bark glowing red, the salt-and-pepper peel of the ash.

It is down to its embers when Rosie begins to sing.

Her brother asks her to, at first. Has to encourage her, then plead, until she concedes with a small tilt of the head.

The wind has dropped. The air, without the fire, is like glass, cold and still. And when she sings, it is a sound unlike anything Will has ever known. Choral, and pure.

They listen until the fire dies and their hands go numb, and then they all part ways. Will pulls his helmet on, clips it beneath his chin and kicks his motorbike into gear, thinking that it'll be a one-time, memorable night where he spoke to someone's sister and she sang a strange song and there was nothing more to it than that.

But her voice keeps him awake that night.

And again, the night after that.

He rises late at the weekend. Pulls on a hoodie, trying to ignore his simmering need for a cigarette as he pads down the stairs in his socks. Dave accosts him on the bottom step, pawing at his knees, and Will knuckles his wiry head before he skitters back to the lounge. The dog spends his days curled on his grandpa's old chair. Like he's waiting, Will thinks, for him to come home.

His grandmother is frying bacon in the kitchen. It smells of hot oil and broiling fat; of salt and pork and toast. She trills at him when he passes through the doorway.

Afternoon, she says.

It's only ten, he reasons.

And you're only eighteen once, lad, she says. No point wasting those cheekbones of yours hiding under the duvet.

I wasn't hiding, he says, and he heads for the kitchen table, pours himself a glass of water from the jug.

Amber's been to swim club already, his gran says, her back to him. *And* finished half her homework.

Good for Amber, Will says.

There is a short silence in which the bacon spits, the winter sun blanched on the walls. His sister is nowhere to be seen. Barricaded in her bedroom, he's sure, colour-coding notes with gel pens, organising her life with heart-shaped paperclips.

You look tired, his grandma says. He doesn't answer just yet, takes two triangles of toast from the table and moves to the back door.

I'm fine, he tells her, as he turns down the handle. She is saying something else as he slips outside and closes the door on her, makes his way to the garage.

He feels bad, for the briefest of moments.

Knows she'll seethe for a while, then bring him bacon, later, for lunch.

Inside, he flicks on the lone light bulb hanging from the ceiling. It's a windowless space with a concrete floor, an aerial-pronged radio on his grandfather's old workbench. It smells of sawdust and long-ago diesel, and there's a toolbox in the corner, a pile of unused timber lying on the ground. It is the only place where things feel somewhat right to him, where everything has a purpose, and nobody talks or doubts or expects things.

His new motorcycle stands, stripped back and unfinished, just where he left it.

He lingers in the doorway and eats his toast dry, scanning the floor for the tools he needs. And then he gets to work, without switching on the radio. Just him and the bike. Repainting mudguards, tightening headlamps. Hardly thinking of the Rosie girl while he works.

Only a little.

*

Rosie stays late in the music room. She meant to just practise her scales, to duck out after fifteen minutes. But an hour goes by and then the cleaner is there, with the swirl of her mop on the tiles. Rosie hears the drag of the bucket, the slosh of the water, and says shit, quietly, to herself, before shuffling her sheet music away. She shuts off the light, lets the wooden door thud behind her. Calls goodnight to the cleaner, who is always kind; always smiles at her when they pass late in the halls, like they share some kind of secret.

Outside, it is already dark, and the air feels cleansed, the kind of cold that foreshadows snow. It is not a night for bare legs. For running under strip lighting.

But she promised her mother, and so she goes to the gym. Changes into her kit and sprints on the treadmill, but only for half the time she should, because she forgot, because the music took over, because she was wasting her time, yet again.

The sweat musses her fringe and burns her eyes, and she wonders, as her feet pound the belt, why she is always trying so hard. Who she is trying for. Why everything matters, all of the time.

She gets a stitch halfway and stops, has to lean on the side and catch her breath. She hopes that nobody notices. That nobody's looking at her. And afterwards, she heaves her bag back onto her shoulder, zips up her jacket and begins the short walk home, her hair hanging damp at her ears. Stars scatter overhead, and cars move past her in a stream of head-lights. She counts her steps, and recounts again. Avoiding the cracks in the pavement.

At home, she finds her twin brother lying on the sofa.

You're late, he says, without taking his eyes from the television.

Not by much, Rosie says, glancing at her wrist, only to see that it's bare. She's left her watch in the music room again. Can't write when she's on the clock.

Mum'll be mad, Josh says, and she pushes his head down with her palm, leaves the room before he can throw a cushion at her.

Her mother is not mad; only distracted. She is in the kitchen on the phone, and she holds a finger up at Rosie, her habitual way of saying hello while also saying wait, I'm doing something important, and you understand, don't you, you know how things are.

How was school, her mother asks when she hangs up. She doesn't make eye contact, instead turns around to open the oven.

Good, Rosie says.

And the gym?

Hard.

Well, good, her mother says. It's supposed to be.

Have I got time for a shower?

Her mother glances round, takes in her shining face and uncombed hair.

I should say so, she says. Can't be sweating like that at the dinner table, can you, darling?

Rosie looks back at her, for a second too long, then nods and heads for the stairs.

In the bathroom, she turns the water on so hot that it nearly scalds. Her skin turns a livid red, but she stands there and endures it. Counting, not her steps this time, but the seconds. Elongating the numbers, over and over, in this way that she does – like blood flow, unable to stop.

When she's out, she wraps her hair in a towel, grateful for the steam that hides her reflection in the mirror. Then she dries herself off and wanders to her room, where sheet music scatters her desk and books line her shelves, tattered and tea-stained from being handled so often, trailed over like old maps. Patti Smith. Oliver Sacks. The Sylvias, both Patterson and Plath.

After tugging on some clothes, she lowers her blackout blind. Stands, for a moment, with her hands on the window sill. She is hungry, in every sense of the word. She thinks about walking out of the door, with her hair wet and the snow about to fall, straight into the Norfolk night.

How was school, her mother asks again, once they're all seated at the table. She has dished up squares of shop-bought lasagne, passes the plates to Rosie's father and brother, says careful, they're hot. Rosie takes her plate with two hands, notices that her own square is smaller than everyone else's.

Earth to Joshua? her mother nudges. How was your day?

Good, he says, through his pasta.

Rosie?

I handed in my history coursework, Rosie tells her. And finished a classics paper.

How'd that go?

Okay, I think.

Good girl.

There is a minute more of silence, knives squeaking on plates. Rosie takes a sip of water, and then her mother launches into a story from work, something about her client surrendering to his wife, not putting up the fight that she knows she could win for him. Again, nobody speaks. The kitchen clock ticks. White sauce oozes on their plates.

Maybe it's just too much, Rosie ventures.

Hmm?

For your client. Maybe it hurts, his marriage ending like this. And he just wants it, you know. Over with.

Her mother pours herself another glass of wine, spears a tomato with her fork.

Let's not presume to know his motivations, Rosemary, she says, after she has swallowed. Josh catches Rosie's eye, soundlessly asking her why she bothers, and she drops her gaze to the table. Her father is doing the crossword.

When her mother rises to clear, Josh scrapes his remaining lasagne onto Rosie's plate, and she finishes it, fast, before standing to help, knocking his shoulder with hers.

A sibling thing, or a twin thing.

She doesn't know the difference.

And it's as she's rinsing the salad bowl that a new melody starts up. Like early birdsong, those first, tentative notes that nobody is around to hear. She is barely listening as Josh mentions revising tomorrow with Will White, from his further maths class, because she's trying to hold the notes in her mind.

Repeating them, over and over, before they can fall away.

Marley rings her early the next morning.

Rosie is awake already, picks up on the second ring.

You're up, Marley says.

Couldn't sleep, she says. She wishes, for a moment, that her friend would ask her why. That someone would notice, or care.

I was thinking we could do something tonight, Marley says, instead. Rosie says that'd be nice, but she's got revision to do.

So? *I've* got revision to do. We could revise together, even. Imagine that.

Rosie turns over in bed. The morning light is pale through the curtains, like cloudy water dipped with paint.

You say that, she says, but then you'll put on a film and we'll end up doing nothing.

Inevitably, I guess, Marley agrees, and Rosie hears the smile in her voice, familiar and slightly taunting.

I could do with a break, though, she reasons, swapping her phone to her other hand. She has ink on her palms from her late-night songwriting, all crossings out and attempted riffs.

Good! says Marley. How about we do something this weekend, then? A Saturday night treat, or something equally tragic.

Why is that tragic?

Because we're seven*teen*, Rosie. We shouldn't need Saturdays as an excuse to see each other, or go out, or do something remotely exciting.

We go out! We went out the other night.

Yeah, and all I got out of it was a bag of chips and a snog that tasted of Tic Tacs.

Rosie snorts. She can hear her mother getting ready for work, the drone of the coffee machine downstairs.

Who'd you snog? she asks.

Never you mind, says Marley.

Fine. It'll be someone new next week, anyway.

Are you calling me easy, Rosemary Winters?

Would I ever?

I guess not. But only 'cause you're a vanilla virgin.

Good name for a nail polish.

It *is,* isn't it? And Marley laughs, her big, swooping laugh, so that Rosie has to pull back from the phone. This Saturday, then. I'll buy a mountain of popcorn and a packet of those old lady sweets you like.

Werther's are not old lady sweets.

And we can replay all the Leo scenes as many times as we want. Or the Patrick Swayze ones. I feel like we need some arousing pottery in our lives.

Marl!

What?

Arousing pottery?

Doesn't have to be pottery. Some dry humping to Solomon Burke. Tabletop sex to Berlioz.

I'm hanging up now.

Prude.

I'll see you Saturday.

Knew Berlioz would get you, Marley says.

———

Rosie thinks about what Marley said to her as she walks to school. Josh left early for basketball, so she is alone, her coat zipped to her chin against the cold. She is a virgin, and she is vanilla. She tries not to be. But she can't care enough to be more than what she is, which is, essentially, one of the good girls.

She has never had a boyfriend. She's kissed someone, or rather, was kissed, badly, her shoulders pinned against a bathroom door at a friend's house party. The handle bruised her coccyx, and the boy tasted of over-chewed gum.

She's never been drunk. Never snuck out. Never smoked a cigarette or lied to or even sworn in front of her parents, though she's not sure they'd notice, or mind.

But there is time for all of that, she reasons, as she steps off the kerb to cross the road. Seventeen is just the start. She will work hard, she will do all that she is supposed to do, and her life will be good and right and whole, filled with music and poetry and wine and sex, and life-altering moments that last longer than three minutes, and don't leave her with bruises down her back.

That is her plan.

She has to cross the road once, twice, three times on her way to school, tapping her foot on the pavement until she can stop, and that is when the snow begins to fall. Lightly, at first, more of a fine rain. It clings to her sleeves like salt.

two

Josh tells him he doesn't get it. They are both staring at their further maths textbooks, the snow swirling outside the classroom window.

They are the only two in class, the only two in their year who study this subject. They knew each other before, had shared a few lessons throughout school, but now, in their last year of sixth form, Will supposes they'd call each other friends. His other mates are more break-time acquaintances; they don't ask him questions, or seem to care, at all, about his life, which suits him just fine. But Josh is different.

What's your first choice, then, Josh had asked him, back in their first class.

First choice of what, he'd asked, and Josh had said uni, and so he'd had to explain that he wasn't going.

Josh had looked up from his worksheet at that.

Come on, he'd said, and Will had said come on what.

You're like, really smart.

Thanks.

Seriously. If you knuckled down, mate, you could get in anywhere you want.

And what if I don't want it? Will posed, and Josh had

looked at him then with a crease at the bridge of his nose, like he didn't quite understand.

Now, though, they're both staring at a page of hyperbolic functions and hoping it will make some semblance of sense before the lesson is through. Their teacher, Mr Brookman, has already left. He quite often uses their class as an excuse for a prolonged break in the staff room, and in Will's mind, this works both ways.

Let's just call it a day, Will says.

Josh leans back, tilts his chair onto two legs.

I can't, man. I need to get this before our mock exam.

Why, Will asks, as he sweeps his pens into his bag.

Why what?

Why do you need to get it for the mock? You only need to know it for the real thing, in the spring. You've got ages.

Mocks matter, Josh says, still tipped backwards on his chair. For the provisional offers, and stuff.

Right, he says.

You're really not going to uni?

Nope.

What you gonna do instead?

Work, he says, hauling his bag onto his shoulder. Travel, maybe.

That's cool.

I'm not trying to be, Will says, because this is what people think about him, he knows, with his motorcycle and his school record and all that trouble he got in, years back. It was so long ago, now, but it's all anyone remembers. All they ever want to see.

You still coming over, later? Josh asks.

You still need me to?

Definitely, Josh says, letting his chair drop back onto all

fours. I'm on Crescent Gardens – you can park on the street. It's the white house with the blue door.

Outside, Will makes his way through the courtyard, snow-flakes landing on his hair. The school looks like a chalk and charcoal drawing, shapeless and smudged.

He doesn't give it much thought, the fact that he's heading to Josh's house that night, to help him revise. And that he happens to be the brother of the girl that he can't stop thinking about.

This isn't unusual, for him. He thinks of girls often. What is unusual is the content of his thoughts; nothing about the soft, wet parts of her, the weight of her thighs around his. Just her voice, and her eyes. How intensely she listened, and held all that he had to say.

You're sure you can stay for dinner?

I'm sure.

You're sure you're sure? You've not just assumed?

Gran, Josh *said*, come for dinner.

You won't get hungry?

I doubt their cupboards are empty.

You can't eat like a horse round someone else's house, Amber pipes up from the table. Like you do here.

She is swinging her school-socked feet, scribbling some-thing in a notebook.

Thanks for the tip, Ambs.

It's rude, she adds, with a flourish of her fluff-topped pen.

Home by ten, his grandma says.

Might be ten thirty, he tells her. Depends how long Josh takes to get it.

Remind me who this Josh boy is, his grandma asks, following him out into the hall.

Will sighs as he shrugs on his jacket, pats down his pockets for his phone.

Josh Winters, he says. He's the other kid in my maths class.

Further maths, she corrects him.

Further maths. And he needs help with this module, so I said I'd tutor him, like I told you. He's a meat-eater, possibly a Gemini, and he doesn't smoke weed. I think his shoe size is a twelve, but I couldn't be sure. Oh, and he –

His grandmother cuts him off with a whip of her tea towel.

Home by ten thirty, then, wise guy, she says, and he says yeah yeah, grabs her car keys and shuts the front door behind him.

The house is a similar layout to his own. Semi-detached but painted white, with a perfect lawn and potted olive trees saying things that his gran's front garden does not, with her gnomes and her overgrown grass.

There is no trace of Rosie when Will arrives. Upstairs, all the doors are closed, and he has no idea which room would be hers, so he puts her from his mind and turns to the logic of maths. Something familiar, and consistent, like an engine.

The night is long. Josh takes several hours to understand the system, to accurately answer four mock-exam questions in a row. They eat dinner in his room, at his large corner desk, when Josh pleads with his mother that they be excused – *we're almost there, Mum, please* – and it is close to ten when he sits back, rubbing his eyes, and says he's finally got it.

Took you long enough, Will says, and Josh flicks him, hard, on the arm.

It's confusing, Josh says.

I never said it wasn't.

S'all coming together, though, Josh says, and he sounds almost gleeful as he leans back in his chair, stretches his arms over his head. He is tall and gangling, reminds Will of some kind of cartoon. Limbs too long for his body, like he still has some growing to do.

Gonna smash that exam, Josh says. Get into Cambridge, and boom.

What's boom?

I don't know, Josh says, and he laughs. Just boom. Just the way things go, you know?

I guess, Will says, though he doesn't know anything about how things are going to go. He plans for the next day, the next weekend. The next part he needs for his bike.

Thanks for coming, man, Josh says, after he's packed up his things. Can we do this again, maybe? You're better than old Brookman.

Not hard to be, says Will. He doesn't think Josh needs an answer, but he's looking at him, as if he's waiting. Not taking his eyes from his face.

You can come to the workshop after school, he suggests. I'm behind with my woodwork project, so I'm there sometimes. Wednesdays, mainly.

Maths, further maths, and woodwork, says Josh, ticking them off on his fingers. That's the weirdest combo of subjects.

Will shrugs. Not if you want to be a civil engineer, he reasons.

And do you?

God, no.

What *do* you want to do? Josh asks.

It's late, mate, Will says, because it's true, and because he has no desire to get into this. I'd better go.

Out on the landing, the walls are adorned with childhood

photos; Josh in dungarees, Rosie picking up shells. One of her at the piano. Will feels strangely alert as he follows Josh down the stairs, aware that she is somewhere nearby. He wonders if he'll see her. If she'll say hi.

He wonders why he's wondering this.

Downstairs, all is quiet; just the murmur of the television from the lounge. But after he pulls on his shoes and tells Josh he'll see him tomorrow, he opens the front door and is greeted by a world of white. His gran's car is wedged against the kerb, topped like a Christmas cake, the snow sifting down like sugar.

Whoa, says Josh, as they both squint out of the door. I guess you're not going anywhere.

Mrs Winters is overly apologetic. Says she hadn't noticed how bad it was, that all the curtains had been closed. That she's *so sorry* he has to spend the night here. Will gets the sense that she's sorrier for herself than for him; her face is pinched, two spots of pink high on her cheeks. There is something feline about her, he thinks, as she fusses in the hallway. She is well kept and hard-edged and she looks at him with vague disapproval, like she knows something he doesn't.

They make him a bed on the sofa, and Mrs Winters tells him to help himself to the filtered water in the fridge; her words imply that this is all he should help himself to, and he thanks her, before she heads upstairs.

Comfy? Josh asks, as he punches one of the cushions. He has given him a spare T-shirt, and Will tugs off his school shirt, pulls it on. Josh looks away while he does it, as if suddenly fascinated by the carpet.

All good, Will says.

Cool. Well. Night.

Josh stands there for a moment too long. Goes to say

something else, seems to decide against it, and flicks off the light on his way out. Will hears him clump up the stairs, then pulls out his phone to see five missed calls.

Sorry, he says, as soon as his grandma picks up. I didn't know the snow was so bad.

You're staying, presumably?

Yeah. On their sofa.

Be on your best behaviour, William.

I always am, Gran.

There is a silence. He looks at the glow of the street light, blurred through the slats of the blind.

You know what I mean, she says. No funny business.

Goodnight, Gran, he says, and he hits the end call button.

*

Rosie cannot sleep. She'd gone over some revision before bed and now it is whirling around her brain, snagging on names and facts that she cannot, must not, forget. She sits up after a full hour. Checks some things. Decides that her mouth is dry, that she needs a drink of water.

She pads down the stairs in the dark and jumps when she sees a boy sitting at their kitchen table. William White, the guy from the bonfire. The aloof, brooding boy from school she hadn't exchanged one word with prior to that night.

Sorry, she says, even though it is her house, and even though he was the one to startle her.

He raises his eyes, very slowly, from his phone, his face tinged blue in the light from the screen.

For what? he asks.

I didn't know you'd be in here, she says.

It's the snow. Your mum said I could stay.

I know that, she says. I knew you were here. I just. Forgot.

He raises his chin, as if all the better to look at her. She is keenly aware that her feet are bare. That her pyjamas are a faded pink, and arguably much too young for her. But then she remembers that it is dark; that he will hardly be looking at her feet, or her clothes. Or at her, generally, at all.

I just came down for some water, she says, unable to keep the apology out of her voice.

There's filtered water in the fridge, he says.

My mum told you that, did she?

She did.

God knows why we can't drink water out the tap like everyone else.

Well, you could, he says.

She pauses at the fridge door and glances over at him. She can't work out, in the dark, whether he is smiling, but she thinks she can hear it in his voice. A slight teasing perhaps, which is new to her. Like him talking, all night, by the fire.

All right, she says. I will.

And so she goes to the tap and fills her glass and takes a mouthful, looking out of the window as she does it. The garden is lost beneath the snow. So pretty, she thinks. So perfect and untouched, for such a short while.

So? Will asks her.

So what?

The water. How is it?

Oh. She looks down into her glass. Entirely comparable.

He laughs at this, so quietly he could simply be breathing, and something floats up and through her.

She has thought of him once or twice since the other night. It was odd, to her, that he barely moved from beside her, and she was self-conscious about the way he kept looking at her, even when she looked away.

She's always thought of Will White as detached and stand-offish, despite his popularity and long list of girlfriends. Gold-brown hair, grey, unreadable eyes. It's laughable, to her, that these sorts of people really exist, like in the films she and Marley spend their weekends watching. And yet here he is, looking at her again, in her kitchen.

Well, night, she says, and she turns in her naked feet and heads for the door.

Rosie, he says.

Her name in his mouth.

Yeah?

He has put his phone down, its screen still lit up where it rests on the table. It deepens the shadows on his face, the rings beneath his eyes.

I don't know what I was going to say, he says.

She tilts her head.

I wanted to say something, he corrects himself. But I don't know what.

Okay.

Sleep well, I guess.

I never sleep well, she tells him, because she thinks she should be honest, and because he's being strange, so perhaps she can be her strange, most honest self in return.

Me neither, he says. Not at other people's houses, anyway.

They look at each other across the kitchen, the light silvery soft with the snowfall. The fridge breathes its low, barely there sound.

Are you hungry? she asks.

Always, he says. He leans back in his chair, and for some reason at this moment she remembers that he is a smoker, and that he is undeniably attractive. Two reasons to end this conversation now, to leave him to his phone and his sleepless night. She has a mock exam in the morning. She needs to try to sleep. Her mother would not approve of the late hour or, indeed, of him.

She pours them both bowls of cereal.

They talk until the early hours of the morning. Rosie has turned on the light above the oven, and it bathes the kitchen in gold, the underfloor heating warming the tiles, the slipper-less soles of her feet.

They eat cornflakes with cold milk and she watches him dribble a spoonful down his chin, and this makes him seem less intimidating, especially when he fails to notice. She tells him, eventually, with a small laugh, and he wipes it away with the back of his hand, says that's embarrassing, and when she asks him why he shrugs and grins, his canines pointed, sharp-looking.

He doesn't try small talk. Doesn't ask her about school or subjects or being a twin. He asks her, immediately, why she rarely sleeps, and this is what does it; this is what catches her, places him in her sphere in a way she wasn't ready for.

I just worry about things, she says. Sometimes.

What things, he asks, and she says stupid stuff, and he says surely not, if it's keeping you awake.

All normal things, she says. School. Grades. Life.

One and the same, right? he says, and she wonders if he's mocking her.

I told you it was stupid.

Did I say that?

She says nothing, lifts her spoon out of the milk.

We're taught to care so much about all of that, Will says. Like every decision we make will lead us down a particular path.

22

And you don't think that's true?

Nope. I think we have a path, but it doesn't change based on the decisions we make. It's a path that leads to the same place, anyway.

She sips the milk off her spoon. It tastes sweet from the cornflakes, reminds her of late-night study sessions and her primary school breakfast club, the years spent rising at 5 a.m. so her mother could get to work.

What do you mean, she asks.

What do you think I mean?

She lets his question hang in response to her own, sees his eyebrows rise, just slightly.

Dying, she says.

Right.

Will leans forward in his chair, as though it's no big deal, which she supposes it's not, when you're seventeen. When it's so far away, so implausible.

I figure we're all dying with every day, he says. So we might as well do what we want, before it happens.

He is looking at her as he speaks, and she drops her eyes to the table. There is a crescent of milk, from the bottom of her bowl. She dabs her finger into it, draws it out in a line.

That's kind of morbid, she says, and he shrugs, says it's true.

So what do you want to do, then? she asks him. She doesn't add *before you die*, though she thinks about it.

Guess I'll figure that out, Will says.

Rosie nods, her fingertip wet from the milk.

And what do you want, Rosie Winters?

She looks back at him. He is smiling, again, but barely. The edges of his mouth are lifted, his eyes soft, lamp-like, in the semi-dark. The use of her surname seems either aggressive or affectionate; she cannot quite work out which.

I want all the things you said I shouldn't, she says. To do

well at school. To get good grades, have a good life. All of that.

You think those things will get you a good life? Will asks.

I think they'll help me *get* to the things that will, she says.

He holds her eyes. Doesn't argue, or ask her about it again.

She lowers her spoon, watches the milk ripple.

It is half past three in the morning when she says God, it's late, and Will follows her gaze to the microwave clock and says that technically, it's early.

I should go, she says, rising out of her chair. She rinses their bowls under the tap, and Will watches her as she does it. Her hair is dark and mane-like, falling just beyond her shoulders. He can see her ankles, so pale beneath her pyjama legs.

He doesn't want to be interested. Doesn't have the time or the inclination for that, not if she's going to university. Not if she's Josh's sister. Not if she'll be too desirable, which he's sensing, already, that she would be.

That song you sang, he says to her, raising his voice so she can hear him over the running water.

What about it, she says. She shuts off the tap, turns the bowls upside down to drain. He wants to tell her it was beautiful. That her voice, that she, is beautiful. But it is so far removed from what he would ordinarily say, so daring, even, to think.

I can't get it out of my head, he says.

Like an earworm, she says. She has turned her back on the sink, is leaning against the counter. Looking at him, with those eyes.

What's an earworm?

When you get a song stuck in your head and it goes round and round. I get it sometimes, when I can't sleep. Like my brain's caught on a loop.

Will considers this. Tells her it's nicer than that.

She half smiles at him then, all lips and no teeth. He wonders what she would say if he got out of his chair now, and pressed his own mouth to hers.

I'm going to bed, she tells him.

Night, then, he says.

She doesn't move. He doesn't, either.

It's been nice talking to you, he says.

So formal, she says, still with that half-smile, and then she leaves him, her footsteps light on the stairs. He sits there a while, in the honeyed glow from the oven. So many hours to go until sunrise.

He pretends to be asleep when Josh jumps on his legs in the morning.

Rise and shine, he says, bashing on his side with a fist. Will grumbles, though he's glad it's daytime, glad he can get up and source some caffeine and maybe speak to Rosie again.

Breakfast? Josh offers.

Is the snow gone?

Better than that, he says. It's a snow day, mate.

Really?

Really! No school. Praise the Lord, or whatever deity you may or may not worship.

I don't know how you don't get shoved into walls more often, Will says, sitting up and massaging his temples with one hand. The room tilts with his lack of sleep, with the too-bright-white of the wallpaper.

Just lucky, I guess, Josh says. *And* endearing.

That's one word for it, Will says, and groans as he gets elbowed in the ribs.

Pancakes, Josh declares. You like pancakes?

I guess.

You know what I like about you, Will, Josh says, as he springs up from the sofa. Your boundless enthusiasm.

Will gives him the finger, still rubbing his head. But when he looks around, Josh is gone, and his twin sister is standing in the doorway. Her hair is loose past her shoulders, and she's cradling a mug in her hands.

I thought you might want some coffee?

Christ yes, he says, and he stands and takes it from her, burns his tongue when he drinks. He is suddenly conscious of his bed hair. Crumbs of cereal stick in the craters of his teeth, and he can taste the tar of his breath.

I didn't know if you'd want milk?

Black is fine, thanks.

Did you get any sleep? she asks. He wonders if that's a loaded question, whether she's asking if he was lying awake, thinking of her.

In the end, he says.

A loaded answer.

Rosie crosses her arms like she's cold, though he heard the radiators clunk on before dawn, the water banging in the pipes. She has blue eyes, he sees now. Full, dark eyebrows that match the wildness of her hair. She opens her mouth to say something just as Josh sticks his head out of the kitchen.

Rosie, he says. There's no butter.

Use oil then, she says.

Where's that? The fridge?

She shakes her head, says it's in the cupboard, and Will looks at the crease of love in her face as she turns towards her twin.

He has never looked at Amber that way, not even when they're getting along. He holds the coffee in his mouth before swallowing, and it's bitter, still too hot.

D'you want to go for a walk, he asks her, before he even decides to say it.

Rosie looks back round at him.

Now? she says.

Or after breakfast, maybe.

What is happening, he asks himself, as he watches her question the same thing. Her eyebrows pleat together and she sucks in her bottom lip. Just for a moment, before her face returns to neutral.

Maybe, she says.

Then she walks into the kitchen, leaves him standing alone with his rumpled bed covers, in his not-slept-in T-shirt and boxers. He listens to them talking, the clank of pans, roll of drawers. It is the sound of routine, familiarity. He has distanced himself from these things in his own house, spends most of his time in the garage.

When he joins them, dressed, Rosie is mixing batter, Josh peering in cupboards and foraging for honey and syrup.

Every snow day should start with a sugar hit, Josh says, as he clunks the condiments down on the table. Rosie is quiet as she ladles the batter into the pan.

This one stresses about snow days, Josh says, nodding over at her.

I'm not stressing, Rosie says.

She had a history mock today, he tells Will. And she'd rather be in school, taking it, than sitting here eating pancakes with us.

No, I wouldn't, she says, and she cranks the heat up high. It's just more days to forget everything, is all.

They watch her flip the first pancake onto its uncooked side. The kitchen smells of vegetable oil and yolk, the windows steamed up with the heat. Will offers to help, because it feels wrong letting her cook for them both, and to his surprise she steps aside. He ladles and flips while she slices strawberries from the fridge, fills a small bowl with a mound of sugar. He tries not to notice as she dips a strawberry into it, sucks the grains off with her mouth.

*

The boys head out to do whatever it is that boys do in the snow. Throw packed ice at each other, no doubt, get their jeans soaked, stay out until their fingers turn numb and they can't put their keys in the door.

She is trying to revise. Trying to embed historical facts into her mind, and when it fails, she tries to practise her scales, but they come smoothly, and she is bored within the hour. She thinks back to breakfast, when she is sure that Will kept trying to catch her eye, and in the light of day, she decides that she doesn't understand why. She isn't interesting, and nor can he be interested. Everything felt different in the dark, the room hushed with the snowfall outside. Their feet almost touching under the table.

He'd told her he had a dog named Dave.

That he lived with his grandmother.

They talked about death and guitars and travel plans, Will's fear of rats, her aversion to cotton wool. Not once did he mention his motorbike or his suspension from school, nor did she feel she could ask him about it.

The part she's replaying, though, the part that's distracting her now, is that he told her he couldn't get her song out of his head.

Her song. One she wrote, herself, though there's no way he would have known that.

———

She catches up to them on the playing field. Children dressed in padded onesies drag sledges to the hillock beyond the playground, ridged footprints trailing from their wellies.

They are by the swings. Will is sitting on one, his legs stretched out in front of him. His boots are black leather, like his jacket, and his hair is laced with snow. She is this close to him, can see how it looks like dew, when Josh lobs a snowball at her head.

You came! he says, as it explodes in a puff. He bounds over from his place by the railings, his ears shrimp-pink from the cold.

Just for a bit, she says, dusting the snow off her hair. I needed a break.

Her brother takes her wrists in his hands then, and his gloves are moist, reptilian; the palms dotted with tiny grip pads. Rosie forgot her own gloves, and the air prickles her skin.

That's great, Josh says, and he squeezes, once, to show her he knows how hard it is for her to choose fun, to choose snow, over study. To ease up, like he's so often asking her to. She feels suddenly hot under her coat, wondering what he would say if he knew she had not come out for him or for herself, but for William White, and that she is not even sure why.

They lean on the railings and talk, a little. Watching the kids play, a dog on the field chasing a ball. Josh drops onto his back and makes a snow angel while Will watches from his swing, and Rosie watches Will watching him. Fixing her gaze beyond his head, as though she's looking at the trees.

I love snow, Josh says, when he stops moving.

Will catches her eye, at this, and they share something in that look. Appreciation, she thinks, or affection, for the unapologetic candour – the innocence, even – of her seventeen-year-old twin.

I don't, says Rosie.

Go home, then, Josh says, and for this, she throws her own snowball at him.

Good shot, says Will, and Rosie laughs.

They keep talking, the three of them, for almost an hour. Josh recalls a snowman they made when they were younger, how they hadn't understood it would melt. You cried, he tells Rosie. I think that was you, she says, and it is Will's turn to laugh, though he shares no memories of his own.

When the conversation has slowed, Rosie tells them her hands are frozen.

Put them in your pockets, then, Josh suggests. The snow has begun to glitter in the pale sun, emerging now, from behind the clouds.

I think I'll just head home, she says.

I'll come, says Will, and their eyes meet, briefly, as Josh tells them they're no fun.

They walk side by side across the grass-pocked snow. The trees lining the field are black and bone-like, the snow already gone from their branches.

Never lasts, says Rosie, as they step through the gate and onto the road, now speckled with gritting salt.

Thank God, Will says. The roads would be a nightmare.

And school would stay shut, she says.

Slush, on the verge. More grit beneath their shoes.

I've never met anyone who loves school like you, Will says. Her cheeks flush at this, but he doesn't sound troubled, or even amused. She is grateful they aren't seated at a table, this time; that he is not able to look at her face.

I don't, really, she says. I just like having a plan.

Will is quiet. They approach a bend in the road and have to cross, so that they're not caught by an oncoming car. They cross back, without discussion. There is a song of snow dripping off the trees, sporadic and out of time, like rain.

That's interesting to me, Will says to her.

Well. That's condescending.

He looks at her then, a half-glance, and she keeps her eyes straight ahead.

I didn't mean it to be, he says. The snow still drips and a car drives past, flecking them with sleet.

I just meant that it's good, he says. That you're so. I don't know.

Naïve? she asks him, and he shakes his head.

Assured, he says.

Josh is trailing behind them some distance away. She has the strange, near irrepressible urge to take Will's hand, just to see what he would do, to see if she's reading this thing right, which surely, she isn't. But she can't test the idea, not with her brother in full view behind them.

She keeps walking, beside him. Puts her hands in her pockets.

It's as they near the corner of her street that a truck soaks them both with road water. It is icy cold, a shock, and Will lets out a roar at the same time that Rosie gasps, and they turn to each other with wide and furious eyes, and then they begin to laugh.

Twat, Will says, as Rosie wipes her face. Her fingers turned numb long ago, and the water is somehow colder, painful, even, as she brushes it away.

God, my hands hurt, she says, and Will tells her to put them under her armpits, and she says what? And it is then that Will stops walking and unzips his jacket and takes her hands in his own, placing them under his arms within the folds of his coat.

Cars drive past. Snow shifts underfoot. Will moves closer so that Rosie's palms are compressed, his hands still closed over hers. His shirt is damp, from the truck water or a light layer of sweat, she does not know. She looks up at him and observes, for the first time, the length of his eyelashes. They are longer than hers.

Yours are cold, too, she says, because her heart is stalled and there is nothing else to say, and everything is melting and frozen, all at once.

This'll help, says Will.

Her hands hurt, even more, as the blood rushes back.

She can feel the pulse of it in her fingertips.

On his skin.

three

When Will stops the car in his driveway he stays seated, staring beyond the dashboard, thinking. Specifically, about the curve of Rosie's ankles, and the way she ate with her spoon.

He shakes his head, laughs, a little, at the madness of it. This girl, with her perfect grades and elven ears, whom he had never even noticed before the bonfire. He rubs his eyes, then watches the snow patter off the trees. He decides that he needs some sleep, and is just about to get out of the car when his phone rings. It is Darcy, which surprises him. They haven't spoken in weeks.

William White, she says, as though he was the one to call her.

Darcy, he says. Hey.

What you doing, she asks him.

Not a lot.

I figured. Being a snow day and all.

Yeah.

So.

So.

You wanna come over? My mum's out.

He thinks on this for all of two seconds, and then tells her that actually, he can't.

Why not? she asks. Her fury is stiff and immediate, and he sighs, not caring that she'll hear it.

I just can't, Darce. I'm knackered.

Why, she asks, again. Who've you been with?

I was at a friend's house all night, he says. Doing maths.

She makes a disbelieving noise, something scornful deep in her throat, and he wonders, fleetingly, why everyone expects the worst of him, when he is only ever telling the truth.

Fuck you, Will, she says.

Well, sure. That is what you wanted, isn't it, he asks.

What?

To fuck me. That's the only reason you called.

She hangs up on him then, and he gets out of the car, his boots sloshing through the snow as it thaws.

He sleeps through the afternoon, wakes to the sound of the ignition clicking, repeatedly, on the oven. He promised his gran months ago that he'd try to fix it. He thinks it must have something to do with the damp, because the noise always stops come the spring.

He hauls himself out of bed, takes a shower, then heads down to the kitchen where his grandmother is ladling soup into bowls, his sister bent over her homework.

He lives, his gran says, as he sits down and passes round cutlery. They keep a basket of it in the centre of the table, spoons with patterned handles, leaves twirling around the knives and forks.

I said hi when I got in, he reminds her.

You're right, she says. You are the king of monosyllables.

What's monosyl-bubbles, asks Amber, without looking up.

Syllables, Will says. It means the king of everything.

No it doesn't.

How was your night, his grandma asks, placing the bowls on the table. She's ground pepper onto his, crumbled blue cheese across its surface.

Didn't sleep, he says. But Josh got the gist of the maths, so that's good.

What did you eat, she asks, because this is always her question, no matter where he's been or who he's been with. When she collected him from the police station that time, they'd sat silently in the car for nine long, difficult minutes, and then she'd asked if he'd had dinner.

Some aubergine thing, he says. I dunno, we ate in his room.

In his room? Amber asks.

Put your pen down, Amber, his grandma says. Eat your dinner, now.

Why can't I eat in *my* room?

Because you need to keep your old grandmother company, that's why. So it was okay? Uneventful?

It was fine, Will says.

He thinks of Rosie as he says this, as he dips his spoon into the red soup.

Maybe you could think about tutoring, his grandmother ventures. Will takes another mouthful, careful to avoid his tongue, still raw from that morning's coffee. The coffee that Rosie had made. Held out to him, with her pebble-soft hands.

I don't need to tutor, he says. I've got the garage.

It's not a long-term plan, though, is it?

Not this again, Gran.

Fine, fine. It was just a thought.

I'm going to be a lawyer, Amber says. Miss Brown says I'd make a good one.

I'm sure you would, his gran says.

Lawyers are dishonest, Will tells her. You don't want to be one of those.

Now why would you tell her that?

Because it's true.

Not all lawyers are dishonest, Willyum.

His gran says his name like this, clipped to two syllables, when she's tense or overly tired. On the day of his grandpa's death, he is Willyum. His mother's birthday, too. At every parents' evening, every school report day, Willyum with a sigh, and a tight mouth.

I could be a dentist, Amber says.

Much better, Will agrees, not even bothering to understand the jump. But no need to decide right now, Ambs.

I've got to, she says.

How come?

For my journal, she says. It's got a whole chapter about hopes and dreams, and what I want to be when I grow up. I've been saving my gold pens for it.

He looks at her over his bowl.

You're only ten, he says.

And you could do with taking a leaf out of her book, his gran says.

It's a journal, Amber says. Not a book.

Will stifles a grin, and his grandmother laughs, a soft sound, like cooing pigeons, and then cuts them all some bread.

*

Rosie lies beside Marley on her friend's bedroom floor, a scene they've watched dozens of times flitting across the television. They untwist sweet wrappers and crunch on toffee popcorn, and her teeth feel slick with sugar.

As they watch Jack gazing at Rose on the top deck, Rosie thinks about telling Marley about William White and their encounter in her kitchen. And then the thing that happened, the very next day, where he took her hands inside his own.

And then what, Marley would ask, a sweet halfway to her mouth.

And then . . . nothing.

He had let go, said, better? and Rosie had nodded, and they had walked back to the house, the snow softened to sleet on the pavement. Josh had caught up to them, thanked him, again, for the maths. And then Will had driven home.

On the screen, Leo is still staring, and Rosie takes another sweet, holds it beneath her tongue.

There is nothing interesting to tell, she decides, about her midnight meeting with a boy she barely knows, and a moment where he warmed her hands, because he took pity on her, was perhaps playing a game she had no interest in playing.

What is surprising, though, is how she keeps picturing him while she sits here, with her knees drawn up, her friend rustling through the popcorn beside her.

She thinks about the grey of his eyes.

Imagines him pressing her against her kitchen wall, his face, so close, to hers.

That's interesting, she thinks, as Marley yawns. That, in itself, is new.

I love this bit, her friend says, shuffling upright as Rose clatters along the deck in her blood-red, glittering dress. I wish our lives were that dramatic.

Why on earth would you want that?

It's just . . . me and you, Rosie. We're such *bores*. I can't wait until life is more than orchestra practice and predicted grades, you know?

Rosie looks back at the film, because she does know, but it

feels like there might be something more, already, for her. Something that's changed. She unwraps another sweet, even though she feels sick and thirsty and vaguely worried that she might be rotting her teeth.

When she gets home, full of sugar yet starved, Rosie makes herself some toast. She warms some beans in the microwave, watching the dish rotate, slow and hypnotic, through the glass.

Lyrics come to her then, about the world turning as one, and she wonders if she's stolen them from somewhere or if they are all her own. She scribbles them down on the notepad by the fridge, folds the page into her pocket. Just in case.

Here she is, Josh says, padding through the door as the microwave pings.

Here I am, she says.

How's Marley?

Good, she says. She thinks we're boring.

Who? Me and you?

No, me and her.

Well. That I'd probably agree with.

Rosie rolls her eyes as her brother leans against the fridge, watching as she pours the beans onto her part-burned toast.

Mum's got a migraine, he says.

Again?

Yeah. There's a lot on her plate, what with Josie's maternity leave.

I guess. She has seemed a bit . . . you know.

Tense.

On edge.

Terrifying?

They share a quiet laugh and she carries her plate to the

table, picks up her fork as Josh settles himself opposite her. He takes an orange from the fruit bowl and rolls it between his hands, as if trying to decide whether he's in the mood to eat it.

She'll get through it, Rosie says, as she cuts her toast in two.

Super-lawyer.

Woman of steel.

Steely-edged Samantha, Josh says, and he finally splits the skin of the orange. Steely, for sure. Her and Dad seem so miserable these days, don't they? Her especially.

They don't seem any different to me, Rosie says.

Then that's *really* sad, Josh says. He holds a segment up to the kitchen light. So many pips, he says.

They're fine, Rosie tells him.

The pips?

No, our parents. Christmas will be a nice reset. Like always.

Ah, Christmas, Josh says, and there is a dreamlike note to his voice. I *love* Christmas.

I know, Rosie says, with another eye roll. Christmas, and snow, and good cheer.

And oranges, he says, tilting the one in his hand towards her, as though raising a toast.

She shakes her head, scoops more beans into her mouth. It is warm in the kitchen, and the wind clatters outside the window, throws a handful of raindrops against the glass. She is debating, as she chews, whether there is a way she can work Will into the conversation, but before she can even form the words her brother does it first.

Think I might actually pass further maths now, he says.

Oh yeah?

Thanks to Will.

That's great, she says. She keeps the beans in her mouth for a few bites too long, is struggling, it seems, to swallow. Her brother is watching her. Seems to misread her hesitancy – her desire to seem uninterested – as disapproval.

He's not like everyone says, Josh tells her.

No? she says, keeping her eyes on her plate. Smear of bean juice, scatter of crumbs.

I know he's got a bad rep, Josh says. With his bike, and his bunking off, and all that. But he's all right. He's smart, and he's decent, I think.

Well, good, she says.

What did you guys talk about, on the walk home?

Hm?

You and Will? What did he say to you?

Nothing, really, she says, and her stomach drops as she says it, because she realises that it's true. Josh is silent for a while, stares her down. He's abandoned half his orange.

Nothing?

He's a man of few words, she says, and he laughs at that, says yeah, he is. He reaches over for a crust she's left on her plate.

She looks back at him, her brother. She knows his face better than her own, grew beside him before they both existed. They've spoken about that, before, when they used to make forts out of duvet covers or camp beneath their bunk beds, torches on, blankets piled around them like sandbags. At what point they became human. Were they twins before then? Or only when they developed brains, or hearts?

It's a twin thing, Josh would say, whenever they knew what the other was thinking. But about this, Rosie has never been sure. She knows other twins who seem like ordinary siblings, and it is not ordinary to get cramp when your brother gets injured on the basketball court, or to wake in the night when his breathing changes. Sometimes she'll stir, for seemingly no reason, and know that he's awake, too, on the other side of her wall.

I think you'd like him, Josh says to her, now.

Who says I don't already, she says, and she lets the sentence hang between them, waits for her twin to catch it, to understand.

He doesn't.

Want one? is all he asks, holding out an orange segment towards her, and she takes it. Spits the pips from her lips to her plate.

*

Will is running.

He has been running every other day for the past four years, ever since his break from school, ever since he was told to find a way to channel his anger. He had never thought of himself as an angry person; had not once raised his voice, never punched a wall, lost his temper with a teacher or on the sports field. But a middle-aged expert with a pine-panelled office asked him some questions after it all happened, noted things down, and told his grandma with certainty that anger was indeed the problem.

With solutions, he had said, the S whistling through the gap in his teeth. And running was the only solution, it seemed, that Will could get on board with.

It isn't easy, because of the cigarettes. He's cut down now, barely ever touches them these days, but the damage is done, already, at eighteen.

Despite that, he runs for hours. He does not track his speed or his distance. He doesn't check his watch or try to prolong his stamina. He just runs. Without music, because he likes to hear the blood pounding in his ears. The gush of the sea, and the gulls.

He runs until he cannot. Until his side sears and his knees are screaming, and he thinks, okay, enough.

Today, he is running along the beach. He isn't cold, though it is December; his skin mottled red with effort, his T-shirt patched with sweat. He passes the beach huts, the sandbank with two basking seals. The lighthouse, once white and weather-beaten, at the very edge of the wood.

When he gets home, he showers in cold water to ease his muscles, towels off his hair, pads through to his bedroom and drops, half-damp, onto his bed. He stares at the ceiling, at the outlines of his old glow-in-the-dark stars. He'd torn them down when he was seven, when he'd decided he was too old for such things.

Too old for stars.

Too old for school.

Too old, already, for all of it.

And as he lies there, that feeling creeps into his chest, something he gets from time to time. A slight tightening, like a valve shrinking shut. It hurts, a little, but it's better than what came before. The slicing urge to react.

Will rubs his heart absently now, distracts himself with thoughts of Rosie's voice. He can hear his grandmother moving downstairs, the click-click-click of the oven. He closes his eyes, starts to hum what he can remember of the bonfire song.

Stops, because he feels like he's ruining it.

When the bell rings and the students pour out of the class-rooms, all loud voices and hitched-up skirts and blazer sleeves rolled to elbows, Will wades against the tide. He does not head for the exit, but takes a chance, and makes for her locker.

She is there with her curly-haired friend. Rosie is listening to whatever she is saying, and then breaks into a laugh, lifting her head so her neck is stretched to the light. An abrupt, vampiric desire pulses through him, and he wonders, again, what it is about this ordinary, soft-skinned girl.

Hey, he says, when he is beside her. She looks up at him at the same time as her friend; four eyes rising to his face.

Hello, she says, and she sounds wary. He has never spoken to her at school before. He has never spoken to her friend, either, and some weird social etiquette kicks in as he realises this, the knowledge that girls care about this sort of thing.

Hi, he says, leaning around Rosie and raising his hand.

The friend just stares at him, then seems to remember herself. She says hi back.

I'm Will, he says, and she says yes, she knows, and doesn't offer her own name in return. I tried, he thinks, before shifting his gaze back to Rosie.

You walking home? he asks her.

Yes, she says, slowly, as though it's a trick question. One of her hands is resting on her locker door, the other inside, stacking her books. He watches her withdraw and push the door shut, latching the padlock in place.

I'll walk with you, he says.

You live on the other side of town, she says.

Yeah, but I have to pick something up.

The lie is smooth, easy. He wants it to be obvious.

Rosie says nothing. She looks at her friend, whose eyes are wide, and some charged, silent exchange occurs between them. Will watches it happen, and waits. More kids skitter behind them, shoes scuffing the linoleum floor.

Rosie doesn't give him an answer, exactly. But she tells her friend – Marley, she calls her, and Will makes a mental note – that she'll see her tomorrow, and Marley tips her chin in acknowledgement, watches them as they walk away, heading for the open doors.

They are out of school and in the teachers' car park when Will pulls his bag higher onto his shoulder and tells her he's not heading her way, after all.

Oh? Rosie looks at him sideways.

I'll be at the lighthouse, later, he says. I run on Monday nights. It's on my route.

Okay.

I'll be running past around half four, I think? If I'm not crazy slow.

Okay, she says again.

Just letting you know, he says. It's a nice spot. The sun kind of lingers there, over the sea. You'd like it.

What are you asking me, Will, she says, and that pulse goes through him again, at her honesty, her straightforwardness. He has never known a girl like her. He thought girls liked mystery and unspoken invitations; long brooding pauses and veiled suggestions.

I'm asking if you'll meet me at the lighthouse, he says.

She stops walking, at that. Younger students fork past them, one boy with his tie round his head, swinging his satchel like a lasso.

Why, she asks.

He looks at her then. Into those eyes of hers, so inkwell blue. And he decides to opt for the truth, too.

I'm not sure, he says. If I'm honest.

And this, it seems, makes sense to her.

I'll try, she says, as non-committal as when she said maybe, before. But he'll take it; is used to it, in fact, from the days when he would see his mother. When he was young and hopeful and looked forward to things; when he had stars stuck to his bedroom ceiling.

———

Later, the lighthouse is waiting, but Rosie is not. A mellow light glows above the horizon, the sea black and still as iron.

Will leans against the whitewashed wall, catching his breath. It's a derelict building these days, a tourist attraction used simply as a marker on the survey maps. Disused churches are called redundant, he knows, some useless snippet he's carried all these years. He wonders whether there's a word for disused lighthouses. Vacant, or elapsed. Abandoned.

He stops stretching and breathes in the sea air. The surf rolls and breaks, white-tipped and patient. His hair is damp with sweat, and he is beginning to feel cold. He will give it another ten minutes and then he will jog home, as though nothing has happened.

Which, he realises, would be true.

But then she is there. Zipped up in her coat, a beanie hat pulled low to her eyes. She is wearing gloves today. Finger-less, and sequined.

Hey, he says, and he sounds a little wild, even to his own ears – eager and surprised and a tenor too loud.

Hey yourself, she says.

She looks at him and he looks at her and he realises he has no plan. The sun is setting, which was all he expected. It glimmers like gold leaf on the dark water.

I don't know why I asked you here, he says.

And I don't know why I came, she says back. He tries smiling at her then, and she returns it. Two lines grooved, at the side of her mouth.

It is beautiful, though, Rosie says, and she looks outwards at the view. The sunset is spilled and soft. Waves rolling in, and out, and in again.

It is, says Will. He doesn't look at the sea as he says it, and her cheeks turn pink, her eyes flicking back to him before they dart away. The wind whistles around the lighthouse walls.

Aren't you freezing? she asks, finally, nodding at his pin-pricked arms.

No, he says, and it is the truth; his whole body feels alight. I mean, I will be soon, he reasons. But not yet.

So, she says.

So.

This is weird, she says.

Good weird, though?

Good weird, she agrees.

He asks her if she's hungry, but she shakes her head, tells him she wants to watch the sea. She sits cross-legged on the ground so he follows suit, sliding down to a sitting position, his back pressed against the lighthouse. They watch the dusk turn from rose to black, so gradually that they barely notice.

Josh says he'll pass his exam now, Rosie says. Thanks to you.

I don't really want to talk about Josh, Will says.

Why not?

Because I spend at least an hour a day with the guy.

Well, what shall we talk about, then?

You tell me, he says. What's in your head?

They're sitting further apart than when they were beside the bonfire, and he can't see her face, even in profile; her hat is too low, and she has angled her chin towards the forest. He can only see the curve of her ear beneath her hat. A thread of her dark hair.

You care what's in my head? she asks, after a moment.

Yeah, he says. I do.

She says nothing for a while. The sea breathes against the stones, and a gull takes flight from the sand.

Do you talk like this to all your girls? she asks, when the seagull has gone from view.

Who?

You know, the Ashleighs and the Keiras and the Darcys.

So she knows about them, he thinks, and something sinks

in him, the pain in his chest a sudden stone. But then he realises that this surely means something. That she had to notice, or care.

I don't talk to any of those girls, he tells her.

Sure you do. You took Darcy to the winter dance last year.

She dragged me, actually.

Well, you can't have sat in silence all night.

More or less, he says. And then, before he can think not to, he tells her that being with Darcy doesn't exactly require a lot of talking.

Oh.

Yeah.

Rosie makes a small noise, like she understands and doesn't mind. A light *mm*, as if he's simply told her what day it is. He's definitely cold now. Can't feel his toes.

But no, he says.

No what?

Can we stop answering questions with questions?

If you stop being so cryptic, then yes.

He hasn't felt this upward tilt before; as if everything inside him, the soles of his feet, his diaphragm and his deltoids, are being lifted towards the sky.

No, I don't talk like this to any of those girls.

Oh.

This, he comes to realise, is one of her recurrent words. This girl with that voice, and all of her ohs and maybes.

I had to lie to my parents to come here, Rosie tells him. I don't really go out for no reason, so I had to come up with something.

What did you say?

That I was going to borrow a book from a friend.

Original.

I thought so. Believable, too.

I figured, Will says.

Did you, though, Rosie says, and she shifts to look at him, and it is dark now, the sun dissolved, the clouds an oil spill above their heads. Do you *really* get that? That I like books and school, and music, and not cool music, either – I play the flute and the guitar and the piano. The recorder, too. Full disclosure. And I really, really want to go to music school but I'll probably end up doing history and I'm looking at Oxbridge and I have no time, really, for any of this. For seeing someone. If that's what this is.

She takes a breath, and again, he is astonished by her.

Why are you going to do history if you want to do music, he asks, after a moment. The wind blows in from the sea, lifts his hair, and hers, from beneath her hat.

That's what you got from all that I said?

Aha, he says. Is that a question for a question?

She laughs then, and it is like the trail behind a firework; it sparkles and fades, the silence that follows left crackling.

Fine, she says. I just thought I should warn you.

Consider me warned, Will says.

She uncrosses her legs, puts her feet out in front of her. Her hiking boots look clean and unhiked-in, and he almost asks her what book she borrowed, until he remembers it was a lie she had told. For him.

He walks her home when the cold gets too much; when the dark has sunk into their bones. The cobbles shine in the street lights, restaurant windows misted up from the inside. They pass the local chip shop, and it smells of skinned potatoes and old oil, the queue winding out of the doorway.

Next time we'll get chips, Will says.

And you'll wear a coat, Rosie says.

And I will wear a coat.

Not your biker jacket, though. A proper coat.

What's wrong with my biker jacket?

It doesn't look warm.

So? I'll be the one wearing it.

But I won't relax if you're cold, Rosie says. I'll just keep thinking about it, and it'll be on your mind, too, how cold you are. And it might make you want to go home.

He pauses, at this, for just a few footsteps.

I'm coatless now, aren't I? he says.

Yep. And here we are, heading home.

Will cannot respond to that. He is not sure what is going on between them; neither of them has explicitly said. There has been no kissing, no touching; no baring of souls or skin. They just sat with their backs against the lighthouse and talked, sometimes falling silent, before they would speak again.

Something passes between them, now. The hairs stand like needles down his arms, the sweat blown dry down his back.

He thinks about taking her hand. Almost does.

Then, at that exact moment, Rosie slips her hands into her coat pockets.

It's not practical, she says.

What, my biker jacket?

No, she says, not that. What we were saying earlier, about studying music. I did think about it, got an application for music school, even. But in the end I thought I should do something more transferable.

Will thinks that sounds like parent-speak, but decides not to say so. They stay quiet as they turn off the high street and begin the slight incline towards the ring road, the shops and pubs giving way to cottages with flint walls, televisions flickering through net curtains. Lives, shadowed, through the windows. Plant pots. Photo frames. Figures, moving, like cut-outs.

I always wonder what people do this time of night, Rosie says.

What d'you mean?

Well, it's a weird time, isn't it? Just before dinner. After school, or work. It's like a period of non-time, where you can't do anything real.

Real?

You know. Important stuff.

What's your important stuff?

Gosh, you're nosy.

Will laughs, because nobody has ever called him that before. He wonders if it's like the anger; if it's something that lies dormant, rearing its head only when life calls for it. When a girl with thin hands asks where you think your mother might be, and looks you in the eye when she talks.

Singing. And writing, she says.

Oh yeah? What d'you write?

Songs, mostly. And poems.

He nods. There is festoon lighting strung above them, and the bulbs chime in the wind, knocking together like spoons in a drawer. They feel dangerous, to him, these sorts of conversations. Like she'll soon realise he has scars and anger issues and a history of unspeakable things.

What's yours? she asks him.

My motorbike, I guess, he says. Maybe running.

They turn the corner onto the residential streets. Cars parked in driveways, heavy curtains drawn against them.

And travel, Will says, realising that, once more, he's sharing something he's never said out loud.

Wow, says Rosie, and her voice lifts with interest. Where have you been?

Well, nowhere outside Norfolk, he admits. Which is why I want to go, when I can.

Where're you going to go?

Anywhere, he says. Everywhere.

That's a lot of places, she says, and he tells her she's not wrong.

*

Rosemary Winters, you dark *horse*.

Rosie can't help it; she laughs down the phone. She feels as though she is filled with balloons, a pleasant pressure beneath her skin.

Nothing happened, she says.

Nothing *happened*? cries Marley. The coolest guy in school asked you out, is what happened.

I don't think he's the coolest guy in school.

He is sexy and sullen and he owns a motorbike, for God's sake.

I know. It's a problem.

A problem? Rosie! Marley sounds slightly crazed, as if she's downed one too many energy drinks. Do you think he'll give you a ride on it?

I wouldn't get on it even if you paid me, Rosie says, and Marley sighs.

That's part of his appeal, though, she insists. His motorbike, his *sad* eyes, his dark, dangerous past. You know he got suspended for beating someone up in the school toilets?

That's just a stupid rumour, Marl.

Maybe, says Marley, but can we back up, please? Will White came over and wanted to walk you home. Now. What happened before that?

I was talking to you at my locker.

No-no-no, says Marley, and Rosie can sense her flapping

her hand in frustration. She doesn't need to see her to picture it; her friend, upside down on her bed, feet up against the wall.

Before that.

He just came over one night, Rosie says. To help Josh with his maths.

And?

And we got talking. That's all.

She doesn't know why she's downplaying this, when she wants to sing, to run, to let the sun in her heart pour out of her.

Did he make a move?

No.

Did you want him to?

I don't know, Marl. I'm not sure what he wants. We know what kind of guy he is, right? He's never said a word to me, and then that night at the bonfire –

The bonfire! I forgot he was there!

Well, exactly. He barely said a word to anyone. But then after you left, I don't know, we just started chatting.

And he fell for you. *Hook line.* Why wouldn't he, Rosie?

I thought I was a vanilla virgin?

Well, you are. And that's your secret weapon.

Being boring?

Being innocent and sweet and so intently you, she says, and Rosie can't help but laugh again at the fever in her friend's voice.

Sounds like you're writing yourself a nice little movie script, she says. But the timing's not right, Marley. Really. I've got bigger things on my mind. I need to focus on Oxbridge.

You need to focus on the size of his biceps, Marley says.

They squabble-laugh for another minute and then Rosie's door opens, without a knock. It is her mother. Her hair is twisted up into a towel, her face wan-looking now it's stripped of mascara, her eyeliner wiped away.

Phone off, Rosie, she says, nodding at the space where her clock used to be. She'd asked her dad to take it down when she'd stopped sleeping; when the tapping hands, once so soothing, began to wind her tight like a cog. Say goodnight to Marley now.

She closes the door behind her and Rosie tucks her chin back to the receiver.

You hear that?

Yeah. But before you go, Rosie, let me ask you one thing.

Okay.

Do you like him?

There is a silence, clockless and lamplit.

Because if you do, Marley goes on, then none of the other stuff matters. The bike or the smoking or Oxbridge, or those other girls, or what your mum thinks, or what date your classics exam might be.

Her friend's voice has changed. It is the serious Marley talking now; the Marley who likes to debate ethics, who shows up early to orchestra practice. Who replies with the utmost concentration when her father quizzes her on diseases at the kitchen table, because she is going to be a doctor, like him.

I can't, Rosie says.

But you do? Marley asks.

Rosie doesn't say it, cannot bring herself to speak. And that, she knows, is answer enough, as well as spectacularly inconvenient.

She makes a decision, overnight.

She cannot do this now. She is flattered. She is full of warm air, and she is confused about why he wants her, of all people, to meet him at the lighthouse, to be the person he shares a bag of chips with by the harbour. And she wants to be that person. She wants to hear him talk about travel and running, all his non-plans. She wants him to listen, in the way that nobody else does; like he's actually absorbing her answers.

But those things can wait.

There are other things she has to focus on. Bigger, important things that she's been working towards, for too long. She cannot slip, not now. Not even for Will White, with his cold, assured hands and his sombre eyes.

So grey, and so serious.

She struggles to leave her bedroom the next morning, checking things on a loop, then another. Her clothes, her curtains, tilting her desk chair to the perfect angle, ensuring it feels right. And then she walks to school with Josh and doesn't mention a word of it and spends the day at school with the focus of an aspiring Oxbridge student and then the bell rings, and she waits by her locker, and he comes to her just as she hoped he would.

There are too many people around. Shoes squeak on the floor, blazers jostling past in a haze of blue. Dropped books, banging doors.

Can we go somewhere, she asks him.

His eyebrows rise at this. Like he hadn't expected it, from her. Like he thinks she means something else.

Just somewhere in school, she says, to clarify.

The library? he suggests.

Or the music block, Rosie says, because she can't face being in silence with him, amid the books and the muffling carpets, everything paper-soft and private. She needs stone floors. Piano edges, the brushed brass of music stands.

When they get there, Will pushes the music block door open. It's heavy, panelled in wood, and he has to lean his whole arm across to let her pass. Inside, it is dark, nobody having bothered to turn the lights on in the hall. The mismatched voices of choir practice drift from a nearby classroom, and there are thumps from upstairs, students dragging themselves to their lessons with their oboes and guitars.

I hate this building, Will says.

I love this building, says Rosie.

It doesn't give you the creeps?

All part of its charm, she says, leading him down the hall and past the teachers' office, to her favourite – usually empty – practice room at the back. The window is blocked by an overgrown hedge, so it's always devoid of sunlight, even at midday. She loves the dappled shadows on the old carpets, the slight smell of damp that never fades.

I think we need to revise your definition of charm, Will says, as she leads him through the door. The piano is in the corner. Stacks of sheet music line the wooden shelves, Debussy and Gershwin and Strauss. Her watch is there, too, on the piano stool, after she'd forgotten it again. She sits down and wraps it round her wrist. Will is looking around, at the music, the notes on the blackboard. Anywhere, it seems, but at her.

So this is your hang-out, he says.

Sort of, she says.

It's freezing, he says.

I keep my coat on, usually, she says. In the winter.

Does it always smell like this?

Afraid so.

Then why d'you come here?

I like the quiet, she says, and he nods, like he gets it, and he's making this whole thing harder just by being him, and understanding. She has never known a person like him. Never felt like she's known someone, for so long, when she hasn't.

I wanted to talk to you about something, she says, because that's what she brought him here for.

I'm listening, he says. He's still looking at the blackboard. He goes over and touches the treble clef, brushes his fingers across the whorl of its tail.

I'm not sure this is a good idea, she says.

He says nothing. Doesn't ask her what she means, doesn't throw back one of his usual questions. She can see students walking past the music block, flickers of blue through the hedge beyond the window. The snow is gone. Her history exam has been rescheduled. Her heart is drumming in her chest.

You and me, she says, in case he hasn't understood.

Will still doesn't reply. He rubs the treble clef away with two fingers, leaves a cloud of dust in its place.

Why's that, he asks, lightly, as though he's not really interested in her answer.

A lot of reasons, she says.

Give me one.

Okay. You're you. And I'm me.

I need a proper reason, Rosie.

I'm just not your kind of girl, she says. I don't want to hang off you at the winter dance or sit on the back of your motorbike or fail my mocks because I'm thinking about you.

So don't, then.

Don't what?

Think about me.

That's what I'm trying to say, she says.

So you are, then?

Are what?

Thinking about me.

Well, yeah, she says, and she's getting flustered, thinks, for a heart-stopping jolt of a second, that perhaps she's read this all wrong. Aren't you? she asks him.

He doesn't say anything. Turns around to face her, and leans his back against the blackboard.

You'll get chalk down your shirt, Rosie says. He folds his arms, as if he's settling in for something long and debatable.

I need another reason, he tells her.

Fine, she says. I just need to focus on my exams, all right? I've come too far, now. I need to get the grades for a conditional offer and then, even if I do, I'll be leaving next September, anyway.

So?

Well, she says, and she casts around the room, as though the answer is written on the walls, hanging in the cobwebs on the ceiling. Is there even any point, you know? Starting something?

You tell me, he says.

I am telling you, Will, she says, and there's a heat to her voice now, the rip of a match as it lights; clipped, and decisive. You'd get bored, anyway. I care about school and grades and all the things you've made very clear mean nothing to you. You don't want to wait for me.

Is that an option, he says. His arms are still folded.

What?

Waiting for you. Is that an option?

What do you mean?

I mean, if you get your exams done, and your conditional offer or whatever it is you need, would that change things?

I'd still be leaving, though. Come September.

But there'd be a summer, he says.

Yes, Rosie says, after a short pause.

And until then, what are the rules? That we can't see each other? That I have to hide from you in the halls, stop helping Josh with his maths?

I'm not laying out any stupid rules, Rosie says.

Come on, Roe, Will says, a half-laugh caught in his throat, and it is the first time he calls her that, the first time he

57

shortens her name to something that nobody else has ever, or will ever, call her.

She shrugs, her point lost between them like the clef on the blackboard.

Do your exams, Will says. Get those results. And I'll wait.

His eyes are on hers. His mouth is set, and his tie is loose, his shirt unbuttoned below the collar. The tut-tut-tut of her watch flits in her ears. A tiny metronome, tapping out time.

You'll wait, she repeats.

Yes.

She looks at him, at the burnt gold of his hair, the down that grazes his jaw. He is stirring, and silent, and that warmth is back inside her. Why, she asks him.

He looks straight at her.

You said you think about me, he says.

She nods, once, when she realises it's a question.

Turns out I think about you, too, he says. On my bike. And at the garage. And when I'm cooking, and running, and trying to sleep.

His eyes are like fumes; they fog up the room.

And that's new for me, he says.

Rosie's throat is so dry, she could not speak even if she wanted to. She is thinking that it's new for her, too. That what she did last night, under her covers with him on her mind, that was new, and it felt dangerous, and good, and only a little bit wrong.

So I'll wait, Will says again.

The choir starts up from the other end of the building, a hymn about winter snow. They both listen, until the song ends. Some line about dawn, and morning. He hears the words, and watches her face, and she watches him right back.

four

She didn't say they couldn't be friends. Just that she didn't want to sit on his motorbike, or go to the winter dance. That he couldn't interrupt her exams.

And so they text, occasionally. He waits for her, at first, to reach out to him. She sends him songs, or the name of a place she's seen online, an island or mountain range or a city she thinks he might like, and he writes the names down and puts them in his drawer.

He messages her early, or late at night.

Asks her how she is, how she slept.

He sleeps with Darcy, once, a week after their conversation in the music room, and he thinks about Rosie the entire time and it is awkward and bumpy and it takes him too long to get hard. What is *wrong* with you, Darcy spits at him, her nails dug deep into his back, and he asks himself the same question while he tugs his jeans back on.

*

When Rosie tells Marley that she and Will are not together, Marley seems to take it as a personal affront.

She barely speaks to her for days.

Rosie is hurt by this, but says nothing, and they're talking again by the end of the week. They make plans to see each other on the Saturday, to watch *The Beach*, or *Jack and Sarah*. Rosie says she'll bring the popcorn this time; a peace offering, though she's not sure exactly what for.

And she studies, hard. She goes over everything that could come up in her mocks, staying up late with herbal tea and pages of notes and a slight sense of having started a marathon, the buzz of it, a tremor of stress and satisfaction.

Will texts her, sometimes. She checks her phone before bed, when she's closed her books and brushed her teeth, brought her ear plugs out from her bedside drawer. She tries to be clever in her replies; more interesting than she knows herself to be. And when she turns the light off, she feels fine.

In control, and on the right path, with someone who's noticed and cared.

She falls asleep with no tension in her jaw. Wakes up feeling lighter and readied, like all the tiny grains of her life are stacked just so.

I've got a date to the winter dance, Marley announces one break time.

Rosie is eating a bread roll, pauses with a piece raised to her mouth.

I know we said we wouldn't have dates, Marley says. That we'd go together, as always. But that was just because we never got asked, right? And now I have, so.

She seems defensive, although Rosie has said nothing to make her that way. She lowers the bread, tries to keep her face neutral.

Who's asked you?

Tom Dellow, from my art class.

He's nice.

I know he's nice, Marley says. We've been talking a bit, on and off.

Oh, right.

Yeah.

So, er. Do you like him?

Guess we'll see after the dance, Marley says, and there's a note of finality to her voice, the conversation closed. This seems unfair to Rosie, seeing as she was only repeating a question she herself had been asked. But she eats her roll, takes a drink from her water bottle.

I think it's great, Rosie says, when Marley reaches the bottom of her yoghurt, is scraping the pot with her spoon. We can still get ready together, can't we?

Marley softens at this, makes eye contact again.

Course, she says. I'll blare our favourite tunes while we mix eye colours and crimp our hair.

This is how they would prepare for school discos when they were younger; when winter dances only meant the Macarena and bowls of ready-salted crisps, boys skidding on their knees along the floor. Rosie tells her that sounds perfect, thinking it's fine by her if she wants to go with Tom Dellow, although there's something pulling inside her, an invisible thread, like Marley is somehow making a point.

I'll go with Josh, she says, to make light of it, and Marley laughs. Tells her that sounds about right.

*

The week before school is due to break up for Christmas, Rosie's mother calls her into her bedroom. It is first thing in the morning, when her mum is usually dressed and making coffee, already on the phone, or working on her laptop.

Rosie pushes open the door and the room smells of sleep, the musk of her parents' breathing. Her father is a snoring mound beneath the duvet while her mother lies, small and straight, beside him, her eyes open.

Rosie, her mother says again. She whispers, which means she is not herself.

Are you okay, Rosie asks, padding across the carpet.

My head, she says.

You need water?

And Imitrex.

Rosie comes back with a glass and the tablets, pops them out of the foil for her. She watches her swallow, thinks how she's still so striking when she is sick, and only just awake. Her hair cascades across her pillows, her cheekbones sliced with shadow.

Don't go into work today, Rosie says.

I don't think I can, her mother says. She closes her eyes, attempts to put her glass back on the bedside table; Rosie has to steady it for her.

Can I get you anything else?

Can you just talk to me, for a little while?

Rosie pulls her legs up beneath her so she's sitting on the side of her parents' bed. At first, she rests her hand on her mother's knuckles, but she shifts away.

Too hot, she says, and Rosie nods.

It is wrong to admit it, and so she never has, but she likes her mother best when she has a migraine. It is the only time she seems to need Rosie's company; the only time she slows down and wants to know things, real things, not about school or exams or her weight loss.

It's not about *weight loss*, Rosie, her mother had said, when she'd laid out her new regime. It's a *lifestyle* adjustment. I just want you to be healthy and happy and the best version of you.

She wants me to get asked to the winter dance, Rosie had told Josh in an undertone, and he'd snorted like it was funny, though she had not been the slightest bit joking.

Her mother stays in bed all day; is still there after school. Rosie and Josh cobble dinner together, and their father takes his plate to his office, opting to listen to the cricket on the radio with his feet up on his desk.

So, I've been thinking, Rosie says, twirling spaghetti round her fork. It is raining outside, the drops tapping like seeds falling on the conservatory roof.

Sounds ominous, says Josh, through a too-large mouthful of food.

I wondered if I should get a dress for the dance.

Josh looks at her over his water glass, still chewing.

Yeah?

Last year's doesn't fit that well, with the weight loss, and everything.

How's that going?

Fine, she says. It's only a few pounds.

We could probably pin it, then, he says. If you don't want to go shopping.

I do, though, she says.

You want to go shopping for clothes?

Well. For one dress. Singular.

Okay. Josh puts down his fork. How come?

What?

You've *never* bought anything without being dragged to the shops by our mother, he says. Or myself.

I know. We can't all love scrubbing up, like you.

Low blow, he says.

I just thought it'd be nice, she says, standing up and taking

63

his plate, before he's even finished. She scrapes the pasta back into the pan, clunks the crockery into the dishwasher.

It will be, Josh says, and she can sense him watching her.

I'll just go alone, if it's such a big deal, she says.

Sis. It's not a big deal.

So why are you making it seem like one?

Jeez, Rosie, I just asked a question! I thought there might be someone you wanted to dress up nice for, he says, that's all. It's not a wild idea, now we're seventeen, is it?

Not you *too*, she says.

Huh?

Marley's always banging on about how I'm a virgin and how nobody ever asks me to the dance, she says. When she's never dated, properly, either. And it's not like you've had a long line of girlfriends, Josh.

A silence, then, that stuns them both. Rosie's throat contracts, and something seeps through her, some prickling, liquid heat.

I'm sorry, she says, and sits back down in front of him. She feels suddenly, bodily, exhausted, like she could sleep right here at the table.

What's with the claws, Josh asks. He reaches over and lifts her hand, makes a show of checking her fingernails.

Just stress, she sighs. Exams.

She says sorry, a second time, and he says it's okay; puts her hand back down on the table.

Are your checks bad? he asks.

Not the worst, she says.

They listen to the rain. Rosie lets the heat fade away, waits for her feelings to ebb. She thinks about telling Josh her secret; that she has someone, that she could have had someone. The best one, maybe. And that for reasons that made sense to her at the time, she said no, and he said he'd wait, and now she finds she wants to look nice for him even though he is not hers, and it's irritating, and distracting, and maybe she should just stay home, after all. With no date to the dance, like always.

I'll help you find a dress, Josh says, because of course he will. Because he is kind, and forgiving, and the one who cares about these things.

Maybe a light blue, he says, nudging her foot with his.

Maybe, she says, and she feels like crying, though she has no idea why.

He is the only one to know, and to ask, about what they have coined her *checking*.

It is something she began doing so young that she can't remember not doing it. She thinks it was the night before her first piano exam. She was seven. And out of nowhere, she felt the need to check she had her sheet music packed in her school bag, over and over, as if no matter how many times she checked, she did not trust that it was there.

It spilled into other things. Adjusting her curtains. Touching her door handle and her desk chair. Irrational, necessary, tiring habits that were compulsory, and private, done only at night or when she was alone, before bed.

Josh could hear her through the wall. Saw her, once or twice, and accepted it, and didn't try to change it, or mock her, or question what she was doing. But he asks her, now and then, if she's all right. Something she forgets to ask herself.

*

The school workshop, after hours, is one of Will's favourite places. Like his grandfather's garage, it is quiet and functional, a place he can use both his hands and his brain, and be left alone by other people.

Usually.

Hey Will, says Josh, as he walks in with his satchel banging his knees, his tie loosened, blazer askew.

Will straightens up from his place by the lathe. He is allowed to work in here, alone, because he has a good rapport with the technician. It's officially not allowed because, Will knows, most students are stupid, or heavy-handed, or melt things in the vacuum packing machine and set off the fire alarms, even saw off the tips of their thumbs.

Will has never done any of these things. But he's never had an insistent schoolmate distracting him while he works, either.

Is this still okay? Josh asks, clearly noting something on Will's face. You said I could come revise here, on Wednesdays?

I did, didn't I, says Will, and Josh looks so forlorn that he backtracks, gives him a laugh to indicate he was joking. Sort of.

Just don't distract me too much, he says. I've got to finish these candlesticks, and I've ruined two sets already.

Okay, Josh says, and he sounds serious as he unpacks his books, gets out his worksheets and spreads them out on the workbench. No distracting. Got it.

Will shakes his head, picks up the bases he'd planed flat last week. He still needs to sand them down, but the shape is pleasing, the drill hole in just the right place. He turns back to the lathe, and mounts a stick on the driving centre. One step at a time, like fixing an engine. One thing after another.

What're you struggling with, then, Will asks Josh, as he winds the tailstock in place.

All of it, says Josh, and Will sighs. Takes his chisel to the wood, just once, the noise harsh and sharp and short. He's ruined previous sets with a slip of the hand, or a lack of concentration; getting too comfortable, too soon, and scoring out more than he wants to.

He spends an hour working like this, in careful stages, coaching Josh over his shoulder. He finds Josh watching him, sometimes, when he glances back to answer a question, or is reaching for a new gouge. Like he's more interested in the lathe, or his hands, than the maths he came here to learn.

So, Josh says, after he's finished a few questions, is stretching his long arms above his head. You going to the dance, tomorrow?

Will lets out a puff of air, a non-committal no, as he swaps to the bedan tool. He is not planning on it. Darcy has not asked him this time, and it is always hot and messy and dull, and he would rather spend the night with his bike, or sanding down these candlesticks.

Rosie's getting ready at Marley's, Josh says, so I'm going to Jack's for pre-drinks. Think we'll all get there around eight.

He says it in an offhand sort of way, as though testing him, and Will wonders, fleetingly, if he knows something; if he senses, or if Rosie has even told him, about their non-relationship. Their suspended not-quite-anything.

But then he moves on, asks about more numbers on the page. And Will pretends that this changes nothing, because he is supposed to be waiting, and she specifically said she did not want to go to the dance with him.

He isn't going *with* her, though, if he simply shows up.

He swaps the candlesticks, working more swiftly, this time, confident that he can match the design of the first. It's no good having one that he can't pair with the other; they need to be equal, exact. He'll lacquer them, when they're done. Next time. When Josh isn't here, asking him about matrices, or watching his every move.

———

When the night rolls round, he dresses in a shirt and jeans. Finds some aftershave at the back of the cabinet to hide the smell of engine grease, wonders why it's considered sensual to smell of dried fruit and cedar trees. He doesn't know why he's bothering. Back in the kitchen, his grandma doesn't, either.

I thought you hated school dances, she says, as she stirs a stew on the hob. Will leans over and spoons some into his mouth, careful not to drop it down his front.

I do, he says. The food is hot so he parts his lips, lets the steam curl outwards like smoke.

So are you going with Ashleigh?

Two years ago, maybe.

Then who's the girl with the piercings up her ears?

Darcy, he says. But no. It's just me tonight.

Oh?

Last time, isn't it, he says with a shrug, as he scrapes more stew from the saucepan. Before everyone buggers off to uni.

Everyone except you, she says.

Yep, Will says. It ends at midnight, Gran, okay? So don't wait up.

You're not driving, she says.

How else am I going to get there?

There'll be drink, presumably, she says.

Yeah. But I won't have any.

Like hell you won't.

Gran!

I'll pick you up, she says. I'll be outside the school at midnight on the dot. Any later, Will, and you're walking.

Gran, I'll be fine to drive. *You're* the one who said I can't ride my bike in the dark, so I'll take your car, and I won't —

Have a glorious time, Willyum, she says. Avoid contracting an STD, if you can.

What's an STD, asks Amber, as she wanders into the kitchen. She is still in her school uniform, her panda slippers bug-eyed on her feet.

Sexually Transmitted Dragonpox, Will says.

Urgh!

I know, Will nods. Don't touch a boy, Ambs, not til you're thirty, at least. Or you might catch it.

Off with you now, his grandma says.

So I have to walk there?

Won't kill you, will it?

You smell weird, Amber informs him, as he moves past her to the door, and he says thanks, to both of them, for the continued moral support.

The dance is busy and loud, a jumble of paper chains and disco balls and soft drinks abandoned in cups. Will's name is ticked off on a clipboard, and because he's eighteen – a year older than his peers, due to the year he retook – he's given a token for a beer. He pockets it and grabs a Coke. Heads for the first person he knows.

For an hour, he moves from group to group, talking, not talking, drinking and not drinking. He gives his token to a girl in a red dress who keeps standing too close, her voice tickling his neck. Like it's attractive. Like he couldn't possibly resist. Like her desperation, her hunger to be looked at, is in itself a turn-on.

Get yourself a beer, he says, handing her his pass. And she looks up at him, tipsy from her pre-dance drinks – peach schnapps, it smells like – and blinks, slowly, as though he's paid her a compliment.

Stay right here, William White, she slurs, before she slinks off, and he immediately walks the other way, towards the dance floor; leans against the school stage in the darkest corner he can find.

She's not here.

The hall smells of floor polish and fresh sweat and the sweet, sticky spill of alcohol. This is the room for assemblies and drama class, carol concerts and visitor talks, hours of stifled listening to prayers and fables and rules. He won't miss it; not for a minute.

Wiiiiiiilllllllll White!

A sudden bump of elbows jars him out of his thoughts; an arm is slung around his neck, a body slumped against his own. It is Josh, and he is drunk.

Steady on, mate, Will says.

Sorry, sorry, Josh says, and he takes his arm from his shoulders. Just didn't 'spect to see you!

I was hiding, to be fair, Will says, grinning in spite of himself. Josh looks even more like a cartoon in this state; his limbs are limp, and his hair looks bedraggled, as though he's been standing beneath a sprinkler.

Did you just get out the shower or something? Will asks him.

The shower?

Your hair, he says. It's soaked.

Just dancing, bud! Josh cries, and he grabs Will's hands, tries to pull him onto the dance floor, but Will resists.

I think you need some air, Will tells him.

I think *you* need to dance, Josh says.

How about we get you some water, Will suggests, and Josh throws his head back, lifts his fists into the air and does some bizarre movement that Will is sure, once he is sober, he will not want to remember doing.

Have fun, then, he says, laughing. He backs up, is just thinking he'll get some water himself, when he meets a girl in a blue dress on the stairs by the stage. He stands by to let her pass, and she hesitates, as though she's noticed that it's him.

He is used to this.

Girls acting nervous around him, as though they want to say something.

He purposefully doesn't make eye contact. He worries, momentarily, that the peach schnapps girl will be back with the drinks, and is just about to head the other way when the girl in blue says his name.

He glances back at her, then stares.

Because it's Rosie.

Except that it doesn't look like Rosie. She has clipped up her hair, done something smoky to her eyes, and she's wearing a midnight silk slip that skims her skin, falls all the way to the floor.

Roe, he says. I didn't think you were here.

I didn't think you were, either.

You look. I mean.

She lowers her eyes, and he sees her cheeks bloom with blood, even through the semi-darkness. His eyes drink her up; her bare shoulders, her braceleted wrists.

Do you want a drink?

I've just had one. I was actually looking for Josh.

She holds up a cup of water, and he grins, shakes his head.

I've just seen him, he says. Good luck stopping those dance moves of his.

Oh dear, she says, and Will says oh dear is right, and she laughs, and it is like fireworks again, the spark of it, the small explosions in his gut.

You want some air? he asks her.

———

The night is mild for December. Near windless, with scuds of cloud shielding the stars.

There are a few couples out in the courtyard, so Will and Rosie slip behind the bike sheds, find themselves on the concrete steps outside the assembly hall. It is quieter, out here. The disco lights whirl through the windows, make patterns on the tarmacked road.

Will leans against the railing and holds out his hand, helps Rosie up the steps in her heels.

That dress, he says. Rosie says nothing; bows her head and smooths her fringe, as though trying to hide her face.

You having a good night?

Yeah, she says, and she leans against the railing beside him. Actually, no. I sort of hate these things.

So why d'you come?

I could ask you the same thing.

I came because I thought you'd be here, Will says.

Rosie tilts her head, her eyelids shimmering with silver.

Well, I came because I always do, she says.

Even though you hate it, Will says, and she nods.

Crazy, isn't it? I don't really like alcohol, for one thing. Another cool fact about me, by the way, she says, glancing at him as she says it. I just really hate being drunk.

Sensible, Will says.

I am, Rosie says. Which is so *dull*, I know.

They listen to the music blaring through the wall. The roofs of the parked cars shine in the moonlight, and some girls cackle, distantly, in the courtyard.

Can I ask, Will asks, why it is that you say these things about yourself?

They are standing an inch apart. Her little finger, close to his.

Because they're true?

They're not, though, he says. If you were dull, or you

really cared about not liking alcohol, you would do something about it. Right?

It sounds like an accusation, and she is quiet.

What else don't you like about the dance, he asks her, when
enough time has passed.

Dancing, she says.

A bit of a problem, he says, and she laughs, and it is the best
sound, and his heart skitters behind his ribs and he turns to
face her, puts his hands on her waist. She stops laughing,
immediately.

Is this okay? he asks, and she nods, once, though her eyes
are doe-like, caught in the spiralling lights.

Dancing can be all right, he tells her.

He has slow-danced at all of these things; or at least, the
ones he's been forced to attend. The girls usually take the
lead, nuzzling into his chest as they rotate on the spot. But
Rosie doesn't. She simply looks up at him, like she doesn't
know what to do. Like she's afraid.

Think less, he says.

I can't, she says.

Try.

Will.

Yes?

We're not meant to be doing this.

What, dancing in a car park?

You know what I mean.

She moves with him, though, despite the things she is saying. His forehead is close to hers, and he can smell the sky, the
cold. The autumn scent of her hair; apples and sweet leaves.
She feels somewhat taut, as well as soft, beneath the satin of her
dress.

Rosie, he says. Relax.

That's like saying: Will, be unattractive.

73

He snorts, tells her she's funny. They keep swaying on the steps, his heart thudding like hooves in his chest.

Rosie! Rosie Winters!

Two people stumble around the corner, and Rosie breaks, turns around. It's Marley, and Tom, a guy he knows from his form class. Marley is waving and he hears Rosie sigh, the smallest breath of air, and then she smiles and waves right back.

Hello, she says, as Marley and Tom join them by the railing.

Hi-hi-hi, Marley crows, before taking a glug from her beer. How are we all this *fine* evening?

Fine, Rosie says, and she's still smiling, her teeth like pearls in the dark.

I thought you guys weren't a thing, Marley says, waving her beer bottle between them. She is a little drunk, Will knows; he can see it in her eyes.

Depends what you mean by thing, he says.

Marley's gaze slides towards him, and at that exact moment Tom introduces himself, and Rosie says hi. They talk about nothing for a while. The beer, and when the burgers will be ready. How they'd all have preferred pizza, really, instead.

So let's go get pizza, Will says.

All three of them turn to look at him.

Now? Marley asks.

If you're hungry, yeah.

We can't just leave, Tom says.

It's the last one, Marley reminds him.

Will lets out a small laugh. Marley frowns, and Tom glances at him, too, with a wariness he's seen in guys his age before.

What? Marley asks.

I just don't get why people are so sentimental about this place, he says.

You mean the place we've spent the last seven years of our lives?

I love this song, Rosie says suddenly. She has stepped back from the railing, away from him. Some of her hair has fallen from its bun.

Me too, says Marley, though she eyes Will for a second longer. Then she passes her beer to Tom and grabs Rosie's hands and they dance, together, on the tarmac. Not well, exactly, but effortlessly. Like they've been doing it in bedrooms for years.

You want some, Tom asks, offering him a beer bottle. Will says thanks, and takes it, but doesn't drink. Watches Rosie laughing, as Marley twirls her around.

Bit cold out here, Tom says.

Yeah, says Will, uninterested in small talk. Tom takes a swig of beer, and Will finds himself doing the same, without thinking. The first sip is lukewarm, unsatisfying.

When the song ends, Marley flings her arms round Rosie's neck and looks over at them both. Rosie says something to her, something Will can't catch, and Marley laughs, again, her shrieking laugh. Kestrels, diving, triumphant.

Are you a thing, Tom asks him, as the girls turn back towards them.

Are *you*, he asks, and Tom pauses, the beer bottle lifted to his mouth.

Me and Marley?

Yeah.

Tom still doesn't drink. Watches them coming.

I don't really know, he says, and Will says well then, and then the girls are upon them, smelling of night air and sweat; the warmth of spinning around with their arms held high, styled hair now damp at the neck.

Let's go back in, Marley says, tugging on Rosie's hand.

I'm going to stay out for a bit, Rosie says.

Oh, come on, Marley says. Come and dance.

We just danced.

It's the last one!

I know, but.

She looks at Will, and then over at Tom. Marley pouts, grabs at Rosie's wrists.

One dance, Rosie says, eventually.

So Rosie dances, even though she does not want to. Her mind is elsewhere, outside on the steps with Will who stayed to light a cigarette, but years of loyalty to Marley and her sentiment for this school keep her in the pulsing, body-filled hall of students, with the grinding and the yelling and the slopped drinks and sticky floor.

It is strangely difficult to get away, even though no one is paying her any attention. She feels hemmed in, like what she wants and what she must do are two entirely separate things; that being here, with Marley and her friends, is only right, and there is some invisible fence that keeps it so.

When the burgers are brought out, people flock to the canteen for the cheap bread and ketchup, the heat of soft flesh in their mouths. She bumps into Josh by the napkins. Her twin is drenched in sweat, and there is something manic about him; he has drunk too much, despite not being old enough for the alcohol pass. It's become a game, she guesses; people feeding him more, the drunker he gets. Because it's funny, and innocent. And because Josh is both of those things.

She takes him to the courtyard, secluded now, all the couples relocated to the dance floor, emptying their lungs to Bon Jovi.

What a night, Josh says, as Rosie lowers him onto a bench.

Looks like you've had fun, she says.

So much fun, he says. Haven't you?

Sure.

Liar, he says, and he tries to ruffle her hair; misses, and ends up patting her on the ear. But you look pretty, Sis. In your dress.

They'd spent an agreeable hour in the shopping centre at the weekend, Josh picking colours and holding them up against her. That one, he'd said, as soon as he saw the blue. For your Lorelai Gilmore eyes.

His own are half closed now, which she supposes is a good thing.

You were meant to be driving us home, she reminds him.

I know, he groans. Whoops.

And then he laughs, and immediately falls asleep.

His mouth hangs open, his hair swept to the side, and Rosie wonders, not for the first time, what it will be like to live apart from him. When he is in Cambridge, and she, in Oxford or Durham or York. Wherever she ends up.

At precisely one minute past midnight, the music is cut and the hall lights are lifted. Students pour out into the courtyard, laughing and squealing; Josh wakes, and is immediately sick on his shoes.

Rosie groans. There's a fine in place for vomiting.

She tells him to get up, now, and hobbles with him to the back of the courtyard and past the tennis courts, away from the crowds and the teachers.

You're a pain, Josh, she says, as she half-supports, half-staggers beneath her brother's weight in her heels.

And you're the best person I know, Josh slurs. I'd think that even if you weren't my twin, you know.

That's very sweet, but you're still a pain.

I mean it, he says, dragging his feet. You see things,

Rosie-Roo. You know things, because you watch. All the important things.

He is talking nonsense, and she is barely listening. Subconsciously heading for the car park, because Will might still be there. Josh lumbers alongside her, pressing his head against hers.

You know, he says again.

I know, she says, though she has no idea what he's talking about.

Do you, he asks, and he sounds serious now. The moon is full, leaves a creamy light in the sky, and Rosie ignores him.

They pass the bike sheds and turn into the car park, where two girls are taking last-minute photographs of each other. A group of guys are smoking weed; she can smell the sweet, dank stench of it. Will, it seems, has long gone.

I'm going to be sick again, Josh informs her.

Brilliant, she says, and they pass the smokers in double time as she gets him off school property. When they are a safe distance away, she rests him against a lamppost, and he sinks his way to the ground.

I'll call Marley, Rosie says. See if her mum can drop us home.

Josh nods, and puts his face in his hands.

I have to tell you something, he says. Something I've decided.

Okay?

She is tapping the buttons on her phone, pulling Marley's name up on her screen.

Not decided, actually. You can't decide these things.

She hits the green call button, waits as it rings and rings.

You're not listening to me, says Josh, and he sounds angry, and still very drunk.

I'm trying to get us home, she says. After you were supposed to, remember?

You don't get it, Josh says. He mumbles something else
into his hands, then says he wants to go to bed.

I'm trying to get you there, Rosie says, as she tries Marley's
number for the second time. Once again, it rings out. And
once again, Josh is sick. She grimaces, lets him finish, then
says it looks like they're walking home.

*

His grandma's car is parked a few feet up the road, near the
school gym; the place she always waits on the odd occasion
she picks him up. Because it's raining, or she's on her way
home from the graveyard. He can tell when it's the latter,
from her fingernails, rimmed with dirt; from the slightest sag
of her mouth.

He gets in, waits as she completes her slow, shuddering
three-point turn and begins the descent down the hill. They
crawl past the school entrance, students emerging from the
lobby in groups, sweaty and sparkling with smeared make-up
and body glitter, an excess of rock-hard hair gel.

Did you have a good time? his gran asks him. Her hands are
fixed at ten and two, her eyes forward as the car rolls over the
many speed bumps.

Yeah, he says. He looks out of the window, at the white
limousine parked alongside the music block. Same as usual.
Bad music, bad burgers.

Then what's different?

What?

Something's different. In your voice.

He glances at her, feels the tug of an unwanted smile.

Nothing, he says.

79

Something, she says, but she drops it, and he looks back out of the window as she indicates, turns down a quiet avenue. She'll cut back through the residential roads rather than drive along the high street. It's a longer, darker route, but she doesn't like the roundabouts or the traffic lights; anything to avoid using the clutch more than she has to.

I could drive, he says. I only had a few sips of beer.

I thought you said you weren't having any?

I wasn't, he said, but then you said you'd come get me, so.

She exhales out of both nostrils. He is just about to say that's not a crime, is it, but stops himself at this particular choice of words, when he sees them stumbling along the pavement; that tall, gangling cartoon of a boy, and a young woman, her silk dress trailing along the pavement.

Stop, he says.

Excuse me?

Can you stop the car, please? Those are my friends, he says, nodding out of the window at the pair of them.

Friends, his grandmother repeats.

Let's just check they're okay, he says, and he winds the window down as his grandmother slows, the engine juddering in its low gear.

You guys okay? he asks, as they pull up beside them. Rosie has one arm around her brother's waist, her other gripping the wrist he's slung around her shoulders. She has to strain to peek over at Will, turns to the side in her heels.

Just about, she says.

What's up?

Someone overdid it, she says, and it's at that point that Josh sees the car and says, Will! Rosie – tugging on her hand – it's *Will*.

I can see that, Rosie says.

Hi Will, says Josh, raising his voice and waving.

Hi Josh, Will says back.

There is a suspended, comical moment of no more hellos, broken by his grandmother who asks in a too-loud whisper, is he a sandwich short?

Just drunk, Will tells her. That's Josh. From further maths.

Oh, she says, and she's suddenly interested. The one who needs your help, a lot of the time?

Yeah.

Who's going to study at Cambridge?

Yeah.

The boy who's going to Cambridge, who needs help from my grandson, she says, more to herself than to him. Will rolls his eyes, leans out of the car window.

He all right? he asks Rosie.

He will be, she says. He just needs some sleep.

Get in, he says. Then, as an afterthought, he turns back to his grandma. If that's cool?

She is looking at him strangely, but she nods, once, without words.

We'll drive you home, he says to Rosie.

That's really nice of you, she says, but he's been sick. Twice.

So he's unlikely to be sick again.

You don't know that.

This car's seen worse. Right, Gran?

Unfortunately, she says, and she leans forward, all the better to observe the two on the pavement. Will feels her assessing the situation, the risk involved, if any.

There's a plastic bag in the boot, she says. If you wouldn't mind.

Of course, Rosie says. Thank you.

Will helps heave Josh into the back seat, and Rosie opens the boot and comes back with an old shopping bag, tucks it between her brother's knees.

Any trace of vomit on these seats and you're walking, sonny, Will's gran says, peering at him in the rear-view mirror. Josh nods, his face pale as milk. His initial excitement at seeing Will has ebbed, replaced by a weary silence.

Rosie settles in beside her twin, clips their seat belts in place.

This is so nice of you, she says again.

Least I can do, after you put Will up in the snow, says his gran, and she lurches off in the car, clunking into second gear too late.

Will meets Rosie's eyes in the wing mirror for the shortest of seconds.

Did you have a good night, his grandma asks them, and Will sees her glance back at the girl she doesn't know. I didn't catch your name?

Rosie, she says. Rosemary.

That's pretty.

Thanks. I never liked it much. It reminds me of that rag doll on the canal boat.

There's nothing rag doll about you, his gran says, and Rosie smiles at her, and it is like the sun breaking through the trees. Will feels something move inside him then, if it hadn't already been shifting; like an anchor, catching in place.

The dance was good, Rosie says. Wasn't it, Will?

I already told her it was the same as always, he says.

There is a short pause as their eyes meet again, the engine humming, the dark houses melting past the windows.

It wasn't for me, Rosie says, and it is bold, in front of his grandma, and again, she is a complete and utter surprise to him. He takes his eyes from hers, watches the night passing in the wing mirror. Pavements and front lawns, stained saffron in the street lights.

*

Will's grandmother pulls up in front of her house, gold lights twinkling from their front hedges. Rosie can see the fir tree in the window, the faint glow from the fireplace glinting off the ornaments. Her parents have finally decorated for Christmas, a full four days before Christmas Eve.

What a beautiful tree, Will's gran says, as she parks alongside the kerb.

Thanks, says Rosie, even though it is nothing to do with her. Her father buys the tree each year, and her mother has a very specific arrangement for the decorations. She and Josh learned, fairly early on, that it was best not to interfere.

You spending Christmas at home? Will asks. The car has stopped, but it feels rude to get out so suddenly, and Josh is still quiet, seems comfortable.

Yes, she says. Mum always hosts. We have a party on Christmas Eve, and then a few family members stay over. It's nice. We eat a lot. Play games.

Descend into wine-fuelled arguments, she thinks, but doesn't say, because surely that's normal, for families at Christmas, and not something that needs to be shared.

Sounds like ours, Will says. Without the party.

Hey, says Rosie, you should come.

To the party?

Yeah! It's an open-door kind of thing. We have the neighbours popping in, family friends, even Marley comes sometimes. The food's good. We get these apple tarts from the bakery that I look forward to *all year*. So. Yeah. Just if you want, and you're not doing anything.

She tails off, embarrassed, suddenly, by her uncapped enthusiasm. She sees him glance at his grandma, who nods, a barely noticeable tilt of the head.

Maybe, he says.

And you must come to ours, his gran says.

83

There is a slightly puzzled silence, both Will and Rosie waiting on what she means. The light outside Rosie's front door flicks on at that moment; her mother must have seen the car through the window.

It's just the three of us on Christmas Day, his gran says. But I make enough to feed a busload.

That's true, Will says.

You'll have your own commitments, of course, his gran says. But if you want to join us for Christmas tea, well, you'd be more than welcome. Your brother, too. If he's conscious.

They all glance at Josh, who is asleep again, his head squashed against the window.

That's really kind of you, Rosie says, and the air in the car seems thick, too warm. It doesn't feel normal, to her, to be invited to something as intimate as Christmas Day at a near stranger's house. But it also feels special. Rare. More golden lights, glowing, inside her.

*

His gran parks on their drive and shuts off the engine. The car smells, faintly, of apples.

Are you going to tell me what that was about, he says, as she twists the key and removes it from the ignition.

I was about to ask you the same thing.

What? What did *I* do?

You're always so defensive, William.

You always make me feel like I need to be!

She chuckles, and it sounds like gravel in her throat.

Your friends, she says, with delicate emphasis.

What about them?

That's it. They're friends.

I'm not following.

Never, in all your eighteen years, Will, have I heard you refer to *anyone* as a friend. Even when you were at primary school. You certainly had them. But you never identified them as such.

You sure you're not just paying some weird Freudian attention to the language I use? he asks, and she wheeze-laughs again.

It was just nice, she says. And they seem like good kids.

They are, he says.

Both of them, she says, slyly.

Gran. Spit it out.

I'm saying nothing.

You're implying it.

I am, she says. And I liked her.

He feels suddenly gauche; brushes his palms down the legs of his jeans. The street is still and silent. His sister's light is on. She must be at her desk with her gel pens, doodling a plan for world domination.

I like her too, he says, and his voice is low.

So why not go to the party?

You know why.

No, I don't.

It's just not my thing, is it? Champagne and canapés. A girl's parents.

William White, she says, and her voice catches him hard, like the corner of a tabletop. Don't you dare.

What?

Don't miss out on something good, simply because it's different. I didn't raise you with thoughts like that in your head, did I?

No, he says.

Well, then. Go. Eat canapés and apple tarts. Fall for the nice girl, for once.

You just like that she's got no piercings.

I liked that she looked me in the eye when we spoke, she says. And that she did the same with you.

They sit there together, the way they have so many times before. His grandma is short and squat, but she has always felt so large, to him, especially in this car. Despite being three heads shorter than he is, she somehow takes up so much space, with her knitted jumpers and her unsaid thoughts.

Amber's awake, he says, eventually.

I know. Pushing her luck, that girl.

By writing in journals at midnight?

It all starts somewhere, she says, as she opens her car door. Next she'll be staying out late, sneaking sherry out the cupboard. Loitering in car parks and getting arrested for it.

Too soon? she asks, when Will says nothing. He shrugs. Finds that words still elude him about that night, or that time in his life, in general.

He wasn't right.

He sees that now.

Things had been building ever since his mother left – after she walked out and never came back. Things that he squashed into the thin lines between what hurt and what didn't, just so he could get through the day.

He loved his grandparents. They were always the good ones, anyway, always had the hot meals and fresh sheets and a TV guide which meant he knew when the cowboy films were on. So he didn't miss her, really. Didn't even wonder about her, after so many years of nothing. After the birthday cards and the phone calls dwindled and then stopped.

But things began to get blurry after he started secondary school. He would spend days wading through what felt like deep water, everything in slow motion, and it was only alcohol, a shot of something to sharpen his wits, that could make him feel any better.

He doesn't know how he first discovered this.

Maybe it was his grandfather leaving out his nightly glass of whisky. Maybe he stumbled across the drinks cabinet, simply because he was bored. All he knew was that if he wasn't sleeping, or he felt weighted down, a swig of something grown-up would soon make everything right.

He was twelve years old, at the time.

He drank more. Made some bad friends, bad choices.

By thirteen, he was skipping school and staying out for days and nights at a time, with groups of guys much older than him, into much harder stuff and with much harder pasts than his own. He found that helped with the pain, too. The danger of it. The knife edge he walked, every night he was with them, with their cigarettes and their packets of powder and their proclivity for theft. He stole things, too, when they asked him to. When the zip of alcohol no longer sufficed, and that jolt of energy – that *aliveness* – had to be found in other ways.

He did and saw things that he no longer thinks about.

Things he's buried good and deep.

But that night in the car park – the one his grandma likes to joke about, to pretend it's in the past and not something she is deeply ashamed of him for – that is different.

It's like a dirty, pointed object that he carries beneath his skin; a splinter, or an ingrown toenail.

Something he can pull out and turn over in his hands, if and when he feels the need.

*

Rosie takes Josh a glass of orange juice and some buttered toast, taps on his door with her foot. Inside, she sees the heap of him beneath his duvet, smells the bad teenage boy breath as she crosses the threshold.

She puts his breakfast down, opens the curtains and he grumbles and says no, please, and she says yes, that he's going to be late for school.

Can't do school, he says. Too ill.

I don't think hungover counts as ill, Rosie says.

Last day doesn't count, Josh huffs. We'll just sit around watching Christmas films.

While she knows this to be true, Rosie picks up a triangle of toast and holds it out, trying to tempt him nonetheless.

Is Mum home? he asks.

No. She's at the office.

And Dad?

Finishes at two. He said he'd try to get home early.

Then I'm staying right here, says Josh, and he burrows back beneath the bedclothes, leaves his toast untouched on the side.

Josh, Rosie says.

Mmm?

What's going on? You never drink like that. You never want to skip school.

First time for everything, he says, his voice muffled.

She looks at the mound of him, the wrinkles on his sheets.

You're okay, though, she says, and there is a long, musty pause before he says yes, and so she rises, leaves him to sleep. Takes a slice of toast on her way out.

five

Christmas Eve arrives lightly misted, all beryl sky and frost-covered lawns, a fog that burns off like steam. Rosie's mother has asked her to pick up the tarts, like always, so she gets dressed early, pulls on her coat from the wardrobe. Josh's room is silent, as though he's still asleep. He's been sleeping late every day, since the dance.

Happy Christmas Eve, she says to her parents in the kitchen. College carols ease quietly from the stereo, and there is a pot of coffee on the table, the smell of leeks, creaming, on the hob. Her mother is already dressed, looping napkin rings around the linen.

Happy Christmas, darling, she says, and beams at her, and Rosie holds that, for a moment, before she kisses her father good morning. He gives her the money she needs, and her mother tells her to hurry back, that breakfast is at nine.

Outside, all is still.

Early morning sun, pure and cold and alpine.

She walks to the bakery and she picks up their order, then pauses at the corner shop and buys a bouquet of fresh flowers; reds and greens, splayed like branches from the forest. She thinks about the lighthouse, the view of the sea on a morning like this. She wonders if Will is awake, and running. He has not texted her since his grandmother drove them home. Not confirmed whether he's coming, tonight.

She is supposed to head straight home for her mother's carefully planned spread, but her watch tells her she could make it, and so she heads for the beach. Puts the cake box down on the sand with the flowers, and removes her shoes, tucking her socks against the soles.

There is a single runner on the shore.

One brave, crazy person, swimming in a wetsuit and cap.

She walks down to the water and steps in, inhaling at the rush over her toes, and she has one of those rare moments of clarity where everything feels real and right and untroubled, and the world is open, and there is relief, in her bones, for a while.

On the way home, she decides to text him first.

Merry Christmas (Eve), she types. I have the apple tarts.

Winking face: a semi colon, end bracket. Too much, she thinks, and deletes, before she adds it again, and hits send.

*

Will lifts the brass ring on the blue door, and knocks.

Rosie's dad answers. He is a tall man with thinning hair, wearing a striped shirt with an open collar. Do I know you, he asks, and before Will can answer he laughs fully at his own question and steps back to let him in, says the young ones were in the dining room, last time he saw them. He takes Will's coat, tells him to have fun, then leaves him in the hall, humming as he goes.

Will stands there, for a moment. It is like he has stepped into the film that Amber had been watching when he'd left. Garlands wind up the bannisters, all foliage and twinkling lights, not a shred of tinsel in sight. Everything looks clean and shiny. He can see through to the dining table from here, to a spread of miniature food on platters, guests glimmering in the turned-down lights with golden bubbles in their flutes.

He can't see his friends, so he heads for the food. Picks up a glass of something as he does so, and comes face to face with Mrs Winters. She is wearing a flattering black dress, her hair scraped into a bun. Square shoulders, frown lines. Like a prima ballerina.

Will, she says, and smiles. She has sharp teeth, he thinks; but then, so does he.

Hi Mrs Winters, he says. Thanks for the invite.

I'm not sure I invited you, she says.

Rosie did, he explains, and she says yes, she knows, and tells him to have a good time, then, that there's plenty to eat and drink, although it looks like he's already found the champagne. She leaves before he can retort, before he can apologise or drink it pointedly in front of her; he is not sure which way he'd have gone.

He takes a breadstick and moves into the living room, where, thankfully, he finds them: Josh and Rosie, sitting on the piano stool, their shoulders pressed together. She is in a velvet dress. Drop earrings sparkling in the tree lights.

Her cheeks are flushed, and she is laughing. Goes from serious to joyful, so fast. Then her eyes catch his, recognition crossing her face, and he heads towards her through the tangle of people. Josh is talking to someone on his other side, so they have two short seconds alone.

Hey, he says.

You came, she says.

He's about to answer when Josh turns and sees him standing there, his face splitting wide open in delight, like a child's.

Will!

Hey, man.

What're *you* doing here?

Your sister invited me, he says, after the shortest pause.

Did she, now, Josh asks, and he looks between them, knocks Rosie's knee with his own.

What, Rosie says, and she turns a deep red. Will looks away, runs his tongue along his bottom lip. Takes a large mouthful from his glass.

What you drinking? Josh asks him.

Not my usual, Will says, and Josh jumps up, says he'll get Coke, or beer, that there's pale ale in the fridge.

That'd be great, Will says, thinking it's fine, for one night, to have a few. Josh beams and heads through the crowd.

Another great dress, he says to Rosie, taking Josh's place beside her.

Oh, she says. Thank you.

Sorry I didn't tell you I was coming, he says. He takes another mouthful of champagne, even though he hates the stuff; the way it prickles at the back of his nose.

That's okay, she says. I like suspense.

Really?

No.

They both laugh, then, and he offers her his flute, and she goes to say no, he thinks, for the briefest of seconds, but then something changes and she takes it from him, sips at the place where his lips were.

Sparkly, she says.

Like this house, Will says. It's quite a party you throw.

It's all Mum, really.

You don't pitch in?

A little, she says. Sometimes. But she likes things a certain way.

Like mother like daughter, then.

It is a joke; a gentle attempt at teasing, but Rosie says nothing. Drains the rest of the champagne, then says yeah. She supposes so.

They both watch the room. Women in sequins and satin. Men belly-laughing, all groomed beards and buttoned cuffs and red shiny foreheads.

So are you gonna show me these apple tarts, then? Will asks her.

Have you had dinner?

Nope.

Then let's get a plate. Apple tarts come after.

How come?

Because they're dessert.

And?

You eat dessert after dinner.

Says who?

. . . the world?

Nobody's policing it, are they?

She turns to him, and her eyes are creased with humour, and he feels his insides contract with something other than desire. He likes it, and it scares him.

You want apple tarts first, then salmon or pork loin later?

I want the wildest thing you can come up with, Will tells her.

Rosie shows her tongue as she smiles, curls it ever so slightly in thought.

The wildest thing at my mother's party, she says. That's hard.

You're a creative person, aren't you?

Dessert first is good, she says.

You can't have that one. That's mine.

You're so bossy, she says.

I reckon you're bossier, he says, and she shifts back to face the room, makes an *ummm* sound, her thigh now touching his.

He doesn't hear what she says next because of this.

Will? she says.

Yeah?

How about *just* dessert.

He looks into her face. Counts the freckles, like nutmeg, dusted across her nose.

Just dessert, he repeats. You wouldn't.

Just apple tarts, she says. No, no, wait. *All* the apple tarts.

You've crossed a line, he says, and she laughs again, and that feeling is back, consumes him like the alcohol used to. Seeping everywhere, all over him.

They take the entire plate of apple tarts – puffs, really, the size of plums – and navigate their way to the conservatory. Rosie stops to offer the plate to guests, then makes it to the back door and slips outside. Will follows her, as planned, soon afterwards.

The garden is long and narrow; bigger than his, because they're on the edge of town. It stretches so far back that he can't see the end of it; only the grass dissolving into shadow, hedgerows swallowed by the sky.

Rosie leads him to a square of decking framed by trellis, more lights twirled along the wood. There is a small table and four chairs, and they sit down, the December air sharp on their skin.

We can't keep doing this, Will says.

Doing what?

Meeting only in the freezing cold, or in dingy old music rooms.

Or the middle of the night in kitchens, she says.

Exactly. Can't I just take you out like a normal person?

Nope. I've got my exams, remember?

You've got exams, yeah, he says. And yet here we are. With apple tarts.

He gestures to the tray in front of them.

Together, he adds.

All rules are off at Christmas, she says, picking up a pastry.

I thought there were no rules?

Just eat an apple tart, will you?

She takes another off the platter and holds it out towards him. He thinks, for a second, about eating it straight from her fingers. Wonders what she'd do, if he did.

They really are amazing, she says.

You've hyped them up, you know.

I know.

And things are rarely deserving of such hype.

I disagree, she says. The Beatles. Led Zeppelin. Beyoncé.

That's an eclectic taste in music.

Mozart, she continues, ticking them off on her fingers. Monet. Paris. Peanut butter.

Smooth or crunchy?

Always crunchy.

See, now I trust you a little more on the tarts, Will says, and he takes it from her and bites into it.

The pastry flakes as it should, the apple silk-soft between his teeth. Fruit jam, melting into the lightest layer of custard. He tastes cinnamon, and ginger. The nutmeg of her freckles.

So? she asks.

I'll need another, to make sure.

You loved it.

Let's test again.

Just say you loved it!

It's clearly an important matter to you, Will says, lifting another off the plate. And I want to make sure I give a thoroughly researched answer.

Rosie laughs then, and bites into her own. Lets out a tiny, beautiful noise.

He shivers at that sound.

———

They stay outside as long as they can stand it; four and a half apple tarts each, cold hands, numb toes.

I kind of like it, Rosie says, when they compare their loss of feeling. When there's a warm house right there, and I know we can just step inside.

It's why I like cold showers, Will says, as she stands, picks up the near-empty plate.

God, really?

It's not as bad as it sounds, he says. You get used to it.

How did you even discover that, though? What made you think, one day, I'll just turn this cold and see how it feels?

He follows her back to the house, glad she can't see his face.

We lost hot water one weekend, he says. Boiler broke.

Oh, she says. Then I guess that makes sense.

He says yeah, but he hasn't told her the truth. Hasn't told her that he just stopped feeling, altogether, for an entire month of his life. That he tried some things. Ice-cold showers, the least extreme.

Inside, someone is playing carols on the piano, and the dining room is deserted. The table looks like it's been ravaged by seagulls, crusts of bread left on plates, sauce stained onto the tablecloth. Will grabs a sausage roll while Rosie puts down the plate of remaining tarts, positions it in the same spot as before.

Who's playing, he asks, tipping his head towards the music.

That'll be Dad, she says. He's the one that got me into the piano. Sort of.

You're better, I'm guessing.

He just plays for fun, Rosie says, with a shrug.

And you don't?

I play because I have to, she says. Because I don't feel okay if I don't.

She fingers the linen of the table cloth as she speaks.

Sorry, she says. Marley says I can be a bit intense, sometimes.

He takes her hand then, without thinking, sees that she has a constellation of freckles here, too. Her fingers fold into his own, and he has pulled her, gently, towards him, when Josh walks in and says oh.

Rosie steps back, like she's been burned, just as Will looks up and sees something cross Josh's face.

Hi, he says, but Josh doesn't say it back. He has the blurry look of someone who's been drinking, again. Not quite as much as before, but enough to make him different. Magnified.

Where on earth have you been, he asks.

We've been around, Rosie says. You must have just . . . lost us.

She gives a tiny smile, but Josh just stares at them both. There is a beer in his hand. He puts it down on the side and says, without looking at his sister, that their mum was asking for her. That she wants her to play for the guests now.

Rosie nods.

Josh, she says. Are you –

But he's already left the room.

Well, I guess I should, she says, gesturing towards the music.

Sure, Will says.

Come listen, she says, and he says that he will, once he's eaten something without sugar in it.

She smiles at him, and lingers, as if she's going to say more. But then she slips out without a word, and Will turns to what's left of the sandwiches. He picks one up and peels the bread apart.

Pâté, a voice informs him. Mrs Winters is standing in the doorway, a freshly poured flute in her hand.

What kind, he asks.

Wild boar, she says. Or Brussels, maybe. There were two.

Course there were, he thinks, and he takes a bite, chews it slowly in front of her. She looks remarkably neat for the late hour. Like no time has passed since she put up her hair and applied her make-up, all thick lines and bronze tones and straight edges.

Where are the twins? she asks him.

Roe went to play piano, he says. And Josh –

Roe?

There is a tight smile on her lips. The champagne hisses in her glass.

Rosie, he says, with a shrug.

You like my daughter, then, she says.

Will leans against the table and waits. Not sure if it's a question. If it's any of her business. He has the impression that this woman is used to pulling justifications out of people, and he has none for her.

She's a good girl, she says, and he says he knows.

You're not playing some kind of game, are you, she asks.

What sort of game?

The sort guys like you play, Will. Let's be real here. Let's be adults.

Guys like me?

You're not dating her for a dare, or something?

I'm not dating her, full stop, he says, and his voice is curt, and his heart has turned to rock. The pâté is thick and oily along the roof of his mouth. He hates it.

Ah-ha, she says. But you plan to?

I plan to do only what Rosie wants, he says, and she smiles properly, then, and takes a sip from her flute. Her lipstick is dark red and does not smudge, even as she drinks.

Well, then, she says. That's all I wanted to hear.

The amateur piano playing has stopped.

Merry Christmas, then, he says.

Yes. Merry Christmas, Will, Mrs Winters says, her eyes not leaving his face.

The piano starts up again, and it is different, and softer, and he knows that it must be Rosie playing now. Her mother leaves the room to watch, and he is left with the sandwiches and the lukewarm blinis, a mushroom-rich taste in his mouth.

*

Rosie loses herself in the songs she has written, purely for tonight.

She always starts writing in the autumn, inspired by the smallest things. Pink-footed geese, flown home for the winter. The school cleaner, with her scarred hands, the peeled laminate of her name badge.

They smoke like coals inside her, for a while. She has them written by November. Then reveals them, first heard, on the piano at her mother's party, same as she's always done, same, she's sure, as she always will.

And people listen. Things go quiet; the chatter dies. Her hands move over the keys like she's blind and tracing braille; effortless and a part of her. And when she finishes, there is applause. The clock on the mantelpiece reads eleven, and her father booms Merry Christmas, and there are chinked glasses and air kisses and thank yous and goodnights.

Tonight, after she's done, she turns on her stool and watches as the guests leave. Waits, for her twin brother, or for Will, but neither of them shows.

When everyone has gone and the house is in darkness, when she is in her pyjamas and her teeth are brushed and she has checked her phone for the twentieth time, Rosie turns off her bedside lamp.

She lies there for all of three minutes, her heart thrumming. There is an anvil on her chest, and it forces her out of bed, into her brother's room.

Josh, she whispers.

He waits, as though he's not going to answer. But then he opens his duvet and she gets in beside him. It is bodily warm, and she presses her bare feet into his.

Jesus, he says, nudging her away. Your feet are like ice.

Sorry, she says, and something in her can't quite believe that she is apologising, for this, when he missed her playing — when he's never missed it, before.

Are you okay, she asks, after he says nothing more.

Yeah, he says, into the dark.

You don't seem it.

Go to sleep, Rosie.

He turns away from her, then, but he doesn't ask her to leave. She stares up at his ceiling and then turns away herself, so their backs are pressed together, warm and solid and unmoving.

*

Will wakes, close to 5 a.m.

He feels sick with sugar and champagne. Light-headed, with everything else.

He had listened to Rosie playing, from his place by the dining table. Songs that flowed like seawater from one verse to another. Songs he didn't recognise, and so knew they must be hers.

He did not know what to say to her, about the music.

And so he left.

Easier, that way. Before he ruined things, like he always seems to.

He gets up, though it is still dark, puts on his trainers and leaves the house. It is cuttingly cold outside, but he heats up as he jogs along the street, sticking to the pavements for the lamplight.

He focuses on his breath, the thud of his feet.

Finds himself thinking about his mother.

She liked Christmas. She didn't like a lot of things, but Christmas morning was different, gave her some kind of supple edge. Permission to slow down, to be around instead of out, doing whatever it was that she did. Before Amber was born, when it was just the two of them, she would buy him special cereal, the expensive, branded sort, and they'd eat it in bed out of the box, watching cartoons on the TV.

She liked the Disney ones. Not Looney Tunes. Too loud, she said. Too crazed.

Then they'd head to his grandma's for mid-morning, and she'd sit on the sofa and drink orange juice and it would be the one day of the year when nobody argued, when they'd eat and open a few gifts and maybe walk to the park with his grandpa.

No regrets, she would say, when they'd chink their glasses at dinner, and they'd all repeat her words, even Will, who was only young, and had no idea what regret was.

When Amber was born, though, things changed. They started spending Christmas Eve, and night, and morning, at his grandparents' place, without his mother, and their shared cereal became a thing of the past. Spending nights at home did, too, but he was never told why, and so he never asked.

He remembers her snowflake earrings.

Dangly, chipped things she got out of a Christmas cracker one time, and would wear every year, without fail.

He wonders if she still has them. What she might look like now.

Runs faster, until his lungs hurt.

Merry Christmas, William, his grandmother says when he comes down later that morning, showered, dressed and thirsty.

You too, he says, and he pours himself a pint glass of water, drinks it standing at the sink.

That was an early one, even for you, she says, as she peers in the oven, her bird already roasting. The kitchen smells of meat juices and stock.

Woke up at five, he says. Couldn't sleep.

How was your night?

Good, he says. Decent food.

I'm glad, she says, and she doesn't ask anything more, though he's aware that she's playing him. Because if she doesn't ask questions, he'll end up telling her, eventually. He always does.

I really like her, Gran, he says. He pours himself a cup of tea from the pot on the side. Adds one sugar cube, and then another.

That much is clear, she says, and she slips off her oven mitts, takes her own mug from the counter and faces him. He takes a sip of his tea, which is strong and black and sweet.

I don't have time for girls, he says.

Since *when*? his grandma asks.

As in, properly, he says. I've got my bike, and my travel plans, you know? And she's going to uni in the autumn.

He takes another mouthful of tea. His heart beats slowly in his ears.

She told me I have to wait til her exams are over. Well. *I* told her I'd wait. I don't really know why. I don't, you know . . . want to care.

His grandmother peers at him over her mug, and for once, he can't read her expression. Her eyes are crinkled, like dates. Dark as treacle.

Perhaps you have no time for girls, she says. But you have time for *the* girl.

He wants to roll his eyes at her. Finds that he can't.

You'll figure it out, lad, she says, turning back to the stove. Is she coming to tea, later?

I don't actually know, he says. She didn't say.

Well, she says. Let's see, shall we.

Let's see, he says.

*

Rosie sees his text, late in the day, wishing her a Merry Christmas. Saying he loved the apple tarts. She stares at it, for all of three seconds, then asks her mother if she can go to Marley's.

Now? her mum asks, her eyes glassy with wine. There is classical music playing from their old gramophone, her uncle and father playing cards in the armchairs by the window. Her baby cousin is crawling along the carpet, her aunt hovering above her.

I wouldn't normally ask, Rosie says. It's just she's got this new karaoke game, and Josh is still in bed, so . . .

Karaoke?

SingStar, she says. She got the new one for Christmas.

You girls, she says. You're just a little musical duo, aren't you?

Yep, Rosie says, her stomach winding in on itself, because she is lying, and she's not even sure that she needs to. But she cannot bring herself to tell the truth about this. About him. Not yet.

As long as you don't outstay your welcome, her mum says. Her parents don't mind?

They said it was fine.

Take something, then, she says. One of the bottles in the wine fridge. Or that stollen we never opened? Don't go empty-handed.

I would never, Rosie says, and her mother smiles at her, the symphony in the background lulling her eyes to a slow blink.

Rosie, she says, as Rosie turns to go.

Yes?

Your piano, last night.

Yes.

It was sublime, she says, and Rosie is filled up with those words, and her doubt about tonight, and the self-loathing from the lies, all of it lifts, for a moment, like steam from a cup into air.

She knocks on Josh's door before she leaves. She has taken her hair out of its plaits, letting it fall past her shoulders. Changed out of her dinner dress into jeans, and a soft blouse she would want to be touched in.

Not that she is expecting to be touched, at Will's grand-mother's house.

But she wants to look good. To feel it.

To have him look at her the way he did at the winter dance, like he wanted to drink the words from her mouth.

When Josh doesn't answer, she pushes his door open so the light from the hall falls in stripes across the floorboards. His curtains are closed. He's playing indie music, soft and low, from his computer speakers.

Josh, she says.

He doesn't answer, but she knows he isn't asleep.

You feeling any better? she asks him. He'd had a stomach ache all day; wasn't his usual self when they traded gifts or sat down to Christmas lunch; wouldn't meet her eyes when she asked him to pass the gravy.

I'm going out, she says.

He remains silent, but she senses a shift in his attention.

To Marley's, she says, using her fingers as air quotes. If anyone asks.

Her brother raises his head off his pillow; she sees that his eyes are wet.

Josh, she says, and her voice has changed. Talk to me.

And it is her twin voice; her levelled, serious, I-am-entirely-yours voice, which finally seems to get through. He shuffles to a seated position, opening the duvet as if in invitation. Rosie shuts the door and flicks on his lamp and sits, cross-legged, beside him, so that they're both staring at the wall.

There is something, Josh says, and Rosie says she knows.

Are you okay? she asks. Are you really sick?

No, he says.

Is it uni? Do you not want to go to Cambridge any more? Or have you just fallen behind? I can help you –

It's none of those things, he says, so she falls silent, gives him time.

What's going on with you and Will, he asks her, as if to fill the gap that he needs; some filler, while he finds a way forward. She passes her palm over his duvet cover, an ombré in navy blue.

Nothing, she says.

Doesn't seem like it, he says.

How does it seem?

It seems like I couldn't find you both for an hour last night, he says. And then when I *did* find you, you lied about it. Made out you didn't want privacy, even though you so blatantly did, standing so close, like that.

Rosie blows the air out of her mouth.

I know, she says. God, I'm sorry. I didn't mean to do that.

So then?

So what?

Are you going to tell me the truth?

She thinks he is being overly standoffish with her, for a relatively inoffensive crime. She didn't think he'd care so much about her potentially liking his friend. But perhaps he thinks more happened than it did; perhaps he's hurt that she's not told him all the details, and this is what has stung. That, during their last Christmas together, before they go away and live apart and become different versions of themselves, it seems like she's keeping secrets. And they have never kept secrets. Ever.

Okay, she says. We hung out, a bit. Nothing happened, I promise you. Nothing is happening. But I like him. And maybe he likes me, too. I don't know.

Another lie, she thinks, and so she corrects herself.

He asked me to meet him one night, she says. At the lighthouse. And we talked, for a while, and it was nice. And he does like me, he's sort of made that clear, I think.

Josh is not reacting; not looking at her. He keeps his eyes ahead.

So yeah, Rosie says. It's not going anywhere, Josh. Definitely not before our exams; I said that to him already. So you don't need to worry, he can still coach you in maths. And who knows, by the summer he'll probably be over it, you know? So it might not ever get to a place where it's awkward or anything.

She keeps talking, because she is not sure what is keeping him so silent, and the more she talks the more she thinks she is realising what it could be, what she has always suspected, because she knows him, all of him, down to his cells and his movements and his moods, but he's never said, never shared, and so she keeps saying things to give him time, to prolong this moment where everything feels like it did last night, when she thought he was merely cross about being left out.

It's all fine, she says, because she so desperately wants it to be.

Josh nods, once, and slowly. He moves his palms down towards his knees, as if he's stretching. Exhaling as he does so.

Here's the thing, he says.

Rosie waits. The classical music from downstairs changes track; there is a pause, then a new song starts up, floats towards them up the staircase.

That's all great, he says. For you. Really.

Thanks, she says, because she's so relieved, so wildly and suddenly relieved, that this is all he has said.

It's just, I like him too.

I know you do. But I promise it won't be weird, if things go wrong. You guys can still be —

No, Rosie. I like him too.

There is a silence, their heartbeats sounding as one. It is like something clicks, even as the room slows; like shadows shifting to light on the floorboards. Waking to a day she'd been waiting for.

Oh, she says.

Yeah.

He is still not looking at her. He is studying his hands now, the whitlows beside his fingernails.

Josh, she says. Her voice a breath.

I know, he says. Shocker.

And then he begins to cry, great, lurching sobs she has never heard come from him in all her life, and he reaches his arms out for her and she holds him, like that, with the notes of Whitacre drifting up the stairs, little trees and green forests and so many tears, like the salt from the sea on her shirt. A shirt she had chosen for its softness, minutes before, like that mattered, in any way, at all.

six

School starts up again, too soon. The paper chains from December are still dangling in the windows, scissor-cut snowflakes stuck to the glass.

Will sits through form class and woodwork and takes his free period in the library with his mates, not studying, not keeping it down, not doing any of the things the posters on the walls ask them to do. The librarian huffs at them from her desk.

He did not hear from Rosie after the party. He spent the rest of the Christmas break running, for miles, and faster than usual. Riding his motorbike, accelerating hard, taking corners lower than he should.

When the bell rings to signal the end of lunch, he makes his way to maths.

He's worried about seeing Josh again.

It's no coincidence, in Will's mind, that he found them together in the dining room, seemed oddly troubled by this, and that Rosie then stopped messaging. That clearly, Josh had a problem with it, and Will's not entirely surprised, because he knows a lot of guys, and he's pretty sure that despite their banter and semblance of mutual respect, none of them would want him dating their sisters.

A small, stifled part of him thought that maybe Josh was

different. That he knew Will wasn't the guy everyone thinks he is. He feels irritated, but also kind of bad about it. Isn't sure what to say while they share a desk for the next hour.

But Josh is not there.

It is just Will and Mr Brookman, who actually stays in the classroom for once, running through all the topics that could come up in the exam. Asking him what he wants refresher lessons on this term, as if it's an important question; as if it'll make one bit of difference to anything.

That night is his first shift back at the garage. He sweeps the floor, fits some brake cables, and then rides home on his motorbike, the air slicing past his face like sheet metal.

On the nights that he works, his gran leaves his dinner warming in the oven. She is often reading in her room by the time he's home, early to bed in the winter. But tonight, she is downstairs. Sitting at the table and reading the local paper, Dave curled at the side of her chair.

You're up late, he says.

I guess I am, she says.

How come, he asks her, as he eases his bowl out of the oven. He can just about touch it, if he moves fast. He slides it onto the table, grabs a fork and slumps into a chair.

My hips hurt, his grandmother says. Old age, I suppose.

He takes a forkful of food, looks at her as he chews.

You're not old, he says.

I'm getting there, I'm afraid.

Sixty is the new fifty, he says, and she chuckles, says she was sixty almost seven years ago now, remember?

Will blinks. He can't believe that much time has passed since her sixtieth. There were balloons, and an ice-cream cake, and his grandpa was still alive.

D'you miss him? she asks, as if reading his mind. He has a mouthful of hot potato, and it burns his throat as he swallows.

I don't really think about it, he says.

She raises her eyes to his.

You do, though, he says. Obviously.

Every hour, she says, and he stops eating, at this. She folds the newspaper in half, sets it aside.

But that's the sign of a good marriage, I think, she says.

I'll say.

There is a short silence, just the sound of his own chewing, the buzz from the light bulbs above them.

Speaking of which, she says, and he braces himself.

What's happening with your love life?

Not a lot, Gran.

Well, that much is obvious.

He shrugs, wondering if all teenage guys are subjected to such scrutiny from their grandmothers, and is about to say so, when she asks him what happened, that night at the party.

Nothing, he says.

Nothing, she repeats.

Nope.

Because you seemed high as a kite when you got back. And you've been a grumpy sod ever since Rosie didn't show up on Christmas Day.

Thanks a lot.

Just telling you how I see it, lad.

He picks up his fork again, nudges his dinner round the bowl.

She just never got in touch, he says.

His grandma eyes him. Says that's a shame, but it happens.

I know, he says. I don't care.

Oh, Will, she says, and she laughs, which he thinks is completely unfair, considering. I can't have you moping around like this. Going out like you've got hell to pay, coming back with a face like thunder. Let's do something about this, shall we?

I can't do anything about it, he says.

Nonsense, she says. You always can.

This is just what being a teenager is, he says, spearing a potato too violently, so the prongs clang against the bowl. You win some, you lose some.

I remember, she says. And I also remember, if I wanted something – even if it was just an answer – I would go out and get it.

Their clock chimes its cuckoo song from the front room. Will eats the potato, something building inside him.

It doesn't just apply to teenagers, she says, after a while. My own mum used to say, you get what you ask for, and you land what you look for.

So you went looking for this life, did you, Will asks her.

It is a single sentence, but the undertone is enough. His grandmother sits back in her chair.

I treasure this life I made, yes, she says.

Will spews some air out of his mouth. Puts down his fork.

I'm going to bed, he says, and she says fine, and he climbs the stairs, burning, all over. Because he wants more. Because he doesn't want to sit in a house with old carpets and someone else's kids and a sad little routine where all the days look the same, and he hates that he was her reason for that, and he won't go looking for something he wants when he doesn't know what that is, yet, exactly, when all he knows is it's not this.

That night, he types out a text to Rosie. It is half three in the morning, the same time they parted ways in her kitchen that time, and he is awake, and seething.

Where have you been? he types out, then deletes.

Lighthouse tomorrow, he tries, instead. At five.

And he presses send.

*

Rosie runs on the treadmill until her sides feel like they could tear open.

She has gained weight over Christmas. Like everyone, she's sure. But it hangs around her neck like a task she needs to get on top of; a mistake she's made that needs rectifying.

And as she runs, her mind is full. Not with revision and homework and music, but her twin brother, and how much he cried, and how he's barely spoken to her since.

She turns up the speed on the machine. All her feelings blazing in her limbs, calories shedding off her like skin.

The lighthouse seems lonelier than before. She remembers the sunset from last time, the neon streaks of the sky. Tonight, all is grey and flat. A seagull picks at something dead on the shore.

She is freezing. The sweat from the treadmill has dried on her skin, and she shivers beneath her jacket.

Will shows up soon after her, in his own running gear, his hair damp with sweat, but his cheeks barely flushed.

I go so red when I run, is the first thing she says to him. And you look like you just stepped out of an Adidas advert.

Going red is healthy, he says, leaning on the railing beside her. I'm just pasty because of the cigarettes. And 'cause I drink a lot of Coke.

Is that right, she says, and she curses herself for starting it like this; for saying these irrelevant things.

Thanks for coming, he says.

Sure, she says. I'm sorry for, you know. Going silent.

It's okay, he says, but he's looking at her like it's not.

I just can't do this, she tells him.

This again? he asks.

No, seriously, Rosie says, and she shakes her head, hard, as if to rid herself of her own hair, strands of which are blowing across her face. I don't know what we've been doing, Will. Being friends, really, more than anything. And that's great. That's all we should be, I think.

He keeps looking at her. His mouth has set. His stubble has grown longer since Christmas Eve.

Why? he asks.

Different worlds, she shrugs. Different agendas.

I don't have an agenda, he says.

You know what I mean.

I really don't, Roe.

She is going to have to do it; going to have to lie, just to stop the questions, to turn off this tap they've both been drinking from, for weeks.

I just don't like you in that way, she says. I'm sorry.

He looks so surprised, for a moment, that she almost laughs; doubts he has been turned down before. But she hates saying it, hates swallowing all the things she really wants to say. It's for the best, she reminds herself. It's the right thing.

The wind is brash and batters their legs; Rosie's hair still flecks across her face and neck, and the air smells of that heavy, weighted smell that comes before the rain. There is a special word for it, she knows. Or perhaps that's for after it rains; she can't remember. Will has looked away from her, out towards the sea, but then he steps forward and his eyes latch on to hers. Storm-grey on blue. And then he takes her face in his hands and says just one, enquiring word.

Seriously?

Rosie doesn't move. She can't. And his eyes scan her own, to check that it's okay, that she was lying, just now, and then he's kissing her and she forgets that she's cold, that she came here to end it, because she is thawing, all over, and his hands are in her hair, tracing the tops of her ears, and she can't think of anything except this, and how this is what a first kiss should be, and how no one has ever touched her neck, like this, before.

Everything alight.

Wildfires, inside of her, with the sea and the trees and the damp air, things softening and flaring in a moment that lasts, and lasts, and is over.

Then he stands back, and takes his hands from her face.

Didn't think so, he says, and she tells him he's unbearable, and he laughs. Leans his forehead against hers.

They leave the seafront because of the wind; trace Will's footsteps back through the forest, which shelters them from the rain.

They are talking about albums; the ones they got for Christmas, which seems too normal, after what just happened at the beach; too polite, somewhat shy. They mention Bright Eyes and The Shins. Mazzy Star, who Rosie treasures like sleep, and whom Will has never heard of.

He is walking in front of her, his back streaked with sweat from his run. Rosie has things to say, and things she can't, so she just follows him down the path, silent except for when he asks her a direct question.

She keeps her answers short, basic.

He seems happy and talkative, looks even taller than before. And she is filled up with everything, butterflies and cravings and the thing that just happened.

But her throat is tight.

She wants nothing more than to run home, now, in her tired

trainers, to tell her twin brother all about it. And she keeps thinking how she can't.

Roe? Will stops walking.

Hm?

I asked what you're doing for dinner tomorrow.

Oh. I'm not sure.

I think my gran feels like she missed out, not meeting you properly at Christmas.

Okay.

So d'you want to come over? She's a good cook.

I'm sure she is.

Roe?

Yeah?

What's up? You look all freaked out.

He has turned around to face her, and the trees are tall behind him, the smell of pine and soil and darkness descending all around. She takes a step back.

I came here to end things, she reminds him.

Because of your exams, he says.

And because of some other stuff, too, she says. It's just . . . not right.

That wasn't right? Will asks, and he jerks his head towards the beach. Rosie bites the inside of her cheek. Tells him no. It's very nice, and she's flattered, but it's just not the right time, for her.

We agreed that already, he says. And I told you I'd wait.

Inviting me to dinner is not waiting, she says.

Well, fine, he says. Come to dinner in May. Or June. Whenever the hell your exams end.

Will, she says.

What?

Don't do that. Don't get angry. I've said all this from the beginning.

And you kissed me back, just now, he says. And if I remember rightly, *you* invited *me* to your fancy Christmas party. Don't make me feel like I'm the one confusing things here.

I never said you were —

Can you just tell me what the actual problem is? he asks. Is it your mother?

My mother?

Do you really care that she doesn't like me? Because I don't.

Where on earth have you got that from?

It can't just be your grades, either. I saw last year's, Roe, on the results board. I doubt you need another mark to get into Oxford.

That's not true.

Is it Josh? Was he mad?

No, Rosie says, somewhat louder than she'd intended. It's got nothing to do with Josh.

So what are you so worried about?

Nothing, she says.

Is it the smoking? The motorbike? The break from school that happened *eons* ago?

Yes, she says, latching on. Yes, it's all of that, Will. All of it. You're the wrong kind of person, for me, okay?

Will has his mouth open, as if he'd been forming an argument. But it doesn't come. Rosie watches him as he realises what's she's saying, what she means, and her heart closes up, like a shell.

She waits. Wants to reach out, bury herself in him, take it back. But it's done. The spark in Will's face, his stormy, flecked eyes, has gone. He lapses back to the boy she'd known before she knew him, cool and distant, and still he says nothing, though she can hear so much noise in the silence between them, the lie, the hurt on both sides, because it is not fair, this is not fair, and she wants to tell him the truth, but she can't, and her throat swells as she watches him believe all that she's said. She wants him to yell. Wants him to challenge her. Instead he just nods, swallows it whole, and they stand there, losing the daylight.

seven

Their exams end in May. It is an unusually hot afternoon, and the unlucky ones with papers on the last day are met with spraying soft drinks, streamers thrown on their clothes. Will is one of them. He and Josh had their final further maths paper after lunch, and afterwards, they walk out of school together for the last time.

Things are different between them now. For weeks, Josh had spoken to him strictly about maths, as if Will had crossed some sort of line, betrayed him in a complex way that neither of them ever discussed. This bothered Will, for a time. But then he called Darcy and spent most evenings at her house, went back to meeting friends at bonfires on the beach. He upped his shifts at the garage, went for long, winding rides along the coast on his motorbike. Things were good. Things were fine. He was soon to be done with school. Released, the day he got that slip of paper, no matter what letters were on there.

But today, as they leave the atrium and wander down the path and get sprayed with Silly String, the tension lifts off the both of them. They laugh together. People are shrugging off their blazers, shedding their uniforms. The sun is the colour of butter, and it melts over everything; the pavements, the parked cars, the sixth formers spilling out through the school gates.

Done, says Josh, dusting his hands together.

Boom, says Will, and Josh throws his head back and laughs.

Boom, he repeats. You know it!

Guys, says a voice from behind them. It's Darcy, and Will's shoulders sag. They'd spent weeks fucking in her house when her mother was out, and in his garage, on the concrete floor, when she wasn't. Not once had she complained, until she'd decided she wanted someone to take her to dinner. Someone to go to Norwich with on the weekends, to meet her raucous friends, buy her froth-topped lattes in coffee chains.

Will was not that someone.

They've not spoken for weeks, but in this moment, with the sun beaming down and school finished forever and everyone drenched in lemonade, this doesn't seem to matter.

Big party at Jessica's tonight, she says.

Cool, says Josh.

I won't be touching you with a barge pole, Will White, she says, but she stares him down, as though by saying this, he'll want to touch her all the more.

Understood, he says.

But both of you are invited, all right? Tell everyone. The more the merrier, or whatever.

What's the story there, Josh asks, as Darcy stalks off, and they continue down the hill.

There isn't one, Will says. We hooked up. Then we stopped.

Such drama, says Josh.

Josh, mate.

Yeah?

Are we okay?

He doesn't realise he is going to say it; doesn't plan on asking such a thing. It just comes out. His heart feels light and open with the sun, or the freedom, and he finds that he just needs to know.

Josh looks at him sideways, as if he's going to feign ignorance, perhaps ask him what he means. But he doesn't. They keep walking. Birds warble overhead, celebrating the blue of the sky.

Course, Josh says, and he bashes his shoulder with his own. Asks if he thinks he'll go, tonight. If he should wear his Hawaiian shirt.

*

Summer comes. It is the longest one they've known, and yet it slides by so fast, the academic year refusing to wait. Weeks of iced coffees shared in the park, clear straws, blue drinks that stain their tongues and turn them giddy and loud and happy. University shopping lists; cutlery, saucepans, printed photos of school friends they're certain they'll love forever, never lose touch with, whom they'll see at Christmas and then never again.

Rosie meets up with Marley. They go for walks along the river, takeaway slushies in hand, and she listens as her friend chatters on about Tom. Rosie pretends she's interested and tries not to burst with her own story, the kiss by the sea that she can still taste in her mouth. It still gets her sometimes, when she least expects it, at night as she lies on top of her sheets, or when she's washing her hair, in the bath, and she's naked and wet and alone.

But no. Not allowed.

Not fair, remember, on anyone.

When she's not with Marley, she and Josh spend long afternoons in their garden, listening to her iPod, trailing an earphone each so they can talk, or else listen to the neighbour's shears, the drone of low-flying bees.

They do not speak of what he'd told her.

She tries, once or twice, to bring it up, to see if he's ready to talk more, but he just turns the music up louder.

She has never known him to not let her in like this, and it troubles her, but in spite of the summer holidays, with their exams over and their new lives waiting, they are both continually busy. At their mother's suggestion, they both tutor younger students to keep their brains sharp, and they both still attend their music lessons. Josh trains with his basketball team twice a week and Rosie keeps to her gym regime, so the weeks slip by, results day looming ever closer. And this distracts her. Means the thing that matters, the thing they should really get into, is held at arm's length, like something on her to-do list that she remembers, sometimes, and knows she will have to address, soon. When he's ready.

*

And then the last Tuesday in August rolls round – a Tuesday that happens to be Will's birthday. It is the prelude to his friends' lives changing come September, and his birthday marks something of significance; one last excuse for them to all laugh, and drink, and be young together.

You've got to mark it, mate, someone said to him. I'll bring a keg.

I don't really drink, Will reminded him, which didn't seem to matter.

And so he finds himself, turning nineteen, sitting cross-legged on the grass atop the cliffs at Burwood Bay. Sipping a single beer, and wondering where the months have gone, and how the two people he'd want to spend his birthday with are not here, because they haven't spoken, really, all summer.

They'd both got into Oxbridge, of course. Two out of

three who'd applied. He'd seen them hugging on results day, Rosie in tears, Josh holding her aloft like a trophy.

Will had done fine, too. Had folded his letter into his pocket and gone back to his shift at the garage. He'd seen them both at a house party, soon after. Passed Josh, on the high street, the week before, and kept Rosie, mainly, from his thoughts.

But there is something about the light of tonight.

Candyfloss clouds, the sun meeting the line of the sea and melting to liquid gold, and it bothers him that neither of them is here to see it. So he texts them. Says he knows it's been a while, but it's his birthday, and everyone's out, and she replies first, asks where he is.

He types back and leaves no full stop, so it is open-ended and the start of something, though of course neither of them knows this when she says yes, they'll be there, and Will puts his phone away and feels, for the last time in a long time, a sense of having done the right thing.

*

I'm over him, you know.

This is what Josh says to her as they walk past the wetlands, towards the clifftops of Burwood Bay. The sky is a puffed, marshmallow pink, and they catch sight of a barn owl with its silent wings, swooping over the fields.

Really? she says.

Sort of. As much as you can be over your first gay crush.

It is the first time she's heard him say it. The first time he's identified as such, out loud.

Josh, she says, because she doesn't know what else to say; doesn't think he's as okay as he sounds. They are walking side by side but he is a half-step ahead, so she can't quite see his face. Just the angle of his cheekbone.

There are two major issues with him, see, Josh goes on.

Okay, she says.

He's not gay, for one thing, he says. Bit of a problem.

Yeah, she says. Scared of saying anything more.

Plus he's into someone else, he says.

Oh, she says. Right.

Her heart rate skitters, and something balloons in her throat, because she isn't sure if he means her or another girl, and either way, it makes her feel dreadful.

There is no wind as they walk; just the weight of summer, the smell of grass and seeds and earth. They ended up sneaking out tonight, because they both have to teach tomorrow, after their own early-bird music lessons.

They had asked, at first. Explained it was Will's birthday, and that all their friends would be there.

You *can* go, their mother had said, but I think it's best you're fresh for your lessons, don't you? And when she'd gone to bed early Josh had said screw it, Rosie, we're uni students now, and so they'd climbed out of his window onto the garage roof, like they did when they were kids, where they would go to watch the stars together if Rosie couldn't sleep.

He'd helped her down with his long arms, and they'd set off, giddy with rebellion; Rosie feeling the slightest bit sick.

That person's still you, Josh says now. In case you didn't know.

Her swollen throat eases, slightly, but her cheeks burn.

Yeah, she says. Breathing in, out. Then she says, who knows why.

Don't do that, Josh says.

What?

Don't be so coy. It's annoying.

I'm not, Josh! He's . . . well, he's Will White, and he could have anyone he wanted.

And he has. Historically.

Well, she stutters, yeah.

Until you.

What do you mean?

Well, you're not together, are you? That's probably pretty hot, for him. That he can't have you just because he wants you.

Rosie doesn't reply to this. It feels like some kind of backwards compliment, aggressive, somehow, and she drops her eyes to the ground.

But you're also the best, Josh says, his voice stiff. So maybe he's got good taste, after all.

Thanks, she says, though she still feels somewhat chastised. Things between her and Josh have seemed normal, mostly, since results day. But he has moments when he turns distant, or unfriendly; hours where he lies in his room, or acts uninterested if she tries to tell him about a new song, or a funny thing Marley said.

So go out with him, if you want, Josh says, as he opens a gate, slides the metal bar back on its spring. They pass through, shut it hard against its latch.

Go out with him? Rosie repeats.

Yeah. Don't let me stand in your way.

His voice does not align with his words; every syllable, to her, sounds like an obstruction, solid and with hard edges. She thinks back to catching her thigh on the corner of her bed that morning. The triangular bruise that came after.

You weren't the reason, she says.

Josh has sped up, his strides so long that Rosie needs to trot to keep pace. But he slows, at this, glances round at her with his hazel eyes.

There were lots of reasons, she says. For us not getting together.

Is one of them that you're scared?

Yes, she says, because he's her brother, and he knows it, and she's not sure why he's being so brutal with her, tonight.

Kind of terrified, actually, she says, and this seems to take the spite out of him. He stops walking, turns to face her properly.

You can't be scared of everything you can't control, Rosie, he says.

She shrugs, crosses her arms.

I could say the same to you, she says. Why are you being like this?

You mean why am I being a normal human instead of a bouncing ball of sunshine?

Well, yeah!

Because I'm just working stuff out, Rosie, okay?

I know you are. But why won't you let me help you?

'Cause it's my thing, he says, walking again.

So you keep saying, she says, and once more, she has to hurry to keep up. But you're my brother. And I can't bear that you're hurting.

Rosie, he says, and he laughs, but it's not a good laugh; it stings, like hard spray from the sea. Just focus on your own happiness for once, yeah? Can you do that?

She trails behind him, treading in the trampled grass where his shoes have just been. His house keys clink in her pocket; he always asks her to safeguard them on a night out, because she is reliable, keeps track of things so he doesn't have to. And she's happy to do it. Has never felt like she was interfering, or mothering him, until now.

I'll try, she says. If you do, too.

I'm working on it, Josh tells her. Promise.

That last word sounds more like him; softer, like the long grass beside them.

He had shared more with her, on Christmas night. How he'd never known, like you're supposed to. All those people who just knew, in their heart, in their bones, since they were children; he just hadn't. He'd not felt an attraction to anyone, ever, boy or girl or otherwise, and he'd not worried, or cared, figured it would come with age.

And it did. Flickers, at first, when he was watching a film, or passing someone on the street. And then a boy he sat next to in maths, who suddenly made everything real.

Rosie heard all this, and she held him, and she said she was sorry, she was sorry she hadn't been there, hadn't asked him about it sooner. She'd always suspected, of course. The way you suspect someone will be a great cook, or can hold their drink. Something that's a part of them, but means nothing, really; nothing that changes anything, for you.

Why don't we just tell Mum and Dad, she tries now, as they trail along the path.

Not this again, Rosie.

I just think it might help.

What's going to help, right now, is drinking a lot of cider and sitting with my friends and forgetting about everything until the early hours of the morning, okay?

That's not healthy, Josh.

Oh, and your constant checking is? Don't think I can't hear you creeping around your room half the night, doing those weird things you do.

It is like he has hit her; something shrinks inside her with the shame of it, spoken aloud like that. By him.

The barn owl swoops ahead of them, again. Sandy wings in the half-light.

Sorry, he says. Sorry, Rosie.

S'okay, she says, and they don't speak again as they climb

the cliff path, as the long grass gives way to chalk dust, and they start to smell the fire and the salt.

Up on the cliff, the bonfire reaches and spits. There is leftover birthday cake, shop-bought and too dry and still in its plastic wrapper. Someone is playing drum and bass from a speaker, and she sees a couple rolling in the grass, get a room, a guy calls, and gets a middle finger in return. Josh does what he intended and downs three ciders within the first half-hour, and soon, all the light has left the sky.

It is like the night she first met Will.

Ink black, and intimate.

When she settles beside Marley, Rosie catches Will's eye across the flames, and he raises a hand, but barely, as if he's merely lifting his drink. She wants to go over, but does not know what she'd say, so she drinks red wine from a plastic cup and listens to people talk and tries to pretend she's not aware of him, over there, so intently not looking her way.

She's wearing a dress, with no tights. Wishes, now, that she'd worn jeans, as her naked knees point towards him.

An hour later, she walks to the edge and looks out at the expanse of ocean, just a dark mass, now that the sun has set. There is a sixty-foot drop to the rocks below. They would have family picnics up here, years ago, and she wonders if Josh remembers collecting ladybirds in their lunchboxes, running from the peril of wasps. So many of them, back then. She wonders where they've gone.

It looks better in the daylight, he says.

Will has come to stand beside her.

She turns her head and tries to smile at him, but she isn't sure where they stand; isn't sure if he's forgiven her, for the awful things she said.

I kind of like it in the dark, she says.

Will takes a mouthful of Coke, keeps his eyes on the sea.

Happy birthday, she says to him.

Thanks.

You had a good day?

Pretty standard, he says.

How disappointing.

He laughs at this, and she gives in, too, lets out her own strained smile.

Birthdays should be anything but standard, she says.

In your world, maybe.

And it is subtle, but enough. An acknowledgement of all that she said to him in the forest: that he is not the right guy, for her; that they are from two different — too different — worlds. It storms inside of her, this lie she told, for her brother. A lie Will so easily believed.

I'm glad you came, he says, after the longest silence they have ever shared. Someone squeals behind them; there is the rush of foaming beer, a scatter of people avoiding the overflow.

Me too, she says.

Good news on Oxford, he says.

Oh, yeah, she says. It is.

You're not the tiniest bit gutted about music school?

Rosie's brain slows, at this. Filters through minor details from the last few weeks. The looping around her bedroom, at night. The tapping of her fingernails, the endless counting in one room, and then another. Her music application, still blank, but kept, for some reason, in her desk drawer.

Nope, she says.

That's great, then, Will says. Come have a drink, yeah? D'you think we could try and be friends, maybe?

That depends, she says.

On what?

On whether you can forget all the horrible things I said to you.

Will gives a half-shrug; like he's shedding something from his shoulders, hardly acknowledging this thing that she broke, between them.

It was all true, he says.

It wasn't, though, she says, and her voice tremors with feeling, which is not lost on Will, she doesn't think, from the way that he looks at her.

Meaning, he asks, and it is Rosie's turn to shrug. To suggest something without words.

*

Their night turns after midnight, after hours of talking, like friends. Will wasn't sure he could be near her like this, but it is surprisingly easy; a relief, even. And he is wondering what she meant, by the cliff. If things have changed. If it was only a matter of timing, for her, like she'd always said.

People drift away, come back, then leave for good. Someone is sick from too much cider; the cellophane from the cake ends up on the fire and it melts, smelling of acid and bad decisions. Josh gets louder and louder by the hour. He is blackout drunk; worse than the night of the winter dance, even, and it was funny, at first, but soon people are rolling their eyes, or shrugging his hands from their shoulders; Will senses Rosie watching him from across the flames.

I love you all so much, Josh is saying, with his arms spread wide. There's so much love in me, guys.

Someone laughs; a friend *aaws*, tries to tug on his sleeve to have him sit down. He bats them away, stumbles a little.

How can love be wrong? he asks them; the remaining few, by the fire. How can any kind of love be bad?

He begins to pace up and down, and his face is blazing, like the sunset from before; the one that made Will text Rosie in the first place.

Josh, Rosie says, quietly.

I *love* love, Josh says, more loudly still, and he laughs at his choice of words. Someone turns off the music, out of irritation, Will suspects. He watches with detached amusement as Josh meanders through the last few of them, old school friends, people from assemblies and science and form group, all looking up at him with affection, or fatigue.

Marley is on Tom's lap, and she says we love you too, Josh, and Josh looks round at her and begins to walk backwards, a can of cider in his hand.

You think you do, he says. You think you know a person.

Josh, Rosie says again, and there is a warning note in her voice, and Will hears it, and sits up from where he'd been leaning on his elbows.

You can never know, Josh says. But it's all right. You've made me see that tonight, guys. *All* of you.

He's shaking his head now, and Will wonders if he's trying not to cry, can't work out if he's drunk-happy or supremely sad. Two things, so often the same.

Josh takes one more swig from his can, and drops it. It falls with a thump on the grass.

Come away from the edge, Josh, Rosie says to him, but he doesn't. He keeps stepping back, and then he whirls himself around with his arms flung out, like he's embracing the night sky. People are getting up now, from their places by the fire. Laughter changing to words of God, and shit. Mild intrigue turned to dread.

Someone shouts Josh's name, and Will gets up, his blood, streaming, like a river, and walks towards him with his hand outstretched, says mate, come on, you've had a few.

They latch eyes for the briefest of seconds.

And then Josh opens his mouth to say something but his back foot goes, and it happens so fast that Will isn't sure it's happened, even though he is there, right there, could have lunged for him if he'd tried. People are screaming. Girls, are screaming. And the guys are at the verge and shouting fuck and Josh and there is noise about an ambulance, and the shock has slowed everything, for a moment, the stars out, the sea flat and still and watchful. And Will looks over the edge and he sees it, even in the dark, the angle of those long limbs, the seep of something so wine-like, so wrong, in the sand. And he turns around and he blocks her, because she is running for the edge, and screaming her brother's name.

No, he says, and he folds his arms around her, presses her into his chest. No. You don't want to see this. You do not want to see this.

And she is sobbing and yelling and still saying his name, and he falls with her to her knees, and he keeps her there, like that, as though it is his sole purpose, to stop her from seeing it, as though this can somehow, someday, take it back.

after

eight

Will knows he will never again be able to eat potato salad, after today.

It is cold and slimy and turns to mush in his mouth. Tastes of stifled things, like the words, forced out, by his friends at the lectern. The air felt close as they filed out into the cemetery car park, shared cars to the house, saying nothing.

They all stand together in Rosie's living room, in black dresses and blazers in spite of the late-summer heat. Eyes dry, now. Finger food on their plates.

Will watches as people eat. Forks some into his own mouth, despite not wanting to.

Voices are low and solemn, and it is busy, busier than their Christmas party, even, but people give each other more space, talk and touch far less. Rosie's father looks lost, as if he can't remember why he's here, in this room with all these strangers and friends and family members. His wife is upstairs, hasn't been seen since the service.

And Rosie. Rosie is sitting by the window with Marley, who is holding her hand, won't leave her side. Another black dress. Long sleeves, hair plaited, by someone else, he's sure, that morning.

She looks like you'd expect a twin to look at their other

twin's funeral. Collapsed into herself, but somehow, still sitting upright.

The world has been slow, and weightless, since the fall. Like nothing sits or stands or functions for any good reason. He experienced a similar detachment when his grandpa died – when he had to say a few words at the funeral, and then, right at the moment when he should, he couldn't.

He let everyone down, he knows.

Tar, in his mouth. The world, sunk, under water.

An hour later, Marley takes Rosie out into the garden. He sees them rising from the window seat, the guiding of one girl through the quiet crowd. One of Josh's closest friends is weeping silently in their circle, and two girls start crying, too, because it's like yawning, involuntary and infectious. Will takes their plates, pretending to be considerate, and carries them through to the conservatory where he can see Marley and Roe through the glass, walking the length of the garden.

Outside, the afternoon is gold on his skin, the sky a soft, cloudless blue.

There is an apple tree, a trampoline. A water feature that's not running. He follows them to where the hedgerows part, to an open view of some farmland. Geese, calling, from the fields, as Marley holds on to Rosie's hand.

He hesitates behind them, but then says her name. Marley's head snaps round, but Rosie does not move. He wants to touch her. To hold her other hand, or, if he's really honest, have her hold tight on to his.

The service was beautiful, Marley says, after the longest time.

It wasn't though, was it, says Will.

Marley turns to him again, but still, Rosie does not look round.

What? Marley says.

It was devastating, he says. And stagnant, like all funerals are. Except it's worse, when someone's young, and brilliant.

Marley is moving her mouth as if grinding her teeth; as if she cannot believe what he's saying.

Because he *was* brilliant, Will says. And interested. And considerate.

His hands feel as if they are shaking. He hooks his thumbs into his belt loops.

Funny, too, he says. But not intentionally. He was just too naïve, too nice, almost, for a guy his age, you know? And *that* was funny, to a lot of people. But I thought he was just . . . so different, to everyone. I felt so . . . relieved, around him.

What are you saying, Marley asks, but Rosie jerks her hand, almost involuntarily, as if she doesn't want her to interrupt.

I can't believe he died, Will says. I can't believe we went to a crappy standard funeral where nobody said anything real about him.

Will, Marley says, and she sounds shocked.

It's the truth, he says. Nobody speaks the truth at these things. It was the same with my grandpa, it'll be the same at mine. Roe, he says again. Roe, will you look at me?

She will not; she dips her head to the ground, and he wonders if she's crying, or simply trying not to.

I don't want that to be your memory of him, Will says. Or think that that's everyone's memory of him. He was so much more than those poems and that reading. And your song was great, Roe, it really was. He would have loved it. But he would have loved an entire album of your songs, right? He would have preferred karaoke, maybe, for you to sing live. And he'd have wanted fried chicken, not finger sandwiches. And Christmas music playing when we all walked out, even though it's September.

Stop, says Marley.

No, he says, and he doesn't know why this is so important to say, but his chest is bursting, so he keeps going. Funerals are as meaningful as . . . the hospital room you're born in. It doesn't matter. But Josh *does*. He was charming and idealistic and sort of clumsy, and he knew the missing verses from *Fresh Prince*, and he doodled stars when he was trying to solve equations, and that stuff matters, Rosie, more than a stupid service.

Shut up, Will!

He pretends that Marley hasn't spoken; raises his voice above hers.

Remember your own things, Roe, he says. The real things. Can you do that?

He is pleading with her for something she cannot give, because she likely wants to die, too, he knows, right here at the edge of the field. Half of her, gone, turning to ash, as they stand here, and Josh does not.

Please, Roe, he says.

And when she still says nothing and does not move, he walks back to the house, with Marley holding her hand and the sun sinking beneath the farmland. His heart feels torn open, exposed. Birds, still singing, in the trees.

He's way out of line, Marley tells her.

The sunset clings on for one moment more and then drops, leaving claw marks in the sky. Coral red, and flaming. Muted shadows of dusk.

He's not, Rosie says, and it is the first thing she has said all day.

Marley turns to her then, takes her arm with the hand that is not holding hers.

Well, he could have been nicer about it, Marley says.

People could always be nicer, Rosie says. Her voice doesn't feel right, but somehow, she keeps talking.

I want to remember all those things, she says. The things he said, that no one else did.

And then something happens inside her, something she'd been fearing and tamping down, all day, and she lets out a guttural sound, and it's like ripping herself down her centre.

But I can't, she says. I can't remember anything except him falling.

Her single cry turns to sobbing without tears, the crumpling of herself out loud. Marley shushes her, like a mother might, and she falls apart in her garden, near the trees they had climbed, on the grass they'd scanned for clover, blown dandelions and snowmen, daisy chains and cloud-gazing, and it's true, in this moment she recalls none of it, but Marley says you will, I promise you, you will.

Back in the house, Will cannot leave like he wants to; he has to hang back in the kitchen while other guests linger in the hall. Rosie's mother has clearly come downstairs only to say goodbye to the guests; she stays by the door, as if unable to move, unable to face the remaining mourners in the living room.

He watches as people clutch at Mr and Mrs Winters' hands, whisper well-meaning, useless words. Roe's dad heads out into the driveway with a few of them, for air, perhaps, or because he can no longer bear the walls of his own home.

When the last person has filed out, Will makes for the

hallway too, readying himself to say something equally hollow. But when Rosie's mother sees him, her face does something he's never seen before. Slackens, then contorts. He sees it twice, in fact, because she is standing by the mirror in the hall, reflected in all her fury.

Get out, she says, when he reaches her.

I already was, he says.

How dare you, she says, and it is like her face is carved from wood; like she can barely move her mouth.

How *dare* you, she says, again. After your pathetic, delinquent party that I *told him* not to go to? Joshua does not do this. Joshua listens to me. And then he meets you, and starts needing help with his maths, and sneaking out the house on school nights.

It wasn't a school night, Will says, and he doesn't know why he says it, when she is trembling all over; still talking about her son in the present tense.

What *the fuck*, she says, and it is so jarring, to hear an adult, a composed woman like her, swear at him like this. It stuns him. His blood runs cold.

He goes to apologise, but then she leans towards him, and he has to take a step back.

You have no decency, she says. To come here, today. Then talk to me, like that. Like you have a problem.

I don't have a problem, he says, and he strains to stay calm, to sound it. But Josh was my friend, Mrs Winters. And I'm –

But she lets out a terrible laugh.

People like you don't have friends, she says. You have people you use, to get ahead, or to pull them down into the dirt. I knew people like you at school. You think I don't know what you got suspended for? You think I'd let you near my kids, for a second?

There is a tiny bit of spittle on her cheek. Her lipstick, still perfectly red.

You are *bad* for him, Will, she hisses. And for Rosie. Get out. Now. I want you out of my house.

She is looking at him as though Josh did not fall. As though Will pushed him.

Get out, she says, for the final time.

Fuck this, he says, but quietly, and he slips past her, his insides lodged in his throat.

He knows, rationally, that this is the talk of a grieving mother. But the darker side of him, the part that likes to drink and tighten and drag him into the blurry, swirling places where he feels nothing, that part hears it and beds in. Because he could have caught him. He could have not invited them, that night. Josh could have stayed home, and Will could have done something, or not done something, and things would be entirely different.

His friend could still be here, solving equations.

Doodling biro stars.

*

Once everybody has left, Rosie lies awake, with her heart racing, and dreads what the world will look like in the morning.

Her mother does not wail, like she has on the other nights. She is simply silent. Her father is numb; just seems dazed, by the entire thing, as if he does not believe it has happened. And while she cannot understand the pain of losing a child, Rosie burns with the fact that they are not twins. They may have created him, but they did not grow out of the same cells; did not share hearts and chromosomes and a home since before they were human.

In the black of night, Rosie imagines that she will die,

too. That she can't possibly live, with this eating her from the inside.

And so she moves into his room, and sleeps in her twin's bed, for days. She sleeps as though she is catching up on all of the sleepless nights she has suffered since she was little; since the clock started keeping her awake, and she started counting, and checking, and making promises to herself so that bad things wouldn't happen, and people would not die.

But he died anyway.

He died and she is tired and her parents somehow carry on, get dressed, leave her be, until it just gets silly, is no longer respectable, or normal; her dad opens the curtains and says come on, now, Rosie, time to get back in your own bed, and she agrees until after dark, when she creeps back to her brother's room and presses her face to his pillow. It still smells of him, a little. Is fading, more and more, with each night.

The morning she is to leave for university, she checks, and checks again, until it is so automatic that she is not sure she even checked right.

Her bags are in the car. Her father is in the driving seat, and her mother is calling her down, telling her it's time to go.

Nothing left, but her curtains, and some pictures.

She texted Will, the day before; asked him to meet her by the lighthouse after dawn. He had not replied, but she went anyway, and he did not come. Unsurprising, she thinks, after weeks of no contact. After she would not look at him, at the funeral.

Now, back home, she checks once more. For what, she does not know. She touches her window sill, positions her desk chair at the right angle. The right angle. Right. Right. A little more to the left, and then it's right.

Then her mum yells again, and it forces her to leave, to descend the stairs.

What were you doing? her mother asks, as if she is on a deadline; as if she has something more important to get back to.

Nothing, Rosie says.

Don't dally, then, her mother says, and she kisses the top of her head.

There is a moment when they hold on to each other; her mother's hand on her back, pressing her close, Rosie gripping her mother's elbow. They are not used to hugging, and it doesn't feel like a farewell embrace; it feels like they're talking, through touch, their long, matching fingers saying things for them.

You'll be okay, her mother says, and because she's had to say it, Rosie does not believe her. She thinks about telling her, now, with their faces reflected in the hallway mirror, that she does not want to go.

Her mother kisses her again, brusquer, this time, and lets go of her.

Be good, she says.

Always, Rosie replies, an exchange they've shared since childhood. Her mother smiles, without really smiling, and Rosie walks out of the house.

*

The night of the funeral, Will goes home via Darcy's place.

He fucks her in her garden, because her mum is indoors, and because she wants it as much as he does. I haven't missed you, she tells him, as she bites down on his lip. But I'm so fucking sad, Will.

He turns her sideways, grazes his cheek against the

pebbledash of her house, and thinks, as he comes, how he wishes he could say that out loud; admit that he's sad, too, and use it to justify everything. All the wrong.

You knew him quite well, didn't you? Darcy asks, as she untwists her skirt from around her waist. He zips up, tells her they took maths together.

And wasn't it your party? When he died?

She says it casually, as if she doesn't care; as if she is just confirming something she already knows. He looks at her, but doesn't answer. Keeps looking, until she turns crimson, asks him what.

He keeps that answer unsaid in his mouth. While he runs, and showers, and works his shifts. At dinner, as he forces down food, under his grandma's watchful eye. It weighs on him now, as he pulls the weeds up in his own garden, feels it slung and objectionable round his throat. The grass is wet. It has rained, overnight.

He'd ignored Rosie's message, the day before she left. And that feels urgent and inescapable; it haunts him, pulsing through his veins as he shoves his hands into the dirt.

He lines the weeds on the ground, then he scoops them up as one and throws them into the garden waste. He is sweating, breathing hard, his fingernails black with earth. Then he turns and makes for his garage, rooting around behind his toolbox, lifting the bundles of grease-streaked rags he keeps piled beneath the workbench.

He pulls out a bottle of the clear, sharp stuff that helped, before. Takes gulps of it in the dark, because he hasn't bothered to turn on the light.

nine

In many ways, university is what Rosie expected.

Green-lawned parks and circular libraries, seminars where she sometimes feels lost, and other times, interested. Lectures, with takeaway cups of coffee, the shuffle of papers. Intelligent people, and stupid remarks. Pennies dropped in pint glasses, so that the beer has to be chugged, like tap water.

She likes the computer room beneath her college library. How it's always warm, and hums with the whir of the printer. People head there with a purpose. They come, they go, and she stays and taps out her essays, with the feet of fellow students passing above her, as she works underground, like she's hiding.

In other ways, it is not what she thought at all.

She thought things would be fine, somehow, when she got here. Even when Josh died, some hopeful part of her thought her old problems might still retreat. That her checking and sleepless nights would wither in the light of a new place, thanks to the new friends and faces, the facts she'd fill her days with.

In reality, though, the deep sleep of her immediate grief has vanished, and she spends her time avidly, achingly, awake.

At clubs, in the bar, in a friend's room poring over last-minute reading. And when she has to be alone, she ends up circling her room, touching her clothes, her keys, with just the right brush of two fingers, before she can get into bed. If she goes to the bathroom halfway through the night, she has to do it all again.

She does not know why.

But she has made friends. Good ones. A small group she watches films with, dances beside in nightclubs, calls taxis for when they drunkenly decide they don't want to walk home in the cold.

She starts to drink coffee, because everybody does.

She tries her first kebab, downs her first Jägerbomb.

Has to rewrite one of her essays, for the first time in her life, and cries down the phone to Marley about it, even after everything. Even though nothing like this should matter, ever again.

She tells nobody that her twin died.

That she gets two, maybe three hours of sleep a night, throughout the whole of her first term.

She studies. She drinks. She stops writing songs. She eats very little, and drops a dress size, which she knows her mother will be thrilled about when she goes home for Christmas.

She almost texts Josh to tell him about it.

Then remembers, all over again.

It is early December – Oxmas, they call it – when she decides to stop circling her bedroom and instead leave her building at dawn. She walks around the college grounds in her long coat, watching the mist rise from the lawns.

Some days, she follows the river until her hands turn cold, and that is why she notices him for the first time.

He is on the water, rowing, alone, and she thinks nothing of it, other than how strange it is that someone else is awake at this hour, and she watches him glide by, with his large arms and short hair, his jaw strong and set.

She sees him again, a few times. He catches her eye once, but keeps rowing; keeps puffing air out of his mouth, exhaling on the effort, as focused as she's seen anyone on anything.

She forgets about him.

Goes home for Christmas.

Has a near-silent, terrible time, and breaks in two when she returns for her second term, because everything that was hard before feels harder. She stops sleeping, and her checks increase, keep her up all hours of the night so that she can't remember what came first, the checking or the not sleeping, because one causes the other, and her brain loops, endlessly, at night and all day, in the lectures that she drags herself to, in the dinner hall while she eats with her friends, mostly moving the meat around her plate, eating the carbs, the carrots, the soft, easy-to-swallow things. She feels cold, and shaken, all of the time, like an upturned snow globe. Spinning, and empty, and full.

*

Will has eaten himself sober. It is two in the morning, and he is in the kitchen, picking bread straight out of the cellophane bag, squashing it into his mouth with two fingers.

The hunger had felt real, and sudden. So he came down and started to eat and the world became sharper at the edges.

Hovis Best of Both, apparently.

It's not really the best of anything.

But he finishes his fourth slice, twists the bread back into its bag and drinks some water. That's the key, he knows; drink an implausible amount of water, and everything will be fine.

And things *have* been fine, more or less. He's been working, and running, and not missing school, the routine of registration and lessons and revision he didn't really do, the teachers who pitied him, or fancied him, or treated him with suspicion. He does ad hoc shifts at Moe's Motors, and he runs to rid himself of Josh, and that night, and the sickness in his stomach that doesn't ever go away. When he drinks, the thoughts ease, like the dialling down of volume, or the lowering of a flame on the hob. Still there, but muffled with gin, or vodka, or rum. He drank out of the house, at first. In his garage, or after work, at the beach or in alleyways, like the scum he suspects he might be.

He listens to rock music, afterwards.

Wakes, hungry, and still sick, with no desire to do anything different.

Now, in the kitchen, he is about to run the tap for more water when his phone vibrates on the counter. Violently, like someone's drilling through the wall.

He sees her name. After he has tried not to think of her, for weeks. The alcohol helps there, too, like an old, comforting friend who always knows what to say. It's distracting, puts things off for a while, until times like this, when real life comes knocking, or ringing, at two in the morning.

He does not run the tap. He does not think too hard.

Roe, he says, when he answers.

She says hi, after the longest pause. He wonders if she meant to call.

You're up, she says.

Yeah.

I didn't know if you would be.

Another pause, even longer, this time. He takes the phone to the living room, closes the door, and sits in his grandfather's armchair. Dave gets up from his cushion in the corner, snuffles at his knees in hello, before padding back to bed.

146

You okay? he asks.

Yeah, she says, though her voice suggests otherwise.

How's everything, then, he asks. He was going to ask, how is uni, or how was your Christmas, but neither seemed more relevant than the other. There is so much between them, now. So many months, and so many things. They have not spoken since the wake.

Good, she says. Fine.

Rosie.

Yeah?

Why are you calling?

There is a silence, again, on her end, as charged as a city at night. He can't hear her breathing; there is no scuffle of bed-clothes, no sighing or tread of feet.

I can't sleep, she says. I've tried everything.

Okay.

And I don't know what to do, she says.

Her voice cracks then, and she lets her breath go, shallow and splintered.

His heart floods. All of it, roaring out.

Okay, he says. Okay. How long are we talking? Just tonight?

No, she says.

A week?

There is more silence, and then she says since she got here, and he doesn't know if that means since day one, or day one of term two, but either way, it's bad.

He gets up and goes to the window and soothes her with meaningless things. Talks about fitting clutch cables at the garage, and Amber's sudden fixation with being vegetarian. The trees he can see; how bare they are, without their leaves. How wet it's been, all winter.

He keeps talking, because she is not talking back, and he

tries to picture where she is, what her room might look like; a single bed and a window, her books stacked tall on a desk.

He talks about a manual he's reading. A band he's discovered, how she might like them, the white noise of the tracks.

At some point, she must fall asleep, because her breathing evens, and eventually, when the milky dawn seeps through the blinds, he drifts off, too.

You look like death, his grandma tells him at breakfast.

Cheers, he says.

What's wrong? Are you coming down with something?

Before he can answer, she presses her palm to his forehead, pushes his hair up out of his eyes. You feel clammy, she says.

Just a rough night, he says.

Bad breath, too, she says, as she opens the fridge. He pretends not to care, but clamps his mouth shut, in case she can smell the ethanol.

Did you sleep down here? she asks, nodding at the living room door. She places butter and jam on the table, a carton of juice, and he has a sudden, intrusive flicker of the snow day, when Josh gathered the toppings for their pancakes.

Will?

Yeah?

I asked if you slept down here?

Didn't really sleep, he says. But yeah, I was down here.

His gran hums her understanding, but asks nothing more. She has been gentle with him since Josh's death, and for that he is grateful, and somewhat furious. Like he needs to be handled with care. Like it changes anything. Like he wouldn't rather have her usual, hard-nosed criticism, have life back the way it was.

I'm out tonight, he says, as she slides crumpets under the grill.

Again?

Yep.

Who're you going round with, these days?

People, he says.

No girls?

Lots of girls.

She sighs, and, almost unbelievably, takes this exact moment to mention her, after months of silence and tact and unventured questions.

You lost touch with that Rosie, then?

After her twin died on my birthday? he says, with such a flare of heat, his skin feels ice cold, afterwards. Yeah, I did.

Willyum, she says, and she sounds both sympathetic and reproachful, and he stands up, says he's not hungry.

Rosie starts calling him every night.

Around eleven, when he is in bed, or walking back from drinking on the beach. Wind up, stars out. The sea roaring, somewhere, behind him.

He talks, and she talks back, sometimes, but more often than not she slides into sleep, and he keeps going, for a while, to make sure she stays there.

He tells her so many things. He likes doing it; likes the time with her, even though she is there, and he is here, and the whole thing is sort of messed up. He finds he waits all day for that moment, when his phone will ring. Feels both a sadness and gutting relief, because it means that she still needs him.

After a few weeks, when the frost of February laces the grass in the mornings and he can see his breath when he wakes, she breaks the routine and calls him at dawn.

Where were you, she asks him.

He is rising out of sleep, not following.

I waited for you, she says. The day I left.

He stares up at his ceiling, at the outlines of the old stars. Artex, swirled above him.

And why didn't you say goodbye, she asks. At the funeral.

Will remains very still. He never thought he'd have to answer these questions; thought it would just be something between them, that they could pack down, like dirt.

You're talking me to sleep every night, she says, but there are other things that need saying. Things we should talk about.

He keeps looking at his ceiling; at the shadow of sun on the brushwork. When he doesn't answer her, she nudges, don't you think?

And so he has to go there.

Too much has happened, Roe, he says. I want to be there, okay? I want to help you through this. But I can't see you. I can't just talk to you about normal things.

Normal things, Rosie repeats. *All* you talk about is normal things.

What's normal would be to acknowledge this fuck-off elephant in the room, Will says, and there's that anger, again, so rife and white hot.

Okay? And that is?

That your brother *died*, Roe, he says. And that I have to fucking live with that.

An intake of breath, so subtle.

He can hear Amber brushing her teeth in the bathroom. The gush of the tap, grate of bristles in her mouth.

How *hard* that must be for you, Rosie says, and it is waspish, unlike her, and their rage meets like waves crashing on sand; necessary, and inevitable. The silence that follows stretches and holds.

Neither of them hangs up.

His clock, ticking. The sound of the boiler down the hall.

It wasn't your fault, Rosie says, eventually. Relenting.

I'm sick of that, Will says, and his voice tremors with that sickness. Don't try to make me feel better, for Christ's sake.

She says okay, okay, and she is the one trying to soothe him, now, and he doesn't want it, feels suddenly, insatiably furious with her.

I didn't say goodbye and I didn't come to the lighthouse because I didn't want to, he says.

Okay, she says again.

Is it, he asks. *Is it* okay? Because it seemed like it was okay for you to play games, Roe, to decide when and where you wanted me, to not even look at me, that day, but now you're ringing me at ungodly hours and interrogating me about those same decisions.

She doesn't answer him, so he keeps going.

I just don't think this is a good thing, any more, he says. If it ever was. You were right, Roe. Just focus on Oxford and grieving, yeah, get some proper help, maybe, and I'll go back to doing what I was doing.

He is sitting up now, his body pulsing.

Okay, says Rosie, and she thanks him, for God knows what, and he stares at the phone after she hangs up, wondering what the hell happened, why he said all those things.

He goes for a run. Tries to put her from his mind.

And that night, she does not call.

*

Rosie meets the rowing boy on a night out.

It is a normal, unremarkable evening, where they end up

seated beside each other at a pub, and he buys her a drink, says ah, you're the early bird. He's noticed her noticing him on her walks by the river. He is big, almost unsettlingly so; arms and legs shaped for slicing oars through the water, a nose broken, years before, on the rugby pitch.

He is older than her. In his second year.

He asks for her number, and they go on a date a week later, for a coffee in between their lectures. It is a Wednesday. His name is Simon.

He reminds her of a bear, with his wide skull and large hands, his ready, deep laugh that sounds so certain and full. He drinks no alcohol, eats a lot of chicken and egg whites, tells her about his love of racing and the water. He talks about how easy it is, for him, to get up before dawn, how he's in bed by nine, and his friends all laugh at him for it, but it's the way it goes, when you're on the team, the way it has to be.

He asks her about her own interests and her studies. Takes her coat and hangs it on her chair, like a grown-up. He pays for the coffees. Asks her out, again; this time for dinner, at a place he thinks she'll like.

It is easy, with him. She finds herself folding into his life the way a baby bird might beneath a mother's wing; for comfort, and shelter; out of necessity.

Marley calls her every fortnight, give or take. She is studying medicine like she always wanted, and she works hard and parties harder, sounds like she has a head cold every time they speak.

She ended things with Tom before they left for university, and hasn't had a sniff of romance since, unless you count her getting off with guys in the student bar, and that, she says, is the least romantic thing ever.

What's he like, she pleads, when Rosie tells her about Simon.

He's nice, Rosie says.

A bonus, says Marley.

Better than nice, she corrects herself. Really kind. And good at two-way conversation. But he doesn't ask too many questions, you know? He's like, the opposite of intense. Just really sweet. And kind.

She has said kind twice.

He sounds great, is all Marley says.

Rosie agrees, and looks out of her bedroom window, across the college grounds. There is a pigeon on the window sill of the old library; cornered, with its wings folded. Like it's waiting for something.

And how's everything else, Marley asks her.

Rosie considers the question. Just yesterday, in the Bodleian, she saw a boy who looked a little like Josh. Her heart had rocketed into her mouth and she'd returned to her desk and written a line of her essay before she went to the bathroom and sobbed, silently, in a locked cubicle.

Everything's fine, she tells Marley.

Yeah? You're sleeping better?

Yes, she says, because it's the truth, and because she'd have given the same answer even if it wasn't. So many people, Marley included, have shown her such concern since Josh died – her school friends, her parents, distant relatives, even, checking in with her – and she knows she should feel loved and appreciative. Instead, resentment spreads in her navel, like that pigeon stretching its wings.

Cool, Marley says. That's good.

Where're you at with your cadaver, Rosie asks, moving things along.

———

She did not sign up for a single music class at the Freshers' Fair. She walked past the choir stall, the orchestra stand, the callouts for a capella and Philharmonia and swing band.

Nobody in her new life knows that she sings, or plays.

That music was a part of her, before.

When Will stopped talking her to sleep – stopped talking to her, full stop – she had to find another way to get through her nights. So she started writing poetry again, for the first time since Josh died; only in bed, and only at strange hours of the night.

She found she could combat them both, that way; the sleeplessness, and the throttling of each day, by taking her pen and writing down the unsayable things. Things not made for music, or human eyes; things she can't believe she is thinking, and feeling, and somehow finding the words for.

Ink spots on her sheets.

When she writes, she cannot check things, or grieve.

Cannot think of anything else.

*

Will starts doing more work at the garage, because he asks to, and because he needs the money. He fits batteries, changes cables, but when he asks to be made a proper mechanic, Moe says it wouldn't be fair.

I can't pay you a mechanic's wage, Moe tells him.

Why not?

Because I've got a business to run.

But I've been on the same wage for three years now.

And I never promised you more than that, did I?

So, all year, Will cleans preservative off the new, ready-to-collect bikes. He picks up overalls from the launderette. He greets customers and sweeps the floor and rinses mugs and makes so many coffees he almost asks Moe to cut back on caffeine, seeing as this alone could allow for a pay rise.

He puts all of his wages, bar a little that he gives to his grandmother, into his bank account for a plane ticket. Because he is going, this summer.

He is half gone, already.

He picks up odd jobs around town, fixing things, cleaning gutters and mowing lawns and painting walls. He learns to sand floors, varnish skirting, lay loft boards and wire plugs and do whatever he needs to do to fill his time and earn his way out. In the evenings, he does as he always has; he runs, cooks, a little, when his grandmother does not want to, and he reads and drives and drinks.

No phone calls. No texts or party invites.

None of his old friends are around any more, anyway. Even Darcy went away to some college somewhere, got the points to study health and social care. He snorted when she told him this, mainly at the idea that she could take care of anyone.

He screws women like her, most weeks, one from the launderette, barmaids and baristas and teaching assistants he meets in the pub.

He fights hard to focus on these girls, while he's with them.

Tries to listen when they talk.

On bad days, he lets himself picture Rosie. When he's with a girl, or simply lying in bed with them afterwards, windows open, the curtains lifting with the breeze.

They would lie like this, he thinks, before he can stop himself. Clothes on the floor, clouds skating past the blinds. Her mouth, imprinted, on his water glass.

Ridiculous.

———

He gets in from a ride one summer night, his hair swept back with the speed, his heart stilled with the risk and the stretching, empty roads.

He decides to eat before he showers. Wonders what his gran will have left him, as they so rarely eat together these days; he is never home at the right hours for that, despite her asking him to try. She's usually in bed when he gets in, all the lights off in the house.

Tonight, though, she is in the kitchen. Seated at the table with her hands laced together.

All right, he asks her, and she raises her eyes.

He is about to ask her what's up, why she's looking at him like that, when she reaches down beside her chair and lifts a bottle onto the table.

She does it again, and again, until there are five part-drunk bottles lined up in front of her. Glass soldiers with long, bone-like necks, catching the kitchen light.

Are *you*? she asks him, and her eyes do not leave his face. Are *you* all right?

Will's mind suddenly feels full, and slow; like someone's blown smoke into his ears, fogged him up from the inside.

When did you start drinking spirits again, she asks him.

He thinks about denying it, like his younger self would have, but then he shrugs and asks, does it matter?

Yes, it matters, she says, and her voice wavers, just once.

After the funeral, he tells her.

Which funeral?

Whose d'you think?

Which funeral, Will, she asks, each word like a hole punched through paper.

Josh's, he says.

His grandmother remains very still, but he sees something release in her face. Just under a year, she's thinking. Not an irreversible habit, which it perhaps would have been, if he'd been drinking in secret for years, since his grandpa's heart gave out in the bathroom one morning, his toothbrush still in his mouth.

I want you to pour these away, his grandma says. Right now.

I could just buy more, he says.

Don't do that, she says, and she grits her teeth to keep from crying, and he burns with the sight of it, every ounce of him blaring with shame and hate and fury, for her, for himself, for what she's about to make him do. Don't you dare threaten that, Will. Promise me. On my own withering heart. Right now.

It won't change anything, he says.

We'll get you help, then, she says, and she stares straight at him with her wrinkled, raisin-like eyes. They shrink, when she is sad. Everything about her gets harder, and larger, except her eyes.

They are the eyes she used on his mother.

I don't need help, he says.

Then pour these away.

Gran.

What?

That won't make a difference.

Yes it will, Willyum.

It won't! You haven't got a fucking clue.

Don't you *dare* speak to me like that in my own house, she says, and she stands up, and she is huge and loud and the woman who raised him, and she knocks one of the bottles, slightly, with the arm of her chair.

Shall we take this outside, then?

How can you *joke*, William, right now? How?

Because, he says, and he shrugs.

They continue to stare each other down. She is breathing too deeply, and he finds it strangely, jarringly calm. It is as though real feelings have deserted him. Like he's stepped back, out of his own body, to watch this scene play out.

If you won't stop drinking for yourself, his gran says, then do it for me.

That won't work either, Gran.

I'm not pulling on your heart strings, she snaps. I'm being practical.

Oh yeah?

He leans against the door frame now; lets the hinge dig into the small of his back.

I might need you to drive me to some hospital appointments, she says. Very soon.

Why? What's wrong?

I'll tell you when I know.

But why have you made appointments?

Just promise me you'll be able to drive, if I need you, she says.

You're lying, he tells her, and he can't believe this of her, can't believe she'd play so dirty. She doesn't deny it. He turns his back on her and walks upstairs, and she lets him go, the bottles still lined on the table.

*

Rosie has run out of paper.

She's been writing on discarded scraps from the printer, but there's none left, and she has more to say, so she takes her pen and writes the rest across her wrist, down the entire length of her arm.

The nib tickles.

It feels thin and light, like the end of a feather, and this prompts another memory, another sentence, a time when she and Josh discovered there were real bird feathers in their pillows. Duck down, she knows now, and she writes a whole song about it, for the first time since Josh died, about the softness and the sharp edges, the rain of white fluff stolen from things once living.

In the morning, she does not scrub it off.

She goes to lectures with long sleeves hiding her skin, crammed with the stories she cannot, it turns out, forget.

After a date one night – though is it a date, she wonders, when you are a couple, when you have slipped into each other's lives without discussion – Simon asks her about the songs on her skin.

They have been for dinner, and to see a film. Something mainstream and high budget and dire; Rosie cannot remember much of it. Now they are in his room, with the curtains drawn, his desk lamp bent low in the corner.

She is cross-legged on his bed. He sees the words, peeking out of the gap in her sleeve, the small teardrop of skin beneath the button at her wrist.

What's this, he asks her, and he nods his large, kind face down at her hands clasped around her tea. Camomile. No caffeine, any more.

She tries to retract, but he reaches out and lifts her forearm to the light, turns it over so he can see. She waits for him to smile. To crease with curiosity and questions, but he simply shrugs and says, arts students, before he gives her arm back.

*

It is raining when Will bumps into his sister in the hallway.

His grandma is watching television in the lounge. The

mournful clarinet from one of her soap operas winds up the stairs, as the drops slash hard on the windows.

Oh, Amber says. You're home.

Yeah, says Will. He was heading downstairs for some water; she is on the top step, blocking his way.

We thought you were out, she says.

Well, I'm not, he says.

She still doesn't move, and this is unusual, the most time they've spent together for nearly a year. They have an unspoken agreement; they never go into each other's bedrooms, and have always maintained a healthy distance. It works.

Gran's upset, Amber tells him.

Why? Did someone die in *Emmerdale*?

No, she says. Because you're drinking vodka again.

His heart snaps, like a band, against his ribs. The rain is deafening against the windows.

I . . . didn't know you knew about that, he says.

I know, she says.

He looks at her then. Properly, for the first time in a long while. She seems older than her eleven years. There's a speckle of acne on her chin, and an intensity in her eyes that reminds him of no one; none of the girls from school, not their gran, nor their mother.

She shouldn't be telling you this stuff, he says, when neither of them goes to move. You're too young.

Gran never tells me anything, Amber says. I'm just not stupid.

His eyebrows rise, at this.

No, he says. You're not.

You are, though, she tells him, and he folds his arms, waits for the why. You're actually quite bright, Will, she says. And good-looking, apparently. All of my friends say so.

What's that got to do with anything?

It means you can do things, Amber says. If you wanted.

She sounds like his grandmother and he wants to tell her so, but she keeps talking, raising her voice above the rain.

You could do more than clean bikes and drink yourself sad, she says, and he stares at her, for the last part.

I know you liked that girl, his sister goes on, and that she went away. And I know that boy died on your last birthday.

Dark cloud, beyond the glass.

And that's why you're sad, Amber says. But while those things might *feel* like they're killing you, Will, it's the drinking that will *actually* kill you. Eventually. I read about it. I can show you pictures.

No need, Will says, when he realises it's a genuine offer.

Okay. If you're sure.

I'm sure.

Take my word for it, then, she says. And make up with Gran, will you? she adds, as she finally moves out of his way. I want a sleepover with Abbie, but she needs to be in a better mood before I ask.

Right, Will says, because despite all that she's said, all the things she's seen without him knowing she was watching, she is still only eleven years old.

He tries to stop.

He does.

He pours the contents of the bottles down the sink, like his gran asked him to. Throws them in the recycling and flinches when they smash. He goes for longer runs that strip his lungs of breath and leave his glutes flaring, and he drinks lots of water, smokes a cigarette when he feels the need, for something to do with his hands.

He lasts three whole days.

Then he takes his wages to the off-licence, buys the cheapest spirit he can find and drinks it in the alleyway behind the shop, hating himself because it feels so good.

He walks around afterwards, unable to go home, and ends up in the car park. The one in the centre of town, where things went so horribly wrong, when he was a kid and hanging out with bad people, doing things he shouldn't, because his parents had left him, and his grandpa had died, and now, after all of it, Josh has died, too.

He starts to run; does a lap of the empty parking spaces, looks like an idiot in his cheap shoes, his non-wicking, too-tight shirt. The lights are on in the corner shop across the way. He knows it's catching him on the CCTV. Knows he looks different, older, than when it caught him before.

He ends up in a bar with a pint, and a coaster that he tears into pieces.

A girl makes eyes at him, but for once, he doesn't look back. He can't stop, he has realised. He's always been able to, before. Not wanted to, but been able to. This feels different, more desperate, and heavy. Like he needs to climb out of it before it crushes him; and because he can't stop, he must act.

So the next day, he buys his plane ticket.

Asia, first. Thailand. He likes pad thai, and the flights were cheap, and that is as much thought as he gives it. He buys them using the computer in the town library, prints the tickets using the huge, red-flashing printer. He shoves the paper tray back and forth a few times, and then it's there, ready and waiting, still warm to the touch.

As he walks home, he realises that he is due to fly the day after Josh died. The day after he turns twenty.

Coincidental, he's sure. A strange, stupid old world.

ten

The deathday rises grey and wet, like it knows.

Will has been braced for the chest pain, and because of this, it is absent. He gets up. Finishes packing his rucksack, checks he's got his passport, his ticket, his sunglasses.

He has said goodbye to his grandmother and his sister. Amber is back at school, some early-bird summer camp for science nerds. His gran left at lunchtime for her book club, kissed him roughly on the cheek, held him for a hard, strange half-minute. They do not hug. Not even when his grandpa died, or when his mother left.

They have barely spoken since they both lied to each other, since it all came out in the kitchen. Since she said she needed him for her elusive hospital visits. Since she found his secret liquor stash, and shamed him, pried him open.

So they had their uncomfortable non-hug in the hallway, and she asked him to let her know when he landed, and he said he'd try, and at the door she said Happy birthday, Willyum, before she left him in the hall.

He spends an hour waiting.

Checking the clock, and his bag.

He is travelling into London that night, getting a train to a cheap hotel beside the airport. He is due to leave at three, was going to walk to the station with his rucksack on his back, but it begins to rain, so he books a taxi. Checks his bag again. Sits at the kitchen table, toggling on his phone, with nobody to talk to.

There is an uncut birthday cake on the table.

A single card, from his gran and his sister, propped open by the fruit bowl.

And then, at a quarter to two, there is a knock at the door. Two light taps with the knocker. It is still raining, streaming down the windows in sheets, and when he opens it she is standing there and soaked through, her hair drenched, her shirt transparent with rain.

I couldn't go home, she says.

He stares at her, as if to check she is real, then tugs her in by the arm and takes her bag, shunting the door closed with his foot.

I couldn't go, she says, again, each word strained between her breaths.

And he drops her bag and presses her to him, feels her warmth through the wet of her clothes. She seems smaller, to him, wren-like, even. All wrists and spine and bent wings.

He makes her mac and cheese. She needs salt and dairy; something thick and unyielding, something to weigh her down. He gives her an old T-shirt and a pair of his sister's leggings to change into, and she sits at the kitchen table and watches him cook. He grates nutmeg and dices bacon and pours milk with the utmost care, as though it is her he is touching.

She stops crying somewhere between him adding the mustard and grating the cheddar. He grates more than the recipe says, watches it pile like wood shavings on the plate.

Do you want a drink? he asks, but she shakes her head. He pours them both some water, anyway, boils the kettle for tea.

He hasn't spoken another word to her, and on some level he cannot believe that she is here, in his kitchen, today of all days, but in some ways it feels inevitable, somewhat right.

He puts the macaroni in the oven at three; the exact time he should be leaving for his train, and tomorrow's flight. His heart turns over in his chest, like a stone in his hands, considering it. But it does not feel like a choice, any more. He does not want to go. Not now. He wonders, vaguely, if he'll regret it, but turns to see Rosie at the table with her rained-on hair and her swollen eyes and knows he would swap her for Thailand tomorrow, and the next day, and he can make a decent pad thai, anyway, and the world isn't going anywhere, right, so he puts it from his mind.

They sit quietly while the pasta bakes. When it's ready, he carries the dish to the table and gives her a fork. They eat together, directly out of the Pyrex, the cheese stretching white and hot from the pasta to their mouths.

Don't burn yourself, he tells her, and she nods, picks at the edges. The kitchen is warm, feels almost damp. The windows steamed up from the heat.

I'm sorry, she says.

Don't be, he says.

You said you couldn't see me, and I came anyway.

Will sinks his fork into the food, and it feels both soft and dense.

Things change, he tells her.

She does not ask him if she can stay, but after they've eaten he leads her upstairs, lets her sit on the end of his bed.

So this is your room, she says.

Impressive, right?

I like it, she tells him. I'd always wondered what it was like.

Were you close?

I knew there would be CDs, she says, nodding at the piles beneath the window. And mess.

It's not *mess*. Everything has its place.

Its place on the floor?

As good a place as any.

I like your cactus, she says, as she shifts back on the bed and props herself against the wall. It is a small, potted thing, and try as he might, it continues to live.

Amber bought it for me last Christmas, Will tells her. Said it reminded her of me.

Rosie frowns, as if she cannot see the resemblance.

A prickly bastard, he says with a shrug, and this throws her, and she laughs, sort of, as if wondering whether she can.

Try and rest, he says, and she nods.

At the door, she says his name, and he turns back, his hand on the frame.

Happy birthday, she says.

Thanks, he says, and he looks at her in his childhood bedroom, each as small as the other, one unexpected, the other so ordinary. Her hair, still damp, shines in the light.

*

When Rosie wakes, she does not know where she is, at first.

Small room. Pine forest smell. There are clothes on the floor, a hoodie and some balled-up socks.

It has stopped raining. The morning spills under the curtains, and she never wants to get up, never wants to leave this warm, still space where nothing has to happen. She lies like this, under Will White's duvet, for she doesn't know how long. Then there is a soft knock, and the door opens, and his grandmother walks in.

She puts a mug of tea on the bedside table, opens the curtains.

Morning, my girl, she says, and Rosie sits up, keeps the duvet close.

Mrs White, she says.

Elsie, she says. Unless you'd prefer Miss Winters?

No. Rosie's fine.

Did you sleep well?

I did, she says, and she sounds surprised, almost scared to admit it.

Now, I'm not asking you this because you aren't welcome, Elsie says. Or because I want you to leave, or have any issues whatsoever with you being here. As far as I'm concerned, it's no trouble having you to stay.

Rosie waits, because there is a but in there, and Elsie sits down on the bed.

Do your parents know you're here?

Rosie shakes her head.

Don't you think it would be best to tell them?

They think I'm at my boyfriend's for the summer, she says.

Elsie nods, once, so deeply that her chin almost touches her chest. Rosie chews over that word. Boyfriend.

So they won't be worried, or calling the police, or putting your face on a milk carton, Elsie asks. And when Rosie looks confused, she tells her that's what they used to do with missing kids' faces.

I'm nineteen, Rosie objects.

And still their child, Elsie says, and she lays her hand on Rosie's knee, on top of the duvet. It's a hand covered with moles, years of weather and toil and hardship. Wrought with lines, like a tree stump showing its age.

I won't be here long, Rosie says, though she has no idea how long she'll be there. She hadn't planned to be here at all. Had got off the train to go home, to do the right thing and be with her parents on the anniversary of her brother's death.

Couldn't do it.

You can be here as long as you like, Elsie assures her. It won't hurt Will to stay on the sofa for a while.

Rosie wants to say thank you, to ask her why. You don't even know me, she thinks of saying. But the old woman looks at her like a granddaughter, squeezes her knee through the bedspread.

Drink your tea, she says. So she does.

Rosie spends the long days with Will in his grandma's house. Watching television and reading her books, and eating eggs and toast and roast chicken. The living room smells of furniture polish and the earthy, outdoor smell of a dog's paws. Dave takes a liking to her and often sits by her feet, or lies across her on the sofa.

Dave's a funny name for a dog, she says, as she rubs his wiry head.

Davidstow, says Will, without looking up from his phone.

Is that a place?

A cheese, he says. My grandpa's favourite cheddar.

Rosie smiles, and she feels out of practice; her teeth feel misaligned, her lips cracked and tight. They talk about cheese, for a while. Get into a debate about Stilton, and whether the rind is meant for eating.

The rain is continuous, but they get out for short walks when they can. Stick to the back fields and forest trails, without having to voice that they need to avoid the town centre, in case they run into her parents. They think she is in Oxford, still, working a summer job. Staying with Simon at the weekends.

How's your mum doing, Will asks her one morning, as they traipse through the trees, the ground damp underfoot.

Rosie doesn't answer for a while. She looks at the backs of Will's trainers, the wet mulch stuck to the rims.

She's herself, she says. Times a hundred.

Okay.

She's cold, she explains. Colder, and more distant. For self-preservation, you know.

Yeah.

They keep walking, twigs snapping beneath their shoes.

And your dad?

Heartbroken, Rosie says. He's on antidepressants.

Are they helping?

I don't think so.

God.

There is no God, Rosie says, and it is dramatic, she knows, but also true, and Will doesn't disagree or call her out or say come on, now, Roe, and she loves him, right then, as if she didn't already; it is the moment she knows for sure.

But she puts this away, in the drawers of herself. Remembers Simon, as she follows Will down the forest path. Separating this from that, and all the things that came before.

Tell me about your friends, Will says, one night. They are in his bedroom, with their backs against the wall. Playing cards. Or pretending to, while talking.

My uni friends?

Yeah. I want to know.

That surprises me.

They're in your life, he says, with a shrug. I like knowing about your life.

Okay, she says, and she watches as he collects up the cards, begins to shuffle the deck. There's Lydia, from my course. Really smart, really scatty, really into chocolate milk. She has it on her cereal.

Weird.

I know. But I kind of like that about her. And there's Henry, who lives on our floor. He's studying Biochem, and really looks like he's studying Biochem, you know?

Glasses?

Yep! And this intensely thoughtful resting face.

No preference for chocolate milk?

No, exactly. He eats toast every morning.

I love that you assess what everyone has for breakfast.

It tells you a lot about a person, Rosie says, and there's a lightness in her stomach as he teases her, asks her about the life she's built, without knowing.

She tells him about her college friends and her lecturers, and she almost doesn't tell him about Simon, but she has to, and there is a stilled, suspended moment as he deals out the cards, when she wonders how it will feel; whether it's a good idea.

And Simon, she says, eventually.

Yeah?

He's really sweet. He's a bit older than me. He rows.

That's cool.

Yeah. He is. Well no, he's not cool. He's actually a little dull. Not dull – no – I meant he's just really by the book, in a good way. He goes to bed early. He eats really well, and exercises every single day, and he's a great listener and he just knows what he wants. Which is so great, isn't it. To know that. To be so sure, even now.

She is chattering, and nervous. Will feels it, too. Has slowed his dealing of the cards.

He looks after himself, and everyone around him, she says. You'd like him. He has clean hands, and nice hair. And he's, uh. Well, we're together.

There. She said it.

It hangs, tangibly, in the bedroom air, which smells of her own sleep, her own breath and skin and borrowed clothes.

Right, says Will, and it's not right, it doesn't feel right, and she immediately regrets it, every last choice of the past warped, just bearable year.

What about you, she asks, desperate for reparation.

What about me?

Anyone on the scene?

He glances at her, once, and then drops his eyes back to dealing.

You know me, Roe, he says.

I do, she thinks, and I don't. And either way, it doesn't answer her question.

*

A few weeks into her visit, Rosie tells Will that she wants to be elsewhere. Not because she doesn't want to be here, with him, he understands; but because living in her own life is taking everything she has.

Where d'you want to go? he asks her.

They are sitting in his living room, as is their habit in the evenings, while his gran cooks and Amber stays out of their way upstairs. Will is in his grandfather's chair, Rosie with Dave on the sofa, gazing at the painting on the wall. An old mill, and a river. Reeds, tangled, in the foreground.

Just away, she says. Anywhere.

So let's go somewhere, he says.

I don't just mean the lighthouse or the forest, she says.

I don't, either.

She takes her eyes off the painting and looks at him.

We could be at Norwich airport in two hours, he says. A door closes upstairs; his sister heading to the bathroom, or perhaps the wind catching it through an open window. She lets out a small laugh; a shuffle of her breath.

We can't do that, she says, when he doesn't smile.

Why not?

Because.

Because?

I don't have any stuff.

You have your passport, right?

Yeah. My passport and my bank cards and my toothbrush.

Then we can go.

Where? she asks him, after she's held his eyes, seen that he isn't joking.

Away, he repeats back at her. Anywhere.

They book five days in Montenegro because it is the cheapest flight that has two seats left, and they both know, roughly, where it is.

Rosie may have packed her passport out of anxiety – too precious to leave behind, even in a locked room on campus – but she has little else. Nothing for the blazing sunshine and oven-hot heat of the tent Will has packed. She buys supplies at the airport; bright flip-flops, T-shirts blazoned with flag-filled hearts, a pair of sunglasses that flick high at the edges and, Will tells her, make her look like a bug.

She puts them back, and he says no, in a good way, and she asks him how looking like a bug can be a good thing, and he lists all the beautiful insects he can think of, right there in the aisle of the Sunglass Hut: butterflies and queen bees and dragonflies and she says okay okay, and takes them to the till.

The flight is smooth and Rosie sleeps while Will stares out of the oval window. He has only been on a plane twice before; on a school trip to Scotland, and a family holiday to Portugal that he barely remembers. There was a fish market, and the unwelcome paste of suncream on his face. He ate a lot of spaghetti. Looked at some boats with his grandpa.

He was absorbed by the view from the plane then, too. That sense of being so high and moving so fast, without actually moving at all.

When they touch down, they hire a small, scratched-up car, and they drive the thirty miles to a village where Will has read there is a lakeside campsite, which turns out to be no more than a scrubby field shared by three raggedy sheep. There is a toilet block with one working cubicle and insects spattered to the mirror and a single tap for drinking water which, a hand-written sign informs them, doubles up as a spot where they must wash their feet. *NO SAND IN MAN'S TOES*, it says on the door.

There must be a beach somewhere, then, Rosie reasons, as Will unrolls the tent, starts to clip the poles together.

Just over the mountain, he says, and he nods towards the hills.

*

The ocean calls to them; they agree that's how it feels. They read by the lake and eat the biscuits they bought at a corner shop on the way in, and then they pack a bag and walk the long, shady route up and over the hill to get to the Adriatic Sea. It is just before noon. That way, Will explains, they'll spend the hottest part of the day out of the sun. Rosie is surprised he has thought of such a thing, and she lets him lead the way, because she has never had that before; never had someone plan things for her. She has always been the planner. The worrier. The watch-for-sunburn-type organiser. She likes that she is unexpectedly here, in a European country she never thought she would see. She likes that she is not having to think. She likes the shade of the trees and the airport clothes that don't fit her and the way she is hungry, again, at unscheduled times of day.

It occurs to her that she should text Simon and tell him where she is, but then she'd have to tell him she is not at home with her parents.

That she's with an old friend.

She doesn't want to worry him, and everything feels so removed out here, so foreign, so far away from everything back home. She is not a liar, but she is exhausted, and relieved, and so warm and soothed in the shade of the trees that look so different out here. She inhales the scent of pine needles, and cones. Switches off her phone.

On the beach, there is a shack where they buy lemonade and figs and sandwiches. They eat and drink and swim and talk, sometimes, but don't talk, mostly, letting the sun trail across the sky, relying on it to tell them what time it is, when to move. She lets the warmth dry the salt on her skin, on the fine hair of her arms.

It is so hot. Almost airless, back in the tent. But she can breathe.

*

They drive to a mountain viewpoint, pass a cobbled village with a car park and a rubble of old ruins. They don't discuss it, but instinctively change their plan; Will pulls up, pays for parking, and they walk up the hill, looking at the market stalls, the trinkets and spices and swathes of painted scarves.

It is like they have crossed out of Europe and into the Middle East. The heat is closer up here, and soon their top lips are beaded with sweat, the cooking smells from the tavernas as heady as the sun. Will sees Rosie touch a necklace of brass and turquoise, something handmade and imperfect, and she smiles at the lady who offers it out to her, shakes her head, thank you, but no.

They wander through the ruins of the long-gone village and then sit under the terrace of a taverna, order sparkling water which comes with mint and ice. There are fresh hunks of bread in a wicker basket. Lemon slices, salt shakers. They order tomatoes that glisten like rubies, diced cucumber drowned in yoghurt.

I like it here, Rosie says.

Good, he says.

Don't you?

I do.

Good. It worked out, then. This spontaneous plan of yours.

I'm not sure something can be a spontaneous plan, he says. Bit of a contradiction, isn't it?

Rosie raises her glass in acknowledgement, takes a sip of her water.

Well, I'm glad the non-plan worked out, she says.

I never plan things, Will says. And life more or less goes okay.

They don't say anything for a while, because they're both musing on how this isn't entirely true. How the worst thing, the most not-okay thing in both of their lives, occurred, because the world is cruel and unpredictable and things just happen, sometimes, and their understanding of this is what brings them back together, over and over, in spite of it.

I think about him, Rosie says.

She says it without emotion. A fact, like how the rain is coming in, that night.

Every day, I'd imagine, Will says.

Every second, it feels like, Rosie says. Unless I'm with you.

Will lifts his eyes to hers and they look at each other for too long and then she blushes, her cheeks flooding with colour. Like a plum, or a peach.

He has a chance, here, in this moment, with the light and the lemons and this opening between them, and he does not take it.

Oxford's not a distraction? he asks.

And Rosie, too, takes the way out, because it is less complicated, and because too much has happened for them to undo, and she says sort of, but it also gives her a lot of time to think, you know, a lot of alone time in the library and her room and watching really bad student theatre.

I sort of zone out, sometimes, she confesses. I know I should be concentrating on the essay, or the play, but I just find myself going over things, like what it would be like, if he was here. Or, just, things he said. Things I never told him.

A hoverfly hums over their bread basket, and the heat seems a degree warmer despite the shade of the terrace. Sunlight dapples through the overhead vines, makes the water jug glint on the table.

There can't have been much you didn't tell him, Will says.

Rosie isn't looking at him any more; her eyes are vacant.

Not a lot, she agrees. But there are . . . some things.

What things, Will asks, and she smiles, even though she is sad, and doesn't answer him right away.

He'd have liked this, she says.

Yeah?

Sitting here, with you, she says.

Her voice is strange; far out, like her eyes. Will shrugs, his chest loosening as she pours him more water.

I'd tell him about my OCD, she says.

The hoverfly is back, and Will tracks it while listening to her every word.

I'd tell him that's what it is, she says. The thing he knew about. The thing that got worse, and better, but was kind of constant, since we were kids.

Like hand washing? he asks her, and he keeps his voice even.

No, she says. Nothing like that. It's subtler.

Light switches?

No.

Okay.

A lot of counting, she says. A lot of straightening things, and checking things are there, or locked, or off, or how I left them. It keeps me up at night, sometimes. I went to the doctor at uni about it. And he said that's what it was: obsessive compulsive disorder.

Yeah, he says. A kid at my primary school had it.

Really?

Really.

Well, she says. Her face is still pink from earlier, her hands folded, in her lap, like she's afraid he'll try to hold one.

Is it, he tries. Then he tries again. Is it . . . stressful?

She takes another mouthful of water. Puts her glass back down.

Not really at the time, she says.

No breeze. Condensation, streaming down their glasses.

But over the years, she says. It's got . . . exhausting.

Will nods, because he doesn't need the full picture to understand. He thinks of telling her about his numb days, and his drinking, and the dull pain in his chest, even the thing that happened in the school bathroom that he tries not to think about, but instead he tells her something else, something not quite as bad, but still awful.

I robbed a woman, he says.

Rosie's eyes seek his out, slowly, like she doesn't connect these words with him.

Well. He recalibrates. I was there, when a woman got robbed, in a car park. I knew it was going to happen. They'd planned it, the guys I was with. And I didn't do anything to stop it. The police came, and they all ran, and I didn't.

Why not, Rosie asks, after a pause. Will takes his time to reply, holding himself abnormally still.

I deserved to be caught, he says.

But you didn't do anything.

Exactly. I did *nothing*. I didn't even try to help her. They took her bag and her dignity, Roe, and I don't care if I was just fourteen, I should have said no, or gone for help, not just kept watch, like they asked.

Who were they?

Just some guys I got mixed up with.

Bad guys.

Really bad guys.

A rare breeze channels through the street, lifts Rosie's hair at the ends. Their empty plates gleam on the table.

You're not a bad guy, Will, Rosie says, and she puts her hands back on the table, as if in surrender, so he could take one, if he wanted.

They both drink more water, parts of their selves now out and floating in the close, ever-thickening air. The tomatoes, when the waiter brings more, taste startlingly sweet.

Her bag and her dignity, Rosie says, with a slight smile. Who even talks like that?

———

At night, they sleep together without sex, and it is the most intimate thing he has ever done with a girl. He can feel the heat coming off her on the roll mat beside his. She is sleeping through the night, and this, to him, is a quiet triumph that they don't acknowledge. She snores, a little, and clacks her teeth, hard.

Do I snore, he asks her, and she looks panicked and says no, do I, and he lies and tells her no. That she talks, a bit, sometimes. What do I say, she asks, and he smiles and shakes his head, all the better to let her wonder.

The shower is more of a dribble, and the cubicle is mostly occupied by insects, so they bathe in the river. Don't look, she says to him, and he promises he won't, and pretends not to as he lays out their towels on the grass. She lifts off her vest and stands in the water in her underwear, washing her underarms, her legs, round her neck.

The sheep watch her, too. Chewing their grass.

Will goes in afterwards with his trunks on, and there is no splashing or swimming together, no romantic notions of this turning into something more than what it is.

They wash, walk, drift in and out of sleep.

Exist, in tandem, and ask nothing more of each other.

*

They overdo it, one afternoon, and get sunburned so badly that they struggle to sit on the chairs at the beach café. The backs of their thighs feel raw, like uncooked meat, which is ironic, Will says, seeing as they've actually been roasted.

They'd been reading on their stomachs all day, and while they'd been careful to apply suncream first thing, they'd become lax, were too absorbed in their books, too bronzed and relaxed to care. It had crossed Rosie's mind, at one point, that the backs of her legs felt sore, that perhaps her lower glutes were burning. But she couldn't reach those spots properly, and she wasn't about to ask Will to touch her there; even though he'd do it, she was sure, if she asked.

She had to reread the same page of her book three times, after that. Had to focus on moving on, from wherever her thoughts were leading.

She's got very good at this, over the summer. Shutting things down, and thinking of Will as something more than a friend, but unromantically so, an attractive second cousin, almost. Someone off limits, but still nice to look at. And that was allowed, surely. She's certain that Simon will have spent his summer at the rowing club, noticing the girls in their short dresses and sunglasses as they cheer him on, flirting over their Pimm's and their picnics, their freckled, sun-kissed legs.

That's normal, she thinks, as she watches Will fold his beach towel and place it on the plastic seat. Completely fine, she decides, as he does the same for her, and they both sit down, gingerly, the pain more bearable against the cotton.

We'll need to buy aloe vera or something, Will says, after they've ordered their drinks. To put on the burns, later.

Rosie is wondering how they would apply lotion to one another's skin in such places when the barman arrives, puts their drinks down in front of them.

You want to eat, he asks, in his broken English, and Rosie says we always want to eat, and the barman laughs, the full-bellied noise they've heard every day since they've been here. They order a tuna salad to share and the barman says you here on honeymoon? Or just summer break?

Rosie splutters, and the barman is teasing, she can tell; simply wanted a reaction. Will takes a sip of his drink. His hair has turned lighter in the sun.

Surely he marry you soon, he says, turning to Will as he takes the menus. Girls like this? Not so many of them, no?

Um, says Rosie, just as Will grins and says sadly, she's not his to keep. The barman laughs again, but then seems to understand what Will has just said.

You're not, the barman says, pointing between the two of them, ah, what is it called?

We're not together, Rosie says.

Not in the love? the barman says.

Not in the love, no, Will says, and laughs. Rosie feels something flash inside her, at the sound, or the sentence that came before.

This makes no sense to me, the barman says, and he clatters off, towards the next customer.

Will and Rosie's eyes meet across the table.

Well, Will says.

Yeah, Rosie says back.

You're just not my type, he tells her, and she stares, but then laughs herself; balls up her napkin and throws it at him.

*

I think you're my best friend, Rosie tells him, on their last night.

They are lying side by side in the tent. It is stiflingly hot, their skin tight from the sun and the sweat.

Don't tell Marley, she says, after a while.

Will snorts, says he wouldn't dare, that he's a little bit scared of her. This makes her laugh, and then she is crying, and he has no idea why, and he sits up to touch her and she says no, don't, can he just get her some water, please, and so he leaves the tent and does as she asks. He fills up a plastic bottle, the same one they've been refilling since their flight over, the stars thrown like salt across the sky.

He gives her a moment and then heads back.

She is on her side, facing away from him, and when he settles inside the tent she says that she's had the best time, and she
didn't know she could have that, still, and she feels so relieved
and so guilty, and how can she be both?

He gets it, and says so, as he lies back down beside her.

It's okay, he says, and she says, just before she falls asleep,
that he's lying, that he always makes her feel like things are
okay, when they're not.

He says he's sorry, even though he isn't, and soon, her breathing changes. She doesn't snore, for once. Hasn't touched the
water he brought her. He listens to her breathing and thinks of
her awake and looping, obsessive and hurting and trying to
cope, and the love he feels is bigger than anything he's felt
before, bigger than his anger and his pain, his desire and his
fury, and this, to him, is entirely new, and the right thing, he
knows, is to keep it to himself.

eleven

It is still raining when they get back to Will's house; has been raining for the full five days they've been away, his grandma informs them. And then, one morning, shortly before she is due to go back to Oxford, it stops.

She is awake in Will's bed, listening to it on the paving slabs outside, when there is suddenly silence.

She decides right then that she is not going back. She is seized by the certainty, feels like something is pouring out of her, and before she can rethink it she phones her mother.

Darling, she answers, like always.

Hi Mum, she says. How are you?

Busy.

Yeah.

Are you just calling for a chat, Rosie? Because I might call you back tonight, if I can?

Rosie pictures her in their home kitchen, making coffee. Scrolling through overnight emails with her long nails.

I just wanted to tell you I'm not going back to Oxford, Rosie says.

There is no emotion in her voice.

But you're in Oxford, her mother says.

I'm not, actually, Rosie says, because she wants her to care;

wants her to know, for a cruel, unexpected shot of a second, that she has been a bad mother, all year.

There is a pause. A recalibration.

Where are you, then?

With a friend, she says.

Not with Simon?

No.

Rosie, her mother says, and she finally seems to have her attention. What's happened?

Nothing, she says. I made friends, I studied, and it was fine.

But it's killing me, she does not say.

There is a hard silence on the other end, so still and clear, she thinks for a moment that the phones have disconnected.

You're being ridiculous, her mother says, eventually, and Rosie feels her throat swell, everything she wants to say rising and lodging. Her mother waits for her to crack.

Mum, is all she can manage.

Where are you? her mother asks her, again.

A friend's, she repeats, because she does not know which word she would use for this house, this place, this boy she keeps returning to.

Right, her mother says, and she tells her to wait, which is ironic, because that's all Rosie feels like she's doing these days – waiting for something, though she does not know what.

*

Will wakes to the September light slanted on the living room floor.

He has slept downstairs the entire time Rosie has been here, although all he has wanted to do is sleep beside her.

He almost did, a few times.

Thought about getting up, in his boxers and T-shirt,

padding up the stairs and letting himself into his own room. She would be awake already, or perhaps she would stir. She would see him, and shift up towards the wall, and he would lie down beside her and his fantasy would end, because that, in itself, was enough.

But he stayed on the sofa, mainly because his grandmother would kill him if he didn't. And because Rosie has a Simon.

Simon. So biblical, like a bored, irrepressible exhale.

He loathes him, mostly in the dead of night, when he tries to picture what he might look like. Fights him, in his head, in empty car parks.

In the daylight, though – in the morning, with coffee and clean teeth and no street light shadows – it makes sense, to him, that she would have someone.

Someone gentle and good, and university educated, who did not invite her brother to the cliffs that night. And if he and Rosie are destined for never – destined for friendship, and card games, and annual, undiscussed visits around his birthday – he thinks that maybe that's okay.

Maybe that's better, for the both of them.

He is frying eggs for breakfast when there is a violent jab at the doorbell, three, four times, so it resounds for far too long in the hall.

He hears his grandma shuffle to the front door, then the tight, recognisable voice he'd know anywhere.

He turns off the hob. Waits to see if he can hear what's being said; briefly considers slipping out of the back door. But he steels himself and moves through to join his gran, whose shoulders are hunched in defence.

Where is she, Mrs Winters says, as soon as she sees him.

You should know, Will says, and his gran shoots him a look.

She's upstairs, she tells her.

When she said she was at her *boy*friend's, I didn't think she meant here, Mrs Winters says. She is dressed in a long coat, despite the late-summer warmth.

Mrs Winters, his grandma says. Why don't you come in? We can go and fetch Rosie and –

I do not need you to *fetch* my own daughter, she says. She can come downstairs with her things and I am going to take her home. Tell her I'm here, Will. Please.

Seeing as you asked nicely, he says.

He ignores, for one ruthless moment, that she is a mother who has lost her son; he wants her to hate him that little bit more, because it is savage, and satisfying, and he has nothing to lose.

Please come in, his grandma repeats, as he turns and heads up the stairs, and he hears her refuse again. He feels strangely calm and controlled as he ascends. He has not drunk a drop of alcohol since the night that Rosie arrived; hasn't felt the need to.

He opens his bedroom door without knocking and stops when he sees Rosie's midriff, the curve of her left breast. She is getting dressed – her arms reached high, a vest skimming over her stomach.

Shit, he says, turning his face away. Sorry.

It's okay, Rosie says, and she sounds like it really is – unbothered that he might have seen things he shouldn't have. She is tying her hair up while looking at him, the morning pouring through the window behind her. A drained, white sky. No birds or breeze.

He momentarily forgets why he is here, and then remembers, like a needle in his side.

Your mum's here, he says.

She lowers her hands, her hair high in its unfinished bun.

My mum?

The very one.

How did she know I was here?

I assumed you told her.

Well, I didn't.

Sixth sense, maybe, he says, and he's joking, but Rosie nods.

I guess I should go, then, she says.

Do you want to?

Rosie lifts her chin and doesn't look him in the eye. She glances out of the window instead, at the wide garden with its scrubby patch of grass.

No, she says.

Then stay.

I can't.

Why not?

Because – I don't know, Will, because you're sleeping on the sofa? Because your grandma needs her house back?

We don't care about any of that, he says.

You will, she says. Eventually. It's already been weeks, Will. I'm sorry, I should have gone ages ago.

Do you have somewhere you'd rather be?

That's not what I mean.

What do you mean, then?

That it's not right, is it? Hiding out here, like this.

That's what you're doing? Will says. Hiding?

Rosie takes her eyes from the window and shrugs, like she doesn't know. She looks better than she did when she knocked on his door in the rain. Fuller around the face and eyes. Rested, and more like herself.

I have to go, she says.

Then go, he says.

*

The drive from Will's to her own house is short, but feels long. Eight stretched, hard, silent minutes, with her mother's windscreen wipers swiping back and forth.

When they stop, her mother gets out without a word and heads up the driveway, and Rosie sits in the car and looks up at her house. It is much the same as when she left it a year ago. A blue front door. Potted olive trees and a perfect lawn and her own bedroom window beside her twin brother's, staring at her from the first floor.

Inside, it smells of home.

The same photos on the wall.

Lock the car, will you, her mother calls, and Rosie takes the keys from the dish on the side, points and presses the button so that the car doors clunk.

Then her mother says her name.

It's not angry or impatient or relieved. It sounds like a question, almost, so she walks into the front room, sits down.

You're tanned, her mother says.

A bit.

Not from the Norfolk sun, I doubt?

Lydia's house in France, she says, because Montenegro is her secret; something she never wants to share. And so she lies by omission once more; a new habit of hers, since Josh died. Since things broke, and no one could fix them.

Why were you with him, her mother asks.

Rosie does not expect this question. She was braced for why she isn't going back to Oxford, or why she didn't come home this summer, or why she was only eight minutes away, for weeks, and didn't even tell her.

All these things, and yet she asks her about Will White.

He's my friend, she says.

Rosemary.

What?

Let's be adults here, she says, and it's her favourite phrase, a sentence she's used since Rosie was by no means an adult; eight years old, maybe, and asked to grow up and be reasonable.

Okay, Rosie says. Isn't it possible for two people of the opposite sex to be friends?

Oh, Rosie, I'm not an idiot, her mother says.

I don't know what you want me to say, Rosie says.

I want you to tell me why you were with him, her mother says, and her voice is fired up now, full of the feelings she tries so hard not to show. Why, Rosie, after everything? After that night? After you've moved on, and met Simon, and are handling everything so beautifully?

Rosie looks at her mother's strained face. Her cheekbones, so pronounced.

It wasn't his fault that Josh died, she says, and her mother simply stares at her, for so long that she has to speak again. Josh was . . . he wasn't himself.

You think I don't know that, her mother asks. You think I wasn't aware?

Rosie's throat swells. Fingers, tingling. She wants to ask her, *you know?* but she cannot dredge up the words.

He was distracted, her mother says. And miserable. Ever since he started revising with that boy. The Joshua before William White would not have snuck out the house, drunk himself to oblivion and fallen off a cliff edge. I just know it.

Her voice, still ablaze.

Rosie's heart on fire.

He was gay, she says, aloud.

Her mother's face slackens, for half a second.

What?

He was gay, Mum. He told me. And he was just – adjusting. That's why he was acting so different. It was nothing to do with – I mean, his dying, or the drinking – had nothing to do with Will.

Why are you defending him, she asks, and Rosie cannot believe she is asking this, after what she has just told her.

They sit in the living room, after that, for too long. Her father is not home; Rosie realises this after an embarrassing amount of time, and even then she does not ask where he is. She feels hot and sick, as if she's colossally betrayed her brother.

Wonders if you can betray somebody who's dead.

Gay, her mother repeats, eventually, with less ferocity in her voice.

Yes, says Rosie.

He was miserable, she says. I was . . . right, about that.

Yes, Rosie says. And then, because she wants to vouch for him, her imperfect, joyful human of a brother, she says that he wouldn't have been miserable for long. He would have been fine. He would have told people, when he knew what to say, and he would have found love, and been happy, and even more himself.

I thought he *was* himself, her mother says.

Rosie remembers the way the walls seemed to shine with a new light; folding back on themselves, shadows shrinking, when Josh told her the truth. It didn't matter, one bit, but she wanted him to know that, to feel it. In the same way, right now, she leans forward and grasps her mother's hand.

It was bad timing, Mum. That's what I think. And I've thought about it a lot.

Her mother is rigid. Holds herself like a rock.

You can't leave Oxford, she says, eventually. Rosie cannot believe it. She feels as if the floor has dropped out from under her, and something is opening, beyond the window, a sense of space rushing between them.

It seems they will not revisit the gay thing, or the Will thing, or any of the things that need revisiting.

Think of all the things he can't have, Rosie, her mother goes on. You've worked *so hard*, for so long. You can't let anything get in the way of that.

Rosie holds her eyes, acknowledging the truth of this.

But you won't, her mother says. I knew my son, and I know you. Even after this past year, I knew you'd be at that boy's house, if you were not where you'd said you'd been. I should be angry with you, for that, Rosie. But I'm not.

Rosie swallows, even though she is the one who is angry, and she wants to say so, throw it all out of herself and into the room, but she cannot grasp where to begin.

You've been through a lot, says her mother, in a softer voice; a voice reminiscent of migraines. I know that. I'm so *proud* of you, Rosie, and I know I don't say it a lot, but it's a given, and you're doing so well. D'you know, when I'm struggling to get up in the mornings, I just remember how you're coping with it all, how mature and diligent you are. And then I put my suit on, and go to work.

Rosie blinks at her. She feels caught between two different conversations with the same person. So burned and hurt, but full of such love and tenderness, she could melt.

You struggle to get out of bed? she asks, after a moment. Her mother gives a one-sided shoulder lift.

My son died, she says.

And Rosie watches as she breaks, in front of her, for the first time since the funeral. Her mother's face crumples, for one, surreal moment, and then she is straight-faced and staring at her, hard, as though trying to keep it together.

Mum, Rosie says, and she goes to put her arms round her, but her mother shakes her head so fast it's like she's hurt her.

No, she says, please don't, Rosie.

So Rosie doesn't. She leans back, lets her mother collect herself, her own throat tight with tears. She has often wondered how her mother has managed through all of this, because whenever she's tried to ask, she just moves the conversation on, or says something vague, and clipped, as if Rosie has insulted her by asking. But Rosie has always hoped that she's coping, somehow. Hoped that she allows her father, at least, to care. To hold her at night, and reassure her, show her she's not alone.

Except she is, Rosie thinks, as she runs her thumb over her mother's fist. When it comes to the one and only thing that matters, she is entirely on her own. Just like Rosie is half of a twin, now; here is a mother, without her son.

Stupid, her mother says, after a while, dabbing at her face. She didn't even cry, not properly, but her colour is up, her cheeks blotched with pink.

It's not, Rosie says.

What were we saying, her mother asks her.

I don't even know, Rosie says, and they share a rare moment of peace, the light mellow, on the wall. She is still holding her mother's hand.

You do what you need to do, Rosie, her mother says, and her voice is normal again. Rosie's heart skips with uncertainty, or triumph; she cannot tell.

You can *think* you don't want to go back to Oxford, her mother goes on, not looking at her. If that's what you need, for a while. But you will. Because you do the right thing. And it's the right thing, Rosie. You know it is.

Rosie absorbs her mother's words, then slowly takes her hand away.

Something sinking in her, like a stone.

———

She calls Marley, that night, and tells her she's home. She comes straight over and they lie on her bed and talk, with their feet up against the wall, like they used to, and Rosie is startled that her friend's hair is dip-dyed an electric blue, but that she is otherwise, reassuringly, the same.

Her mother pauses in the doorway on her way to bed and asks Marley how med school is going.

It's going, Marley says, with a shrug.

You don't like it?

I love it, she says, but it's a lot to learn. I can't help thinking I'm going to kill more people than I help.

There is a strange, fluid quiet between the three of them.

Nature of the job, Rosie's mother says, after the most delicate in-breath. Goodnight, girls.

Shit, says Marley, when they are left alone again, after her mother has closed the bedroom door. I didn't *think*.

It's fine, says Rosie.

I joked about killing people in front of a mother who just lost her son, Marley says. It's not fine. I'm a moron.

You aren't, Rosie says. And she didn't just lose him. It's been a year.

Marley turns her head to look at her. She has a Drumstick lolly in her mouth, and it makes her look young and vulnerable, like a child sucking her thumb.

A year isn't that long, Rosie, she says, with her tongue around the stick. It's still going to hurt like hell.

Rosie feels the retorts rise in her throat, but she lets them go, because it's easier, and she is too tired to be angry. Of course it's going to hurt. Of course every hour without him is going to siphon the cells off her, but she's trying, goddamnit, and she wishes the world would let her.

So, Marley says, after an awkward and loaded moment,

where she pulls the lolly out in one long string, like gum. Do I get to meet Simon soon?

If you visit Oxford, then sure.

You could bring him to Edinburgh. I could take you to all the cool curry houses and we could listen to folk music and eat deep-fried Mars bars.

Do they actually do that in Scotland?

No, but we could if you wanted to.

They listen to the rain on the window. It is late, and it sounds louder now that her parents are both in bed; now that the rest of the house is in darkness. The light from her lamp-shade bathes them in pink, everything blurred at the edges.

Folk music sounds good, Rosie says.

Let's do it, then. But I'll come to Oxford, too. You like it there, right? Your friends are nice, and – you're – you know.

Rosie waits, because she does not know. Marley clears her throat, puts the Drumstick back in her mouth.

As happy as you thought you'd be? she says. After everything?

As happy as I thought I'd be, Rosie repeats, and she says it aloud to see if she can understand what Marley means, but instead, her friend takes it as an affirmation.

Good, she says. That's good.

Yeah, says Rosie.

The rain taps, like feet, on the windows.

Simon calls her the next morning while Marley is still sleep-ing, her mouth parted, curled hair spread on her pillow. Rosie has been awake since four, listening to her friend's deep breathing.

She slips out of bed and leaves the room before she answers, wondering why he's calling so early. They usually speak just before bed; a warm, sleepy exchange about their days, before they say goodnight. Simon has presumed, for the last few weeks, that she's been staying with her parents, and Rosie hasn't been able to bring herself to explain otherwise.

Hey you, she says, once she's accepted the call.

Morning sunshine, he says, and his voice is too loud for the hour, for the silence of her house. You know what day it is?

No, she whispers, in an attempt to make him do the same.

It's the day before I get to see you.

Oh, right. Yay!

She has never said yay in her life, but it felt appropriate, though she feels suitably stupid afterwards. Simon doesn't seem to notice.

What time are you coming back, he asks. I'll meet you, help you unpack the car.

Won't you have your own unpacking to do?

All done, he says. I got here yesterday. Wanted to get some training in before lectures start.

You have the whole of noughth week for that. Lectures don't start til first.

Thank you for explaining how our terms work, Rosemary, he says. I'd forgotten, being in my third year and all.

Sorry, she says.

I'm joking, Rosie.

I know.

So what time?

What time what?

What time are you arriving tomorrow?

Oh, she says. I don't know. I haven't really thought about it.

Well, when you do, he says, can you let me know, please? I want to see you. And to impress your parents with my undeniable charm.

Right, she says, because she's forgotten that he hasn't met her parents yet.

Rosie, he says again.

Yeah?

You're away with the fairies, he says, and her body turns to water, because that is something that Josh used to say.

*

Will does not drink when Rosie leaves. He does not book another plane ticket, either. Instead, he gets a job at another garage in town, and Moe is so annoyed that he rings him up and offers him a step up, with more cash.

You should've said you were getting itchy feet, he says, and Will shakes his head, disbelieving.

But he takes Moe's offer and trains, finally, as a mechanic. He knows things, of course, knows more than he has ever let on, because his grandpa taught him, and because he's been building engines since he was old enough to make tea, and watching his grandpa do it before that.

He is soon earning a good enough wage that he can leave his grandma's house. He views a flat without telling her. Closer to the coast, in a block that looks derelict from the outside. If he leans really far out of the kitchen window he can see the edge of the harbour. There is seagull shit streaked down the panes, Coke cans wedged in the gutter. It comes unfurnished, but with a working oven and an ancient, crackling fridge.

He says he'll take it.

He speaks to Rosie roughly once a week. She talks a lot, he thinks, without managing to really say anything, so that he's always left filling in the gaps. He tells her stories about the garage and she tells him about her friends and her weekends, and he pretends to be blithe and engaged and not in the least bit jealous.

He misses her singing, and he tells her this one night, when she's home from a date with Simon, is pouring herself some water in the shared student kitchen. He hears the tap running, the fill of it in the glass.

I don't really do it these days, she says, and he hears her moving from kitchen to hallway.

You did at mine, he says, remembering her quiet voice in the shower, the hum of her passing between rooms.

Not properly, she says. I don't . . . sing properly, any more.

I knew it, he says.

How did you know, she asks, and he thinks she's smiling, even though it must be uncomfortable, the fact that he's caught her out. That she's made a choice, and it's wrong, and he's not being polite about it.

I could tell, he says.

Yeah, but how?

You won't believe me if I say it, he says.

Go on.

I'll tell you if you'll sing for me.

No, Will.

Why not?

Because firstly, she says, and she lowers her voice, so that he knows she's right outside her door – in the porch that links with another person's room. He hears the scrape of her keys, the thick clunk of her lock.

Door shut. Voice back.

Firstly, she repeats, it's close to midnight, and everyone is asleep.

Sing quietly, then.

And secondly, she says, as though she hasn't heard him, it would be weird singing to you down the phone. Like one of those sad cat mums who asks for the phone to be held to her cat's ear when she goes away, so she can sing it a lullaby.

Cat mums, Will says, and he laughs because it's ludicrous, and because he still sort of knows what she means.

She is mute on the end of the phone, but he is sure he can hear her smiling now; feels it stretching through the receiver.

Those aren't good enough reasons, he says, and the silence that follows is indecipherable, this time. He waits.

I just don't want to, she says.

What, sing to me?

To anybody.

He hears the gentle knock of glass on wood. The flump of her body on her bed.

Well, if you change your mind, he says, and they move on.

They talk like this, nowadays. Like friends. And between their calls he does his best to forget her, to live a life she isn't part of, day to day, which, he reminds himself, she isn't. She chose to go back. She chose to stay with Simon, the guy he asks after, to sound interested in her life and uninterested in her, and she tells him almost nothing while somehow still answering his questions. They send each other photos and songs and texts at normal times of day. She sleeps, it seems. Sometimes in Simon's room. And Will brings women back to his own apartment, with a fridge stocked with Coke and ketchup and protein shakes. He flips through television channels and walks into town in the evenings, sometimes, to watch the seagulls and pretend he has somewhere he's going, somewhere he has to be.

*

Rosie has been dating Simon for two years. Two years of lectures and essays and skipped lunches. Late nights, shared pillows, films half-watched.

Two years of him not knowing about Josh.

It is a Sunday when she tells him. They are lying in bed together, and it is his rest day, which means he is not out on the water, for once. His arms are around her, holding her to his chest. Hairless, and smooth, like the hull of a boat.

She'd had a bad dream. Woken up and thought, momentarily, that Josh was still alive, and Simon asks her what's wrong, and so she tells him everything.

Or at least, the everything she can bear to tell.

That she had a twin brother. That she loved him like she hasn't ever loved anybody, and that he died, one night, just before she came here. Dead before he made it to the hospital. Dead as soon as his skull smashed on the rocks, so far back from the tide.

She talks like it is all she is able to do. No emotion and no pause; a river, pouring out of her, until it isn't.

Simon lets her run dry, and then he says my God Rosie that's terrible, and he just holds her, and asks no questions, and it is then that she thinks she might marry him.

*

Will's grandmother comes over, unannounced, most weeks, with some groceries and judgements and any excuse to check up on him.

I can shop for my own lunch, Gran, he tells her, as she unpacks tins of soup onto the counter.

Pot Noodle is not a lunch, she tells him.

I don't eat Pot Noodle.

You do. I saw it in the bin last time I was here.

So I had one Pot Noodle, once. After a night out.

Well, there you go, then.

I smoked pot once, too, he tells her. Does that make me a pothead?

Will, she says, with a sigh. You're so contrary, you know that?

So I've been told.

Never been any different. Just like your mother.

There is a stilted quiet after she says this; one of her accidental slips that she makes, sometimes, when they have more or less agreed never to speak of her. His gran opens a cupboard and starts stowing the soup cans inside, and he pretends she said nothing.

Are you busy Wednesday afternoon, she asks him, when enough time has passed that her voice is normal, the soup all lined in a row.

Working a shift at Moe's, he says. Why?

Any chance you could shuffle?

Probably, he says. How come?

I might need you for something, she says.

Okay.

So just keep it free.

You'll have to give me more than that, Gran. I don't think my grandmother needing me for some secret mission will go down too well with the boss.

Moe knows I'm the boss, his gran says, and she winks and puts the kettle on. It begins to rattle almost immediately, too little water to boil after his morning coffee.

I'm having my first round of chemo, she says, as though she's merely pointing out the seagull sitting on the roof.

Will is taking out a teaspoon for their drinks. He will think, later, that if there was ever a time to drop some cutlery, that would have been it. Fingers numbed, the clash of metal on the tiles. But he just holds it in his hand, the cheap, plastic handle unremarkable against his skin.

Chemo, he repeats.

I'm afraid so.

For what, he says.

Oh, Will, you know what chemo's for.

What kind, he says, and she sighs again, as if he's being difficult, and he can tell she does not want to talk about it, that her whole body has closed off the way it does when she is sad, or tired, or thinking about his mother.

Lung, she says. Which, if you ask me, is the most ridiculous thing about it.

But you've never smoked, he says.

I know. That's why it's ridiculous.

I never smoke in the house, Will says, and the terror is so real and red and tidal that he has to sit down – to grab the chair from his tiny fold-out table and fall into it, so hard that the wood creaks with his weight.

No, his gran says, gently. You don't.

There is another moment of quiet – not stilted, this time, but stretched, skin-tight. The seagull outside the window takes flight, its wings huge, pterodactyl-like.

How long have you known? he asks her.

Not long, she says. I knew something wasn't right, so I've had lots of tests. Been passed from pillar to post, actually, for months. But now they know.

Will nods, feels his guilt fall, then rise.

Could it have been Gramps' cigars? he asks.

She sighs, again, but this time without sound. He sees her shoulders sag a little lower, and then she turns to him, and her eyes are resigned.

Could have been, she says. But more likely, Willyum, it's just one of those things.

He swallows.

Nobody's fault, she says.

When he doesn't move, she steps towards him and prises the spoon from his hands. Asks if he wants sugar in his tea.

*

Rosie has put off introductions for too long. Her parents tell her this every time they speak, and Simon brings it up, too. I'm starting to think you're ashamed of me, he says, with a playful wink, and she laughs, and simultaneously panics.

So when she goes home for the weekend of Mothering Sunday, she takes Simon along with her.

They'd packed their bags, caught a train. Held hands up the driveway as they approached.

He has been polite and gracious and complimentary about her childhood home and her mother's cooking and her father's crime fiction collection, and she feels like screaming with the niceness of it, with how much she wants, for some strange, inexplicable second, to have violent sex with him on her bedroom floor.

This thought comes to her at dinner. As Simon smiles at her over the salt and pepper mills, passes her a dish of carrots.

She shoves her chair backwards.

I have to go, she says.

Darling? Her mother raises her eyes, her own fork halfway to her mouth.

I ordered something for dessert, she says, and I've just realised I forgot to pick it up.

But I have dessert, her mother says. I bought a trifle.

Yeah, but – it's Mother's Day weekend, and I thought I'd do something special, Rosie says, and she's walking to the hall as she says it, taking her coat from the cupboard by the door.

Darling, her mum says again. We're eating.

Can't it wait?

Her dad, this time. Paused as he's topping up Simon's wine glass.

No, Rosie says. I won't be long. I've had enough, anyway.

You've barely touched your beef.

See you soon, she says, and she takes herself to the front door, hears their nervous laughter, her father saying she's always been this way, I'm afraid, Simon. There's no getting through to her, when she gets something in her head.

She traipses to the bakery, because she has lied, and now she has to come back with something to cover that lie. Her rage, her hot, rising waters, have subsided again, and she almost laughs at herself. There is no air in that house. There hardly ever was, but the small talk and the clinking forks and Josh's empty chair drive her near crazy, now, every time she comes home.

She thinks she loves Simon, and she knows he loves her, but sometimes she wants him to look at her like he could eat her; wants him to touch her in a way that means she feels wanted, instead of just cared for. But he sips wine and talks and smiles with all his teeth and passes carrots across the table.

She does laugh at herself now. Wonders whether it's hormones; what Marley would say, if she told her. I wanted him to fuck me upstairs, with my parents eating their roast beef on the good china, she would say. On my flowery childhood rug.

She tries to hold on to this image, now she's outside.

He would never. And she would never, either.

The day is mild, even warm; there are flowering trees and picture-book clouds, families walking by as she heads to the nearest line of shops. A hair salon, and a café that's rarely open, its faded laminate menus stuck to the door. She stops outside the bakery to assess the window display. Pink cupcakes. Farmhouse loaves. Piped celebration cakes covered in roses, the sort of thing her mother would never choose.

She goes in and she buys one.

And when she steps outside with the cake box she almost drops it, because Will White is standing there, leaning on the brick wall between the bakery and the salon. He hasn't seen her, and she cannot fathom why he would be here.

She says his name before she can stop herself, and he looks up, as surprised as she is. She has never seen him look like that. Always so cool and unaffected, so ready for anything.

Roe, he says, and she feels a wash of something warm. Hey.

Hey yourself.

What are you doing here?

I'm home for a few days. Mother's Day, she says, indicating the cake box, and he raises an eyebrow.

Didn't think your mum was the cake-eating type, he says.

Isn't everyone the cake-eating type?

She struck me as someone who would rather abstain, he says, and he is right, but she doesn't say so. She asks, likewise, what he's doing here, and he nods towards the salon.

Waiting for my gran, he says.

Rosie peers through the glass, and sees her sitting in a chair. She smiles at her little frame, her greying, recognisable bob.

How is she?

Will doesn't answer right away, and she glances back at him, impatient. She's conscious that she needs to get home; that her boyfriend and her parents are waiting. And she's annoyed, too, that she would rather stand here in the street, with him, even though they haven't spoken in weeks.

Their friendship has swollen and shrunk and ballooned again, over the past year. Sometimes they talk once a week, and sometimes life gets in the way and they slip into mutual silence before one of them reaches out again. That's how true friendship works, she thinks. Like her and Marley. She is distracted, cutting bodies open and partying until four in the morning, frequently rescheduling their calls so she can spend the day with her head in the toilet.

But with Will, Rosie reflects, things are slightly different. Will might be quiet, sometimes, but he is always there when she calls. Not once has he rescheduled. And now he is here, and holding himself differently; like he's being pulled up from the crown of his head.

Will? she says.

She's sick, he says.

What?

Cancer, he says.

Oh.

Her *oh* is an intake of breath – a shocked, sad, it can't be, but it is.

Oh God, she says, and she wishes she wasn't holding the cake box, wishes she could reach out and touch him.

Yeah, he says.

Is it . . . is she going to be . . . ?

Too soon to tell, he says. She's having chemo.

Well, that's good.

Is it? She's seventy and being pumped full of poison every other week. Her hair's falling out. She doesn't want to eat. She's dropped a stone and just sleeps, constantly. It's like she's a fucking shadow.

Rosie blinks at him.

But it's giving her a chance, right, she says.

Yeah, Will says. Yeah.

She knows it, without him having to say; can see it in his eyes. He has written her off, already. He is waiting for her to die.

D'you want to . . . go to the lighthouse, for a bit? she asks.

He glances at her, and then back inside. She can see him calculating whether he has time. Whether he can make room for Rosie in his life, today, now that everything has changed.

There is a young couple leaning on the railing when they get there. Hands interlocked, nuzzling noses and necks.

How dare they, says Will.

Don't they know who we are? Rosie jokes.

We should leave a sign, Will says.

What, no one near our lighthouse?

Bugger off, basically, Will says, and she laughs out loud, and he smiles, a little, and she is so relieved she almost hugs him, but the cake box stops her. She has some time, she thinks, before she has to head back, so they walk further on, to a bench that looks out to sea. The ocean is choppy today. Waves, determined and deep blue, rolling fast towards the shore.

I didn't know you were back, says Will.

It's just for the weekend, Rosie says. Family stuff, you know.

Yeah.

Is Mother's Day weird for you?

He seems to consider her question; watches a family picking their way across the beach in front of them. Two young children in bright wellington boots. A mother, a father. Hand in hand.

Not really, he says. I think about her at odd times.

She doesn't press him, and so he goes on.

Mostly when good stuff happens, he says. Like when I got my mechanic qualification, I sort of wanted to tell her. I know that's sad. Just a learnt behaviour, like when you get a gold star on your shirt at school.

Oh, yeah! Rosie says. I got so excited about those.

I'm sure.

That's not sad at all.

I don't really think about her when bad stuff happens, he says. She made hard things . . . harder. She never even came to my grandpa's funeral. Her own dad.

Rosie did not know this. She feels pulled in two directions — half panicked, thinking she should get back to her own family, yet desperate to stay here, as long as he needs, especially while he is saying these things.

Sometimes I think I see her, Will says. Out on the street, or when I'm running. But it's never her, obviously. Just a random woman. Same age, wrong face. It's not like I'm pining for her, looking for her on every corner, or anything. It's just one of those things.

He falls silent, as if remembering the last time it happened, and in that moment, Rosie really wants to touch him. Wants to hold his hand, or push his thick, golden hair out of his eyes, as if to say, I see you, even if your mother does not.

So to answer your question, he says. No, I'm not thinking about her, right now. Not before you asked, at least.

I bet she's thinking about *you*, Rosie says, and he makes a derisive sound, and she feels hurt by this, his rejection of her empathy. She swallows the lump in her throat, and he says nothing more about his mother.

How are you, anyway, he asks.

Fine, she says, thinking that fine actually means half-dead; nothing to report, nothing new or exciting or good.

Just fine?

Just fine, she repeats.

Still with Simon?

Yep.

Still on track for your First?

I think so.

S'all coming up Rosie, then, he says, and she knows she should laugh, but she is still reeling from the news about his grandmother; still hurting, as if she's her own.

Can I visit? she asks him. Can I come see her, sometime?

He looks at her, and his eyes are full.

She'd like that, he says.

They sit together, watching the water. She asks him how Amber's taking it, and he says like Amber; turning to facts and figures, writing numerous lists. She tries to ask him about normal things, too, work and running and a recent album she thought he might have heard, but she gets the sense that he's struggling to respond, so she falls silent, lets him be. The afternoon has dipped to early evening when he says his gran is probably done, that he should go and drive her home.

When they get back to the salon, Rosie says his name. Puts the cake down and hooks her arm round his neck, standing on her tiptoes.

She wants to say, I'm sorry, but she cannot speak.

He cradles her in return and she thinks she feels something slip in him; that height she'd noticed, that pull-up, slackening like a snipped puppet string.

Can we get coffee, before you leave tomorrow, he asks her, without pulling away, and she says yes, of course, without thinking.

*

That night, Rosie texts him to say she's bringing Simon, and is that all right, and it's not, so he doesn't reply.

They are due to meet an hour before their return train. He makes sure to get there first, sits at a booth by the window. It needs cleaning, has handprints smeared up the glass.

He feels agitated, and spreads his fingers on the wood of the table. He wonders how his gran is feeling, if she can be a reason to bail early. And then they walk through the door, him after her, and he takes in the person she says that she loves, the one she lost her virginity to, spends all of her spare time with. He is tall, and muscular, and clean-shaven.

They spot him, and head for his table.

Ah, the famous Will White, Simon says, and he comes forward with an arm outstretched. Will goes to shake his hand but instead the guy folds him into a brief embrace, clapping him on the back. Will is embarrassed that he didn't expect it, and embarrassed that he is embarrassed by it. They break apart, and his face feels hot.

I've heard a lot about you, Simon says, and Will says oh yeah? And when Rosie shoots him a look he says, uh, you too.

All good things I hope, Simon says, and Will wonders if he's being clichéd on purpose; if he's embarrassed, too, or threatened. Rosie is standing beside him, watching Will with a strange expression on her face. Alert, and ready to bolt.

What's up with you, Will asks her, when Simon goes to get their drinks.

What d'you mean?

You've got a little fawn face on.

What?

You know. Bambi.

No, I don't.

You don't know Bambi?

Of course I know Bambi! But I don't have a fawn face.

You can't see your own face.

Will! For God's sake!

What? Why are you so on edge?

I just want you to get along, she says.

Okay, Will says. Weren't we getting along?

It's too soon to tell, Rosie says.

Well, exactly. Give us a chance, at least. Let us drink our coffee, chew the fat.

I hate that expression, she says, and he says he knows, and then Simon is back with the coffees and too many sugar sachets and he bumps into Rosie's arm as he sits down, his frame too big for their booth.

So, Will, he says, as he distributes the drinks. Rosemary tells me you're a mechanic?

Will raises his eyes to his; muddy brown, and, it would seem, genuinely interested. Which annoys him.

What is this, he asks. A job interview?

Simon blinks, then grins. He stirs his Americano, clinks the teaspoon against the cup.

She said you were kind of surly, too, he says, and Will sees Rosie tense as she lifts her own cup to her lips.

Surly? Will repeats.

Excellent word, I thought.

She does have a great vocabulary, says Will.

One of the many things that attracted me to her, says Simon. Is that so?

Okay, Rosie says, too loudly. Shall we start again?

Both men look at her, if only for a second, before flitting back to one another. Simon is still smiling, though perhaps less genuinely.

I like you, Will, he says. I like that you've got my girl's back.

Will says nothing. He forces himself to remain still, then remembers he can drink his coffee; that this would be a non-confrontational, even sociable move.

Always, he says, once he's swallowed.

Well, good, Simon says. Anyone who's a friend of Rosie's is a friend of mine. If you want, he adds, and it is boyish and humble and a bit pathetic, and Will pities him then, because he really has no idea.

There is an awkward moment of no talking.

Rosie, looking into her tea.

But if *we're* all good, says Simon, breaking the silence with his booming, private-schooled voice. Then all I need now is Marley's approval.

Good luck with that, Will says, and Simon laughs, and it's a nice laugh, full and appreciative, and this annoys Will, too, because he wasn't being funny.

You don't need anyone's approval, Rosie says.

Nice to know, Simon says, and he takes her hand and squeezes it on the table, and then he asks Will something about motorbikes, and the rest of the hour is perfectly pleasant, though Will's blood beats in his head.

*

He tries to fix the clicking ignition on his gran's oven.

Thinks, if he spends all night on it, he'll crack it.

He does some reading online, adjusts a few things, makes himself coffee after coffee, to stay wired and awake. He finally thinks it's there, at around three in the morning, and he doesn't even question why he started the job so late, why he couldn't just do it in the daylight.

His gran fries up some bacon the next morning, and the clicking is still there.

*

Rosie is true to her word, as he knew she would be.

Weeks later, after a few late-night texts, she comes by the house, alone.

She'd made some excuse and caught a train and knocks at his grandma's door, because he told her he'd be there, if she came.

His grandmother is thrilled. They hug, and she says she looks brighter, and too thin, and Rosie says that's what Oxford will do to a girl, and they laugh some shared female laughter and she says let's eat, then, let's eat.

Will cooks for them. Fish and vegetables, cooked in lemon, because he's read that Italian nonnas swear by citrus, claim it's what keeps them alive. His grandma doesn't eat much, despite her own insistence, and Rosie doesn't seem to want to, either, but they pick at their plates for something to do, for an interruption between the questions and the cancer talk. His gran seems happier to tell Rosie the details that he himself has asked for; she is methodical and thoughtful with her answers, doesn't hold anything back.

The radio is on low. Country music, desperados waiting for a train, as his gran outlines her chances, the odds that she's dealing with.

You'll beat it, Rosie says, and there is a ferocity to her voice that catches him off guard.

Let's hope so, my girl, his gran says, and Rosie reaches for her hand and holds it and Will has to get up to clear their plates.

They play cards by the fire. Dave curls up at Rosie's feet and they stop talking about cancer and things feel normal, for a while, like they did two summers ago.

His gran asks her about Oxford, and her friends, and even Simon, which is unexpected and awkward, though she pretends that it isn't, looks mildly at her and sips some tea from her mug.

He's lovely, Rosie says. And Elsie says well, good. And Rosie reddens and asks her what she's reading, and they swap notes on a book that's too long but worth every page, something about a man and a passport, and he tries to concentrate, he really does, though he wants to drink, or run, or do something he'll regret.

Late in the evening, he walks her back to the train station. His gran said she should stay, but she said she needed to get back, that she has an essay to finish.

She left gifts; a jar of Oxfordshire honey, and sunflowers she put in a vase. So yellow, wide open like faces or planets or ripe, freshly grown vegetables. They seemed gaudy to him. Smug with enforced cheer.

Thanks for coming, he says, as they walk. She really loved seeing you.

I loved seeing her, too, Rosie says. I'm sorry I haven't come by, since, you know. That summer. I'll come more often.

Because she's dying?

No, Rosie says, and he doesn't know if she means no, that's not the reason, or no, she isn't dying. But then she says, because I want to.

They walk in silence along the busy roads. It is a Saturday night. People are going places, doing things. After she boards her train, he will go back to his flat and watch mindless television, maybe call the girl he'd hooked up with last week.

Simon really liked you, she tells him.

Her voice is light, non-committal.

Huh, he says.

He lets her words hang there, and she seems flustered when they arrive at the station, her eyes bright and her cheeks too pink from the short walk.

See you, then, she says.

Yeah. See ya, he says, and they do not embrace, and for a reason neither of them can quite voice, after she's spent an afternoon with his sick grandmother, held her hand, made her laugh, there is no gratitude or tenderness but a disconnection, a pain so deep and private they cannot broach it, and she boards her train and Will turns his back, without watching it pull away.

twelve

Rosie has a nosebleed on her wedding day.

She has only had two in her life. One on the first day of secondary school, during the fire drill, and the other some years later, on the same day she started her period. The school nurse told her it was like her body wasn't sure where to bleed, and she'd laughed at her own little joke, and Rosie felt something else leak out of her, then, something vital and self-preserving.

This third nosebleed is not the nightmarish scene she'd read about in bridal magazines. She is not yet in her dress. It is early, her mother and bridesmaids still sleeping. She is twenty-four years old, and she is still Miss Winters, for now, and she's sitting on the edge of the bathtub watching the light change outside the window, grey lifting to milk-white, when she feels a wetness on her top lip. She reaches up to touch it and draws back, her fingertip startlingly red. And that is it; it doesn't flow or drip or stain the tiles.

She wipes her nose on a sheet of toilet roll, and then her mother knocks on the door, says, Rosie, are you in there?

*

When she'd told him she was engaged, he'd said he was happy for her. Three times.

He was standing in the street, queueing for a bag of chips, his breath white on the air, as she told him the news he'd been waiting for. Then he hung up and took the chips home, let them turn cold in the paper.

His grandmother cried, when he told her.

What, he'd said, and she said nothing, just wiped her face with the tissue bunched at her wrist, her hair wispy but grown back, in patches.

Don't, he'd said, and she'd asked don't what, and he said just don't, and he walked out and phoned a girl and spent the next few weeks in her flat, drinking and smoking and dabbling in things he said he never would, again.

On the day itself, he almost storms the wedding; or at least, he thinks about doing it, and that is nearly the same thing. He knows the ceremony is at two, keeps looking at the clock. He makes a coffee, a long, luxurious version usually saved for weekends or when he has women to stay. He drinks it in his kitchen, looking over the rooftops. Clogged gutters. Lichened slate. It's an astonishingly hot day and it's another hour closer to her vows and something in him is taut, like a guitar string that smells of nylon and rust, the swollen tips of her thumbs.

He was invited. Not to the ceremony, but to the reception at some barn on the outskirts of Norfolk, a relatively short drive away. He was even granted a plus one. He did not RSVP, and Rosie did not ask him to, and he still has not decided whether he is going when the time to shave and dress and leave comes and then goes and he is still in his kitchen, in his jeans, staring at a shred of sea.

He was going to give her the Montenegro necklace, one day. The one she looked at in the market, which he bought, later, when she wasn't looking. He has kept it, all these years, in its creased paper bag. The chain has darkened, a little, but the stone is still the colour the sea was, that summer, so he takes it to the beach, when she is probably saying I do or I will or in sickness and in health, and he throws it into the waves, like they do in the movies, and it does not make him feel a single bit better.

He wants to drink. Really drink. But instead he makes a decision, and for once, it feels like a good one. For once, his chest eases, like a valve has opened. Air, escaping, in a rush.

*

Vol-au-vents. So fun to say, she thinks, though there is nobody to share this with, even though the hall is filled with people she knows and loves, and many that she doesn't.

There are roses, and gypsophila, and table runners and sparkling wine and warm-hearted speeches and lemon sole sprinkled in dill. Bridesmaids' dresses in royal blue, because that was Josh's favourite colour.

It is everything a wedding is meant to be, but Will's absence is like a missing tooth. Something she worries at, all night, without giving it proper attention.

Her dress is beautiful and too tight. Her mother laced it up the back for her, and it should have been a tender moment, but they were mostly quiet, stressed about the fit, and instead of focusing on her husband-to-be in the ceremony she was thinking about how Josh wasn't there and neither was Will, and that was her decision, not to invite him to the first part, to their intimate and graceful ceremony. A harp entrance. Religious readings, even though they're not religious, because it's only right, Simon had said.

She has spent her life trying to be only right, so she did not argue, did not care, even, very much, because the words were nice, and surely that was the point.

All day, they talk and stand and drink. They hold each other for their first tilting slow dance, and she thinks about the night she was seventeen, in the teachers' car park, the current between her and Will and the urge she had to both touch and not touch him. It felt dangerous, and this, she thinks, is the opposite. She feels steadied in Simon's arms. Propped up. With Will, she never knew where she was, how he might make her feel.

She realises, as she slips off her garter that night, with her husband undressing beside her, that she has spent a lot of the day thinking about a man she barely sees. It must be because she loves him like a brother, she concludes, after all this time. And she's lost one of those already. So she phones him the next morning, while Simon is in the shower.

He doesn't answer, so she keeps trying until he picks up.

Rosie, he says, and he so rarely calls her that, and she hasn't heard his voice in so many months, that she smiles, and tenses, both at once.

Hi, she says.

What's wrong?

Why would something be wrong?

You called me like six times.

Well, you didn't pick up.

He says nothing. Light falls through the blind, skirts her splayed fingers on the bed sheets.

What's wrong *your* end? she asks him. Why wouldn't you answer?

Rosie, he says again, and he sounds tired.

I just wondered where you were last night, she says.

The silence weighs them down, like snow.

I just couldn't, Roe, he says.

Oh, come on, she says, and her heart quickens, and she reaches for humour like a life raft. I know posh food and string quartets aren't your thing. They're not really mine, either. But it was my wedding day, Will.

Silence. Snow. Cold hands, not so long ago.

Right, he says.

It was . . . weird that you weren't there, you know?

Weird, he repeats, and she thinks she can hear him raising his eyes to his ceiling, opening his mouth as if he's angry, holding something back.

Will? she says.

I think we're done, Rosie, he says. I'm leaving.

Leaving?

I'm moving, he says.

Where to?

The North.

How rugged.

I guess. Rent's cheap.

She hears Simon shut off the shower in the bathroom. The water, faltering.

Are you going soon? she asks him, ignoring what he'd said, before. Can I see you before you go?

I don't think so, Will says, after another pause. Like I said, I . . . think we're done.

Shadow, beneath the bathroom door. A cabinet, opening and closing. Simon does not emerge, and she does not hang up.

Take care, he says, and she says wait, and he does, and she says what do you mean we're done? What . . . were we doing?

The sun pales on the bedspread. Clouds, moving, beyond the window.

I don't know, Roe, he says, and it's the name he gave her, and the same small thrill lights in her stomach, before he says, I really don't know. Do you?

*

He follows his plan and goes to Leeds, but he doesn't like it. It's busy and cold and full of people he has nothing to say to, kind of like Norfolk, but with more rain.

He soon moves to a town in the Yorkshire Dales, instead, and that is far better. Still cold. Still wet. But quieting, and with quiet people, and a job he lands with a garage owner who asks no questions and likes his handiwork and pays him a decent wage.

It's just for a while, he'd told his gran. For a change.

Her chemo was over, and she had survived, and she understood and let him go and he knows nobody and drinks one-off ales in the local pub and volunteers for Mountain Rescue after two weeks, not knowing what he's letting himself in for. But he hears them chatting by the bar, sees the hills outside his bedsit window and thinks, why not. He runs. His legs are strong. He has time to kill and nothing to care about.

He needs to pass some kind of test, which he brazenly thinks will be easy. But the inclines are steep and the ground is pocked with rocks and he has to train his body to move differently, to endure in an entirely new way. They make him carry heavy packs, force him to revisit navigation, after the little he'd learnt from his grandpa. Safety is paramount in the hills, which is a new concept, to him. It is, oddly, not a place for risk-takers; they try hard to make this clear.

After a year, he is made a prospective member, and called out mostly for sprained ankles, tourists walking in plimsolls who get tired and embarrassed and emotional. He gives them flapjacks and hot tea and they make it down the mountain and he goes home and reads cookbooks and looks up new running routes on his Ordnance Survey maps and his heart feels fine, for a while, as if it's beating beneath a drawn curtain, taking time to rest.

One time, when the weather is bad, the sky as white as the

hilltop fog, they take a while to find the couple who'd raised the alarm. Eventually, though, they reach them. Two women in their late forties, one of whom has slipped on the scree, and he flares up when he sees them, because one of them looks so impossibly like her.

He spends so much of his time unseeing Rosie Winters, he had forgotten this nostalgic fear – the jolt of seeing a person, of around the same age, who looks like the woman who birthed him. Same shade of red hair, same limber arms. Never, ever the same face.

Sometimes, when he thinks about her, he wonders if she's died.

And he doesn't know how to feel about that.

One night, he is ordering a round for his rescue team, his face fired with the wind burn from the hills, and there is a girl at the bar.

She looks at him like a lot of girls do, so he knows she'll say yes if he offers to buy her a drink. She has short dark hair and sharp, even darker eyes. A twist of jade at her throat, looped on a piece of twine.

It's from New Zealand, she tells him, when she catches him looking.

You're Kiwi?

I wish, she says. I spent a year there, after uni.

Skydiving and stuff?

God, no. Just living. I sold tickets for boat tours.

Sounds thrilling.

It kind of was, she says, shrugging. I like boats. And any-thing's better halfway across the world.

He tips his drink at her for that, and sits beside her on a bar stool, ignoring his friends as they jeer at him from behind.

She can drink. He nurses his single pint, but she doesn't comment on this, which makes him like her, and they talk about travel and home and underrated things that make them both laugh, a little. She likes cats, and late nights, and horror films. She doesn't eat meat or coriander. Tastes like soap, she tells him. She has a sister, and a mother and a father who are separated, but still live down the same street.

Is that weird, he asks her, and she says people who make vows and then never see each other again is weirder. She is pale, like milk. Reminds him of the weather up here.

What's your story, then, she asks him, as the bell rings for last orders. You got a mum? A dad? A one-legged dog?

No to all three, he says, and so he gets into it, and she's so interested and matter-of-fact that he keeps going, and he even tells her about Roe, spilling all of it to this woman he doesn't know but senses he can trust. That he moved here, really, to cut loose, and he wishes there was another reason but there it is, the truth, stark and bent like the dead trees on the side of the Yorkshire roads. She listens to every word, swirling her wine in its glass.

So you're in love with a girl you've never even slept with?

Worse than that, he says. With a girl I've only kissed once. Eight years ago.

He does not repeat the start of her sentence.

I'd say you just love the idea of her, then, she says. You're pinning everything on something you've never even had. Something that's not real.

You reckon? he asks, and he stares at her, desperate for this woman, this stranger, to be right, so he can suddenly, finally, in his mid-twenties, become unstuck.

I do, she says, and he knows as he watches her tip her drink back, the way her fringe falls to the side, that she will be important to him, somehow.

Her name is Jen. She has a tattoo of a fern on her hip bone, he finds out that night, as they remove each other's clothes, and she tells him that is real, and that, and that, as she guides him to touch her in places that make him crave and blur and forget all other things.

His sister comes to visit for the first time since he moved up North. She has spurted upwards like a bean shoot, all elbows and kneecaps and shoulder blades.

You're a teenager, he says, and she says obviously, and he goes to hug her and she says, um, what are you doing?

Greeting my little sister, he says, as the train eases out of the platform and trundles onwards.

Then greet me, she says. No touching.

How are those intimacy issues going? he asks, and she rolls her eyes, says she's hungry, that he'd better still be a good cook.

She seems to like Jen, as much as Amber can like anybody. They live together now, which he hasn't told his gran yet, and the evidence of living with a woman is everywhere; her razor on the side of the bath, the low-fat yoghurt in the fridge; clean, dry tea towels, folded on the kitchen counter.

At first, Amber says nothing, though he sees her taking it all in. She slopes off to the guest room and seems happier at dinner, when Jen shows an interest in her studies, and she gets a chance to show off about her grades and her swimming, and her new plan to be a human rights lawyer.

Or an oncologist, she says, and Will looks at her across the table as he tears some bread with his teeth.

Because of Gran? he asks.

Because it pays well, Amber says. And I'd be good at it.

Jen is looking at her, too. She swallows some wine and

then asks if they really have the same parents, and it's meant to be an affectionate joke, a compliment, which works on Amber — she snorts, and takes a half-shy, half-smug glug of her lemonade — but Will is quiet for the rest of the meal.

In bed that night, Jen asks him what's up, what she's done. Will exhales, wondering if he can be bothered to share.

We have different dads, he tells her.

Jen's eyes search his own. She is facing him in bed, her hair fanned black on the pillow.

I didn't know, she says.

Amber doesn't, either, he says. She's too young to remember that my dad had left, already.

Jen touches his face and asks if he wants to talk about it and he says no.

I didn't know, she says again. I'm sorry.

No need, he says, and he means it. He rolls over so he's lying flat on his back, scoops his arms behind his head.

She's a good kid, she says. You did a good job.

My grandparents raised her, he says. I did nothing.

Rubbish, Jen says. She idolises you.

He actually laughs at this.

Seriously, she says. All these things she says, and does. She's trying to impress you.

She's trying to outdo me, Will counters.

She wants to make you proud, Jen says, and he finds this hard to believe, but he doesn't say so; lets her have her sentimental family vision, if it's what she needs to see.

Love you, Jen says, when she is close to sleep, and he is still looking at the mildew on their ceiling. He tells her he loves her, too, because it turns out it only takes practice, and meaning it — and feeling it — has nothing to do with anything.

———

They take Amber out walking. See the skylarks on the fells, climb over stiles, order tea and cake in small, slate-roofed cafés. She takes photos of unremarkable things like thistles and phone boxes and sheep, and asks him about Mountain Rescue, and talks, mainly, about her friends and her coursework and her desire to study at Warwick.

The morning she is leaving, she asks him how he's doing.

How d'you mean? he asks. He is making them both coffee in his kitchen. Jen has left for work, and it is the first time all week that they are properly alone.

Like, how are you *doing*? Amber repeats. Are you drinking?

Socially, he says, after a pause.

That's all right, then.

Yeah, he says. It is.

Gran worries to death about you, she says.

Don't say that.

Why not? It's true.

The death part, he says.

He grins at her to show he's only joking as he puts her cup down in front of her. He can't quite believe she drinks coffee now. That she's nearly as tall as him.

She's still in the clear, Amber says. She has another check-up soon, but she's good. Cooking casseroles and baking bread. She's even whistling again.

Oh dear, Will says.

I know. It's infuriating.

I remember.

But I do kind of like it, now.

I know what you mean.

I heard you talking through the wall, she says, out of nowhere. She holds her coffee up to the light, as if checking to see what brand of mug he has in his cupboards. Details she'll report back to his grandmother, no doubt.

Okay, he says.

And I already know we're half-siblings, she says. At least, I'd assumed.

He cannot look at her. He doesn't like how casual she sounds; how untroubled.

Right, he says.

I don't think it matters, though, she says.

No?

Nope. Both our dads are absent, so fundamentally, they mean nothing. And our mother is absent, but shared, at least. You're pretty much all I've got, she says, thoughtfully. Apart from Gran, and she won't be around for long.

Ambs.

What? You need to get used to the idea, Will, that people die.

I know they fucking die.

You don't! You don't confront it, or properly let it in. It's why you drink and run like a madman and try to kill yourself on that motorbike.

What?

I saw you, sometimes, she says. Taking corners like you had a death wish. People from school called you Suicide Will.

Will stands up so fast he cracks his knee on the table; he feels the bruise burning around the bone, the creeping of his blood.

I'm just saying, Amber says, as he turns away, runs the tap for something to do. I feel like you need to – I don't know – *process* things. I'm doing psychology A Level, and –

Process things, he repeats, and his voice is high, disbelieving. Christ, Amber. I'm a fucking adult. Some shit things have happened, okay, but I'm fine. I'm all right.

But are you *happy*?

Water running. Fingers, underneath, to check the heat.

No one's happy, he says.

That's just not true, Amber says. For goodness' sake, Will,

this is what I mean. You can't go through life like this. You need to talk to someone about Mum, and Grandpa, and your friend who died.

I talk plenty, he says.

I saw her, she says, changing tack so quickly he can't grasp what she means.

Mum? he asks.

No, not Mum, she says. Your girl. Rosie.

A pause. Sun, stilled, on his shoulders, as he stands with his back to her.

Rosie is not my girl, he says.

Well, whatever. She was home with her boyfriend.

Husband, he says.

Whoever. They were at the pub with some old school friends. You'd probably know a lot of them.

I don't care about any of this, Amber.

You don't care about Rosie Winters?

Why are you telling me this?

Because, Amber says, and she takes a deep breath, and is quiet for so long that he has to shut off the tap. It has filled the washing-up bowl. Teeters, on the edge, water slopping into the sink.

I was saying that you're all I've got. And I was saying that I want you to be okay. And I feel like the only time I've ever seen you close to okay was when that girl was around. Not that I liked her much, she adds.

Something sparks in him.

A fuse, blowing out.

She was mopey, Amber says. And so *floaty*, like she wasn't really there.

Her brother died, Will says.

Yeah, Amber says, and she has the decency to pause, again, to pretend that must have been hard for this girl she barely knows.

But when I saw her, Will, I felt like I should tell you about it, and that's why I came all the way up here. Not that it's not been nice to see you. Sort of.

Will has his hands in the sink water. It is so hot that it scalds.

Is she pregnant? he asks.

No.

Another spark. He takes his hands out of the water, slowly, sees the raw, meat-red of his skin.

She's miserable, Amber says, and she waits, lets that hang in the air.

Her eyes are *hollow*, she goes on. And she's stick-thin. She wasn't drinking wine like everyone else – she had water, and when she went to the bathroom, she was in there for ages, Will. Like, ages. I almost went to check on her.

Why are you telling me this, he asks, again.

I thought you'd want to know, Amber says, with a shrug. Clearly, I was wrong.

Clearly, he says.

I just think, she says, and she stands up, takes her empty coffee cup to the side, that you only get one life, you know? So what's the point in spending it miserable, or inert?

Inert, he repeats.

Yeah. Good word, isn't it? I am soon to be a tertiary educated young woman, Amber says, and she looks smug again – but also different. Something else in her eyes.

So get over it, she says.

What, you being smart? Or me being miserable?

Both.

She smiles at him then, without teeth. Just hitching her lips on one side.

And for the record, she says, as she retreats, heading to the hallway to start packing her things. I did really like Jen.

He notes her use of the past tense as she stalks into the next room, but there is no spark, no fuses blown, no flame in his stomach.

He upends the bowl. Watches the water flood, then drain away.

*

Rosie does not go far, once she's married. She and Simon did not want to live in London but craved the lights and youthfulness of a city, so they settled for the centre of Norwich; close to home, but different enough.

Different from what? Simon had asked her.

The place where I see Josh on every corner, she'd not said.

And so the place she could not bear to leave.

She gave him some vague answer, and Simon thought about it, said it was like a bigger, less beautiful Oxford, why not, and so they bought a penthouse flat, wide and glassy with a view of the river and a feasible commute to the airport, the capital, the rest of the country, for all the adventures they planned to have.

He has a senior position in investment banking, and Rosie, somehow, ends up in management consultancy. Unplanned, but stimulating enough, with long hours and high wages, a good pension and health benefits, and family days where all her colleagues have picnics or ride go-karts or play badminton in tennis whites.

She does Pilates and cardio classes and counts calories and cooks, badly, for Simon and sometimes their group from university who have remained close and jovial, and connected only, it seems to Rosie, by their ages and their salaries. She buys chia seeds and soy candles and anti-ageing cream, on her mother's orders. She fits into clothes she never thought she'd be able to, and she puts them on and feels exposed and unlike herself, instead of sexy or beautiful like she expects. She has dabbled in therapy. She cannot meditate, though she has tried. She checks things, still, on a loop. She is a wife and a daughter and no longer a sister.

Wonders if she can be a twin, still, without him.

She still writes on her skin, in private, when she's waiting for a client to join a video call, or if she's travelling in a taxi back from the office and something comes into her head that she will not be able to hold on to. This is her favourite part of any day, this stealing of a moment. Crafting a sentence, or stanza, and feeling, for a time, like she's standing in sunlight.

She means to write it all down properly, to transfer it to a notebook, and sometimes she does, and sometimes she forgets and the poems or scraps or lines, whatever they are, smear off her arms in the shower. Ink washing down the drain with the grime from the city, the sweat from her treadmill sessions, the shower crème she lathers all over her strong, bony, unrecognisable limbs.

Sex, with her husband, is sometimes nice, and occasionally awkward, and often makes her shiver in the wrong kind of way. He is away with work a lot. He is sweet and tender when he is home, and for this, she feels grateful and guilty as hell.

One evening, after she has shaved her legs in the bath, she is rubbing moisturiser onto her calves. Simon is out at a conference, and she has to make herself dinner, without him. She thinks, briefly, about slathering her body butter onto a cracker, and biting into it. How thick and creamy it would be.

It has been so long since she has tasted sugar.

So long since she has allowed herself anything that even remotely resembles love.

———

Marley calls her every month. She is pregnant, now; seeing another doctor, a neurologist, in fact, and living in London and taking on that eclectic, caffeine-laced energy that all Londoners have, a fast-walking, tube-catching, ramen-eating verve that makes her friend feel like a gust of swirling wind when they speak. She is ambitious and direct and still interested in Rosie, but Rosie feels like she can't keep up with her; like she's observing her through those brass opera glasses you get in theatres, simply watching from far away.

Her friend seems happy, if incessantly busy. Rosie wonders if she's satisfied, if all their hard work and rule-following and good grades at school have paid off, for her. If she even gets time to think about it.

Rosie is the opposite. She has too much time to think now, after a time when things just happened, when she wasn't herself, and she let things play out, without thinking.

Most unlike her, she muses, sometimes, in the dead of night, or when she's walking to the gym in the rain. But it's not all bad. She's writing. She's earning. She's got floor-to-ceiling windows that let the sunlight in, and a good husband who smells of soap and brings her tulips and says he loves her, every day, before they turn out the light.

She does not feel satisfied, but she feels safe and calm and poised, and that's okay, because that's what she'd needed. What she needs.

She gets a text near midnight, when Simon is home and sleeping beside her. She wasn't tired when they got into bed. Has been writing her poems down, the ones she washed away earlier that day and is now trying to retrieve.

When her phone buzzes and she sees Will's name, she does not open the message right away. It has been so long since she saw it, like that, on her screen. They have not spoken since she got married, and he told her they were done, which sometimes, she thinks, is completely fair, and at other times, makes her so mad she wants to stamp and scream like a child. Like a broken-hearted teenager. Even though, she reminds herself, her heart was not his to break. They were close friends. They were not meant for more. She knows this, now, and is happy with Simon. Happy with her lot.

So she ignores the text for a while. Observes, as her therapist would advise, what happens in her body; what spins and pulses and rinses her out.

She finishes writing, thinking that maybe she won't read it until morning. Closes her notebook. Stares at the moonlight, on the wall.

Wonders who she's kidding, and opens up the message.

She scans it too fast, at first, has to slow down and reread. He asks her how she is. Says he's thinking of coming home to visit, and would she and Simon like to get together. That he's bringing Jen, who he lives with now, and who he's sure she'll like.

It is the most ordinary message, so she doesn't understand why it infuriates her. Why she has to get out of bed and do a core class down in the living room on her laptop, holding herself stiff and tight and clenched.

Will wants to see us, she says at breakfast.

She says it casually. She does not care. She sips her sugar-free juice.

Will White? Simon says, not looking up from his magazine.

How many other Wills do we know?

Simon doesn't answer; he takes a mouthful of his smoothie

and keeps reading. She marvels, then, at how much he reminds her of her father doing his crossword. Letting important things pass him by.

What should I say? she asks him.

What do you want to say, he asks, and she wants to throw her juice at him for being so reasonable and companionable, all the time.

I don't feel like I know him any more, she says. I don't think I care about seeing him.

Then say we're busy.

But could we conceivably be busy for the whole week he's down? Is that rude?

Rosie, Simon says, and he finally looks up. You're over-thinking this.

Sorry, she says, because apologising is a reflex, like flinching away from an open flame.

Would a drink with him be so bad?

No. It wouldn't be bad.

It might be good. Clear the air between you both.

What do you mean, she asks, and her whole body hardens, until he says you know, since he let you down with the wedding, and all.

Yeah, she says.

He might even want to apologise, he says. For missing it.

A few years too late, she says.

Better late than never, Simon says, turning a page. So she says maybe, and dithers about it all week long.

Her cowardice takes over the day Will is due to leave, and she finally texts him back. Says she's sorry that she'd missed his message – that Simon was away and she was on a conference but next time, yes, definitely, it would be nice to see him, no kisses, a pause, then a follow-up text, two small letter Xs, either affectionate or cancelling out her lies, she is not sure, and he himself does not reply this time, and for that, she is relieved.

*

Quiet things ensue. Calm days. Marriage, and partnership, and restful, regular sleep. Will falls for the landscape of North Yorkshire, even more than the coastline back home, and Rosie likes the routine and certainty of her days, a newfound strength she thought she would never find, but here it is, without her realising, one morning, and still there, the next and the next.

There are good days, and not so great days. Rainfall, in Yorkshire, that lasts a full week, and cold snaps in Norwich that turn Rosie's hands numb, make her think of things she doesn't want to think about, snow days and lighthouses and storm-grey eyes.

I love you, you know, she says to Simon, when this happens, a thread of panic wheedling through her.

I do know, he says back, and they carry on, this way, and everything is steady.

*

It is a raw winter's night when Will gets a call.

A thirty-four-year-old male is reported missing, was last seen heading for the hills. He's not in good shape, they're told, so Will heads out into the sleet with his team, carrying ropes and survival bags and warm gear, the urgency driving them uphill more than the strong winds behind them.

His team does not seem worried, and so he isn't, either. It is first thing in the morning, and the dark is the opposite of dark – a whiteout of unfallen snow, weighing heavy in the clouds. Will's own heart rate is up because of the weight of his pack and the force of the gale, but he is not struggling; he is focused. Pumping with the edge that running gives him; that hit of speed and danger, like clear, hard alcohol, which he has not touched since that rainy knock on his door, so many summers ago.

His own foot skids on a sheet of rock, and his heart jolts, but he rights himself.

All right? asks Jim, the officer behind him, and Will says yeah. Because he is all right. At this moment, everything is all right. They take another nine, ten steps. The wind is roaring, ocean-like, and the sleet has finally stopped.

He does not hear or see a single thing to warn him. He is in front, and it has already happened. The man had made the decision, tied those knots, taken the step that was required. A single step. A single tree branch.

One moment, Will is looking for a missing person, and the next, he is not.

Dammit, Jim says, under his breath, but Will hears him, and realises he must be stupid for not having expected this. For not expecting it to stare him in the face, one day, in some form, in a different county under a different sky, but with the outcome successful, this time, for the person who wanted it bad enough.

Terror. That thing he has always felt, but kept down.

It comes for him, on the hill.

Things get numb and blurry, after that. He wants to drink, desperately, but he tells Jen in a moment of clarity and she does her utmost to prevent it. He spends his days in the flat, and goes to work and completes his shifts with as little interaction as possible. In the evenings, he takes his motorbike out, because it is the only thing that makes him feel anything at all.

He thinks about what Amber said.

What they called him at school.

He thinks about that day in the school bathroom, with the smashed mirror and his cut head. People assumed he'd attacked another student, and that was easier, more understandable. Nobody, least of all himself, would know what to do with the truth. That he had cracked his own skull multiple times against the glass, to see what would break first.

He thinks about the woman they robbed.

Josh, and the edge.

His mother left. His father was never there. His grandpa died, and his grandma will, and the missing man, with his khaki trousers and unlaced boots, the man they did not find in time – he was gone, too, and nothing Will did or could do would stop any of it.

So he rides, and he lies in bed, and he says very little, and he lets whatever it is inside him take him down, down, down.

*

Rosie goes to see Marley and the baby. She takes an assortment of gifts from herself and Simon but also her parents, wrapped in tissue paper and dotted with ducklings. Marley asks her to open them for her, sunk into the sofa cushions with her tiny person nestled on her chest. She looks exhausted. Content. Dishevelled, like a bud that's late to open.

She tells her in detail about the birth, and Rosie holds the baby for a while but is so startled by the weight of her that she soon hands her back. Sunshine tips through the windows and warms the room. Rosie takes off her jumper, refreshes their drinks.

I can't believe you're a mother, she says, at some point.

Me neither, Marley says. I wasn't meant to be until I was thirty-three.

Oh, really?

Yep. I had a plan. A Rosie Winters plan.

Rosie smiles as she lifts her lemonade, tells her to go on.

I was going to marry Trev at thirty, Marley says. Finish my residency and start trying. I figured it would take me roughly a year to fall pregnant. So yeah, I'd be popping her out at thirty-three. Not twenty-nine. This is all a bit . . . soon.

What happened, Rosie asks.

Skye happened, Marley says, looking down at her little human. She seems unconcerned that it is too soon, that her plan had a timeline of its own.

So will you marry Trevor, anyway, Rosie asks her. They are both staring at Skye, her sleeping face and hammy hand, resting on Marley's collarbone.

Someday, Marley says. If he asks.

Of course he'll ask.

There is a pleasant silence. They listen to the sigh of traffic outside, the shuffle of the blinds in the breeze.

Did you feel any different, when you married Simon? Marley asks her.

Rosie takes another mouthful of lemonade. Different how, she asks.

I don't know. You tell me. I always thought a wedding would be necessary, you know, and special. But now we have Skye, I just wonder whether anything can be more special than this. More binding. You know?

Sure, Rosie says, though of course she does not know, because she does not have a child. She and Simon have talked about it, once or twice. She feels no desire to be a mother, though she has never admitted such a thing, hopes that it'll set in, one day, without her noticing.

So did you feel a change, when you got married?

Yeah, of course, Rosie says.

Marley waits, and Rosie drinks more lemonade. It is tart and already flat, leaves a film of sugar on her teeth.

It solidifies your commitment, she says. It was nice to do that out loud, in front of everyone.

Nice, Marley repeats. She is watching her in that way that she does.

Wonderful, Rosie corrects herself.

Rosie, Marley says.

Yeah?

Are you all right?

. . . yeah? Why?

No reason, she says. You're just so . . . on edge.

Haven't I always been?

They smile awkwardly at this, thinking that it's both sad and true. Skye mewls and Marley rearranges her on her chest, and soon, she falls asleep again.

You're skinny, too, Marley says.

Finally, says Rosie. Marley pulls a face; not denying it, but not approving of her response, either.

It's just Si's healthy lifestyle, Rosie says, with a false laugh. It's hard to be married to a rower and still eat dairy and bread.

But you're all right, Marley says.

I'm completely fine, Rosie says. Really.

She goes over this lie as she rides the train home. Because the fact is, she has never been completely fine; can't remember a time she was ever fine, and that was even before Josh died.

Josh.

His name, like a lost lucky charm. Still shining with hope

and good things, but also laced with something irretrievable; a yearning that gets her nowhere.

She sees him in the mirror, sometimes, in the shape of her own ears and the angle of her jaw. Both of them a little funny-looking; he, with limbs too big for his body, sure to grow handsome and refined with the years he was never given. And she, never quite right. Eyebrows too thick. Forehead too broad. Almond eyes, blue, but sad.

She misses him like a vital organ.

Sits up, sometimes, in the middle of the night, because she thinks she can hear him coming down the hall, even though he never set foot in her apartment, would have probably hated all the granite and the grey, the lack of plants and music and cushions.

When she gets back from Marley's she skips dinner, brushes her teeth because that makes it easier to convince herself that she's eaten. Then she checks the windows are closed, three times – a smooth night, really, all things considered.

Once she's in bed, she phones her mother, without thinking about it. A reflex, when she feels down, or confused, even though it so rarely helps.

Darling, she answers, and Rosie says, Mum.

Are you all right?

Not really, she says.

Oh! What's happened?

Nothing. Nothing.

A silence.

I think that's the problem, she says. *Nothing* has happened. I think I'm bored, Mum. I feel stuck. And tired, all the time.

Are you eating properly? her mother asks. Do your breasts hurt?

I'm not pregnant, Mum.

Are you sure?

Yes. That's not why I called.

You called because you're tired?

Rosie holds her breath, looking at her drawn curtains, the scattering of face creams on her dresser. She wonders where her books went. Her records and notebooks and her stacks of Post-it notes.

Yeah, she says. I guess.

Well get an early night, darling, her mother says. And just watch it. It could be anaemia, or something. You might need some supplements.

Maybe, says Rosie.

Darling?

Yeah?

You're just bored because you're bright, she says. Start looking for new jobs, if you need to. You've been at your company long enough. You probably just need a change.

Rosie agrees. She thanks her mother, though she doesn't know what for, and hangs up. The face creams seem to stare at her, like they don't know what she expected. So judgemental, standing in their straight line.

Soon after, Simon texts to say he'll be late, that she shouldn't wait up, and even though she is already in bed she feels a flash of righteousness, like she's allowed to be angry at the man who loves her and cares for her and plans their weekends with the diligence he shows almost everything: rowing, sex, weight-lifting, Scrabble. He touches her wrong, but it is still touching. He supports her through her quiet grief and her constant checking, and holds her strange, tapping hands when she is nervous because something bad is happening on the television.

In time, she slips out of her anger and sleeps, dreamlessly. The same way she moves through her days.

long after

thirteen

Seasons of good, and bad, and totally fine.

Sleepwalking.

Routine-making.

Life passing like cars. Smells of petrol and bleach and instant coffee. Chest pain, fresh tulips, calories burnt and units consumed and late-night noodles out of a pot.

Good sex; bad sex. Rude waiters, and crying women, and long phone calls with relatives that expect it but have nothing to say, talk only about the washing, the neighbours, the things outside the window.

They do not think of each other. Often.

They do not.

Until, one bright day, at the top of a hill he has climbed, Will takes a photo of a view he has never seen before. Like he used to when he was a teenager, on his long runs by the coast. Photos of clouds and silhouetted seabirds, and sunlight doing bold things. This time, the sky is the clearest blue he's ever seen, so clear he can see as far as the Irish Sea, which hasn't happened in all the time he's lived here. He captures it, for Rosie, without pausing to think, and feels good, and light, for one clear moment.

He is hiking back down, the summit behind him, when the weight returns to his chest. Because he will not send it to her.

They have not spoken for nearly two years. He does not want to draw her in again, doesn't want to go there, even though he so badly wants to hear from her, to read her words on a screen, and he is furious with her, for that. For making him want something he shouldn't. So he keeps the photo on his phone, a reminder of the good things, the light things, that they must not share.

Last time they'd been in touch — when he'd reached out to check on her, more than anything, after what Amber had told him — she had ignored him. Or seen it, and opted not to respond until too late. Either way, he feels quietly enraged at her cowardice, or worse, the fact that she no longer cares. So he fumes, and stays silent, because he doesn't want to know her reasons, is not sure he could handle it if they were to cross texts, or send Christmas cards, in case he finds out she's happy without him in her life, moved on and married and detached. So he says nothing. Just rages, day in, day out, apart from the odd occasion he sees a sky like that, and things feel right for a while.

It is all less beautiful, on the way down.

Rosie plays on his mind, like the sunlight on the stream beside him, running parallel to the edge.

He knows this thing between them will always hold some temptation, some kind of magnetic pull that neither of them can quite break. An addiction, he thinks, as he descends, passes another lone hiker who nods to him, says morning. And like any addiction, you have to learn to manage it. It's a moment of weakness, when he sees something and wants to share it with her, an urge that crops up out of nowhere, even though he is calm, and managing, and getting out every day, as if he can walk off the bad feelings, because Jen says it is good for him, that she notices a change in him if he does.

He does it to please Jen, more than anything. To stop her worrying. And because there are seconds – literal seconds – when he is walking, stopping to drink some water or watching figures atop the opposite ridge, when he does feel a change, and it is such a relief, so pure and real, that he knows feeling numb won't last, that things are going to be okay.

The urge to send Rosie photos comes, and goes, like this.

Out on the fells, he can make these kinds of choices. To see, and not send. To think, but not do. Back at home, in his flat with Jen, everything feels too bright, and hard. The sun, catching the edges of the TV screen. The unwashed bread knife on the chopping board. Fork tines. Nail clippers. The nick of Jen's dental floss, cutting at her teeth in the mirror.

After the night on the hill, he quit Mountain Rescue. He works and socialises and walks alone, like this, to make it through each day. Nobody presses him about anything, the way they did after that unspeakable time at school, and the year after Josh fell. His gran, his friends, his girlfriend – they all let him function as he needs to, without questions and without criticism. His depression – because that is what it is, he knows now, what has plagued him since his early teens, the need and the numbness and the chest pain – has finally got a reason for being.

The doctor put him on medication.

It hasn't changed a thing, but he's living, and he's cohabitating, and he's not one of the bodies on the mountain and that, he thinks – on his better days, when the lights are dimmed and the noise is level, and he finds small flickers in things like the smell of Jen's hair or the thick buttering of bread or the call of the larks in the pale morning – that is only a good thing.

He has a ring that he keeps in his sock drawer. Something his gran gave him that belonged to her late sister, or some other meaningful relative he'd never asked about. I'll trust that you'll give this to the right person, she'd said, handing it over when he'd last visited. I meant to give it to your mother, she'd said. But, you know. Someone else works, too.

He does think about proposing to Jen, sometimes. But they've been together for more than four years now, and she's often scoffed at the concept of weddings and marriage, all that tradition and paperwork. She wouldn't like the ring, anyway, he knows; too delicate, too fussy, with its interwoven strands and deep-set white stone. It doesn't look like her.

She takes him into the hills, most weekends. They walk and scramble and boulder, in the wind and rain and rare, pollen-heavy heat. She swims, too, in the cold, shallow tarns, often going in completely naked, calling back at him to join her, though he never does. He just watches from the shore, listens to the splash and dives and shrieks of her, as they carry across the water.

She is proactive and, it seems to him, always in motion, in a way that keeps Will moving, too, stops him from thinking too much.

In the evenings, they play cards together and watch box sets and he even stops running, to spend the mornings in bed with her. Hiking doesn't keep him in quite the same shape, though he finds he has no energy to care. Much of him wants to give up and get fat and start smoking again.

Don't you dare, Jen had said, when he'd shared this desire with her. My friends are jealous, and I like it that way.

As she'd said this, she'd moved her hands down towards his groin, slid them across his lower abs. They were still there, beneath a soft layer of skin he'd never had before. That's the meds, he'd said, his voice bitter. That's turning thirty, Jen had said, before she took him in her mouth.

He does not know how she knew this. He'd been with Jen

for more than two years when she suddenly clocked that she did not know his birthday, and he'd told her that was because he didn't celebrate it. How woke, she'd said, and he'd said nothing, let her believe it was because he was too cool, or unsentimental. Anti-consumerist. Clinging on to a golden youth he would actually much rather forget.

*

Simon goes to the kitchen cupboard and takes down the first-aid kit while they argue, again, about nothing. Arguing with Simon is a quiet and stalled activity; to an observer, it would hardly look like they were fighting at all. To Rosie, it is exhausting, and endless.

He removes some ibuprofen from a pack while she badgers him, swallows two tablets before he pours himself a glass of water.

I just don't see what's wrong with it, he says to her, again. I thought you liked your parents.

I *do* like them, she says.

Then what's the problem?

The problem is I want to spend some alone time with my husband, Rosie says, and she cannot believe she is having to explain this to him, yet again. We need that, Si. Don't *you* need that?

I don't feel like I do, he says, and I suppose that's the issue, Rosie. I feel as in love with you as I always have.

That is not what I'm saying.

What, then? What's wrong with inviting them along?

When you said let's celebrate our anniversary, I thought you meant me, you, maybe some wine. Not a family gathering where I need to worry about how revealing my dress is, or whether I can order a cocktail.

Why couldn't you order a cocktail?

I could. But if I didn't, she'd think I was pregnant. And if I did, she'd raise her eyebrows, or mention the calories in the fruit juice.

I'm confused, Simon says, and he's rubbing his temples now, as if the pain has intensified. Does your mum want you to order a cocktail or not?

This is a hypothetical cocktail. We're not even at the restaurant yet.

I know, but hypothetically.

Simon, this doesn't matter!

You're the one that said –

I'm *saying*, she says, that I don't want to have an anniversary meal with my mum and dad, okay? I want to go with you. Alone.

Simon looks at her over his water glass.

But I've asked them now, he says.

Right. And we can't un-ask them.

Well, we can. I can say there was a misunderstanding.

No, you can't. It's done.

Sorry, Simon says, and he sounds so helpless, so dazed by one of his frequent headaches, that she decides to let it be.

To Simon, it seems, six years of marriage calls for an upmarket restaurant with too many forks; dauphinoise and jus and some sort of three-bird special, the greed of which turns her stomach. Rosie looks down at the menu and doesn't want any of it. She thinks about how she would rather be cooking a vat of spaghetti at home. Throwing it at the wall, to see if it would stick. Eating it with a spoon and a twirling fork and getting ragù down her chin. Someone kissing it off her. Garlic and heat, and unwashed pans in the sink.

That's what she thought sharing a life might look like.

Moments of need, and lust, for each other, and places, and books and food and music. But she and Simon do not even listen to the radio. And they have never really been anywhere; he is always too busy with work, too tired at the weekends. She is not sure he even knows that she was a musician, once. That she still writes songs when she can.

The waiter brings over a bottle of sparkling wine and they order their starters. Her mother lays her napkin in her lap and her father asks her husband about the hours he's working and Rosie slips her heels off under the table, because the straps are cutting into her toes.

How's Marley, her mother asks her. The light drops from the chandelier, glitters off their wine glasses.

Good, Rosie says. Struggling a little, in this heat.

They say your second is always bigger, her mother recalls, nodding. She'll be the size of a whale soon.

Don't write that in your New Baby card, Rosie says, and her mother laughs, a forced tinkle like a fork on china.

What about you, she asks her.

What about me?

How are you, Rosie. You don't really tell me anything these days.

Rosie reaches for her water. She lets the surface of the glass moisten her palm, which feels slick, and far too warm. She'd chosen to wear a high-necked dress, and regrets it.

There's not much to tell, she says.

You look good, her mother says, and this surprises Rosie so much that she glances up at her, to see if there's a catch, or a but.

You look good, her mother repeats. But you don't look as though you feel it.

Tired, Rosie says, shrugging. That's all.

Are you sleeping?

Depends.

Do we need to get you to a sleep specialist again?

No, Mum. It's fine.

I do worry about you, darling.

You don't need to. I'm fine. I'm . . .

She considers finishing her sentence truthfully. Perhaps it is the low light, the safety of her husband in deep conversation across the table; perhaps it is the rare moment in which her mother has asked her a real question and seems to want a real answer.

But then the waiter arrives with their tiny wide-rimmed bowls, ceviche and gazpacho and tartare.

I used to play piano, Rosie says that night, to the bedroom ceiling.

Simon is in their bathroom, doing whatever it is he does before bed. She has already shut off the light, and the gold spills from their en-suite across their new carpet, just touches the foot of their bed.

I know, he says, his voice measured around his razor. She hears the swill of it in the sink, before he raises it back to his skin.

Do you?

Sure. There's that photo, in your parents' hall.

She realises he is right; a shot of her as a five-year-old sat on the piano stool, her feet not yet touching the floor.

Well, I miss it, she says.

Oh yeah?

She doesn't respond. Waits until he comes out of the bathroom, flicks off the light and eases himself into bed. He smells of shaving cream, their bergamot hand soap.

You should play, then, he says. I'd love to hear.

Would you?

Of course.

Why have you never asked, then?

Because you never mentioned it?

Rosie sighs, because she is angry, and she feels bad about it.

Happy anniversary, then, Simon says, and despite every-thing, he falls asleep within minutes. Light breathing, catch of air through his teeth.

She glares at the ceiling. She can't help it. So much about him annoys her these days. It annoys her that he gets so many headaches. That he weighs himself daily. That he brings her tulips, even though she doesn't particularly like tulips, the way they droop one by one, like they've given up, their necks broken over nothing.

There was a time when this was a good thing.

She remembers telling Marley, over a glass of wine, that this was one of the reasons she was marrying him. Because he got rid of the sad tulips, without her having to ask.

The sad tulips? Marley had asked.

Yeah. The ones that droop. He takes them away, leaves just the happy ones standing.

Oh *stop*, Marley had said. That's too adorable.

But now, this beautiful thing, this kind, understated ges-ture that they'd never even discussed, annoys the hell out of her. Like he's trying too hard. It bothers her that he is a better cook than she is, even though he never makes dinner, and that his breathing is nasal when they're watching television. His chest, once so wide and safe, seems to have shrunk, which makes her feel wrong, too big.

He sleeps well, and Rosie tries to.

She counts the light switches while she lies there.

Thinks about how he is still gentle and patient and loving,

but he does not hold her hand, so much, any more, when she taps and clicks and has to check they've locked the front door six times. Seven, maybe eight.

Everything's fine, Rosie, he tells her, with a strain in his voice. Everything's fine.

*

The doctor is looking at him over his glasses.

Will looks back, because he's not sure he heard the question.

I asked if you'd consider counselling, the doctor says. I know we've discussed it before, but it's an avenue you're yet to explore. Worth a go, perhaps. I can get you twelve sessions on the NHS, in this same surgery.

Will nods, as if he's considering it.

Maybe, he says.

The doctor sits back; steeples his fingers.

How are you sleeping? Any nightmares?

Fine, and no, Will says.

Are you sleeping more than normal?

No.

Do you know what's normal, any more, Will?

It seems a rude and accusatory question, so he doesn't answer. He lets out a puff of air, like he's offended, but not bothered.

Are we done? he asks. Look, Doc, I'm grand. I'm not wanting to overdose or hang myself off trees. Progress, right?

He is trying to keep his voice even. The doctor eyes him as he speaks.

Progress, he repeats, after a long, clock-filled silence. There is a metal ball apparatus on his desk, and Will has the desire to lean forward and get it started – to watch the steel knock on steel, make something move, fly through the air.

You appreciate, the doctor goes on, that we need to be mindful of a person with a history like yours. And if the medication isn't enough –

It's enough, Will says.

But if anything changes, the doctor says. If you begin to feel worse, or have any of those old urges. Any thoughts, even.

Like throwing myself off a cliff? Will asks.

Well, the doctor says. Or cracking your head against a mirror.

Will crosses his arms.

That was once, he says.

And still a concern, the doctor continues, looking back at his screen. Using his index finger to scroll through all the godawful details, no doubt, the story that Will wants to delete, or forget, but which gets dredged up every damn time.

Yes, Will says. I attempted suicide in the school bathroom. I was young, and stupid, and I failed. So here I am. Taking my meds. Feeling fine.

You're feeling fine, the doctor repeats.

As ever, Will says. He reaches over, this time, lifts the silver ball and lets it fall. They both watch it start something; watch the other end raise and knock back, tiny noises, like nails on wood.

Glad to hear it, the doctor says. He types something on his keyboard.

Jen is waiting for him outside.

All good? she asks. She has shopping bags in both hands, is wearing sunglasses so he can't see her eyes. He's always hated that.

Yep, he says.

Any updates?

Nope.

Talk to me, she says, as they turn and head for home, past the graveyard and the kebab shop, the traffic lights, the square. It is a quiet day in town. Retired folks ambling about; no bikers or hikers or tourists.

I am, Will says.

No, you're not. You used to. But now you're all . . . clammed up.

Well, I'm feeling clammy, he says.

He takes one of her shopping bags so he can link his hand through hers. It is not like him to do this, but he knows it'll get her off his back.

It works. She shakes her head and drops the subject. They walk in silence the rest of the way home, and in the flat, the sunshine is bright, bounces off their wooden floor.

It's like a greenhouse in here, Jen says, as she unloads the shopping, so Will opens the windows and closes the blinds. He lies on the sofa and shuts his eyes and pretends he's fallen asleep while Jen witters on, and he thinks she finally buys it because, after a while, she goes quiet.

But then he feels her shadow. She sits on his chest, wraps her legs either side of him, and he gets an erection, in spite of himself.

Jen, he says. I'm knackered.

Too knackered for this? she says, and she takes off her top and her bra and amuses herself with his jeans for a while, and it is good, and distracting, and it is all over in fifteen minutes, quick and dirty and raw. Her heart flutters against his own as she lies on top of him afterwards.

Now, she says. Talk.

Jen, he says, and he struggles up from beneath her, but she is strong, clamps her calves down around him.

What did the doctor say? she asks. If we're partners, Will,

and not just roommates, then you tell me this stuff, okay? That's the rule.

I didn't know we had rules.

Well, we do. I'll just be your roomie, though, if that's what you want.

He doesn't answer. The sunlight stripes across the floor, through the gaps in the blinds, iridescent as it catches the brass wheels of the furniture.

Look at me, Jen says, so he does.

What did they say, she asks him, again.

They checked I was fine, he says. And when she keeps looking at him, like she knows there is more, something blows in him – another fuse, another implosion – and he goes there, decides to give it to her, if that's what she so desperately wants. See if she can handle it, the fear, the terror, the distaste of all that he has to say.

He has never told anyone. Not even Rosie. But Rosie did not need him to say it.

I tried to kill myself, Will says. When I was a kid.

Jen says nothing.

Not properly, he says, as the shame tightens in his chest. I tried to smash my head on the mirror in the school toilets, after taking a few too many painkillers.

She is still looking. Still straddled, across him.

It's why I was suspended. Except it wasn't really a suspension. It was time off, to recover, or whatever. Everyone at school thought I'd attacked someone and got in serious trouble, and I sort of preferred that story.

Sun, barred, on the floorboards.

The fridge heaves behind them in the kitchen.

So he was just checking, I guess, Will says. That this depression isn't going down that route.

And is it, she asks. Her voice is normal, somehow.

Nope, he says. It's why there was nothing to say.

She is still looking at him, but he won't meet her eyes; looks instead at her pierced ears, the mole at the base of her neck. There are parts of her he still doesn't know. As if he looks, without seeing. Struggles to remember the small, incredible details of a person who matters, but doesn't seem to know him, either.

And mostly, that's been a relief.

Jen swings herself off him, after a while, and sits beside him on the sofa.

For what it's worth, I'm not surprised, she says. I can tell the difference between sadness and real shit.

He shrugs.

But I hate that you've felt so much pain, she says.

It is an abnormally emotional thing for her to say; they are well matched, because they don't share their feelings, don't show affection unless they're having sex — sometimes, not even then — and it is jarring. Like accidentally biting down on a fork, the metal hard between his teeth.

It's not really pain, if that helps, Will says. More a sort of . . . nothing.

Even with the meds? she asks.

So far, he says.

Maybe you need a higher dose.

Jen, he says. Please leave it, all right? I'll figure it out if I need to.

But —

If you want to be *just roomies*, he says, then keep pushing.

It is cruel and unfair of him, but it has the desired effect. She gets up and leaves him to his fake nap on the sofa, his jeans still around his knees.

*

Rosie finds herself staring up at her mother's office block. She has not been here since she was a child, when she was too ill to go to school one day, and her mother brought her to work. Sat her on a chair, gave her a book, and told her to be good and quiet. She managed it, for an hour or so, and then vomited in the waste-paper basket.

She squints at the glass doors. Remembers the acid, the half-digested cereal. The chrome finish of the bin, so cool beneath her hands.

It is a tall building, with floors of lawyers and bankers and insurers. Important people with important jobs, and important leather furniture. Orchids in the lobby. Brass buttons on the lift. She presses floor 5 and waits, her heart thrumming like a sparrow's wings.

Her mother is where she expects her to be, in her glass-walled office sealed off from the rest of the floor. She moved in when she made partner; Rosie had helped her pick out her lamp and potted plants and rug, things to make it her own. It had been an exciting time. Her mother had seemed happy and fulfilled. She was kinder, for a while. Asked good questions.

Right now, she is on the phone, and Rosie waits for her to finish, watches as she turns to her computer and clacks on the keys with her long nails. A mousey girl in a crumpled suit rustles past with papers and wired, caffeinated eyes. A phone rings somewhere down the hall. Then she bumps her fist on the glass, watches the reaction as her mother looks up. Her face goes taut; she rises from her desk as Rosie pushes open the door and closes it, gently, behind her.

Rosie, she says. What's wrong?

Nothing, she says.

Your dad? Simon?

Everyone's fine, she says.

Are you pregnant?

God, Mum, Rosie says, and she lowers herself into the chair in front of the giant desk. The view out of the window is wide and lustrous. More glass buildings. More people at more screens. And further out, a hazy fade of the city; the river somewhere, beyond the concrete.

I am not pregnant, Rosie says. That's sort of part of the problem.

You're infertile, her mother says.

Jesus, Mum.

Well, why else would you show up at my office unannounced?

Because, Rosie says, and she raises her voice, unintentionally. Because I wanted to ask you about divorce.

She does not look at her mother's face as she says it.

The city traffic roars beneath them.

For a friend? her mother asks.

Yes, Rosie says. Then, no. I don't know.

*Rose*mary. You can't be serious. Every couple has difficulties. That's what marriage is − it's compromise. It's living through the worst. It's binding.

Says the divorce lawyer, says Rosie.

It's a last resort, her mother snaps. And you don't exactly strike me as someone at the end of her tether, darling.

Rosie looks up at her, completely astonished. Her throat swells; that old pressure against her voice box.

What's going on? What's changed?

I don't know. That's just it.

Talk to him, then, her mother says.

I've tried.

Then try couples therapy. Have a baby, even. If you need IVF, your father and I −

That's your advice? Have a *baby*?

Lower your voice, Rosie. You're giving me a migraine. I just thought, if there was an underlying issue –

But babies are the issue, too, Rosie presses on. We should want one, by now, shouldn't we? And we don't ever discuss it. He doesn't even want to go on holiday, but he seems so stressed out, all the time. We're just on this hamster wheel, Mum.

What's the exact problem, Rosemary? You need to tell me that before you come here asking for a divorce.

I'm not *asking* for a divorce, Rosie says. I just wanted to talk about it. To find out our options. See how often it works out, maybe. In your experience.

Her mother sighs and raises her bony hands to her temples.

He's so miserable, Rosie goes on. He's always tired and bored and uninterested in me.

That's marriage, her mother says, and it takes Rosie a second to realise that she's not even joking.

It shouldn't be, Rosie says.

Well it is. It's managing.

I don't want to just manage, Rosie says.

Oh, Rosie, her mother says. You always were an idealist.

Just like Josh, they are both thinking, though neither of them says it; and he, her golden boy, was never criticised for it.

Her mother turns back to her screen and clicks her mouse. Rosie resists the urge to walk out, keeps her feet rooted to the floor.

Your father and I aren't happy, her mother says, eventually. Haven't been for years.

Rosie stares at her.

But nobody is, she says. The *successes* are the ones who choose to stick it out. And you're not a quitter, Rosie. You never have been.

You and Dad aren't happy?

We tolerate each other, her mother says. Which works, for us. He's a good man. He respects me. And I like him, most of the time. Wanting anything else is a fairy tale, Rosie; I've been in this business long enough to know that.

You're not happy with Dad, Rosie repeats. Something seems to crumble, every time she says it. She knew her parents weren't the best of friends. But she thought, after all this time, there must be something she didn't see. Hands touched, under the duvet, at night. Whispered stories about their days. Comfort, and grief, and unity.

Happy is what you make it, her mother says, and Rosie looks out of the window, at what little she can see of the sky.

Look, Rosie, her mother says, and she sounds impatient now. Why exactly did you come here? You didn't really come to ask about divorce papers, did you?

No, Rosie says. Still looking at the sky, the impenetrable cloud.

Well, then. Promise me you'll work on it.

More work. More effort. It looks as if it might rain, and she waits for it, just for a few more moments. When it doesn't fall, Rosie slides her bag back over her arm, stands up from the mesh chair; the one that she'd helped her mother choose, all those years ago.

Simon is in bed when she gets home. It is early afternoon, and he is hot, the duvet flung back.

Feeling rough? she asks him.

Yet again, he says.

Maybe it's stress. Can you take some time off work?

Work doesn't *feel* stressful, he says.

Then . . . is it us?

260

No, Rosie. Why would you ask that?

She feels terrible for suggesting it, then. For feeling the opposite.

Just thought I'd check, she says.

That's very polite, he says, and he rolls over to rest his head on her arm, his cheek stubbled and prickly. He has no idea, she thinks, and the guilt feels like a sword sheathing itself inside her; huge, and pointed; put away.

Maybe you should see a doctor, she suggests. Could be a thyroid thing.

He makes a noise of agreement, and they lie together in the low daylight. Their bedroom smells of their marriage; folded pyjamas and hand cream, bed sheets she should wash more often.

Do you want dinner, she asks him, at some point, and he murmurs no.

Do you want *me*, she asks, and he snuffles, rather than laughs; doesn't answer. She waits a while, lets the darkness encroach across the carpet.

I want things, she says, into his hair.

Like what? he asks her. He sounds as if he's near sleep.

I want to leave management consultancy, she says.

Okay, he says.

I want to play music again.

All right.

Piano. And guitar. I think I want to teach.

Then teach, he says.

It is as easy and as complex as that. No arguments. No questioning, or discussion, or conflict. She does not know what she wanted. Some kind of fervour, or fire, she thinks, beyond his body heat.

You should row, she says.

He snuffle-laughs, again, before his breathing changes, and

then he sleeps on her arm, like a child. Pins and needles, tingling, in her palm.

*

Will is at work when he gets a call from his sister.

He is changing the oil on an old Triumph. The radio is on, and he will never again be able to listen to the surf guitar and close harmonies of the song that is playing. The potato salad of the music world.

Will, Amber says. It's Gran.

She okay?

She died.

Two words. Two words he'd expected, all those years ago, when the cancer got her, when she fought and her hair fell out and the light mostly faded from her eyes. Two words he does not expect now. Not while he stands here on the oil-marked concrete, with his coffee going cold on the workbench.

What, he says.

It was painless, Amber says. In her sleep. Old age.

But she wasn't old, he says.

Will.

Are you sure? Have you called an ambulance?

His sister ignores him, says, just get here, okay, and there is something in her voice that means he cannot argue; cannot check or confirm or deny. He turns off the radio. Says he's coming. But as he leaves the garage, he still does it, can't help himself; he dials his grandmother's number and listens as it rings and rings and rings.

The house is too quiet. There had always, irrefutably, been sound; the fire in the grate, the television on low, the ignition clicking or the wind clattering against the blinds. But the windows are shut. The oven, the TV, the fireplace, all dead.

Dead.

It is a word that does not feel like a word. Like when he reads something, over and over, and it just stops looking right.

He and Amber had parted ways at the hospital. She had a seminar the next day and needed clothes for the funeral, so she caught the train back to Warwick. I'll be back soon, she'd assured him, her eyes holding on to his. Like she was the older sibling. Like she would guide them through this.

He moves through the house, checking for clues to construct his grandmother's last hours, but there is nothing untoward. Her bed clean but unmade, where the paramedics had lifted her out. Her book on her bedside table. He picks it up, opens it to where her bookmark is wedged against the spine. It's a story about a girl and a long-lost love. Bad dialogue. An even worse cover. He touches the page where she would have done, before she turned out her light.

He has a missed call from Jen, checking on him, he's sure, on her lunchbreak. But he does not call back. He goes to the garden and pulls up weeds, trims back the little tree where Dave was buried, all those years ago. He remembers his gran calling him, so choked she could barely speak, as if Dave were a child, and not a dog. He snaps twigs, snags the skin of his hands on the bushes as he cuts them back, because it is what he would do, for her, whenever he came over.

It is so wet outside, he thinks, which is weird, when it hasn't been raining. So wet and goddamn aggravating, getting in his eyes.

Amber is true to her word and catches a train back to Norfolk a few days later. The funeral is soon. Too soon, it seems to

Will, mainly because they did not ask for a post-mortem. It won't change anything, Ambs had said, and he guessed she was right. She was nearly eighty, and she died in her sleep. Nothing more to it than that.

They have to do all the things you do when someone dies. Go through her things. Her drawers, her paperwork, her stash of old records to select music for the service.

I've no idea, Will says, as he stares at the vinyl in his hands.

About what? Amber asks, not looking up from her screen. She is crafting an email to the funeral home, answering questions about flowers and coffins and things that don't matter, because she's dead, but for some reason they need to try to care about such details.

What songs to choose, he says. Do we want happy, or mournful? Her favourites? Or something bland and funeral appropriate?

Definitely not the latter, Amber says.

No, he says. No.

What about the song she danced to at her wedding?

How do you even know what that was?

I asked once, she says, with a shrug. Will nods, and swallows. He never asked her those sorts of things.

So I have a question, Amber says. She closes the laptop lid and looks at him.

Yeah, he says, expecting something about finger food, or poetry readings, or where to host the wake. Here, he thinks, so they don't have to pay for a badly lit hall with cheap carpets and smoke-stained ceilings.

Do we invite Mum, Amber asks.

A silence. A car heaves past the window. Diesel, instead of petrol; he knows by the sound of the engine.

Why would we, he says.

Because she's Gran's daughter, Amber says. She should know that she died, at least.

She didn't come to Grandpa's, Will says.

And she might not come to this one, either, Amber says, and she starts to plait her hair, splitting it into three before overlaying each strand. But it's not our choice, I don't think. It's hers.

Why even ask me, then, Will says, and his heart is kicking.

Because we don't *have* to invite her, she says. If you think it's a bad idea.

I think it's a nothing idea, Will says. I wouldn't even know how to get in touch with her, Ambs. So go ahead, if you think you can.

I have her email address, Amber says.

He looks up at her, at this. The records feel heavy in his hands. His sister looks right back at him, waiting.

How? is all he can manage, after a moment.

Gran, she says.

She was in touch with her?

No, Amber says, and she finishes plaiting her hair, starts to undo it right away. She just had the email, and said I could use it if I wanted.

When?

A few years back. She said it was my choice, at the time. And I think this is Mum's.

Big of you, Will says.

What is?

Giving her a choice. Like she deserves it.

Amber turns to the laptop again, opens the lid and tells him to think about it. He says he doesn't need to; that she should do what she wants.

———

The day before, he goes running, for the first time in months.

He runs through the forests and along the roads and across the wind-strewn cliffs. He sweats, and swears, and hates how hard it feels, and listens to his own breathing as it rips through his lungs and catches in his throat. He runs on the wet sand on the beach. Pauses at the lighthouse, which feels all wrong, and makes his heart thud faster as it looks at him with its glass eye and asks him things he doesn't have the answers for.

When he gets home, he lies in the bath until his fingertips turn soft, and he looks at his nakedness and he thinks of all the things he never asked her, the woman who actually raised him, scolded him, loved him in spite of all he did and didn't do. And he wonders what the hell he should do next, beyond this bath, and the funeral, and he dreads the life he's built and how little he cares about it, and he sickens himself with the contempt he held for his grandmother's own shoebox days, with her books and her casseroles and her accidental second family, but at least she had something, he thinks, at least she had things she thought she wanted.

He pulls the plug when Amber asks him, through the door, what's wrong. Says that he's been in there a long time.

I can't believe she died, he says.

The suck of water, clouded with soap.

I know, Amber says.

They stay like that, on either side of the bathroom door, as they listen to each other and say nothing.

fourteen

The day is overcast, at first. Bleak cloud, diluted sun.

Despite feeling like it, Will does not wear black. He has asked the guests not to, either. Instead, he buttons up a blue shirt, something his gran bought him one Christmas, and he combs his hair, like she would want him to.

He and Amber get a taxi to the crematorium because neither of them feels like driving, and both of them feel like drinking, later. His standalone beer awaits.

They get there first, as planned, and the guests arrive in pairs or alone, elderly friends from her book club or her old job, a few even from her school days. She never left Norfolk; she grew up, lived and died in this town. Raised children, twice. Made friends. Met her husband, and lost him. Kept going, because that's what you do.

Jen pulls into the car park, looking oddly out of place, to him, outside of Yorkshire. She has driven down this morning, taken time off work to be here. They embrace, and he smells the tea tree aroma of her hair, the vague, lemony scent of her car freshener.

You're okay, she says, a reassurance, perhaps, or a question he can't answer. She takes his arm like a girlfriend should and they walk in together, the two of them and his sister, and the room seems so small with its wooden benches and pinstriped carpet, and he wishes they could have the service outside. It is mild enough. Scudding clouds, sun breaking through before it withdraws again. Birds, and mown grass, and trees.

There are no windows in the crematorium.

Amber goes to talk to the celebrant while Will thinks about the name, and how inappropriate it is. Because this is not a celebration. He hates it, and he hates himself for agreeing to it, he needs air, and he tells Jen he's going to the bathroom and he breaks out of the windowless hall and he finds a bench, hidden from the car park and the entrance and all the faces he should know but does not.

He puts his head in his hands and decides to miss the service, to just have his own memorial right here, with the daisies speckled at his feet and the wood pigeons shuffling across the grass, no hymns, no sad, meaningless overview of her life measured in years and jobs and paragraphs, but Amber comes to get him, says it's time. He wants to ask her if their mother is here, but at the same time, he does not want to know.

He looks up at her as if to say, do I have to, and in the strangest moment, though perhaps not so strange for the occasion, his sister holds out her hand.

He takes it and stands.

Her palm is cool, like his own. Chewed fingernails, and split lifelines.

It is mostly a blur, until the end, when something happens. They have sung – mouthed, mostly, in Will's case – the final hymn, something about sunrise and shadow, and then her name is called.

Will is in the front row, beside Jen, who is beside Amber. A sad show of family, he thinks, as he tries not to look at the coffin.

And now one of Elsie's young friends, the celebrant says, is going to sing a little something for us. If Rosemary Winters would like to come on up?

A slow-down.

A shift on his own axis, while everyone sits and waits, looking down at the order of service, or else watches this woman tread down the aisle with her guitar, her wide, doe-like eyes beneath her fringe.

His heart halts.

It is like seeing a ghost, or a mirage, and he does not believe it right away.

He wants to say something, but the words are stuck, so he turns to his sister, who is looking straight ahead and holding herself oddly still.

She knew.

She knew, and he does not know what to feel.

Jen looks at him sideways, and he turns his face to the front. Roe is arranging herself on a chair, takes a moment to tune her guitar.

The room watches her take a breath. And then she begins to play.

Will has never seen her with her guitar, before. Her fingers flow over the frets, and he waits, unable to breathe, himself, until she starts to sing.

She looks different. Fuller, and softer, than he remembers, her hair chopped and shaped. But her voice – that voice – is the same. Still touches him in a way he didn't think possible, now, on medication that numbs the numb, leaves things muted and bearable and bland. But it lights something in him. That same old match, struck.

She is wearing a blue dress.

No earrings in her ears.

He does not recognise the song. She sings about early

mornings and apples, something clear, hanging in a window. He suspects it is one she has written, especially for this moment, and it is beautiful, and haunting, and it comes to an end too soon.

Nobody applauds, because it is a funeral.

But the stillness does not break, even as she returns to her seat. No shuffling of papers or clearing of throats. No focus, any more, on the celebrant's closing words. Everyone taken in, by this girl and her voice and the lingering quiet.

Will cannot believe her.

Cannot believe what's inside him, today, of all days.

The wake is at the community hall down the road; a shabby square of a building that smells of stale beer and snooker cues, the sweaty peel-back of cling film. It is a joyless, shadowy space, but many of her friends' wakes were there. Her husband's, too.

We won't want to host, Amber had told him, and he'd argued with her about it, but now, as the guests stand to leave, he is grateful. Bodies creak and shuffle. He can't imagine having them crammed in the house; touching her things, outstaying their welcome. Taking up all the air.

He stands, too, but tells Amber and Jen he'll meet them at the hall. That he just needs a minute. Jen protests, says she'll stay, but Amber takes her elbow and guides her out, still, he notes, not looking at him.

When the room has mostly emptied, Will sits back down and waits. Because she has waited, too. She has waited, and she comes down the aisle, settles herself on the row behind him. Breath of blue, like the sky they cannot see.

The coffin hasn't moved. They did not opt for that moment where the curtains close or the turntable spins, and there is a definitive end to the proceedings. Just leave it where it is, they'd said, and so it is still there on the table, with its polished wood caught in the room's flat light.

Who makes coffins, he asks, and Rosie shrugs. He sees it out of the corner of his eye.

A carpenter? she ventures.

You don't think there's a niche form of carpentry for it?

I guess there must be.

A coffin-maker, Will says, and Rosie says yeah, that maybe it's a nice job, really. Crafting something so personal, for a stranger.

She has chosen a chair one back and two down from his own. They both look at his gran's coffin and try to form words, until the celebrant says he's sorry, folks, that there's another service in ten, but to take all the time they need.

All ten minutes of it, you mean, Will says, and the celebrant looks confused but then laughs in apology, stammers in a way that Will is used to, when he does this; when he asserts himself, like that.

Let's, says Rosie, and she nods to the door.

A familiar, slight dip of her head.

It is spring, but still cold, like the season hasn't quite found itself. If seasons could have voices, Will muses, then April would be a whistle, light and non-invasive, like the tight-lipped buds on the trees.

Your song, he says, as they settle on his bench from before.

Yes, she says.

Did you write it for her?

She looks at him, as if surprised he's had to ask. Her pupils are so wide and black, he can see his own face reflected back at him.

Of course, she says.

He has to swallow, at this. Has to turn away.

271

I'm so sorry, Will, Rosie says, and she puts her hand on his own, after the shortest deliberation – he feels it hover and then lower, the warmth of her palm as it closes. Her hands are so delicate, still. Such thin, lovely fingers, and he never even thinks of words like lovely, and it embarrasses him, and he feels pathetic, and angry, all of a sudden.

I didn't know you were coming, he says, as he takes his hand away.

Rosie blinks.

Really?

Really.

Oh. Well, Amber invited me.

Did she ask you to sing?

Of course. I wouldn't have . . . presumed.

But you didn't think to tell me you'd be here?

I figured you knew I was on the invite list, Rosie says, and there is a heat to her voice, a disbelief at how accusatory he's being. I assumed you'd have other things to worry about, without me . . . messaging you hello.

Sparrows flit in the hedgerows. A mower, somewhere beyond the graves.

She died, Rosie, he says.

I know.

If any time called for a message, he says, it was then.

I'm sorry, she says again, and her voice is like breath, the wind in the elms. He does not want her to say sorry. He wants her to hold his hand again. He wants her to leave. He wants her so badly, he thinks his heart might give out.

Roe, he says, and he is not looking at her.

No yes, or murmur of assent. More breath; more wind. More of everything, when she is around; white sun, blinding his view.

I'm so fucking glad you're here, he says.

You are?

You're the only person I wanted to see. I actually thought that, this morning, when I woke up and realised what day it was. And now you're here.

She is quiet for the longest time. The mower stops, then starts again. The sparrows have gone, and he wonders if she will get up and leave, too.

Let her, he thinks. Let her go.

Why is it so hard, to let her go.

You said you didn't want me in your life, she says to him, eventually.

I never said that.

You did.

Think back, Roe. I did not say that.

You didn't *not* say that, she says.

Stop avoiding what I've said.

What, that you're fucking glad I'm here? God, Will.

What?

Even when you're saying nice things, I feel like you're angry, she says. I never know what you want from me. Just like when we were seventeen.

Are you kidding me?

What?

You're the one who didn't want *me*, he says. Remember?

I've never not wanted you, Rosie says, and she seems to say it without thinking, not intending to put it out there, so raw, in the clear April air. The words hang between them, like forbidden fruit. Bruised, but unripe.

I don't get you, Will tells her.

And I don't get you, Will, she says, and her voice is trembling. Aren't you with Jen?

And aren't you with Simon?

No, she says, and that single word is strong, and fierce.

Come off it.

I'm not, Will.

Since when?

Since recently.

But you married the guy.

Yeah. We're still married.

So you *are* with him.

What are we even doing, she says, and she stands up now, in a gust of dress and long coat. You're with Jen. We're adults. We haven't spoken in forever.

Twenty-nine months, Will says.

What?

We haven't spoken in twenty-nine months.

She stares at him like he's sworn at her again, called her something inexcusable. His sudden anger has soared into something else. He cannot explain it. He is at his grandmother's funeral. His girlfriend is half a mile down the road, eating crudités and making small talk with cousins he's never met, for him, and only him.

We can't, Rosie says, and her voice is strained, like water being wrung from a cloth. He lets it fall, all that she does not say splashing at their feet.

I didn't say we should, he says, and he looks around, at the grass, at the headstones set deep in the earth. Something ruptures. He wants his gran. Wants to talk to her about this, or have her talk some sense into them both.

I just wanted to tell you, he says. Just once.

And still, he does not tell her, but it seems she does not need him to.

I should have told you every day since I knew it, he says. But I was young and stupid and scared and I'm still a lot of those things, Roe.

She is quiet again.

Roe?

I don't know why you're yelling, she says.

I'm not.

You are. It sounds like you're furious with me.

He looks at what he can see of her face, her hair grazing her cheekbones. He wants to tell her that love and fury so often feel the same, to him. That his skin burns for her. His blood crawls, and that doesn't feel safe or nice or quiet; it feels like rage.

I'm not yelling, he says.

Not any more, you're not.

This wasn't the way this was meant to go, he says.

What, today? The funeral? Or us?

All of the above, he says, and something thaws between them, then. Birds, singing. Shift of sun through the cedar trees.

Will, Rosie says.

Yeah?

I . . . I think we should talk about this. But not now. Not here. It's Elsie's day, you know. Let's just go and remember her.

He feels so much towards her, then, that he nearly spills over. He draws his hand around his face, says the wake isn't far from here, and Rosie nods. They rise from the bench and begin walking in silence towards the car park, but then there is a noise, like footfall, which makes Will turn back towards the bench.

Someone, approaching.

A woman, of the right age. With the right face.

*

Rosie takes sandwiches and cocktail sausages and stands in the corner and picks at her plate. She has felt herself soften, these past few weeks, as she takes in bread and pastry and puts sugar in her tea. So many years of nuts and proteins and low-fat alternatives, but now she feels the closest to nourished that she can remember. She is not thinking about calories, or hardening, or lessening, or holding on for five seconds more. She is thinking about how she is teaching, now; her students, and her songs. How she's writing on paper again.

She recognises faces at Elsie's funeral. People from her hometown, the library, the bakery. But she doesn't truly know anyone except Amber, who seems intent on speaking to everyone but her. She doesn't mind. She works her way around her plate, waiting, because she left Will in the car park with his mother.

Her gut feels knotted. She keeps watching the door, hoping that he will walk through it and be all right, or at least something close to that.

Three miniature sandwiches down, and still, he has not shown, and that is when Jen comes over and says hi.

Hello, Rosie says back.

Her blood simmers in her veins. She feels guilt, and dislike, and shame for both.

Your song was decent, Jen says, and Rosie hears Will's inflection in her voice, the way you mirror the words of someone you live with, without meaning to.

Thank you, she says.

So nice to have proper music, and not just hymns.

I'm glad, Rosie says. She lifts a sandwich off her plate, then puts it down again.

You're Rosie, right?

Yes.

Will's best friend?

Not sure he'd say best, she says. But we were friends. A long time ago.

Jen watches her, and Rosie is about to comment on the weather or ask about the breadsticks when Jen cuts to it, and Rosie sees the kind of woman she is.

He talks about you, you know, she says.

Rosie raises her eyes to Jen's; this woman he shares his life with. Solid black hair and narrow features, a twirl of jade at her throat.

Does he, she asks.

Not a lot, Jen says. But enough.

There is a ripple of laughter from near the bar, too loud for the occasion, and both women look over to see two men clapping each other on the back. They keep watching the strangers, and Jen keeps talking, her voice level.

I know he had a thing for you, she says.

Rosie burns red; takes her focus away from the bar and drops her eyes to her plate.

I just don't know if he still does, Jen says.

And Rosie's throat closes in on itself, like it does when she has no idea what to say, when there is no right or wrong, and no room to be either. She tries to swallow; reaches for her water glass on the side, when there is a shunt of colour and noise and they see Will storm into the hall, heading towards Amber. Oh shit, says Jen, as Rosie thinks the same, and then his girlfriend is gone from her side.

Rosie puts her plate down. A few people are looking, because the commotion is tangible, even without any shouting; Will is angry, and he is saying things in a low, rough voice, and Amber is holding her chin high, as though she'd been braced for a fallout.

Rosie makes a choice and heads for the exit. She strides past Will and his sister and the funeral guests, wide-eyed and watching, and then she's out of the hall and in the car park, and the air is colder than before. It smells of frost and wet tarmac. Ashen sky, in puddles on the ground.

And as she walks towards her own car, she sees what – or whom – she had hoped to see. The woman who abandoned her son, because life was too much. Bailed, because it was easier, because it was wild and freeing and the opposite of how

Rosie has learnt to be. She watches as this wild, absent woman with her long copper hair turns the keys in her car, so that the engine growls alive. She watches as she keeps both hands on the steering wheel and places her forehead, oh so briefly, between them. She watches as she cries, for a while.

*

Jen takes him to a bar. She gives Amber the keys to her car to drive home, and the two of them get a taxi to a country pub in the middle of near-nowhere, on a road out of Norfolk, with brick walls and local draught ale and low, twilight-style lighting. So dark, it's near impossible to read the menus.

But Will does not want to eat.

Double vodka, he says to Jen, and she says no, he can have one beer, or a soda and lime, and he wants to smash his fist into the small wooden table they're seated at, but instead he stares at his hands.

So much, for one day.

She comes back with his soda, her own glass of wine like a fishbowl in her hand, and they sit and drink, the murmur of the pub washing over them. Not being numb, for once, is unsettling for Will. Things poke at him like needles, and he's trying to figure out what hurts the most when Jen speaks.

I met Rosie Winters, she says.

I met my mother, he says back.

She lowers her eyes at this, and he's jabbed with another needle, violent satisfaction, he thinks, then a stab of guilt, because he told Roe some things he did not intend to, today. Implied, maybe. He does not know what he was doing on that bench, nor does he know what he's doing here with Jen.

D'you want to talk about it, Jen asks. She is swirling her wine the way she did on the night he first met her.

There's nothing to say, he says. She came. We talked. I told her to go.

Laughter, and voices. The shove of the pub door.

Was it . . . awful? Jen asks.

It was what I'd always expected, he says. She wanted to hug me, at first, then she got defensive and tearful, like I owed her something, like I was an arsehole for not collapsing into her open arms.

That's shit, Jen says. That's really shit.

She said she thinks about me, Jen, he says, and some spittle flies from his mouth, like an old man, and he doesn't care. She *thinks* about me. As though that excuses every fucking thing.

It doesn't, she says.

I'm not even talking about missed birthdays or Christmases, he ploughs on. I'm talking about *years*. Holes, in my life, where I didn't have a mother. And what that felt like, after my dad had already left. Jesus *Christ*.

He slams his fist on the table, and some men at the bar look over, and he wishes they'd start on him, wishes he'd have a reason to break something, a glass or a bone or a nose.

Amber knew, he says, his voice snapping, like a guitar string. She knew she was coming. My mum replied in advance, for the first time in her bloody life, probably, and Amber could have prepared me – she *should* have prepared me – but she thought it was *better not to tell me*.

If she had told you, Jen says mildly, would things have gone any different?

Don't take her fucking side.

I'm not. If there is a side to take, Will, I am on yours. Every time.

She is calm, and he feels his insides simmer, at that.

I fucking hate her, he says.

So you should.

279

I hate her, he says again, and he is being a child, he knows, but Jen nods.

They drink some more. Will downs his soda and feels that chasm open in his gut, an endless, unfilled well.

One vodka, he says.

Not a chance, Jen says.

More murmuring; more burning; pins in his hands and feet and eyes.

Can we talk about Rosie now, Jen asks.

Will takes his empty soda glass and rolls it around on its base. It leaves a ring of water on the table, and he keeps rolling, drawing a wet arc onto the wood.

If you want, he says.

I'm just going to say it, she says.

Okay.

I saw the way you looked at her, she says. While she sang.

Okay, he says again.

And I don't think I can go on hoping that you're over her, she says.

He keeps rolling his glass. Look at her, he urges himself, but he can't. His rage settles. They have changed gears, now. Upped their speed; a new focus required. He lifts his eyes to her face.

She is trying not to look at him, either. He has so rarely seen her cry, and he realises he has always liked this about her; appreciated her stoutness, her unsentimental way of moving through the world. It's pacifying, and uncomplicated. He likes her skin, too, its near-translucence. He often wondered, when the morning bled through their window, how a woman could be so pale, so paper thin.

Strong, somehow, but transparent.

I don't need to know any details, Jen says. But I can see it in your face, Will. And at the risk of sounding like a goddamn diva, she says, her eyes flaring, I just, you know. I want someone to look at me like that.

Will stops rolling his glass.

And I'm not coming between that, either, she says. She deserves to know how you feel, still. After all this time.

He cannot believe it is unfolding like this. He was prepared for anger and accusations, an argument that saw her storming into the car park so that he had to follow, or order a drink at the bar. But this: this steals the breath out of him.

I'm so sorry, he says, because that is all there is to say. They sit together with their empty glasses and the low-lit bulbs in their domes, the mirth and hubbub of other lives happening all around them.

At least we never got married, Jen jokes, raising her glass to him.

She did, though, he says.

And while she doesn't answer him, he sees the hurt in her face. That even now, as they're ending, he doesn't have anything to say that isn't about Rosie. He feels a sudden, wrenching sadness. Wants to reach out and touch her, apologise, change the things he cannot change.

I had a ring, you know, he says, after a while.

I know, she says. I found it in your sock drawer.

And you never wondered why I hadn't asked you?

Not really, she says, cupping her glass with both hands. I knew your heart wasn't in it. I knew, when we started all this, that you were in love with someone else.

Somebody laughs, elsewhere. Doors swinging, waft of hot chips.

Bit of a red flag, I suppose, Will says.

Yeah. I think I liked the challenge, Jen says. Thought I could change your mind. Which was arrogant of me, I guess. But it would've been *so* sexy, if I'd managed it.

To undo my undying love for someone else?

Yeah, that, she says, and he's relieved to see that she is no longer near tears. But also, to just . . . set you free from it all.

He has no words, for this. He knows he should buy them more drinks, but he also doesn't want to stand and break this thing they're cradling; this fragile, near dying thing they've passed between them for five whole years.

Would've been fucking hot, he agrees. She gives a wild laugh, but it sounds like something else, a cough, or a sob, maybe, and she puts her wine glass down and stands up and leaves, all too fast, all coat and boots and noise.

And that's it.

That's it.

*

It is disquieting, to Rosie, being in her childhood bed. It feels too narrow and she cannot sleep without the mass of Simon beside her, the familiar, habitual weight of him. They have not spoken, as they'd agreed. She packed a holdall and came to her parents' house, in some stupid, broken outreach of yearning that only made her feel worse.

You disappoint me, Rosie, her mother had said, when Rosie had told her why she was there.

A voltage of pain, and something harder, like a nail, passing through her.

Upstairs in her room, she did not unpack. It felt easier and less permanent not to. She will get her own place soon, and decorate it in her favourite colours; have a musical instrument in every room, and books, lots of books.

She sinks towards sleep with these pinboard plans, and then she jolts awake, like she's forgotten something.

She gets up, checks that she has her purse, her passport, her keys, then she gets back into bed. Watches as the night lightens to dawn, the shapes changing from deep mauve to the fairest cloud-like blue. And just as she's drifting off, she jolts again, and this time it leaves her burning, like someone has tipped molten wax on her skin.

It is then that she reaches for her phone.

You said I never wanted you, she says, when he answers. And I was a stupid, scared teenager, too, Will, for reasons that don't even make sense to me now. I know it doesn't change anything, but I just – I needed you to *think* I didn't want you back. That's why I said no, that time, in the forest.

There is background noise; some sort of muffled wind, as if he is outside.

I shouldn't have said what I said, she says. I didn't think it would have such a lasting impression on you. It was just easy, to play the good girl card.

What are you saying, Rosie, he asks her. It still sounds as if he is in the thick of a crowd; on a high street, or at a port, somewhere bustling despite the early hour.

Rosie takes a breath, looking at the teenage posters on her wall; three faces who sang about colliding and still believing.

I'm saying it was a lie, she says. And I just wonder how things would have gone, sometimes. If I hadn't said it.

There is a short silence. She hears a shuffle, as if Will is moving the phone from one ear to another, or finding a more sheltered place to speak.

You're talking about that time you told me I was the wrong kind of person for you?

Yes, she says, and she feels her chest clag with the cruelty of it, even though she remembers her reasons. Josh, crying, in her arms. And something else, something sterner; a hook, in her heart, that holds her back.

More noise. A squeak, like shoes on a hard floor.

That was a lie, he repeats, as if he's checking what she's said.

Yes, she says.

But your brother dying was not, Will says.

I know, she says. But –

You couldn't even look at me afterwards, he says. I know why, Roe. I get it. And we can try this thing, we can pretend it's okay and that you don't see him when you look at me or that you want to be over it, we can *try*, but I swear to God, Rosie, it won't work. He died, and it was because of me, my invite, my birthday, no matter how you try to spin it, and that's why we dance around this thing, that's why I never chased you and why you never wanted me to and why you're still not sure, even now, that this is what you want.

Rosie breathes into the receiver. His voice is tightly wound, about to break. So brittle, after holding back, for so long.

That's what you think, she says. But –

No, he cuts in, again, and she hears the chiming over a loudspeaker and realises he's at an airport. No, Roe. I ended things with Jen, last night. I fucking ended things with the woman who's stuck with me through depression and my gran dying, and for what? Because she knows I'm not over some-one who doesn't even want to *be* with me?

She tries to cut in, too, but he keeps going.

I will never, ever be okay with Josh dying like that, Rosie, he says. And you won't, either. So let's just stop whatever this is, between us.

I do see him, when I look at you, Rosie breaks in. She is breathless with adrenaline, with the need to finally say it.

Right, he says.

No, she says, and she shakes her head, violently, forgetting that he can't see her. I see him when I look at you, okay, but not for the reasons you think.

He finally, mercifully, does not respond.

He was gay, she says, and it is some sort of joyful, heartfelt firework of truth that she sets off down the phone.

What?

Gay, she says again. He'd only just told me. And he – uh – he'd fallen for, well – you. Obviously.

She is sitting on her bed, her bare feet beneath her. She feels cold, but she cannot move; holds herself still, in the moment that's unfolding.

And I just wanted him to be okay, she says. I wanted him to figure that stuff out, first. Before we broke his heart, you know? And then he died.

She says it, just like that; as hard and clear as the fact of it.

He died, she says again, and I . . . I didn't know how . . .

He was gay, Will repeats.

Yes.

More silence. More white noise from the airport. She wants to ask him where he's going; wonders how long he's going for.

You were protecting him, Will says, after a while.

I should have told you sooner, Rosie says.

Yeah, Roe. You should have.

Would that have changed things, she asks.

What things?

A question for a question, she says, and he says don't joke, Rosie, not now, and he sounds distant, is still processing, she thinks, on the other end of the phone.

I'm so sorry, she says. For not telling you. It just . . . didn't feel like my secret to tell. You know?

Will does not respond to this, and Rosie waits, too long. Another fluid, female voice sounds over the loudspeaker at the airport, announcing something she can't quite make out.

Roe, Will says, and she says yes.

Thanks, he says. But I have to go, now.

And he hangs up.

fifteen

The doorbell rings.

She is alone, the duvet tucked beneath her arms as she stares at the ceiling and thinks. Her parents left for work hours ago, and still, she has not got out of bed.

It rings again and she curses the postman and his packages and his insistent, infuriating desire to do his job.

Leave it on the damn step, she says, aloud, and immediately feels rude and embarrassed, even though nobody can hear her, as she pads down the stairs to the door. She turns down the handle and swings it open and goes to say thank you to the uniformed man with the outstretched parcel.

But it is not the postman.

He is standing there, in his leather jacket, with his harsh cheekbones and his bronze hair and his burning, endless eyes.

They share a single heartbeat and then he says he'll never travel the world at this rate, and he steps forward and takes her face in his hands, those rough, mechanic's hands, and he keeps looking at her like that until she pulls him into her, with her mouth on his, and he tastes, to her, the way he did before.

*

They end up on her parents' staircase. The carpet burns their backs and there are teeth and sighs and nails, but a softness, too, a melting.

The colours of them, beneath their clothes. Skin that nobody else gets to see, and wanting the other person to touch it, so badly, to have it as their own, and it is teenage years and lucid dreams and desire that feels so raw and real that it cannot be allowed, surely, it can't. They say each other's names, just once, and then again, and they both half laugh without sound, as if they'll scare it away if they are anything less than silent, but they can hear each other, still, and that's all they want, all they have ever wanted, if they are honest, if they cut through the noise that came before this, all of this. Her hair, like willow, falling between them. Strong arms, and bent, soft, downy legs, unshaven and uncaring.

She presses her mouth to his collarbone and he groans, softly.

Shadows, from the trees, on the wall.

They cradle each other, and between their rushing blood and their thrumming hearts there is something neither of them has known before. That unreachable, implausible place. Bonfires, crackling. Imploding. The sun rising, permanent, and blinding, if you look straight at it, if you're so bold, so wanting, so goddamn, unbelievably lucky.

And then quiet.

Perfect quiet.

We can't stay here, Rosie whispers, afterwards.

She is wrapped around him, the mid-morning light grazing their foreheads, catching the copper-gold of his hair.

No, he says. He kisses her again, so long and drawn-out

that she thinks she might come, right there, but then he draws back, says he knows a place they can go.

*

Will stirs, for the next few days, as if in a dream he does not want to wake from.

He lies still and tries to hold on to it, but then he hears Rosie breathing and his heart launches upwards, like a whale out of water, sudden and graceful and huge.

They are sleeping in his old single bed. Neither of them felt right moving into his grandma's room; not until they can change a few things. Rosie insisted they buy new bedding, at least, and he agreed, though they have not yet left the house.

It has been days of drifting, and discovering. Making coffee but drinking only half of it. Mapping each other's skin, the soft, hidden parts of it, and tangling their limbs and hands and hair in bed, in the shower, and once, on the kitchen table.

This is, Rosie says one time, breathless in his ear.

Happening, he says, and she shudders into him, and he thinks he might die with the pleasure of it, and he dares not think beyond the next touch of her, the next note from the birds outside; the crests and the sparrows and the geese they can hear, sometimes, in the slipstreams over the house.

*

He was gay, he says, one night, as they're facing each other in bed. Imprints of her, all over him. Her eyes look like orbiting moons; pulled into his, wide and white and unearthly.

Yes, she says.

I had no idea, he says. But now you've said it, I can sort of believe it. You know?

288

Maybe, she says, her favourite word, and it is like she has retreated from him. No real movement or pulling back, just something less than before; she seems reticent, and he curses himself, inwardly, for raising it.

Did you know? he asks. Before he told you?

I'd wondered, she says.

He nods. Watches her face fall, as if remembering things he was not a part of.

I don't think he'd mind, he tells her.

Mind what, she says.

This, he says. Us. If that's what you're worrying about.

What made you think I'm worrying about it?

Because of what you said, he says, and he props himself on his elbow as she rolls away from him, tucks her long, dark hair behind her ear. About not wanting to break his heart.

I'm not worried about that now, am I, she says. He died.

He looks at her looking away. Moonlight falls through the still-open curtains, the room shifting between silver and shadow.

Aren't you, he says.

He doesn't say, I know you. And I know this thing you've carried for years does not suddenly lift, in spite of everything. In spite of getting all you knew you'd wanted, but thought you could not have.

Maybe a bit, she says, and her voice is hoarse with the strain of not crying. He gathers her hair, laces it over her shoulder. Leans in to kiss her collarbone, the shallow, pooling dip of it.

She is more rigid than he has ever known her to be.

I don't think he'd mind, he says to her, again. But I still feel sort of weird about it.

She nods, and sinks back down again, the pillows creasing beneath her. She smells of soap and duvets and breakfast tea.

I guess I feel bad, he says.

I do, too, she says.

Both of them thinking, all of the time, and folding in on each other.

*

After four or five days, Rosie makes them leave the house.

We need air, she says. Supplies.

So they walk into town for milk and eggs and other basic things, though they crave nothing but each other, and she feels giddy, like the seventeen-year-old that first fell for him, and it is stupid and embarrassing and so all-consuming that she doesn't even care.

They talk about school, and dinner, and terrible television. The sun pours over the pavements, creamy yellow, like buttermilk. So warm, for late spring.

It is in the supermarket queue, as Rosie unloads the groceries onto the conveyer belt, that she realises she is still wearing her wedding ring. There is a shift in the speed of things, for just a moment; as if someone is taking something from her, and she has to try and hold on to it.

She packs it all into her tote bag, pays, takes her receipt. She walks down the exit aisle, thinking she should process the divorce, soon; they'd both left the paperwork, because there was no rush, and it was exhausting, to separate, to even make that choice. I'll be in touch, she'd said, and Simon had said yes, he would, too.

Outside, she asks Will to get some bread from the bakery and while he's in there, she twists the band off her finger, zips it into the coin pocket of her purse.

The sky is a graze of grey.

Her reflection, in the glass.

She waits to feel shame or regret but there is nothing, nothing she confronts beyond the golden-haired, wolf-toothed guy who comes out of the dinging door with a loaf in his hands and says ready? and she says yes, yes I am.

Tell me something, she says that night.

About what?

Anything. Something that happened while we weren't in touch.

That's a lot of things, he says, and he closes the cookbook he'd been reading, slots his bookmark in place.

It should be easy, then, right?

Okay, he says, and he puts down his book, raises his hands behind his head while he thinks. She wonders how he is even more attractive than when he was eighteen. Tucks her arms across herself, and watches him. He has not shaved in several days. There is honey-blonde dandelion down, all along his jaw.

Well, he says. I was chased by a badger, one time.

A badger, she echoes.

An angry badger, he says, and she laughs, a tremor of disbelief and alarm.

You were not.

I was. On a Mountain Rescue call.

Rosie laughs properly, now, and it makes him laugh, too, and they stay horizontal on the sofa, tickled by the story or each other. When they settle, she asks him why it was angry.

Aren't badgers always angry?

I don't know. I've never met one, she reasons, which sets her off again. Her ribs ache. She feels bruised, out of practice, and so relieved. His calves, pressed against hers.

Your turn, he says. You tell me something.

I wasn't chased by any woodland creatures, she says.

Disappointing, he says. But not essential.

All right, she says, and she's still smiling, doesn't think

much about it when she says, um, I lost my appetite, at one point. I don't know why. And I did some therapy. It was sort of helpful, and sort of awful.

Will holds her with his eyes.

In what way?

Lots of ways, she says. I went because of Josh, obviously. But we barely spoke about him, really. It was mainly about goals and my mother and what I did and didn't eat, and my OCD, and everything. Which I suppose was important.

Will is not touching her, apart from his legs leaning on hers. His hands are still behind his head, elbows out, as if he's sunbathing in the lamplight.

I think we were meant to be unpeeling things, she says. Layers, you know. But I was too impatient. I wanted to jump straight to Josh, and be fixed, and get out to my spin class.

Spin class?

Another thing I did, for a while. Which was also kind of awful. I remember one time, the instructor was yelling at me to pedal harder, and the lights were flashing, and I thought, wow, I really hate this. I stopped going, after that.

Thank God, he says, and she says yeah, and they are momentarily quiet.

He is still looking at her, with his hands behind his head.

Did you do anything that wasn't awful, he asks her. In all that time?

She half smiles, at this, though she doesn't think he was joking.

The wind roars, outside, like the sea. It is due to storm around midnight. She has been looking forward to it; the noise of it on the window panes, later, when they go up to bed.

Sad, I know, she says, after she has no answer for him, and he touches her properly, then; leans forward, takes both of her wrists in his hands.

You're a lot of things, Roe, he says. But sad? No. No way. Even after everything, you're a light, Roe. A goddamn beam of light.

She feels embarrassed under the intensity of his eyes and his words. She burns, all over. Her face, and neck; between her legs.

Who even talks like that, she says, her voice like breath against his.

Laughter, again, between them. Softer than rain, the cloth of their bookmarks.

*

He does not wear pyjamas to bed. Just boxers. She starts to wear his clothes without asking, takes a T-shirt from his drawer, pulls bed socks up to her shins.

He asks her how she can sleep with socks on.

She asks him how he can't.

It is like being at school again, the pull and the fizz and the heat of it all, when it is just them, in a different decade, the way they always were.

*

Summer brings the tourists. The coast is littered with families and fishermen, and still, after two months of being together, they go to the lighthouse, most days.

I'm singing again, she tells him, as they walk along the sea-front towards it. Driftwood lies like bleached bone on the shore. The air smells both fresh and rotten, all foam and washed-up weeds.

So I've heard, he says.

Not just in the shower, she says, and she laughs, and it is so

293

easy and she thinks of how different she feels, right now – not weighted down or boxed in, but torn open.

And not just at funerals, she says. But at work. They've asked me to take on the choir.

She left her consultancy job just before she and Simon parted, began working as a music teacher at a Norfolk girls' school. She teaches piano and guitar, helps with the admin of school concerts. It is not world-changing work, she realises, but it feels life-changing. For her.

When she told Will she was playing again, and getting paid for it – albeit badly – he looked at her like he wanted to swallow her whole.

That's so great, he says now, as they pick their way across the sand.

It is, she says. It feels kind of right, you know? It was my choice to quit music, obviously. Even though it didn't feel like a choice. It was like I had to learn to breathe differently, if that doesn't sound too weird.

It doesn't, Will says.

But now, it just feels like . . . how has this not been my life the entire time?

The sand crunches beneath their shoes. Grains, pushed sideways, leaving their footprints behind them.

He says he knows, and she is embarrassed suddenly, because she realises what he means. Her cheeks redden and she stoops down to pick up a shell so that he doesn't see her blushing.

She watches him as he walks on, turns, waits for her. He is so tall, so strong and weathered. William White, on his medication, with his hurting heart and deep, sad eyes. Hers. Every splintered, scar-healed part of him.

She keeps the shell. Puts it on their bathroom shelf.

———

When they get home, windswept and with cold hands, Will boils the kettle for tea, and then he leaves her, to go and trim the garden hedges.

I didn't have you down as the hedge-trimming type, she says to him, and he shrugs, says it's for his gran, and she nods.

She still does senseless things for her twin. Or with him in mind, at least. Too many things. She still buys his favourite cereal, and goes to see films he'd like, ones she couldn't care less about. Sometimes it's hard to untangle where Josh ends and she herself begins, what she really thinks and feels about something, whether she is trying to honour him instead of herself. It was like this when he was alive, and has become blurrier since he died.

Just little things.

But it's those things that make up a life. That make up a person.

She hears the back door shut, out in the kitchen. It is strange, being alone in the house without Will, and without his gran or his sister knocking around upstairs, like the summer that she stayed here. She listens. Settles in the armchair by the window and does nothing except look through the open curtains. Absorbing the quiet, like a warmth, on her skin. A mother walks by with a pram. A man, with a whiskered dog in a coat. It is a clear bright day that matches her heart, as if everything inside her is lifted.

So she takes a pen and begins to write.

It is so rare that her songs come so easily, and she feels young again, a person with no mistakes or tragedy in her life. Something flowing through her, from some other place. It is like floating in water, or standing in the sunlight or the snow.

The snow.

There's Josh, again, and she wonders where exactly he

comes from when he's attached to these strands, thinks there must be something separate to the mind, the heart, the gut. And is it memory, or is it the soul, and what might a soul look like, if you could touch it, if you could dance with the light and the dark of it.

She keeps writing, as the hours fall. When Will comes in from outdoors and begins to cook dinner, the oil shimmering and spitting in the saucepan, drawers rolling open and closed, water running, knife on wood as he chops.

You like spinach, right, he calls to her. She says yes, without really registering what he's asked, because she is elsewhere, even as she's in the armchair, in this house that saved her all those years ago, and is saving her again.

She finishes it, before they eat.

Wishes she could play it for Will, or for Josh, maybe, if she really believes he is watching, somehow, up and away or between worlds, because he loved physics, after all, and he knew there was more than just life and death, didn't just ponder, but knew. Yes, she'll play it for him, or that part of him that is her, so maybe, just maybe, she'll end up playing it for herself, after all.

*

Something has changed, or begun, or simply begun again. Every moment that Rosie is not at work, or sleeping – or not sleeping, with him – she is writing.

Will watches her without comment, with her sheet music and her fountain pens, the cheap notebooks filled with graph paper so she can draw out her own staves. It feels as though he's been given a window into something private, and he knows if he questions it, even with well-intentioned interest, that nothing good will come of it. He is happy to exist around her, when she is writing. He cooks and cleans and takes himself off for hours at a time to tinker in his garage. That is his own personal art, in a sense, though it does not remove him from the world in the way it seems to with Rosie. Mechanics root him in the here and now. But with Rosie and her songs, he sees a transcendence. A change.

She has always been an attentive person.

It's what caught him at the bonfire. The way she looked deep into him and listened, even though she did not know him then. And that attention has never wavered, until now. Because when she is writing, all of it falls away. The focus she reserves for everything and everyone else just disappears, and he thinks that, actually, this is a side to her he has not yet seen. All that energy going where it's supposed to.

She hums, sometimes, or moves her lips.

Hair tied back from her face, legs tucked sideways as her fingers tap, or count.

She goes somewhere he is not able to follow, and he lets her, and it is a joy, a privilege, to be able to give her that space and time and make no demands of her. He loves it even more, he thinks, as he turns a page of his cookbook, or puts a mug down by her elbow. That version of her. Before she returns, blinking in a daze, as if coming back to earth and reminding herself of the world. His feet up, crossed at the ankles. Her novel on the coffee table. Them. Their things. Night sky, velvet beyond the blinds.

Rosie brought her guitar to his gran's house, and she has her voice, but something seems to be missing. She starts staying late at the school, sometimes, to make use of their piano, play her songs the way she intends them to be played.

Is that okay, she asks him, calling him up when she's meant

to be leaving and he's got water boiling for dinner, oil glopped in the pan.

It concerns him, that she thinks she needs to ask.

But it does make him wonder. He has an idea, and it is hard to let go of, so he takes to the internet on the nights she's still out, and after a couple of weeks he finds just what he's looking for. It's only a short walk away, cash in hand, a thanks mate, be careful with it, yeah, and he wheels it all the way home, up the kerbs, across the roads, as if it's a completely normal thing to do, to roll an old piano down the street.

It needs restoring, a little time and care. The woodwork is deeply scratched, and pools of ancient candle wax, spilled long ago, have hardened on its lid. He takes it into his garage and touches the keys to try its sound, and while he knows next to nothing about music, it's clear that it is desperately out of tune; the keys feel stiff, and slow, click like joints beneath his fingers. The overtones are impure, as the seller had explained, but somehow, that didn't seem to matter.

He knows she'll love it.

The swirling design on the wood panels, and the delicately turned legs, which remind him, loosely, of the candlesticks he made in sixth form. The deep brown of the wood, so different to the shiny black of the piano at her parents'. He digs out his toolbox, spends hours watching videos online to understand how to take it apart, remove the front panels, get to the soundboard and the tired strings and the hammers and dampers and pins.

It looks forlorn inside. The metal rails are dull and tarnished, the felt withered in places. He spends a long time just looking, and figuring things out, like he did when he would watch his grandpa with the engines, when he had nothing to contribute, no skill or experience, but a desire he couldn't articulate.

Just him, with a project, in his garage.

An itching in his palms.

When he hears Rosie's key in the door, he throws a sheet over it, just in case, though she rarely comes out here, is scared of knocking his bike over. He turns off the light and heads inside, where she kisses him hello, shoes off, hair down, and they eat dinner and talk about their days and he burns with silent pleasure at the thought of her piano waiting for her, on the other side of the wall.

*

The days slip into late August, towards the day they both dread, every year. Will's birthday; the day that Josh died, and their lives split into before and after; what should have been, and what was.

They do not talk about it. Will gets up, earlier than usual, and goes running, and Rosie pretends she is asleep when she has in fact not slept all night, not properly, has been drifting in and out of dreams since dawn.

When he's been gone a good while, she gets up and makes breakfast. Something a little special, jams and croissants and fresh juice, Will's favourite biscuits on a plate. She calls her parents, as she always does on this morning, and her father answers. Hard day, she says, and her dad says isn't it, and they share some things about Josh, his habits, things they miss or still remember. The smell of his socks, after a basketball game. The way he would crack his knuckles, or hide his vegetables under his knife, when he was little, as if no one would notice he hadn't eaten them.

They laugh, the only way they are able to on this day, and at Christmas and Easter and any other occasion he is no longer here for: quietly, and with so much love and hurt in their hearts, it feels like they might choke on it.

Shortly after she's hung up, Will gets home, his face red

with effort and the early, already-hot sunshine. He walks into the kitchen and sees the breakfast things and asks her what she's done, and she says nothing, really, that it's just breakfast, for his birthday. But he shakes his head, says no.

No? Rosie repeats.

I don't celebrate my birthday, he says.

Will.

No, Roe. I never have, after everything, and you *especially* don't need to make a thing of it, just because you're here. Seriously. Let's forget it.

Will, she says again, but he backs out of the room, starts up the stairs for a shower.

Rosie sits at the table for all of three seconds and then pushes her chair back to follow him. He is already under the water when she heads into the bathroom, no steam, because he still showers in the cold.

Josh would hate that you don't mark your birthday, she says.

Will is squeezing shampoo into his hand, runs it through his hair. It looks so long when it's wet. Turns a dark, dirty blonde, like the pine-pocked Montenegrin sand.

I'm sure you're right, he says, as the water pours all over him. Down his back, between his strong, runner's thighs. Rosie watches him from the door frame.

So let's do something today, she says.

Can't, Will says. I'm washing my hair.

Don't be annoying, she says, and she watches him rinse, lather up, rinse again. Then he shuts the water off, rubs it out of his eyes.

Pass me the towel, will you, he says, and she does as he asked, watches him wrap it round his waist and step out of the tub. She has a moment, even though it is the day that it is, even though her heart aches like a cracked rib, where she feels elated. Because she is here, in this bathroom, with Will White, and he is the most beautiful thing she has ever seen. She actually thinks that to herself, and nearly laughs out loud.

Will sits on the edge of the bath and says that she can't change his mind on this. That he's thought about it a lot, and it's better this way. Unless she needs to acknowledge it, somehow. Not his birthday, she understands, but her brother.

The bathroom window is cracked open, and she can hear a bird rasping in the garden. A magpie, she thinks. So harsh, and unlovely.

I think about him daily, she tells Will. So today isn't any different.

Right, says Will.

A normal day, then, Rosie says, and Will looks so relieved, so grateful, that her heart aches even more. She stands aside, lets him pass her into the bedroom, and thinks how all the old songs are true, how love is so often just pain, still four letters, the flip side of the same feeling.

*

After five months together, they are walking to the beach when Rosie grabs Will by the arm and pulls him into the doorway of a high street shop; some place filled with hanging signs and seashell frames.

What, he says, as she peers around him, her nails dug into the crook of his arm.

She shushes him, and holds still. An elderly woman comes out of the shop so that they have to step to one side. Treated myself, she says to them, holding up a paper bag and continuing on her way. She has a walking stick, and Will watches her hobble away from them until Rosie steps back, looking flushed.

Who did you see, then, he asks her.

My dad, she says. Which means my mother's probably nearby, too.

Right, he says.

God, Rosie says, and she presses her palms to her eyes. Sorry. It was a reaction.

It's okay, he says.

No, it's not. I'm such a coward. We're not doing anything wrong. They know that Simon and I aren't together.

But they don't know about me.

No.

Does anybody?

She tilts her chin upwards, as if sighing at the sky. Someone else moves into the alcove, asks if they can get past, and Will gestures towards the pavement. Rosie steps out of the doorway and they walk back the way they came; in the opposite direction to her father, he presumes.

I'll tell them, she says. I promise.

I don't actually care whether they know or not, he says. Unless it would change anything, for you.

In what way?

If they're unhappy about it, would that mean you would leave?

She stops, mid-step, and looks alarmed.

Of course not, she says. That's not – no. Of course not.

He leaves her to mull over his question, because her repetition shows she has not actually considered it. He keeps walking, and she follows. The light is clean and fresh, a day for drying linens on the line. A sheet-stripping day, his grandma used to call them. Bright sun, a steady breeze.

Nobody knows about you, either, he reasons, as they edge away from town, rejoin the backstreets that'll take them towards home. But I never told anyone about anyone. I figured it's nobody's business.

No, Rosie says, as if she's trying to agree.

You didn't keep Simon a secret, though, he says.

No, I didn't.

And how'd that work out for you?

Rosie doesn't say anything, and Will bumps into her side, as if to bring her back.

Rosie, he says. It's okay. I'm saying it's fine.

I should tell people, she says. I want to. But I also just . . . don't want to ruin anything.

I get that, he says.

And not because I care what they'll say, she says. My parents, or my friends, or whatever. But it's just not been that long since Simon. And none of them will understand that it's been even longer, for us.

A red kite sweeps low overhead. It cuts behind the rooftops, disappears.

They'll assume this is just a fling, Rosie goes on, when it's not. And I feel good about being happy, and I just want to enjoy it a bit longer. I'm so scared of it going away. So the fewer people that can interfere, or disturb this . . . this thing that we have, is just a good thing, I think. You know?

Will knows. He thinks he should tell her not to be scared, that there's no reason to be, but he knows too well how she feels.

D'you know what I mean? Rosie prompts, misreading his silence. Another bird, then. A blackbird scoots from the top of a flint wall, flits along the grass verge.

You're saying I'm not your rebound, says Will.

You're definitely not my rebound.

Well, okay. We might need to regroup, in that case.

Why?

I thought this was just a casual thing.

She laughs, then, her sparkle laugh, and loops her arm through his own. Leans against his shoulder.

I've not even told Marley, Rosie says, as they follow a bend in the road. But she's been so busy with the new baby, and everything.

You'll tell her, Will says. When it's right.

He knows this is what she needs; openness, and space, without imposed timelines or rules. It has felt like one long summer since they found their way back to one another, and that is no time at all, really, not after all the years he has waited.

And besides, he has kept Rosie a secret, too, which is easy when he and Amber aren't speaking, and he's meant to be off travelling the world. In Vietnam, by now. Yet here he is in Norfolk, again, with the same girl, again, rushing nothing, just letting life happen. He's applied the same, unhurried strategy to the question of her divorce. Hasn't asked her when, or how; just assured her she'll know when it's time. It is unsettling, being so stimulated, so eaten up with desire, for a woman he really cares for. He wants to shield her, and shelter her, but let her find her own way, too, with certain things.

They are turning down his grandma's street when he sees that she is smiling to herself, her arm still in his. He asks her what, and she shakes her head, a little jerk, no. But he presses her, and she shrugs, a shy smile still at her mouth.

I wish I'd done everything on earth with you, she says.

The street is quiet. No cars, or closing doors. Just them, and her voice, on the linen-dry wind.

It's not mine, she says. The quote. But it's beautiful, isn't it?

He nods, but barely, because he is not used to such talk.

And I feel it, Rosie says, still with that smile of hers. I was just thinking that I feel it.

*

Will got home early, has been waiting by the living room window, and there she is, walking down the pavement, her school satchel in hand, her hair tucked beneath a scarf so it looks like she has a short bob instead of her long, wild mane.

He takes a breath.

His feet are tingling. He laughs, a little, because he wonders if this is what it would feel like to propose.

He has a vision of the ring his grandmother gave him, but then Rosie's key is scraping in the door and he feels his heart ricochet in his ribs, and then she's by the lounge doors, putting her bag down, loosening her scarf and turning to him and then stopping.

She is still, for just a moment.

What's this, she asks.

It's yours, he says.

She says his name, the sound higher than her speaking voice, a note of both shock and joy. It is a wonderful sound. He has an image of her as a girl at Christmas, or wandering into her first music shop.

Come and look, he says, and he touches the top of the piano in invitation, and she comes forward, still holding her scarf. He takes it from her, frees her hands. She looks and looks and says nothing, and his excitement begins to waver.

She reaches out and traces the design on the panel. Something Victorian, vines and whirling leaves, which he had conditioned and then stained. He'd re-upholstered the piano stool, too, bought a new fabric he thought she might like, filled all of the scratches and dents and sanded them back to smooth.

He is proud of it, if he lets himself think about it.

But Rosie isn't saying anything.

I know it's old-fashioned, Will says. But I read that early

1900s was a good time for pianos, that they got a bit mediocre after that? And the guy said this one was 1920s, so I thought it was probably decent. Not that I know anything about pianos, obviously. Maybe I should have asked you first.

Still nothing. Her hands, trailing across the lid.

It wasn't in great shape, Will admits, but I've tried to restore it as best I can, and it had good bones, you know. The strings needed replacing, and it's got new felts and keys, so the soundboard's back to how it should be. Apparently the bass is better in these pre-Depression pianos, because they're that bit bigger. And this one's like fifty-four inches, or so. So yeah.

He swallows. She still has her coat on, has stopped touching the wood; is standing with her hands by her sides.

Don't you like it? he asks, and she turns to him and her eyes are full of tears and light and she says his name again, and he watches her, wants to see her, remember her, like this.

Colour stained in her cheeks.

I, she says. I don't even know what to say.

Just play, then, Will says, and she looks stunned at this idea for all of five seconds, and then she unbuttons her coat, sits down on the stool and lifts the lid.

He watches her take in the keys, for a moment. Sees her lay her hands in place, as if checking that they can be there.

A pause.

And then she plays.

*

How did you know, she asks him, later. They have eaten dinner, showered, are lying in bed with the duvet folded around them.

Know what, Will says, into her hair. She is pressed into

him, her back curved along his stomach, his knees tucked alongside her calves.

What I needed, she says.

Will is not sure this is a real question. He thinks it might be her way of simply telling him what everything has meant to her. Not just the piano, but all that time apart, the months where they did not speak, gave each other space, tried to heal in their own, separate, fruitless ways. How he never forgot her. He never knew they would find their way back to one another; never dared hope it would happen. But life continued, and there she was, and here he is, for her.

He was right; she does not need an answer, because she falls asleep before he can respond. Lying with her reminds him of their last night in the tent, the night she cried, told him life could be good again, and that she did not understand how.

*

Half a year of this.

Hours of talking, and eating, and piano playing, shopping and sleeping and not sleeping. They have moved into his grandmother's room; redecorated, changed the bedding and the curtains.

He makes her coffee before work, milky and with a half spoon of sugar, his own black and bitter. They drink it in bed with the blinds open, the sun falling on the opposite wall. We should put some pictures up, she suggests. I prefer the sunlight, he tells her, and she smiles, says nothing. Lifts her coffee cup to her lips.

He kisses her, deeply, at the front door, every day before her short commute to school. It leaves her breathless, leaves him hard, and they have sex most evenings, as soon as she gets home. In bed, on the sofa, and again on the stairs, which gives him a fairly severe carpet burn one time. I'm too old for this, he tells her, as he inspects it in the bathroom mirror that night. Just making up for lost time, she says, and he grins at her, marvelling at how much she can surprise him, still, with the things she comes out with.

It is all too perfect, of course.

Too right, for a life of wrong.

She gets a phone call one day, six months after she moved in. He is making eggs. Stirring slowly at the hob, wondering whether he should start to make his own bread. Fill their home with the smell of wholegrain and comfort, when he hears her on the stairs, and he knows it, already, from the fall of her feet.

Simon, is all she says, when she walks in.

He turns the gas off and puts the spoon on the side. Turns around to look at her.

What about him?

He's ill, she says. Really ill.

A roaring, in his ears. He is a terrible person; he wants to tell her he doesn't care about this man, this fellow human being who once loved the woman he always has — that nothing matters, now, but this, but them, their kitchen and their eggs and their mornings drinking coffee. Simon can die, for all he cares, and it's ruthless but in that moment it's true and he wants to say it to her, to make her feel the same.

He asks her what she needs to do.

I need to . . . go to him, she says, and her voice isn't apologetic, but firm. I'm still his wife.

Technically, Will says, and she nods, repeats the word. Technically.

Do you have to go now? he asks, and he knows it's meaningless in light of everything but he gestures at the eggs, at the plates he's laid out on the table.

I should, she says, and she won't look at him, won't even meet his eyes, and he is suddenly so angry he cannot speak. She leaves the kitchen and he grips the side of the counter, waiting.

Prisms, splintered, on the chrome of the sink.

The burn of it in his eyes.

And then she is back, with her bag at her feet. He leans against the countertop, watching her. Takes his coffee mug from the side. She comes over, folds herself into him, and he holds his breath. Won't inhale. Won't smell her hair or her skin or her early-morning sleepiness, a smell he has come to rely on.

I'm sorry, she says into his shoulder, and then she is gone, and he waits until he hears the front door close before he throws his coffee cup to the floor, watches it shatter into a hundred shards, the explosion of it on the tiles.

sixteen

Rosie goes to him, her husband. The man she has not spoken to in seven months.

The man she spent night after night with on a single university mattress and in their queen-sized marital bed, who soothed her to sleep in his large arms and bored her with his endless kindness and commitment and unwavering certainty about how their lives should go.

They would spend hours at the gym together; toning, strengthening. Him running in front of her along the river, telling her to keep going, that she was doing great.

With him, she was always doing great.

And she is sickened with herself now, and the euphoria she had found outside of him. With Will. With the breakdown of the structure they had built since that first coffee Simon bought her in the Student Union café, when she was still so sick with grief, so unendingly awake. He took her hand, and her coat. He propped her up. And so she goes to him, and she shuts down everything she is feeling about other things, and other people, and she climbs back into that tight, wraparound skin she knows so well, before she knocks on their old front door.

———

Simon tells her about Hodgkin's lymphoma in their living room, with a teapot on the table, something herbal, the colour of urine. She wants milk and sugar and Yorkshire tea. Custard creams. She cannot stop thinking about biscuits, and she is queasy, with how surreal it all feels. Her sofa. Their sofa.

This man she should know, sitting on it, with his dulled, red-rimmed eyes.

They drink their tea and he lists things like enlarged lymph nodes and extreme fatigue and how he thought it was stress, at first, because of – well, them – but when the night sweats started he got the bloodwork done and the scans, and that was it, his diagnosis, and all Rosie can think of after the custard creams is the artist she studied at school, Howard Hodgkin, who painted Mumbai weddings and raspberry crumble and red mornings, and she should be asking Simon smart, attentive questions, but all she sees are streaks of colour, artworks she'd not understood. Brain, looping. The touching of window sills; tilting of internal chairs.

Simon is calm all afternoon. Matter-of-fact, his gentle self. But after dark he tells her he is scared, and he cries, and she holds him in her arms and is reminded of the time that Josh came out to her in his bedroom; that similar loss of what to say, but an instinct to show up, so fully, that there is nothing, no one, that would see her anywhere else.

She thinks about Will's grandmother.

How she beat it, and died anyway, after all.

You're young and fit and you're going to be fine, Rosie says, for herself as much as him. Numbers glare at her from his fitness watch. It has been hours; has felt like hours. He twists himself round to look at her.

When I found out, Rosie, the first thing I thought was, why on earth did we do this?

She wants to hang her head, but she forces herself to look back at him.

I'll cut my hours, Rosie. We can sell up, move to the country. Move to Bali, even. Whatever you want. We can have kids, or not. I'll make more time for you. We'll be like us again. I promise.

We were always like us, Rosie thinks, in the dark.

Simon, she says, and she tries to extricate herself, peel back from the weight of him.

I love you, Rosie, he says, and for the first time in their years of knowing one another, his voice is fierce. I should *never* have let life get in the way of that. So I'll survive this, and I'll put it right.

Simon, she says again.

Yes?

We were apart for a long time, she says. We ended things. And. Well.

You're not wearing your ring, he observes.

Her heart freezes over; spreads like frost down her spine. Shame, burning cold.

We both thought it was over, Simon reasons. We'll have both . . . done things that married people aren't supposed to.

He folds his fingers in hers. They feel clammy, like the backs of her knees.

Let's agree not to go there, he says. I love you. This is just about the worst thing I could imagine happening, and all I could think was, why is Rosemary not here?

But —

I get it, if you don't feel the same. I get it, if you don't want to be married to me. To this, and all that it comes with.

Simon. It's not that.

Then give me a chance, Rosie? Give us one more chance?

He is still looking up at her, and his face is so pleading and good, and she has loved him for so many years, and she made a vow, and he could be dying, and there is no question of right or wrong, here, for her. She knows what she wants to do. Who she desperately wants to be.

In sickness and in health, she says.

Til death do us part, says Simon, and she says oh, God, please don't.

The days after are leaden, and slow. She endures them, booking chemo dates into her diary, pouring herself into laptop research for outcomes and statistics, but then, inevitably, she calls him.

She can't not.

The fear and the regret and the sinking of it all is suffocating, and she needs her best friend, as selfish and awful as that makes her, her skin crawling with the plague of it.

He does not pick up, so she tries again.

In the end, she leaves a voicemail.

Will, she says. I know I'm the last person you want to hear from right now. So hang up, if you need to, okay? But I just need to talk, to someone. To you. It's cancer. He has cancer. Lymphoma. And I can't actually believe that. I can't be*lieve* it. My brother died, and your gran, and now this? How much bad luck can one person witness in a lifetime?

She gives a stupid, strange laugh, and she is trembling, really trembling. Her hands don't feel like her own.

He's my husband, Will, she says. And I know we parted ways, and I know that . . . we . . . but I just can't, any more. He might be dying. And I have to stand by him. I have to be his wife, you know?

She pauses, as if he is listening, to give him the time to absorb.

I have to do this, she says. I do. And I don't want you out of my life, Will, I never have. But it's your call. Okay? Okay.

And she hangs up.

Marley comes as soon as she asks her to, with her toddler in a pushchair, the new baby in a sling, and most importantly, a takeaway menu in hand.

Order whatever you want, she tells Simon.

I don't really feel like eating, he says, and she says all the more reason to order what you want, Si.

Then she asks questions and listens and reassures them both, dandling the baby on her knee, telling them exactly what his own doctor has said, echoing the figures and recommendations and timelines they expect. Skye plays on the carpet with what looks like a pair of balled-up socks, and the street lights come on outside as they eat noodles and sticky rice and chicken drowned in coconut cream.

If you're going to get cancer, Marley says, then this is the one you want to get.

So they say, Simon says.

He is twirling his chopsticks around, barely touching his food. Rosie, by contrast, has devoured bowl after bowl. Something cavernous has opened inside her since the not-quite-divorce. She wants salt and comfort and soft, warm things to fill herself up with. She listens to Marley's words as if they, too, can nourish her, as though knowledge and facts can somehow bolster them against this, like they can build an immunity among the three of them, here, in this living room, with sheer revision and repetition of numbers and body parts and stages and cells. Rosie is good at exams. She is good at knowing all there is to know, and putting in the effort that's required for the best outcome. She believes, for the short, quiet time that it takes them to eat dinner, that things are actually going to be okay. And okay is all she wants. All she should ever have wanted.

How are you doing, Marley asks her, as she shrugs her coat on in the stairwell, and Rosie buckles Skye into her pushchair.

Just – trying, Rosie says, as Skye kicks out. There!

She clips her in, and Skye pouts.

No, Marley says, as she buttons up her jacket, one by slow, tortoise shell one, the baby still asleep in her sling. How *are* you. With all this.

Rosie looks at her friend from her squat by the floor, Skye now tugging at her hair.

I don't really know, she says. I guess I feel . . . focused. Like I just need to get him through his first chemo, and then we can go from there.

Good, Marley says. That's a good way to think.

Good, Rosie echoes.

But I didn't actually mean about the cancer, she says. I meant that you guys were separated. And now you're not. And I get why – cancer changes things.

It really does, Rosie says, as she tries to disentangle her hair from Skye's fist.

Just know that I'm here if you need me. Not as a doctor, or a second opinion, though obviously I'm here for that, too. But I'm still your friend first, Rosie. I'm here if things are hard, all right? Outside of cancer.

Rosie glances into the flat, at what she can see of the kitchen; Simon is clearing up, stacking the dishwasher with plates, banging around as he always has, with his large limbs and heavy hands.

Shall we, she says, and she nods at the lift doors, and between them they guide Skye's pushchair inside, take the seven floors down to the lobby. Outside, the night is clear and strewn with stars. Their breath clouds silver in the air.

Rosie waits for the glass door to close and feels the truth rising like a cough, up and through her, and then she turns to her friend and says that she slept with Will White during the separation. Not just once. A lot. That they were sort of, together, she thinks. For months.

Marley's eyes get wide and her mouth slackens. Rosie puts the heels of her hands over her eyes, presses them into the sockets.

What do I do, Marl, she asks.

Okay, okay, back up, says Marley. Will White. From school. Who you sort of stayed in touch with but then lost contact, because he didn't come to your wedding, 'cause he was still utterly in love with you – *that* Will White?

Yes. Though I'm not sure about the love part.

Whatever, Marley says, and she shakes her head, as if to clear the warm, sleepy fog of too much Thai food. So, you were together. For *months*? How many months?

I don't know. Like five or six. I was kind of living with him.

Kind of living with him.

Yeah.

How do you *kind of* live with someone?

What do you –

Did you have a spare toothbrush in his bathroom, Marley asks, or did you rarely go back to your own place?

I didn't really . . . have my own place, Rosie admits.

I thought you were staying with a colleague, after you left Simon?

I didn't leave Simon. We left each other.

Marley waves her hand like that's insignificant, then shushes the baby, who has started to mewl.

But no, Rosie relents. That was a . . . cover-up. I went from my mum's, straight to Will's grandmother's house.

Mamma *Mia*, Marley says. After all this *time*?

I know.

It's like a movie, Rosie!

A movie where the husband gets cancer so the heroine stamps on the hero's heart and walks out?

Marley's smile fades.

Right, she says. Right.

What do I do, Marl? Rosie asks again. Should I tell Simon? I wanted to, but he said he's been with other people, too, and we don't need to talk about it.

Well, then. I think you're fine.

But it's Will, you know? Not some random guy.

He's definitely not some random guy, Marley says. He's *the* guy.

Stop it, Marl.

You're the one that called him the hero!

There are no heroes, okay? There is just me, and them, and the right thing. And I'm with Simon. I married him. And he's – he's got to be okay.

Her voice cracks, like glass, under the night sky.

Okay, Marley says. I get that. I do.

Rosie's arms are bare, and she feels cold, but she welcomes it. She wants the discomfort, the reminder that it is not so much effort to endure, after all. This life of cold hands and long falls and wanting, so much, that it burns.

Cinders, in the grate of her.

Rosie, says Marley.

Yeah?

Are you . . . is this what you want?

Rosie doesn't look at her friend; she stares upwards, instead, at the pinpricks of white so far above them. Light years away.

Looking back in time, at millennia gone by. Josh told her all about that. The physics of it.

I have to put Simon first, she says. I want to.

But do you love him, Rosie?

Yes, she says, fiercely, and without pause.

Okay, Marley says. I just needed to ask. But it's okay, Rosie. Don't.

Because apparently, Rosie is crying. She brushes at her face, rubs at her stupid, leaking eyes.

Okay, she says back, and she wants to stamp her foot in fury, tug on her own hair like Skye, and scream, with her face tilted upwards and the apartments hushed around them, people looking out of their windows, alarmed, by the noises she would make.

Okay, she says again.

Marley grips her shoulder with her steady surgeon's hand.

You're okay, she says, and it is as if the word has lost all meaning, and yet still Rosie holds on to it, like a lifebuoy, a truth they can speak into being.

*

Her songs do not dry up, this time.

They gush out of her, like broken waters, as soon as Simon is sleeping. And he sleeps a lot; in the day as well as through the night, and for the whole weekend before his first chemo, which is plenty of time to write. Plenty of time to sit on the window sill of their flat and bleed lyrics under the gaze of the city lights, the traffic moving below.

Will is probably awake, too, she knows.

He kept similar hours to her.

An early bird, and a seasoned insomniac, both led by the things in their heads.

She makes a list of what she thinks might keep him awake.

She writes a text, and deletes it.

She drinks water and coffee and stays wired and functioning, with her pen nib fused to her notebook, the lamplight on the not-blank pages, the crossings out, the found words and rhythms that flood out of her. Oceans of it. Outpouring.

*

Will thought about taking a bottle of vodka to the cliffs and drinking himself numb. But that was it: a thought. He paces the house, instead, battling the urge to head to an off-licence. There is no drink in his grandmother's house; Amber emptied the cupboards as soon as their gran died. He hates her, for this, and is unequivocally grateful. Roams around the living room, like an enclosed big cat.

He hasn't slept since she left.

Wonders if she's managed to.

But after he's thrown himself into his grandpa's armchair and his eyes are closing, just as he finally gets near to some kind of shut down, his phone rings and he lurches up as if there's been a break-in, his heart thundering in his ribs.

It's an unknown number. A scam, or cold call, he thinks, as he presses the green button and waits.

Hello? a woman's voice says. Hello? Is this Will White?

Speaking, he says.

Oh, cool, she says, and a shot of recognition goes through him, the sound of a schoolgirl he once knew. It's Marley, she confirms.

Marley, he repeats.

Rosie's friend.

I know who you are.

Right, well, I'm sorry for calling so late. I just wanted to touch base.

Okay, he says.

I know about you and her, she says. She told me, tonight, and she's . . . she'll hate me for ringing. It's none of my business.

No, says Will. It's not.

You never liked me, did you, she asks him, and her voice has changed, mild curiosity mingling with distaste; like the time he tried caviar.

You never liked me, either, he says.

Not really, she says. But Rosie did. Does.

Will says nothing. He sinks back into his grandfather's chair, stretches his legs out in front of him.

For all the good it does, he says.

I know you know her like I do, Marley says. Better, even, I'd imagine. So I know you already know she's just trying to do the right thing. She's so moral. Like, annoyingly so. What she wants . . . doesn't really count. Not even when we were kids. When we had sleepovers, right, she wouldn't eat any midnight snacks because we'd already brushed our teeth. She's that kind of person, Will. She has rules that rule her. And it doesn't dictate how she feels about you. Just what she does.

Will is looking, unseeingly, at the living room he grew up in. The wood floor and downtrodden carpet, with its tasselled rug, ravaged by the dog. There is dust on the fireplace. Thick, slanting cobwebs, cloaking the poker and tongs.

I think what she does is the most important thing here, he says.

Marley is quiet. He hears a baby crying in the background.

Just don't be too hard on her, she says eventually. She's so hard on herself already, you know?

Thanks for the advice I didn't ask for, he says.

He hears her sigh. The baby cries louder.

Nice talking to you, Will, Marley says. As ever.

Will snorts, hoping she catches it before she hangs up. Then he throws his phone across the room where it bounces, uselessly, on the opposite armchair. His grandmother's, with her tartan blanket still draped over the side.

*

Rosie rubs Simon's back as he vomits into their toilet bowl, the fan flicked on and the window open. It is cold outside, but they need the air. The taste of sky and wind and good things.

All she can do is soothe him with her hands, these small gestures of opening windows, saying it's all right, over and over. His shoulder blades feel like bird bones under her fingers. Delicate, and unhuman. Like the seagull skeleton she and Josh found, once, on their local beach. They buried it, gave it a funeral.

Simon heaves once more and then groans, lowers his face to the floor.

Let's get you in bed, Rosie says, and he says no, he wants to stay here.

Then let me put some towels down, she says. I can try and make you more comfortable.

He says no, again, and his eyes are already closing. The first round of chemo had seemed too easy, almost jovial. They'd taken magazines but not read them, instead opting to talk to the other patients, learning their first names, hearing their stories. It was an oddly optimistic atmosphere, and Simon had felt fine.

Two days later, he did not feel fine.

Now, Rosie looks at him curled on the bathroom tiles. Then she stands quietly and leaves him to rest, with the noise of the fan and the sounds of the October night carrying through the window. A dog barks. Car horns, scuffing leaves, and low, distant engines.

She makes a cup of tea and doesn't drink it. Chooses a book, only not to read it, and is staring into space at the kitchen table when she hears another sort of engine. A deep, growling sound, the guttural revs that still, even now, flip her stomach. She has one of those moments where she knows something is about to happen, and she watches time, as if it is a tangible thing; sees it seep through the lamplight and the shadows cast by her furniture, nothing moving, holding its inanimate breath.

Her phone rings, and she answers, says his name.

Which number d'you live at, he asks her.

What?

Which number flat, he says. I'm outside and I don't know which buzzer to press.

You're outside?

Yeah.

You want to come in?

Or you could come out, he says.

She hesitates, though stalling is the last thing she wants to do.

I won't touch you, he promises. If that helps.

I'll . . . buzz you in, Rosie says, and she does, and then she immediately regrets it and takes her keys and walks out and down the stairs.

He is already halfway up. Wearing his leather jacket and carrying his bike helmet, and looking okay, and sober, and calm. His steps are long and sure, even in his heavy boots. The boots she knows and loves, somehow, and how can you love someone else's shoes, she wonders, as she watches him ascend.

When she is close, he hears her and stops, one floor below.

Holds her still in his eyes, and then shrugs, like the eighteen-year-old version of himself.

Wolf teeth. Unshifting gaze.

Sorry, he says to her.

What for?

For taking so long, he says.

They eat cereal in the kitchen, just like they did before, when Josh was alive and the snow was falling and they barely knew one another. It is inconceivable, to her, that there was a time when this was true. She has never especially wanted a child, but sometimes she wonders, if she did, how it is that she does not know them yet. And it is like this with Will.

Tonight, they keep the lights low, their voices even lower.

He's sleeping, Rosie tells him, and he nods.

Has he started chemo?

This week, she says.

Shit.

Yeah.

I can come back, he says. Another day.

But she shakes her head, passes him a coffee. His hands seem cold from the ride; they look red and a little swollen.

You should really wear gloves, she tells him.

You should really sing for a living, he says.

Huh?

Don't tell me how to live, he says, and I won't tell you, either.

Wow, she says. You got cranky.

I've always been cranky.

No, you haven't.

I have. When I was young and attractive, it just seemed more appealing, I think. Seductive.

Is that right?

But it's actually been crankiness all along.

You are a prickly bastard, she says, remembering the cactus, and she splutters at her nerve, and the memory. It takes Will by surprise, too, and he grins, then snickers at her own laughter. She thinks she wants to cry.

I know it's weird, he says, and he pours himself more cereal, the rush of grains raining into his bowl. But I'm trying to be a better human. More like you. Or Josh.

Rosie nudges her spoon around. She wants to tell him she is trying so hard to be good because she is not; that it is not effortless, for her, like it was for her twin. That she wants things she shouldn't, and makes terrible choices, and hurts people despite trying not to.

You're already a good human, she says.

Thinking, the one that keeps me up at night.

In all the right ways.

Will crunches with his mouth closed, looking at her across the table. Then he tells her he's going to be there, for all of it. Whatever she needs, or Simon needs. He knows they have closer friends than him, but he's flexible, with his shift work, and he can drive, and he has no ties, no girlfriend or family. So he can be a friend. He wants to be a friend.

Traffic breathes through the latched windows. Rosie puts down her spoon and takes his hand, with the day dying around them, the burn of auburn clouds. And when he shifts away, she lets him go.

This is bad cereal, he tells her, after a moment.

I know, she says. Sugar free.

They both take another mouthful, chew and swallow.

It's Simon's, she says.

He nods, and they keep eating.

———

She does not explain to Simon about Will; simply says to him, during his next round of chemo, that he's going to drive them both home.

We got back in touch, Rosie tells him, while he's hooked up to the wires, the life-saving poison flowing into his veins, and he accepts it without question. Afterwards, he greets Will, tired but smiling, says it's good to see him, and then he sits quietly in the back, looking out at the roads as Will drives them back to their flat.

He says thanks, as he gets out of the car, and Will says it's no problem.

There is a moment when Rosie senses Will wanting to say something else. She sees his eyes in the rear-view mirror, drinking in this new man, so different to the young, muscular one he met in the coffee shop, when she hoped they'd be friends, all three of them, when she thought life would go another way.

Call if you need, Will says, and she says she will. She does not invite him in, this time. She takes the lift up with her husband – something they'd not done once, in all the years of living there, unless they had suitcases and were coming back from the airport – and she makes him decaffeinated tea and they do easy things like sitting, or napping, the television muted in the background.

One day, though, he is so sick that she is frightened.

He cannot even keep water down, and his skin is like paste, but she has back-to-back lessons that day, and she's already missed enough work as it is, and he tells her to go, that he'll be fine. She wants to call his mother, but he says no. A family friend, then, his best man from their wedding, but he refuses that, too, says he doesn't want anyone to see him like this. That everyone's busy, has work, their lives. That, again, he'll be fine.

I might call Will, she says, from the door. Simon makes a sleepy noise, an agreement or another refusal, she can't be sure.

But he has nothing to lose, with Will. They don't know each other; there will be no emotion, no pitying eyes or obligation, which she knows is Simon's worst fear. And so she calls, on her way down the stairs. It is a blanched day, everything dull and fallow, the stairwell mordantly cold.

It's a lot to ask, she says, as soon as he answers. But could you come over? I've got work, and he's in bed, but just in case he needs more water or something happens, I just –

I'll be there, Will says.

And she says okay, and he says okay back, and then he's gone and she's out on the pavement, and her mouth feels too full of teeth.

*

Will knocks on the door, thinking that if Simon's awake, he'd probably rather answer it. Five seconds. Six. When nothing happens, he takes the key from under the doormat, as Rosie instructed, and lets himself in.

He hadn't really looked around their flat, before. It is spacious and expensive-looking, larger than his gran's whole house. Floor-to-ceiling windows let in more light than he is used to, the River Yare gleaming like a silver ribbon below. Their furniture is shiny, and hard. A city dweller's pad, filled with glass tables and chrome handles and a television screen wider than his kitchen table.

He stands by the door for a while, listening, but Simon does not seem to be up. He walks forwards, swears, then doubles back, takes off his shoes and leaves them on the mat. He looks out of the wide windows. Peruses their DVD collection, finds nothing he'd be remotely interested in watching.

And though he does not mean to, he ends up snooping;

looking in their cupboards, the fridge, the bathroom cabinet beneath their marble-set sink. Gold taps. Pearly-white hand sanitiser. It reminds him of a hotel, which leaves him feeling sad, and strangely, somewhat satisfied.

At lunch, he makes them both sandwiches, a task he doesn't expect to be as difficult as it is. There is some seeded bread in the freezer that seems older than the margarine he finds at the very back of the fridge, so yellow and smooth, it's as though no knife has ever been near it. Sundried tomatoes in the bottom of a jar, and a block of cheese with fine grate marks, clearly only ever used for cooking. He slices it up and toasts the bread, trickles the tomato oil over the top to turn it golden and oozing and less cardboard-like.

Two plates.

Butter knife, left in the sink.

He pads down the corridor to the bedroom and taps on the door with his foot. When he pushes it open, he finds Simon sitting up on his pillows, looking at the wall. There is another television in here. Paintings of blue things; abstract splashes and coiling waves, bordered with mounts and thin frames.

You're up, Will says.

Oh, Simon says. Hello.

Rosie told you I was coming, didn't she?

In a roundabout way, I think, Simon says. I'm not very good at listening, these days.

I made lunch, Will says, and he hesitates in the doorway, some deep disinclination keeping him out of this man's bedroom. He thinks about shoving the food across the floor, leaving him to it. But he is sick, not in prison, he reminds himself, and so he crosses the threshold and hands him the plate.

A sandwich, Simon says, and he sounds bemused.

Yep.

I don't . . . he says, and then he falters. Takes it from him.

You hungry? Will asks, as he seats himself in a chair by the dresser, his own plate balanced on his knee. He watches as Simon inspects the bread, takes a bite, then visibly relaxes.

Must be, he says, through his mouthful, and Will raises his own sandwich in a false toast and they eat, teeth gnawing, the air thick and smelling of sleep.

Will looks around as he chews, without really wanting to. Some dark fascination takes over, like needing to look at a car crash, or a wild animal attack, despite everything that's wrong about it. Simon and Rosie's bedroom. Their private space, with its sage walls and photo-filled frames, mostly snaps from the wedding he never attended. Her dressing gown, on the door. Contraceptive pill on the nightstand.

His heart is beating too slowly. He realises, as he takes his final bite, that he does not know what Simon knows, about anything.

How d'you feel? Will asks him, when they're done.

Like I have cancer, Simon answers.

That bad, huh?

I wouldn't recommend it, he says, but he smiles, and Will sees the stretch of square jaw from all those years ago, the pleasant face of this pleasant guy he's spent so many years loathing.

He has wished him dead, many a time.

Which troubles him less than it should.

So nice that you and Rosie got back in touch, Simon says, and Will braces himself. Wipes his mouth with the back of his hand, the oil lucent, like spilt water.

Yeah, he says.

It'd been a while, hadn't it?

Years, Will agrees.

She missed you, Simon tells him. She never said, but I could tell. I'm glad you got over, you know. Whatever it was.

Me too, says Will, after the longest, most dreadful pause.

Rosie isn't a proud person, Simon says, sinking back into his pillows. But she's principled. She feels things deeply, and takes a long time to forgive. I like that about her, though. She's sincere, you know? And I like sincerity.

Yeah, Will says, though he doesn't know why Simon is telling him this.

So she might have been distant, Simon says. But she came back. She reached out, when times got tough. And that means more than the distance, I think.

Right, says Will. Then, just as it looks as though Simon might close his eyes, he says, I do know all this. It's why I'm here.

So nice she has you, Simon says, his voice fading, already, into unconsciousness. He mumbles something that sounds like the word brother, and Will stands up, takes the plates, and pauses at the door. He wants to tell him he is not the brother, here. That nothing about him is brotherly. A savage, boorish part of him wants to say that Rosie has never been a sibling, to him, that he's read it all wrong, and it's embarrassing and pathetic and he wants to see the carpet burns he has, the white scars of them on his glutes from the sex they had in the house they shared, more than once, where she'd borrowed his shirts and cut his hair and laughed with his grandma in the greenhouse. Geese, calling, in the mornings. Her hair, like apples, after a shower.

But he doesn't. He leaves him to sleep.

Goes to wash the plates, in their giant marital sink.

Later, they play cards. When Simon emerges from the bedroom and says oh, you're still here, and Will says he promised Rosie he'd stay, that she'll be home soon.

I can look after myself, you know, says Simon.

I know, Will says. But he does not move, and so Simon shrugs, and there is a pack of cards on the shelf of the coffee table, staring at them with its smug, cobalt-blue outline of a king. Shall we? Will asks, and Simon says sure.

Will shuffles the deck. He likes the logic and order of card games; it reminds him of maths, in a way, or the maintenance of an engine. Such a variety of outcomes, but with resolutions, definitive ways forward. He used to play with his grandpa. And his gran, when she was having her own chemo, so long ago now, though he can still smell the rust, the sourness, of that time, the coppery odour of blood and bodies and split fruit.

Simon does not smell like that, yet.

His eyes look bruised, and his hair is mussed from the hours in bed, but otherwise he seems himself, though Will realises, as he deals the cards, that he has no idea who that is.

Rummy? he asks him.

Simon says sure, again, and Will wonders if he ever has an opinion on anything, and they play in silence for a while, the slap and scuffle of the cards the only sound as they sit on opposite sofas. The living room floods with the setting sun, warms their wrists as they play.

What's with the art, Will asks him, when he feels he has to speak.

Hmm?

Simon looks up, and he sees that it has taken every ounce of his concentration to be able to play their game. He has not read their silence as awkward, or loaded. He is simply struggling to focus.

In your room, Will says. All the water.

Oh, he says. I used to row. And sail.

You don't now?

Not since Oxford.

Will says nothing. It is a familiar story. One he abhors, and

330

one that makes him a hypocrite. He still has travel brochures in his old flat, the pages folded down, circled treks and waterfalls and ancient wonders he's never seen.

Why not? he asks, when he can't help himself.

I got a job, Simon says. And a mortgage, and a wife. I want to teach her to sail, one day; I always said I would, but it never happened. No time. City living, you know.

Will does not know, because he has only lived on the coast and in the Dales, and his time outside the garage was spent hiking and rescuing and running in the mountains, along the cliffs, in the rain and the shining sun.

Like Rosie's music, he says, after a long pause. Another card laid on the table.

Her music?

Yeah. She stopped, didn't she. For years. No time. City living. All of that.

I suppose so. But she's teaching again, now, I think.

You think?

His voice is harsh, sarcastic, and he should recover it, but he can't. He doesn't know what to say, or how to take those two words back. Simon may be sick, but he is not stupid. He lowers his cards and looks at him, and Will waits.

You still don't like me, Simon says.

What?

You didn't like me, when we first met. That much was obvious. And then you and Rosie lost touch and I figured it didn't matter. But now you're here, and you still don't. Can I ask why?

The sun falls through the high windows, like molten brass.

I'm genuinely interested, Simon urges.

Will exhales through one cheek.

Okay, he says. There's a list.

Blimey, Simon says. After just one coffee?

Well, Rosie and I talked a lot, remember, he says.

Simon nods, his face mild, as though this is only fair.

I thought you were – are – hugely privileged, and a bit of a drag, Will says.

Simon stares at him, and then his face breaks. Will steels himself, thinking he must be offended, angry, even, but then he sees that he's laughing.

A drag, Simon repeats.

Yeah, Will says. Just a bit dull. Nothing to you, really. Beyond your money and your manners.

I do have money and manners, Simon agrees, and he's still grinning. What else?

This is weird, mate, Will says. You really want me to keep insulting you?

Simon has put his cards down, and he rubs his hand along his jaw, stubble like lichen on his chin.

People don't tell me how it is, Simon says. My parents are wealthy, and privileged, like you said, and they're great, but they're also people who never, ever let me believe I couldn't do anything I wanted. All I had to do was ask. Live. Then I went to public school, where my teachers projected the same message, and then Oxford landed me a job that meant I was earning a lot of money, very quickly, with a team of people who do what I tell them. I've never had to think about that not being the norm. Ever. I've never had to think about life not being plain sailing, because it has been, so far, and with relatively little effort.

Will hates him, a little more, despite his self-awareness.

I think I'm an all right guy, Will, Simon says. I care about people, and things. But I'm only just starting to realise how . . . *blinkered* I am.

Because you got cancer, Will says.

Exactly, he says. And because my wife left me. Well. Maybe

332

we left each other, I don't quite know how we got there. But that wasn't plain sailing either. And I didn't know why. Because nobody had prepared me for that. Nobody ever tells me what they really think.

Forgive me if I'm all out of sympathy, Will says, and Simon grins, again.

What else, he says. I want to hear it.

Will pauses, and then relents.

I thought you were smug, he tells him. And patronising, but because you were nice, it was a subtle sort of patronising. Not arrogance, exactly, but an ignorance, almost. And I thought you looked at people without really seeing them. You saw a pretty, intelligent, pocketable wife in Rosie, I think.

He stops himself before he says more.

I did, Simon says, and his grin has faded now. That's true. But I see a lot more than that, too.

Do you?

Of course.

What do you see, then?

That's pretty personal, mate, Simon says, and Will shrugs, stares him down. I love her, Simon says. I really do. I don't need to explain why.

But you let her live a life where she's not herself, Will says.

What do you mean?

She doesn't *create* anything, Will says. She doesn't sing or play or write.

She never expressed an interest in those things, Simon says.

It doesn't matter, Will says. You let her get smaller, and thinner, and even quieter than she was. I bet the in-laws love you.

Simon sits back, his face no longer genial.

They do, actually, he says.

I don't know why we're even talking about this, Will says.

I asked you why you didn't like me, Simon says. And you were kindly answering.

There's nothing kind about this, Will says.

Actually, Will, Simon says, it's the kindest thing anyone's done for me in weeks. I've been getting a whole lot of nothing from everyone. Old friends, and colleagues, and family members, who are scared to even look at me, and don't know what the hell to say.

Will gets the impression that it's the first time Simon has said hell.

And I get why, because they're in that same bubble, Simon explains. Where they don't ever have to face things. Where things don't go wrong.

Newsflash, Will says. Things will always go wrong.

There is another pause. A plane beelines through the dusk, streaking a neon trail across the windows.

Thank you, Simon says. Honestly.

Will looks at him, trying to work him out, when he realises he is still holding his cards. He puts them down, leans back on the sofa.

You're more interesting, now you have cancer, he tells him.

Every cloud, Simon says.

*

Rosie is walking home. She never learnt to drive, and she didn't want to wait for the bus, and when she calls Will he says they're fine, that she needn't rush.

This is a new concept, to her. She feels like she's always rushing.

She walks through the city, past the cathedral, looking up, out of habit, to see the peregrine falcons, but they're not there. She keeps walking. She has to stop, at one point, and tap her foot three times on the kerb, and then she curses herself and walks on, under the cleft autumnal clouds.

What'll happen if you don't tap or touch, her therapist had asked her, once.

Nothing, Rosie had said. I know it makes no difference. But that doesn't stop me feeling like I have to do it.

Or what, the therapist had asked, and Rosie had clamped her mouth shut because, once again, she wasn't being heard; because she knew the outcome changed nothing. So she left, and kept touching and tapping and stepping when some internal force told her she needed to. It happens less, in adulthood, she's noticed. But since Simon's diagnosis, the urges come out of nowhere. Touched window sills and tapped door handles and syllables, counted, in her head.

She is minutes from home when her phone rings. It is her mum, who so rarely rings her first that she assumes the worst. A dead dad, or another cancer, this time in her mother's bones or breast or blood.

Mum, she says.

Hello darling.

What's up?

Nothing's *up*. I only wanted to see how you were doing. How Simon is.

Really, she asks, and there is a confused moment between them, her response not what her mother expected.

Really, she says, after a while. How's the chemo coming along?

Fine. As fine as these things are, I guess. He got sick this morning, just like the doctor said he would.

But you still went to work?

Learnt from the best, didn't I, Rosie says.

A bus rattles past; the bus she could have caught, if she had waited. It is so noisy, all fumes and wheels and rumbling engine, that she does not notice the prolonged silence down the phone.

Was I such a bad mother, her mum asks her. Rosie has just reached the door to the flats, and she pauses while searching for her keys.

No, she says, as a reflex. Why would you say that?

I know I'm difficult, her mother says. I know that, Rosie. I know I pushed you, and wanted the best for you. But I always thought you understood that.

I did, Rosie says. I do.

Then why are things like this, she asks, and for the first time, Rosie hears a hint of something new in her mother's voice. Sadness, or desperation. Panic, pushed down, between the edges of her words.

Rosie turns back to the street and watches the bus trundle onwards. The cars, moving. Pavements, coppered, in the dying sun.

It is her instinct to deny and smooth over and reassure, but she looks at her hands, one clutching the phone, the other holding her bag, a satchel she'd found buried in a second-hand shop. It is so battered. Permanently bruised, where patches of the leather have rubbed away.

Because I came to you about Simon, Rosie finds herself saying. Before his diagnosis. And you just turned me away.

Another silence, stretched between them.

I gave you advice, her mother says. I told you what I would do.

It was bad advice, Rosie tells her.

Well, her mother says, flustered. Rosie battles herself, for what feels like several minutes. Stones, bulging, in her throat.

How's Dad? Rosie asks, eventually.

Fine, her mother says.

Simon'll be fine, too, Rosie says, and then because there is something wild in her now, something that thinks to hell with it, she tells her that Will's been with him all day.

Will White, her mother says, slowly.

The very one, Rosie says.

I didn't know you were in touch.

It's a recent thing, Rosie says. He's being a friend, to us. Me and Simon.

That's good, her mum says, and it sounds like her mouth has got really small, like her words have to find their way round her teeth. Rosie knows she's dying to say that surely they have better friends, people who know Simon intimately who could be there with him, but she doesn't, because that's the whole point.

I also got a new job, Rosie tells her. The air is warm with exhaust fumes and the lack of wind, wrapped around her as she speaks it all aloud.

Oh?

I'm a music teacher now, she says. Classical guitar, and piano. Some singing. That's why I was out, today.

Oh. Rosie. That's – that's lovely.

It is lovely, she says. It's really lovely. The pay is terrible. Like, godawful. But I don't really care. No: I don't care one bit.

Why are you doing this, Rosie, her mother asks, after no silence, this time; a hardening, instead, a refusal to play this game.

Why was I not doing it, Rosie asks back. The sky, so red, above her, as her mother does not answer.

*

Will gets to know Simon in a way he has never known another person. He learns what sort of light will make him feel lethargic, and requires him to close the curtains. What colour he likes his bananas to be, before he'll eat them. He finds out exactly what temperature the heating should be set to, at varying points of the day; he is overly warm in the mornings, and often too cold after lunch. He wears slippers in the house, like an old man, which he insists he did even before his diagnosis. I hate getting stuff on my feet, he explains, when Will mocks him for it. And when Will asks what he means, he says you know, dust or hair or water splashed on the floor, and Will says wow, you do have problems, and Simon says he reckons he'd take cancer over dirty feet and they laugh about it, together, in the kitchen.

He finds out other things, too. That he takes honey in his camomile tea, but only past midday, as if sweetness is a treat reserved for afternoons. That he is an only child, and is scared of heights, and reads a lot, about politics and philosophy.

What do you read, Simon asks him, when he's scanning his bookshelves, one day, Will boiling the kettle from the kitchen.

Not a lot, Will says.

Come on, Simon says. Everyone reads.

I read motorbike manuals, Will says. And cookbooks.

Simon nods.

And travel guides, he adds.

You like to travel?

Will just smiles at him, for this. Turns his back to pour the boiling water into their cups, wondering if he can like something he's never done, put on hold, missed, perhaps, altogether.

I don't, really, Simon says. I know that's kind of dull.

I'd expect nothing less, says Will, and Simon grins, tells him he's a bell end, and the term takes them both by surprise, throws them back to school, and they snicker, at first, and then laugh so hard that Simon says oh man, it hurts, which makes them both laugh some more.

*

And this is how it goes. Weeks of a sick husband, and a best, unexpected friend, coming to spend time with him when it's needed; to drive them both to and from the hospital, to stay with them, sometimes, for dinner, or to hang out with Simon while she works.

She is so grateful she feels like her heart might rise up and out of her. Organs held out to him, like offerings.

He asks for nothing, except better butter. She restocks the fridge and watches him, sometimes, when he smokes on their balcony, wondering how he never smells of tar or tobacco, but pine trees and soil, a faint trace of petrol.

She remembers the clarity of him; how he tasted of fresh water.

The hills they climbed in the shade of the Montenegrin trees, and the tomatoes they popped in their mouths, the removal of real life as if it had been cleaved off, for one week, one summer.

You're smoking again, she says to him once, at the door.

Not really, he says. Just sometimes.

Simon says he likes him. That they've found the opposite of common ground; intrigue, and a grudging respect, and Rosie turns to him in bed and says she doesn't want there to be a grudging anything, and Simon laughs, touches her face, tells her she is the sweetest person he knows.

This is a word used to describe her, so often. She is beyond bored of it.

*

Will ends up going to chemo with Simon, one Thursday. Rosie has a school concert that she can't get out of, even though she tried, apparently, asked if she could skip it – but Simon insisted she go, and Will, for once, agreed with him.

He knows the drill; spent a lot of time in a cancer ward with his gran. They don't play cards, or read, or even listen to music, because Simon is too exhausted. This is his fourth treatment, and his hair has thinned, his eyebrows shed into pale lines.

They simply watch the room and the patients, the pools of daylight on the hard floor. It has been a wet winter. So much rain and wind.

D'you know what's funny, Simon asks him.

What's that?

I think, all things considered, you're probably my best mate.

Will feels a sharpness go through him, as if the poison has been hooked up to his own veins.

I know we don't share stuff like that, Simon says. But cancer makes you sentimental, so just give me this one.

All right, says Will.

It's funny, isn't it, Simon continues. We barely know each other, and you're Rosie's friend, really. You didn't even like me. Don't, even. But I'm just sat here, and thinking, that actually, apart from Rosie, there's nobody I'd rather be sitting here with. And maybe that's a bit sad, I don't know.

Will just looks at him. He has no idea what to say.

My parents came over, last weekend, Simon goes on. And I love them, you know, but they were just awful to be around. They made me feel like a kid again, or like I was elderly and incapable, like I'm a feather they mustn't knock down. And my actual best mate, Jon, he calls, sometimes, and it's awkward, and he asks how it's going, which is nice, but we don't talk any more about the things I want to talk about. The rowing, and the rugby, or even his kids. Like cancer is catching, or something.

Will is still looking at him. He has some colour in his cheeks, while he tells him this. He's styled his hair, for chemo, made an effort that Will can't understand. A little gel, so that his hair sweeps to one side, like a lifeguard, a pretty boy from a different life, on the water.

But you're different, Simon says. We can talk about anything. And nothing. And it doesn't feel uncomfortable, whether we're at home, or here, or wherever. You know?

Will simply nods. One slow dip of his chin.

Either way, Simon goes on. I guess I'm saying thanks. And no matter what happens, with all this, I hope we can, you know. Stay in touch.

Simon is observing the room while he speaks, as if his request was simply asking for a glass of water, or getting Will to slant the blinds shut, keep the sun out of his eyes.

We can do, Will says, when he finally finds the words.

Good, Simon says. And Will thinks he should tell him, right then, about him and Rosie, and not just the shared house and the carpet sex but all of it, every year of it, the bonfire and the dance, how he was there when Josh fell, and how it's kept them apart and together for all this time, because Simon deserves to know all that before he thinks he's his friend, but it's too late, it seems, and he is a coward, and he ends up staring at the scuffed shoe marks on the floor and feeling, for the first time in a long while, like he does not know himself, or what he cares about, and it is unnerving and disloyal and he wants, desperately, to run. And keep running.

I take pills, he says.

Simon takes his eyes from the other patients.

Really? What for?

Depression, or whatever, Will says. They keep me on a level, I guess.

Sure, Simon says, and he nods.

You should row again, after all this, Will says. If you can.

You're all about other people pursuing their passions, aren't you, Simon says, and Will doesn't like the way he looks at him, then.

I preferred it when you were dull, Will tells him.

Simon laughs, but barely. More of an inhale. They stop talking after that, and watch the room, and Will feels warm, and sick.

Will stops at Rosie's school and picks her up on the way home from the hospital. She is bright-eyed, her cheeks pink. She looks happy.

How'd it go, Simon asks her from the back seat.

Wonderful, Rosie says, and she's breathless. They sang *so* well. The solos were near perfect. I feel so – I don't know. Proud.

Will had been thinking, alive, that she looks alive, but he drives in silence as Simon says you *should* be proud, Rosie, and he drops them off and declines their invitation for dinner, says he'll see them again soon.

It is as he's driving home that he has the urge to talk to someone.

Someone who knows him, and might care.

Her number is the first in his contacts, and he calls her on the hands free, sat in the Norwich traffic with the night closing in. Bright red and green of the lights. Engines, biting, near stalling.

Hello, his sister answers, and she sounds uncertain.

Hi Ambs, he says.

Hello, she says, again. He drives. She waits. He clears his throat.

Been a while, he says, eventually.

I'll say, she says.

Sorry about that.

No, she says, as if she doesn't want to hear it, or it simply doesn't matter.

How's the PhD, he asks.

Good, she says. And then, are we speaking, now, then?

Looks like it.

He imagines her nodding. Recalibrating.

I have a question for you, he says.

Go on, she says.

Do you think everyone has a thing? Like, something they're meant to do? I don't mean some grand vocation, or anything. But do you think we all need something to, I don't know . . . anchor us?

Amber is quiet, for the shortest of moments, and then she says well, obviously.

Huh, says Will.

But that's the quest, isn't it, his sister says. People don't always know what that is. And that's why they run. Or drink. Or gamble. Or have affairs or switch careers or suffer from anxiety.

That's cheerful, Will says.

Well, you asked, she says. And you've done a lot of those things, to be fair. But you know your thing, Will. You always have.

Do I?

Think.

Ambs, all I do these days is think.

Think harder, then, she says.

Will has merged onto the dual carriageway now. Cloud hangs like fog, concealing the stars.

Just ask yourself what feels like home, Amber says, and he says okay, but doesn't; he just keeps driving. He can hear her typing in the background. A sentence, then silence, before another. Shuffle of pen on paper.

He drives and she works. The road slips behind him, headlights and red brakes and empty hard shoulders, when he asks her, eventually, how their mother is, and she says oh, who knows, that they only check in every few months, that she's gone to India, or something.

She's the kind of woman who gets elephant tattoos, she tells him.

Got it, Will says, and they share a moment of muted laughter. Silence, taut and punctured, knowing smiles between siblings.

Half-siblings.

As if it matters.

He wonders, as he turns off the motorway, why he is no longer angry with her, and then decides not to question it.

He has spent his life feeling angry.

It has eaten him up.

Why're you asking, anyway, Amber asks, as he pulls past the sign to their hometown, street lights glowing along the pavements.

About Mum?

No. About anchors.

I . . . don't know, he says. I just . . . don't know anything, any more. I don't know what I want, or what to do next. And that's never bothered me before.

Amber is no longer typing.

Jen's gone? she guesses.

Long gone.

And Rosie?

He remembers the funeral, Roe up front with her guitar, the way his sister would not look at him.

Back with her husband, he says. Her dying husband. Who is, incidentally, someone I quite like now, even though I still despise him, in principle.

Amber clucks her tongue.

Tricky, she says.

A pickle, he agrees, as he pulls onto his grandmother's drive, turns the key to kill the engine.

Couldn't you have just married that awful girl? Amber says. At least you knew where you stood with her.

Who d'you mean?

You know, what's-her-name. Dolly, or Vanessa.

Those names are pretty different, Ambs.

The one with the nose piercings and lacy thongs.

How do *you* know she had lacy thongs?

Gran found some once, in your jeans pocket, she says. I remember because she told me no self-respecting woman ever wears anything less than sensible pants.

That's true, Will says. And chastity belts, remember.

Will, she says. I'm twenty-four years old.

And still a practising virgin, right, he says, and she sighs, says whatever.

Everything – and nothing – has been said, but he does not end the call. He sits with his sister, who is miles away, and she sits with him a while longer.

I should, she says, when he keeps sitting, and not talking.

Yeah, he says. Okay.

And when they hang up, he rubs the knot in his chest, sitting in the darkened driveway, alone.

seventeen

Cancer free.

The doctor has said these words, and Rosie has made her repeat them, three times. Simon laces his hand in hers and they sit there in the oncology office, married and stunned and hardly daring to feel the euphoria of what it means.

The chemotherapy has been as successful as we'd hoped, the doctor is saying, and she is smiling, and calm, and Rosie thinks how strangely similar the slowing of the world is at these words, the same, somehow, as the endings and the lost, irretrievable things she is more accustomed to.

As we said all along, the doctor goes on, with her white teeth and her bobbed hair, you're strong and healthy, Simon, and we caught it early. You'll still need to finish your chemo sessions, but it's —

But you got it all? Simon says, and it is the first time he has spoken since they sat down. The cancer's gone?

It's gone, she confirms, and she is patient, explanatory. But it's like finishing a course of antibiotics; you'll still complete the other sessions, and we'll need to see you every eight weeks after that, to check in. But this is good news, Simon. This is the news we wanted today.

So . . . I don't have cancer any more, he says, and the doctor says that's right, and they cry, the both of them, on each other, and the doctor sits behind her desk and Rosie loves her, this woman she does not know; in that moment she loves her more than Marley, and her mother, and Will's gran; she is indebted and in love and Simon is living, undeniable and permanent, in her arms.

Outside, the day is fair and bright.

Cold, beyond belief.

We should celebrate, Simon says, as they walk down the street, arms looped, half dazed. They feel jet-lagged, or as if they've both woken from a prolonged, shared mirage. That can happen, Rosie has heard. Married people can hallucinate the same thing, in bed at night. When their REM sleep cycles align, somehow, like the intertwined roots of their lives.

Of course, Rosie says. What shall we do?

Dinner, Simon says. And wine.

Done, Rosie says.

With Will, too, Simon says. And we should go to my parents' place, this weekend. Surprise them. And when the chemo's over we should go away, just you and me. Somewhere hot. We could go back to Mauritius, even? Have a second honeymoon?

He is animated, talking with uncommon speed, and Rosie is relieved, finally, to hear that energy back in his voice. She always liked that about him. The joy and the ease of him; his enthusiasm. Things she had missed for so long.

The springtime sun is high and hazy. Pigeons scatter as they walk, their shadows short beneath them. She should talk back, match Simon's delight, but all she can think about is how he wanted Will there, first and foremost, and what that means, and how much harder this just got, despite being all she'd wanted.

The restaurant is high-ceilinged, all linen tablecloths and gleaming cutlery and domed, copper lighting. Small, delicious plates descend the length of the menu, and Simon says he's ordering all of it.

But you don't eat red meat, Rosie reminds him, as the waiter retreats from their table.

You do, though, he says. And Will does, I'm guessing.

He's coming, then?

Who knows, with that chap, Simon says, and he gestures for her hand. She passes it to him, and he rubs her thumb with his own.

It'd be nice for him to meet someone, he says, and it is a vague comment, a conversation starter that, she realises later, is the end of things.

Or perhaps things ended, long ago.

Why? Rosie asks, and Simon looks puzzled.

Because it would be nice for him, wouldn't it? He wouldn't be the third wheel then. And we could do more of this. Go to dinners. Be real friends.

We are real friends, she says. He took you to chemo when everyone else backed off. He drove us to appointments, and he switched shifts, and he put up with a hell of a lot, actually. More than we can ever thank him for.

I know that, Simon says, and he is frowning, a little. Still holding her hand. I'm just saying it would be nice to do more stuff with him.

And why does he need a partner for that?

He doesn't, I guess, Simon says. I was just . . . thinking out loud.

Rosie is about to answer when the waiter brings the bread basket. Warm rolls, seeded and seasoned; this was their favourite restaurant, when they first got married, a place for special occasions, and on special occasions, Rosie would allow herself to eat bread. She would smell it, first, before taking a bite.

Tonight, she takes a roll and splits it open and pulls

fingerfuls of the soft dough from its centre. She wants to stuff the feelings out of her. Stifle the unsaid things with a cotton-like gag of the mouth.

Did you and Will ever, you know, Simon asks.

He is watching her eat the bread, and she knows he sees it, the frenzy in her hands.

What do you mean, she asks him, and the darkness of the restaurant seems suffocating, suddenly, and she wishes the lights were up, that she could look him straight in the face, burst up and out of herself, for once.

I mean, did you ever have a thing? I sort of thought you might have.

When did you sort of think this, she asks, and her voice is tight, and Simon sits back, because it has answered his question.

I'm not accusing you of anything, Rosie, he says. I don't mind.

Well, I mind, she says.

A candle flickers between them in its glass orb. Floods their tired, drawn faces.

She opens her mouth and then Will says hey, sorry he's late, the traffic was murder, and he drops into the chair between them, at the side of the round, white-clothed table.

Simon lets go of her hand.

No problem, he says. We've only just ordered.

Will nods, says it better not be a salad; that he hasn't driven all the way to Norwich for a couple of radishes on rocket leaves.

He is teasing, Rosie knows. Gently ribbing the man he has come to think of as a friend; something that both troubles and pleases her.

The food's good, Simon says shortly, and Will glances her way, then. She avoids his eyes and pours wine. Slops it, accidentally, onto the tablecloth.

So, any reason we're having dinner in this fine establishment at one second's notice, Will asks, after the waiter has taken his drinks order, and still, neither Rosie nor Simon has spoken.

Yes, Simon says, and he smiles, but without showing his teeth, and Rosie can hear his energy has gone, once more; leaked out of him, like the oil from the olives on the table.

Will raises his water glass to take a swig, but pauses when Simon does not go on. A group arrives at the table beside them. Chairs grind along the floor. Sequins and high heels and low laughter, invading their non-saying of things.

I'm, uh, Simon says, when they're seated.

You're . . . ?

I'm an idiot, I think, he says, and Rosie says Simon, please.

Will puts his glass down.

What's —

Tell me, Rosie, Simon says. Because I was just curious, before. But now I'm more than curious.

It's not interesting, she says. Can we just do this another time? Why don't we talk about what we're actually here for?

Because, Rosie, Simon says, I've lost a lot, over the past year. And I'm starting to wonder whether it's more than I'd actually realised.

Rosie knows that Will is watching the two of them, though her eyes are fixed on Simon's face. She knows he is wondering what he has walked into, and she wants to think of a way through this, a way that is right and kind and inexplosive, but her mind has turned to water. Clear and still, like that in her glass.

Okay, she says. Okay.

Okay what, Will asks, and neither of them looks at him, and he says that maybe he should go.

You might want to stay for this, Simon says.

And then the first courses arrive. Small ceramic plates, gold-flecked and catching the candlelight, a question of more wine, shaken heads. Will's soda and lime is placed beside his napkin, still folded on the table.

I was just asking my wife here, Simon says, when they are left alone again, whether she and you were ever more than friends.

And Rosie can't help it; she stands up.

We were, she says. Okay? We were. But we're not now, because I chose you. And you only chose me back because you needed me, Si, and you know what? That's fine. Because I need you, too; but not like this. Not with drama in a restaurant, when Will is a good friend, and came all the way here for us, and today is a day we've all been hoping for. So let's not ruin it, okay?

You keep saying okay, Simon says. But it does not make it okay.

Look, mate, Will says, and Simon holds up his hand to silence him, and for a staggered, whirling moment, they all find that it works.

What bothers me, Simon continues, is not the *fact* of the thing. It's that neither of you told me, which says there was a reason not to.

It was just, Rosie says, and she shrugs, still standing, her hands splayed flat on the tabletop.

She wants to take back time.

Take back all of it, and none of it.

I'll meet you at home, she says. I'm not doing this here.

And she does the boldest thing she can ever recall doing, and walks away, even though she is wrong, even though she owes Simon everything and the man next to him even more, and she gets her coat from the cloakroom and she heads down the many flights of stairs, alone, lets the maître d' bid her goodnight and begins the cold, star-strewn walk home, her breath white on the damp air.

*

Will looks over his unfilled wine glass at the man whose wife he's had.

Or who has the wife he was meant to.

We should eat, Simon says, and it is the last thing Will expects, but after Simon lifts a plate, scrapes some onto his own and starts to pick at it with his fork, he follows suit. The food is rich and buttery, and the restaurant is oppressively dark. He hates it when he can't see what he's eating.

I don't want to argue, Simon says. I'm too tired for that. I was never good at it, either. And I sense that you probably are.

When the mood takes me, Will concedes, as he pushes a paste-like something around his plate. Simon forks something into his mouth. Chews, and swallows.

Rosie's easy to read, Simon says. Always has been. She's a terrible liar, and she shows her emotions in her eyes. Have you noticed that?

Like a deer, Will says, and Simon says yes.

They eat more small things. Take small bites, and say nothing for a while.

The bread's good, Simon says. Did you have any?

Will shakes his head, and Simon says he'll catch the waiter's eye, get the basket refilled.

This nice guy thing is really starting to grate on me, Will tells him.

I thought it might, says Simon. He shifts some sauce onto his fork.

Can we just say whatever needs saying?

And what does need saying?

352

Don't do that, Will says.

Do what?

Answer questions with questions. Rosie does it.

Does she?

Can we just . . . have it out?

I don't want to have it out, Simon says. I want to enjoy the nice meal I'd booked to celebrate being cancer free. And then I want to go home to my wife of seven years and tell her that none of this matters, because it's nicer for all of us. But I've realised, Will, that even though you've essentially lied to me, for weeks – my God . . .

He rubs his eyes, takes a moment.

All this time, Simon goes on. You've lied, skirted the truth, insulted me, actually, without me knowing. But there's one thing you did say that's true.

Which is, Will asks, after a tight pause.

That things go wrong, Simon says.

They have stopped eating. Laughter, and voices; the hum of enjoyment around them. Will runs his index finger along the edge of the table. Back and forth, and back again.

Look, says Will. Things went wrong with me and Rosie years ago. Several times. It's sort of . . . a thing we do. We fail, but we stick around, because she's . . . well, I'm . . . we're friends. Good friends. I tried not to be, for a while.

Simon does not say anything. He's staring at his plate, as if willing it to refill.

You could try and be friends with her, too, Will says. If this is too much, the lies, or secrets, or whatever. But I don't think you'd have much luck.

Simon meets his eyes, for the first time all night. His white wine gleams in its glass.

You love her, he says.

Will holds his gaze.

Tells him he has tried not to.

Their plates sit, untaken, on the table, and Simon drains his wine, pours more. He offers him the bottle, and Will declines. Droplets perspire down his soda glass.

I just thought you were like siblings, Simon says. That's how it seemed to me.

That's because you don't pay attention, Will says.

Don't be an arsehole, Simon says, and Will feels a savage triumph, because he wants the rage, welcomes it, even, can handle fire with fire. This is all so placid. So disconcerting.

If anyone's the brother here, Will says, and he lets it hang.

What d'you mean?

You're just like him, Will says. Sort of.

Like who?

Oh, come on, Si, Will says. This is your *problem*, see? *Every*thing comes back to Josh. You know, her twin brother, who died? Fell to his death? Smashed his skull and bled out on the beach right below us, nearly half our lives ago?

Simon says nothing. His face has gone slack.

It's destroyed her, Will says. And you don't even know it.

She, he says, and he clutches the stem of his wine glass. Twirls it in his fingers. She . . . never wanted to talk about him, much.

Right, says Will.

Oh God, Simon says, and he drags his hands across his thin, cancer-lined face. Will watches him do it, and his anger dies. Things slow, for a long, rolling moment.

She chose you, Will says, even though it kills him, and he wants to upturn the table, to throw the tiny plates at the solar-shaded windows. Simon keeps his face in his hands.

I've never met anyone like Josh, Will goes on. But you're pretty close, Si. Friendly. Unassuming. Kind, and fair, and full of this, sort of, relentless energy. Annoying as hell.

You think she married me because I'm like him?

I don't think she realises it, if that helps.

The waiter appears then, to take their plates, asks them how everything was. They both say good, though Will remembers none of it; he has no idea what he's eaten, and is hungry, still, for something he cannot identify.

Like I said, Will says, when they are alone again. Nobody's quite like him. But you fill a hole, for her, I think.

He stands up, because there is nothing more to say, and as he turns to leave Simon says, just tell me, Will, when it was. Was it years back, or more recent?

Will asks him why that matters, and Simon shrugs. Says he's not sure that it does.

Both, Will tells him.

He should apologise. He should say sorry, to this man, this good, well-groomed, just-about-living man, sitting alone at the table with his warm wine and his ruined evening. But he will never apologise, for her. No regrets, his mother used to say, and it is the one thing he has tried – failed, indubitably – to live by.

Oh, Will says, as he makes to leave. Congrats on, you know. The cancer news.

Simon raises his glass, in acknowledgement.

Broken things, between them, that Will cannot – even if he wanted to – take back.

As soon as he steps outside, Will starts to run.

The air is the brittle cold before snow; he had not checked the weather for the drive home, but it doesn't matter, because right now, he is running, and he thinks if he knows anything, he knows where to go.

It takes ten minutes to reach the riverbank and then he

speeds up, dragging long, heavy breaths of the night air as his heart pounds with his feet. He feels something hot and joyous flowing through him, which seems wrong, after all that's happened, but it's Rosie, and it's him. Currents, fast-moving, like the river gushing beside him.

He catches up to her on the bridge. She's standing at the parapet, looking out.

I told him, he says, when he reaches her.

She's wrapped in her coat, her hands stowed beneath her arms. The river flows fast and steady and black.

Told him, she repeats, as if from far away.

About us, he says.

The river, rushing, like the tide.

I also told him he fills a hole, for you, Will says, because he wants her to bite, wants her to disagree, to finally tell him the things she hasn't.

He doesn't, though, Rosie says – and it is there, she has said it, at last. She keeps her face turned towards the river, away from him, and he finds he wants to shake her. Grab her arm and force her to look at him, speed up this long, arduous thing between them.

He doesn't?

No. I thought he did. I wanted him to. I really, really wanted him to.

She takes her hands to her forehead, tugs her hair behind her ears. She is still, and upright; like a dancer, he thinks. He sees her mother in her then, for a second; that strength, that hardness.

I'm half a person, Will, she says.

No, you're not.

I am. The moment the doctor told me he'd died, I felt it – I felt something detach, and I'm half empty, and nothing helps. Eating doesn't help, and starving doesn't help, and therapy and marriage and music and cured cancer – none of it ever

helps. I don't know who I am, or what I want, or what anything means, any more.

How theatrical, he says, and she says fuck off, Will, and
then she finally looks round at him, surprised.

Sorry, she says, immediately.

Don't be, Will says, and he's angry, but also kind of laughing. Jesus Christ, Roe. You're the person you always were.
Believe me.

Cars pass on the road behind them. White noise, in their
ears.

I don't know what I'm doing, she says, so quietly, he can
barely hear her.

Did you ever?

Well, yeah. I thought so.

Getting good grades doesn't count, he says. Nor does marrying a nice, boring boy who doesn't eat real butter.

Don't, Rosie flares, and there it is again, that triumph,
flaming inside of him – he wants her to yell, and he wants to
yell back. He wants contact, and raised voices. He is sick of
tinkling spoons on ceramic, shared cereal at night, unanswered
texts and false friendship.

Goddamnit, Rosie, he says. Why the hell have you stayed
with him? Can you tell me that? I thought, after everything,
he must have something – and I figured I could live with that,
maybe, if it's what you really wanted. But if you're standing
here and telling me he doesn't, after all these years? Then
why, Roe?

I don't know! she says, and she seems fraught. He's – *good*!

Good, Will repeats.

Yes! He's good and kind, and there needs to be more people
like him, she says, and she sounds feverish now, her words
coming fast and deliberate. And it's not his *fault*, Will. It's not
his fault that it's not enough.

So it's not enough, Will echoes, and it shoots through him, the fury and white-hot joy of it, but Rosie's face crumples, and she asks him why isn't it, Will, what's wrong with me?

He should not answer, but he is angry, and cold.

A lot of things, Roe, he says. You're indecisive, for one. You let other people choose for you, over what you want, and that's not just sad, Rosie, it's fucking spineless, which is the opposite of what you actually are. And you have this false perception of what's good and, I don't know, *proper*. Like it matters. You don't live your life the way you should. You never speak out, to anyone, least of all your mother, who frankly could do with being put straight. You don't sing, any more. You deny yourself everything. You rob yourself, Roe. Every second of every hour, you're forcing yourself into some kind of box, and it's fucking painful to witness, but you do it anyway because you don't know any different, and nobody's ever told you not to.

Snow is falling now. It drifts down, lands in her hair. She is looking at him as he rants, her hands back beneath her arms.

But in spite of all that, Will says, there is not a single thing wrong with you, Roe. With any tiny part of you.

Her eyes, on his. Blue, and ocean-deep.

I made a vow in a church, she whispers, as the snow floats around them. He says he knows she did. And then she says he's her husband, and she loves him, and he says, not in the way you should.

He does not say all that he wants to. That she is meant for more. That she should have someone who burns for her; who crawls beneath her own skin.

I think, he says, that you need to figure some things out, Roe.

She looks at him with her fawn face; it breaks him, a little, but he can't not do this; can't keep doing it, either.

I'm not saying choose between us, he says. You need to work out *what* you want out of life, Rosie. Not who.

They stand there, in the sifted dark. Lights glimmering on the water.

And through his anger and relief, he finds he still wants to kiss her. His hunger so real and cavernous that he wants to take her inside him, somehow, to drink her up; swim deep in the low, dark red of her.

Instead he says, this thing we do, Roe. Let's not do it, any more.

Will –

No. I tried to be a nice guy, just your friend, or whatever, but I can't. I'm sick of waiting, and hoping, and thinking about you all the goddamn time. Not just these past few months. Ever since that bonfire.

Her eyes are as open as her mouth, and he steps back, because he wants to consume her, or cradle her, or both.

I'm serious, Rosie. Go be married, or not. Go write music, or not. Sing, don't sing, open a fucking late-night cereal café, for all I care. Just figure out what you want. And I'll go and do the same.

But –

Stop, he says, more loudly than he intends to. Just stop, he says, and with everything he has in him, every last good fibre or breath or feeling, he turns and he walks away, from her, from them, from all of it, and he knows, deep down he knows, that it's finally for the last time.

eighteen

It is a long night, after the river.

A long few nights.

Rosie goes back to Simon, though she knows she cannot go back in any real sense. They talk, for days, and she tells him everything. He expects her to move right back in with Will, but she can't, not after all that he said; not now she knows that he's right, about all of it. She always thought she knew what she wanted, but it turns out she'd just been following rules and structures and ideas put on her by her mother, by Marley, by old movies; some sense of right and wrong she formed so long ago, she can't even remember doing it.

She can't keep it up, she knows.

Can't let this life be her own.

Can't keep using Will as a comfort blanket, like she always has, the boy with the wolf teeth and the rough hands and the bad birthday.

She'd told him, by the river, that Simon wasn't enough, and rather than take her in his arms he'd told her he was done; and that, strangely, was the most freeing thing he could have said to her. No need to choose between one thing, or another.

No right, and no wrong.

Things are broken open, and waiting, and she knows, now, what she has to do.

When she and Simon finish talking, she moves out of her marital home, for the second and final time.

Late nights, and tears. Emptied drawers and sodden shirts and things packed into bags. Books, dog-eared and faded from the sun on the shelf, squashed into a holdall and brought with her, like children she cannot be parted from.

I am doing this, she tells her mother, when she moves home, just briefly.

I am fucking doing this.

She has never sworn, aloud, in front of her.

She has never done a lot of things.

This time, she stays with her parents for two nights, while she gets her things together. She tells the school she is going, and they are kind and supportive and she has to resign, because they can't cover for her, can't hold her job indefinitely.

That's okay, she says, and it is.

She touches the photograph of Josh in the hall, before she leaves. Wishes he could come with her. Wishes she could hear his voice, if only for a second. She would give so much of herself, just for that, still, and that is why she knows she is doing the right thing.

*

Will begins to dream about his grandfather. He did this a lot, when he first died. They do things that they never did in real life. Things like fishing off the side of a rowing boat. Building things, together, out of wood and hammers and nails.

They do not talk, in these dreams.

He thinks he's forgotten the sound of his gramps' voice. Wishes he could forget Rosie's, too, if he could have a say in such things.

He dreams, and he wakes, and he goes to a group, sometimes, when the days are hard, when he wants to turn to the bottle or something worse. Things embedded in his past, mostly. But there is a line, he knows, a thin, pliable line, like the fishing wire he twists round the hooks in his sleep, and he does not want that line to unwind, despite all his years of tightening.

It's not like the TV shows.

No, I'm Will, and I'm this. No heartfelt storytelling or revelations. Mostly, it's a lot of listening, and allowing. Making eye contact, sometimes, with people he does not want to.

There are biscuits at the break. Orange squash, watered down like at school, and he laughs at this, at the supposed circle of life. Everything leading him back to sour milk and cheap bourbons and tea and coffee and juice that nobody wants, and yet everyone drinks, because it's what you do, isn't it. It's what you do.

*

Rosie has always loved the mornings, even when she wasn't sleeping. Especially then, perhaps. The light so liquid and gentle, as if saying, it's okay, you can get up now.

But now things are different, and to her surprise she has found an affinity with the late nights in Vienna. A romance, almost, when the day bleeds to dark, and the cobbles start to shine in the street lights.

It is then that she lines her eyes with pencil, slips on a dress and walks down the iron stairs in heels that make her feel like a woman who knows what she wants. At this bar. In this place. Making up for lost time.

Before she begins, she always closes her eyes, a ritual that is not obsessive, but necessary. And then she plays, and the diners either listen or they don't, and she finds that she does not mind, has stopped noticing, even. It's just her and the grand piano.

No dead twin. No ex-husband.

Her hands, finding themselves, all over again.

When she is not working, she walks, and she thinks. Exists, in the city of music, as if breathing here is healing, and harmonious, as if the daylight itself will soak into her skin, the way it touched all the composers who lived here before her, crossed these roads, turned their faces to the same sun. Centuries of music, hanging in the air like heat. She had never dreamt of living abroad, but there is something about the pull of this city that felt right when everything else collapsed.

She returns to her favourite restaurant most nights, the one that clings on to the sunlight at the edge of the square, horses' hooves and Bavarian and wine pouring, all around, as she reads or drinks or writes or eats. Some days, all four, together.

Mostly, she sleeps in after her shifts in the bar, then spends the late mornings in the coffee houses with her books and her sheet music. She eats strudel, daily. She takes her shoes off in the museum quarter and treads in the grass and does not visit any exhibitions. She goes to so many concerts she loses count.

She calls her parents, rarely, and Marley, often. She even rings Simon, sometimes, and they talk naturally enough, about his check-ups and their divorce papers and his mother, and her mother, and she is glad to do it, but she is gladder when they hang up.

She writes in real, leather-bound books now.

Not on her wrists, or on loose paper, or on napkins that she loses. The poems tumble out of her like fallen leaves, flying every which way so that she has to chase them, almost, catch them with her pen.

It is some kind of magic that she had once forced herself to forget.

So many things, forgotten and found.

So much to fill herself up with.

There is a man, even. A gorgeous, olive-eating, dark-eyed man who is younger than her by a couple of years, who waits tables and plays violin and does not kiss her in the daylight. They get coffee, and go to concerts, and then they go back to his or hers and blur between the sheets in a strange, satisfying tangle of sex and cigarette smoke, in his hair, on his skin, along his jagged back teeth.

She says no, when he offers her one, afterwards.

He smokes in bed and they might kiss, for a while, as if they're both somewhat hungry but unbothered about eating. And then he dresses and leaves her, and it might be several days, or a week, until they do it again.

She sleeps well, once he's gone. Or she writes about it. The smoke smell. His pointed chin. The pegs of her, stretched and held.

*

Will tells Rob to book in the Honda, that there's space out the back, but to be careful with it.

Rob nods, and Will sees in his young, unshaven face that he wants to tell him he's always careful, that he doesn't need to say it. Will does, though. He can't help it. It is his own name on the line now; these early days rely on word of mouth and reputation, and any scratch, any dink, could be the end of his good run.

And it turns out he cares about that.

He logs the customer's details and is about to follow the kid into the workshop when the door goes, again, and his sister walks in, tall and skinny and bare-ankled. She looks like she could be working in his garage. Leather boots and patched overalls, *dungarees*, she tells him later, when he comments. Glasses with lenses so thick, it's a wonder she can see.

Amber, he says. Hi.

Am I interrupting? she asks.

No customers right now, he says, and she says that's not good, is it.

I've had plenty all morning, he says. D'you want to see the books? Check my finances from the last twelve months?

That won't be necessary, she says, and she's looking around now, at the limited stock he keeps, the engine oil and spark plugs, the bulbs and brake cables and inner tubes.

I don't know what any of this is, she says, and he tells her she doesn't need to. She also says that it smells weird.

That'll be the exhaust fumes, he says.

Want to swap petrol for paninis? she asks, and he looks at his watch, says all right, to just give him two minutes. Out the back, he washes the grease off his hands, tells Rob to watch the shop for an hour. The kid looks at him, terrified, but determined not to say so, and Will likes him a bit more, for that.

Outside, the wind is low. Clouds layered like basalt.

So, how is it, running your own business? Amber asks, as they head down the gravel path towards town, their shoes crunching on the stones.

Good, Will says. Busy.

You named it after Grandpa, she says, and her voice is light, offhand. He shrugs, says yeah, and that is all they need to say.

She never questioned him staying in Norfolk either, after

they'd sold their grandmother's house. He couldn't have told her why it felt right, even if she'd asked. Something to do with the proximity to where his grandparents were buried, perhaps. Where he'd realised he had roots, after all, after thinking he'd had none.

They find a table in the café on the corner and order sandwiches with mugs of tea. Old boys greet him by name, and the waitress winks at him, brings him extra bacon on the side.

You'll get fat, Amber tells him. You're not eighteen, any more.

Just eat your roll, he says, so she does, and she tells him about her training, and her new boyfriend, whom she's not sure about because his voice is too loud, and he drinks far too much water.

Yeah, hydration's a turn-off, Will says, and she looks at him and says seriously. He laughs at this, but she does not. She is wiping up salad cream with her crusts. He feels a shot of something like tenderness, or pride, as she does it. A rising, in the pit of his chest.

Where are you staying, he asks her, when they've eaten.

Your place, she says.

Right. A heads-up would've been nice.

I had some leave and thought I'd be spontaneous, she says. Why, what's the problem? Got a woman living there?

No woman, he says. No women.

Good.

It is, actually.

They order more tea, listen to the conversation between the two men at the next table. A debate about horses, and numbers, and luck. They both look out of the window a lot, rather than at each other. The sea is slate-like beyond the window. Seagulls stand on the harbour wall, sardonic and alert.

It's weird, not having Gran's house to come home to,

Amber says. She is handling a sugar cube as she talks, angling it between two fingers.

Too weird? he asks her.

No. It's good, obviously. To have the money.

Know what you'll do with yours, yet?

She curls her lips in a don't-know. Says she'll buy a flat, she guesses, when she knows where her training will take her. Put it in an account with good interest, maybe.

Don't go wild, he says, though she does not get the joke, and she puts the sugar cube in her tea and says she doesn't know why she just did that, that she hates sweet tea, and so he swaps his mug with hers, promises he hasn't drunk from it yet.

Amber stays for the weekend, though he barely sees her because he's working. The garage is finally breaking even, and he has been working harder than he can ever remember. He knows full well that it is a distraction in the way of alcohol, or running, or riding his bike so fast he almost comes off at the hairpin bends. But it is not dangerous, this time. It is sustainable. And that's all he wants for himself, it seems; something constant.

They order takeaway and sit up late and talk, because that's what they do when they see each other, these days, and after two nights of it they are done, and she goes her own, academic way and they barely speak for weeks until she shows up again with her news and her watchful eyes and her annoyingly pertinent questions. He sees his grandmother in her, now, and this is both pleasant and strange for him. She is not the kind of woman who would get elephant tattoos. She is not the kind of woman who would walk away.

You found your thing, she says to him, just before she

leaves, and he shrugs, says maybe. They are sitting in his car, the rain like spittle on the windscreen.

You seem good, she says. Better.

I'm still on the antidepressants, he says.

I know. And what I said still stands.

He nods, says he is, and she gets out at the train station and he watches her go, wondering if this is as good as it gets, and if so, it's okay, really, it's fine. It's better than a lot of things.

He'd told the truth about the women.

There are none.

He found he did not want them, in the same way, after the carpet burns and the scrambled eggs. After the good-guy act, with the chemo and the sandwich-making and the small talk. Some guys in the pub like to mess with him about going soft, or bent, or dying lonely with a house full of cats.

I don't like cats, is all he says, supping from his single beer, or his soda with its chunk of cheap, too-old lime. So tart, and effervescent, settling only when he swallows.

And don't say bent, he tells them. It's fucking offensive.

And they *ooh* and *err* and he lets them.

He cooks even more, these days, like he's stockpiling for winter, or the end of mankind. Low-cost, stew-like meals, mostly, with glugs of olive oil and blackened skins. Brown rice. Torn herbs. Full-bodied coffee that he grinds by hand and drinks in the morning and at night, and sleeps worse for it, probably, but not so bad that it matters.

And he swims. Every day, in the sea. It's good for his tight muscles, and he can do laps in the shallows before or after work, and it costs nothing and makes him feel strong and wild and a part of something bigger than the seaside town he never left.

He always meant to.

Somewhere along the way, things happened, or they didn't. So he swims, and he works, and things are.

He thinks of her, sometimes.

Rosie Winters. The girl he lost, several times over, for several good reasons.

She crops up at moments that seemingly have nothing to do with her. When he's pushing his trolley down the supermarket aisle and he sees a burnished tower of apples, red and ripe. When he's pouring milk into a saucepan, or he hears the pitch of a certain note when he flicks past a song on the radio.

He sees her mother, one time, from the car park at the harbour.

She is queuing for the butcher's and does not see him; he stays in the driver's seat for a while, and waits for her to be gone. She is on her phone, her handbag clasped beneath her arm. She looks much the same, just older. Deeper frown lines, he imagines, from a distance.

He wonders if she would know him, if he got out of the car. If the hatred in her eyes would have dimmed, even a little.

He sits in his car and observes her as she waits, with her hard face. Like an elbow, all points and edges. He wonders, not for the first time, how it is that a woman like that could have reared two children like Rosie and Josh, but then he thinks of his gran and his mother, and the unborn seeds of nieces and nephews and sons and daughters he might not yet know, and he lets go of something clenched in his gut as he watches her step into the building, sees her pointing with her elongated nails, the butcher nodding, taking something from the counter and wrapping it for her, gently, in his gloved hands.

*

One night, Rosie finishes playing, with the restaurant near empty and the waiters carrying glasses back to the kitchens, plates in the crooks of their arms. The room sparkles as if it is Christmas, even though winter is ending. Little gold lights and leftover wine, all crystal flutes and mirrors. She savours the scene, for a moment. Then she closes the lid, and is gathering her sheet music when she feels rather than sees someone approach.

You play so beautifully, says a young woman, at her side. She has long black hair and square shoulders. A wide mouth, sincere and serious.

Rosie smiles and thanks her. She does not know what more to do; nobody has approached her like this in all the months she has been playing here. It is her job to serenade, to entertain, while the wine is poured and the food is eaten and the hum of conversation ebbs and flows. But her shift is over. So she faces her, this intent woman, dressed in black. No makeup. A tiny mole, on her cheek.

Rosie will remember this about her.

I am writing my thesis on the last song you played, the woman says. Her English is somewhat stilted; Rosie suspects it is not her first language, and nor is German. She must be a student here, she thinks. She has that sort of look. Curious, and hopeful, and thirsty for things still within reach; Rosie had known that feeling, long ago.

She is thinking this at the exact moment that the woman asks her which arrangement she was playing, by whom, and Rosie feels her cheeks bloom with colour. Oh, she says. No one's. Just my version.

The woman blinks.

Are you studying, too, she asks her, but Rosie shakes her head.

Just working, she says.

Did you study, before?

Yes, but not music.

The woman nods.

You should think about it, she says. Rosie smiles at her, again, and they talk a little about the arrangement; she shows her the sheet music, when she asks, says she can keep it, if she likes, that she has plenty of copies.

The woman touches her shoulder in thanks, walks out of the bar with Rosie's music, and later that night, Rosie finds she cannot sleep. She sits up in bed, with the windows open and her phone in her lap, and considers how she has walked past it, many times. The largest music university in the world, with its ochre brickwork and arching doorways, the Schloss-theater she'd so often dreamt about.

Mozart had performed there.

He'd walked these streets, sang and played and taught piano in this city.

And Rosie had come here, thinking that would be enough, to be around such tradition and history and meander through it all. To attend the concerts and write fragments of her own songs, play classical music late into the night.

She hadn't, however, foreseen the students. The best musicians from all over the world, who congregate here, with an openness and a vision and places at the music academy. They are her long-ago peers, she knows. The people she'd never met; the person, perhaps, that she'd missed the chance to be.

She'd felt something she thought was sadness, every time she saw them, but she knows now that she was wrong. That it is not melancholy at all, but a longing. That deep, silent pull she has felt ever since she was a child and her father sat her down at their piano and showed her that she could make sounds with her own hands, magic that matched the music she'd heard elsewhere, in the swirl of the sea, the leaves in the forests, her brother's footsteps, light on the stairs.

So that night, after the woman with the mole and the black hair, Rosie learns everything she can about what she has always wanted. She reads up about the institution she can see from her window. Devours the descriptions of two courses, in particular, writes down the names of the professors, makes notes on the entrance exams, and feels a heat inside her, an inflation, she thinks, all of her molecules bouncing and rocketing and colliding, even when the sky begins to lighten.

She is still in her dress, from the night before.

She puts on a jacket, collects her notebook and pens and locks the apartment door behind her, heading for her favourite place in the city.

It is a fifty-minute walk, and when she arrives, she remembers that it isn't exactly beautiful, the *Leuchtturm*. Iron stairs wrap around the outside, tourists standing before it and zooming in with their phones, their miniature, hand-held cameras. Flashes of white, foreign chatter. There is a patched circle of grass, and a nearby bench that's empty, but Rosie settles herself on the ground and sits with her back against the wall. She gets a view of the water, that way.

She sits, and she watches, and waits.

It'll come to her, she is sure.

If she is quiet and patient enough.

She prepares. Plays her way through the nights at the piano bar, with a new, renewed deliberation, as if she's got something to prove, or perhaps, somewhere else to be.

It is like she has growing pains in her hands and feet.

She is thinking about how she could put this into words when Simon rings her, one night, an hour before she needs to be at the piano bar. She puts him on speaker phone so she can continue applying her eyeliner while he talks, staring herself down in the mirror in a way she had, until recently, always avoided.

They say their hellos, and then Simon cuts to it. Says he has found some of her jewellery in a drawer, wants to know if she'd like it back.

Rosie asks him to describe it to her, only for them to realise it is not hers, after all.

Well, that's awkward, Simon says, down the phone. It must be . . . someone else's, I guess.

One of the women you had while we were apart, you mean, Rosie says.

Yes.

I don't mind, Si, she says.

Of course you don't, Simon says. Why would you, after what you were up to, yourself?

Rosie takes a breath, listens to him exhale. He says sorry, and she puts down her pencil, says it's fine. This is what they do, now; try to stay pleasant, attempt some sort of halfway friendship, only to clip each other with hard comments or occasional digs, treading a line that neither of them knows how to walk.

D'you think we should, Rosie says. She doesn't need to complete the sentence; doesn't need to voice the idea that they should stop speaking, now their divorce is through. That it's better, and smarter, even though it feels like they're giving up. Cheating each other, somehow. Again.

Yeah, Simon concedes. I do.

There is a sad, overdue silence between them.

I'm thinking of staying in Vienna, anyway, Rosie tells him, as if that'll make it easier on them both.

Oh yeah? How come?

I want to study music, she says. And this is the best place for it.

Uh-huh, says Simon. Makes sense.

She doesn't respond, at first, but he is quiet for so long that in the end she asks him, what does?

You, wanting the best, he says.

Rosie lets out her breath, unaware that she'd been holding it.

It's a compliment, Rosie, Simon tells her, but after they say goodbye, for the last time, she is not so sure that it was.

*

Will runs the Norfolk marathon, one day. Just like that.

Although it's not just like that, he knows, because he has been training his whole life, without knowing it, and he is fit and strong after years of hiking and running, the daily swims he has come to love.

The water, slicing his skin.

There, every day, without fail.

But he is in the pub when someone tells him they've dropped out of the race, got injured, and before he knows it he's agreed to take his place and he is there the next morning at the start line, in his old running shoes and shorts and cursing himself for not eating properly the night before, no carb-loading or lean meats or whatever the other runners are conferring on, and he thinks screw it, when did he ever eat anything but what he wanted, anyway, and then the horn sounds and the race begins and they all start moving, in a wave, a great surge of nylon and calves.

Nothing matters, when he is running.

Still, after all this time.

He forgets that he didn't eat right and he forgets that he

hates jogging beside other people and he just follows the route along the coast, runs from Sea Palling to Sheringham, down the open roads, listening to his breathing, like always, no music or interruptions or clock-watching. His limbs, meeting the earth.

He is used to running twenty miles most weekends, but the final six almost kill him. He actively thinks this, at one point, when he hits the famous wall. That this could be it. He feels like he could drown under the weight of himself, the impossibility of the next step, but it still comes, somehow, and comes again, simply because he won't quit, because there's someone in front and behind him. Strangers, cheering him on, even though they don't know a thing about him.

So he keeps going.

When he finishes, drenched in sweat and every bit of him hurting and feeling fantastic, he whoops, out loud, with the other runners, claps them and thinks, out of nowhere, that of all the people under and above the blue and cloudless sky, he wishes his grandma were here.

He gets a silly little medal, on a silly striped ribbon.

He puts it on the kitchen counter when he gets home, and takes a shower before he cooks dinner, a giant bowl of fresh pappardelle, the radio keeping him company. After he's eaten, he stacks the dishwasher and runs the taps for a bath, even though he's already showered. His limbs and his abdominals ache, almost pleasantly. All he wants is to lie down and close his eyes, soak his muscles in hot water.

He pours a can of Coke into a glass, and is about to head through to the bathroom when the medal catches his eye.

A little lurch, in his chest.

The question of what to do with it.

His gran kept everything, of course. His childhood drawings of cars and motorbikes, Amber's swimming certificates, their school reports; his grandfather's cigar humidor, the hospital bracelets from her own chemo. Books she'd read. Photos, and letters. Pieces of a life, and not just her own; things that made up her entire world. Sentimental, and stupid. She'd have been the first to say so.

Will takes the medal off the side and feels the weight of it in his hand. He can hear the bath running, the water rising in the other room. He pads over to the shelf next to the television, towards the only framed photograph that he owns.

He doesn't know anything about it, really, where it was taken or who took it; how he even came to possess it. It captures his grandparents, young, pre-children, standing on a boat, white railings and a body of water behind them. She is smiling, adjusting his sun hat as he stands beside her, his eyes part-closed in gratitude.

Will looks at the two of them, then props the medal against the frame.

Sentimental, and stupid, he knows.

The months slip by, as they tend to do. He gets up every morning and jogs to the sea, swims and then runs home, showers, makes a strong, tall coffee in a Thermos that he drinks on his way to the garage. He services bikes and orders new parts and jokes with Rob and Ryan, the new mechanic he's hired to manage the workload.

He sometimes thinks, as he locks up and lowers the shutters, that if this is all there is, he'll take it.

He considers getting a dog.

A retired greyhound, maybe, who could run with him on the beach.

He checks flights, now and then, wondering if he'll finally do all the things he thought he wanted to, but he has his business now, and it would be difficult to leave it, and Amber might need him, maybe, though she's never needed him in her life, and he forms a long list of excuses that make him feel old, and responsible.

If he's honest, it's because he likes it.

The routine, or the calm, that means he has not felt his heart pain in the longest time. He does not know what has lifted it, exactly. Years of medication, maybe. Or the exercise, or living alone, without a woman, or the peace he's made with the things he did and the people who left and the way the sun keeps rising, regardless.

He misses some things.

Some people.

Knows, though, that that's just the way of things, and he prefers the balance, the rest, unexciting and mundane and, it turns out, all that he seems to need.

And good butter, of course. Decent coffee. He was raised by a woman with priorities.

*

Different days, now. Separate coastlines, split sections of the same sky, but still morning coffee and evening meals, bread toasted when it's gone stale. Scrape of butter, gloss of jam. Moisturiser for their hands. Hers, each morning and night, and his, because they're older and tougher, like animal hide, from the garage and the tools and the grease.

There are things that mean something, friends and laughter and nourishment, and things that just happen, because that is living without tragedy, routine-led, more deliberate. Showers, shaved underarms. Pianos and engines. The one he restored, in his basement, because he didn't know what else to do with it. They think about it, sometimes. Once, even, at the same time, when a song they'd liked plays over the credits of a film they both see, and it leaves them warm, and half-sad, and reflective.

But they are themselves. Full of spaces that don't need to be filled, imprints in the mattress and the carpets of the houses they no longer live in, getting on in ways they had wanted.

Will thinks this to himself, as he locks his garage up one night, and hopes that Rosie is thinking it, too, feeling it, in that period of non-time she'd talked about once, just before dinner and after school or work, where you can't do anything real.

Who even talks like that, he thinks, as he heads to the shop. Picks up some milk on his way home.

*

And then, at the end of summer, that day rolls around again, unnoticed by everyone but felt deeply, like a war wound, when he wakes.

He is closer to forty than eighteen, now, and he counts back, as he does every year. Not in candles gained, but in years that Josh has lost.

He wonders what he might have been, as he grinds his coffee by the sink.

What life would look like with him in it.

Strangely, he finds that he thinks of him as a mid-thirty-something, too, as though the ghost of him has grown older alongside him. Long limbs, salt-and-pepper hair. Less bounce, more of a slow, seeping appreciation in his movements; creases near his eyes, hands trailing along the flint walls of their hometown.

But he wouldn't be in Norfolk.

Bristol. Berlin. Los Angeles, perhaps. Somewhere with colour and conversation and live music; tech centres, with slides and ball ponds and sleep pods.

He would still doodle stars while he worked. Still be curious, about everything.

Will drinks his coffee, skips his swim, and then works through the day, like always. No cards, no cake, no texts from anyone but his sister, and even then, he does not reply. He repairs motorbikes and serves customers and teaches Rob how to check tyre pressures and then he closes the shop and takes himself to the seafront for a bag of chips and a cigarette. It is the one thing he allows himself, on this day.

He thinks about dying, for a while. An abstract, undramatic thought, like a low-flying gull; wondering how it might feel, where you might go.

And though he is feeling mostly well, these days, there is a feeling he cannot shake with medication or daily swims or uncelebrated birthdays. He has found it to be true, what people say: that time can heal, but he has also found that it cannot wipe muscle memory. The weight of that dread, the doom felt deep in his chest. So he smokes his cigarette and he digests his deep-fried dinner doused in vinegar and he is wallowing in the sheer pleasure and self-loathing of it all when his phone begins to ring.

And when he answers, he keeps eating his chips, because that seems like the only thing he can do.

It's me, she says, eventually.

It's you, he says.

He looks out at the shoreline, at the waves lapping and retreating. The chips are warm through the paper, and he can taste oil and salt, the off-white grease of the newsprint.

I . . . know I shouldn't be doing this, she says.

Will does not speak. The potato steams hot in his mouth.

But there's this lighthouse in Vienna, Rosie tells him. I go there when I need to think, or write. I've got a thing for lighthouses, I guess.

You're writing?

Yeah. Sort of.

How do you sort of write something?

Well, I don't know if any of it's any good.

It's still writing.

I guess.

What're you writing?

Songs, mainly. Do you. Uh. Want to hear some?

He catches the question as he looks out at the water, and then bundles up the remaining chips in the paper, throwing them into the nearby bin before he takes the steps down to the shore.

I'm listening, he says.

She is quiet then, for a little while. He picks his way along the sand, and the evening is windless, and he waits for her, with his heart too large for his chest. Fragments of shell beneath his feet. Pebbles, driftwood, rope.

This is weird, she says.

You refused to do it, before, he says.

That was back then, she says, and she pauses. And it is your birthday, after all.

Afterwards, he heads for the lighthouse, and they talk.

The light is failing. Strips beam from beneath the cloud, gulls flying out to the horizon. So far a journey for so late, he thinks, as she tells him about her piano, and this man that sits, every day, with his cigar and his coffee in the corner of some grand café, how he wears a fur coat and says nothing to anyone. How she's tried to guess his name.

She talks about the rounded sounds of Bavarian German, the pavements, the street lights, the meat. He tells her about his garage, when she asks, though he keeps it short, would rather she kept on talking.

But he finds, with a little coaxing, that he does want to share things with her. About his meetings, and his swims, how things are enough, but not.

He wants to crack down the centre of himself, and launch his phone into the waves, and press it so hard into the side of his skull that it hurts. That line between joy and fury still exists, for him, as real as breath, and bone.

He keeps walking. She is talking about Mozart now, and horse-drawn carriages. Drinking her coffee with cream.

The sky is yellow and pale, a strip of sundown that meets a wall of cloud, like the Rothko postcard his gran kept stuck to the fridge. It feels like it might storm, later. He draws closer to the lighthouse as Rosie talks, and it stands like it always has, tall and white against the dusk. Everything smells of soil and salt, wet sand, oddly sweet. But something feels markedly different, in the way that some nights can: the bonfire, the fall, the night his mother left or his grandmother died or he poured all the vodka down the sink.

And he knows why, before he even sees her.

His heart lifts, without any real reason, and then there she is, sitting on the steps, the railing between her and the sea.

It is Rosie. He knows, even from a slight distance, by the way her legs are bent. The contours of her features, elfin peaks through her hair. He stops walking, watches as she worries about his silence. One moment, two. Then she senses him, looks up, and they both stare at each other for a while, the phones still held to their ears.

Bright eyes. Skittered hearts.

You're here, she says, down the phone.

I am the one who lives here, he says. I thought you were abroad?

I was, she says.

He hangs up and moves closer, but slowly, as if it might have consequences that he cannot prepare himself for. Shatter the semblance of calm he has built. Blow him open. Unquench that thirst he has, for her, and everything he does not have.

She seems thinner, again, her face matured and drawn. More freckles, from the European sun; keen, blue irises despite her late nights. He thinks about her drinking coffee and writing songs by her own lighthouse and he feels that same pride, again, that swell of something so good, it aches.

She puts her phone down.

Hello, she says, as if to restart.

Hey.

I, uh . . . I'm not in Vienna any more.

I can see that, he says. You visiting your parents?

No, she says. No, they don't know I'm here.

He nods, and puts his hands in his pockets, waiting. She seems nervous. Keeps touching her hair as if to smooth it behind her ear, even though it's already in place.

Here's the thing, she says. I decided I wanted to go to music school. Not just any music school, though: *the* music school.

Okay, he says. Which one's that?

The MDW.

In Vienna?

You've heard of it?

I saw the brochure on your bookshelf once, Will says. He doesn't say, I was looking at your things, when you were out and Simon was in bed, and it didn't pass me by that it was shunted between the sheet music that you never threw away. That he'd pulled it out, seen she'd folded down the pages on voice and piano and composition. That he'd considered, for a long, rogue moment, leaving it out on the coffee table.

Rosie nods, as if it's completely normal that he would have noticed something so private. So tucked away.

Well, I applied, she says. And I didn't expect to get in.

But you did, says Will.

Yeah. I got the email this morning.

He feels a shift inside of him; a light, barely-there wind, changing direction.

That's brilliant, Roe, he says. That's really great.

Thanks, she says. It is.

They hold each other's gaze.

I turned it down, she says.

She does not take her eyes from his face as she tells him this. Hands in her lap, in his pockets. The two of them, blue-black, against the burning cloud.

Why? Will asks her, after the longest time.

It would have meant a few more years in Vienna, Rosie says.

You don't like it there?

Oh God, I love it, she says. It's got such poise and magic and history, in every wall of every building – even the lamp posts are pretty. I think you'd like it.

I'm sure.

But I just . . . don't want to live there, any more.

A beat, between them. The tug of the sea.

He takes his hands out of his pockets and sits beside her, then. Sees the scuffs on her shoes from where she's walked along streets, down iron steps, across bridges he doesn't know the names of.

He can smell her shampoo.

The apples.

He remembers the first time he saw her fresh out of the shower, with her hair hanging long and wet. It is dry now, has grown beyond her shoulders.

So here's the thing, she says, and he waits.

It's been wonderful, she says, and it comes out slowly, as if she's scared of forming the words. All of it – the music, the freedom, the time alone. But you're not there.

Will daren't look at her. He keeps his eyes forward, on the sun.

I shouldn't have left, she says. When things ended with Simon, properly, I should have stayed, and fought for you. But I really believed what you said.

What did I say, he asks her.

That I needed to work out what I wanted. But when I got that acceptance letter today, I just . . . realised I already knew.

His heart has lifted, his pulse fluttering like the wind in the pines. Rosie laces her hands around herself, rests her chin on her knees. Early thirties, and still she seems so young. He wonders how he looks, to her. He feels so much older. Funny, how he's so often thought about dying, but never about growing old.

I don't expect anything, she says. Not after everything I did, or said, or didn't do. But I'm here, if you want me. I'm not going anywhere. I don't need the best music school in the world. I don't want to shoot for things that bleed me dry, any more; I want things that fill me up, and I don't care what they are, as long as you're there, and I'm there with you. I want to make you breakfast, Will. Meet you at home, every day, and share car keys and toothpaste and surprise you with birthday candles.

She turns her head towards him then, and her face is soft and earnest. He knows that face. He's seen it before. Over shared macaroni, and in a stifling-hot tent. Tickets bought and stairs climbed and doors unlatched in the rain.

Toothpaste, he repeats.

Whatever flavour you want, she says.

She is teasing, trying to soften the strangeness of the moment, but he cannot even think to laugh.

You should go to music school, he says.

I'm going to, Rosie says. Just not in Vienna.

He nods, once, and fights the urge to touch her. Her hand, or face, her slender, freckled wrists.

Never again, he'd promised himself. Never again would he touch her, or get close to her, in case his heart couldn't take it.

But now she is here, beside him, and never has already been broken.

I think about you all the time, Will, Rosie plunges on. And I know I don't deserve to. I know we had our chance, and I blew it. More than once. But I wish I'd just stopped, for one damn second, and realised I was trying to do the right thing for everyone else, which just made everything wrong, in the end, you know?

Will does know. But he hears these things as though he's asleep, and being pulled back to wakefulness. Dragged by the ink of the tide.

I know it seems like I didn't choose you, ever, Rosie says, when all I *wanted* was to choose you. And I'm sorry I never said that to you. Even if we're only ever going to be friends, that's okay, I think, but I just wanted to be able to say it. It's all I can think about, now; that you matter, more than anything, to me. And I never even told you.

Another beat; another wave, breaking on the shore.

I ruined our chance, she says, again.

They keep sitting by the lighthouse, him and Roe. The girl

with that voice, the girl who listened, who clawed her way into him without trying.

His hands, on the concrete, are cold.

I don't believe in chances, Roe, he says. I thought you knew that about me.

She unclasps herself, then, and turns towards him. Her eyes are the deepest blue, and he's never told her how beautiful they are, he doesn't think. Never said the things he should have, or asked her the things he needed to know.

There is only what happens, he tells her. What is and what isn't.

And as he says it, her face fills with all that he has dared not look for: certainty, and something else, that word, four letters he has felt and wanted and held, and she reaches out and touches the lapel of his jacket with those slender, piano-playing hands.

So what happens, she asks him.

What do you think, he asks back, though he knows her answer, now, as the sea stretches ahead of them and the geese call from over the trees. Coming home, maybe, or taking off from the nearby fields, two things that are one and the same, really, if he takes a second to think about it.

Acknowledgments

Firstly, I want to thank my fantastic agent Ariella Feiner, for taking a chance on me and this novel. Thank you, Ariella, for believing in me, advising me so brilliantly, but mostly, for trusting me to write this book. Thanks also to everyone else at United Agents: Molly Jamieson, for her keen insight on the first draft, and the wonderful Amy, Amber, Yas, Eleanor, Lucy, Jane, Alex, and Anna.

Thank you to my impeccable editors: Clio Cornish, my kindred spirit at Michael Joseph, for the letter that changed everything, and for immediately understanding the sort of story I wanted to tell. To Pam Dorman, for her unflinching eye and decisive, much-needed wisdom, and to Jeramie Orton, for her continued warmth, curiosity and organised notes.

Thanks to all the incredible people at Penguin Random House, both in the UK and US, especially Ellie Hughes, Steph Biddle, Kallie Townsend, Courtney Barclay, Emma Plater, Christine Choi, Sara Leonard, Yuleza Negron, Chantal Canales and Marie Michels. To Lee Motley, Elizabeth Yaffe and Lili Wood, for the gorgeous cover art. Thanks also to Louise Moore, Brian Tart and Andrea Schulz, who were behind this book from the beginning, and to the added hard work of Riana Dixon, Emma Henderson, Stella Newing, Claire Vaccaro, Tricia Conley, Tess Espinoza, Randee Marullo, Kate Stark, Mary Stone and Lindsay Prevette. To Shân Morley Jones, for her patience and diligence. Thank you, as well, to all my international editors who wanted to share Will and

Rosie with the world – I will forever be touched, surprised and delighted.

Thank you to Richard Skinner and my pre-pandemic writing group, for all their feedback on a previous project which meant this novel could take shape. Special thanks to Gaurav and Kathryn for their kindness, friendship and support beyond the Faber classroom, and to Tamar, for all of this and more.

To the early readers who told me to keep going: Justin Coombes, Kirsten Norrie, Jason Gaiger, Georgia Stephenson, Savannah McGowan, Georgia Taylor, Flic Box, Rebecca Hilsdon and Emily Griffin, among others. Huge thanks to the late Brian Catling, who gave me permission to dream big and write bold, and to Liesel Thomas, who read a lot, cried a lot, and gave thoughtful feedback on the novels that didn't quite make it.

Thank you so much to those who answered my questions: Kelly Degaute, for delving into the realities of Hodgkin's lymphoma; Ollie Henson, for sharing his experiences of Mountain Rescue; and Bella Chipperfield and her father, for their notes on music, wood turning and piano restoration.

I cannot explain how deeply thankful I am for Emma (Lane) Green, for all her love, spirit and happy tears, and to Jessica Lockyer-Palmer, for her guardianship and unswerving encouragement. Endless gratitude to my brother, who believed in me, always.

Thank you, as well, to my parents. To my dad, for his granular knowledge of motorbikes and the many hours he spent on story time (in particular, the blue balloons). To my mum, for the midnight bookshop visits and all those special trips to the library – and to both of them, for the car journeys spent listening to Danny.

Thanks to Elizabeth Gilbert for every single, joyous word in *Big Magic*.

To Kate. For so much.

And finally, I want to thank my husband. For the time and space he gave me to write, in the early mornings, at weekends, on holiday, and during several long, cross-country drives. Thank you, Clive, for never questioning any of it. For ensuring I survive on more than just porridge and tea. For not once dismissing the energy I spend elsewhere, or asking too much, or too little. I would not have written this without you.

JACK TEMPLE

BOOK 2

Medicine Man

Healing with the
Crypto Power
of the Hebrew Word

FINDHORN
Press

First published in 2002

ISBN 1-899171-49-5

British Library Cataloguing-in-Publication Data.
A catalogue record for this book is available from the British Library.

Co-written by Susan Hill

Layout by Pam Bochel
Cover design by Thierry Bogliolo

Printed and bound by WS Bookwell, Finland

Published by

Findhorn Press

305a The Park, Findhorn
Forres IV36 3TE
Scotland
Tel 01309 690582
Fax 01309 690036
e-mail: info@findhornpress.com
findhornpress.com

TABLE OF CONTENTS

Introduction

Permit me to introduce myself. Readers who already know me are excused: you can skip the next few pages and go for a walk, take a bath, eat something delicious or enjoy some other brief diversion. Since my first book, *The Healer*, was published a few years ago I've gained a lot of new friends and patients who already know something about me and my background, so this introduction is pitched primarily at new readers who may want to know a little about me before they feel the trust and faith that will help them benefit from my forms of healing.

Having said that, I do suggest that even readers who are already acquainted with my work glance through this introduction. So much has progressed and developed in the last few years, such extraordinary new findings have been built upon my original foundations, that I hope that some of my existing patients will want to learn how much more I can help them in the future.

Jerry Hall, the model and actress, was kind enough to write:

'Going to Jack Temple was a life-enhancing experience. He cured me, my sister, my mother and my children of all of our ailments. He is a genius miracle worker.'

Sarah, Duchess of York, wrote:

'I am stronger than I was, thanks to Jack, and I am 100 per cent behind him and his work. If there weren't people around like Jack Temple who are prepared to stand up for what they believe in and fight for it, where would the world be?'

And the late Diana, Princess of Wales, to whom I had given a special crystal after a series of treatments, sent me a note of thanks:

'I will always treasure it and keep it close to my being at all times.'

Eminent politicians, various members of the aristocracy, a judge, a general and countless other people distinguished in public life have been to my clinic. But no one patient is any more important to me than another and to say that the 'ordinary' people I see matter just as much would be misleading because I don't think in those terms. No one is ordinary. We are all unique and *extraordinary*.

My methods do not involve complex exercise, diet change or other disruptions, far less the surgery and commercially manufactured drugs which I so deplore. Things begin, and grow from a simple glass of pure water from the supermarket – not from the tap, or filtered, or carbonated.

In some ways it seems astonishing yet in others completely logical that these leaps of knowledge have taken place so recently. Advance of any kind – scientific, medical, cultural or artistic seems to flower in bursts. That's why historians use terms like 'the Renaissance' or speak of 'the Industrial and Agricultural Revolutions' in describing how a short spurt of blooming can skew ideas which had seemed to be set in stone for centuries. I feel much the same way about the new ways of healing which have been revealed to me in the past few years.

This new book will show how any reader can utilise for themselves the giant strides I feel I have made during the closing years of the old millennium and the opening two of the new. My mission is to inspire and to show how any physical or emotional unease can be at least arrested and possible reversed by following my simple advice. Case histories will speak for themselves throughout and I'll do my best to spare you too much complex theory and research: it is, after all, a good part of my job to clearly describe what you need to know to enable you to help and heal yourselves. That's why a little bit of autobiography is relevant here: to trust my advice you need to know how, where and why I assembled it all.

In the past few years I've become a bit of a star-gazer. Not in the familiar astrological sense (although star-sign considerations have affected my interpretations), but in a practical sense – as the gardener I was and always will be. With the sun, moon and star energy I trap and collect in specific grasses, herbs, flowers and leaves grown carefully within my stone circle and labyrinth in Surrey I have found that I can assemble the makings of tinctures which will relieve scores, even hundreds of disabilities, from the mild to the severe. Furthermore I utilise the wisdom contained within the Old Testament, what I now call the Crypto Power of the Hebrew Word, to tailor my remedies for each individual patient.

I'm building three further circles in the grounds outside my clinic in Surrey to create more growing space for these healing crops. Some of the new remedies derive from journeys made to distant lands, especially to Argentina, where I have found an extraordinary wealth of hitherto untapped healing strength.

By dowsing, as always, I've learned how to make an incredibly potent food enhancer, a few drops of which will release the taste and nutritional potential of even the least promising foods. I've learned how to crack the gene code, so that many patients need not be saddled with any unwelcome or unhealthy genetic inheritance. I've learned so much more about the dangers of vaccinations – particularly for babies and children – and I have corroborated evidence about how this aspect of my work has rescued children from autism.

I believe I've helped the lame to walk, the barren to conceive and the sad to smile. I've been able to reflate the lungs of children previously condemned to a life constricted by asthma. I've even seen the bald pates of middle-aged and elderly men begin to spring hair growth again and, thanks to my recent work with cell renewal, seen the skin of a fifty-year-old recover the unmarked elasticity of her thirty-year-old self.

My new methods – including this understanding of cell-renewal – have saved older patients from unnecessary surgery and amputations, and others have reported an extraordinary revival of spirit and emotional health. I've seen the skin and muscle tone on patients' faces and bodies soften, yet simultaneously tighten, as I've rid them of ageing particles. I could go on – but the personal stories interspersed within chapters here tell their own tales.

I think it's worth noting here, at this early stage, that where the vaccination of children is concerned there's evidence to support the idea that the little ones actually need to go through that sequence of childhood disorders as each illness flushes out some all but inevitably inherited minor toxin and leads to a noticeable growth spurt. It should go without saying that the way these childhood illnesses are managed is of utmost importance, as I will explain later, but in today's bleached and over-clinical world there is a tendency to forget that some bacteria are benign, friendly and positive.

All this new work has built steadily on the findings of a lifetime spent working on the land, respecting our soil and all that springs from it. None of my principles have changed – and I still often tape my tablets to a patient's body so that toxins can be drawn out through the skin – but there *has* recently been an exciting series of developments which enables me to offer faster healing and a deeper range of solutions.

If all this seems daunting and complicated let me say that chapter by chapter all will be clarified and illustrated, and I'll offer practical suggestions whenever I can about how you can look after yourself better, so that, with any luck, you'll never have to visit a professional.

I like to keep things simple. For instance, think of your skin as a mackintosh, the most efficiently protective cover-up ever devised. It not only keeps you dry and warm inside, but any rash or change of texture alerts you to some internal problem. Take notice and since the skin, like all good mackintoshes, breathes, remember that poison can be extracted through its pores much more efficiently than via drugs and antibiotic medicines which disturb our natural internal harmony of friendly bacteria dealing with invasive ones. The simple promise I offer is that your permanent healing will begin with a glass of good quality bottled water instilled with both ancient Crypto Power wisdom from the wise Hebrew texts and benign, super-strong stellar energy.

I'm well over eighty and you must permit an old man a little vanity when I say that few people would believe me. I work six days a week from first light till dusk, sleep well, eat well, enjoy good wine and bright conversation. I drive as fast as the law will allow and feel fitter than I ever have. I like long walks and stimulating travel. There is *nothing* painful, restrictive or joyless about the healing methods I expound.

But if you'd seen me twenty years ago you might have imagined that I was a rather tired and slightly overweight businessman on the brink of a sluggish retirement. A little golf, maybe, to stave off that heart attack, the occasional luxury cruise with indulgences to invite one... If you'd met me as a much younger man you'd have been unlikely to bet on me collecting my pension. Even at the age of fifty I was refused life insurance, so dicky a wicket did I seem. Never as a child, a young man, or a steady, family-orientated father and businessman did I look like a chap who'd go the distance – and beyond. Afflicted by serious digestive, bowel and skin complaints at various times of my life since boyhood, I never imagined that I'd enjoy the stimulating life and broad horizons that I see today.

Ironically it was the very ill-health that prevented me from serving my country as a young man when war broke out in 1939 that spurred me towards what has become my life's work.

Frustrated almost to the point of anger and humiliation, I learned that there *was* something I could do for my country. Britain was in danger of being starved into defeat, so people were needed to work on the land. Thus this puny young man left his family home in the East End of London and became an apprentice farm labourer in Surrey, living in a hut and subsisting on bread and cheese and swede and other fast-grown crops. I married and became a family man in little more than a shack. After the War, having learned a bit about agriculture, I was helped by various post-war grants, became a market gardener and prospered. My wife Blanche and I built the family home in Surrey and many members of our family are with me there still – coming and going, as happens in family life.

But even though my market gardening business prospered and I was, I think, a pioneer of organic cultivation in Britain, I was becoming a bit of a paunchy old chap who'd done his bit, done his best and that was that. I became (I think) a respected member of the local business community. But I didn't always feel all that well and it wasn't until the 1970s that I started to make the connections which underpin all my work and theories today.

That's when I first became a dowser and to this day I use a silver pendulum as a starting point in identifying the unique trouble and singular remedy for each of my patients.

By chance I had come to respect the importance of organically grown foodstuffs and became active within the Soil Association, an organisation often dismissed at the time. And I learned much from reading and writing for journals such as *Here's Health*, a magazine which has proved to be hugely prescient and influential though regarded by many as cranky at the time. Believe me, I've endured so many jeers and sneers over the years that these days I almost take them as compliments. Becoming a healer happened little by little after that, particularly after I began to see how early homeopathic treatments and my own could sometimes work in partnership with traditional National Health Service wisdoms. After I'd started to fix my own health, largely by diet, and people began to ask for my advice, my confidence grew and I dared, ventured, to take on a few patients in a rather informal way.

Now I have a busy clinic and a long waiting list of clients, I don't advertise so I can only assume that word of mouth accounts for its enduring success. I hope that I'm not a man of fixed ideas and that my methods have developed and improved over the years. I've had princesses, duchesses, stage-stars and supermodels in my consulting rooms, couples desperate to conceive, chronic asthmatics, migraine sufferers, anxious people with cancers for which previous orthodox practitioners had insisted surgery was essential. I've enabled depressed people to come off chemically artificial drugs. I've seen the lame walk and the terminally ill die in dignity. I seldom, if ever, speak of 'cures'. I'm not a doctor, after all. But experience has shown that what I offer has brought relief, reversal and sometimes arrest of all manner of problems.

Make no mistake: I take little personal credit for all this. I am, after all, a beneficiary of natural healing and perhaps it is 'pay-back' time. I remain utterly certain that the soil, the seeds, the seaweed, the skies, the rain, the frosts and snows, the roots and the barks and leaves that mulch down into our soil – and soils and rocks all over the world where I dowse for specific remedies – contain all the answers we need. These days I also thank the energy of the stars, which pours such healing power into a single leaf, petal or blade of grass – which dowsing guides me towards – and the extraordinary coded messages contained within the ancient Hebrew texts and the glass of water which is set upon the circle of paper.

People have some odd ideas about fasting – a practice which has been pivotal to my work. It's not cranky, it doesn't have to be extreme or uncomfortable and it is central to the success of my work today, and as many people seem to achieve their first glimpse of the importance of homeopath-based medicine through the prism of diet and food, I thought I'd explain that aspect of things here before we dive into other pools of knowledge. This is warm and gentle pool to swim into, for fasting, cleansing the body, need never be some torture of days on end. You can do your body a big favour simply by missing as few as two consecutive meals. Healing somehow works more efficiently and faster if the body has had even a short time to rest from the demands of the digestive system.

I can't recommend too highly the principle of cleansing and de-toxing the body with this rest from solids and especially those seasoned with spices and additives. We can all enjoy well-seasoned food most days. Junky additives should be eschewed every day if possible. I don't advocate the kind of fast (sometimes suggested by others in the name of rapid weight-loss), wherein over long, bored and anxious days or even weeks of deprivation, the body's systems become alarmed and convulsed, the breath becomes foul, and muscle and bone strength is diminished. But perhaps for one day a week, or even for half a day, you could sip only correctly infused water and juices. The body needs to rest sometimes, that's all. Imagine if it had to deal with Christmas lunch every day – or even every week. (I don't see the post-prandial nap as being a particularly healthy thing because I want my food to give me strength and energy, to keep me awake and alert, not to make me feel torpid.)

But what about the Mediterranean siesta I hear you cry? Well, it should be remembered that the entire way of life of the Italians and the Spanish differs from that of us who live in northern Europe. In southerly climates it's just too hot to work in the afternoon and even modern air-conditioning has failed

to change the habits of centuries: after an early start when the
air is fresh, a good lunch is followed by a snooze, and shops and
offices shut down; back to work when the evening is cooler and
then home or to a restaurant for a dinner far later than is
normal farther north. People may say all sorts of things about
the wisdom or otherwise of these traditions – but the health of
Mediterranean people tends, on the whole, to be better than that
of those of us who live in brisker climes. Diet plays a part in
this. (See Chapters Eight and Nine.)

Speaking of diet, the less said about fasting as a slimming
tool the better. This book isn't primarily to do with weight-loss,
although those who have a few pounds to lose will almost
certainly do so if they exercise, eat and drink correctly. They
will probably find that skin tone and texture improves, as mine
has. But this is a happy side-effect and judgmental attitudes as
to what exactly defines beauty don't much interest me,
Standards vary so much from age to age, culture to culture.
Many of us realise that the prosperous Western ideal of
extreme slenderness would seem strange in other parts of our
planet where a firm plumpness is considered to be far more
attractive than limbs like reeds and bones like razors.

I didn't know whether to be amused or horrified when I
heard that these days in China – only recently exposed to TV
shows such as those set on Californian beaches – a profitable
new industry for padded ladies' knickers has emerged. Hard to
imagine this happening in the West, where most women worry
if their bottom is too big, but in certain regions of China
wherein women have been genetically programmed to be
narrow-hipped and generally slight, the sight of those curvy
TV blondes has made them feel inadequate.

Good health, long life and freedom from pain and
disability is what concern me. Anyone so blessed will almost
certainly generate such airs of relaxed confidence and
strength that the issue of weight will barely be considered –
unless it is to wonder if there is something unhealthy about

those super-thin people who have worked so hard to display their bone structure and unwittingly damaged and malnourished themselves in the process.

There's only a single vowel between feast and fast. We all enjoy, and perhaps need, the occasional indulgence. Nothing wrong with that, but I first came to understand the importance of regular fast days when, as a young man, I was afflicted with something then known as barber's rash, as it was caused by being shaved by a blunt, rusty or otherwise infected razor. Don't ask me to recall why a working-class lad like me was going to a barber's for a shave: I simply don't remember. But I do remember how my whole face became encrusted with seeping, weeping sores for the next four or five years. You may imagine how severely this disfigurement affected a teenager's confidence, particularly since I already suffered from less obviously debilitating stomach and digestive problems. At one point, after about four years, a liquid German dye solution was applied and this worked like a dream – but only for a week or so.

I was married by then and Blanche, my wife, urged me to consider a 'nature cure', as it was then known. In desperation I consulted a Major Austin. He recommended a change of diet and regular fasting. He warned that it might take ten years to restore my skin to normality after all the suppressive and other medicines I'd been prescribed and taken in desperation. Well, he was right and he was wrong: in following his advice my skin cleared completely within weeks. With my self-confidence thus boosted I was able to address my work in the fields of Surrey with renewed vigour and I've never looked back. I had learned the crucial importance of fasting for one day each week and absorbed my first glimmerings of the most vital message: nature can cure.

No one talked about allergies or food intolerances in those days. Even twenty years later when I picked up coral poisoning whilst swimming in tropical waters in the West

Indies and was decreed as having contracted Crohn's disease, my medics advised surgery to save my life. But by then I had become a dowser and was used to fasting one day a week. Although antibiotics had made my right leg swell to the size of an elephant's and my bowel functioned merely to drain away all my body fluids, thus rendering me dehydrated, I avoided an operation. Dowsing by blinking (in the absence of a pendulum, I was able to get my eyelids to respond to my questions and eventually identify how and where I could be helped), I saved myself by a form of self-healing. I'm not suggesting that anyone can achieve this so quickly – although it always amazes me to observe what humans are capable of in desperation – but those years of coming to trust my dowsing skills and my own instincts certainly saved me from enduring (and not necessarily surviving), complicated surgery.

It is when we are at our most fragile and vulnerable that the temptation to give up or give in is the strongest. Anything to end this pain and discomfort, any new means, however strongly we might have resisted such procedures before. I cannot stress too often or too strongly how powerful the body's own healing mechanisms are if only we will find them, listen to them and trust them – or entrust our health to a healer. We must never give in or give up. Rarely will the body let us down, if only we let it heal us in its own way and in its own time.

Invasive bugs and germs do their worst within already damaged systems, as I found out in the West Indies. If the body is already healthy and immunised by natural defences it will have little need to resort to the sometimes savage remedies of thoughtless orthodox medical techniques. To underestimate our inherent immunities or to neglect the easy ways with which we can strengthen them is folly indeed.

✳ ✳ ✳

We can all count on our fingers the obvious places through which the body receives sustenance and discharges waste. The nose, the eyes, the ears, the mouth, the rectum, the urethra and the skin itself are all vital receptacles and carriers. But I have learned that there are seven other places upon the body where essential health messages may be received, and these seven entry points of vital energies are called the chakras. Interference by suppressive orthodox medication can damage or ruin the positive, natural healing forces that they absorb. Moreover, I have realised that each one of these healing 'staging-posts' is influenced by energy beamed into plant and herb matter from particular stars.

I never treat a patient until I'm sure what I'm doing and this means using my own body as the guinea pig for any new theoretical practice as a matter of course. Study, experiment and practice have shown me which plants respond best to those individual cosmic forces and I have thus cultivated tinctures from these plants and can then dowse to apply them exactly where an individual might most benefit from them. I use the Crypto Power of the Hebrew Word to help in my identification. The method is to identify the relevant crypto verse and then place the herb on top of the words. The pendulum will resonate immediately with a clockwise gyration if the selection is correct.

The seven vital access points for stellar energy do not correspond to visible entry and exit points on the body, like lips and nostrils, but they are just as crucial. They are known as the chakras (see pages 26–30 for further information) and are located at:

- The top of the cranium
- The brow
- The throat
- The heart
- The spleen
- The solar plexus
- The base of the spine

These are the seven places where good, health-restoring energy can be received and from which illness can be extracted. These energies are quite separate from and different to those which we derive from food although ideally they come to work together in harmony.

Healing energy donated by the stars and planets is absorbed independently and will cut off the negative energies the body may have received from unsympathetic medications or environmental pollutants.

✳ ✳ ✳

In my garden in Surrey I have a labyrinth as well as my original circle and the new circles under construction.

The labyrinth is not like a maze with trimmed but dense, high hedges where you can become lost – great fun though such places are. My labyrinth is a plain, flat, scrubby area, with shallow ditches dug out in a precise formation to catch the energy that certain benign stars bestow, and I am careful about the plants which I cultivate there. Some patients simply sit there, rain or shine, and receive healing, as others do nearby in my original small (perhaps fifty yards in diameter) circle of sacred stones. From both special areas I harvest special herbs, grasses and flowers which are added to the gleanings of stellar-enriched clippings.

Then it is off a few yards to my little laboratory to perfect my tinctures and use them as the basis for healing. The next, and crucial, stage of my work is to dowse and be guided, whenever I see an individual patient, by the wisdom of the Crypto Power. It really is very simple and later I will tell and show you how much of this can be done at home. All of you can benefit: I'm utterly committed to the idea of self-help where possible because I'm well aware that it's just not practical for everyone to reach a healer as easily as they can make an appointment to see their GP.

Almost concentric circles like those of my shallow labyrinth can be dug in your own back garden or even fingered and curved into a pot of earth on your window sill. Forget all that you might dimly remember, here, about the fearful and fateful undergrounds of Greek mythology. 'Labyrinth' is just a word and a practical device you can use to pull down the graceful balancing energies burning above. They are beaming by to help, perhaps even to save us. That natural labyrinth spiral is all around us – from the creature protected by the snail's carapace, to the lines on the pads of your fingertips, to the swirl of cream you might sometimes treat yourself to in coffee or soup. Telescopes prove that it's there in the way that distant constellations, like those that famously encircle Jupiter, arrange themselves in certain humming, circular movements. Music of the stars, indeed.

We in the West have come belatedly to understand what Hindus and others in the East have appreciated for centuries. Better late than never: it's time to realise that aspects of our medicine can join with the cosmic circle and link with the earthly intelligence of homeopathic knowledge to help us heal ourselves and retain or regain our place amidst the stars.

✳ ✳ ✳

I'm a great believer in the power of apparent coincidence. Actually I don't really believe in the idea of serendipity, or happy accident. My dowser has always guided me to the exact place where I needed to locate a specific leaf, even if it was contained within a tangled field a continent away – or over the river to the next county in England, for that matter.

The way I came to see, on a visit to Israel a few years ago, how my existing work as a dowser and healer could link up with star energy seemed coincidental, but I have no doubt that some higher guidance dispatched me there for that purpose. Dowsing for something quite specific, crystals, had lead me to Tel Aviv. I found the crystals I needed for the purpose of radiating 'distant healing'. But I found and learned much else besides, there and in the outlying region. Much of this book derives from lessons learned there, so close to the epicentre of all the Hebrew wisdom.

❋ ❋ ❋

It's important that, amidst this glorious stellar promise, we remember that we live on planet earth. To bring us back down to the shirt-sleeves and coal face of everyday pain and reality I would ask you to consider or imagine a country ditch or urban drain, thick with dubious slurry and blocked with cess and unfriendly fungi. For this is what our bodies may have become – pretty or handsome on the outside, perhaps, but truly ugly within and disconnected from the forces which can help us to return to some natural and universal equilibrium. Vaccinations, which we allowed our children to endure as a matter of course or queued for before getting some holiday visa, may well have contributed to nameless and numberless ailments. Indeed, they can programme us to be vulnerable to a range of disorders for the rest of our lives. The very household cleaning things we thought were protecting us, the cosmetics and synthetic clothing fabrics, let alone the foodstuffs which we may buy from supermarkets with misguided confidence, as it all looks so clean and bright in there, have all made a negative contribution to our health and potential longevity.

The sympathetic systems within can fight back but need our co-operation. Even damaged organs can be renewed if we listen, notice outward signs of disorder and take care of them. Try to have faith and belief that the chemical and surgical solutions which you may have trusted in and relied upon can be rejected and dismissed.

Is it not logical to attempt to become, once again, part of the universal structure, just as you were when you curled so warmly in the womb? And might you not owe it to your newborns or future children to cleanse yourself of any contaminated matter that you might pass on to them?

In a later chapter I will address and explain as best as I can the vigorous debate currently concerning genomes and other relevant genetic issues. So complex is the entire DNA question that I can merely hope to simplify things and refer readers to distinguished science writers like Steve Jones, Colin Trudge and Matt Ridley if they wish to grasp all the complexities. Suffice to say here that I have the greatest respect and instinctive sympathy with ideas which suggest that our genetic destiny is preordained.

But I also believe – indeed now know – that very often a bad hand of genetic cards delivered at conception or birth can be somehow cheated or corrected and that we need not live or die with a faulty genetic inheritance. With understanding, common sense, hope and faith we can all of us live as long and strongly as we wish to.

I'm not one to advocate a Balkan style life, subsisting on yak's milk and twigs if the aim is merely to attain a record-breaking age. Far better, I think, to live rather longer than that biblical three-score-and-ten and live every year to the full. The Old Testament does at times suggest that the elders survived into their seventh or eighth century. I have no worries about this – only a certain doubt that anyone would *want* to do so. Another sixty years will do me fine! As I see things, it is the quality of life which matters most, not massive duration. So if a man or woman should return to the soil and earth after a fulfilled life, having lived to see their grandchildren play and having enjoyed a peaceful and painless old-age of a reasonable span, I think that's great. It is the person who collapses and gives up at retirement age and feels no joy in life, only pain and worry, that concerns me, as well as the children who may be doomed to follow in those dread footsteps.

I mentioned earlier how a visit to Israel a few years ago seemed to steer me towards what I now consider to be the absolute refinement of my life's work. Well, perhaps not 'absolute' because, just as I urge patients with pains and worries to be positive and never give up hope, I can't be sure that my working and healing journey is over. I hope I will always remain open and receptive to new challenges and solutions.

It was in Jerusalem, guided there to seek a single, specific leaf, that a friend unwittingly showed me how the wisdom of the Crypto Power of the Hebrew Word could be incorporated into my work. Through that meeting I came to see how if I dowsed the Old Testament whilst concentrating strongly on a particular patient's specific problem, I would be led to a verse which contained healing wisdom. The Hebrew version of each and any verse of the Old Testament is sometimes arranged in the circular fashion, shown on page 19.

Within this drawing lies the key to your long, healthy and, with any luck, happy life.

The next thing I learned was that if a simple glass of good quality bottled water is placed upon such a circle, healing power will infuse it. If the circular diagram is xeroxed eight times (or more, depending on what the pendulum suggests), so that the glass may stand on a sort of pad, the power is all the greater. And if a single drop of tincture made from a plant steeped in star energy is added to the water, its healing power is phenomenal. This also works with a plate of any food: when a single drop of tincture is added after the remedy has rested on the layers of the Hebrew mantra the food is purified and nutrients released – even from the sort of junk you really shouldn't be eating at all. When placed beneath proper organic food, however simple, the dish becomes a feast, bursting with healing nourishment. You can easily do this yourself, at home.

Thus a tremendous union seemed to form between my existing work as a dowser and the healing that was there to be tapped within the Hebrew Word. I have rarely felt so excited in my life. The idea of merging and harnessing these two great benign forces seemed both revolutionary and logical, so my work immediately adapted towards refinement of the techniques. I had learned how a sip of this water could release within the body the healthy enzymes we all need to fight whatever ails us. This coupled with my new understanding of the chakras and the vital entry and exit points on the body enabled me to know where to place the tablets I made from tinctures of distilled plant and star energy.

Dowsing techniques will become clear as the book proceeds. You will soon learn how I'm guided to the correct leaf or mineral matter and how I then create my tinctures and apply the tablets I make from them and you may, I hope, be inspired to take such steps yourself. It's not private property. Indeed, there is a whole world of healing out there for anyone to tap into. I happen to hear a little chime ringing in my head when I'm somehow called upon to dowse – and so might you. This is just an extension of listening to a hunch or a gut feeling – but with a different application.

Suffice to say here that whilst I was already fairly certain that my work contained mysterious forces to the good in the

> ### CRYPTO POWER OF THE HEBREW WORD
> ### USE UNDER FOOD AND DRINK
>
> *Take 8 xeroxes of disc 17 illustration below.*
> *Cut them out and place all 8 on top of each other,*
> *fasten with micropore tape.*
>
>

past, I now know that those powers and forces have amplified immeasurably. There is nothing to *see* except results. I cannot explain this power but I have utter faith in its wisdom and benign influence because I've seen those results. I have seen the strengthening of weak bones as the vital calcium, magnesium and phosphates start functioning again. I've seen slack skin regain firmness. I've seen disease and disorder retreat. I've seen unhappy people begin to smile again. I've heard about gurgling new babies where parents had despaired of conception. I've even heard a tired old dog bark and gambol like a floppy puppy... but that's another story.

And for me it all starts with that faint chime in my head which tells me when and where to dowse.

I do hope that here in this introduction I've given you a sense, an idea, of some of what my new book seeks to explain and celebrate. I also hope it might lead at least some of you towards adventures in dowsing and healing of your own.

CHAPTER ONE

The Labyrinth

A labyrinth is not a maze. But it is amazing. Unlike a maze which was cultivated above ground with high hedgy bushes and trees to encourage frivolous and deliciously flirtatious little mysteries, a labyrinth was a dark place, mined underground, often containing the most dread secrets and knowledge. In Greek mythology the Labyrinth was built for the Cretan King Minos to house the Minotaur, a half man, half bull monster who fed on human flesh. Ariadne, the King's daughter, helped the hero Theseus find his way through the darkness of the Labyrinth by giving him a ball of thread which he unwound as he entered. He then killed the Minotaur and rewound the thread to find his way out.

My labyrinth in Surrey isn't a bit like that. You could trudge over or around it on a dry summer day or a muddy winter one without necessarily realising what extraordinary steps you were taking. Small stones are there at each of the seven essential turning points, places where energy is at its most intense, seven places where star power is focussed right into the earth here at home. The stones are of the same age and share the DNA of those distant spheres and I dowsed for them after a study of a simple little paperback book called *The Night Sky*. Then the fact that I found my stones easily and locally simply strengthened my belief that we are all part of the same universe. It's as simple and logical as that.

In my most recent researches I found that configurations of sevens kept coming up: the stars, the colours which they emanate – shown to me by one of my students – the colours of the rainbow, the days of the week, the curved branches of the holy candelabrum of the Jewish faith... my seven narrow pathways. Thus an interest in the science of numerology was ignited, as you will see.

THE HEALING LABYRINTH

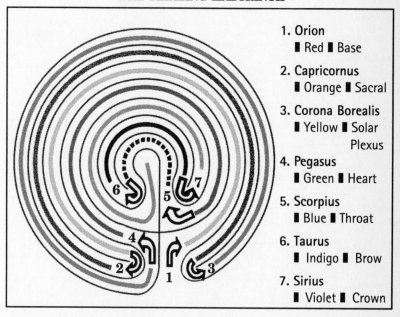

1. Orion
   ■ Red ■ Base

2. Capricornus
   ■ Orange ■ Sacral

3. Corona Borealis
   ■ Yellow ■ Solar
   Plexus

4. Pegasus
   ■ Green ■ Heart

5. Scorpius
   ■ Blue ■ Throat

6. Taurus
   ■ Indigo ■ Brow

7. Sirius
   ■ Violet ■ Crown

It's a smallish area in the grounds just outside my clinic, close to the circle of Priscilli stones I arranged some years ago. Shallow ditches were dug in the Surrey soil, with the guidance of an inspired friend, Ken Church, from Wales. We spread the narrow paths between the gently mounding edges with simple pebbly gravel.

In a way it will replicate what has been possible within my stone circle for years. And where that's concerned, I have always told patients that they can, if they wish, arrange a tiny circle of stones at home and sit on a chair placed over it to experience the benign power of the stones. Sadly, such simplicity isn't as practical with a labyrinth – as the business of the walking and turning is vital – but anyone with the will and a small back garden can construct their own providing they have learned to dowse for the plant matter and stones.

You see, a few years ago – after a lecture given at The British Society of Dowsers – I came to realise that many human disorders are rooted in a simple flaw connected to physical balance. We tend to walk in straight lines. Roads and railways are built to go 'as the crow flies' as much as natural terrain will allow. Tunnels and bridges are constructed to facilitate this, all in the perfectly reasonable interests of speed and economy.

Yet nature is all curves, coils and spirals. Think of a snail, the boles on a tree trunk, the tangle of roots beneath the soil. Rivers meander and tides are cyclical. Think of your own body, which contains few straight lines or right-angles. Bones, even the spine, are subtly curved and have flexible joints. The human digestive system is a wonder of bending, rounded masses. Elementary mathematics teaches us that there can be no such thing as a perfectly straight line because ultimately any line will curve back to source and starting point: it's in the very nature of the spheres. I saw that we needed to re-introduce physical balance by walking a curved path at times. I don't fully understand why this should be the case, but I have seen results and so have patients who have walked through my labyrinth and I believe that I have been able to convey my instinctive faith to them.

Many cases of physical malfunction can be corrected by taking this effortless stroll and by applying remedies based on cosmic energy which I dowse for.

This, I realise, is a very bold claim. I suppose it should be qualified by the reminder that the vast majority of human ailments are relatively mild and minor and I'm not promising miracle cures for every life-threatening illness. In fact, as patients and past readers will confirm, I don't promise 'cures' at all. What I can activate and promote is the body's ability to heal itself. Once you realise that illness can only take hold in a diseased body, that bugs, viruses and invasive diseases simply cannot survive in a system already primed to be healthy, you will grasp the core principle of my healing.

We all have a deep internal intelligence, a kind of personal bush telegraph whereby one part of the body will communicate with all the others, silently rallying strength when and where it is needed. You take this for granted, of course, just as your nose knows how to breath and your feet know how to walk. These are givens. We don't ponder upon them – we watch TV instead, walk the dog, cook lunch, go to work or otherwise get on with our lives. And this is how it should be. But remember that hugely efficient internal network next time you or your child sustains a graze and the blood obligingly coagulates to form a protective scab, next time you eat or drink something so toxic that you excrete or vomit almost at once, next time your skin creates a blister to cushion you from further dangerous sun rays or chaffing new shoes... Then there are your most basic hungers, thirsts and other needs: a craving for sugar or salt at times, for water, for sleep. It is all so obvious but somehow often overlooked that these are urgent physical demands we are obeying.

The labyrinth, then, is no more and no less than a device to enable us to become re-tuned, readjusted, to the messages playing along those bush telegraph lines – so curved and apparently complex, but so simple, really.

My labyrinth is carefully arranged to contain a number of sharp bends, the kind drivers may refer to as 'hair pin'. At each of these turning points there is a small stone lodged in the earth and pretty much grassed-over. Every stone connects to a specifically dowsed-for star or constellation and – coming from the same immensely ancient organic root – it attracts cosmic energy and a vibrant colour from a 'sister' star. However extraordinary this may sound, it was simplicity itself to dowse for the stones my labyrinth needed. That I found all of them from nearby stone masons and even garden centres close to my home only proves to me how close we really are to our natural and universal energy sources.

As someone who has often and willingly obeyed my dowser's instinctive directions and flown thousands of miles to locate a single leaf in the search for an essential component for some remedy needed by a particular patient, sourcing the rocks close to home was undeniably convenient, but not a lazy option. If need be I would have had them shipped home from the other side of the world. It didn't surprise me that this proved to be unnecessary, as we are all fragments of the same moment of creation – all life on earth and all life elsewhere in the Universe. I was as likely to find what I needed, where rocks were concerned, in Surrey as in Sacramento.

* * *

My profound belief that sometimes you can somehow flick a switch and turn negative or static energy into positive has seldom been so clearly illustrated as by the speed with which this exponential development of my existing work took place. The need for the labyrinth and my certainty that I could harness the power hit me almost like one of those cartoon blows to the head which suddenly restore memory or, in my case, bring enlightenment. I have learned to trust certain instincts – about people, about something as simple as the weather whilst I sniff the air, above all about healing. The pendulum is just a physical extension of those mysterious instincts which I was gifted with and I believe all gifts should be received with gratitude and used with grace. The New Testament expresses this with wise concision in the parable of the talents. If blessed with such luck do you hoard it like a nervous miser? Squander it like a fool? Or use the talents or gifts and by doing so spread their bounty and generate wealth – in the broadest sense – anew? Guess which instinct mine has always been.

I was busy at my clinic and quietly encouraged by my success rate, working with my belief that the time at which some disorder set in – whether it was in your lifetime or during that of one of your ancestors – can be dowsed for and the system corrected back to replicate the optimum health which existed before.

I'm still like a builder or a plumber, really, in that I have a skill which enables me to locate a problem and then to fix it. (It sometimes amuses me that surgeons in orthodox medicine often seem pleased and proud to be known as Mr This or Mrs That, rather than as plain Dr Whatnot. The fact is that the 'sawbones', as surgeons were called in the past, were considered to be little better than butchers and thus unworthy of the doctor's prestigious appellation.) So sometimes I'm just a simple technician, often releasing blockages, clearing the drains, fixing the boiler, mending the roof and addressing the foundations and structural faults of the house – or body, in my case – exactly like any other craftsman.

But once I formed the idea of creating a labyrinth at home I foresaw how my methods could be accelerated and successes intensified. I harvested a small quantity of grass from tufts growing at each of the sharp bends and then used these samples to lead me to a sympathetic stone. Each sample of grass contained a different energy and all I had to do was to dowse, placing the grass on the stone which I thought might be the 'match'. If the pendulum gyrated strongly I knew that this stone was the one needed for that particular sharp bend. Time-consuming, certainly, but not – as people say these days – rocket science. Yet this practical discovery showed me how the ancients knew that the labyrinth could be a kind of telescope, a means by which to read the stars.

To confirm the accuracy of my findings, I stood on or next to each stone before it was positioned and then placed my finger over the chakra entry point on my own body which is linked to that stone. The pendulum only gyrated when I touched the right place. Once all the stones were positioned I repeated the test and this time the pendulum gyrated at an even higher speed. Moreover, when a phial filled with 5 ml of ethanol was placed on each of the stones it became charged with star energy within a few minutes. In later tests each bottle and its contents only responded to the correct chakra point on the body.

The base tincture amounts are tiny but may be constantly recharged on their 'home' rock. Once the energy is identified and bottled it can serve for many lifetimes. One pure solution can and will deal with an indefinite number of patients' worries and can be infinitely refreshed.

The result is that a tiny glass bottle containing ethanol and resting on the appropriate stone does indeed become supercharged with extraordinary healing energy. I feel that this is simply another example of the circular way that life has, whether it is the revolution of the spheres or the turn of the seasons. I still use the trusted methods described in my first book, *The Healer*, to extract toxins and blockages from a patient by taping homeopathic tablets to the correct – and sometimes surprising – point on the body. The difference today is that when I am dealing with the chakras I use phials of star energy in place of tablets to recharge each point of the chakra triangle.

All of us have these seven receptive places – points on the body where healing can really start. Each chakra connects to a specific star, planet or constellation. That number seven does keep coming up – on your face and head there are seven visible exit and entry points. But the chakras cover the body systems in a different and vastly more subtle way and I have seen how an understanding of them can bring back to life bone, tissue and organs that might have otherwise have been deemed to be dead or dying.

I think of my labyrinth as a star trap. In an astonishing way its nearly concentric circles seem to capture and hold the healing wisdom and power of many aeons and tell me that we all remain part of the same universe, dependent on one another for our growth and survival. It is no more and no less than an incredibly powerful and – relatively – gigantic magnet which pulls in invisible filaments of strength, just as a small magnet in a schoolchild's physics lab attracts iron filings.

At each crucial turn, where the path may seem to double-back, the little stones I have set there contain exactly the same DNA as that of a distant planet or constellation and they somehow communicate with each other to create a healing force when captured by stones on these twists of the labyrinth in Surrey. The stars which are present are:

1 Orion	4 Pegasus	7 Sirius
2 Capricornus	5 Scorpius	
3 Corona Borealis	6 Taurus	

Each one, I found, corresponds exactly to one of our chakra energy reception points and each emanates its own inner physical colour, something which one of my students helped me to understand. This is not to be confused with Kirlian photography, which was developed decades ago in Russia and which records in colour the auras that surround all of us, giving indications of inner health. Nor should we confuse it with the spectrum of rainbow colours with which we are all happily familiar. (There may be some link to these glorious colours which nature creates – whether it's in a rainbow arc above us or a filmy puddle of oil in a rut in the road, but I'm not yet quite sure what the connection, if any, may be.)

Look at the drawings on pages 28 and 29 to see how the chakra entry points influence the health of specific areas of

THE SEVEN CHAKRAS

ALL CHAKRAS

Some triangles of influence are broad and squat; others are narrow and more obviously pointed. The areas that each triangle influences may overlap, but since each triangle has independent energy, it will not be affected by, or affect, the work within or power of other triangles.

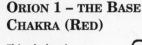

ORION 1 – THE BASE CHAKRA (RED)

This chakra is fundamental and its entry points are close to our intestine at the front and above the sacrum, just above the rectal region. The triangle is formed by linking upwards with places close to the shoulders. Any problems related to the arms, hands and wrists are likely to be solved via an examination of this chakra entry point.

CAPRICORNUS 2 – THE SACRAL CHAKRA (ORANGE)

Indicates any problem connected with the spleen, which plays an important role in the body's immune system. The chakra entry point is at the front of the body and the area of influence extends downwards towards the left hip.

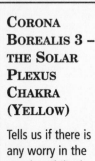

CORONA BOREALIS 3 – THE SOLAR PLEXUS CHAKRA (YELLOW)

Tells us if there is any worry in the navel, umbilical area or reproductive system. The chakra entry point is near the abdomen.

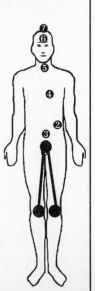

The Seven Chakras, continued

PEGASUS 4 – THE HEART CHAKRA (GREEN)

Tells me that there may be something to correct in the heart or with the entire cardiovascular system. Everyone knows how important the heart is: it is our physical and emotional engine room. But perhaps too few of us realise that optimum health can depend on the comfort zone of the flats of our feet.

SCORPIUS 5 – THE THROAT CHAKRA (BLUE)

Located at the throat and larynx. Obviously, a signal here will alert me to possible respiratory problems including asthma and other breathing-related disorders, many of them, as ever, innocently inherited. You'll see from the drawing that a problem here can reach right down below the knees to the shins and may be treated there.

TAURUS 6 – THE BROW CHAKRA (INDIGO)

This chakra doesn't simply connect to our mental health; its influence stretches right down to our toes where remedies may be applied. Our feet contain amazingly accurate maps of general health. Remedial action taken here can have astonishingly beneficial results bearing upon areas of the body far away.

SIRIUS 7 – THE CROWN CHAKRA (VIOLET)

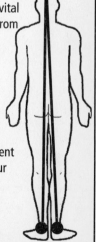

Has a narrow but vital area of influence from the crown to the heels. Thus, if your pain or other disorder is in the legs, it is very likely that your salvation is to be found with treatment higher up – on your head, in fact.

the body. A roughly triangular shape contains the strongest area of influence of each chakra.

As you can see from the triangular lines on the diagrams, each of the seven chakras influences an almost 'enclosed' area of the body. A disorder in the heart or chest may well be rooted in a malfunction of the foot – something as simple as ill-fitting shoes, so you needn't always worry, although it's obviously prudent to take even the slightest concern seriously. Following the lines of the drawings you will see that a digestive problem could have its origins in the upper arms. This could be some muscular strain or a bruising – even an old fracture that you'd all but forgotten.

And of course the damage may have been genetically inherited and your problem today could be the result of a 'ghost wound' donated by a forebear. Chapter Five touches upon such conditions.

Look again at how the lines of the triangles connect and you may be shown that trouble in the shins or some scalp or skin disorder may be corrected by attention paid to the backs of the lower legs... and so it goes.

> Case study... Case study... Case study... Case study...
> She was only in her mid-forties but there were times when SB feared she was developing Alzheimer's disease. Doctors had suggested that she had ME – often a shorthand for 'nothing to be done', since this disorder is as yet so little understood.
>
> 'I felt so dizzy, disconnected from objects and people when I was in conversation. I could hear what people said but I couldn't quite engage. It was almost as if I'd drunk too much and I had to make a special effort to be steady. If I put something on the table I'd feel the need to concentrate on the action with exaggerated carefulness. I just didn't feel wholly 'there'. I also had pain and aches all over my body and energy levels were alarmingly low.'
>
> I identified a problem with the cerebral spinal fluid which connects with the brain. Any cerebral damage,

shortage or blockage is going to have ramifications all over the body. I dowsed to discover that SB's base chakra was red and placed the tablets on the correct meridian. Her problem had been caused by the drug Septrin, taken after the birth of her first child when a urinary infection set in: it had literally left poison in her brain. SB herself remembered how unwell she had felt after just one dosage was administered. I was able to restore brain health to the strong levels she was born with and prescribed the usual food drops to maintain the recovery. Her back pains were relieved as the meridian lines formed by the base chakra triangle were strengthened.

'My energy has returned, the aches have gone. I feel normal again – almost born again.'

I do realise that for some readers the concept of this extraordinary human geography may be hard to grasp, but it all happens to be in complete sympathy with the homeopathic paths of healing I have been treading for years and with my belief that Eastern, Western, homeopathic, complimentary and orthodox medicine can co-exist for the greater good if the patterns and similarities are recognised and addressed.

Everything in nature connects. Circles, coils, cycles and curves ultimately control us.

Thus if your shoulder hurts it could be because you're asthmatic and the way to deal with this might well be to dowse the spleen and treat things there... A problem with your heart and blood pressure could connect to some disorder below the knee – a sort of domino effect. Every single organ, bone, muscle or tissue in the body will connect and respond to star energy. It is simply a question of dowsing to find where exactly the problem lies and then reaching for or creating the correct remedy for treatment. That I often, these days, find the text of the Crypto Power of the Hebrew Word essential as I identify an individual's problem is covered in separate chapters

We need to experience the occasional sharp bend in order to jiggle, unsettle and then correct things within. This is rather different from the ideas about a short, sharp shock for social miscreants once so beloved of some of our politicians. It may have closer links with those stories you sometimes read in the tabloids, of people recovering apparently hopelessly lost use of limb or sight if they have some severe shock or trauma, or of the seven-stone mother who manages to lift a large car in order to rescue her child trapped beneath it. I don't know. I've given up trying to analyse or fully understand sometimes. But I have learned to trust my instincts and intuition. There truly are 'more things in heaven and earth'... as Hamlet reminds Horatio. At times I wish I could understand and explain things with greater clarity, but as Shakespeare reminds us, some things remain beyond our understanding. All I have is my absolute trust in the evidence I see when patients recover or are restored after following the guidance offered so freely by the stars.

Case study... Case study... Case study... Case study...
EW is an old friend. At any rate, she's been my patient on and off for over twelve years. She's in her late fifties now and has had a lifetime of throat and sinus problems and she's also suffered from back pain. After treating her in other ways and, I think, relieving her discomfort, I recently saw that she needed the help of the Scorpius place in my labyrinth and that with the help of the 'blue' power of that stone and the application of a homeopathic form of phenol, she would soon begin to feel dramatically better.

'I first went to Jack with pains in my neck, having hurt my shoulder. I'd been to a physiotherapist who told me I'd never be able to hold a pen again, which was disastrous news for me professionally. Jack treated this with crystals for my back and just stood by me with his hand on my hurt shoulder. The pain lifted at once. My weak spot must be my back because that's where his tablets are taped these days even if he's treating one of my recurrent throat or sinus problems, but he dowsed and cleaned out my immune system beforehand. Previously a doctor had offered me medicine containing steroids, which I rejected and I'd also been told that only surgery could open up the sinuses and that even then there was no guarantee of a cure. In the meantime a side-effect was terrible headaches. I've been to specialists who didn't impress me much and was sick of enduring these throat and back problems even though, in a way, I'd learned to live with them after so long and kept them under control with various nasal sprays. But I hated the idea of antibiotics sloshing around my body and have every confidence in Jack's methods, mysterious as they are.'

I dowsed back through the generations but found that on this occasion my patient's problems were rooted in phenol poisoning sustained as a result of her premature birth. EW's life-history of throat and breathing problems stemmed from this and I treated her along the fifth, or Scorpius chakra, which links to the knees, where I also applied some tablet pads. She also puts the star drops on her food and we're both hoping that a lifetime of enduring such chronic ill-health is now a thing of the past.

As I have said, if you walk a labyrinth like mine the simple paths require you to trace a sharp turn whenever the paths curve back upon themselves. Then some essential balance is restored and perhaps some daunting physical mystery will right itself. But this is by no means the sum of it: within my labyrinth are stellar energies which become alive and dense with a cosmic force which creates strength and health with every step as the power beamed from a specific star makes contact with the small stone embedded there on my little patch of earth. The small rocks with which my labyrinth was fashioned and 'land-marked' simply respond to the call in a way that astronomers and many other people cleverer than I cannot quite account for. I simply dowsed for them and marvel at the response and results

Case study... Case study... Case study... Case study...
It's hard to believe now, but before World War Two brown
bread was considered vastly inferior to white. It was
another of those silly social things – white bread was
thought to be more elegant and, well, refined. One patient
of mine, NR, has reason to regret this as she inherited a
dietary intolerance because of the bleach used in that pre-
war flour. Her spleen had thus been damaged.

'I had all sorts of ongoing aches and pains and I'd seen
many alternative healers as well as my GP. I knew the
problem was somehow connected to eating disorders and
possibly allergies, rooted in my solar plexus, which is close
to one's emotional centre. But I also began to worry about
possible heart problems ahead, as my father had died after
heart failure at the age of fifty-nine. I had a scan and
nothing amiss was found, but I still felt wretched most of
the time.

'Then I heard about Jack and went to see him. It was
incredible. Almost the moment he asked me to stand within
his stone circle I felt recharged with energy right down to
my toes. It was almost instantaneous. Jack also placed
tablets on my solar plexus and forearms. All that stomach
acidity seemed to vanish.

'I know life is stressful and my work brings its fair share
of strain, but I now know how this can be managed and I
feel so well again now.'

In NR's case I restored homeostasis by applying bleach
tablets and phials made from the energy of Capricornus
gathered from the orange section of the labyrinth to the
solar plexus chakra point.

We need this cosmic energy every bit as much as we need
nourishment derived from food although it is an entirely
different form of nutrition from that we extract from good food
at mealtimes. When it enters our body through one of the
chakra reception points this nourishment connects to what is
known as 'the sympathetic system' and begins to work a sort
of magic which is both mysterious and practical. Wouldn't

even the most sceptical person agree that there is a logic in
feeding back into the body fragments of pure energy that link
precisely with our physical make-up at the time of universal
creation?

Readers of my first book, *The Healer,* and any patient of
mine, past or present, will know that I distil my clippings and
stone or mineral pulverisings in pure alcohol before drying
and hardening the matter down to make the tiny tablets
which are central to my work. The little tablets are not taken
internally but taped to the skin at the correct point. The
chosen place has often surprised my patients – if their
problem concerns the back the tablets may well be taped to
the legs... If there is trouble in the stomach or digestive
system I might well apply the remedy to the foot... The health
of our body is ruled by the meridian lines which may not
always seem to be directly connected to the source of pain. In
this aspect of my work I share many ideas with the
practitioners of homeopathic acupuncture and all these
aspects of my practice continue to work in perfect harmony
with my most recent findings.

As well as the tablets which release their power through
the absorbent conduit of the skin and overcome invasive
internal antibodies, the drops of star energy-infused tinctures
that I might now ask my patients to add to their foods are a
completely new way for me to compound and expand upon the
healing processes which I have now been developing over the
past four decades. Any hostile presence beneath the skin –
however svelte and youthful you may appear – can silently
wreak terrible damage. Seldom is it of the patient's own
making: most disorders are inherited and genetically
programmed. The water that your grandmother innocently
drank from a tap fed by lead pipes can explain your infertility
or your headaches, your persistent backache or your lung
disorder. Any sense of guilt or personal responsibility for
illness is pointless and in itself unhealthy, I believe.

Case study... Case study... Case study... Case study...
Sometimes I see gratifyingly fast results. PD is a
businessman in his fifties and had suffered from low back
pain and shoulder stress for over twenty years. Many
sessions with chiropractors had brought only temporary
relief. PD experienced relief from pain within five minutes
of an application of my tablets and the pain did not return
for some time. He tends to come back for an 'MOT' every
now and again and that's all he needs now that I have
identified his homeostasis level and have been able to treat
his spinal weakness with phosphorus boosts as well as
remove the ill-effects of old antibiotics.

'I'd spent some years in the armed forces and had been
obliged to have numerous inoculations during my duties
abroad. Also, years ago, I worked on a farm and came into
contact with organophosphates in the form of sheep dip. I
consider myself to be someone who has an open mind and
I'm very receptive to spiritual ideas and alternative methods
of healing. I had certainly come to believe that taking drugs
to relieve my back and shoulder pain was not the answer.
My problems do sometimes recur, but I'm not a pushover
and I wouldn't have returned to Jack to be dowsed and have
the tablet 'poultices' applied to my shoulders and lower
back if I hadn't come to trust the results – I wasn't
converted instantly. I accept that to some extent my back
and shoulder problems are caused by my chosen lifestyle
and habits. Now I know how to take personal responsibility
for relieving them.'

※ ※ ※

Is it so strange to accept that we're influenced by the energy
of the stars? Ever since human history has been studied or
recorded, the ruling power of the sun has been acknowledged.
Equally the cycles of the moon have long been known to drive
our tides and emotional states. The stars are measureless
millions of miles more distant but perhaps this merely means
that it takes their force that much longer to reach us. More
prosaically it may simply be that because the stars are, to the
naked eye, just tiny twinkling dots, rather than observable

orbs, we have underestimated their importance. I'm no astronomer, but I have come to realise that their beams – and millions of them do beam upon us although certain specific stars and constellations have greater power than others – supply just as much benign force as our closer planetary neighbours, the sun and moon.

As soon as I realised that I needed seven types of rock with which to construct the labyrinth – seven different stones which would connect to seven specific stars and constellations – amazingly, perhaps, after dowsing, I found all seven within a short drive of my home. I always, incidentally, preface any request to my pendulum with the word 'accessible'. As I noted earlier, I would willingly have flown across the world to find the right rock, so distance wasn't at issue. I just ask the dowser to guide me towards material I can practically access, not some stone buried within the foundations of a living building or a bush clinging to edge of a dangerous ravine in a remote mountain range.

By now I was coming to understand the complimentary balances of sun, moon and star energies. I realised that to absorb the proper nutrients from our food, especially those that remain in the hybrid foods which have been cultivated in artificial or otherwise unnatural ways, we should sprinkle them very lightly with the clear and tasteless essences derived from plant matter grown within the labyrinth and circle and harvested, preferably, around the time of the full moon.

ROTATION OF ESSENCES

MOON, SUN AND COSMOS DROPS	Over a three day cycle, take 1 drop in juice or water on waking, e.g. day 1: Moon, day 2: Sun, day 3: Cosmos. Then repeat cycle. (Essence in 25% ethanol)
FOOD DROPS:	At the beginning of each meal put 1 drop on first mouthful. (Essence in 25% ethanol)

These drops release all available energy from even the most dubious foodstuffs and make wholesome organic foods taste even more delicious as well as extracting such healing power.

Thus taken, the energy of the stars links up with the chakra system within the body and harnesses the food's correct nutritional energies. But apart from obtaining the essences which I create, there are practical ways that you can entrap star energy at home, and constructing your own circle is just the beginning. Moreover, if the whole field begins to exert a grip of interest you could join or form a dowsing club. You'll find it very sociable and will meet a range of people with very varied aims. Not everyone who dowses does so for health's sake: plenty of keen dowsers seek archaeological evidence if history is their passion. Others just like a treasure hunt. We've all seen people with divining rods on the sea shore, hoping to find Spanish dubloons as they walk the dog!

✳ ✳ ✳

We have learned a little about the chakras and how pivotal a study of them has recently been to my work as a healer, but here's some more information. By now you know that I aim to harness energy from the stars to match each individual's chakras and I can do so by calling in cosmic energy to my labyrinth. It is there for the taking. Then, with the complimentary forces derived from the plant matter grown within the adjacent stone circle, I can get to work. And I do so with as much enthusiasm and excited anticipation as I have ever felt about my job as a healer because I truly believe that relating and applying cosmic energy to the seven chakra entry points on the body can revolutionise human health and well-being for ever.

Case study... Case study... Case study... Case study...
When he was sixteen MN was doing fine. His mother
remembers the day he ran excitedly up to his school in
Newcastle to discover his GCSE results. Two years later, he
couldn't hold a pen. He has lost his sight, his hearing, and
the use of his legs.

This silencing tragedy is the result of a condition
known as neurophylomatosis two, diagnosed in autumn
1998, a disorder so rare that MN's case has attracted the
concerned interest of at least forty doctors, including
Chinese practitioners and top specialists. None of them
has been able to suggest anything much beyond surgery
to remove the tumours which have flourished in his brain
and spine, but as his mother says, this recourse offers no
solution as new tumours would probably grow. She was
told, however, that without surgery her son would
probably die.

'He seemed perfectly normal before the onset of the
disease, apart from being a little clumsy, perhaps, which I
put down to a difficult birth. I took him to our doctor
when this awkwardness seemed to worsen.'

With horrible rapidity the condition escalated as
tumours developed. MN's parents travel down to the
Surrey clinic about once a month and I keep in touch
with them by phone between appointments. He has such
an evil, unjust and almost wily illness, with new tumours
growing in places far away from the areas where I had
treated existing ones with taped-on tablets. I also
suggested that a different star tincture should be put in
MN's bath water every day, in a weekly rotation, and
some improvement seemed to coincide with this, as a
drop from each of the seven star chakra remedies was
faithfully given. Sometimes I feel almost as despairing
as his parents must, since there isn't always any
discernable improvement... and yet at other times there
seems to be some hope, not for complete reversal or full
recovery – we cannot hope for too much – but for the
restoration of some quality of life. At any rate, three
years have passed since the boy was given three months
to live.

But his mother speaks generously of the progress he has made since he became my patient.

'I believe Jack has kept my son going since 1998. He's kept his spirits up and strengthened his will to live. Around Christmas in 2000 Jack had told us on the phone that he couldn't suggest we come down for a few weeks because he was still at a loss about what to do next. In so far as he can communicate distress now, my son made it clear to us that he wanted to go, that he felt better after those visits. It was very difficult for us to explain why there had to be a short delay.

'On a strictly practical level I know that Jack has probably already saved his life because his small intestine became blocked. With systems like that shutting down and all remaining physical balance lost it didn't just seem that my son was going to die – it seemed as if he *wanted* to. Apparently some fresh area in his brain had become damaged. Jack fixed that with the drops which we now put onto his food. Since he's been taking them his bowel function has been normal and he is to some extent restored. In fact I would say that Jack brought him back to life and continues to keep him going.

'We're grateful, of course, for all the interest that has been shown in my son's case by all the other specialists nearer home and will continue to value their advice. We would never dismiss the opinion of a specialist in any field because we have to retain hope and keep every door open. But I have to say that so far Jack has helped more than anyone else. Recently one of the despairing specialists, on seeing that his most recent tumours had not grown any larger – as had been expected – had the generosity to say "keep on going down to Surrey". We will.'

I include this terrible, humbling story of bravery, optimism and parental devotion for a number of reasons.

It is I who should be grateful to the MN's family for their continuing faith in me and their patience as I keep working to find ways to ease and improve his quality of life – not always as fast as I would wish, but it is cases like this that inspire me to keep looking and studying. MN's progress seems to be steady rather than dramatic and it depends on the build-up of the carefully devised remedies as they are administered to separate parts of the body. Building up too much strength in one physical area before the whole of his body is ready to cope with that aspect of recovery would be pointless at best and dangerous at worst if a weakened system was traumatised by a rush of energy in one area. So despite my wish to see faster results, and his family's hope for rapid progress, I have to take things step by step.

His mother's practical and pragmatic attitude towards working with – not against – people in other fields of medicine is to be applauded and may help lead to what we all hold in common: the ideal of sharing all healing knowledge. Lastly, I am simply inspired by the determined character of MN, this promising, normal boy – not necessarily destined to become a rocket scientist - just an average lad with a life of normal expectations.

NB: whilst this book was in preparation brave MN died, slipping away in a calm and peaceful sleep. Doctors had told his devoted parents to brace themselves for the worst and most violent form of brain death, so his dignified departure may have been of some comfort to them. I do hope so and hope also that the family of this remarkable boy will be able to find some peace of their own.

✳ ✳ ✳

We cannot see electricity, but we know it exists. We cannot touch fear, but we don't doubt its power when its cold finger touches us. And neither do we doubt the power of hope – so tangible sometimes that we can almost hold it.

Similarly, contained within the surfaces of the labyrinth's shallow, curved pathways is a concentrated wealth, a whole universe, of cosmic power for healing. Perhaps it will always remain a mystery of sorts – for who are we to attempt to fully understand and deconstruct the awesome, ancient mysteries of the stars? But we can dance to the music of the spheres and take confident steps towards health, strength and regeneration. Let me be your guide to the maze and your dancing partner through the labyrinth until with your own confident steps you can stride along without a guide.

CHAPTER TWO

The Circle

Not so long ago I had a patient who knew he was terminally ill. There really wasn't much more I could do for him other than help to make his last months as comfortable and peaceful as possible.

This brave and cheerful chap, beyond any hope of real recovery, used to come and sit in my circle during the months, years even, before he died. I'd often look up from my rooms at the clinic and see him sitting there, still and apparently calm. The fact that when the time came he was ready and at ease was confirmed to me when I heard that he had asked that his ashes should be scattered within the stone circle. The peace there had really helped him deal with things, enabled him to face his death with dignity and without pain. I like to think that he is there somehow – watching and blessing.

All life is circular. I considered it both an honour and appropriate that my patient's ashes should join the soil and stones, grasses and herbs which all make their contributions, along with the seasons, to the ever-turning wheel of human life. He'd felt blessed and happy there and I like to think that part of his soul still resides there, benignly enriching this mystical, almost magical area.

The circle is a place of life, of hope and of renewal.

We all know that if we keep our eyes, ears and minds open we can keep on learning every day of our lives. A great truth is rooted in this cliché, as in most clichés, but it isn't always easy to be alert to change and progress as one grows older.

Where expanding and developing and learning about stone circles are concerned, however, it has been an effortless pleasure for me and I hope to pass on exciting new knowledge here. Readers of my first book, *The Healer*, may remember that even then I had a stone circle outside my clinic, a place of spiritual and physical nourishment which had already become crucial to my work. The labyrinth was created close by soon after the beginning of the new millennium. Once again it is my teacher – I learn all the time.

Henry Ford – arguably a capitalist monster who bears some responsibility for our planet's declining ecology – remarked that whether he was eighteen or eighty a man was as good as dead if he had closed his mind to new ideas. In this, if nothing else, I am with the godfather of popular motoring.

They are wise, those small rocks, and far from simply resting peacefully amidst the grasses and herbs, they continue to impart new knowledge and to teach me how best to work with them. I've long believed in the healing properties of much plant and vegetable life but these forces are almost newcomers to the field compared with the concentrated sun, moon and star rays integral to certain fathomlessly ancient rocks. And I always knew that my rocks contained healing force – I just didn't realise how much until recently.

I'm lucky enough to have acres of land outside the clinic and I'm planning three more circles. Now I can grow more herbs within these new circles to keep up with demand. Some healing plants are hardy and grow unstoppably – mint and lemon balm spring to mind – but others can only be cultivated and harvested in minute quantities, so extra space within the magical shield of the new circles of Pembrokeshire stones will be needed. It will take about three years for the plants to grow into their full strength but even in the early seasons I will be able to gather a little – at the correct time of day and month – and create new remedies which can be endlessly recharged.

The central concept to be grasped here is that when the universe was formed it was in a state of perfect purity. When a meteorite from a distant star is embedded here on earth and can be located and dowsed or if rock of comparable age and purity can be dowsed for and utilised in the creation of my medicines, all that uncorrupted strength is released. And since human life originally sprang from and thus shares the same DNA as the old stones, there is an instant compatibility – rather like belonging to the same blood group.

It is at the root of my work to restore my patients to the moment when, in their genetic past, they were at their strongest – however far back in time I need to search.

I realise that for some, this general idea may take a leap of faith to grasp: after all, are we humans not warm and flexible whereas a rock is quite the opposite? However, that point of view represents a very limited attitude about what is actually 'alive'. The measurable forces which rocks can emanate are just as vibrant as any human aura and, in the main, a good deal more powerful. They bestow this life force into plant life close by and with my recent, greater understanding of the importance of the stellar energy they redistribute, I've been able to develop even more effective treatments. Just energising an innocent tablet with stellar energy seems so natural and simple to me – working in a tiny laboratory with the most simple tools. I'm still rather baffled by the ideas and trust of people who still have more trust in the commerce-driven laboratories of the faceless European multi-national companies.

On the edge of the centre of the circle is a relatively large stone which I call the '100 per cent healing point'. Sixteen slightly smaller rocks mark the rim of the circle and each represents an area of body or mind. The healing point attracts sun and lunar energies and sends 'messages' out to each of the outer stones, where its power blends with their own. I've seen and proved how the stones themselves and the grasses they

NEOLITHIC HEALING CIRCLE

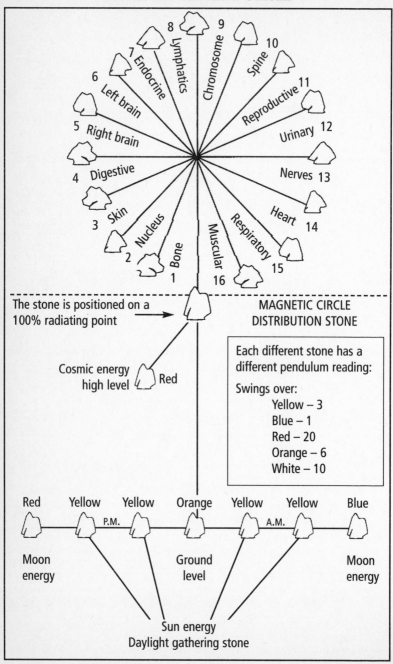

encircle have massive and almost mystical healing prowess. Some plants are low-growing and nestle close to the earth, others reach higher towards the energies and the healing point but all are influenced by the stones as well as by the light and only recently have I begun to realise just how powerful such energies are. Energies from the sun and moon tend to be concentrated near the ground whilst the force from more distant planets and constellations influences those plants that grow taller. After about three years all the plants will be charged with awesomely maximum powers.

As I go along I tend to snip, clip and cull the leaves just before full moon, usually at dawn or dusk. Into pure alcohol these clippings go, each bottled separately according to the sixteen segments of the circle. In time, six months maybe, I will have forty-eight separate tinctures – sun, moon and star.

Case study... Case study... Case study... Case study...
SF couldn't remember when she hadn't been depressed. As a child she would weep inconsolably – the mystery of her misery only adding to it. She had been born with a slight spastic disability but this hadn't stopped her from achieving a university education, which says much about her inherent strength of character. She went on to have a career as a computer programmer, to marry and to have three children. But every day she was haunted and blighted by depressions which led her to seek advice from many different kinds of doctors and healers. She had come to assume that food allergies were at the root of her problems.

I believed I could help SF but knew it would take time. She agreed to this 'investment' and simply sat outside my clinic in the circle, whenever she could, for a year, whenever the weather was fine enough. She sat on the junction of the fifth and sixth points of the circle, gradually gathering strength and energy. Only then, once her brain was restored and receptive, could I begin to help her in a more strictly practical way but I knew that anyone who had displayed such tenacity would probably respond well to subsequent treatment. SF has this to say:

'I did get help, so I suppose things were controlled, but it was never quite enough. My mood never seemed to lift for long. After a lifetime of receiving psychiatric help, an acupuncturist even told me, frustratingly, that I wasn't ill enough to be worth treating This wasn't helpful for me, my marriage or family life. Then I started to see Jack and sat in his circle for an hour or two at a time. I won't say that the results were instantaneous, but one day after seeing Jack I felt a sort of spiritual lift and I've never been in the depths of depression since then.

'After my children were born I'd been told that I was suffering from post-natal depression. Perhaps I was, but since I'd been smitten with these dark moods ever since I could remember I wasn't prepared to accept them as a result of pregnancy, pure and simple. I was drinking a little too much and crying all the time. I began to see why people committed suicide.

'I really think that Jack saved me from killing myself or ending up in a mental hospital. My depressions were threatening to break up our family. The more therapy you have, without anything doing any good, the more depressed and hopeless you can become.

'I had his tablets taped on and nothing much more complicated than that. All I know is that I found being within the circle hugely calming. It was wonderful not to be treated like some routine neurotic and, now, to be able to work again and enjoy my family life. I don't know how he does it. All I know is that what he did worked for me.'

Most of my stones originally came from Wales after I was deeply affected by the large circles at Gors Fawr, in the Priscilli Hills of Pembrokeshire. I researched their magnetic and vibrational fields by dowsing and in discussion with another healer and decided to create my own circle at home. I dowsed for rocks of similar age and type as the Welsh ones. 'Mine' weigh about five hundredweight each – pretty hefty if you and six other strong people were to try and lift one but really small in comparison with the ancient circles in the wild, let alone the majestic splendour of Stonehenge in Wiltshire, the most famous sacred circle of them all. But it is not the size of the rock that matters – it is the nature of the energy it emanates that counts. My circle is about twenty yards in diameter, but tiny pebbles containing the correct energies could be arranged in a circle under a chair at home and the potential for healing could be considerable.

Any circle automatically divides itself into the sixteen segments and any dowser can delineate the dividing lines which prove, apart from anything else, calm and pleasing reminders of how the circle is functioning. There's no need to be too fussy about the stones you use as markers – virtually any will do, they are all as old, or older, than the hills, after all.

Recently I added more seats and resting places so that people can absorb the stones' energy as they sit at peace within the circle. There are many ways to utilise the benign vibrations within the circle to very simply address specific disorders. Someone with a fracture, for instance, will be asked to sit within the segment radiating bone energy, with tablets made from an appropriate leaf or flower or herb later attached to the injury.

About those sixteen segments: each has a specifically dowsed-for stone at its outer edge and each one of these segments and stones represents a particular part of the human body or aspect of human spirit. These, in turn connect with the chakras. The chakras (See Chapter One, about my labyrinth) being only seven in all, 'overlap' into the sixteen areas influenced by the stones – all working together harmoniously.

Some people come to me with shining, optimistic trust, others with a weary pessimism bordering upon desperation after a dozen failed treatments elsewhere. And sometimes I encounter old-fashioned scepticism. This I can usually deal with by demonstrating how something as simple yet agonising

as muscle strain or weakness near the hand or wrist could be
mended. I seek to show that in a little test. I might ask the
cynic to stand in the section of the circle connected to heart
strength and hold his arm out. With one finger touching his
heart I use the other hand to touch, but not push the arm. It
remains rock steady. If the we both move to another section of
the circle, however, the arm just flops down when touched
because we are in a different area of energy. This rush of
strength to each of the sixteen body parts will diminish if my
hand is removed from his heart or the wrong section of the
circle stepped into. This somehow goes against the commonly
held scientific view that 'you can't prove a negative'.

In my earlier book I drew the comparison with those
electronic devices people use to open their car doors without a
conventional key. We all have our own inner electricity and if
the device's battery is flat, the owner merely has to hold the
device under their chin to recharge it. Much the same happens
within the stone circle when someone with a heart short of
energy – like the flat car key gadget – can stand in the right
place in the circle and become recharged at once. Never
underestimate the importance and influence of our own
electricity. It's there, just as surely as the stuff that ensures your
TV works or your bath water is heated. Remember that in the
early days of wireless people used to keep their windows open
so that the waves could enter the house: they couldn't yet grasp
the concept of such invisible power. And it wasn't so long ago,
either, that people in less 'civilised' parts of the world thought
that a fragment of their soul was stolen if someone took their
photograph. The point I'm making here is that an instinctive
faith in, wonder at, the strange but strong, intangible but
inviolable powers resides within us all, just beneath the skin,
however sophisticated and modern we may think we are. You
have that power too – your body is alive with it.

I take clippings of the grasses and herbs growing near the
rocks in each segment of the circle at very specific times,

having found that they contain maximum power at or just after full moon. The time of day is important, too – very early in the morning or at dusk. It took me several months of experimentation to work it all out and, as always, I dowsed myself and 'test-drove' the remedies before I was sure they were ready to be offered to my patients. The grass is harvested over a period of several months by which time it has been influenced and nourished not only by energies emanating from the head stone but by the celestial energies as well. Just in passing I should mention that lovely though newly mown lawn grass looks and smells, it is very different from the tiny amounts I garner so carefully from my circle.

These grasses are first dried, like hay, on brown paper and then chopped and steeped in pure alcohol and become permanently charged with the correct healing powers to deal with almost any human disorder. Once the tincture is adapted to tablet form it is ready to begin its work. Some readers will already know that I believe strongly in the principle of using the skin as the most important vehicle for repair. Thus tablets are taped onto the correct part of the body to extract toxins and, if necessary, to subsequently replace the poison with some beneficial matter.

A crucial part of the process is to surround, at full moon, the harvested and dried grasses with four pieces of local wood, for which I will have dowsed, each placed upon a xerox of the appropriate verse from the Old Testament – for which, again, I will have also dowsed earlier. This procedure intensifies the power of the final tincture by 1000 per cent.

By this means and those described earlier, I now create three incredibly powerful new medicines – enforced with moon energy, sun energy and star, or cosmos, energy – from apparently simple stones and humble grasses. Many of my tried and true remedies, formulated years ago, remain in my pharmacy and still do sterling service, but these new ones exemplify the newest steps forward in my quest for healing. As

I have said, all the tinctures are most generally used to infuse the tablets which I tape to the appropriate part of the patient's body; not always the obvious place, as a study of the chakra triangles in the previous chapter has shown. However I also always advise the use of 'energy enhancers' which involves the lightest sprinkling or drop of one of the three essential essences in strict rotation of sun, moon and star in the morning drink. The energy boost so achieved is remarkable, as many patients have told me. But I knew this already as I was my own guinea-pig for six months before I offered these enhancers to anyone else.

*There'll be much more about the effect of these energy enhancers on nutrition, but suffice to say here that as a bonus, they not only extract every last atom of nutrition from even inferior food, but also make it taste better – in the case of organic food, **even** better.*

The body's systems work in parallel with the ancient holistic and homeopathic methods which I have long respected and wherein the body's meridian lines are a kind of map which show the connections and links between every area on and inside the human frame. Meridian lines have an acute intelligence which responds to what is good for them and excretes – or rejects even faster – foods or medicines which are either useless or actually damaging. The harvested grass clippings may well look unremarkable to the untutored eye, but with all that they contain, they are as potent as any drug expensively developed in some Swiss or North American laboratory, infinitely more effective and, perhaps above all, will *cause no harm*. Chemically manufactured drugs create as many disorders as their makers claim they relieve.

Any patient, or potential patient, of mine who retains faith in some of the orthodoxies of conventional medicine and thus has some doubts about my methods should remember that many of the big international drug companies buy the entire national harvest of certain herbs and plants grown in some parts of the world – thus having a devastating effect on the ecology as well as the economy of the area – and use plant extracts as the basis of the medicines they produce in a chemically tampered-with way. The simple aspirin derives from matter taken from a willow tree and all the opiates, natural and unnatural, have their origins in plant life. Think of eucalyptus, of rosemary, rue, thyme, sage and all the other healing herbs the Romans used and which were cultivated in England's sixteenth century gardens... So in this respect I don't have to ask even the dubious to take very big leap of faith: it is clear and logical that healing begins in the soil. And deep within and beneath the soil, of course, feeding their energies upwards, are stones as ancient as history and containing acids, proteins and other vital life forces for us to tap.

Volcanic stones and mud are particularly rich in healing powers because they have been thrown up from the earth's epicentre and are dense with benign energy. Remedies made from meteorite rock or crystal, thus, are infused with even older strength.

I've had to deal with more than my fair share of cynics, but it's amazing how cynicism can lessen when a glimmer of well-being shines ahead after the utter failure of twelve or twenty earlier forms of treatment. It doesn't take many of my cynics long to agree that the pathway to divinity is more likely to be lit by the stars than by strange glows emitted by GM foods and commercially produced drugs. And although people might scoff at the idea of mud baths and facial mud packs these are no more or less than an extension of many of my ideas. Quite why such commercialised enterprises are usually dismissed as hokum and vanity rather than given a measure of credence defeats me. Maybe we should consider the impulses of certain animal species – the 'lumbering' hippopotamus, for example, a creature which has survived genetically intact for thousands of years. That survival may owe much to the mud in which the animal instinctively anoints itself. Nor should we forget that some of the earliest known human remains were preserved for our anthropologists' analysis in a Danish bog where the mud contained enzymes of startling purity.

My twenty trainees will ensure that soon there will be enough practitioners qualified in my methods to be available to everyone. Look at Chapter Eleven here to see how my little 'academy' is rigorously training students in the art and science of becoming dowser-healers, well placed to advise or practise all over the country and beyond.

The calm good sense and trust in nature at the core of my methods of healing don't prevent me from researching the most modern ways of expressing them. I've become interested in radionics, by which in taking a clipping of hair or fingernail from an unwell person, I can create a magnetic field and within that 'broadcast' anywhere in the world, calling out for a solution and often receiving transferred healing. This is particularly useful if a patient is abroad or otherwise situated too far away to see me or another dowser-healer in person. The fact is that, just as the entirety of a limb which has been partially severed by amputation will appear in an X-ray, the complete blueprint of health is contained within these tiny fragments of hair and nail and I can 'prescribe' from afar on the basis of these personal bits and my pendulum remedies derived from circle-grown plant matter. The patient's 'records' are surrounded by four phials of healing tinctures, often based on crystals or derived from meteorites.

Interestingly the force within the clippings dies if the patient does. Occasionally I have learned with sadness of a patient's death by dowsing after sensing cause for concern. Invariably I later learn of their demise and know that the tiny phials containing their clippings must be cleared away.

The star, sun and moon energies are connected to the stones of my circle and the herbs and grasses within it connect to the very first commonly acknowledged life-forms, amoeba, and contain the same pure proteins as such awesomely ancient creatures. So when we are lucky enough to be struck here on earth by a passing meteorite from some distant constellation we can be sure that the rock is vibrant with the same uncontaminated life-force. I have a fragment of meteorite, given to me in Tel Aviv but originally from the Soviet Union. I have a small piece of solidified mud found three miles beneath the surface of the earth in the Norwegian Arctic Circle at a place called Heidron, and know that this, too, is pure and bursting with ancient healing energies. I also dowsed for some volcanic lava near Washington DC in the United States. The three components all represent pivotal moments of our planet's creation. When my pendulum is placed over any two of the three it remains still, but when I gather them together it whirls wildly in response. It is as if it has recognised a fusion of the powerful earthly beginnings which first churned in a kind of primeval soup and then evolved into all forms of life on our planet. It will be interesting to see what healing remedies can be devised by combining the correct balance of all three.

I would ask readers new to my work to refer, if they can, to my first book, *The Healer*, in which I explained at greater length how the vibrations and magnetism created within a stone circle can work. And I think it's actually helpful to scupper the idea that only grand and majestic temples like the one at Stonehenge count. Isn't it rather reassuring to know that smaller and apparently 'lesser' stones can contain and release considerable power too. In fact I managed to persuade Mrs May Estler to produce a complete set of stones and cloth printed with the outline of the circle, with all its sixteen segments defined, along with other crucial information. Therefore anyone will be able to lay the cloth on the floor at home and then sit in a chair over the stones and take healing from aeons of ancient force and wisdom. So you don't even need a garden to have your own stone circle.

Of course, if you do have space outside and can arrange a circle large enough to sit within, so much the better as that way you may also benefit from the emanations of any grasses and herbs you may have planted there, as well as natural light.

> Case study... Case study... Case study... Case study...
> GL was already a dowser himself before he came to see me, so perhaps he was predisposed to be receptive to my methods. None the less, severe back problems had taken him to herbalists, acupuncturists, reflexologists, osteopaths and a chiropractor before he read about me and made an appointment. GL is over seventy now and has been retired for some years from a series of stressful jobs. But shortness of breath and recurrent heart problems were robbing him of the pleasures of a well-deserved retirement. His greatest sorrow was that he couldn't even enjoy his golf any more. I dowsed to find that his problems connected back to a tetanus injection years ago and to cortisone treatments and various other inoculations that an army career had demanded. Later he had a hairdressing business and was surrounded by fumes generated by the many dangerous chemicals used in the salon. After dowsing I taped tablets to his feet for a mere twenty minutes, having divined that Pegasus was his chakra. I was pretty pleased with his progress, but will let GL speak for himself: 'He's brilliant. All my tiredness has gone. The first time I went back on the golf course after Jack's treatment I got a hole in one!'

GL's heart disorder was taken care of with tablets charged with cosmic forces which had beamed into and then cradled in rocks. As I have said before, I believe that all life on earth could have started with a single cell, lodged in the centre of a configuration of rocks, all generating the same cosmic energy that has made us – and, if need be – can make us well.

Sometimes the most complex-seeming mysteries can reduce to a single simple truth.

Perhaps the best way to prime yourself for the sort of good health you will come, with luck, to take for granted is to have

FOOLPROOF DOWSING FOR BEGINNERS

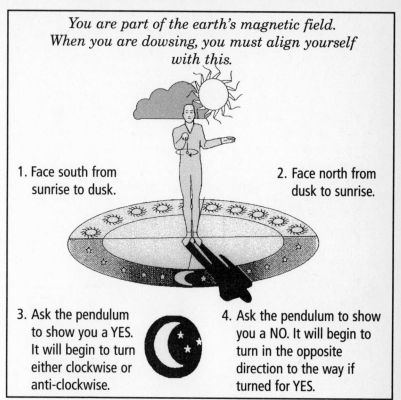

You are part of the earth's magnetic field.
When you are dowsing, you must align yourself
with this.

1. Face south from
   sunrise to dusk.

2. Face north from
   dusk to sunrise.

3. Ask the pendulum
   to show you a YES.
   It will begin to turn
   either clockwise or
   anti-clockwise.

4. Ask the pendulum to show
   you a NO. It will begin to
   turn in the opposite
   direction to the way if
   turned for YES.

some rocks of your own at home. If you can, join a dowsing
society and learn how to divine them or simply make your own
pendulum with something as simple as a thimble and ask it
the 'yes' or 'no' questions. It really is a very simple process.

Then on a day when you don't feel quite well, rest in bed
(no one seems to respect bed-rest anymore; it's unbeatable if
you are really low, old-fashioned though some might think it).
Have lots of pure water within reach, a book or magazine to
dive into, some fruit, the telephone... and above all ensure
that your indoor stones are nearby. Remember that you are
doing friends, colleagues and yourself no favours if you don't
permit yourself and your body to recover from those little
disorders that can sometimes become serious. By such simple

means your body will begin to mend itself in a far sounder way than any drug-induced torpor could. I was truly appalled to note some recent advertising campaign, advancing the use of a commercial flu remedy which suggested pretty boldly that someone else in the office would gladly step into your shoes and steal your job if you were weedy enough to take a day off work. I'm writing here, of course, about some brief, low-level set-back, not chronic or life-threatening illness.

For advice about dealing with those you'll need to read on and learn about the rudiments of my most recent and revolutionary work. In the meantime, consider again the circle and the total logic it contains and remember that with any pebble casually picked up on the beach you hold a piece of the universe in your hand.

CHAPTER THREE

The New Gene Power

As this chapter is going to contain a little bit of condensed science I thought I'd help you to play yourselves in with something both astonishing and amusing: our genes play melodies and each of us emanates a unique tune, which can be heard and registered by a skilled dowser. This silent singing is unlikely to form the notes of a Gershwin song or a lovely Schubert *lied* – being more like whale song or the 'noises' heard from space.

The music of the spheres has long been recorded by astronomers. Human bodies also emit tones, conducted by our genes, which give signals relating to health and well-being. Happy and euphonious noises indicate balance and strength, as one might expect, whilst anxious or even honking sounds can alert the dowser to some malady.

The popular seer Betty Shine has also recognised this phenomenon, relating that a few years earlier a Japanese geneticist had seen that genetic patterns of living cells could be converted into musical notation. He realised that genes not only contain a blueprint of human life but carry a tune. The scientist found rhythms akin to lively Viennese waltzes or baroque chamber pieces. I can't say I've heard anything as melodious as these, but I'm with Betty Shine when she asserts that sad and sombre noises seem to be issued from people whose cells are cancer-ridden whilst light and cheerful notes are detected from a healthy body in positive working order. And I'm with the Japanese geneticist who likened these life-enhancing sounds to birdsong – sounds which obey no conventional structure of musicality but which seldom fail to lift the heart.

But now I must address some less light-hearted and entertaining aspects of what our genes have to say and do. Over the past year or two we've heard or read a lot about developments in genetic sciences which allow animals to be cloned, parents to select a specific foetus from an artificially created multiple pregnancy and, of course, foodstuffs to be genetically modified. I have followed this whole debate with intense interest.

In the spring of 2001, when Britain's farmers were crippled by an outbreak of foot and mouth disease, the domino effect of poor husbandry was felt across the nation's other industries and the entire economy, not just in butcher's shops and supermarkets but in whole communities. The hotel trade was blighted; all horse racing was suspended for the duration; road hauliers, used to driving cattle and sheep across the Channel, spoke of bankruptcy; manufacturers of camping gear and outdoor clothing were hit hard and the price of imported meat rocketed. (Yes, someone always profits from such disasters.) It got worse: the tourist industry upon which so many of Britain's loveliest rural and farming areas depend, studded as they are with lovely historic houses and gardens to visit, was also set to slump for the summer as overseas Britain was widely seen as a nation under siege and no place to plan a holiday. When election plans were postponed it did indeed seem as if there was a state of emergency akin to that in wartime.

I'm not claiming that if all meat was organically reared and farmed there would be no swine fever or foot and mouth disease but I'm absolutely certain that instances of such outbreaks would be far fewer and then be more efficiently contained. One day I hope the British will finally realise that they ultimately pay a very high price for the cheap foodstuffs they have come to demand. We've long passed the age and stage when war-time restrictions and the old public school ethos urged us to eat what we were given and be grateful for it. In any case, this was later often an excuse for lazy food preparation and stinginess. Most people are more satisfied with a small plate of something delicious and wholesome than with a great bowl of muck and no number of exhortations about the plight of starving millions in distant continents will make poor food more appetising to reluctant children exhorted to clear their plates, nor to their discerning adult friends.

As a supposed nation of animal lovers it is extraordinary that the British can countenance the conditions that animals endure in order for cheap meat to be put on their plates every day. Modern – but not so very advanced – farming methods have ensured that overcrowding and inadequate supervision of livestock mean that terrible contagious cattle diseases spread far more quickly than they otherwise would.

Colin Trudge, Research Fellow at the London School of Economics, has said, 'It's surely time to rethink agriculture completely, from top to bottom. When we buy cars or houses we don't simply buy the cheapest – we demand quality and we are prepared to pay for it. Why can't we apply the same criteria to our food? ...But everyone – politicians, supermarkets, consumers – wants the costs brought down so that the workforce is cut.'

That reduced supermarket workforce, by the way, accounts for the twenty-minute wait at the check-out. Now, think about this. How much are you paid an hour? Divide it by three. If you add that sum to your supermarket bill you may wonder if next time you won't choose to buy slightly more expensive foods at proper shops where there are no queues and you know that what you are buying is safe and sound. And pish tish, I say, to supermarket 'reward' cards which award you exactly half a penny for every pound you spend. What a very cheap way this is for the supermarket giants to conduct their market research, quite apart from the fact that in using these cards you are placing a good many of your personal habits and preferences on record. Perhaps *that* helps to explain all that escalating junk mail and the unwelcome catalogues which in themselves account for massive stripping of the world's timber resources as the supermarket chains sell on your details to mail-order companies. All patterns of life are circular – but this last example speaks of a downward spiral...

We should begin to see the patterns and the links and realise that little happens in isolation. Even the smallest action or decision will have ramifications somewhere on our planet. Politically this is expressed by the 'joke' that if America sneezes Britain catches a cold. Where your personal health is concerned, the extinction of any plant species – anywhere in the world – will eventually cause an imbalance in that country's economy which will affect our own. And that can lead directly to short cuts in husbandry and manufacture of foodstuffs and to a reliance on 'cheap', chemically-based medicines instead of natural ones.

Like many others, I have my reservations about some of the potential uses – or abuses – of the new genetic knowledge. But it exists, cannot be unlearned and we must not now be King Canute-ish about resisting the advancing tides of science. As recently as autumn 2000 it was reported in *The Times* that 'genetic therapies that alter the genes passed to future generations are not yet safe and should not be attempted' and the article went on to mention 'irresponsible scientists' who plan to use techniques which amount to human genetic modification. So I know that in some quarters I will have an uphill struggle if doubters continue to confuse my work with the experiments of the multinational laboratories.

Having said that, I know that we do not need to go down the path of cloning sheep or transplanting animal organs to human beings. This is fundamentally wrong for every species involved in the process and there is an alternative. It is based on genetic research, certainly, but it is more natural and more

effective than anything devised in a laboratory. Thus whilst I
study and embrace the ideas at the root of genetic modification,
I have found different ways... Remember that the term
'genetic' applies just as much to plant and other organic matter
as it does to animal cells and that stones and crystals contain
DNA just as surely as bones, blood, hair and nails.

Indeed, where human health and nutrition is concerned I
suppose the current debate has influenced and encouraged me
to develop my own ways of cheating inherited genetic disorder
and I have begun treading some very exciting new paths.

I was inspired, if you like, during a visit to the National
Portrait Gallery in London. Looking at picture after picture of
members of the same family, painted over hundreds of years, I
was struck by how a nose, a brow, the shape of a mouth or even
that of the hands can be replicated over generations. Most of
us don't have that sort of record to study – the family
photograph album may only go back a generation or two – but
in pictures of families grand enough for members to have been
painted century after century we can see extraordinary
genetic inheritances.

It got me thinking. If the dominant genes in a family
produce the same bone-structure generation after generation,
why wouldn't the inherited genes also hold records or
blueprints for every other aspect of physiology and health or
potential for disorder? There must be a family memory of all
this contained within the blood, tissue, bones and genes, just
as real as the holiday snaps pasted into the photograph
album. And within that code is an intact genetic memory of
unblocked, undamaged genes, as well as damaged ones and I
have become ever more certain that I can remove the screen of
genetic blockage, so that the healthy gene is unmasked and
reactivated.

It seemed so obvious. The 'Hapsburg Lip', in any case, has
been noted by many distinguished historians and often said to
exemplify the decline of the Austro-Hungarian Empire. In

portrait after portrait of members of the Hapsburg family in the nineteenth and preceding centuries a characteristic shape of mouth was observed – as was the steady lowering of physical and moral strength of those imperial giants. Dubious marriages between cousins and even half-siblings have been said to account both for the pronounced physical resemblance from generation to generation and a parallel descent into physical and mental weakness.

Much the same took place in ancient Egypt during the centuries when the king was only permitted to marry and mate with his sister. Thus, it has been convincingly asserted, did the powers and achievement of a once great civilisation erode. So you see I have only been building on ideas already well established by the most respectable scholars!

I reckon a generation to be about thirty years. Over three hundred years and ten generations an average individual's gene pool today will contain the DNA of about of twenty forebears – in an average family little or none of it inbred. The fact is that I can dowse far before and beyond that, to forebears of thousands of years ago, but sometimes that's a concept that people find hard to grasp. But however far I dowse back to learn about the genetic moment when any or all functions of the ancestor's body were in prime health, in an attempt to restore that condition to a patient today, I have to do it in two stages, which is only logical when you consider things.

Think of your birth gifts as a hand of cards. Life's a lottery and some people glide through it having received the jackpot of good looks, good genes, good health and good luck. Few people are so blessed – or cursed: I sometimes wonder if being on the receiving end of too much good fortune might one day backfire and a sort of corrective balance be restored based on fairness and natural justice. Myth, legend and history – right up to today's colourful tabloid newspaper stories – abound in tales of the tragedy that so often overcomes apparently perfect lives... It's not that those of us not so richly blessed actually welcome such misfortunes. Usually the reverse is true: we love to believe in fairytales because therein lies the hope that the magic wand could touch our shoulder as well. But human nature is not always saintly and sometimes people find themselves thinking that the glorious but doomed person simply flew too close to the sun... The German language donated the word *Schadenfreude* to describe this feeling and our very own Oscar Wilde once had a character in one of his plays remark that nothing upset him more than the good fortune of a friend.

Anyway, here you are with *that* nose, *those* eyes and the stumpy legs your mother always deplored. You may not know it yet but you have that uncle's talent with the pencil and paintbrush, that cousin's fear of cats and some great grandparent's propensity to drink too much at times or to become too easily angered. And yes, you also have the same gentle tolerance as one sibling but have been denied the maths gene that enables a brother or sister to deal with complex figures so effortlessly.

You're a muddle, you're unique, you're YOU

I used to think that whatever you were blessed or saddled with at birth or conception is going to affect you for the rest of your life. From the instant that the most fundamental 'boy meets girl' encounter took place, that is, when your father's sperm met your mother's ovum, the cards were dealt and the dice were loaded, that however much you may rail and fret, envy others and resent your 'deal' there's nothing to be done about the basics as the broad health of both parents is planted into the embryo at the moment of conception. Ancient blockages to perfect health will be formed at the same time as equally ancient tendencies to be artistic, musical or a brilliant scientist. Ideally all systems will be functioning and thriving at 100 per cent. But the likelihood is that things are far from perfect in one or another department, that the child will inherit this or that balance or imbalance and that over generations this deterioration of system efficiency will accelerate by about 20 per cent per generation.

Obviously I trust that none of my past patients feel ill served now that I've revised some of my ideas and can dowse back to correct flaws inherited from the ancient past. I can only emphasise that help I was able to offer then was based on my open-minded quest regarding ways to improve my methods and that this latest finding is simply a continuation of that desire to keep on learning.

Because now I know better. I have recently realised that we are *not* bound for life by that conception hand of cards and that, to a large extent through a deeper understanding of the function of the thymus gland, we are not trapped within that direct genetic inheritance. This is truly a breakthrough of enormously exciting dimensions and with the help of the distinguished teacher of physiology and anatomy, Gillian Lim, I have reached a better and more optimistic understanding of *homeostasis.*

Gillian teaches at one of London's best new universities, in Kingston, just south west of central London. With her help I have now realised that even if the birth or conception levels of strength of the parents cannot be changed or improved upon for the newborn, enlightened science and dowsing can break through this barrier in later life. You don't have to settle for the lowered homeostatic levels that your parents bestowed upon you. And I don't seek to muddle or confuse any patients with daft ideas about the search for physical perfection. Leave that to the quacks, I say, although I hate to see them prosper at the expense of people often already sick with worry.

Case study... Case study... Case study... Case study...
Three-year-old JT was diagnosed as having cerebral palsy and her parents were informed that their daughter had no hope of a long or normal life. She couldn't speak or walk. She couldn't even hold her head up, such were her muscular

problems. There was an absence of correct DNA and RNA from the moment of conception.

Her mother takes over the story: 'After doctors here had all but written her off we took her to the States where some specialists identified E. coli stomach bacteria in addition to everything else and recommended surgery. We were about to arrange this back in England, with some reluctance, when we took her to see Jack.

'We were sceptical at first but then he cleared the stomach disorder through dowsing and his tablets, so our daughter did not have to endure surgery. The E. coli had been inherited from residue of medicines I had to take for a heart condition as a child, and he cleared that. Doctors at the hospital where she was due to have the operation were astonished when they saw how the condition had vanished. Then he set about the cerebral palsy. Our daughter – who had been consigned to life as a vegetable – now talks and crawls. She's obviously longing to walk, as she loves it when we hold her up. She's so lively and has now been admitted into a mainstream nursery school, so she socialises with other children. When we hold out a book she reaches for it, so we hope that reading will be next.

'I felt that we only had half a child, much as we loved her, but that now the other half is being reclaimed. Jack's brilliant. She always had terrible frustrated rages but she's much calmer now and when she does express frustration it's just because she's impatient and longing to reach the next stage. We go to Surrey from Sheffield every month and every month my daughter's mental and physical progress is measurable.'

As I've noted, the key to my new understanding resides in a little fellow called the thymus gland. It really is our controlling influence and if this small gland is in good health the quality of both our physical and spiritual lives will be in optimum harmony. Every other system is placed out of kilter if it isn't functioning properly. I now know how to correct a faulty thymus with the aid of the healing power of the Crypto Word.

What this means in practical terms is that all our other glands and the entire endocrine system itself, which directs the health of our hormones, emotions and many physical functions, are dependent on a healthy thymus. Our energy, reproductive kit, skin, hair, looks in general, mood, digestion and practically everything else will do as the thymus tells them. This gland conducts a whole orchestra of other vital physical instruments, registering any fault in our immune system and having a profound effect on the way we can call up energies from our past lives. For it is within our thymus that our soul resides and although it physically shrivels at the point of death, its power and energy never rests.

It's important to understand the difference between past lives and reincarnations: Reincarnations form the magnetic aura around our bodies and a fault here will create 'ghost' malfunction in our physical bodies. Past lives, by contrast, relate personally and directly with our spirit and soul. These will return time and time again and reside in the thymus. (See Chapter Five on auras and 'ghost illness'.) If the previous owner had a diseased body, then disharmony will occur in the thymus of the new owner of the spirit/soul. To get to the heart of this work, so to speak, I address my client's thymus and by this means I have been able to arrest all manner of disorders which previously defeated me with some patients – from all things glandular to PMT, persistent headaches, certain back problems and depressions.

We've already touched upon the physical resemblances which can pass down the generations. Few of us have a problem in accepting those genetic influences: indeed, we often welcome and embrace them. I'm still not quite sure why many people find it harder to accept that psychological and illness-related disorders should not similarly be our inheritances. Is it not marvellous news that by dowsing it's possible to trace back through four or five, ten or eleven and more genetic legacies, correct faults in order to cleanse and strengthen the current physical body and soul?

Think of it as a left-luggage locker in some ancient railway station: decades – perhaps centuries – ago some forebear had some heavy baggage which they stowed away and forgot about as they continued their journey. The baggage remained, unclaimed, and possibly becoming heavier. Now a descendant still carries it, without quite understanding bleak moods or tendencies towards a range of physical disorders. Within dowsing lies the key to that old locker, and the chance to banish all the old demons.

For people skilled in dowsing, the practical thing to do is to dowse for the correct verse of the Crypto Word, set a glass of purified water on the verse and drink the water twice a day. This immediately increases energy in the thymus and thus in the entire glandular system. (Please refer to Chapter Six on stem cells for further detail, as our stem cells, chromosomes and genetic legacies are all so closely linked.) I know this sounds complex, but let me reassure you by saying that of all the thousands of verses in the Hebrew Word, there are a mere forty-six to be dowsed for and they will have healing messages for each of us.

Already I have scores of patients showing visible signs of improvement since I addressed their thymus and I've come to see how the spirit force in that little gland can control so much and can be brought into service as a short cut to the improvements achieved by so many of my earlier remedies.

It's so obvious that we should try to model ourselves on the strong – and we can all access this old inner strength. Remember that you wouldn't be reading this today if you weren't the result of generations of strong genes, survivors. Isn't that a comforting – even inspiring – thought?

As ever, I conducted experiments on myself before I had the confidence to apply this new therapy to patients. I dowsed down through eleven generations of my own to find where my greatest spirit force resided and now I know that this power will see me through for another sixty years or more. There are younger souls in transit and much older ones. Sometimes it's a matter of centuries (never less than two hundred years) and sometimes the soul may be three or four or more thousand years old. You may have heard that expression 'he/she is an old soul', casually used to describe a young person who somehow emanates something very far from youth – as usual, popular idiom is rooted in some instinctive truth. So, by analysing when the thymus of a particular forebear died I can return the present body – and perhaps spirit – to optimum potential health.

Case study... Case study... Case study... Case study...
Do you remember what they always say about working in a sweet shop – that being surrounded by all the erstwhile tempting goodies quite puts you off them, especially if the wise shopkeeper has advocated a 'help yourself' policy? Well, maybe it was a bit like that for KD, who has worked at my clinic for five years and remains a stalwart of my staff. But it was only fairly recently that she decided to see if I could help her. KD, who was then sixty, I soon realised, had a thymus in need of care and attention.

'I came to England from Germany in 1961. Maybe it was something to do with change in climate but that's when my arthritis began, and I had a couple of falls, as well, which caused wrist and foot fractures. Eventually my GP put me on HRT (Hormone Replacement Therapy) and I'd been taking it for fourteen years before consulting Jack. I'd got kind of used to it but really, I knew I shouldn't have these bumps and lumps on my breasts. They kept an eye on me and I was assured that there was no real problem, but the cysts didn't go away. I also had the poor sleep, hot flushes and other symptoms that HRT is supposed to spare one. My doctor advised me to carry on with it but as soon as I saw Jack he said I should stop taking it.

'I soon realised that the HRT had simply been masking my arthritic pain, because it came back as soon as I stopped taking it but Jack has dealt with that and with the flushes and so on as well. One aspect that worried me a lot was my osteoporosis, which HRT is supposed to manage. I have a genetic history of this condition and because of the fractures and fear of more breakages I'd become wary about walking around outside when its slippery or frosty in case I took another fall. Thus one is denied the simple pleasure of a winter walk outside and you even become worried about a simple stumble indoors. My hip was also giving me some worries and I had pains in my hands, feet and shoulders despite taking lots of calcium. Swollen legs, too. It was like having toothache in several different parts of my body at once. The stress of all this was also, of course, in itself depressing and debilitating.

'So I did the obvious thing, at last, and asked Jack to have a look. After he'd identified my thymus trouble there really wasn't much to the treatment. It was kidney trouble that had caused the swollen legs and this problem – along with the rest – seemed to disappear as soon as I started drinking the charged-up water and taking lots of Vitamin E and the food enhancing drops on my food. After dowsing down through about ten past lives he's fixed my homeostasis levels, most of the pain and feelings of weakness have gone and I've stopped taking HRT. I really do feel well again these days – so much stronger both physically and mentally'.

Then it's time for me to look briefly at the patient's aura – and this shouldn't seem too odd since even the most cynical will usually accept that a person can exude an aura of power or sex-appeal or calm or negativity or gloom. A clouded aura or one still heavy with ancient disease must be cleaned up. By dowsing the aura I can discover how far back I need to search. Some old wounds or diseases loiter for as much as fifty or sixty thousand years

I don't offer to begin genetic corrective remedies until I have managed to restore my patient to the level of homeostasis they had at birth or conception. After that we can see how far back we want or need to investigate. The essential balance must be restored before further work can begin, however. People born with a lucky handful of cards – or strong genes – may need no further therapy. But with most people, once I have identified the body part or system that needs priority treatment, I can begin healing right away and will finish my work as soon as the patient is restored to their optimum possible strength.

But it's important to remember that even if someone is restored to 100 per cent of the strength they were born with in any one of the body systems, that does not necessarily mean perfect health as that 100 per cent will only reflect the best that an immediate forebear can offer and there may well be plenty of room for improvement if the forebear's system was only functioning, for instance, on 60 per cent of optimum power. The worse case I ever saw was that of someone who was struggling to manage on a mere 1 per cent of potential strength – all that parents had been able to donate.

Case study... Case study... Case study... Case study...
There were many reasons why RS should feel stressed and unwell. In particular, she had dealt with first the decline and then the death of both her parents and had all the horrible practicalities to cope with afterwards.

'I felt so ill. I could barely climb four stairs without feeling worn out. My GP and all the many Harley Street specialists I consulted put this down to emotional exhaustion but I knew there had to be something more. I do consider myself to be sympathetic to and in touch with subconscious forces, so when the word "poison" kept crossing my mind, I took it seriously. When I first saw Jack he immediately said that I was being poisoned and identified the cause as being the essential oils I put in my bath water.

'This did strike me as being a sad irony, since the only rest and relaxation I seemed to have had for ages were regular deep soaks in lovely warm baths infused with these supposedly beneficial unguents.

'Anyway, I gave them up and came back to life. I'd been putting on weight through comfort eating coupled with the fact that these bathtime poisons were preventing me from absorbing proper nutrients in the right way. All that has now normalised and I feel like a different person.

'Once when I was at the clinic I'd left my poor ailing old dog in the car. He didn't have much of a life left and with his severe digestive problems more than one vet had said that his time was up. As you can imagine, after the trauma of my parents' deaths this was the last thing I wanted to cope with. I just mentioned it in passing to Jack. No animals except guide dogs are allowed in the clinic but Jack suggested I went outside and held up my dog so that he could dowse him through the window. He immediately deduced that the old fellow had lived in an old building and had been poisoned by lead, probably in the water pipes. Spot on. Anyway, he gave me some drops to add to his food and suggested a calcium supplement as well. My dear old dog's condition cannot be reversed, he is fifteen years old, after all, but whereas before he seemed close to death he is now as perky and contented as any dog could hope to be, despite failing eyesight and hearing.

'As for me, I will always return to Jack whenever I need an MOT and have actually been inspired to become a dowser myself. An added bonus is that, at fifty, I feel better and know I look better, than I have in years'

I can measure the entirety of physical health and correct it. I recommend that patients return every six months or so for a topping up of the restored strength but this isn't always essential. When patients come back for follow-up treatment I will dowse to find how many ancestors I need to go back to find the one whose health was perfect in one respect or another and then dowse for a 'shape' which fits the person. It could be circular, oval or rectangular: my pendulum will guide me. It's hard to explain why these shapes matter but I know them to be an essential part of the new healing process and hold the shape in my head as I take written notes. Having identified the correct shape I dowse for the matching chapter and verse which contain the prime number appropriate for the patient and the mantra relating to their forebear. The Crypto Word, after all, is closely linked to the equally ancient science or art of numerology.

Bottles of pure, unadulterated pills may now be charged up, along with two natural plant substances – these will vary from person to person and might be readily available in my laboratory stores or might have to be freshly dowsed for – and the formula is complete.

I have basic natural remedies which can deal with hundreds of disorders, from respiratory to renal. It is the addition of genetically empowered matter which makes the remedy specific for individual patients.

Right at the beginning, as I approach this healing, I need to learn about both the male and female lines which have, over a long time, fed into and influenced the genetic make up of my patient today. So first, over a few sessions taking a matter of weeks, I question and dowse the left-hand side of every aspect of a patient's body to learn about the male history and then I turn to the right to discover their female genetic history. Don't ask me why this has to be the sequence, but I have learned by trial and error that the male side must be dowsed first.

An interestingly beneficial consequence, or side-effect, of this has been to see how as the first side of the body is dowsed and correct genetic balance restored as blockages are removed, it becomes noticeably more healthy-looking, pliable and youthful. I am always my own guinea pig and have seen how the skin on one side my face and the back of one of my hands became softer, more flexible and less lined than the other. Even the eye on the 'male' side of my face seemed to become enlarged back to a more youthful size as bags and wrinkles lessened and the delicate muscle tone there was restored. Enlarged veins on my left leg have vanished, leaving the skin pale and clear – in marked contrast to the knotty, darker appearance of the other leg. The 'female' side catches up, of course, when treatment is completed. Now I have twenty or more patients who report the diminishment or vanishing of bags under their eyes or of a slack jawline on one side of their face and can't wait for the other side to match this seemingly miraculous regeneration.

I must reiterate that my work is pitched towards health, not beauty, but surely this is a valuable aspect of the treatments even though they are devised primarily to address a health disorder. We all know that when we *look* well, look our best, possibly even knowing that we appear younger, this is likely to increase psychological health and self-esteem in a way that might not be easily measurable but which certainly exists. For the appearance aspects, treatments may have to be boosted every six months or so – although the internal health balance will have been permanently restored. But with no knives, drugs, anaesthetics or other trauma (including the massive trauma of receiving a plastic surgeon's bill), this seems to me to be a much gentler and saner way of making the most of whatever physical attractiveness nature was kind enough to bestow.

Case study... Case study... Case study... Case study...
HM, now forty-eight, spent twenty-five years in Africa where, by his own admission, he abused his body with excesses of alcohol and drugs like LSD. He'd also picked up a recurring virus, with rather malaria-like symptoms, that even the Hospital for Tropical Medicine in London was unable to stem. By dowsing I learned that he is a relatively 'young' man, with only ten previous lives. Over the past year or so I've been working to correct faults that he's inherited from two of them, but many of his problems derived from invasive substances and medicines taken within his own lifetime. As HM says:

'I'm a committed Buddhist, quite in tune with ideas of mind, body and spirit interacting, and I've had a long-standing interest in holistic and homeopathic medicine. But

I'm also something of a cynic and I won't just swallow alternative therapies wholesale: they have to work. When I first saw Jack the lingering effects of my years in Africa were still troubling me. Sometimes my skin would break in eruptions the size of side-plates and I could actually see threads of poison flowing out from them, below the skin. I had terrible fevers too. Nothing seemed to help until I started seeing Jack.

'I was always tired – not the sort of weariness you expect after hard physical exertion or even mental effort – and as a law costs draftsman who sits in front of two screens all day, I know something about how exhausting mental concentration can be. No, this was a vague but deep and very debilitating fatigue, all the more worrying because I couldn't understand the cause. I also had such pains in my feet that I shuffled about like an old man.

'Jack dowsed for what might have been inherited causes and treated me accordingly with his taped-on tablets. The malaria-like symptoms have certainly lifted since then. He thought my foot and fatigue problems could connect to Septrin taken in the past ten years and he was spot on. Apparently there was some blockage in my lymph drainage system and this has now been fixed. As for my feet – he wrapped one end of a longish silver chain round my feet, one foot at a time, and curled the other end of the chain around some little phials of poison. Almost instantly the pain in my feet vanished, as if called back into the poisons from whence they had come. I won't say this total relief was absolutely permanent, but what I have now is a kind of dull memory of pain rather than the pain itself.

'I was also troubled by bladder and prostrate problems. For these Jack asked me to sip water from a glass which had been charged by resting it on a sort of mandala, copied onto paper. Within five minutes pain in these areas was gone. This, obviously, is something I can do at home, especially as it has helped to control the inexplicable mood swings I often suffered. I gather that this is part of the procedure for cleansing my body of fault lines inherited from previous existences.

'Frankly I'm bemused by all this and don't begin to grasp quite what Jack does. But it works for me so I'm hardly going to argue.'

HM is not unique in his cheerful bafflement: I can't always offer explanations as scientific as some of my patients – and the occasional sceptic or critic – would like. I adhere to Hamlet's dictum that 'there are more things in heaven and earth' than we can necessarily hope or expect to understand. Some mysteries are better left that way if you have trust and faith in their benign powers, as I do.

Science cannot explain love, fear, despair or joy. Why should we expect it to explain every aspect of healing?

CHAPTER FOUR

On Homeostasis

The word *homeostasis* may be fairly new to me, but the term has long been used in orthodox medical circles and simply means 'balance'. I've learned so much about it, about how it mirrors my own methods and how those methods can marry with the work conducted in medical schools from Gillian Lim, Senior Lecturer in Applied Biological Sciences at Kingston University.

Our working together came about when four years ago I contacted her university to see if any teacher there was interested teaching the students I am training to become dowser-healers about medical anatomy and physiology. Gillian agreed to give the idea a chance and has now become pivotal in my seminars relating to dowser healing. (There's more about all this in Chapter Eleven, where Gillian will speak for herself.) My work with her exemplifies how sometimes my work can bridge and dovetail with the latest researches in orthodox medicine and the way it is taught. Homeostatis is concerned with the way good, healthy genes can be knocked-out, or masked, by blockages and how it is possible to remove those impediments which interfere with the restoration of optimum genetic health. Here is what Gillian has to say about it:

Homeostasis concerns equilibrium and balance.
I was interested to see that Jack never promises a
cure as such but works towards enabling the body to
heal itself. My university is very open to the study of

*fields of complementary health and its not
impossible to imagine that one day classes in
dowsing will be offered there, just as reflexology and
aromatherapy are taught. At the moment I try to
give Jack's students a solid grounding in anatomy
and physiology, for without a clear understanding of
how the internal systems of the body work, dowsing
may be less effective.*

*It may be a while before dowsing becomes a part
of the general education of medical students and
therapists – but that time might well come. In the
meantime it's instructive for me to work with these
student dowser-healers. We can learn from each other.*

For some time I have been able to tell patients that via
dowsing I can return many a physical and mental function to
the prime state it was in at the time of their conception – thus
removing damage that may have been sustained in any
number of ways since then, particularly through well-
intentioned vaccinations, non-organic diet and the unthinking
use of chemically devised household items. But even at
conception things may not have been perfect in every respect
and understanding homeostasis has helped me to see how I
can dowse back through the generations to correct genetically
inherited disorders, having first divined to see how strong
each system was when the patient was conceived.

Furthermore, my work used to centre upon remedies
derived from the DNA of trees and other plant material. This
is still very important, but with homeostasis I can be much
more efficient and tailor my remedy more precisely for the
individual, wherever in the world they may be, whereas my
earlier methods were more geographically restricted.

I just keep asking the pendulum to give me a 'yes' swing
when I ask it how many generations I need to research back.
Two... five... fifteen... thirty? And so on.

I have learned when to stop, when I know that there is no need to dowse further back or point in doing so. As I have said before, perfection is a subjective concept and not always, ironically, an attractive one. If we were all 'perfect' the wealth and breadth of human diversity and the achievement it brings would be diminished. We'd all be much the same and fewer physical or intellectual challenges would exist. I simply aim for a realistic balance wherein all the systems work in harmony and some systems will inevitably play a slightly stronger tune than others and I believe it would be fairly pointless as well as time-consuming to keep dowsing for total, elusive perfection. It would be irresponsible to lead people on. Until recently it was impossible to cheat the odds you were born with or improve on them dramatically. Now it is. In the homeostasis I might see a deficiency of zinc, calcium or hydrogen – all of which could lead to serious disorder in later life. I must address each deficiency separately, dowsing back as far as it takes.

Even if a young patient's homeostasis could be brought to reach 100 per cent, I never apply this sort of healing to anyone under eighteen years of age, especially if there are obvious birth 'defects' present, because development of any genetic inheritance may well continue into early adulthood. I know when to start, as well as when to stop.

I need to find each adult patient's prime number and, consulting the old numerology, I dowse for this in the usual 'yes' or 'no' way. The numbers are unique to the patient but will always finish with a 1, 3, 7 or 9, and are thus unique to the forebear with healthy genes whom I will have already dowsed for and I will have noted their personal gene number. It's important for patients to realise that whilst the actual words contained within the Crypto Power of the Hebrew Word may well speak to them with a significant personal message, so far as I am concerned it is the numerology of the dowsed-for verse that enables me to heal.

I hope you will take it on trust that the science of numerology is central to my work. I *know* it to be relevant, but so complex a science cannot be explained in a few sentences. There are many books to refer to if you'd like to learn more. Suffice to say here that each Hebrew word has an allocated number and the total sum of all the individual's numbers is the one which contains the power.

The sentence which corresponds to the prime number I have sought will be dowsed so that I can ascertain how many times the mantra or verse needs to be xeroxed and then rested in a low stack beneath phials of plain, untreated tablets which will then be charged with energy. Absolute precision is required here: recently I attempted to help someone in this way without realising that a single sheet had become lodged in my photo-copier. No healing vibrations were observable until I realised my mistake and added the missing sheet to the little pile of mantra copies. Then the power immediately infused the tablets I had prepared for that patient.

I use pure, unadulterated sugar tablets, prepared for me by Dr Nero Sahab whom I have worked with and trusted for about twenty-five years. These days I use only tablets made from crystals derived from organically grown cane sugar. These vehicles of healing energy are far more expensive than tablets derived from milk or beet sugar but hold the energy indefinitely and carry none of the risks of transferred pesticides. Once applied with the trusty transparent but sturdy microtape to the correct body meridians the healing power hits the correct spot at once – be that bone, tissue or organ.

I'm sometimes amused when I read or hear about the power of those patches that people place on their skin as they try to kick a nicotine habit. Good luck to them and I have real respect for this method of conquering an addiction. It's just that I was so soundly derided, until recently, when I maintained that good health can often be more effectively achieved by putting healing substances into the body via the skin's energy points rather than orally.

So, to summarise how I set about things in the first place:

- I find the prime number applicable to each patient by dowsing the Crypto Power of the Hebrew Word.
- The matched energy contained within the ancient text is transferred into tablets made from pure sugar and sometimes into subsequent homeopathic supplements.
- Healing cosmic energy is absorbed as a consequence.

I should mention here that if you are travelling, on holiday or business, it is wise to keep any homeopathic remedies in your hold baggage, rather than taking them with you into the passenger area of the plane, strange as this may seem. Or you could pack them in layers of bubble-wrap. Whether these medicines have been personally prescribed or simply bought from a health food store, they are likely to be damaged by the process of going through that screen they employ at airports now to make sure that you're not a gun-runner or other explosive expert.

At Heathrow once I had an absurd experience that only seems faintly amusing in retrospect – at the time it was infuriating. A uniformed official insisted that I put my tablets through the electronic screen and I refused. Things became quite heated and I was eventually able to demonstrate to her by dowsing that the tablets which *had* passed through the machine were damaged. The same principle applies to bar-coding in chemists or supermarkets: that seemingly innocent and simple X-ray can destroy most of the healing in the packet or bottle, so do try and see if you can pay for those goods without having them 'swiped'. It would be wasteful and perhaps tragic as the healing power is always swiped away.

If we accept 100 percent to be the perfect potential optimum functioning strength of each of our physical and emotional systems and yet are conceived with any one of these systems struggling at 90, 70, 50, 30 per cent or even less, it will take a little time and some patience to restore each system to a realistic maximum power, even with the aid of dowsing. The separate sympathetic systems, as defined by the chakras, need to be addressed individually and they don't always work on an identical time scale.

Firstly I need to ascertain exactly which elements are missing and then dowse for the genome number to discover the time when that particular aspect of the system was in perfect working order. As always I ask a series of questions which will elicit a 'yes' or 'no' from the pendulum. My intuitive subconscious now comes into the equation as the vibrations are measured and logged by the pendulum. Is the problem located above or below the chest? The knee? Which knee: right or left? Do I already have a remedy for this? If not, is one accessible to me? And so it goes on. However with my new knowledge of the Crypto Power of the Hebrew Word I can now tap a new source of healing without the need to travel.

The merest twitch of the pendulum could open a door to centuries of new and, for me, undiscovered knowledge. In all I could ask the pendulum to give me fifteen answers in as many seconds and yet the patient may only be aware of a very brief, painless and calm (I hope) examination. In a way my dowsing and the information I derive from it is a kind of Morse code. Quick little flashes of data are registered in a language I happen to understand but I don't expect they'd make any more sense to an outside observer than Hungarian or some cryptic World War Two coded mystery. Anyway, I write notes as I go on or immediately afterwards. Although one of *my* genetic rewards has been an excellent memory, I prefer to keep meticulous written records for each patient.

If I have an appropriate remedy in my laboratory stores that patient is in luck and I can devise treatment for them at once. If, however, I need to search for a particular plant or mineral it may take a little longer. Some searches are fast and short, others take more planning – such as the incredibly useful journey I made to Argentina early in 2001 because I was directed there for a plant search. Before I went I had no idea what I would be looking for or what I would find. But I had been directed there by the pendulum as it hung over my atlas and I knew where to go and what to do. That resultant remedy will prove to be of crucial use to countless future patients, I know. Whilst in Argentina I was asked to give a number of talks about my work so – who knows – perhaps the healing message is spreading faster and farther than I could ever have dreamed.

I should also add that new and exciting though I believe these advances in my work to be, they absolutely complement the trusted foundations that continue to form the cornerstones of my practice. I will stress again that no one who sought help at the clinic before I began developing these new techniques need fear that remedies offered to them in the past have been rendered inadequate now. Indeed, I'm still using many of the constantly rechargeable healing tinctures I first created years ago. But it is the nature of any vibrant research to seek to move onwards. After all, patients I treated ten years ago were the beneficiaries of whatever was newly learned then.

Sadly, there's always a danger in any science or other field of endeavour that others operating in the same field will mock or sneer if they feel either insecure or overly competitive – usually one and the same in my experience. I feel very strongly that scientific, and particularly medical, knowledge should be shared, crossing boundaries and barriers of discipline, nation and commerce, and it truly worries me that people working, striving, to achieve identical ends in the field of health should feel compelled to dismiss the work of others who may simply be searching for the same target via a different route. The case of my friend Sylvia Caplin, who you will meet several times in these pages, presents a remarkably graceful but sadly rare example of how collaboration between apparently conflicting disciplines can work in harmony.

Having virtually accepted, with some reluctance and dread, that surgery was necessary to remove her colon, Sylvia consulted me beforehand and I did what I could to help. Soon afterwards Paul Toomey, her Consultant Colarectal Surgeon at the Ashstead Hospital had the courage and decency to write to her:

> *I was amazed to see the complete resolution of your pneumatosis. Please pass on my congratulations to Jack Temple and anyone else concerned with this remarkable resolution... I do not think the diagnosis is in doubt.*

I would refer some of those doubters to the way that even in clinically 'ordered' societies, such as those in modern Germany and Austria, some of the ideas I espouse are accepted and granted proper respect. For instance, I understand that it is part of the legal building regulations, as we would describe them in Britain, for the surveyor to check to see that the house or office being sold or planned is not built on a line of negative energy. In Austria dowsing is routinely used to deflect negative vibrations caused by the voltages from high-speed trains. In the former Soviet Union studies were made to see if by dowsing mind-reading could be drawn into the business of international espionage – but perhaps that's another story.

The fact that in industry, politics and commerce dowsers are discreetly employed to comment and advise upon whether or not oil exists in a certain field, where exactly a vital dam in the Third World may be leaking or where a 'lost' ship may be located on the sea-bed should all indicate that the skill and value of dowsers is recognised in all sorts of fields beyond the strictly medicinal. There are about 1500 members of the British Society of Dowsers – many of them involved with healing. There are undoubtedly thousands more who are harmless hobbyists, hoping to find something interesting or even valuable as they walk the dog along the beach or the Downs with a dowsing rod at weekends.

I'm well aware that sometimes too much information can confuse rather than clarify, so let me simply say at this stage that a study of the homeostatic mechanism for each patient will involve a search for the need for light, the demands for correct body temperature and the correct individual balance of chemicals and minerals which will bring about the efficient functioning of the vital glandular networks. The blood, once restored, will feed positively into every cell and re-empower each of them, whether it affects the bones, the skin, the brain or, vitally, the heart. The immune system, also, can often need correction and a counter-attack on the aggressive white blood cells which can cause anaemia as well as a range of emotional problems.

Fear of flying, claustrophobia, problems with hostile neighbours, insomnia and marital difficulties are just a few of the emotional troubles that homeostasis can address. And if the problem is strictly physical, like high blood pressure, I will attempt to correct a strontium deficiency or, if the problem is rooted in cholesterol, restore balance of the B vitamin inositol. Someone suffering from multiple sclerosis will probably have a magnesium blockage which can be corrected with applied erbium or neodymium. Skin problems often respond to boosts of sulphur, zinc and vitamin C.

Case study... Case study... Case study... Case study...
AN is seventy-four now but looks younger than she did when she first came to see me some years ago with a portfolio of niggling worries which had built into a very heavy case. Her daughter, who had been to see me earlier, with a gynaecological disorder had urged her to give the clinic a try. I found that all the troubles, from shoulder pain to eye irritation, stemmed from the poisoning caused by

blockages brought about by medicines which, from childhood, had inhibited her natural homeostasis levels. After dowsing AN I taped some tablets around her knees to extract the toxins and advised her to fast one day a week whilst 'feeding' her stomach meridian line with a paste made from Forceval dietary supplement. Her genetic strength is now at least as good as that with which she was born.

AN recalls with good humour how she had a slight moment of embarrassment when the bandages sagged around her ankles at her local supermarket. 'But this was nothing. I had thought I had some ordinary allergy and had no idea how complex the real problems were. All the muscular problems were connected to RNA and DNA genetic histories which Jack dowsed for and cleared. He fixed things and I wouldn't go anywhere else. I feel better and I know I look better – and younger.'

ONE DAY FAST

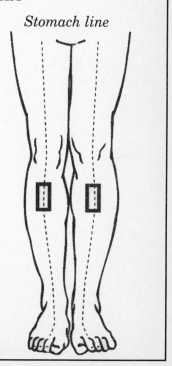

Stomach line

1. *Drink spring water charged on sheet 74 all day.*

2. *Mix the whole packet of Forceval-Protein into a paste.*

3. *Divide equally into two and use muslin to make a poultice.*

4. *Place anywhere on the stomach line on each leg.*

5. *Hold in place with a bandage or plaster.*

6. *Leave for five hours.*

So it was with a sense of triumph that I came to see that whereas in the past twenty-six years I had felt that I could confidently dowse back 'this far and no farther', homeostasis and the found prime number now enable me to seek far beyond the constraints of potential health flaws that may have been inherited at conception. I was sometimes frustrated by the fact that my earlier healing methods seemed effective up to a point but were somehow stifled, until I understood this new concept, going far beyond my earlier work.

It hasn't all been roses. I've had to deal with the fact that sometimes, whilst observing the rules of homeostasis, the strength of one aspect of a patient's system may diminish as another improves. That's why the process is relatively slow, so that each aspect of health is addressed and adjusted individually. I won't begin gene therapy until I'm pretty certain that the patient is as cleansed as they can possibly be of toxins acquired at conception, birth or more recently. After cleansing comes the homeostasis work and only then, if necessary, gene therapy which can search into the distant ancestral past for healing. The atoms which form us are the building blocks for good health, as are the neutrons and protons – all so strong but also prone to damage from drugs and toxins. Even a single lapse into eating some convenience food, an application of suntan lotion or wearing some man-made fibre can set you back.

We don't live in an ideal world and however well-intentioned my patients are, few of them are perfect. (Naturally I applaud the ones who are!) That's why the twice-yearly cleanse and toxin-fighting session is often advisable.

* * *

It's important at any time of life to be receptive to the new or refreshed, and not to cling exclusively onto old methods, however trusted they may have been. One must see existing knowledge as a springboard for the new and now that I know that I can dowse back many thousands of years to seek the root of genetic good health I don't waste my time or that of my patients by concentrating any longer than I need to on the biological conditions which pertained at the moment of their conception. This isn't to suggest that I've revised any of my firmly held principles concerning the damaging effects of chemicals, vaccines, artificial fibres or poorly cultivated foodstuffs and so forth. Observing my earlier suggestions can only help to retain the health and strength which working with homeostasis can provide.

My own family provides good evidence for my ideas about diet and vaccinations. None of my three kids was vaccinated for anything even though back then in the 1940s and 1950s inoculation was almost fashionable and parents like Blanche and I were criticised, if not reviled. None of the children suffered and are now all blooming in their late middle-age. All of *my* babies – children born after their often despairing parents consulted me at the clinic – thrive similarly. As for me – the notes taken at my local GP surgery over the past sixty years don't even amount to half a page. The pharmaceutical giants have made no money out of me. Just remember that disease cannot take hold in a cleansed and toxin-free body. Even dreaded illness like meningitis just don't stand a chance, let alone a raft of allergies and less worrying illnesses. It's as simple as that.

Horrible though it may be to contemplate, the fact is that disease actually feeds on certain medicines and antibiotics. It develops wily ways to cheat the chemicals and other agents in the drug. The disease seems to be winning so more and stronger medicine is prescribed. All the while there is a build-up of useless or even dangerous and undischarged drugs in the body. I think the wheel has turned and that just as it took fifty years in Britain for the experts to agree that some aspects of our education system were better in the old days, it now looks

like my long unfashionable ideas about diet and medication
are being taken seriously at last.

Having ascertained how many generations I need to dowse
back to find an unblemished record of a healthy forebear, I
then dowse for the correct prime number for that forebear to
feed into the patient. When I have found it – it is always
upwards of a million – I need to draw my diagrams around the
number. Upon this simple paper pile I place four phials of my
untreated tablets and by trial and error dowse to find which
two elements of plant matter are needed next. It is *always* two.
They could already be here in my laboratory – nettle, plantain,
bark or comfrey – but if I do not have them to hand I will
dowse again and be guided by the pendulum as to what I need
and where I must go to find it. Then, at last, all six little
bottles will be charged-up by a quick study of numerology and
the Crypto Word, the tablets are mixed together and healing
can really begin.

I used to attach tablets to the patient's body with
microtape so that the healing force could enter the body
through the skin, but now I twist the tape into a kind of rope
which is gently bound to the patient's ankle and kept there for
about ten hours. Ladies travelling on foot or by public
transport are advised to wear loose trousers or a long skirt if
they do not wish to attract curious glances as they make their
way home! Evidence of healing usually begins within two
weeks but many patients report some improvement in only a
matter of days. In any case, I prefer, if possible, to monitor
progress after a week or so, or when a quick appointment can
be slotted in. Almost always there is already evidence that the
new genetic strength is taking hold even if the superficial
evidence is no more and no less than a greatly improved
pliability and clarity of skin tone.

If I feel that I have reached the limits of what a particular
forebear can offer, I will dowse again and see if, after all, an
earlier ancestor can be called in for help. Sometimes my

results are gratifyingly fast but at other times the patient must wait a little longer. And here's another interesting and inspiring account from a patient:

> Case study... Case study... Case study... Case study...
> Just after her hysterectomy, at the age of forty-nine, TC began to find breathing painful and the left side of her body hurt, particularly the breast, which actually throbbed. She also suffered from debilitating mood swings. She had been placed on Hormone Replacement Therapy but was not happy with it. Apart from anything else it seemed to have caused weight gain.
>
> 'I was on HRT for two years and wanted to get off it. I tried homeopathy but was still prepared to wait for an appointment with Jack as I continued to feel dreadful. It took three months for the pains to lessen and I had to track down cotton bras – not easy – but well worth the trouble as I'm now feeling so much better and I'm overjoyed to be off HRT.'
>
> I dowsed and deduced that TC's problem resided in her spleen and her chakra was the second chakra, Capricornus. Hers was a relatively easy case to address but, as she has said, the results were hardly instantaneous. In the first place I taped some tablets to the front of her shoulders and asked her to stand over the appropriate chakra stone in my labyrinth for a few minutes. Her spleen gene had been damaged by bleach poisoning at the moment of her conception and later nylon poison that had lodged in her already weakened spleen. Extracting the residue of these poisons was a good start. I was also able to supply some tablets of my own devising as an alternative to TC's HRT. Altogether a good result: her condition had hardly been life-threatening but it had been life-diminishing and that can be chronically lowering to live with.

As I wrote in Chapter One, we all have chakras, those seven entry points for the possibility of a recovery like this, however slow, since they enable healers like me to access the sympathetic system that is there to be both tapped and fed into. And never forget that the 'food' the chakras need comes from the cosmos. That nourishment is *at least half* of what your body needs. (See Chapters Eight and Nine for more about the food you should choose to ensure maximum genetic and planetary power from what you eat.)

In the early weeks of treating a patient I will have asked myself whether, with my dowser, I have the ability to find a way for the makeup of flawed genes to be mimicked and replaced by healthy ones, including the gene P53, which is often associated with cancer. For a long time I have wanted to see if I could construct a kind of master-gene which would protect against all forms and strains of the disease.

I should make clear here that the gene-codings I apply to my work do not always conform to the labels applied by orthodox scientists and medical practitioners. But I have borrowed and developed their idea of identifying a specific gene and investigating its relevance, in the first place, for individual patients. I dowse for the numbers I need and these invariably connect to the numerology of the Crypto Power. The fact that often a basic finding has wide application to other patients only strengthens my belief that the work I am involved with today has universal potential. My work always begins with the careful examination of the needs of a particular patient, but patterns have and do emerge and these tend to confirm my basic precepts.

It's early days yet, but I can report that one patient whom I have treated with my own P53, obtained with the help of my dowser and the Crypto Power of the Hebrew Word, has tumours which have reduced in size in the six months she has been treated here. When they saw X-rays indicating a retreat of the illness, rather than the expected advance, her regular doctors were astonished – delighted, but astonished.

Another cancer patient, a young mother, came to me after her doctors said they could do nothing for her, except offer chemotherapy which would merely have prolonged her life for

a short time whilst severely reducing the quality of the time
she had left. They did not think surgery was an option, as her
cancer was already advancing aggressively. In the face of such
hopeless news, these doctors also evinced annoyance when she
and her husband said they might seek further opinions. And
so she came to me. After the initial consultation and the
creation of a P53 tincture, she came down to the labyrinth
several times a week and sat by the centre stone, where she
could absorb the energies of the number seven chakra, sirius.
(Do refer back to Chapter One, which deals with my labyrinth,
if you need a reminder of how these star energies work.)

Since I don't want to present myself as a miracle-worker it
is only fair to report, with regret, that this time my treatment
failed, despite a bright start. This patient had been dependant
on morphine to control her pain and my treatment is
incompatible with such drugs. After a while she could bear her
pain no longer and returned to morphine and chemotherapy
and I wish her well, literally. Who could blame someone
suffering like that for reaching for, resorting to, a pain-
numbing relief?

I do have my own equivalent of codeine – an everyday
painkiller for severe but not chronic pain, but it wasn't enough
to ease the suffering of this patient. In less dire circumstances
I suggest that for headache, toothache or other nasty but
temporary pain a plain cotton handkerchief should be dipped
in cold water, wrung out and laid flat on the appropriate body
part, covered with a warm towel, and that the handkerchief be
refreshed as often as necessary. The toxins causing the pain are
thus drawn out of the body. The patient should dowse to
ascertain the correct connecting body area for the compress – as
usual it may be far away from the painful area.

∗ ∗ ∗

I plan to re-create the genes which are associated with all common physical defects, especially life-threatening ones.

Every nutrient in the system – by which I mean essential vitamins, naturally produced chemicals and so forth – not absorbed food as such – has a protective gene. It is when this gene is damaged that viruses enter the system and the body's ability to absorb the nutrient is blocked. If, for instance, the gene I term Z67 is interfered with, the body cannot produce or utilise zinc and so the nerve-endings suffer. (I always label the genes in my own way – readers should understand that my terminology may not match that of the scientists.) When there is a problem with gene Q61 there will be a copper deficiency and kidney problems. Without a properly functioning gene P73 there will be an iodine blockage and thyroid troubles will follow. And so on...

Problems with the heart, the lungs, the bladder, the skin, the spine, the stomach and digestion, the bones – every part of your body – can be traced to a mineral or vitamin deficiency. This is not really news. What is new is the way I am now able to inhibit these shortages by allowing the body to produce its own defences naturally, all with the help of the hitherto unlocated protective gene. You'll see below a simplified table of what harm 'natural' shortages can do.

So, to emphasise, I now regard it as a priority to dowse and with numerology and the Crypto Power of the Hebrew Word find a way to deal with every single possible gene blockage so that the protector gene can do its vital work. This is far more effective and logical than attempting to deal with the virus attacking a damaged gene, as by the time a virus has taken hold it may be too late to save the full, healthy function of the gene.

How these blockages occur in the first place I really do not know. Often I believe them to be genetically inherited. In any case, a combination of the pendulum, the ancient text, the mantra and, *always,* those two herbs which I will have dowsed

Deprivation	Malfunction
Copper	Kidney
Iron	Liver
B12	Liver
Kali Mur	Stomach
Selenium	Heart
Thorium	Lungs
Potassium	Skeletal muscles
Sodium	Small intestines
Iodine	Thyroid
Erbium	Brain
Neodymium	Brain
Magnesium	Nerves
Samarium	Sexual organs
Nickel	Eyes

for form the basis for treatment every time. The Hebrew Word verse, of course, will contain the prime number essential to procedures. The logical development of this aspect of my healing work is to identify if a patient has inherited a self-destructive or otherwise flawed gene. This could cause programming, a sort of predestined tendency, to have addictions, ranging from nicotine to opiates, alcohol to antidepressants.

If I can break that cycle by cracking an ancient genetic code and removing the genetically flawed gene and then replacing it with a perfect mimic, I'll really have made a breakthrough. As I work and research the human body, time is on my side – its extraordinary, holistic genetic memory is there for me to study and learn from. Even in conventional medicine, if X-rays are taken of an amputee the shape of the missing limb will show up on the photographic plates, so powerful is the residual and remembered aura of the whole body. We have all heard of people who report aches and pains, tingles and itches in an amputated limb. Each cell somehow knows what and where its correct place in the total balance of the body should be and acknowledges the lost limb which now renders the whole incomplete. And you know by now that it is my mission to help to enable all of us to help ourselves to attain – not perfection, for that is folly – but completion, or the best that each of us can possibly be.

Crucial today to my work and my healing is this exciting and ongoing understanding of homeostasis – defining and divining the birth balance of any individual and basing my work – whether slow and steady or swift and satisfying – on that.

CHAPTER FIVE

Of Auras and Ghost Stories

I'm constantly challenged and excited by the new. It's not that I feel I need to keep abreast with every fresh, faddy development nor that when I embrace a new idea it means my earlier work is in any way rendered less valuable, but I like to keep my mind on the move. It's fatal – sometimes literally – for any healer to continue doing this *this way* or *that way* just out of a habit that might verge on complacency or laziness.

However only recently, at a seminar in Sussex, the enduring validity of some of my established methods and their ability to be enhanced by the use of my new methods was demonstrated.

At the seminar we showed how a person's aura could be captured by Kirlian photography – that technique which I described at some length in my first book. Everyone radiates energy – benign or troubled – and this form of photography, pioneered in Russia some decades ago, records the otherwise invisible magnetic human aura. In a controlled demonstration we showed that one particular person was radiating very weak energies. Then a clipping of her hair was placed in a tiny bottle of pure alcohol and crystals (from the batch which I had travelled to Tel Aviv to find), were arranged round the phial. Two hours later the 'guinea pig' was photographed again and it was astonishing to see how her energy levels had been restored.

What made this experiment unique was that the phial containing hair clippings and its surrounding crystals were placed upon a xeroxed representation of the Crypto Power of the Hebrew Word and strength was transmitted upwards from the Word. The verse chosen, or rather dowsed for, was of specific use for that particular body system. Each disorder will require a different verse and often these will vary from individual to individual. As the body is brought back to its optimum functioning state it will be enabled to heal itself.

Within any single person's aura there can be traces of no fewer than 140 previous incarnations, not our own but other lives. It remains both a challenge and a source of excitement to dowse through these genetic memories to find the moment in ancient history when a patient's aura reincarnation problem might have been spawned or, indeed, when the genes were clear and can be brought forward for healing today. Remember that if all your ancestors since, say, the Norman Conquest in 1066 were crowded into your living room (a generation generally being calculated at about thirty years), there would still be standing room for a good few more.

Many physical ills can be controlled or even cured by understanding and utilising the power of 'ghost images'. If the reincarnation suffered some accident the residual effects will be carried forward as 'ghost wounds'. Thus if the old injury was in the knee, the present carrier will always risk weakness there and by dowsing back working with a patient's aura, I can usually correct things for the patient and for future generations. I dealt with this aspect of healing at length in my first book, but it remains important today and I want to develop it with the extraordinary new methods which have been revealed to me.

We should never confuse the auras of other, past lives which enwrap and surround our bodies – sometimes protectively, sometimes not – and everything they tell us about inherited fragilities and disease, with matters of the spirit and soul. Certain emotional legacies – a tendency to be fearful, resentful, even violent – can cause an internal disharmony which causes our thymus gland to become out of kilter. When this happens the thymus will not produce enough of the T cells which protect the body against the effects of viruses and bacteria. As we now know, an agitated or dysfunctional thymus gland will also affect the endocrine system, the heart, the eye sight and the efficiency of the frontal lobes, all leading to endless treatments for separate ailments in conventional medicine.

It is most important that we should realise that our soul and spirit is housed in the thymus. The spirit contains the memory of each individual's past lives and it's sometimes part of my job to help rid the patient of trauma or bad baggage – emotional as well as spiritual, to the extent that the two can be separated – that should have been left behind many, many

CRYPTO POWER OF THE HEBREW WORD
TO RESTORE SOUL TO HARMONY

כָּרוֹת בָּתֵּינוּ אֲרָזִים רַהִיטֵנוּ בְּרוֹתִים:

Song of Solomon, Chapter 1, Verse 17

Place a china saucer over the circle. Place a covered glass of still water on the saucer. The water (not tap water) will become charged. Keep a glass of water permanently on this power circle, drink and replenish the glass as needed.

years ago. The thymus contains our soul and spirit and if a blameless life had been lead all will be in harmony for the next incarnation. But who leads such a life? There is usually some unresolved business of the soul to carry forward and correct. Again the Crypto Power of the Hebrew Word has helped me to deal with such problems. I reproduce here a chart which should help anyone who feels they may need to be rid of any such unwelcome legacies from past lives. This is all you need to do – remembering that fresh water restores a flagging thymus function:

Twice a day place a small glass, half-filled with fresh bottled (not tap or filtered) water on the circle illustrated. (Take a xerox if possible.) Leave it for about ten minutes to 'charge' then drink the water and after doing this daily for two months that old, destructive poison will have been flushed away.

Sometimes we may welcome communication from friendly, even loving, spirits. When someone dies their spirit or soul, located in the thymus, does not vanish. It will come to live in another being – not necessarily at once – and can often be reached. Gifted mediums, so often the butt of mockery and accusations of fraudulence, can indeed reach and communicate with the souls of the physically dead. Responsible mediums have brought comfort to surviving loved ones who often need to know that their lost child or friend is happy or calm wherever they are and are pleased to be contacted.

This is such a complex, still mysterious field that to offer much explanation is beyond the scope of this book, but obviously faith does come into things. I certainly believe that contact with the spirit world is possible and usually beneficial. I emphatically do *not* believe that anyone is punished in this life because of some unresolved transgression that some spiritual forbear has passed on. The very idea of amends for ancient 'sins' needing to be made in the here and now would be simply ridiculous if it wasn't also morally repellent.

Case study... Case study... Case study... Case study...
I have a very special patient, C, who lives in Wales. He's
been seeing me whenever possible for the past six years
although, as you can imagine, the round trip would be
stressful for any healthy person, let alone someone as shy
and troubled as he. C is in early middle-age now and life
has not been kind to him. He has recently given up even
part-time self-employment in order to concentrate on
recovering his health. C is so crippled by shyness that he is
virtually unable to interface socially – a tragedy, really,
since the support of friends can be so vital. I believe that all
this is rooted in the negative influence of other lives, and
between us we are slowly but steadily committed to finding
a balance which will allow C to enjoy a fulfilled life at last:

'I last went to see a general practitioner over twenty
years ago. I gave up hope for any help from that quarter
then. Now I regard Jack as a trusted friend – at least he
wouldn't have me sectioned as the others might. I do feel
we're making progress and I also accept that it will take
time after a lifetime of living in such a limited way. I know
he gets results – I feel better after every meeting with him.
It used to take me a week to recover from the emotional
exhaustion but it's getting faster.

'Jack think it relates to a BCG vaccination I had when I
was about thirteen. I think it also connects to bullying I
received when I was a youngster. Whatever – I try to help
myself between appointments. And Jack gives me hope.'

In Chapter Seven you will read the whole alarming story
about needless vaccinations, but it is worth mentioning here
that tuberculosis – against which the BCG vaccine was
devised – is approaching epidemic proportions in Britain, with
an 11 per cent increase in reported cases of TB in the year
since spring 2000. Inner cities, especially London and some in
the Midlands, like Leicester, are hit harder still. I'm afraid this
tends to support my view that the vaccine has not conquered
the disease and we must look elsewhere for prevention of this
killer.

We all are or should be surrounded, from the tops of our skulls to the tips of our toes with an invisible protective 'membrane', our aura. The celebrated writer H E Bates, author of *The Darling Buds of May,* amongst other classics, wrote in his memoirs of being considered lucky because he was a 'caul' baby. He was referring to the early-twentieth-century country mid-wife's conviction that a child born enclosed within this thin, tangible, web-like film was born lucky. Of course, it could easily be argued that Bates, who survived a Spitfire fighter's war and went on to become a writer of considerable renown was indeed lucky. But I hope you take my point: we all have a film or membrane, visible or invisible, which guards us. If I see that this membrane, the aura, has been punctured in any way, for whatever reason, I set about repair – as always by dowsing and, these days, with reference to the Hebrew Word.

On a lighter note, perhaps, the aura reincarnation also controls our need for what is now called 'personal space'. I've seen it often enough. A lack of energy, both physical and mental, caused by damage to the membrane can have immediate and damaging psychological effects. Just the 'simple' matter of feeling deprived of personal space and privacy, whether in a crowded bus or train, in the office or at home, can be caused by damage to the membrane which can be repaired if the individual's natural need for personal territory is restored. I now regard dowsing back to find the genetic point when the membrane was optimally protective and strong as a very important aspect of my work. Some aspects of emotional and physical harmony can be corrected if the patient's magnetic field is placed back in balance and I have found that a simple dowsing of the tops of their feet and some subsequent homeopathic tablets often helps enormously.

On the subject of personal space, a friend tells a story which connects to this. He was having an after-work drink in a pub near his office and left his briefcase by his feet near the curved bar. A colleague with no sensitivity to or understanding of the notion of personal space engaged him in conversation and he stepped back a little. She persisted, an unhappy woman with many grudges and general miseries, to air to a sympathetic and kindly ear. (I should stress that the woman was not a close, dear friend enduring some sort of temporary crisis but a 'professional' malcontent in search of a target for an account of a series of her regular woes.) By the time he wished to leave for home he'd been stepping back so often that his briefcase was many yards away at the other end of the bar.

This little anecdote tells us much about the power of the aura: his mostly benign, almost to the point of altruism, was actually weak in the face of an aura strengthened by bitterness and unresolved anger. Innocently collared, he had been exhausted by the force of his colleague's negative aura.

Maybe this sounds heartless, but we have a duty to ourselves and those who depend upon us to be self-protective. Once a child learns that their hand will hurt if they put it in scalding water they will somehow remember parental admonishments and never do so again. As adults we should avoid people and situations which damage or exhaust us and remember that the power of a negative aura can be invasive. Life, sadly, is too short to be saintly towards everyone and sometimes we must try and be brutal – to excise, when we can, potentially negative personal forces from our lives.

I am reminded of the advice of William Morris, the great nineteenth-century designer, writer and thinker. In the context of domestic space, he said something like 'keep nothing which you do not know to be useful or believe to be beautiful'. In the very broadest sense this dictum may well apply to personal relationships: don't clutter your life up with people who depress you. Not even the dearest friend can be a life-enhancing companion all the time – it would be rather tiring if they were – but at any rate, unless you actually are a saint, save your emotional strength for those who really matter.

✳ ✳ ✳

I see no reason not to suppose that birds and animals have souls just as humans do. Indeed, in some societies and civilisations, arguably more advanced than our own, animals and birds were or are sacred, and to return to life one day as the soul within one of these holy animals was as much as a mere human could aspire to or pray for. There is also the belief that a less than perfectly virtuous life on this earth could hold the threat of 'downward karma' and return, or reincarnation, as a much lesser creature. (And, believe me, this animal soul or intelligence goes far deeper than the 'he understands every word I say' assertions of some doting pet-owners.)

Animal spirits, just like human ones, need to rest between incarnations and what's partly wrong with animal husbandry today is that in many instances the tired or damaged spirit of a recently slaughtered beast is returning to reside within another before problems related to the onslaught of viruses, bacteria and an agitated thymus have had time to repair and restore. Certain modern farming and breeding methods more or less ensure that generations of sheep and cattle will be progressively weaker and prone to infection.

A lot of lip service is paid to the idea of animal rights and dignity. It's about time these issues were taken more seriously and perhaps this will only happen when human beings – who depend so much on animals – for their soap, shoes and warm clothes as well as their food – realise that this is simple, old-fashioned self-interest.

The carefully ordered archives of the Soil Association and the Biodynamic Organic Agriculture Group provide records of many farmers raising herds of disease-free cattle year after year, generation after generation without resorting to vaccines or antibiotics. But sadly these farmers have, to date, been largely ignored by governments and scientists who pay perhaps a little too much respect to the doctrines of Louis Pasteur, who grasped the nettle of immunisation, little realising that, taken too far, this could

have devastating and destructive consequences for both
animal and human society.

When early in 2001 Britain was in the ghastly grip of the
foot and mouth epidemic which affected cattle across the
land and soon spread to Ireland, Holland and Germany,
although no one knows where this wind-borne plague
actually originated, I was struck by how much a holistic
approach to the disaster could have ameliorated things:
governments should have woken up sooner to the fact that
the effects of the disease penetrated virtually every aspect of
society and commerce. This was strange because in the
sphere of business and stock markets it has long been
accepted that if New York sneezes London catches a cold.
Why wasn't it realised that if the agrarian economy of a
nation suffers *everything*, from the price of a lipstick to the
traffic in cities, is affected. Years ago the science fiction
writer Ray Bradbury advanced the idea that if a species of
butterfly in the Pacific Rim became extinct, it would cause
the industrial economies of the West to falter. The man had
broadly holistic ideas ahead of his time.

It is scandalous that Europe's innocent livestock have been
deprived for many years of much holistic veterinary science
and healing because it was decreed, in Britain at least, that no
one could practise holistically without first qualifying in the
conventional way. I'm not saying that this in itself was
misguided but I do suggest that these strictures could have
conspired to make many people feel that holistic healing only
really counted if the veterinarians had proved themselves
with a 'proper' training beforehand.

As in medicine for humans, veterinary research has been
based on the premise that illness is caused by bugs and
viruses which can only be staunched and stemmed by the use
of vaccines and antibiotics. But whilst humans have the
freedom of choice to bring children into the world without
breeding them for any specific purpose, farm animals have no

such luck, being reared for human consumption and to conform to economic demands rather than to have a pleasant existence, free to express themselves. One is reminded of some comedian's astute question: Would turkeys vote for Christmas?

But time will tell. I do remain optimistic that holistic methods – so fast and safe – can even now provide most of the answers we seek and need.

I do retain trust in the marvellous ways of healing I've developed over the years, but these are the building blocks and springboards – as ever – for something new. The new development which inspires me most at the time of writing and which we will consider in the next Chapter is the discovery of stem cells – or rather the new understanding of their importance.

CHAPTER SIX

The Stem Cell Revolution and Beating the Genetic Chromosome Blueprint

Stem cells are the 'mother cells' which control the activity of every other cell in the system and it is the study of them which most excites me as I write. Their existence has only recently been identified and their function as a kind of breeding ground for all other cells understood. We each have a mere eighteen sites where they are located, nine on each side of the body.

Stem cells are located above our ears, by the temporal lobes; in the middle of the upper arms; under the arms – the bra line for women; on the side of the thighs (mid femur); on the top, or dorsal, aspect, of the feet; on each side of both the umbilical area and the pubic bone. Two more reside at the base of the spine and a final pair under that little V-shaped recess at your throat, the manubrium bone – and that's it.

These few cells really are our masters, self-generating new stem cells or whatever new cells our body calls for, releasing blockages, enabling renewal and the smooth servicing of every physical and mental function. Thus it's obvious that there may be trouble ahead if blockages or faults occur in the stem cells themselves. I'm now committed to seeing how these vital cells can be kept in optimum health and order.

Stem cells form the basis of the body's blood and immune systems but can grow into other cells for any part of the human body – muscles, organs, nerves, skin or bone. Already research is underway to see if they can be used to replenish ageing skin tissue and thus prolong life and, presumably, youthful beauty.

Early in the summer of 2001 there was an explosion of controversy about the function and power of these stem cells. As with all medical advances, it just depends how wisely the science and the new knowledge is used. Thus, when concern, bordering upon outcry, was expressed about their use in the treatment of Parkinson's disease in the United States (where it had been thought that cells taken from aborted foetuses could replace the damaged brain cells which caused the characteristic Parkinson's symptoms of failing motor skills and intellectual function), I was not surprised, but my faith in the use and power of stem cells remained undiminished.

Incidentally, when this outcry took place – and leaving aside the dubious practice of utilising foetal matter – a number of Parkinson's sufferers went on record as saying that they would take any risk, take any medicine however untried it was if there was any hope of relief and release from the cage of their illness. I found this combination of bravery and folly rather humbling: who are those of us who do not suffer from any crippling disease to judge the choices of those who do?

A more constructive use of these cells may be that being developed at Bradford Royal Infirmary in Yorkshire where the idea of storing and freezing blood from a newborn's umbilical cord originated. The idea is that if, in later life, that child shows signs of developing a disease like diabetes or multiple sclerosis, stem cells from the stored umbilical blood can be used to repair damaged or mutating tissue. Dr Derek Tuffnell, a gynaecologist at the hospital, has said 'If a child or adolescent gets a disorder, for instance, leukaemia, their stem cells will give us the means to replenish their bodies with healthy blood

STEM CELLS – TOTAL OF 9 PAIRS

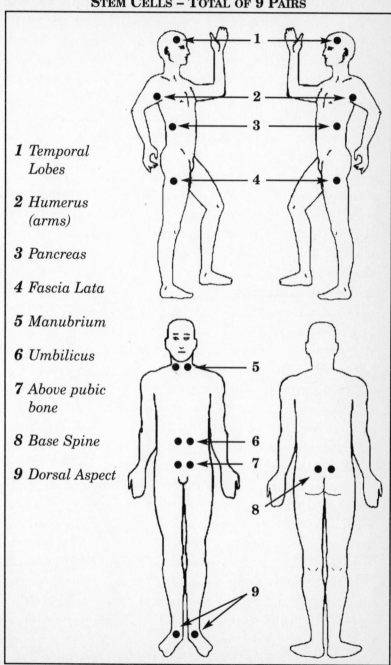

1 Temporal
Lobes

2 Humerus
(arms)

3 Pancreas

4 Fascia Lata

5 Manubrium

6 Umbilicus

7 Above pubic
bone

8 Base Spine

9 Dorsal Aspect

and save their lives. It might not be a cure for everything but it's likely to be a significant improvement over other options.' This particular option would only be helpful for sufferers up to the age of twenty, but at least it utilises the personal physical property of the individual concerned and does not involve a raid of some bank of anonymous foetal matter.

Even so, I'm not entirely in agreement with this because I believe that the healthy cells are already there, stored in a body bank and waiting to be withdrawn or released. But the fact that the principle is gaining such attention is interesting and you can see why I'm so enthusiastic about the responsible use of stem cells in the treatment of illness. And so it's vital that the mother cells themselves are kept in good repair, so that normal cell renewal can take place and effect healthy body maintenance. The importance of these cells is reflected not only in protection from life-threatening disease but in the management of everyday pain such as that caused by arthritis and rheumatism.

It was while I was in South America, early in 2001, that I was alerted to the potential healing power of our stem cells. The timing of this happened to coincide with the opening of a wide debate within the international scientific and medical establishment, but I am never surprised by such synchronicity: sometimes it seems as if there are invisible ideas or elements in the air waiting to be reached for by those with open eyes and minds at any particular moment. A clairvoyant woman advised me to study the area at the base of the spine and by dowsing someone else I was able to see that whilst a perfectly natural process of cell death and renewal was taking place with that patient, the 'powerhouse' of renewal was indeed located there at the lower back. Upon my return to England, and fired with enthusiasm, I quickly located all the other sites.

I also learned that the stem cells in the feet control our brain's natural dopamine. Dopamine is a hormone which influences mood and feelings of well-being. It has been chemically replicated in pharmaceuticals such as the drug L-Dopa, long used to treat Parkinson's disease amongst other conditions. When the natural supply of this hormone is restricted people often turn to the artificial highs of alcohol or cigarettes – or worse. It is even thought that the onset of Alzheimer's disease is caused by a deficiency in dopamine. There are scores of good reasons to respect your feet and take care of them. This recent finding suggests that, whilst we cannot address a deficiency here as easily as fungal infection or a fallen arch, we should never dismiss any pain or discomfort in the feet. A reflexologist can identify a place on the sole (rather than top, or dorsal aspect) of the foot which connects to every single organ or tissue elsewhere and this revelation about dopamine is in synch with that trusted form of healing.

A technique called metamorphic therapy was developed as a spin-off from reflexology as early as the 1960s and was originally intended to be of help to autistic children. Even now there are still few skilled practitioners but the benefits can be felt by anyone who is able to find one. The idea, very close to many of mine, is that the human life-force and energy is focussed and directed towards the release of emotional blockages. Like me, metamorphic therapists believe that from the moment of conception (or before, genetically), traumas are held within the memory of every cell and only when the negative memories are released can the patient realise their full potential. Gentle massage of the foot, hand and head releases the bad cell memories into the ether and allows benign ones to begin restorative work on the psyche. Many report an amazing upward curve of mood and attitude after such treatments and this can only aid physical recovery, as well.

I have found that clearing a blockage of the stems cells on the dorsal aspect of the feet enables the brain to trigger the resumption of its production of dopamine and of melatonin,

agreed by everyone, it seems, as essential for clarity of mind.
Commercially produced compounds of melatonin are available
over the counter in the USA as a defence against jet lag.

What may start as simple absent-mindedness – such as
frequently forgetting where you left the car keys or leaving a
room to fetch something and then, seconds later, not
remembering what it was – should never be dismissed as it
could signal the onset of Alzheimer's disease. But I have
actually observed sluggish brains coming back to life, memory
restored or at least improved by the simple use of herb-based
medicines which stimulate our body's natural supply of
dopamine. I have never been asked to dowse a patient in a
coma – surely the most extreme form of memory loss since the
person has no apparent sign of memory of self or of life or of
consciousness itself – but would be very happy to see if
dowsing can raise the dormant spirit and life-force back to
sentient responses. There's a clinic in Germany where doctors
claim a high rate of success in this field and I will watch their
work and results with interest.

Doctors George Foster and Bradley Stringer, researching
brain cell tissue at two British universities, believe that a
dopamine deficit is at the root of so many different disorders,
including Parkinson's and Huntington's chorea, that the use of
genetically modified dopamine-producing brain cells could
alleviate the suffering of thousands. Their work has been
welcomed by the Parkinson's Disease Society but I cannot help
worrying about the use of foetal matter in this research. We
cannot stem the tides of science, nor should we wish to, but I
hope that science can also discover more natural means of
relieving the symptoms of such diseases. I find the very idea of
this use of foetal matter as disturbing as the use of urine
taken from pregnant mares in the preparation of hormone
replacement therapy for menopausal women.

*On a practical note I have observed that when the stem
cells in the humourous area of the upper arm are cleared,*

patients with stiff, painful and arthritic fingers and other joints immediately become more flexible, mobile and pain-free. When the stem cells in the dorsal aspect of the feet is cleared, patients who had been depressed experience a lifting of mood at once.

I'm forever questing for and open to new ways of building on my work even if it might seem that earlier findings have been 'thrown away'. Actually no patient need worry that treatment they received a year or more ago was inferior – as my results will testify. It's just that I see my researches as a steady sequence of supporting building blocks. Where my research has taken me today will be seen, I'm sure, as yet another building block in a few years time. Right now, at the time of writing, I'm also looking carefully at how the chromosome structure influences our health. Our genes are merely components of the chromosomes and it is there that I look ever more frequently to find ways of restoring a person's health to 100 per cent of the homeostasis they were born with. The genes will take care of themselves once the chromosomes have been managed.

Nigel Hawkes, science writer for *The Times* writes: 'As so often in science, a peak is conquered only to reveal a still more daunting one ahead. Those who believed that elucidating the genome would provide the key to understanding everything will have to think again.'

I certainly never presume to understand more than a little bit, fragment by fragment, and attempt to build on what I've learned over the years. And once again I'm turning to the Crypto Power of the Hebrew Word here and dowsing the texts to make activated tablets which include two distinct herbal ingredients in their make-up. I have observed how these medicines play an important part in correcting any genetic imbalance, cellular disorder or damaged organ.

Each patient is shown how a glass of water over a wad of xeroxes of a dowsed-for verse of the Crypto Word contains extraordinary power– this even before the tablets including the two special herbs have been added to the equation. I demonstrate the power of the Word quite simply by placing a compass on a flat surface and waiting a few seconds whilst the needle settles at its customary due north point. When the same compass rests upon a single slip of paper containing a verse from the Hebrew text, the needle invariably swings away from due north by between 10° and 20°. I repeat the experiment with bottles of treated and 'virgin' tablets and the results are similar.

Remember that the human body, also, has its own magnetic fields, different ones for separate parts. In my work I seem to be able to release specific fields of energy which send messages, in a holistic way, to other parts of the body. If one area or system has been corrected, the other bodily networks tend to raise their game, so to speak, so that all levels of health rise. This miraculous positive adjustment is a clear example of the body's internal intelligence – the same basic common sense that causes us to cool with perspiration when we are overheated, to stifle appetite when our stomach is upset and to rest when we are tired.

The reverse, sadly, is also true. I've observed how a whole physical system can be lowered because one aspect of it is ailing. This silent communication between bodily functions is an incredibly important aspect of the entire field of holistic healing. Understanding that this internal physical intelligence exists is the first step towards ensuring that all systems are levelled up, rather than dragged down. It is a matter of being aspirational about our health just as we might be about every other important value in life and society, from education to housing to spiritual calm – and that is all part of what used to be known as the Wealth of Nations – a wealth and deep prosperity which doesn't entirely depend on money.

I've been treating four generations of a local family for some years now, helping the grandmother, D, recover from the

ME which was threatening to cripple her business as well as her own health, and subsequently saw each of her three daughters through potentially difficult pregnancies. All four had to have old vaccines lifted before they were well enough to advance in health. All three of the younger women have gone on to have lively children who are not only in perfect health but who all seem to be outstandingly gifted and full of confidence as they keep on achieving at school. None of the kids ever seems to fall ill much and when they do they recover fast, as their mothers follow my cold-compress/liquid diet advice if the temperature rises above 98.4°F. It gives me real pleasure to think that I may have played a part in this three-generational family success story.

Ideally every organ, bone, tissue and muscle should work in harmony with all the other inhabitants of the house we call our body. This peaceful and productive co-existence could be compared to the relationship we have with our neighbours next door or down the road. You might not be forever popping in to borrow a cup of sugar or to interrupt a family meal or conversation, but you know that you can depend on them in any emergency or even to take care of the pets or post or garden if you are away for a while. And you can trust them to do the same for you. All our body bits will swing along nicely in the ideal neighbourhood: but the 'neighbourhood watch' will take care of things if there's any kind of irregularity. This happy system of mutual supportiveness is the natural way of things, but we must all be watchful in case some failure of one system or another suggests to 'the neighbours' that standards have dropped and there's no point, thus, in keeping things up to scratch.

A friendly balance is essential. Any imbalance will be revealed if the individual's homeostasis is out of kilter – even if only one single system is damaged, whether temporarily or more profoundly. Any such disharmony will send messages all round the body. So in the first place I look at each system individually – the heart, the pancreas, the digestive tracts –

but always with the certainty that fixing a problem in one of those areas is going to holistically prove to be of benefit for the entire system.

Brick by brick I try to build and learn. That doesn't mean that I always have a perfect understanding of how things can heal, nor, always, do my patients, but we work on it together. So long as the patient accepts that taking drugs is seldom the answer – that these chemical interferences can often artificially impede true healing, as the body is confused by substances which can prop up a suffering system rather than restore it – we have made a good start. After all, what is the point in prolonging the agony of the living dead?

Understanding how the stem cells work can often mean the difference between life and death. Staying at a health hydro in the USA, I once met a cancer patient who took matters into her own hands and fasted for a hundred days. I wouldn't advise this, but it was her decision and she succeeded in starving her cancerous cells to death and the healthy stem cells were able to revive and multiply to aid her ultimate recovery. Fasting need have nothing to do with religion, any more than observing the Crypto Word does: the fact is that apart from some devout Christians who are restrained over Lent, few people today fast for religious reasons. Fasting for health reasons makes more sense to me and most other people, I think. Equally we refer here throughout to a Hebrew numerology system simply because it responds to an alphabet, as does the Arabic one. But the wisdom is for everyone.

Whatever creed we follow, if any, we all have a spirit and a soul. Look back to Chapter Five to see how the heavy baggage or intense trauma carried on from some past life, or several past lives, can be finally healed in this one.

The simple truths to remember about our stem cells are that when our immune system breaks down we are more vulnerable to cell mutation and the possibility of cancer. Strong stem cells will fight back. The least we can do to help them in this battle – or even to avoid a battleground in the first place – is to avoid synthetic clothing and as many household and 'cosmetic' chemicals as possible and to follow an organic diet. (See Chapter Nine, Helping Yourself.)

Case study... Case study... Case study... Case study...
I'd been seeing VR for several years. She lives nearby so it wasn't hard for her to get to see me if I had a slot. She asked me to address a vague but nonetheless troubling raft of worries ranging from loss of libido to a general flagging of energy. There was never anything specific that I could do to help except suggest ways that these things could be managed and somehow tolerated. VR herself said she wasn't actually depressed but one may conclude that her continued interest in my healing methods spoke of some hope that things might improve:

'I knew I needed extra vitamins and I took them. I'm over fifty and most women of that age expect to feel some changes but there was this constant constricted feeling in my chest that hadn't been helped even by the diet specialist I'd seen. I couldn't complain about about anything specific. I just knew that things weren't quite right.'

Maybe the very fact that VR could not attach her general malaise to a specific and identified illness or disorder added to her unease. Sometimes it's easier to live with illness without guilt if you've been informed that a specific condition has caused the worry. And maybe that's why sometimes people who feel pretty awful but don't have a label for their illness, a name which elicits sympathy from their friends and family, sometimes resort to 'negative attention-seeking', wherein the vague but ghastly illness is called an ulcer, a heart murmur or diabetes or whatever. Because that way their plight is noticed and support is offered... VR wasn't like that at all, but you'll take my point as she takes the story on:

'Since Jack identified a blockage in my chest, relating to a stem cell dysfunction, and placed his tablets under my arms, telling me that there was an old disorder there, relating to something so long ago that there was no need or reason for me to blame myself, I've felt so much better.

'I feel freed.'

VR's remarks are very astute. No one should feel guilty or self-pitying about admitting to even the vaguest of malaise. Horrible cloudy feelings that must somehow be dealt with, even though you don't know why they have flopped into your life like a heap of old blankets or fallen through the roof of your equilibrium like a shower of bricks, are often even more alarming than some recognised disorder that you may fear but at least understand how to identify and address. A stem cell clearance offers much help to others, like VR, who had or have a dark cloud to lift. It can be as simple as that.

It's almost as if there are certain genes, not gainfully employed, who hang around the street corners of our system with little to do but make mischief. I call these parasitic genes who, having no useful function, have been rendered unemployed. But they still carry the memory of disease and poison and must be flushed out. Their presence in the system will inhibit the absorption of vitamins, tissue salts, bone marrow renewal and correct organ function. So it is my job to identify where and what they are and to break the chain wherever they are lodged, so that a healthy chromosome balance may be restored. Healthy cells as well as poisons are lodged inside the parasitic genes and I must take care not to remove the beneficial matter. The human system normalises itself once the correct balance is achieved and will self-generate healthy stem cells – so there is no need to introduce them artificially.

I have a list of twenty-four parasitic genes to dowse for; for example the one I connect to the potato poison, which can rob the body of potassium.

So far I've found that most of my remedies are made from plant matter found in the Cordoba region of Argentina, Camarthen in Wales and the Isle of Skye, but as my work proceeds apace I don't doubt that I will see that tablets can be made from herbs, flowers and grasses gathered elsewhere in the battle with these parasitic genes.

TABLE OF PARASITIC GENES

Leprosy	Pleura Bacterium
Malaria	Bronchial Bacterium
Amoeba	Flue Jabs
Rickettsia	Organo Phosphorus
Heroin	DDT
Anthrax	Vodka
Small Pox	Gin
Diphtheria	Potato Poison
Ricin (Castor Oil)	Ergot
Nerve Micro-organism	Aluminium Sulphate
Microplasma	Formaldehyde
Alveoli Bacterium	Mercury

These days I can hasten the old, trusted like-with-like homeopathic procedures to extract poisons by dissolving the whole chain of cell disorder in one procedure. After dowsing to locate the stem cell blockage. I apply homeopathic like-with-like tablets (which could contain antibiotics, steroids or histamines to replicate the root of the toxicity) to the site of the stem cell and affix the pad with microtape. But these pads will also contain tablets derived from the magical Cordoba herb I found in Argentina. Then I place my middle finger on the 'bandage' and silently order the first link in the chain to be destroyed. A quick check with the pendulum will tell me if the link is broken. If so, I go on to the next link and so on until all five links in the chain have been broken. A correct swing of the pendulum will indicate that this stage of the healing work is completed. Then I dowse again to check blood purity and hope and expect to see that the debris of dismantled chain cells are already collecting to be discharged as body waste and that the system is well on the way to being cleansed.

It seems to work and however many sceptics who may cry 'bunkum' I have a fistful of patients who will testify to the efficacy of this system of cell renewal. People used to think that anyone who spoke to plants or trees was crazy and yet today evidence shows that vegetable matter responds warmly to a positive human voice. I don't doubt that I'll endure some flack and hilarity about this most recent of my healing routes. I don't mind; I've coped with it before, and by the time I hit my century I'll be surprised if this principle of stem cell renewal isn't an generally accepted aspect of conventional medicine.

I treated S, my young patient with cancer in this way. Her tumours reduced in size as stem cell renewal enabled fresh new cells to literally eat her cancer away during a period of remission. In the end her cancerous cells proved to be the stronger but she died peacefully and without pain, having lived for eighteen months longer than her hospital doctors had expected. And her life was full to the last – she drove, enjoyed holidays and took pleasure from family and friends before the cancer finally took her.

Case study... Case study... Case study... Case study...
Another patient, RN, was diagnosed with untreatable and incurable cancer – which had spread to his lungs, amongst other places – in the early spring of 2001. He was told that his life expectancy was a mere month or two. His wife had been to one of my seminars so he came to see me and he visits every week. One year and two months later, we're both cautiously optimistic about the continuing stability of his health. Perhaps bearing in mind Mark Twain's remark about there being only two certainties in life – death and taxes – RN says:

'I've never been ill apart from mumps when I was nine and indigestion when I was forty. After a career as a medical scientist, very non-stressful, particularly in recent years when I've worked from home, I was considering retirement when I felt a slight muscular strain in my back. It was this which sent me to my GP for the first time in years and which proved to signal my condition. The shock was unimaginable, of course, but added to that was my sense of having been abandoned by the profession in which I had worked all these years. The attitude seemed to be that as I could not be cured I was a hopeless case. Orthodox doctors seemed to have forgotten the distinction between cure and healing and yet I feel that I am receiving true healing from Jack. It includes tablets taped to parts of my body, food drops, absent healing (during which Jack can send benign 'messages' to me via dowsing a clipping of my hair preserved in pure alcohol in a phial in his laboratory), meditation and 'picture healing'. This last involved Jack dowsing art books until a particular image seemed to 'speak' to me. It was a Dali drawing. Then I was photographed with the drawing and back at home I rest a glass of pure water on the photograph.

'Who can say how these things work, or why, or for how long? I do know that I feel better than I did after hearing about my condition. I drive, I go for walks, I feel quite calm and emotionally uncluttered. When I first saw Jack he simply said 'I don't see death here'. Obviously I hope to be around for some time yet and in the meantime I appreciation being treated as a patient rather than a condition.'

When the poisoned chain is broken the damaged cells go into the bloodstream and their toxins are soon naturally excreted. If there's a danger that the patient will feel unwell during this brief period I'll give them a remedy devised from spirulena and a herb from Nepal, which hastens cleansing and brings balmy relief in the meantime. Most would agree that a very short period of 'toxic shock' is a small price to pay for the entire cellular system having been brought back to life. Feeling rotten for a day or two is always manageable if you know the reason and know it will pass. People should never resort to painkillers or other medicine from the chemist and I always warn my patients what to expect.

A physical system which has suffered any sort of trauma – whether a difficult birth, a road accident or an emotional shock

– will respond to any treatment I offer much faster and with greater hope of permanent recovery if the chromosome balance has first been corrected. Everything genetic and cellular springs from this. Every week, with every patient, I learn something new. It's my job to find how best to treat and serve my patients and they, in their turn, help me to further advance my healing methods as I monitor their progress and results.

I now know that each of our many genes is controlled by a chromosome and this makes my work simpler in some ways, and faster. A failing or ailing system can be revived and corrected, so to speak, by a flick of the correct switch. But I must never interfere with the patient's homeostasis because if that is lowered in any single respect the entire physical mechanism will drop to create a balance, even though this will be a negative plateau. Thus I must be careful to dowse and seek information that applies to any one specific disorder and correct this without throwing other complementary systems out of kilter. I generally dowse for the level of homeostasis, or fusion, the particular body part, organ or system had at the moment of the patient's conception and work onwards from there.

Recent work and careful experiment has convinced me that there is even yet more healing to be achieved by lifting, through dowsing, constrictions on our chromosomes – genetic barriers to optimum health – and addressing directly our genes at their best. I used to think I was saddled with working on the genes inherited at conception and making the best of those. Now I know how to dive and dowse deeper and clear even the stem cells of genetic blockages.

I was frustrated when I saw that renewed energy and power that was released after the stem cells had been cleared had nowhere to go. There had to be another layer to lift and with the help of the Crypto Power I have learned this lesson.

I have learned that every person, every body, passes through seven vital stages of growth, times when they are either flexible and open to benign influences or at risk of being affected by lowering ones. These stages and ages are

- At conception
- At fifteen
- At thirty
- At the age of fifty
- At five
- At twenty
- At forty-five

These days, when a patient comes to me for help and healing, I dowse back to the nearest past moment in the list of stages and can restore them to the health they had then. As we age and things slow down – even amongst the strongest and fittest among us – the age of fifty is the last moment in the progress of the human genetic blueprint that is worth addressing. And this, of course, is marvellous news for my older patients to whom I can now restore the general health, skin tone – and in the case of some balding gentlemen – hair growth that was enjoyed when they were younger. A patient aged forty-four, moreover, can expect to be restored to the broad state of health and appearance they had when they were thirty.

Those seven stages are the crucial ages for health – times when our personal blueprint or passport is stamped. I was in despair when I felt that it would be hard to get beyond, uncover, the chromosome inheritance that we'd all been given by our parents. It still seemed that we would either be blessed or bedevilled by that hand of cards we were wished with at the moment of our conception and it would be a slow slog to crack that genetic coding. Now I know that the chromosomes were simply masked and that the mask can easily be lifted. The smooth texture of the skin on the back of my hands and the hair growth on my previously bald pate were testimony to this as I experimented and I've already begun to show patients how they, too, can be regenerated even if they inherited from their parents some damage related to drugs, vaccines, surgery or trauma.

There's no revolutionary new practice. I dowse, work with the ancient text and create the correct tablets to be taped onto the correct place on the body of the individual patient. Just an extension of what I've been doing for years, but what an exciting development. We are all controlled by brain impulses, and understanding the tangle of the neural path and the waves sent all round the body was a great challenge which I hope and believe I have now met. The brain, of course, does not merely set our moods and intellectual activity: it dictates everything else – when we want to eat, sleep, weep, when we are likely to be vulnerable to virus or disease, when we feel strong or defeated, when we deal with pain or suppress it. Knowing that just beneath the layer of genetic potential was a cleaner, clearer layer for most patients and learning how to access it has been incredibly important in my work. I call the layer cleared in this healing work layer C. I then reach layer D and then begin to see startling results.

I don't want to overstress the cosmetic aspects of this because health and strength interest me more than appearance and beauty. But, of course, most people might like to return to the moment in their lives when they were fittest and thus, probably, looking their best. That moment dictates, for all of us, our levels of energy and health for the rest of our lives.

Case study... Case study... Case study... Case study...
I love my cynics: they are such a cheerful challenge. One such is WL, a London accountant in his late fifties who even now, after successful treatment, says that the jury's still out, at any rate about the way I've dealt with his stem cells. Nonetheless, he speaks eloquently of the help he's received:
'I used to get bad colds all the time, Infections that could put me in bed and away from work for as long as two weeks. I used to resist the temptation to say it was flu, but these colds were still so lowering and debilitating that friends and colleagues came to expect them of me and

make 'amusing' but actually very unfunny remarks about my vulnerability to these things. I felt these viral infections were really mucking up my life

'A friend suggested I saw Jack. I'd seen many doctors and healers before about these respiratory ailments which had tracked me since childhood, and was fed up with basically being told to live with them as they were not life-threatening. I didn't think this was good enough and by the time I first saw Jack in 2000 I was ready to try anything. It was with some cynicism that I allowed him to place tablets on my ankles and under my arms but the truth is that I haven't had a cold since. It's as if there were a line across my chest above which I could always expect to fall foul of any passing virus and suffer badly from it. These days the worst I suffer from is a slight sore throat.

'You could say I remain amazed. That's the cynic in me because a true believer would be unsurprised. And I'm yet to be convinced about the stem cell business and if I fell ill with something else I might well want to hear what the orthodox medics had to say about it. But time will tell and in the meantime I'll give Jack the benefit of the doubt: I accept that in life there may often be things which we don't fully understand. At the moment I just know that I feel very much better'

In dealing with the chromosomes to correct disorder I usually consult the Crypto Word and, with the help of two herbal additions, create tablets which I place on the pulse side of the wrists for about six hours. This tends to immediately enable the chromosomes to regain energy needed to combat illness and disorder, especially if body temperature is lower than it should be. As a committed believer in the human body's power to manage and heal itself by means of utilising its own resources, this makes perfect sense to me. It's almost as if I was that mechanic again – merely applying the leads necessary to jump-start a very efficient engine that is actually already primed to look after itself with a little encouragement.

I can't stress too often how important the holistic aspect of all this is. It's something the chromosomes and genes instinctively know, adjusting, correcting, compensating throughout the body in a never-ending see-saw during which they strive to achieve that perfect, steady, level balance. But it's like the painting of the Forth Road Bridge in Scotland: refurbishment at the first end has to begin again long before the work has finished on the far side. The 'workforce' never rests. It is expert, however, at deciding upon its priorities and knows that in fixing a major worry lesser disorders will be enabled to restore themselves as the entire system is strengthened. Any specifically diseased or poisoned organ needs to be addressed directly and separately.

Importantly, I never attempt to restore a chromosome imbalance until the rest of the body is healthy enough to receive and respond to those corrected genes and cells. That's why the process sometimes can be a gradual one and takes a little time.

I can make a whole mental map of the body's network of stem cells in a thirty-second dowsing session. Now, knowing how they co-exist and co-operate with our chromosomes, I can really get to work – as never before.

CHAPTER SEVEN

About Vaccination
and Needless Needles

Many adults have feelings ranging from mild fear to extreme terror about vaccinations. People unfortunate enough to live within a culture of recreational drugs will say 'I'll try anything, but no needles'. Others will endure prolonged dental surgery without anaesthetic because they dread the injection more than the pain of the electric drill. Some people say they've toyed with idea of having a small tattoo but balk at the idea of the process. Often the mere thought of the needles involved deters many people who would otherwise confidently give acupuncture a try.

Why? Most vaccinations are over in microseconds, cause no more than the merest pinprick scratch of discomfort and seldom leave bruising. Could this widespread fear of the injection, often seemingly illogical, derive from some traumatic childhood memory, from innate, instinctive common sense, or from both?

Think about it. How truly awful it must be for babies to endure the series of injections they are usually subjected to in infancy. The whole process will probably be forever linked with the anxiety of a parent, the brief but baffling stab of pain, being cold, perhaps, if being undressed was necessary and, most profoundly, the after-effects of strong drugs being introduced into a tiny bloodstream and fragile body. No wonder many adults have learned to dread the syringe.

Perhaps, for the wrong reasons, this dread is entirely appropriate. For the irony is that vaccinations of every kind have caused much more illness and disorder than doctors and pharmacists may claim they have averted.

As the complete immune system is transferred from mother to baby after birth, it must be clearly understood that if the umbilical cord is cut before the cord ceases to pulse, then baby

VACCINATION AGAINST SPECIFIC ILLNESS CAN RESULT IN OBSERVABLE PATTERN OF SIDE-EFFECTS	
Glued Calcium Enzyme	Babies will have a weak bone structure.
Glued Selenium Enzyme	Babies will suffer a weak heart.
Glued Copper Enzyme	Babies will suffer defective kidneys.
Glued Germanium Enzyme	Babies will suffer tumours, cancer.
Glued Aluminium Enzyme	Babies will suffer neoplasms, cancer.
Glued Para-amino Benzoic Acid Vitamin	Babies will suffer moles, cysts, skin cancers.
Glued Vitamin B6	Babies will suffer anorexia.
Glued Vitamin B5	Babies will suffer burning legs.
Glued Tissue Salt Sodium	Babies will suffer fluid retention.
Glued Tissue Salt	Babies will suffer breathing problems.
Glued Essential Fatty Acids	Babies will suffer from dry skin.
Glued Elements Erbium or Neodymium	Babies will suffer MS.
Glued Fat Enzyme	Babies will suffer overweight problems.
Glued Carbohydrate Enzyme	Babies will suffer from a lack of energy.
Glued Lithium Enzyme	Babies will suffer from violent mood swings.
Glued Gold Enzymes	Babies will develop a brain that can become criminal.

will have an incomplete immune system. It is those babies that suffer the debilitating diseases that vaccines cater for.

It is cruel and unnecessary to vaccinate babies that have been given complete immune systems. Every vaccine, in my experience, interferes with body enzymes. A certain number of enzymes will become glued and unable to carry out their individual function. If the enzyme programmed to target magnesium becomes glued, then that baby will always be hyperactive.

The avoidance of vaccination, particularly for babies and children, is central to my principles of healing. The body's natural immune system is stronger than any chemically devised solution and, quite simply, a healthy body cannot accept and will not receive the invasive elements of disease.

The case of polio, a once-dreaded disease now mercifully all but unknown, throws up an interesting question. Protection from the illness was usually administered via a sugar cube steeped with the serum and this would suggest that the carrier fluid in a vaccine is more to blame than the drug itself. But one cannot generalise and my jury is still out here. At the very least it makes me wonder why the sugar cube method of protection has not been more generally adopted.

Most vaccines lodge initially in the right hemisphere of the brain which causes, in men, a blockage and reduction in their intuitive thinking. A book like this is not the correct forum to address all the social and emotional problems that this might connect to, but who can deny that heavy weekend drinking, road-rage and frustrations otherwise expressed in drug abuse or worse might, arguably, be linked to the restrictions of the brain's more thoughtful side? Statistics suggest that more men fall prey to these behavioural patterns than women.

Women tend to be much more intuitive than men and vaccines do not appear to affect them in the same way. Vaccines seem to have affected the female right hemisphere

too – but a quick glance at the tables of university results in
Britain suggests that even today male students specialise in
and excel at the scientific and structural subjects whereas
women do better in the arts.

Of all the post World War Two vaccines offered so widely
and hopefully, the worst – in my opinion – was the BCG jab
given to every child to protect them from tuberculosis at the
age of thirteen or so. At this age, when the young body is in the
throes of transition to adulthood and thus particularly
vulnerable, I believe it to be almost criminal to introduce the
extra strains of dealing with what amounts to a legitimised
poison. Natural body fluids cease to flow and the absorption of
vitamins A and B6 are impeded by the presence of the serum
– just when the brain needs them most. In my view a good deal
of the stress and depression observed in adolescents could be
attributed to this.

Later in life liver and respiratory problems can be traced
back to this particular inoculation and the blockage of
vitamins A,C and D which it seems to cause. Endless chest
problems, colds and lip-sores are the very least of it. Arteries
thickened with cholesterol may at least make doctors alert
and worried but how much more preferable if these disorders
had never been allowed to take hold?

I'm afraid that the happy notion of dealing with these
kinds of problem by taking whacking quantities of vitamins is
almost always laughable, reminding me of bolts and stable
doors. You might as well save your money because the basic
problem now resides within the fact that the body is unable to
absorb vitamin supplements, so apart from their psychological
benefits, you might as well flush them away in the bathroom.

The manufacturers of such pills and tablets, meanwhile,
are doing very nicely indeed as they prosper on our fears of
illness and hopes for long life.

Case study... Case study... Case study... Case study...
PR lives in Aberdeen, so it was something of an effort for
her to bring her two-year-old son J to see me in the
summer of 2000. As it happened the little chap needed a
second session with me and I was able to fit them in the
next morning. J had been diagnosed as having meningitis
when he was only eight weeks old and had had various
vaccines. His mother had no criticisms about the way her
boy was treated before, but after consulting me she says
how happy she was to take home a restored son after the
terrible fright and to watch him develop normally. But I'll
let her take up the story:

'My son was a lovely child. If we worried about
anything it was just that he was almost unnaturally quiet
and well behaved. Nothing else about his progress after the
meningitis seemed at all unusual until he started saying
"head hot" all the time. When I think about it now, and
realise that my little boy had this constant burning
sensation in his head but could only express it when he was
old enough to have learned the words, I worry about what
he must have endured before we took him to see Jack. How
frustrating it must be for a child to *feel and know* a disorder
but be unable to communicate. "Head hot" were some of
his earliest words.

'Our GP had been helpful and supportive, but when we
read of Jack's work in a newspaper we thought we owed it
to our son to see if something else could be done. We were
getting more and more worried, as any parents would after
something like the meningitis scare. Jack dowsed him and
placed the tablets on his arms and legs. He actually
extracted toxins from J which, apparently, related to
smallpox jabs that one or other of his grandparents had
received years ago and this damaged gene had been passed
on. Only 30 per cent of potential brain strength was
working for J then and the blockage there meant that he
could have become dyslexic in later life. Of course with
such a little boy, it was too early to say then whether that
problem was manifested.

'I don't really understand how Jack does the trick, but
after the very first session J started saying "No head hot".

After that he seemed to move into himself, somehow, and express much more of the normal devilry one might expect of a toddler of his age. It's not that J had been withdrawn or terribly quiet or anything, but he was quiet enough to make us alert to some potential problem. Afterwards I realised, as his speech developed, that he truly knew the difference between "hurt or sore" and "hot".

'When we took him back to Scotland we joked that J had had a "personality transplant", he was so much livelier and mischievous. Maybe some parents would have envied us our unnervingly quiet, calm, polite little boy – but we knew that something wasn't quite right. We'll always be grateful to Jack for this complete transformation.'

I do know that wherever residual matter from a vaccine lodges – whether it is the drug itself or its carrier fluid – there is trouble ahead for that part of the body. It could be the liver, the intestines, the stomach, the colon, the lymphatic system, the respiratory system or any other function. It's hard to know where to begin as I attempt to explain the many evils of vaccination. For instance, it can actually cause or aggravate asthma, as stifled muscle tendons block the benign action of genes and bone is weakened and breathing difficulties arise in the chest area as the muscles find it harder to grip and adhere to bone. Spinal weakness and joint pains are often the result of vaccinations made years ago, again blocking the working programme of the genes.

We have to remember that the body is a perfectly designed entity with its own closed circuit tailored for human protection. Any invasion or intrusion into this system is likely to short-circuit it. I can dowse and then remove toxins in adult systems, originally cased by needless vaccinations, but far better, particularly where babies and children are concerned, to avoid them altogether. Any vaccinations which block the function of genes that protect the health and strength of bones should be outlawed.

For instance, the stomach is connected to the brain by the vagus nerve which in turn links to the part of the brain which controls the tongue. Recently I saw two young children, aged three and six, both of whom had speech difficulties as well as constant colds and low energy levels. Their distraught mother thought she had somehow saddled her son and daughter with a genetic inheritance, but their problems were rooted in anti-diphtheria and tetanus injections they had had at the age of three months. By dowsing I was able to extract the toxins from the vagus nerve and both children are now speaking normally for their age. Proper energy levels have been restored and they no longer suffer from endless cold infections. It took several sessions over time to achieve this. Ironically the mother's initial thinking was on the right track, however, as any vaccination damage sustained by parents can and often is transferred on to children at the moment of conception.

In another relatively simple case, I saw that the antibiotic Septrin, often prescribed to young asthmatics until recently when it was withdrawn from general usage, may have damaged generations of children irreparably, Like many other carelessly prescribed drugs and medicines it can pass on a legacy of genetic flaw from parent to child. In relatively simple cases of inherited poison I can usually remove the toxins from small children.

> Case study... Case study... Case study... Case study...
> LJ is a remarkable woman, with considerable inner strength, as the story of her survival attests. She should explain things herself:
> 'My childhood was spent in Indo-China, then in the grip of terrible war. There was no escaping the sight, smell or sound of it and I grew up in a traumatised state of permanent fear. My body responded to this by failing to absorb nourishment from food and at the age of nine I was covered in scabs and sores and weighed only 2 stones. I barely drank the water there but, sadly, as I didn't

experience much concern or kindness in my childhood, nothing much was done for me. My kidneys, of course, were also damaged.

'I grew to be 5 feet 4 inches but still only weighed about 5 stones. I'm fifty-seven now but until the age of forty-five I didn't really feel I had any life. I saw lots of healers and alternative practitioners but only one homeopathic doctor was really helpful. Mostly I was dismissed as a neurotic anorexic. Once I was put on a drip but my body couldn't even cope with that "nourishment". It blew up at first but couldn't excrete properly and I remained in great pain. When I read of experiments which took place in Nazi concentration camps I'm afraid I'm reminded of what was done to me in the name of medicine. People seldom realise how simply agonising it is to be severely underweight. Malnutrition is torture. When I came off the drip I took on the appearance of a shrivelled apple – and felt like one. Things like barium meals were of no help, either. That I'm now a robust 6½ stones is largely due to Jack's help.

'After years of what I call "aggressive medicine" it was a great relief to be treated by Jack. He identified at once that there was a blockage in my cranium and that this affected my spine. For years I had felt as if my brain was a half-filled jug, with water sloshing around whenever I moved. Jack explained that this derived from faulty DNA compounded with viruses picked up in the East. It seems that as I had grown my brain had actually lessened in size, hence the sense of compensating fluid there. He seemed to understand the roots of my problems right away and set about extracting the residue of penicillin and all the vaccines which had shattered my immune system and rendered my spinal fluids inadequate. Tablets were fixed along crucial meridian lines to effect my recovery. That's all corrected and gone now and Jack restored health to my kidneys by dowsing, tablets and his food drops. Beforehand my bodyworks couldn't support proper digestion. I feel that life has suddenly, finally and joyfully opened up for me. After my very first treatment at his clinic I felt a huge sense of release and relief.

'It's the awful truth that I used to think of doctors as torturers, not healers. Jack has restored my faith and made me feel, at last, that I have a real intellectual and physical life!

* * *

The body's systems and organs are connected to the brain via nerves and meridian lines. It might explain why I can get to grips with a bladder problem by looking first at my patient's ankle or heel. I don't like to upset or trouble my patients, but half the time as I nod sagely and make notes I already know where to start my healing. That's not to say that I'm not listening, simply that it's unrealistic for me to expect them to know or understand as much about the body's mechanisms as I do.

Think about that vital and complex fusion point in the brain, for instance, where nerves and meridian lines intersect and share information which is then transmitted all over the body. It's like spaghetti junction and air traffic control at Heathrow combined. Any poison in the system will slide through it and be spread to other parts of the body if we don't make sure we are rid of them.

The MMR vaccination – an inoculation supposedly designed to protect against mumps, measles and rubella – became the subject of massive controversy early in 2001 when it was revealed that there were strong links with the vaccine and the onset of autism and the development of colon problems. Defenders of the inoculation maintained that these claims were erroneous and that any perceived link was invalidated by the fact that all babies who received the jab were properly monitored. In fact this monitoring was far from satisfactory as it only lasts for six weeks after the injection and in my observation the signs of tragic side-effects may not become evident for some years. Some 'experts' dithered around a daft compromise and said that there should be three separate inoculations, each less of a body shock for a tiny infant and making it easier to assess the effects of the three different serums. Some injection or immunity is better than none, they argued.

Case study... Case study... Case study... Case study...
I was attempting to demonstrate some aspect of this healing at one of my weekend seminars and by coincidence that day one of my associates, an acupuncturist had brought his wife two sons along and volunteered the boys to be dowsed as models in my demonstration. The older boy was eleven and he's autistic. His younger brother is dyslexic – but they'd come to the clinic on a day out, not as patients. Their mother, takes up the story:

'We were amazed to see what could happen during such a short time – not a proper appointment or consultation – just a few minutes. Our oldest boy is a lovely child but obviously he has special needs and we hope that Jack may be able to meet them. Our younger son has difficulties of his own and we worried that perhaps he was upset by all the special care we need to give his brother. At any rate, the boys weren't getting on at all well and this only added to the stresses and stains which all of us as a family had to deal with.

'I can only say that I'm astonished and delighted to report that after those very few minutes with Jack, the boys began to be trusting and affectionate with each other in a way we'd never observed before. Something mysterious seemed to have been eating away at the basic good nature of the children but they are now much happier and calmer. My older son is a tall, rangy boy but he's become less pale and his face has filled out – I'd call it all miraculous. He was always in a world of his own, rather distressingly cut off from us, but he seems more integrated within the whole family now.

'Obviously it's very early days yet where the autism is concerned but we'll be seeing Jack again and I've every confidence that both my sons can be helped further. We noticed such an immediate change in our youngest son after Jack worked on his head for a few minutes. The poor little chap complained of a severe headache for most of the next day, which upset us, of course, but since then he's been brighter all the time.

'Jack explained to us that the MMR vaccine and various other jabs the boys had received as babies could account for their separate difficulties. I know he's already lifted out quite a few of these toxins and there may be a way to go yet. So far we are all thrilled with the results.'

When our children were young in the 1940s and 1950s none of them was inoculated. When the nearly inevitable illnesses of childhood struck, my wife and I nursed them through with a gentle regime of fasting and liquids, trusting their natural immune systems would do the rest and only reintroduced solid foods when the child's temperature had remained steady and normal for twenty-four hours. Over fifty years later all three have remained hale: indeed they seem to have been primed to shrug-off the kind of minor disorder that can flatten others. All parents should seriously wonder whether, in the long term, the injections they inflict upon their children are doing much more harm than good. I realise that this will take a leap of faith for many brought up to implicitly obey 'doctor's orders' and to accept that vaccination is so essential that they are risking their children's health if they do not blindly accept the received wisdoms. I can only reiterate that the opposite is true.

Bowel cancer and sleep disorders as well as tumours, autism and many other problems are associated now with the MMR vaccine. One problem may be that some parents consider mumps and measles to be tiresome, inconvenient but inevitable disorders of childhood whilst others hope they can be averted entirely by inoculation. Neither group is quite right: mumps and measles used to be, and could still be, killer diseases. But there are better ways than immunisation to avoid them and the long-term dangers of injection must always be considered in parallel with the understandable parental wish to spare the child the upset of the illness, disruption to education and so forth.

Old-fashioned as it may seem today, I believe that one parent should stay at home to care for their sick child, insisting on time off from their place of work if necessary. Nothing could be a better investment in the future – in the broadest sense – than caring for a sick child.

I have a real worry about the orthodox medical profession's tendency to collect together all disorders, particularly where children are concerned, and pronounce that one single inoculation will fix things. They really should take a deeper interest in the background of the child and its parents, and consider diet and other factors. Apples are not the same as pears and comparisons are ludicrous: so is the idea that every patient will respond in a positive way to some expensively researched new drug. Many things might influence a child's likelihood of contracting an illness. But the great international drug companies are all too keen on promoting the idea of their magic bullet cure-all jabs. Increasingly I see their magic bullet as a terrible time bomb.

Apart from anything else these inoculations tend to give parents a sense of false hope or confidence. They fail to understand the potentially lethal consequences of a stacking up of vaccine residues in the body. By the age of eighteen a young person could well have enough residual vaccination poison in their system to undermine their health forever. Apparently mysterious illnesses like ME are often rooted in such vaccination overload, as is the meningitis, which every parent dreads. How ironic it is to learn that many diseases are actually caused by inoculation. Poor diet compounds the danger of the onset of any number of diseases.

In the nineteenth century people often had large families, possibly following the example of Victoria, their Queen, but possibly also hoping that of their seven, eight or nine infants, three or four would survive into adulthood. Then as now, better ways than immunisation existed to ensure the survival and health of young children. But the long-term dangers of vaccinations must, of course, always be balanced with the understandable parental wish to do their best and spare their child the upset of illness and disruption to their education. I understand all that.

But as the debate rages on we must ask ourselves whether the interests of the drug companies and medical establishment are being served over those of patients. In January 2001 a consultant gastroenterologist at the Royal Free Hospital in London said in a published paper that tests of the MMR vaccine had been inadequate and did not address the complex issue of fears about its effects. A spokesman for the British Medical Association countered by saying that there was nothing new in this paper – with the suggestion that alarmist views were being expressed. I applaud the scientists and doctors who have been brave enough to express concern about the perceived medical wisdoms that seemed to be set in stone and I welcome the debate as it surely means that fewer people will automatically turn to procedures which were up till now regarded as infallible.

The fact is that residual matter from any vaccination cannot be excreted and remains in the intestine until it makes is way upwards to the cranium, which controls every single bodily function and dictates its efficiency.

The vagus nerve which I mentioned earlier links the intestine to the brain. A malfunction here could be serious enough to affect intellectual strength. To grasp that basic physical functions, such as the power of speech, hearing or simply breathing or sleeping comfortably, could also be affected is almost worse, somehow. Yet none of this worry or discomfort is necessary and as you'll see from Chapter Nine Helping Yourself, there are many safe and easy alternatives.

Any injection is potentially harmful, some more than others. But removing the toxic residue of the MMR vaccine is relatively easy, as is the task of ridding the body of the legacy of the BCG injection which supposedly fights tuberculosis.

It has become clear to me over the years that the harmful side-effects of vaccines are not caused by the physical presence of the drug but by the body's *memory* of it. My experience has shown that by removing a vaccine-induced blockage by the simple means of taping a small bottle containing blank homeopathic tablets onto the area where the residue has accumulated, I am extracting a magnetic memory of the substance which forms the base of all vaccines. These unhappy memories can lodge anywhere in the system, making mischief. They will even find their way into the human genetic structure. Eventually the body will in turn rebel and illness results as damaged genes are prevented from fulfilling their programme of renewal and restoration. Much of this damage can be repaired by sipping water activated by a short rest on sheets of the Crypto Word containing the appropriate verses. (See page 99.)

For example, gene N97 controls the entire system of bone modelling. I believe that this vital gene is blocked by the BCG vaccination which purports to protect against tuberculosis and was routinely given to young British teenagers, as I have already noted. A far more likely result is that bone density will suffer and over time such conditions as arthritis and osteoporosis will develop since bone and joint function are so closely linked. I believe it to be almost criminal that this injection is so gaily given to children in the name of good health. While it may be some time before evidence of bone disorder is apparent, a tendency to develop eczema and other skin complaints can take place almost at once. And those children's children are already blighted to suffer in similar ways as the gene pool has been tampered with.

Case study... Case study... Case study... Case study...
I had to dowse back twenty generations to get to grips with
DF's problems. Her bone density was incredibly,
dangerously, low. She felt sluggish and depressed and ached
everywhere. A series of previous practitioners had dismissed
all this as a thyroid problem but she wanted to get to the
root of whatever the matter was and came to me. I
recognised at once that she had a severe calcium deficiency
and that her bone modelling was faulty and with my recent
researches I found this condition quite simple to correct
with taped tablets and food drops after dowsing.

'Now I wake up full of energy and optimism. Before I
was absolutely desperate. At first I thought the idea of the
taped-on tablets was pretty weird but I was ready to try
anything. As well as my health, my sense of humour
recovered pretty quickly too – I was meeting a friend at
Christies, the auctioneers in London, and she remarked on
the "bandages" around my ankles, about which by that time
I was quite without embarrassment. "It's an Irish suicide
attempt", I told her with a laugh.'

✳ ✳ ✳

The distinguished micropalaeontologist, Dr Viera Schieber,
has delivered learned talks and papers all over Europe, in
Australia and in the United States and participated in the
post-graduate GP training debates concerning vaccination.
She writes humourously of those, like her, who were born
before 1940. Here's a summary:

We are the survivors. We were born before
television, before penicillin, polio shots, xerox,
plastic, contact lenses, credit cards, split atoms,
laser beams and ball point pens, before
dishwashers, air conditioners, drip-dry clothes...
We thought fast food was what you ate during
Lent and a 'meaningful relationship' meant
getting along with cousins... We existed before

> *laser beams and artificial hearts, before penicillin*
> *and polio shots... We who were born before 1940*
> *must be a hardy bunch when you think of the way*
> *in which the world has changed and the*
> *adjustments we have had to make... but, by the*
> *grace of God we have survived.*

I sometimes wonder if recent folk memory makes people still regard inoculation as somehow advanced and miraculous. When I was a young man TB used to be the dread disease of the poor in Britain. Few could afford to rest and recover in Alpine sanatoriums where the air was pure. There was often almost as much social or class stigma attached to it as worry about the illness itself and older people will remember this, just as *their* parents reminisced almost sentimentally about London fog. These days, with dietary, sanitary and environmental conditions greatly improved, the disease does not have to be regarded as controllable only by a needle. This isn't to suggest for a second that tuberculosis is not a serious and often fatal illness. In fact in the spring of 2001 there were alarming outbreaks amongst schoolchildren in London and in England's Midlands and then in Aberdeen. That we seem to be going backwards, that TB is statistically on the rise, only serves to reinforce my point that inoculation is *not* the answer.

Any vaccine left in the intestine will make its way to the centres around the ear, where the vagus nerve connects via the brain stem; this meridian influences every aspect of our physical and emotional needs and all sorts of essential physical functions. The messages transmitted by it inform and alert the blood, nerves, bone marrow and every other guardian of our mental and physical health. Think of this place in your brain – that most complete and perfectly designed machine – as your friend. You'll have read or heard about all the scares and dangers related to tetanus, diphtheria, TB, autism, typhus and may well have become worried enough to conduct further research.

The tragedy is that for many adults these awful conditions were regarded as being a miserable but inevitable result of weak or damaged family genes. It takes a little time and faith but all that can be fixed. I know it's an extraordinary concept to embrace, but try to keep faith with me as so many patients have over the years.

There is one simple and clear, plain and easy way to escape from this bewildering muddle: trust in your body's natural defence systems and absolutely reject the 'fast fix' of an injection.

Something called modelling has come under scrutiny recently, even in the most revered and august medical journals, and rightly so as it is an important matter. Modelling is concerned with both bone density and the way that the bones support flesh and tendons. Bones need to be kept supplied with calcium to maintain strength and – in the case of children – growth. If bone density is impaired the tendons and ligaments which support muscle are unable to grip properly and the end result is their inability to properly support the flesh. This sequence happens when a gene controlling the calcium-building process is blocked. An easily grasped example of this is the way that if muscle tone around the rib cage is under par, the chest bones are weakened and breathing difficulties like asthma can set in. There are more asthmatics in Britain today than there were a hundred years ago when no one had heard of clean air or pollution. Otherwise healthy children can be programmed to become asthmatic in adulthood because of some medicine that a parent unwisely took before they were born

I'm sorry to say that the TB vaccine administered in childhood has also been shown to be associated with the onset of many bone-related problems in later life. The serums have interfered with the vital absorption of calcium, so mature women in particular will be prone to osteoporosis and all the risks and worries that having fragile bones can bring, as calcium taken in food and drink is simply excreted since the body is unable to utilise it.

Between 5 and 10 per cent of bone mass is remodelled every year – less as we grow older. This renewal is essential to maintain homeostasis. Most importantly, poor cranial health in the 'control centre' will affect every physical, hormonal, glandular and emotional function and, as I have said, the legacy of any vaccine will make its way to the brain eventually.

Perhaps the worst situations I have seen are those when I see that residual matter from some vaccine – any vaccine – has lodged in the small intestine, which is connected to the thigh. This is when I fear that the onset of cancer is a real danger. That area of the body connects again through the brain and the network of meridians to the eyes, bladder, spleen, kidneys, stomach and blood circuit. It's not impossible to extract the toxin from the thigh and I always feel 'not a moment too soon' when I locate it there. Vaccine residue can make its way to the thigh marrow via the small intestine. The result here will be loss of stomach muscle control and the development of a paunch – neither healthy nor attractive for men or women.

Quite why the bone marrow in the thigh seems to be the place that the unfriendly vaccine residues aim for remains a mystery to me. But each week or month these days I seem to be guided to unravel some maze that had defeated me for years. Thus I fully expect to crack this particular conundrum before long.

While you wait remember that someone, somewhere, is making a fortune out of the technology behind the dialysis machines that hospitals struggle to raise funds for. Furthermore, millions of adults are spending fortunes at gyms, hydros and spas, worrying themselves silly or sick about lost muscle tone even as they joylessly jog or pointlessly pilate. All the hassle and expense could be avoided by the simple extraction of these pernicious old poisons.

So my message is that however rightly we may worry about exterior pollutants, which are often unavoidable in modern life, the real pollution has been passed into generations of human bodies by vaccinations which effectively disempower blood, bone and muscle from co-existing and operating in correct harmony.

Sadly, I must assure you that no injections are better than one, two or three. No programme of carefully considered and timed vaccinations will ensure a life free from disorders ranging from the so-called common cold to tetanus.

But you *can* protect yourself and your family. And this vital aspect of your health can be achieved without any vaccination. Most importantly, you can protect your children from illness for life without forcing them to endure either the long- term or short-term trauma of the needle. I have already made the point that we are all born with a perfectly designed internal immune system. 'Use it or lose it,' as they say.

I must report that I have seen conditions ranging from asthma to bowel cancer inherited from a parent. We must never dismiss or underestimate the ferocity of a destructive force in the system – whether inherited or accidentally acquired.

We can actually become almost as addicted to injections as any sad crack or heroin user. The more inoculations we receive, the harder fight do the white corpuscles, antibodies and alien viruses put up. They become immune: we've all read about alarmingly intelligent flu strains which resist and cheat even the most powerful antibiotics. The more often we introduce these alien, chemically produced medicines into the body systems, the faster will the agents of disease adapt. I have even seen signs of childhood disorders like rickets and whooping cough – thought to have been conquered decades ago by diet and drugs – taking hold again today as diet deteriorates. Antibiotics are seen as an automatic cure-all and people have bought the idea that an injection is often the only way to prevent disease.

Case study... Case study... Case study... Case study...
R is the father of a five-year-old child who received all the usual injections of infancy in good faith. As R relates things, his son was a perfectly normal baby and toddler, perfectly horrible at times, of course, but perfect. And then around the age of eighteen months the boy seemed to regress, lose all his social and language skills, become not just 'a handful' but a tragically disruptive child who seemed to be consumed with frustrations and anger. There appeared to be no joy in his tiny life. His parents were naturally distraught and sought medical advice. Their horror could only increase when they heard that their son was autistic. They heard about my clinic and in their desperation thought they'd at least give it a try. R remembers:

'I was inspired with confidence the very first time we visited his clinic. In the foyer there was a notice board but instead of showing letters of gratitude from celebrities (of which I'm sure he has many), there were cuttings from newspapers and journals concerning the MMR debate. It should go without saying that Jack had no knowledge of the purpose of our visit. I think that sometimes one has to take a leap of faith and after all we'd been through I was absolutely inspired to trust in what Jack said and did, even though I didn't presume to understand how it all worked.

'When he saw my son he immediately began to speak of enzyme dysfunction, toxins in the blood which prevented toxins from draining away from the brain. Jack speaks very simply – which may have sometimes allowed scientific professionals to jeer – but I have read enough learned journals and papers to realise that once their complexities are deconstructed, they often say much the same as Jack. Another thing which inspired my confidence right away was that Jack didn't hedge his bets. He would say "do this and that will happen and then we'll move onto the next stage..."

He didn't cover himself by saying any of this was dependent on factors beyond his control. And he said it would be a steady process and progress rather than an instant result.

'So we began seeing Jack regularly. He didn't waste any time or delve deeply into our past beyond saying there may have been some inherited genetic weakness and tendency towards susceptibility to adverse reaction to vaccinations in my son's case. What Jack said about our son's inability to control his bowels, the damaged gut which interfered with his natural ability to absorb nutrients and properly deal with waste, the neurological disorder which prevented him from developing social and communicative skills all made perfect sense. He explained that the malfunctioning blood cells were too congealed to reach the outer layers of the skin, which explained the boy's pallor. The same problem with blood cells was preventing his intestine from working properly... Step by step every aspect was clarified.

Tablets were taped to his legs and arms, along the relevant meridian lines, over six sessions in a year and a half. He was also attending a nursery for children with special needs at this time. We parents had special needs of our own as the whole process had led me to take my eye off the ball, so to speak, professionally, and things became pretty dire. I'm pleased to say that all is now well in that department but if nothing else the experience of fighting for my boy's health forced me to prioritise. Nothing else mattered. Nothing is as important to us as his health and recovery and I can't imagine that any practical or professional setback will ever bother me much in future. Naturally I hope that no such event occurs – but I don't now have any real fear about my ability to deal with it if it should confront me. One puts things into perspective.

'The poor little chap had to endure endless examinations, dietary upheavals, mysterious, although well-intentioned, persons looking him over. A fungal infection? We can fix it. Vitamin deficiency? Let's try this. Homeopathy? Fine, we'll go down that route too.

'Now my boy attends a regular school and, like any proud dad, I'm delighted to hear from his teachers that he's not only exceptionally bright and reading well for his age, but exceptionally sensitive, by which his teachers mean that he's unusually aware of the sensitivity of other people – not that he's thin-skinned and selfish. He leads a pretty normal life altogether, with lots of friends and displays all the usual complexities of a growing child: sometimes he's adorable, sometimes irritating. This is exactly what we once hardly dared to hope for. Fortunately my wife and I almost retired from social interface during the two or three years of his crisis and allowed our friends to believe that we were simply preoccupied with a "difficult" child. Thus we believe that no unfair, unjust stigma of autism will attach to him.

'We watch his diet, and put Jack's food enhancing drops on his plate; he drinks the energising Crypto Power water and takes homeopathic tablets without comment or notice. He still has some food intolerances but these are easy to deal with, no big deal. You can imagine how to say that we are overjoyed about all this is an understatement.

'Sometimes when we saw Jack in the past he'd say that we might have to wait for a week or two before improvement could be observed. He didn't promise miracles and so we came to trust him absolutely and confidence in his work was steadily increased. He never let us down and within those periods we always saw progress. A smile, then some clearly formed words, then a noticeable difference in the bowel function that caused our son so much more distress than it caused us... I report with regret that all this is so different from the responses we had to deal with when dealing with the orthodox medical establishment. They may have endless doctorates and years of theses and scientific qualifications, but most of them were prepared to write my son off, consign him to a lesser life. In a rather matter of fact way Jack made it clear from the start that he could fix things and that was that.

'I'm aware that some might cry "bunkum" simply because they don't understand how someone like Jack can achieve these results. Well, even after all this, I don't understand either but I don't feel the need to question his instincts and his sure, calm touch.

'I've asked Jack not to use our names for the book because I don't want my son to be stigmatised in any way, even though he is now so well. One day I'll tell him about those lost years of his childhood, years which he mercifully does not remember now. When he's old enough to consider having children of his own I will explain things to him but I have some confidence that by then the medical establishment will have caught up with Jack's ideas and that half of what I tell him will seem like some daft tale from the Dark Ages. I hope so.'

When the boy's specialist observed his remarkable advances she told his father that while ethics prevented her from actually referring other patients to me, she would happily henceforth refer them to Richard who could, in turn, tell them about me and my clinic.

Despite years of study and research I do not yet know whether the harm done by vaccinations resides within the serum itself or the 'carrier' vehicle within which it is suspended in that syringe. That vehicle could be a tincture of formaldehyde, aluminium sulphate or some mercury derivative. All I am certain of at this stage is that the residue of any vaccination will lodge within the lower intestine and thus influence the processing of any consumed nourishment and impede its journey towards the blood supply and that it will eventually make its way to the brain – the organ which effectively controls all our functions.

I know from long experience that certain key enzymes cease to function once vaccines are pumped into babies. Each enzyme has a job to do and if there is any blockage or deprivation the baby will soon prove it with colds and fevers. The enzymes are the workers which transport nutrients wherever in the body they are needed but if something is amiss with the task force it has to be called back to base and the inhibitors perform the function here of aborting pointless enzyme missions by plugging themselves into holes which are part of the enzyme structure. Now joined, the enzymes and inhibitors return to 'base', ploughing through the gluey vaccine that had recently been introduced into the bloodstream. Fixed together like this, the enzymes and inhibitors effectively neutralise any hope of nutrients reaching the baby's needs, when the colds and temperatures occur.

When nutrients that the system needs are prevented from travelling around the body, little by little every essential function will suffer. Believe me, you'll soon know it – by the stress you will feel – if your magnesium supply is being blocked. You may develop a dry cough or other lung disorders is you're deprived of thorium. If Vitamin 12 is glued up your liver won't work properly and heaven help your kidneys if the system's copper supply has been restricted. Enzymes and inhibitors work tirelessly to ensure that none of these things happen.

I don't want to overly complicate things here for my readers. Many if not most of you will be car drivers. But only some of you will take a keen interest in the complex ways of the internal combustion engine. Most, I suspect, are happy enough if the car gets you from point A to point B without breaking down or needing anything more than a petrol fix. So just trust me here, look upon me as the mechanic or the AA man who has the expertise to fix your motor if you break down on the highway.

So stand by now for the good news, after so much worry and gloom. Sheet 74 of the Crypto Word can undo this sort of damage over a matter of weeks. When a glass of pure bottled water is rested upon it for fifteen minutes and then drunk the enzymes will, gradually, become detached from their inhibitors. A couple of egg-cup sized drinks per day will do the trick for toddlers.

Case study... Case study... Case study... Case study...
'I was always brought up to query things, to ask why? if something happened – good or bad.' MK's searching attitude to life made her incapable of simply accepting that, in her

late twenties, she had ovarian cysts, and that they should be surgically removed. She didn't like the idea of an operation and she wanted to know why she had been saddled with the problem in the first place. I explained that they connected back to anti-tetanus jabs she'd received as a girl. We were both thrilled when, just by binding some tablets on her fourth finger, the cysts shrivelled and moved away.

'I'm a schoolteacher and had been on the contraceptive pill. It helped a lot with my acne and no teacher wants to face a classroom full of spirited children with a spotty face. But I didn't want to stay on the pill forever and even when I was scanned and the cysts were identified and I was in great pain I resisted both the idea of surgery and a return to the pill. I did some research of my own and found out that first-born daughters – of which I am one – are statistically more likely to develop ovarian cysts if they were born with a forceps delivery, as I was. This tied up with what Jack told me.

'He identified the cause of the cysts as having a direct association with an anti-tetanus jab I had when I was a child and the "booster" some years later. The residue of this particular serum remains near the hypothalamus gland near the temple – exactly the spot where the forceps would have gripped my head when I was born. So perhaps the combination of the two things triggered the cysts. That serum also has a tendency to cause back problems and I certainly had those but Jack's treatment has lifted them. He saw that I had a calcium deficiency causing a bone density weakness. Firstly he placed tablets at the base of two of my fingers and then I had tablets taped to my forearms and ankles. Then they were applied to my ring finger and this treatment really seemed to see off the threatened illness.

'I also have a great osteopath. Between them all my problems have retreated and my general health has improved enormously. So far as the ovarian cysts are concerned, a second scan showed that they had gone and I believe I have Jack to thank for this.'

Case study... Case study... Case study... Case study...
Another patient, BN, now fifty, has been coming to see me
for about ten years. She'd been suffering from ME, only
slightly less understood then than it is today, and she was
frustrated by a series of unsympathetic doctors who had
just told her to buck up or prescribed antibiotics which
ultimately did no good at all.

'It was getting me down but the illness itself wasn't
causing the depression although I was exhausted and felt
physically sick a lot of the time. I had to take a year off
work. I was taking vitamin supplements, going to a health
club and generally trying my best but I couldn't seem to get
better and the antibiotics just made things worse. Jack saw
that I was suffering from bleach poisoning – probably from
all the household cleaning stuff I used all the time, and
from residual damage caused by the BCG vaccination
against tuberculosis I'd had when I was about thirteen. He
lifted these poisons and I felt so much better that I didn't
hesitate to send my daughters to him when they needed
help, for different reasons.

'One daughter was pregnant and had not been getting
along well. We were worried about the baby and Jack even
suggested that she had a scan. She was unwilling to do so
but Jack did removed poisons from diphtheria, TB and anti-
tetanus injections. Apart from needed gas and air, she was
able to have her baby naturally and her son has not had any
of the childhood vaccinations. Jack has removed any
possible residual damage by placing his tablets on his little
shins and advising on the use of bottled water.

'My other daughter was having bladder problems a
while later when she was pregnant and a colposcomy was
recommended. She too was unwilling to endure this
interference, so opted for treatment from Jack instead, and
tablets were placed upon her bladder's meridian line. I was
waiting for her when she bounded out of the loo at his
clinic and said she'd just had her first pain-free pee in
months! She went on to have a natural and pain-free
delivery.

'I have other children and we all rely on Jack, taking his
food enhancing drops as a matter of course, apart from

anything else. He's given me such confidence that you don't need to succumb to the pressures of the medical establishment if you want to get well. There is another, natural way, as an alternative at least. There may be some things, practical matters like broken bones, that I'd discuss with a conventional doctor but for anything more complex I'd trust in Jack's methods.

'Basically I feel that the good health of generations of my family has now been corrected under Jack's care. My grandchildren are doing so well at school – outstandingly so – that I suppose I *would* naturally feel great pride. But their levels of health and achievement must be connected to the way we all look after ourselves now.'

Any residual vaccine in the brain could occasionally retain the power to block the work of the inhibitors and prevent friendly enzymes in the body from protecting healthy cells and thus allowing them to do their work. In these instances the vaccination serum is doing the work that it was programmed to do – to knock out perceived enemies within the system. But it is indiscriminate and will often, thus, knock out or damage friendly enzyme material.

For example, if I see that enzymes of Germanium, Aluminium and PABA are blocked because their inhibitors have prevented healthy enzymes from doing their work, I know that a pre-cancerous or cancerous condition is inevitable. In other less life-threatening but nonetheless distressing conditions such as the onset or aggravation of eczema, I can see that the natural supply of iridium, zinc and sulphur is blocked and correct things accordingly.

Those old vaccines will have entered the bloodstream through a vein but finish up in the intestine and the brain. They cannot be excreted. The most common problems connected with residual vaccines relate, thus, to the stomach and to the lymphatic and brain functions. Hiatus hernias and prostate cancer are on the rise as a direct result, I'm sure, of unnecessary vaccinations and the way these inhibit the body's proper absorption of minerals, tissue salts and vitamins. Too much acid in the stomach can lead to ulcers. In extreme cases the remains of vaccination fluid can lead to Crohn's disease and the agony of violent diarrhoea, which may progress towards colonic cancer, a colostomy and dependence on a colostomy bag.

Residual matter lodging in the brain can cause severe headaches and a weakening of the intuitive brain function in men and blockage in the structural or logical brain function in women. It can be seen to have associations with ME. And all these malfunctions are – for want of a better expression – for life. Unless, that is, they can be lifted and the damage undone.

By some happy, if not miraculous, coincidence I and many of my short-sighted patients have found that, as a bonus, this gentle and simple sipping from water charged on my Sheet 74 has the effect of cleansing the fluids in the eyes of many pollutants and irritants associated with a society lodged within and worsened by petrol and diesel fumes, by households and cupboards loaded with dodgy cleaning agents and synthetic fibres.

But I'm a realist. I don't even imagine that anyone can presume to alter a complicated lifestyle by one finger-wagging session or even several. I have faith in the intelligence of my clients and respect the fact that, in their own time they will probably come to realise that all the seemingly separate aspects of my work weave together with the benign beams of the cosmos to help us all. In many cases it will probably only then be that the aerosols, deodorants and hair sprays, the shampoos and the tanning lotions are either discarded or used with much more thought. At the very least I hope they won't be hoarded, for such products have a limited life-span, just like food. Counsel of perfection is to junk the junk four months after you bought it – certainly four months after the seal was broken, however much remains in the bottle or tube.

That, incidentally, is a big argument against the supermarket's gimmicks of 'buy one get one free'. That second item is going to prove far from free if you do the right thing and chuck it out before it has gone off. Similarly, unless you *know* you're going to consume or otherwise use household products or foodstuffs fast, don't buy the bulky 'economy'-sized packages. Much better to buy smaller bottles or packets and use them while they are at their best. Less of a storage problem, that way, too. I realise that it's pointless to hark back to some sentimentalised golden age during which we shopped each day for our household's immediate needs – but we may have gone too far in the opposite direction.

I'm a pragmatist too. Much as I would like to see women abandon nylon tights I simply know that they won't. All I can constructively suggest is that tights with a cotton gusset are chosen – much cheaper in the broadest, longest run, even if things like all-cotton bras are hard to track down. But do remember that if enough people ask for such items the manufacturers will eventually wake up: it makes good business sense for them. That's precisely why organic food is now so much more widely available. Equally, as I know that however effective my remedies are, I can't compete with the promise of beauty in a pot, I will advise clients who insist on using makeup to buy from the companies who promise organic purity.

* * *

It will come as no surprise to anyone with a knowledge of reflexology that the soles of the feet contain a whole map of the body and any physical ailment will connect by meridian to a precise place on the foot. Where the extraction of poisons from vaccines is concerned, I have seen great results after a bottle of untreated homeopathic tablets has been placed on the area between the two smallest toes connected to lymph drainage. One patient told me that she had hitherto been mystified when any bladder or bowel problem seemed to express itself with ankle pain: she just knew there had to be a connection.

Such remarks steer us back to the place and position we always understood. It is up to us, as individuals, to choose. What we feel in our bones, skin and water is often a surer barometer of what is best for us than the fancy promises on the box or label of some expensive medicine or cosmetic.

Happily one of my more straightforward tasks is to remove the residual toxins that well-meant vaccinations have left as potentially lethal calling cards. I've been doing this for years but now believe that I can do so more effectively.

In the past I relied on the organic wisdom of trees and plants and the generally wholesome and effective remedies that could be derived from them for anyone whose ancestors connected somehow to the same soil and vegetable DNA. Now that I call upon all the stars of the cosmos to help me in my healing, the new power can be directed, with the aid of my stone circle and labyrinth, more precisely towards the healing of anyone on our planet.

A 'little' thing like glue ear in children can be easily healed. Glue ear, caused by toxins in the lower bowel or small intestine, isn't so trivial when that kind of persistent infection leads to hearing loss or, in adulthood, tinnitus and the terrifying loss of natural balance that ear disorder can bring. The 'invisible' disabilities are every bit as serious as conditions which cry out with obvious, sympathy-gathering signs of illness, such as bandages, crutches or even wheelchairs.

So we know, however reluctantly, that we're never going to take a needless injection again and that we'll always spare our children or grandchildren this needless horror. But what about us, now? What about cleansing the system and making good the damage? Here's how...

I dowse to find what toxins have entered the body via vaccination and to find the correct drainage point. A pad of tablets, perhaps steeped in tincture derived from the cosmic energy stored in the heart stone at the centre of my labyrinth, is taped to that point and the poison is drawn out. An eye problem will be resolved by tablets applied to the bladder meridian line at the back of the heel. The liver spots, potential skin cancers and vitamin B deficiencies caused by some distant anti-tetanus injection can be dealt with in a similar fashion.

So *trust* that fear of needles. It isn't irrational at all. On the contrary it is rooted in common sense and a very basic instinct for survival. The adage 'less is more' is applied to many areas of life and it has never had more truth than when applied to the dubious business of vaccination.

I very much hope that by the time this book is published memories of the foot and mouth epidemic which paralysed Britain the spring of 2001 will have faded. Or do I? On reflection I think I prefer to hope that, even though the crisis will have passed, that some lessons will have been learned and will be imprinted forever.

As disease among cattle raged there was a furious debate about whether or not they should – or indeed could, with any benefit – be vaccinated. Many advised against this measure for a range of reasons. I felt very strongly that it was no wiser to vaccinate our livestock than it is to subject children to inoculations when the distressing consequences may not be realised for years. Good farming and animal husbandry have served our own and every other community well in the past and it isn't too late to see careful, caring methods of nurturing our food supply imposed again. If silly laws can be passed to restrict seed propagation, wise ones to protect our cattle can also reach the statute book.

As with humans, germs and viruses can only thrive in an animal's system if it has already been weakened. During this entire pitiable debate there was a danger of looking at things through the wrong end of the telescope: raising cattle organically, in small herds, is far preferable to the mass-production which leads to mass-destruction, and is much cheaper in the long run. It was noticeable, even during that crisis, that organically-reared herds were largely free of the disease – and thus even more tragic for those wise farmers to see their beasts slaughtered. It was such a terrible example of widespread ignorance and short-termism.

I hate to say 'I told you so' but this time I must.

CHAPTER EIGHT

Life's Hard and Then You Diet

It's not going to be easy. We all know that. Cold turkey here has nothing to do with Boxing Day lunch – in this context, the phrase and the phase that all addicts endure in order to conquer addiction is hell. Drugs, alcohol, cigarettes, chocolate and certain other foods – the agony of withdrawal from physical and psychological dependency is much the same.

People report insomnia, hives, ill-temper, depression, constipation... Family and friends close to someone who is attempting to kick any serious addiction should try to be as supportive and tolerant as possible. The addiction may well have been an 'innocent' one rather than dependency on a hard drug and thus it is sometimes imagined that getting clean is, as they say, a walk in the park. Don't imagine any such thing: getting off some hard drug like heroin is awful and requires masses of support, but getting off lesser drugs and fighting less threatening addictions still need lots of coping strategies that friends and family can supply.

I deal with the business of fasting in Chapter Nine, so there's no need to repeat much of that advice. In fact I'd like this chapter to emphasise the positive and the possible and to assure you that many of the things you may like to eat are not only permissible but also beneficial.

I rather like the fact that the great British snifter, the gin and tonic, was basically invented by colonials out east in the nineteenth century as a defence against malaria – it's all the quinine in the tonic. Some might argue that this was the single most enduringly positive achievement of the old empire-builders.

The principles I advance concerning fasting do actually apply to anyone attempting to lose a bad habit. Self-discipline comes into it, a sense of goal or target – whether this relates to weight-loss, improved general appearance, social and professional skills and success or simply the bank balance.

In this chapter, however, I am principally concerned with guidelines relating to what we eat. Diet, of course, is not merely to do with weight, but realistically I know that many of my readers are going to be mainly concerned with losing excess poundage and I hope I can encourage them. My interest in helping patients to lose weight springs less from much daft evaluation of what might or might not represent 'beauty' than from my certainty that an adult body maintaining a correct weight is likely to be a healthy one. That good or improved looks follow is just a happy coincidence.

We must also remember that physical deterioration isn't always rooted in poor diet or lack of exercise. It can be attributed to all manner of genetic inheritances and blockages or simply our genes running out of steam as we grow older. In my case careful diet, fasting, exercise and other sensible practice had kept me almost artificially fitter than I had a right to expect – given my birth genes – for many years. But eventually that strength began to give out.

About twelve years ago I was a wheezing OAP, around three or even four stones overweight and with a fistful of other problems ranging from stiff joints to insomnia, let alone tired-looking skin and a condition akin to psoriasis. All this despite the fact that I'd kept to a healthy organic diet, with occasional fasts, for years. The fact that I was fat and sluggish was to do with my genetic inheritance – and that's what I tackled. Today I'm back to my fighting weight of around eleven stones again, sleep like a peaceful baby, have the energy of a man half my age and – as photographs prove – look years younger.

I can't attribute all this to my diet, but I know it has played a major part in what sometimes seems to me to be a positive regeneration after I had *regained control of my body*. And I seldom feel that I am denying myself anything. I share a bottle of wine with a friend if I feel like it, have something sweet and sticky for desert now and again (the body can send out messages about needing sugars, you know), I eat red meat, but seldom now, and white meat and fish so long as I know it has been properly farmed. I always put a little of my stellar enhancing drops on my food in order to extract all available nutrition from it.

I also ensure that I take plenty of organic freshly pressed grapefruit juice and sea salt – in my daily bath water. I alternate between the two and know that my skin absorbs their nourishment just as surely as some emollient cream might sink into a thirsty face. Occasionally I'll have a very hot salt bath, wherein the pores are opened and toxins drained through the combination of steam and dissolved sea salt. But this is something that I would recommend you take under supervision – at least have a friend close at hand – as it's not unknown for people to lose consciousness.

Another thing which I recommend for people with stubbornly sluggish bowels is occasional colonic irrigation, but only if herbally based fluid is introduced into the rectum by a qualified expert and the technique is employed as something of a last resort if all else fails. The practice got a bad name a few years ago when it became known that some people were relying on regular 'colonics' as a means of controlling their weight. It should *never* be undertaken for this reason, nor, for that matter, should any other form of bowel relaxant. A healthy bowel, dealing with correct diet, will empty itself naturally in the usual way. Do remember that whilst ideally this will be every morning, not everyone's system works that way, so don't panic and take any extreme measures if the bowels haven't opened for two or three days and certainly don't book into an expensive clinic for colonic irrigation unless you must. It's ironic that a seized-up colon can be caused by the very worry about not being 'regular'. It was not for nothing that our old friend Sigmund Freud categorised some personalities as being 'anal' partly because they fretted about every little thing and simultaneously repressed their emotions as well as their rectal sphincter.

Curiously, these anal types tend to be extremely fastidious and tidy – perish the thought that some healthy enzyme derived from honest, organic soil or dirt should be allowed into their house or physical system. That this absence of general psychological tolerance and fear of disorder of any kind tends to inform their whole nature has been a study deemed worthy of many notable books.

Try to relax, don't worry – it might never happen, lighten-up... Many of us have been subjected to this kind of unhelpful bar-room or building-site philosophy in our time. Of course, one cannot will oneself to be carefree and cheerful. How nice it would be if that were possible. But at least where our bowels are concerned we can help them to function regularly with a decent diet and absolutely not with a confusing bombardment of pills and powders, which will at best result in some fast relief – not necessarily exactly when or where you might prefer it – and at worst with a colon rendered too lazy to remember what it is supposed to do naturally.

> Case study... Case study... Case study... Case study...
> CR, from Kent, has been my patient for a good few years.
> She's happy in a stable marriage now, but badly overweight
> and carrying with her a raft of disorders, some of which
> derive from a period when she was miserable and anorexic,
> and others from an old accident which damaged arterial
> flow, from irritable bowel syndrome and from ME. Recently
> there's been a breakthrough and I really think that all these

problems can now be sorted out. We've stuck together, with a mutual faith that things can be mended and CR's impressive faith, persistence and open-mindedness is now paying off.

'I've always accepted that there's such a thing as a "crisis of healing", in that fixing something in the system is likely to cause something else to react. I've never been surprised when I get headaches or skin eruptions as my body discharges toxins and I've never felt that treatment isn't working if it needs to take its time... Like everyone with ME, I was chronically fatigued and Jack set about dealing with this. And like many other people with this horribly debilitating condition I despaired as doctor after doctor dismissed it. At least I was too old to be told that I was suffering from the insultingly named "Yuppie flu": highly pressurized younger people in demanding jobs can seldom have found this easily delivered label at all helpful. Anyway, without prompting Jack somehow knew – or rather dowsed to find out – that I'd had that accident ten years earlier and explained how a problem with blood flow was at the root of my headaches, neck stiffness, depression and the rest. Things have been fixed one by one, little by little. I was on a downward spiral before. A year ago I was still under a cloud and couldn't even watch a TV programme or read a newspaper. Conventional doctors had just said I was depressed and needed Prozac.

'I just eat sensibly and put the food enhancing drops on everything these days. Jack says that eventually the weight problem will self-correct this way. I've already lost my cravings for chocolate and don't even enjoy wine any more. I've recently noticed that scars from an operation a few years ago – they never really healed and remained as bumpy red lines – have all but vanished. A recent photograph, compared with one taken when I first started seeing Jack, proves how my appearance has improved, especially my face which is no longer saggy and "jowly". It's better than having had cosmetic surgery.

'He's dealing with genes that may need to be brought forward eight hundred years, so I shan't expect overnight results... We just know that my blood pumping is faulty and that when it reaches my head it is slow to leave. I have every confidence that when this problem is solved I'll feel completely well and I accept that along the way the "cure" may create its own disorders and these will need to addressed as we go along. So far I'm very happy with my progress. I feel it's a question of mutual faith: he's determined to see me well and I'm determined to let him'

Case study... Case study... Case study... Case study...
Another patient who has spoken of the 'healing crisis' is NY. She lives in Buckinghamshire, is in early middle-age and, like a number of other patients, works in the field of complementary medicine. She is training in cranio-sacral therapy. She came to me largely, in the first place, because her teeth hurt.

'I take the long view about healing and accept that sometimes things need to get worse before they improve. I'm sure they will and I'm prepared to give it time. I'd already had all the poisonous mercury fillings extracted from my mouth but I knew something else was still wrong. Jack says my thymus is weak and I'm having treatment to strengthen my T cells. Like anyone else I'd have loved an instant solution, but I know my entire system to be a particularly sensitive one, so I accept that I may have to wait a little longer and, in the meantime, perhaps deal with some emotional problems. But I can say – even early in this treatment – that I already feel a great deal better. I take the food enhancing drops and am sure these are helping too.'

A simple thing surprised my friend Susan, who has helped me in the preparation of this book. She noticed that I almost always slabbed butter on my bread, certainly spread it quite thickly. She describes herself as a 'butterholic' and would rather have one slice of bread generously buttered than three thinly smeared, rather have one small baked potato with lots of butter than a larger one not quite buttery enough.

I explained that this instinct is not merely normal, but healthy. These fake and phoney butter substitutes and margarines taste really horrible and are made from derived industrial waste, artificial flavourings and fats which will do your heart and blood circulation no good at all. By all means take your polyunsaturates in the form of olive oil when you cook or dress a salad, your Omega 3 and 6 oils in capsule form if you cannot get hold of the cod, fresh sardines or halibut to grill. These latter oils should be taken as supplements in 'raw' form and not used as a cooking agent, as heat destroys most of their nutrients.

Don't deny yourself the simple pleasure of butter on your toast or in your cooking because it's been demonised. Why do younger-looking people have a nice plumpness to their skin? Because a subcutaneous layer of healthy fat has been retained. Anyway, no one sits down with a half pound of butter on their plate and cuts away with their knife and fork, do they? Be moderate, but never deny yourself an innocent healthy pleasure without very good reason.

You know that olive oil is good for you, that it promotes a healthy heart. Dipping good bread into a special oil is a wonderful treat with a taste evocative of the Mediterranean. But there's no need to go mad and buy fancy bottles of costly extra-virgin oil for everyday cooking. Use an ordinary supermarket oil most of the time, or groundnut oil, if your dish requires the fat element to be tasteless, and save the best quality oil for special meals and for dressing salads.

Eat as little salt as possible – about a quarter of a teaspoon a day is enough for me. Sea salt flakes or crystals are better than that refined 'easy-pour' stuff and the best salt of all is Malden. It's relatively expensive, but again one only uses tiny amounts at a time and because it is saltier than the others, you use even less. I am, however, aware that the individual's actual *need* for salt can vary (as opposed to the demands of a blunted palate), which is why I'm irritated by both the ignorance and arrogance of certain restaurateurs who refuse to put salt and pepper on the table as they feel their food is already perfect and that to add seasoning would be to insult the chef. Remember that just as many vegetables contain natural sugars, plenty of other foods have a natural salt content, so you shouldn't need too much more. Both an excess of salt and a shortage of oils can lead to a hardening of arteries.

As for sugar – well that's just about the easiest nut to crack if you'll pardon a mixed metaphor. The availability of unrefined sugars of palest cream granules to darkest brown ones is extraordinary these days, as is the range of honeys we can easily find without even making a detour to the health food shop. I know some people don't feel they've had their sweetness fix if the sugar comes naturally through fresh fruit or vegetables: that's often a psychological matter related to the business of self-reward, about which I will add a little more shortly. It's almost as if they've bought wholesale that 'naughty but nice' idea and taken it a little too far, so that they have an actual *need* to feel naughty. I'll stop the amateur psychology here, but I bet what I've just written has rung some bells. And I'll add that a little dish of proper Greek yoghurt with a dollop of organic honey and a scattering of toasted almonds or pistachio nuts is one of the most satisfying and ambrosial deserts ever devised.

Remember that millions of people – maybe you're one of them – decided to cut sugar out of tea and coffee. Tough for a couple of days perhaps but soon the taste of either drink is often repellent if it's sweetened. Those who still prefer a sweetened taste will find that less than a teaspoon of good honey will suffice. Never, ever, resort to those nasty little carcinogenic sweetening tablets: not only will they fail you in your resolve to re-educate the palate to appreciate the true flavour of whatever you are eating or drinking, they will be actively doing you harm. Wine enjoyed in one's early adulthood – often the sweeter German or Italian ones – tastes quite horrid once the palate adjusts to vintages which are drier yet somehow richer. The public relations company hired to research and help to improve the poor reputation of German wines in the United Kingdom found that young people weaned on colas and fizzy pops gravitated towards the sweeter wines as a rite of passage into adulthood. From Lilt to Liebfraumilch or Lambrusco, cola to Riesling or sweet cider in one sugary curve, but these are areas where many people can recognise how they gradually, imperceptibly almost, lost their taste for the wickedly sweet.

Recent research at Harvard Medical School in North America has suggested that chocolate cravings may be genetically programmed. It has been known for many years that chocolate can create a mild 'high' but these days instead of feeling weak-willed as they submit to a craving, chocoholics might be able to attribute their longing to an inherited sweet-tooth gene. So far definitive experiments have only taken place with mice, but Dr Gopi Shankar of the Mount Sinai School of Medicine says the gene activates a receptor which 'recognises the sweet content of food and initiates a cascade of events which signal to the brain that a sweet food has been eaten. If your parents had a sweet tooth then you probably will as well.'

> Case study... Case study... Case study... Case study...
> Z, who has known Blanche and me at the clinic for years, became understandingly worried when her seventy-five-year-old father began to experience fits after a holiday in Italy. A consultant recommended that a new heart valve was needed, but even after this bypass operation the fitting resumed.
>
> 'My father was also taking about twelve tablets a day, including six of phenaton to control the fits. But he still felt sick all the time and looked awful. I really feared that he would die soon. We took him to Jack who prescribed the food enhancing drops and taped the tablets on his forehead and arms to remove the traces of zinc and castor oil poisoning which were the cause of the onset of my father's condition. Dad now only takes two tablets a week and he

fasts once a week. The whole quality of his life has been
restored, he walks strongly now and there have been no fits
since June 2000! Z now intends to take any problem in the
family to me.

I heard recently of a successful career woman who is
grossly overweight but who has a ten-year-old daughter as
lithe and slight as an elf. She was already quite porky before
she became pregnant in her mid-thirties but has ballooned
since the birth of her daughter. She puts her weight down to
the well-meaning parental command to clear her plate when
she was a child. Psychologically she felt she was being a good
girl if she ate everything up and even asked for second
helpings.

She's not a qualified professional, but with inspired
amateur insight, she has striven to ensure that her daughter
will not see the family dining table as a battlefield, that she
will not grow up to have neuroses about food. Her daughter is
allowed, indeed encouraged, to eat what she likes, pretty much
when she likes, even though she may only toy with some food
as the cheerful conversational aspects of family meal times
take place. The child likes pasta and cheese, bananas and
yoghurt. So be it. Last year it was bread and baked beans, next
year, God help her mother, it may be lobster and guava fruit.
Whatever – the young girl is given and wolfs down what her
body craves and there are none of the table tantrums that can
lead to eating disorders like anorexia and bulimia when eating
and mealtimes have become associated with stress and
adversity.

The daughter, by the way, slender as she is, is strong
enough to play hockey for her school, is bright, perky, clever
and very keen on dancing.

Another younger friend remembers how she was deterred
for life from certain root vegetables – swede, turnips, parsnips
– because of the way they were cooked at home when she was

a child. To this day she will not touch them, nor sprouts nor any of the other vegetables she feels her mother murdered in the kitchen all those years ago. However often she reads that, properly cooked, these vegetables can be delicious, the memory of the food which grew cold on her plate and made her gag before she forced some more down endures. The legacy of poor or poorly cooked or unseasoned food can remain with us forever. It never fails to astonish me that so many people failed and still fail to make basic foodstuffs tempting by something as simple as the addition of some fresh herbs grown in a pot on the window sill or outside the back door.

I can half-understand why for some cooks in the 1950s and 1960s the idea of the packet stuffing, the stock cube or the canned soup seemed so thrillingly modern, sophisticated – promising a variety and exoticism absent during the recent war – and 'labour-saving'. But was it really? The tragedy is that it is often this basic ignorance and laziness that has put people off good food cooked properly at home and pulled from a garden if there was one.

Whilst absolutely accepting this, I have to think back to those post World War Two days when my three kids sulked a bit if they were offered yet another meal based around foods we'd grown at home. Blanche and I found that they managed to eat up if we made it clear that there would be no ice cream, cake or other sweet thing if they didn't. I'm not quite sure why, but some things don't seem to change. Anyway, none of my children had tonsillitis or appendicitis – illnesses that were almost *de rigueur* for kids in the fifties and sixties – and if their school records were dug out it would be clear that they seldom had to stay at home through illness. I do attribute this partly to the fact that they were never vaccinated for anything, were put on a diet of liquids if their temperature rose above 98.4 degrees (it's asking too much of the body to require it to digest solids at the same time as it works to fight a fever), and to the fact that we ensured they formed the habit of eating salads and fresh vegetables as a matter of course.

By now I need hardly repeat that organically reared meat is vastly superior in every way to that taken from animals and poultry reared in horrific, unhygienic and malnourished conditions. There have been enough food scares in Britain over the past decade or so to convince everyone, surely, that (leaving aside the vital but separate issue of animal cruelty), we owe it to ourselves and our children to choose organic foodstuffs. The British are paying a high price for the 'cheap' chicken and mince and the dubiously economical sausages they've demanded in recent years. An animal terrified and traumatised as it is pitched towards death in the abattoir will understandably go into some sort of muscular spasm and the subsequent toughness of the meat reflects this. And a little later on in the food chain that tough meat is 'tenderised' by any number of additives in bottles of muck for the domestic kitchen and in pre-prepared supermarket meals, which are not called junk food for nothing.

Beef is a relative newcomer to the Japanese diet and tends to be regarded as a luxury food, akin to Dover sole or the finest game in Britain. Consequently it is seldom eaten there but relished all the more for that. Perhaps it's got something to do with the fact that Japanese beef herds are pampered with massages every day, so that the animals are contented and their flesh tender. They are prepared for their last long journey to the slaughterhouse with a final massage to relax them into their next life – having at least enjoyed a pretty pampered one here on earth.

✻ ✻ ✻

Ever wondered why so many brands of cake or biscuit in the supermarket have unmistakably Scottish names? Well, there's long been a fine and noble tradition of fine baking in Scotland

and this must account for Scotland being the biscuit capital of the world, with more consumed per head than anywhere else by a Royal Mile and, coincidentally perhaps, one of the world's worst records for heart disease. Giving a baby sugary gloop from cans or jars or a child a biscuit is a fast, cheap and all-too-often welcome snack. Thus do children grow up with a 'sweet tooth' which they find hard to shrug off in later life. It's got nothing to do with any addiction-forming sweetness in mother's milk, as has sometimes been suggested.

In post-war Britain it was likely that a general fondness for sugar and sweet tastes was encouraged by those well-intentioned brown glass bottles of orange syrup which were issued free to children because of their vitamin C content. Given that the 'juice' was so highly sweetened I shudder to consider damage done to developing teeth as well as the negative education of young palates.

The Scots are also keen on deep-frying – even serving deep-fried haggis, often cooked in ancient, cheap and blackened oil, and strangest of all, the deep-fried Mars bar, served with chips and salt and vinegar. Mmmmm!! Well, once in a while I guess, but with a high percentage of the national diet characterised by this muck with nairy a green vegetable except for the tinned mushy pea, there really is something to worry about there – a country which conversely produces some of the best fruit, grains, fish and meat in the world.

Take some heart. Even a diet with a significant amount of such foods can be redeemed by the food drops which alert the system to recognise even tiny quantities of nutrients – such as carbon and vitamins – in meals like this and absorb them.

Incidentally, dozens of my 'other children' – kids who were conceived after their parents had come to me anxious to get really fit before having children or desperate because they seemed to be unable to start a family – have all enjoyed similarly perfect health. My records and the testimonies support this. And the happiest result of all, perhaps, is that those kids are not going to pass on any awful dietary inheritances when they have children of their own.

At the most profound level, children who have been pumped with all the routine vaccines as babies and then raised on a diet of cola, crisps and processed proteins will lead less healthy lives than those who were spared the inoculations and programmed to enjoy nicely seasoned and cooked organic foodstuffs. It's sometimes a question of basic and benign education. For instance, Susan has a young niece who likes Smarties as most kids do. Rosemary, her mother, metes them out one at a time, so a small tube lasts for weeks. If someone gives Janie two of the little chocolate buttons the child thinks that she's won the lottery.

Sometimes I think it's helpful to think of the body – whether it's yours or that of your child – as if it were your house, your home: it *is* in a way, since you live inside your skin. Any responsible householder knows that their property must be properly maintained in order to remain safe and sound and preserve its value. That might mean tiresome things like decoration inside and out, servicing of heating systems, dredging of guttering, airing and cleaning. You all know what I mean. Unless you're keen on DIY it's usually a bore. Equally the car owner knows that the motor needs an MOT every few years otherwise the car might be dangerous to drive. Once cracks appear inside or outside the walls of the house, or the persistently coughing car doesn't like an early start on a cold morning, then its time to take action.

I hope I can help the metaphoric MOT to go well and to advise about how you might sort out your house if you've neglected things for a while. Everyone with a mortgage will have been told tirelessly that this is the biggest investment they are ever likely to make. I beg to differ. The greatest and most important asset we have is our health and our body and looking after it should be seen as every bit as important as protecting the value of bricks and mortar.

Here's a simple example. All of us need to consider our liver, that wonderful flushing and cleansing organ. Although most people know that excessive alcohol can damage it, we sometimes forget that even non-drinkers need to be watchful and there are some people whose middle livers fail to absorb essential oils, fatty acids and the vitamins A, E, D and K. If you're worried about this, simply place some granules of the vitamins in question (just pounded up tablets from the local health shop will do fine), in a glass of water which rests on a dowsed-for verse of Crypto Power text (see illustration on page 99) and drink it after five minutes. The power of these vitamins will probably go straight to the feet and thence, via the meridian lines, upwards towards the heart. Many a potential thrombosis has been avoided by this simple means.

And here's another thing you can easily do at home: dowse for some stones to make your own private indoor circle at home. You don't need to travel far – after all, you're not looking for majestic rocks here and the chances are that the stones you need can be found in your garden or somewhere locally where you go for walks. You can then arrange these little stones in a circle under a chair at home and whilst sitting above them, whatever remedy you take with your food, or otherwise orally or have taped to your skin, will have a much more powerful effect. Again, under test conditions, Kirlian photography has proved this.

I see myself, crucially, as someone who can be called upon to deal with those worrying physical structural cracks, subsidence or whatever. I look straight at the foundations, not the decorations. The way things look can be important – and a gage of primary health and its possible neglect – but as in most areas of life, what matters most is what doesn't show.

Case study... Case study... Case study... Case study...
VT was nearing retirement but was nonetheless a very
active man, with a photographic business and hobbies
which included conducting an amateur band until a few
years ago when pains in his calves and feet led him to seek
a specialist's advice. He'd had a heart attack a few years
before that but had recovered enough to resume work and
to travel – especially to the United States; however recent
history had made him watchful about his health.

'The consultant delivered the bombshell that I'd had a
thrombosis and that I might have to lose both my legs.
Firstly they said they needed to amputate my entire left leg
and told me to prepare for the other leg to go. My daughter
told me about Jack Temple and, in desperation, I saw him
over about a month before the surgery in the wild hope
that he could save both my legs. Well, Jack was very frank
and said I'd left it too late to save all the left leg, even
though he did his best, but that he'd try to help me keep
the other one. In the meantime I'd been able to negotiate
a delay of the proposed surgery and, with Jack's faith,
found the nerve to insist that the hospital gave me another
pulse test in the limb they planned to amputate. This was
unheard of, as once pulse has been lost it is never expected
to return.

'Jack was able to restore blood flow to my left leg
above the knee and as a result I did not lose that entire leg.
I did lose part of my left leg, but perhaps less of it than if I
hadn't been to Jack. Thanks to Jack I can still lead a pretty
active life and drive a car. I really believe that he saved my
right leg as well as my left thigh.'

It troubles me to consider the millions of pounds wasted
every year in Britain alone by people buying expensive
vitamin and mineral supplements. Most of these can't do you
any good as the pill or capsule can't function in a body which
has forgotten how to use them. Thus they are just wastefully
flushed out, at great expense. With a correct diet the body can
send a signal which alerts the system to utilise and process

the contents of these tablets – but if you've been eating junk there will be no such healthy collaboration. So don't imagine that a week of burgers and other junk can be corrected by some daily multi-vitamin. Of the brands available, the only one I endorse – always in conjunction with sensible eating – is Royal Life's Mega-Multis. This is only the third commercial plug you'll find in this book and I write as someone who is bombarded every day with glossy leaflets and samples from the health food industry.

A very good reason why I trust the Royal Life brand is that I recommended them to a cancer patient of mine who was also receiving chemotherapy treatment at London's Royal Marsden Hospital. As her hair grew back faster than anticipated and her fingernails became long and strong again, her hospital doctors were delighted to accept that the tablets may have made a contribution to this. Anyway, I understand that they advised the local pharmacies to stock up. So I would say that if you live life on the run – grabbing a sandwich here and a rushed station snack there – and if you really must take a dietary supplement, these are the ones to choose.

Sometimes I'll dowse samples before chucking them in the bin but usually I know the company in question of old and have reason to doubt their marketing strategies. The fact is that dietary supplements may work as placebos for some people but even that is dangerous if the capsules lull them into the idea that its now OK to overindulge in food which has almost no nutrition at all. Hybrid foodstuffs have little enough nourishment in the first place and the body won't absorb it any better just because you've taken a multi-pill for breakfast. I may make an exception about vitamin E supplements, but that's about it. Good food and my stellar-based food enhancing drops are all that anyone should need.

Case study... Case study... Case study... Case study...
DW and I are old friends. She's sixty now and about to retire
to Devon – which after an adult lifetime in London she still
regards as home. I gather than she intends to at least
consider becoming a teacher of my holistic ideas. Better,
she maintains, than spending her retirement in knitting and
fidgeting. DW first came to see me in the mid-1980s, long
before my clinic was built. A colleague had suggested she
consulted me because nothing had seemed to help her
stomach pains.

'The pains were just awful. I'd be hunched over my desk
in agony. Medicine I'd been given to deal with ulcerative
colitis didn't help at all and although this condition is
sometimes known as "irritable bowel syndrome", I was
certain it was something more than the almost trivial
matter which that label implies. I worked in a bank with lots
of younger people and I knew that, with help, I could
function just as efficiently as the others. But I did feel I
needed help to deal with the terrible gut pain, pain that
made it hard for me to straighten up if I'd been seated at
my desk for too long, and Jack offered it.

'I'd had some chest problems before, and trouble with
my eyes that Jack had said were caused by contact with
rubber, petrol and other pollutants. These cleared years ago,
so I was quite receptive to the treatment he suggested
when I went back and said my stomach was painful. Now I
take the food enhancing drops with every meal and feel so
much better.

'Maybe it's a coincidence but I went through "the
change" without any of the horrors women are lead to
expect, believe that my memory has actually improved –
despite the warnings that it will probably fail as you grow
older – and altogether feel that treatments taken for some
specific disorder have helped my whole system recover and
work together as well as they did when I was much younger.
I won't say that he's a miracle worker because it's an act of
faith on both sides, but I can date my physical and
psychological advancements to those early days when I saw
Jack in his house. I've had to keep up with the young ones
at the bank where I work and I really feel that, having been

rid of certain problems, I've been right up there on my toes.
'I do as I'm told and drink the charged water every day.
I may not fully understand why it makes me feel so much
better and optimistic and positive but I just know that it
does and when I go back to Devon I'll take that all with me,
even though it might not be practical to see Jack so
regularly. It would be marvellous if I actually could start to
teach down there, but we'll see...'

When I was a younger man and founding my market
gardening business, I was capable of shifting twelve tons of
potatoes a day without any help. I could also deal with a
hundred bales of hay. I was young, driven and strong and I
needed those four square meals a day in those days to
accomplish my work. Our needs change with age and activity
and it's foolish to adhere to a regime that, for whatever reason,
no longer makes sense for you.

We often read of athletes who need to consume 12,000
calories each day to enable them to row, swim, run, lift weights
or even fence at their best. And we often read about how all
that muscle quickly turns to fat when competitive athletic
demands wind down. A new kind of dietary education is now
required. I find it interesting to see that these days footballers
and other athletes, even boxers, train on carbohydrates and
that today a huge steak before a match or event is considered
damaging to performance, as the body concentrates its
energies on digesting such heavy proteins. This suggests that
there was wisdom in the admonishments of old-fashioned
parents who forbade their children to swim for an hour or so
after lunch on the beach. In any case, professional athletes or
keen amateur ones must usually unlearn the habit of eating
massively calorific meals of whatever type when they ease up
on their sport.

Few of us ever need to meet such strenuous demands and
the idea of the three or four squares has really rather gone out

of fashion, and rightly so. Three meals, maybe, but not all of them need to be substantial for most people. When I was younger there was a mantra which dictated that we should all breakfast like a king, lunch like a prince and dine like a pauper. All very well if you rise at dawn to do some heavy labouring, and I rather embraced the cliché of those 'descending' meals in the past. I feel rather differently now and believe that for most people a light breakfast is best, especially if it contains the power elements of star drops in some vegetable juice. Both tea and coffee are stimulants and the latter, in particular, can fill you up. If you really can't manage without it, then add a drop of the star tincture to the brew. Sometimes a spoonful of flax seed oil or avocado oil is a good idea in the morning. Whilst neither may be exactly delicious in themselves they can be hidden or disguised within a bowl of organic cereal or fruit salad if that is how you like to break your fast and both will contribute to the body motor's efficiency.

Then lunch can be a little more solid, depending what you need to do later in the day – in other words, not so tiring on the digestive system as to induce weariness in the afternoon. Don't eat standing up or on the run if you can help it. The digestive system needs oxygen, brought by the blood, to process food properly. If you're rushing about or even just leaning against a counter, that oxygen is diverted to other muscles and this can lead in the short term to stomach cramps or indigestion. In the long term, if this mode of eating has become a habit, it can completely skew the entire digestive system.

I rather approve of people having their main meal in the evening if it makes sense for their lifestyle. An early dinner, almost a reward for a full day's work, is not only nutritious and likely to promote deep and contented sleep, but psychologically important. Sit at the table with friends and or family if you can, enjoy their company, relax, savour the food.

It may be stating the obvious, but families whose members 'graze', pick away at things from the fridge, grab a packet of something to heat in the microwave, call for a motor-bike pizza delivery at midnight and almost never sit down to eat with others in the house are really missing out, and not just in a dietary sense. Perhaps this is why even the most fashionable chefs and restaurants acknowledge the importance of Sunday lunch – often the only time that the family will eat together all week.

Even if you are by yourself this process of self-respect whilst choosing, cooking and eating matters. Perhaps it matters especially if you are by yourself… Feel the fatigue slip away. Enjoy that lovely sense of a good day completed. Pour out the extra half glass of wine you will probably be too sleepy to finish before you retire for a good night's sleep, eager to greet the morning, maybe, instead of facing the day with a vague sense of unease and evidence of a sluggish digestion.

Whatever you choose to eat, however low in nourishment and/or high in additives it might be, if for some reason you have no choice on that occasion, a drop of my food enhancing tincture will release all available nourishment and vastly improve flavour, too.

Well, that's how it should and can be. Naturally the 'weight' or balance of your meals will depend on your lifestyle. Someone who rises at dawn to face hours of heavy manual work, possibly outside in the cold, will need fuel to kick-start them, probably a combination of energy-supplying carbohydrates and proteins. For them breakfast may well be the most calorific of the day. A sedentary office worker may need no more than a fruit or vegetable-based drink or, as I've said, even tea or coffee and a drop of energy-enhancer in such liquids, too.

Certainly I don't think people should eat if they are not hungry. Apart from anything else, eating without appetite

means swallowing without the essential lubricant of saliva
and the digestive juices and this in turn leads to poorly
digested food and strain on the stomach, intestines and colon.
However, even if you don't feel hungry you still need
nourishment, which is where and when 'power juices' and
added cosmic energisers are so useful.

I'm well aware that this flies in the face of conventional
wisdoms regarding eating patterns. What's new? I've spend a
working lifetime countering conventional advice about health
and nutrition. And I can't remember when I last had a
headache, toothache, joint pain or cold, even when all around
me other people seem to be succumbing to some virus or other.
At times like that my trust in our natural immunity seems
well founded.

You'll know by now that I recommend organic foods
wherever possible and practical. Despite the slight extra cost
it remains a bargain in the long run. It is the non-organic
foods which, literally, cost the earth as well as harming the
planet's human visitors. Don't be fooled by labels like 'farm
fresh' or 'naturally pure' on vegetables, eggs or meat. These
are usually meaningless and misleading. Look for the word
'organic' and/or the Soil Association's endorsement. The
supermarket chain Iceland deserves a special mention here as
they sold and promoted organic foods long before many of
their so-called upmarket competitors and in 2000 the chain
announced that all its own-brand frozen fruit and vegetables
were organic and would not cost any more than the other stuff.
This brave experiment was ahead of its time, sadly, and
overestimated the general British consumer's common sense.
The scheme lost the company so much money that they had to
abandon it.

But gradually the principles will take hold and in the
meantime choosing genuine organic foods where you can find
them, and paying a little more, will help you to recover or
regain control of your body – your most precious possession.

Case study... Case study... Case study... Case study...
EA was only twenty five when severe rheumatoid arthritis
was diagnosed. Neither her doctor nor a specialist nor
various homeopathic practitioners were able to give her
much hope of improvement. To be so physically debilitated
is depressing at any age but for a very young woman it was
especially so. As her gene pool was in many respects
exhausted when she was born, I dowsed her left side back
thirteen generations to find the genetic moment when this
aspect of her health was potentially strongest. It was on
those healthy genes, brought forward, that I was able to
hang her treatment, having dowsed down through
generations of her 'foremothers'.

    'I don't quite know how or why it works but I
definitely feel better. There's been a real, steady
improvement over the past two years. All my joints were
swollen and aching. Sometimes I could hardly get out of
bed. I kept going to my job in an office – but only because
I'm stubborn, I think. Jack puts the tablets on my arms and
legs – not necessarily specifically where the pain is – after
dowsing me. I take the food drops and drink the energised
water that's been standing in a glass over the Hebrew
Word. It's all a bit of a mystery to me but I don't mind that
as it seems to work'.

I've already said a little about fasting, but will repeat that
a short spell without solid food is far from the biblical forty
days in the wilderness. Just choose to go easy once a week,
even if it's only for half a day. Watch for and listen to your
body's language. A body which sweats a lot is getting rid of
toxins in its own way and should be allowed to get on with it;
so much the better if you have a slight temperature for a short
while. Don't eat if you feel unwell – remember that no sick
household pet will touch food unless and until their system is
ready to cope with it. When you perspire in this way your body
is burning away and discharging rubbish. That probably
accounts for your slightly raised temperature. Don't try to

suppress this – you're being alerted to give the whole system a rest and the most you should do is cool the system with cold compresses on the forehead. Just as we should try to see pain as a friendly warning that something somewhere is amiss and take remedial action, any kind of fever is our body's way of alerting us to some kind of blockage and of begging us to allow it to have a rest from processing solids, so that it can deal with the problem in its own way.

The same is true of the mysterious skin rashes which some of us suffer. They may look blotchy and unattractive but try to see such outbreaks as the system's friendly and self-regulating way of extruding toxins. I have to agree that it's a bit of a shame that these rashes so frequently appear on the face – but perhaps we wouldn't notice them so quickly and take remedial action if they erupted elsewhere. In Chapter Seven I note that children actually *need* to endure the stages of mumps, measles and chicken pox, as after each of these illnesses there is a growth spurt. This really is relevant to what I have said just now as it illustrates how the body regulates itself, deals with toxins and makes ready for improvement and advance.

As Dr Schieber pointed out in Chapter Seven, we live in a rapidly changing world and not all those changes are for the better. But it's no good thinking back to some past golden age – there probably never was one anyway. There's very little we can do as individuals to control the quality of the air we breathe in the streets or the ions that zip and zap between every household or office where there's a computer, a mobile phone or access to the internet. Sadly, unless you've all the time or money in the world, you probably can't even always ensure that the clothing you buy in high street shops is free of some damaging chemical hidden within that mysterious '5 per cent other fabrics' you see on the label of the 'pure' wool or cotton garment. But you *can* control what you eat and what you eat will influence every area and aspect of your life and well-being.

The body has a self-healing mechanism. Poor diet serves to de-programme that mechanism and render the body more vulnerable to attack from illness of any kind. So whether you diet because you need to lose weight or to meet the requirements of sustained good health, try to think of the diet as a rather exciting challenge. There's a world of great food out there – quite a bit of it could be cultivated at home, as well as masses of it prepared and cooked there. Eating well in a restaurant isn't always quite the same thing and although you may want to dowse the food there, go easy. Since a restaurant meal is often a celebration of some sort, 'eating well' in the broadest sense – atmosphere, companionship and other pleasures – is sometimes as important as the food on your plate.

If you can, take 8 xeroxes of the disc 17 illustration on page 19; cut them out and place them under your plate or glass in a restaurant. It will purify whatever you are eating or drinking there.

I've mentioned the 1973 Seed Act elsewhere in this book but make no apology for reminding readers that this act effectively robbed us of the means to absorb nutrients contained in foods. Hairline fractures and easily broken or strained ankles are a warning that not all is well with our absorption of carbon. Hybrid foods simply cannot compare to foods produced from seed pollinated by bees and insects – which is why I developed the food enhancing drops you will also find several references to here.

A prescient old Beatles' lyric proclaimed that 'you are what you eat'. Well, which would you rather be, an additive-laden biscuit, all brittle and crumbly, or a shiny, fresh cherry? A piece of tough, leathery meat or something nimble as a leaping trout, or as peachy as beautiful fruit ripened in the sun?

CHAPTER NINE

Helping Yourself

There's so much that you can do to help yourself become or remain well that this chapter can only skate across the surface of some very strong ice. Nonetheless I'll try to offer a few suggestions and examples here and leave you to pick up scores of other pointers elsewhere in the book.

I've already made the point that sometimes too much information can confuse rather than clarify. I assume that most of you will read the newspapers and watch the TV news. Since every week there's some new development in the GM debate – whether it concerns food scares or human cloning and frightening (or exciting, depending on your point of view), embryonic research, I'll assume that you will follow the scientific developments which you feel relate most closely to your own lives and then will rely on instinct and common sense. You'll have to be on the ball to keep track of the government-funded genome report, the privately funded researches often in the news and the new books which seem to be published every week. The speed of scientific advances being so breathtaking, this time next year there may well be some new boon to cheer us or a fresh threat to worry us, but innate good sense will transcend either of these.

And in any case, studies which we are told will only be tried, tested and proved in many years aren't much use to people who want to see some results now, or at least soon.

Everyone knows how much more positive and less lowered they feel about any problem or worry once they have done something practical. In many cases accomplishing a simple, single act or task can flick some psychological switch, so that the next step – and then the next one after that – becomes much less daunting. It's a bit like starting a crossword puzzle: at first you may be completely baffled but then you manage one clue. Those letters enable you to get the next few because you have at least a toe-hold... Then all the others become increasingly easy – almost obvious. One good result can give the encouragement needed to keep going. This, again, is no more and no less than everyday common sense.

One vitally important thing that a mother can do to help – not herself, or at least not directly – but her newborn, is to insist that when her baby is born the umbilical cord is cut correctly. That is to say that it should not be severed at once, not until the pulse there has finished. That may not even mean any time lapse before the baby can be placed in her arms and will certainly spare the child a lifetime's raft of disorder. As a matter of fact, I have even wondered if it might not be of immediate psychological benefit for the new baby to establish a tiny period of contact with the mother, in her arms and against her breast, before the lifeline he or she has known for nine months is severed.

All too often that cord is cut a few seconds too soon and the health and energy forever generated by the umbilical centre, which we know as our belly-button, is impaired forever. As I believe it to be a mother's duty to do all she can to ensure the future health of her child, I try to insist that all my pregnant patients observe this advice or brief their partner to do so for them in the delivery room. We are all born with thousands of body parts and systems designed to interact in harmony. This practice is a very simple means of ensuring that the child is properly programmed for the best possible start, given all the other variables, such as possible inherited genetic imperfections.

I can deal with problems caused by the failure to cut the umbilical cord at the proper time, but how much better if those problems had not been there in the first place.

You will already know how much store I set by the weekly fast. For quite a few years I have eaten nothing for one day a week and drunk only good quality bottled water, and I urge you to do the same. You might begin with a half-day fast during which either the midday meal or the evening one is missed. Even a full day of fasting soon becomes no hardship at all for most people, especially if they already have problems with obesity. These days, what suits *me* best is to eat nothing solid at breakfast, have a light lunch and eat my main meal in the evening. You will soon learn what works for you.

Sometimes the main point of mealtimes is to break up the day, to signal a period of rest or relief from boredom or to provide a stimulating contrast. Try to find some intellectual, emotional or spiritual nourishment to enjoy instead of food. I remind those of you who have endured long-haul flights that the tedium of the journey was sometimes only relieved by the prospect of the next plastic tray meal: it wasn't that you expected to enjoy it much or even that you were hungry. It was probably only something to do in an enclosed environment where options were strictly limited. It's no coincidence that the major international airlines attempt to sell their tickets on advertisements for the excellence of their 'cuisine'. After all, none of them can guarantee to get you there an hour faster or to arrange that you be seated next to your fantasy travel companion.

When fasting your body should be simultaneously nourished by a little *Forceval-Protein* powder taped to the stomach meridian line on the lower legs. Look at the sketch on page 87. This product is available at all good chemists, health food and homeopathic shops and is one of the very few brand names you will find specified in this book. The powder was designed to be taken with water as a liquid food containing a high balance of vitamins and mineral nutrients. I have observed it to be most effective if the powder is mixed into a paste or poultice, placed as pads in muslin and then taped to the skin where benefits can be best absorbed. This way the cleansing benefits of the short fast are unhindered by even simple digestive complications. For 'solids', a tablet each of birch ash, black shilajit and ginger powder could be sucked four times a day.

A system that has thus been cleansed and detoxed on a weekly basis is going to have improved muscle tone anyway and prime energy levels will be restored. So trips to spas and hydros, subscriptions to expensive gymnasiums, exercise bikes, personal trainers, rather daft special clothing and other gear will all be rendered unnecessary. Good health can be so much simpler than all that commercially driven pressure.

Some time ago I was asked by an anxious father to look at his daughter. She'd been diagnosed as having cancer and was only expected to live for a few more days. She was floppy and too weak to even eat without vomiting. The only treatment her wasted, damaged body responded to was the morphine they gave her to relieve her pain. Given the hostility I've often encountered when dealing with the medical establishment, I was rather surprised when her consultant made no fuss when her father said I was going to visit and treat his dying daughter. Perhaps he felt she was beyond help and hope and was simply humouring the father.

Anyway, I immediately fastened powder poultices to the meridian line stretching from her stomach to knee and told the parents that these 'bandages' should be changed every two hours. Days passed. After ten days the girl was sitting up in bed and enjoying the company of visiting friends. I'm sad to report that twelve days after that her heart gave up and she died. In the meantime I'd established that the cause of her cancer had been caused by handling melons treated with pesticides during a holiday job on a farm.

This story is recounted not only to underline the points about pesticides and so forth but to emphasise that I'm not a miracle-worker and that sometimes disease is beyond my reach however hard I try to arrest it.

But in another instance an adult cancer patient who expected to live only a few more days came to my clinic, again with the consent of his consultant. I put a paste of the Forceval-Protein powder and water on his stomach meridian line, dowsed to find the correct Crypto Power text upon which to place the spring water he was allowed to drink and then told him to fast for eighteen days. His pain retreated and within less than another five weeks he was back at work. I had not realised at the time of treating him that this patient's spinal cord had been damaged by radiation given to him earlier to treat his cancer. I'm afraid that I could only help this patient to enjoy a short new lease of life. His cancer was rooted in lamb he had eaten years before – meat that had been affected by organophosphate pesticide. That's common sheep dip to you and me.

Case study... Case study... Case study... Case study...
Unjust criticism is always hurtful, however thick we reckon our skins are and however often it must be endured. One is never quite inured to it.

Recently a young woman, married to a doctor who worked in a group practice came to see me, troubled with a general malaise. When I heard that he was a doctor I invited her husband, waiting outside, to join us for the consultation and he observed silently as I dowsed and drew my conclusions about the patient's health. I deduced that her problems had been caused by her father's contact with that greenish-yellowish paraffin-based jelly used as a heavy-duty cleanser for the hands and so forth. I'm sure you know the brand I mean.

The following day I received a remarkably poisonous letter from the husband, accusing me of being a charlatan and describing my work and ideas as 'bunkum' and 'preposterous' and 'quackery'.

Well, you can't please everyone, I guess, but it did occur to me as I read the doctor's violently critical screed, that it was a bit odd that his wife had chosen to consult me when she had instant access to a range of practitioners in the surgery where her husband worked... Anyway, I put this uncomfortable experience behind me and was only reminded of it when a year or so later I began treating CM, the young mother of three, who had been informed that she had hopeless, terminal, inoperable cancer.

CM grew up in Spain, where her father was a mechanic. Throughout her childhood she played and loitered in garages and workshops where that very same yellow-green gunge was used every day to cleanse oily hands and faces... I'll let her husband continue the story:

'After some vaginal bleeding and a pelvic examination in 1999, my wife had a complete hysterectomy. A few months later a scan revealed nodules on her lung and we were emphatically told by the oncologist that her cancer was spreading and incurable. Surgery would be pointless, we were told. Chemotherapy would merely prolong the agony, he said. She was given only months to live and the specialist suggested she enjoyed her last months and need only return to hospital when she was clearly very ill. He was very negative about the idea of us seeking a second opinion or even considering alternative medicine.

Actually my wife felt fine and we weren't prepared to accept this bald prognosis. After scans and blood tests, a clinic in the USA suggested surgery on both lungs, a procedure which would cost about £50,000. They recommended that we consult someone at the Royal Brompton Hospital in London, who gave conflicting advice: he said that surgery would be of no use to her (she was still feeling fine apart from the worry about all this).

'Then we saw Jack for the first time and he offered treatment for her lung nodules. A few weeks later, when we went back to our original oncologist for X-rays, he was astonished to see that the nodule had become smaller. We had been in a hopeless sea of despair and the whole experience has made us see so-called specialists and experts as irresponsible, ignorant and proud, whereas we always look forward to seeing Jack and have every faith and confidence in his work.

'I'd seen Jack on TV some time earlier and once when I was praying the memory of this came into my mind so we tracked him down. As I said, my wife hadn't been feeling unwell but Jack did detect residues from a rabies vaccine and other jabs including pethidine she'd had during childbirth, as well as identifying the effects of the petroleum-based cleaning jelly and he removed these after dowsing and applying his tablets. She takes the food enhancing drops and drinks the energised Crypto Power water – in fact the whole family does these days.

'We still can't be sure about the future and my wife is still monitored and X-rayed regularly. But she feels fine and whereas a couple of years ago we were given no reason to have any hope at all, we now feel very optimistic and have absolute trust that it is Jack we have to thank for this.'

Tragically, this patient's remission only lasted 2 years. During a well-deserved holiday her family insisted that she must seek medical advice for a developed cough. A heavy dose of antibiotics was prescribed and my patient passed away a month or two later.

Naturally I'm tempted to mention this to the other doctor who'd been so dismissive about the after-effects of that cleaning jelly stuff. Perhaps he'll read this and have the sense and humility to be less dismissive of 'charlatans' next time he encounters one.

✳ ✳ ✳

You have a murderer in your kitchen if there is a microwave in the corner.

That bulky box which takes up so much space and sends negative ions into the atmosphere of your home every time it is switched on is actually causing food to die and decompose before you eat it. Eating microwaved food is little better than poisoning yourself, simple as that. It can destroy the life force in even organic foods, as I discovered during an experiment with fresh beans some years ago.

I once lined up ten of my strongest students and challenged them to resist the downward pressure of my little finger whilst they held a green bean. Nothing doing – my little finger exerted no strength against them. Then I gave the macho men another bean to hold and repeated the test. This time each hand collapsed under the pressure of my finger. Both beans were fresh from my organic garden, but whilst the first had been cooked in salted water, the second had been microwaved. In a similar test about thirty years ago, at the first Festival of Mind, Body and Spirit in London, when I was first expounding my beliefs concerning organic foods, I offered £20 cash to anyone who could twice resist the pressure of my hand. In those days £20 was really worth having. To some it still is, of course. Anyway, a number of burly soldiers, policemen and other confident chaps accepted my challenge, raised their arms and twice grasped a carrot, fully expecting to grab the £20 note. It drew quite a little crowd – and I never paid out a penny... One carrot, you see, was shop-bought and tainted with chemicals and the other had been organically grown.

Around the same time some fellow alerted me to a simple machine he'd devised which could be wired up to the mains and clipped to the leaves of a plant. His aim was to deduce whether or not vegetables felt pain when they were handled. A supermarket lettuce was heard to squeal in alarm whilst the organically grown one tugged from my garden gave a little gurgle of pleasure, indicating that the organic leaves were happy ones, full of life.

Now I realise that tales of the laughing lettuce are likely to consign me to the rank of crank – after all, the organic fellow-lettuce was destined for the salad bowl too – but he'd had a happier life, is all that I'm suggesting. The same applies to that box of plump red berries which have been irradiated to give them a week's shelf-life in the supermarket cabinet.

They're organically dead long before you get them home.
Really fresh fruit is only fit to eat for a day or two after
harvesting. So the choice is yours: eat poison at your
convenience or shop more carefully and maybe slightly more
often. Personally I'd rather go without or eat only small
amounts of really delicious foods than buy the cheap stuff,
which can sometimes turn out to be expensive rubbish.

The point I made just now about the microwave, and the
little stories of happy lettuces are not entirely flippant. They
all support my view that this is one household device you
could easily dispense with and should. Rethink the idea that
food has to be on the table within minutes and remember that
some of nature's 'fast foods' are just as quick to prepare and
taste a million times better. How long does it take to boil a
perfect egg and prepare some good bread and butter to go with
it? You can grill a piece of fish in less than four minutes, too.
You know perfectly well that good vegetables or salads need
take no longer. And who in their right minds would consider
blasting a piece of meat or a cake mix in one of those cursed
machines?

❋ ❋ ❋

Not another long lecture here. Most readers will already know
by now that one of the easiest and most effective ways of
prolonging and improving health is to banish aerosols,
detergents, artificial fibres, cosmetics, lead and petroleum
products, plastics and chemical drugs from their homes and
lives. If you can't quite cut them out at least cut back and
expose your children to them as little as possible. Of course,
the area in which there is often massive room for
improvement is that of diet. Happily this is an aspect of things
which almost everyone accepts and which most people find
easy and practical to adapt to.

Case study... Case study... Case study... Case study...
FB is a professional therapist and as such has knowledge of and access to any number of complementary and alternative therapies as well as all that is on offer through the National Health Service. Thus I take it as a particular compliment that she has become a patient of mine. There was a rather appropriate *balance* about this as FB, now fifty, initially heard about me through an interest in and research on labyrinths. At the same time she was experiencing high blood pressure and a severe viral disorder of the inner ear, rather like tinnitus.

'I couldn't walk straight, my sense of balance was completely shot and my blood pressure had gone through the roof. It was absolutely terrifying. I'll never be sure if the blood pressure problem was a result of the fear, but in any case, three years later – when I was able to get to see Jack – I'd seen a homeopath and the balance problem was less severe but I still felt very unwell. My father had undergone serious heart surgery in his 50s and I was almost fatalistically programmed to worry that this was some inevitable genetic destiny. It also seemed almost preordained that my researches on labyrinths coincided with Jack's construction of his own and his study of how the sharp turns on it can restore balance.

'When I first began to speak to him and receive treatment I had a marvellous sense of "Now, at last..." I finally felt when I first discussed things with Jack that I was in the right place. Jack identified a problem in my sympathetic nervous system that may have connected back to dentistry I underwent in 1989. Anyway, I was dowsed and had tablets taped to my skin. I put the star drops on my food and I followed Jack's advice about nylon tights and underwear, finally tracking down items which were all largely made from cotton.

'Today the ear problem has receded and my blood pressure is normal. Just as importantly, perhaps, I am no longer fearful about my long-term health. Jack has given and inspired me with a great sense of confidence. Every time I see him I feel better. This isn't through any mystic or psychological trickery – I'd never fall for that. I've quite

simply been helped by quiet, practical advice and
treatment. It has worked for me so I have no worries about
Jack's unconventional methods.'

✳ ✳ ✳

In their recently published book, *Cosmetics Unmasked,*
American chemists Dr Stephen and Gina Antczak confirm
what most women already knew, namely that most beauty
products offer unsupportable promises. 'Claims such as "for
sensitive skin" and "hypoallergenic" should be strictly
regulated, if not discouraged', they warn. Expensive products
are seldom any more effective than cheaper ones and women
should remember that they buy into a fantasy, a daydream of
perfection when they shell out.

Chemicals in make-up, face creams, bath gels and so
forth can dissolve the outer layer of skin cells and increase
risk of damage by ultraviolet radiation as well as penetrating
deeper into the dermis where they can do further damage.
Even 'natural' cosmetics and bathroom bubbles are suspect
as they need to be stabilised by distinctly unnatural
preservatives. The Antczaks dismiss as myth the idea that
products containing vitamins will nourish from the outside,
counter free radicals and so forth. 'Proteins cannot be
absorbed by the skin, hair or nails and cannot repair or
improve body tissues.'

They go on to point out that chemicals in food, washing
powder, scent and cosmetics can exacerbate asthma and
psoriasis, amongst other conditions. And beauty-related
products can go off just as surely as food, so unless you want
to slap mould, bacteria and fungal material on your face and
body, chuck out any product that's been hanging around the
bathroom or dressing table too long or which has changed in
colour, consistency or smell.

✳ ✳ ✳

In 1973 an act of Parliament that I consider to be perfidious was passed. Too few people remember it now, but we are all affected by it every single day. It was called the Seed Act and in the wake of Britain's recent membership of the European Community it compelled all growers and farmers to conform to a uniformity of cultivation that has affected not only the size and shape of the tomatoes in our shops but in the grain with which our cattle are ultimately fed and our daily bread.

Even the much beloved common swallow and starling would testify to this if they could. Early in 2001 a spokesman for the Royal Society for the Protection of Birds explained a 20 per cent decrease in the population of these species by saying that the quality of the seed which the birds peck at to survive had dramatically declined.

So concerned am I about this – for humans as well as birds – that I am planning to construct three more circles with stones from Wales and plant them out with special herbs which will not only attract the bees and other insects but will encourage the propagation of the kind of herb which I can make into tablets to eat with food.

I believe that a stone circle can form a kind of replica of the human body and contain 'references' to match every part and system. I've held this belief for decades and initially had the conviction to demolish my commercial greenhouses to make space for my original stone circle. Today I've never felt more certain that herbs and plants, grasses and rocks contain the missing link between human health and longevity and nature itself. They contain supplies of extra energy that can help to improve almost every aspect of life, from peaceful sleep to agreeably tiring sport. Properly dried and used at home in the preparation of food and healing remedies, herbs are life enhancers and can sometimes be life savers. The obverse, I'm afraid, is that you can chuck out all those little supermarket tubs and bottles of dried herbs right now – yet another way to help yourself – as they're a waste of space and money, have no nutritional strength and are useless as flavourings unless you like the taste of taste of dried grass clippings in your food. Herbs and spices are often irradiated in order to kill off pests and thus prolong their life. Dowsing informs me that such herbs – even potted ones bought expensively in supermarkets – have no food value whatsoever.

I estimate that it will take a little while before the plants within the new circles can soak up all the stellar energy, are seeding properly and may be harvested. But it is the only logical way. We are *all* creatures of the earth, after all, and that Seed Act affects each of us. However, I remain an optimist. Some things are worth waiting for – like the asparagus bed in the garden that will take five years to bear spears. But when it does, and you can tug fresh asparagus every spring thereafter you will forget the few years when the bald patch seemed to be a waste of garden space.

Just as nature would soon reclaim even the busiest motorway if no traffic thundered along it for a while, natural foodstuffs cannot be obliterated by acts of Parliament alone. The Seed Act was passed in the interests of trade and commerce, not in the interest of the consumer and it has had a devastating effect on our diet and health. Diabetes is on the rise as food is artificially sweetened; additives and chemicals, preservatives and other 'supplements' don't just damage the natural taste of food but rob it of energy and nutrients and in some cases actually poison it.

Some of the best food we could possibly eat has been outlawed: to meet the Brussels' directives vegetable seeds must be registered and each variety must demonstrate that it can conform and maintain stability over annual maintenance and inspection. There is a fee for this and many traditional varieties of fruit and vegetables were only cultivated by farmers and gardeners who did not produce enough to justify the cost of registration. Yet without this registration the varieties became illegal. Thus, within a very short space of time, varieties which had survived and flourished on their merits for centuries were rendered extinct. I regard this as little less than tragic.

Those rock-hard English salad tomatoes of a uniform shape and size which suits the supermarkets (which coincidentally exploded in size and number in Britain during the 1970s), 'ripened' in artificial greenhouse conditions, bear very little resemblance in shape, size, colour or taste to the irregularly shaped, knobbly, sun-ripened giants you can still buy in Mediterranean markets. The same applies to the shiny, tasteless and watery peppers we import from Holland or the pretty, evenly matched but curiously bland dwarf beans which are expensively flown in from Nigeria and Kenya. Regarding these last there was a terrifying TV programme recently which showed that hundreds of ill-rewarded African farmers thought that Tesco was actually a foreign country, as all they knew was their entire crop was destined to be freighted there. If true, this story serves to illustrate how it is not just diet but whole ecologies and national economies that have been affected by the wretched Seed Act.

Many people in Britain seem to have bought wholesale the notion that strawberries in January, asparagus in March and 'new' potatoes all the year round somehow exemplifies the fact that these days we all inhabit a more open and cosmopolitan world. Well maybe we do – but if anything this food engineering in itself speaks to me of a more closed, controlled and limited world. And a less healthy one. By the time that fruit has, so to speak, had its air-fare paid, its 'hotel accommodation' in some warehouse covered and its 'cosmetics and fashions' expenses met, so that it will look nice in its styrofoam box, it will not only be ludicrously expensive (even though the original producer or farmer did not see much profit), but it will be well on the way to decomposing. Why on earth would anyone choose to eat such foodstuffs? The answer

is that the consumer in Britain has seldom been given much
choice in recent years.

The taste of the foodstuffs has been altered. Even more
importantly, more and more food intolerances and allergies
have been observed since the Seed Act began to dictate what
we might eat. As seed cultures have been developed in
laboratories all over Europe and chemically tinkered-with
strains have been introduced to satisfy the supposed demands
of consumers all over the continent, the natural character of
the resultant foodstuffs has been altered to the brink of
deformity. And the damage in the food chain does not simply
apply to genetically engineered fruit and vegetables, but to
cattle and poultry feed and thus to our animal proteins as
well.

*The ultimate self-help is not saintly or particularly
altruistic. It's enlightened self-interest which has the happy
side-effect of helping other people and the environment as well.*

We cannot absorb nourishment from foods which our
bodies do not recognise – in other words from foodstuffs which
have been cultivated without the ecological contributions of
insects and bees, which have no place in the laboratory. Our
bodies just weren't programmed to absorb nutrients from
foodstuffs which have been cultivated in an artificial way. This
explains the increase in food intolerance as the entire system
weakens through an inadequate supply of zinc, magnesium,
selenium or any number of other vital minerals, as the body
struggles with, amongst other things, these alien foods. It also
explains the enormous increase in sales of dietary
supplements, sweet things, stimulants and vitamins: people
just know they are not getting proper nourishment from their
meals and look elsewhere.

The most frightening fact is that the heart will, quite
simply, stop if there is an absence of sufficient chromium in
the system. We used to be able to rely on getting these supplies
from properly grown food. That means food which has been

grown organically or from animals which have been reared organically. Every single seed counts. Properly cultivated seeds, pollinated by bees and insects, for example, have a mysterious ability to absorb and then pass on a derivative of carbon. A deficiency here can make bones weak and hinder the repair of hairline fractures – those silent, secret injuries which can, in turn, prevent the meridian lines from carrying their messages of healing across and around the body.

At a recent seminar I asked all in attendance to test their meridian systems by touching a special, indicated, place on their heads. Five of the group found that there were problems with their lower intestine – hitherto unsuspected. One woman discovered, via hairline fractures located in both fibula bones in her leg, a gall bladder disorder that I was shortly afterwards able to connect with an accident which had taken place sixteen years earlier. This woman plays tennis several times a week and must have an enviably strong constitution since her gallbladder was all but destroyed. She admitted that she often suffered from indigestion but had thought this was so trivial as to be almost normal. In fact she was receiving very little nourishment from her food because of the dysfunctional gall bladder. A single drop of my food enhancer placed on the tip of her tongue before eating fixed this.

Over time any organ or other body part suffering from a lack of energy supply from its meridian line will fail. The very least anyone might expect then are allergies and food intolerances, fatigue and depression. All horrible – and all avoidable.

All this underlines the supreme importance of choosing to eat organically.

Just in case you needed reassurance that my views are not merely those of an old fellow whose ideas are a bit cracked, let me refer you to the celebrated young chef Allegra McEvedy whose restaurant in London's Notting Hill is one of the busiest in the capital. I will condense what Allegra has written in her

REACTION POINTS WHICH CAN BE USED FOR TESTING FOOD AND OTHER SUBSTANCES

HOW THE TESTS WORK

Each of the points illustrated are linked to organs.

Foods or substances injurious to any of these organs will cause the pendulum to go into reverse, if, while holding the pendulum over the food or substances being tested, the middle finger of the other hand is placed on any one of the points illustrated.

- Point 1 is linked to the gallbladder
- Point 2 is linked to the stomach
- Point 3 is linked to the large intestine
- Point 4 (either point) is linked to the bladder
- Point 5 is linked to the small intestine
- Point 6 is for testing the reaction of hair to shampoos and dyes

Because the body system works on the cross-over principle, all the points to the left of the face will give a reading to the right side of all organs.

All the points to the right side of the face will give a reading to the left side of all the organs.

All the points illustrated on one side of the face will have equal points on the other side of the face.

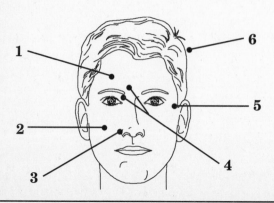

book, *The Good Cook* (Hodder & Stoughton, 2000) in a way
that I hope she will forgive:

> *When is a tomato not a tomato? When it's a*
> *herring... the agrochemical companies... have*
> *come up with the perfect tomato by implanting*
> *herring DNA ... Some fish have evolved to*
> *withstand very low temperatures because water*
> *gets pretty cold, so if you implant a bit of fish*
> *gene you can create a tomato that isn't damaged*
> *by frost... A bit of a worry for vegetarians and*
> *anyone else who stops to think about the*
> *consequences... You can't tell the birds, insects*
> *and the wind that it's just a trial period... so they*
> *just carry on with the job... of transporting seeds*
> *across the land. That means that unless GM sites*
> *are banned...we will all be eating GM foods*
> *without knowing it.*

Allegra goes on to deplore the use of antibiotics in food
production. I couldn't agree more and am heartened to see
that influential young chefs such as she have the courage to
shop and cook for their restaurants in the correct, ultimately
sane way. She concludes – and once again I condense her
words a little:

> *Organic food is more expensive. How could it not*
> *be? But the bigger the industry the more prices*
> *will fall. Buy what you can afford today and*
> *tomorrow everyone will benefit... most*
> *supermarkets now are toeing the line... buy it for*
> *no other reason than it tastes better.*

Thank you, Allegra. All good sound and solid common
sense here. But sadly the likelihood is that even those trugs of

organic veg of yours were seeded from plants that began life after the wretched Seed Act.

There are some effective things you can do to supplement even an organic diet and certainly to counter some of the damage sustained by a non-organic one. A single drop of my star remedy on food – whether it's at home or in a restaurant, can restore most of the energy you need and recharge the damaged meridians. And of course you can dowse in shops before you buy, restaurants before you order and in your own home to learn whether the food you are considering is fit to eat.

✳ ✳ ✳

I've already written a bit about the hairline fractures that many people have without even realising it. We should all be eating foods which help to strengthen our bones, along with allowing some absorption of carbon. Without this, a tiny fracture can scupper processing of nutrients.

Vital internal communication lines of healing along the meridians will be blocked even if you are unaware at first of the damage.

Internal organs can even begin to rot if the body cannot absorb carbon. That carbon contains and records the very memory of life is evidenced by the fact that carbon-dating has served archaeologists in recent decades as they have studied ancient bones and plant matter. But these fractures can be dowsed for at home and then you might be surprised to learn – like the lady with the damaged gall bladder – that however healthy you feel or considered yourself to be, that one or more meridian line is being obstructed from peak performance. A single drop of star energy tincture on food or placed on the tongue will release all possible nutrients and can restore the carbon balance and begin the wider correction processes.

Each time a child takes a heavy tumble in the garden or playground, let alone has a serious fall, some hairline fracture could be sustained. Dowse to check and take remedial action. This is certainly preferable to a long wait in the Accident and Emergency department of the local hospital and the likelihood of pain-killing injections administered there. A metal plate might even be inserted to help fractured bones to mend if the fall was deemed to be severe. As a parent do all you can to resist this, however distressed you and your child may be and however confident and well-meaning the hospital staff.

For the sake of generations to come it is essential that any fracture which disturbs a meridian line, preventing vital communication from destination to destination in the body, should be identified and removed before a genetic memory can be formed – a memory which will otherwise be passed on and on

* * *

Bear in mind that, in the main, people in Britain were healthier forty or fifty years ago. Without seeking to sentimentalise any mythical golden age, people who could not afford to visit or call out the doctor at the slightest worry relied much more on natural remedies before the National Health provided state-funded medicine for all. Moreover, it has often been recognised that Britain's wartime austerity diet – meagre rations, especially of meat and other proteins, supplemented with garden-grown foods – was better for the population than the plenty of today.

So I have fabulous news for my older readers: many of those who grew up on the restricted diet of the last world war and its aftermath have been primed to be much stronger and healthier than their children or grandchildren. But everyone can make a significant difference to their current and future health, and that of their family, by eating organically at the small extra expense.

* * *

I wish there were magic bullets and quick fixes for every disorder. I will always do my best and have achieved remarkable results. I'm not going to be falsely modest. But when it comes to self-help I can only hope to offer guidance and encourage the confidence that will enable you to do a great deal by yourself, for yourself. And such 'selfishness', ironically, will also help our planet a tiny bit.

Some years ago I was invited to visit a farm in the New Forest, in Hampshire, a place where cattle had been organically raised for meat production for ages – but recently there had been a problem in the health and well-being of the animals. I dowsed and immediately identified a selenium deficiency. The farmer, understandably wanting a second opinion, arranged for one carcass to be analysed elsewhere. It took almost exactly two years for scientists in Edinburgh to form exactly the same view that I had taken in ten minutes. I didn't quite know whether to be pleased by this news or horrified, and I do not relate the story in the spirit of trumpet-blowing but in one of optimism for the hope that sooner or later we'll all see sense.

Similarly I'll mention the awful business of the cervical cancer which has scared tens of thousands of British women in recent years. With so many of them having been misdiagnosed, even after the screenings which all but promised immediate remedial care if something looked awry, many younger doctors are reluctant to offer this screening service in case some error – not necessarily their own,it could have been some clerical bungle – results in a court action. And so the victims of all this are all the vulnerable women who trustingly believed in the assurances originally offered but who might now think more than twice about relying on those orthodox tests.

What they can at least do for themselves is to wear cotton underwear and if they must wear tights, choose with a cotton gusset; eschew creams and sun-tan lotion near that delicate area unless they are known to be free of toxic chemicals; choose pure cotton tampons and the like with great care; and, obviously, observe caution where new sexual partners are concerned. Please don't mistake me, I'm not suggesting that healthy women should live like nuns. But the fact is that the incidence of cervical cancer amongst those who have taken holy orders is negligible and it is also rare amongst women whose partners are circumcised, so we may draw our own logical conclusions here.

I'll close this chapter on self help with a cheerful testament from someone who practices the ultimate self-help:

Case study... Case study... Case study... Case study... WN is a fellow-dowser, so my work with him has been a special kind of 'partnership'. Since he already understood the principles at the root of my work, he was immediately receptive and as a fellow-dowser he has been particularly interested in the beneficial effects of understanding the chakras and the labyrinth. He suffered from horrific migraines, caused by various vaccinations given to him as a child, most particularly from the TB inoculation.

'I had suffered from migraines since I was twelve, and I'm fifty now. I was absolutely flattened by them, days on end. My migraines were the type that come with violent nausea, retching long after there's anything to vomit up. Apart from a general association with stress – which might in itself have been caused or aggravated by worry about these attacks – there was no pattern. Sometimes weeks would pass without one and then I'd have four within a month.

'Years ago doctors tried to treat me with pills, which I don't like taking anyway, and they only seemed to fractionally reduce the time I had to stay in bed. Then I took homeopathic advice and cut out dairy foods and that made a tremendous difference. I still got the headaches but without the sickness, which was a big advance. But then the sickness sometimes came back and around that time I began to see Jack. Recently I decided for myself to cut all yeast from the diet and I put star drops on my food and drink the energised Crypto Power water.

'I still get migraines but these days they are much more manageable in that I can pretty much predict that I will be smitten every nine days. This means I can ensure I'm not scheduled to be travelling or attempting to do anything much at all away from home. I can plan around my migraines and that's made a big difference.'

Obviously WN wants to be completely free of them, and that is what we are working towards. A migraine isn't just a bad headache any more than a cold is flu or indigestion is gastroenteritis. All these lesser conditions are nasty to endure but they shouldn't be confused with their much more flattening relatives. Sometimes I get annoyed when people say they've had a migraine but then went on to do this or that: anyone who is in the grip of migraine is doing well if they can raise their head to be sick in the bowl beside their bed, or cross what seems like the Gobi Desert to get to the loo. However, I guess I must be pleased for those people who are spared such terrible suffering. Anyway, as WN suggests, once you realise what good health and partial release and relief from pain can be like, you resent the bad times almost more than ever.

I've already explained how a simple cotton cloth wrung out in cold water and placed on the brow is the best cure I know for an ordinary headache and how, if in doubt and in the grip of some mildly debilitating disorder, all of us – not just children – should give our hard-working body a rest from solid food for a while. It's taking time, but I think we're getting there.

CHAPTER TEN

JOURNEYS

Travel is said to broaden the mind. Maybe in the past that was more often the case than it is today when 'travel' has become almost synonymous with tourism, often a very different thing. So many people seem to holiday with a subconscious idea of finding fault, of reassuring themselves that there's no place like home and have the 'been there, done that, bought the tee-shirt' mentality that enables them to strike Greece, the Far East, Russia or Chile off their list of holiday destinations with the complacent thought that 'at least I can say I've been there', as if that was the whole point of the journey.

I don't really take holidays as such any more. Given good health and my continuing excitement about my work, I never feel the need to rest and get away from it all for a restoration break. Indeed, even after a complicated series of flights back home from Argentina recently, I was straight back into my laboratory on the evening of my return. Everyone on a long-haul flight should take the simple precaution of exercising as much as is practicable. Even if you're flying cattle-class you can wiggle your feet and ankles and flex your knees from time to time. The danger of a thrombosis is further minimised, of course, if you're in good health to begin with.

The veins in your legs should be in good working order. That means the observation of a sensible diet (for a few weeks before your flight if possible, that is if you haven't been observing it already). One of the effects of the 1973 Seed Act was a reduction in the quality of the wheat most of us consume in our daily bread. Because of this many peoples' livers are not functioning properly and are failing to absorb vital vitamins. My food enhancing drops will correct this at once, but I realise that they may not be available to everyone and many people may not realise that they have circulatory problems in their legs as they begin a long flight.

If disaster should strike it is awful if an important business trip is aborted and possibly even more distressing if a vitally needed holiday is ruined. I now advise all patients who plan to fly to take – as far in advance as possible – a tiny pinch of the synthetic vitamin E d-beta tocopherol in powder form. I have found that this vitamin in powder form is quickly absorbed by the system. It's rare for me to recommend anything synthetic, so you may judge for yourselves how useful I consider this compound to be. It's even more effective if the pinch is stirred into a glass of the healing water and stood on a pad of the Crypto Power text for a few minutes. Vein circulation has been observed to improve almost at once – a very good preparation for flying, with its risks of deep vein thrombosis. I have Kirlian photographs which demonstrate this almost instant response.

At the very least, make sure your system is primed with lots of vitamin E. Take a couple of capsules before the flight if in doubt. Another invaluable tip is to cram a handkerchief soaked in pure water and pressed into a polythene bag in your hand baggage, especially on long-haul flights. As soon as the crew start spraying the cabin to 'freshen' it – a euphemism for a blast of pesticide – hold the handkerchief to your nose and breathe through it for several minutes. You can then discard the hanky confident that you have averted the damage to the trachea which if you are male is often connected to prostate cancer and, if you are female, often to a cancer later developing in the fallopian tubes or cervix. Anyone will be doing their heart valves, also, a favour by this simple measure.

Basic common sense tempers what I choose to eat when I'm abroad and obviously I'll dowse the food in restaurants. I only eat freshly cooked foods and even avoid salads unless I can be sure that they've been prepared and dressed properly. Ice cream and ice cubes in drinks are to be avoided unless I am absolutely confident that the local water is OK and kitchen standards immaculate. And abroad, as at home, I choose fruits and vegetables that have been naturally ripened on the tree, plant or vine, rather than culled half-grown and ripened in artificial conditions. Astonishingly, perhaps, this daft practice can take place in the sunniest of climates as well as our own. Sadly, the fact is that just as our British spinach contains less than 40 per cent of the iron it bursted with fifty years ago, many of those Greek olives or Spanish peppers could have suffered in the same way.

As for destinations, I simply don't travel to places where documentary evidence of certain vaccinations is a condition of entry and I stay out of direct sun. I love sunshine and the relaxed mood it generates as much as anyone, but simply basking in the generally warmed air, perfumed by flowers, fruit and vegetation is enough to give me all that heady sense of heat and benign solar power. Everyone looks better with a flush of colour on their face, but that's enough. We don't want to resemble walnuts or prunes, delicious though they may be to eat.

That my journeys have usually been highly enjoyable is a happy by-product of my main mission, which is always to seek out plant or mineral matter that I know I need to meet the needs of a particular patient (and which can then be used to help others), after asking my dowser and the atlas where I should look. I generally find what I want but also, with the stimulation of a new place and culture, learn much else besides. Nothing in nature is static. Nothing – animal, vegetable or mineral – can defy nature's law of perpetual motion and this is the thrill, the challenge of new places and new discoveries.

Occasionally a visit truly is a 'flying' one and there isn't time, frankly, to learn much about the place or its culture. One such was a flight to Athens on behalf of a cancer patient so sick that I needed to return home the next day, after successfully dowsing for the plant I required to complete his remedy. The patient knew he was ill, but not how serious his condition was, that he had only days to live. I was disturbed to see how heavily dosed-up with morphine he was and when he asked me to take care of him for the next fortnight I agreed. After a week I knew he needed treatment derived from a herb which I would find two hundred miles west of Athens. So I got on the first flight and when I dowsed I was duly guided in the right direction and plucked the few specific leaves that had the healing qualities.

It's not enough to know the genus of the plant and imagine that any specimen will do. I believe there are invisible pipes of healing all over the world, each a few inches wide and each emitting from the bowels of the earth their healing power. The energy might only pass through a few leaves of any given plant or tree, possibly only one leaf, so it's no use charging anyone else with the task of locating it unless that person is a trusted and expert fellow-dowser. As you'll learn later, I'm helping to train as many of these as possible, but in the meantime, I generally grasp the nettle, so to speak, myself.

Anyway, I was able to devise remedies that helped my patient to live for another nine months – time he needed to settle his affairs and prepare himself to die with dignity and a sense of calm.

Once a blind woman was told by a clairvoyant that I might be able to help her. The clairvoyant's message was that I should look for a stone near some yellow flowers at the foot of a hundred-foot high cliff on an island in the Mediterranean.

Offshore would be a rock which resembled Gibraltar. There are many rocky islands in the Mediterranean, but my pendulum hovered around Palma, Majorca and I prepared to set forth. Then, at about the same time and by marvellous coincidence, I ran into the parent of a child I'd been able to help a year or so earlier. She lived on Ibiza and wanted me to spend a holiday there, thrusting an air-ticket into my hand. So that was that and once there in Ibiza I asked her Spanish husband if he could enlighten me about the beach in question. Instantly he knew where I meant and offered directions and I was directed to a remote stretch of coast on the other side of the island.

Sure enough there was the cliff and there were the yellow flowers blooming at the foot. Looking out to sea I saw a rock, in shape and profile undeniably similar to Gibraltar. My pendulum now guided me to a small rock charged with amazing healing powers. 'My' stone must have chipped away from it and been washed ashore. I was able to take a fragment away, subsequently pulverise it and use it in a remedy for the blind lady. I always travel, by the way, with a 'pounding' instrument and a basic homeopathic kit for on the spot work if called for.

I won't claim to have restored her sight, but put it this way: I saw the patient in my home rather than the clinic and she had been in total, sightless darkness. After taking the remedy she was able to make out the diamond-shaped lattice of my window panes. During subsequent visits she saw patterns on the carpet and other details which, she felt, indicated the restoration of partial sight.

Incidentally, this may be as good a place as any to mention that I pay for my airline tickets just like anyone else and – unless I am a visiting speaker somewhere – for my accommodation when I arrive at destinations both mundane and exotic. But the reason I've been able to keep clinic charges largely unchanged for more than ten years now is because few journeys result in only one application of medicine and the costs are thus amortised over treatments to the many. There are also a couple of strictly practical reasons: years ago I was able to sell some land adjacent to where my clinic stands today. With that capital I built the clinic itself, unencumbered by any massive mortgage debt, and this happy situation is reflected in my charges. And of course I know that some patients have less disposable income than others and may even have had to travel from the other end of the country to see me, paying for overnight accommodation as well as fares. But I'm not a charitable foundation and I believe, rightly or wrongly, that people have more respect for something they pay for than something they get for free. However, I never want my healing to be out of the reach of the socially disadvantaged, so I have been happy to keep my charges low.

And when one considers the true price – both in time and money – of NHS waiting lists and most private medical treatments, I think that few people feel exploited or let down, especially when they experience the results of treatments at the clinic.

When I went on a lecture tour to Argentina recently I was also guided to seek nineteen separate plants for use in remedies concerning eye health and sight problems. That whole area seems to be increasingly important in my work. As well as finding them all I had the bonus of finding three essential new crystals and a tree drooping with long red pods. A tincture made from the pod has proved to be miraculous in extracting almost any poison from the body and I can now often circumvent the somewhat laborious procedure of using several different sets of tablets when taping my 'poultices' to a patient's skin.

I was also introduced there to a little-known philosophy of life known as Akashic Records, whose followers can deduce huge banks of information about a person just by knowing their name. This knowledge is not necessarily health related but it does sometimes connect and overlap with my own work. Those blessed with and schooled in this gift say that all the knowledge that has ever been acquired in world history is contained in some vast psychic library relating to each of us and a skilled person can draw down the page, as it were, for any individual and read what their ancient past was and what their future might hold. Just before returning home from that journey I was given an Akashic painting which I was told held some reflection of my very soul. All I can say is that it's now hung in my surgery and many patients are immediately drawn to it. The ideas of that sect are something I intend to pursue for my patients. Altogether, then, a highly productive journey, that one to Argentina, as more than one patient might testify:

Case study... Case study... Case study... Case study...
Being able to read is extremely important to seventy-five-year-old TM. She's worn spectacles for years, but suddenly in late 2000 her eyesight deteriorated rapidly and to such an extent that, after referral to a consultant, she was advised to undergo laser surgery.

'I was very unhappy about this idea but I couldn't continue with my eyesight like this either. The right eye and the left were behaving in different ways, which I'm told is quite common at my age, but it was very frustrating nonetheless. I had such peripheral vision that if I wanted to see someone's face I would have to look over their shoulder – which might have been unnerving for them. Central vision was completely lost. If I tried to write anything down I could only use my left eye and even then I couldn't write in a straight line and individual letters would seem to jump around the page. I could only use my right eye when reading – and that's with spectacles and the aid of a magnifying glass as well.

'The specialist said I had macular degeneration and there was nothing for it but surgery on my right eye. Apparently nothing could be done for the left one. By the time I hear this news I'd been to see Jack twice. He made some tablets from herbs he'd brought back from Argentina

and these were taped first to my ankles and next around my
head, so that it looked as if I'd been in a car accident. Jack
told me that the cause of my problem was some deficiency
in certain brain cells which I had been born with.

'The first time I saw him I could barely the read the
large capital H at the top of his sight test card. After the
second visit, two weeks later, I could read all the letters
down to the fifth or sixth line. When I next saw the
specialist he was astounded by the improvement in my
sight and said that some sort of natural adjustment had
taken place just in time. I suppose he was right in a way. I
didn't tell him about the treatment I'd received from Jack –
but that was certainly a lot more natural than surgery
would have been. I intend to continue seeing Jack to see
just how far this correction can go, as I'm quite astounded
by the improvement so far. Eventually I intend to tell the
specialist about how I've been helped. I think that would be
a fair and responsible thing to do.'

Yet another startling and stimulating revelation during
that trip to Argentina was to see the complex of circular houses
built in a community in the Cordoba region. These houses are
white, well-lit, solid and can be quite large enough to
accommodate family life, with plenty of separate rooms, but
internal walls, also, must be curved. I suppose they are the
southern-equatorial, luxury versions of the more familiar igloo.
Anyway, if ever I build another house for myself it'll be like
that: the philosophy underpinning the building planning
seems to be so closely connected to my conviction that a
rounded, bending shape (as exemplified by the labyrinth and
all the curves and coils in nature, from those of an ammonite,
or a sleeping grass snake, or the rings inside a tree trunk to the
snail's 'house') is far more naturally and spiritually attuned to
general well-being than straight lines and right angles.

We've already seen how in Germany issues of planning
permission for new buildings can often depend on a search
which ensures that the work will not adversely traverse a ley

line. Apparently the curves in these circular houses deflect and defy the harmful and negative energies in the ley lines surrounding them. One resident unwisely installed straight internal walls inside his round house and negative ley energy was able to enter, actually crossing right across the place where his bed was situated. He was able to correct this before any real damage to his health was sustained. Just in passing I'm tempted to wonder if that temple of British counter-culture activity in the late sixties and early seventies, The Roundhouse, has any sort of cosmic connection to this. Those were, after all, days when young people were particularly receptive to benign old philosophies from afar... Oh, all right, I know that the building itself was designed in the nineteenth century to be a huge shed where trains could turn about – but it's an amusing and interesting thought...

People used to scoff at the very idea of living in a dome – often citing the Eskimos as primitives (perhaps forgetting that these native North Americans, with their diet of oily fish and so forth, tended to live long and contented lives for centuries before 'civilisation and progress' intervened and bestowed a whole raft of Western stresses and diseases that they'd never known before).

There's a story about Sir Christopher Wren, architect of the majestic St Paul's Cathedral, built in London after the Great Fire in the seventeenth century, that heartens and amuses me. He was told by the town planners of the day, who were paying his wages, that the great dome could not possibly be structurally viable, that it needed support. Biting his lip, no doubt, the architect appeared to cede to his masters' ignorant whims and duly had four massive columns constructed to support the dome of the church. Only when it was cleaned, over a century later, did the masonry cleaners see that Wren had left a gap of several inches between the tops of those columns and his vast and beautiful dome, so confident was he that this high, curved ceiling was strong and safe. This story may bring to the minds of some readers a famous photograph taken during the Blitz: London is aflame and thick smoke clouds speak of devastated homes and offices buildings, docks and schools all around. But standing inspiringly still and sound above it all, the dome of St Paul's can be glimpsed through the clouds.

On another journey a few years ago, to Israel, I was drawn to a dry river bed, a wadi, where I found the five plants I sought on that journey for my food enhancing drops. Not one to waste time or opportunity, I dowsed to see whether somewhere in the desert I would find plants needed in the treatment of cancer. Dowsing the map, my pendulum directed me to another wadi fifty miles to the north and yes, there I found five herbs needed for my cancer-fighting remedy. So often Tel Aviv has proved to be a place for growth and discovery: herbs and plants, crystals that I use to great effect year after year, the nurturing of strong friendships – this city has offered all these and more to me. That the Crypto Power of the Hebrew Word was formed in this region cannot, I think, be any coincidence.

Luck certainly seemed to be on my side during that journey. A good friend, Dr Ol Anand helped to arrange for the University of Strathclyde, back in Britain, to analyse the properties of one of those herbs. They reported back to me that they believed it could help in the treatment of ovarian cancer. At around the same time I had a patient hugely distressed by news of the onset of this disease. After treatment at my clinic her consultant – who had advocated surgical removal of her ovaries – was astonished to observe that the growths had disappeared. However, and very sadly, collaboration with the university never came about. They could, I was informed, perform similar tests on the other four plants if I was prepared to pay them for their trouble. I declined this offer with some regret. But my pendulum had told me all I needed to know and the fact that one test confirmed my findings left me delighted and I will always be grateful to my enlightened doctor friend who encouraged the test.

Once the owner of a Tel Aviv crystal shop was sitting behind the counter on the day of the week which he normally takes off and I walked in unexpectedly. He showed me a fragment of meteorite which he had recently bought in Russia. Previous dowsings over a map had told me that I need four specific crystals to complete a particular project but meteorites hadn't been on my agenda when I went to Tel Aviv that time. Anyway, there was my friend and there was his Russian meteorite which I subsequently needed. While I was in that shop a man walked in from the street, apparently on impulse, saying he wasn't quite sure why he'd done so but that he had backache. By dowsing him and holding a crystal I was able, at least temporarily, to lift his pain away. Exactly the same thing happened a little later, when a baffled but instinct-driven woman came into the shop: I was able to help her too. My shopkeeper friend also found me a crystal when he was in Romania. I was to find that when I dowsed while holding it in the other hand I could discern if the patient was in danger of developing leukaemia.

I'm a great believer in the power and purpose of coincidence. Actually, I'm kind of with Sigmund Freud here although conversely Freud seemed to say that there was no such thing. I take this to mean that when events collide it's not because of any random chance but because there is a reason, a pattern, a driving force that leads us to a particular place at a particular time... I mention this because when I was in Penang, Malaysia, on another mission to find healing materials – pearls this time – I found myself in a particular shop and amidst the hundreds of pearls. I dowsed and found just a few which emitted the correct energy. Once again the owner, Mohammed Shaffi, was unexpectedly on the premises, having cancelled a flight to visit one of his other shops several South Pacific islands away, without quite knowing why. I noticed he was chain-smoking and asked him why. He removed his shirt to reveal a back riven with the deepest scars I'd ever seen. My friend had been caught in the crossfire of some terrible political street riots and had been very lucky to survive his injuries.

Mohammed Shaffi then allowed me to sift through the hundreds of crystals neatly displayed in trays there as I searched for any with a true healing force. It may be worth noting here that a lot of nonsense has been written about crystals and a lot of gullible people have been cheated when they've bought any old stone, however pretty. That's fair enough if they simply want to acquire an ornament or something that could be fashioned into a piece of jewellery, but the fact is that only one crystal fragment in a thousand has any healing power. Of course there may be a reason why a particular stone appeals to you, some ancient instinct, and I certainly know that wearing or carrying a crystal can generate calm and inner strength. The late Princess Diana assured me that the blue one I found for her in Nepal made a significant contribution to the confidence she enjoyed and displayed before her fatal accident. But I divined this stone for her and all crystals – if they are to be of any use as well as decorative – must be dowsed for and selected to match the individual's vibrational frequency. Anyway, during my dowsing and study of the crystals there that day I was lucky enough to find two fragments of firestone opal which had powers new to me at that point. I was so taken by these fragments that I had them set into a silver pendulum which has ever since been my trusted travelling pendulum and has never failed to guide me towards whatever I seek, however far from home I may be.

✳ ✳ ✳

There is such a thing as a destination without a journey and I have become increasingly interested in a kind of psychic distant healing called radionics. If I have a clipping of a patient's hair I can send them healing wherever they are in the world. The hair clipping, preserved in a tiny phial of pure alcohol is placed within a small circle of crystals brought back from Tel Aviv and I dowse over it. When I called a patient with a bowel problem in Australia after I'd done this she told me she felt an immediate improvement – at exactly the time I'd sent the healing out. Much the same happened for a patient stranded in a New York hotel room with a severe chest problem but a heavy schedule of business meetings that prevented him from flying home at once. I was able to send him relief as well.

Once I was impelled to go to Malta to find the plants needed to alleviate the heart condition of a patient whose tingling fingertips and toes warned of poor circulation and a possible severe heart condition in the forseeable future. That remedy has since been used to help many other patients and just as I tend to be led to Malta to find remedies for heart conditions, it is to Egypt that I've been guided to find ways of addressing other disorders.

Few cities are as steeped in ancient wisdoms as Cairo, but it must be allowed that the capital of Egypt today is a bit of a concrete jungle – not an obvious hunting ground for plants, flowers or herbs or anything much green for that matter. Modern Cairo is an exciting, vibrant place in many ways, but it was towards the city's quiet graveyards that I was drawn.

I've come to believe that diseases have memories and strange as it may seem I sometimes travel to find plant matter that retains genetic evidence of disease in its 'purest' form. And where better for this than a place of burial? Modern drugs and other medicines have distorted the strains of many diseases, TB for one, as they resist, adapt to and sometimes even accommodate the treatment. The disease re-morphs and we've all read about the clever flu viruses which defy vaccines and continue to thrive, ruinously for their human hosts.

So it's important for me, in devising remedies, to find plant matter containing the DNA of people who succumbed to disease before the devilish strains learned how to coexist with the apparent cure. Amidst the trees, shrubs, other plants and flowers in a graveyard containing soil which holds the mulched down remains of the long-dead, I will often find material which somehow *defines* the disease which caused illness and death and then set about creating a medicine which hits the core of the illness. Two-thousand, three-thousand, even five-thousand-years-old, these remains tell me much about strands and strains of illnesses, such as leprosy, venereal disease, typhus, smallpox and cholera. Maybe that sounds a bit sick. But confronting sickness is my job, after all, and at the epicentre of many homeopathic remedies is the concept of treating like with like. Obviously to devise a cure one must understand the disease and much as I oppose today's widespread inoculations and the damage caused by the serums carrying the drugs, I have to accept that this was the basic principle at the root of the earliest vaccinations.

In the burial grounds of two ancient churches in Cairo I found four vital components for remedies I needed to complete and perfect. Satisfied with my tiny harvest and with the burial site leaves safely stowed away, I wandered over towards a nearby vendor, as any tourist might, to inspect his wares. I might tactfully describe that shop as being stuffed to the gunwhales with trinkets and tat of the worst kind and, after dowsing around the shop, I only saw two items with any intrinsic value. I mentioned this to the astonished shopkeeper who informed me that these two items were the only ones actually made in Egypt, the rest of the stock having all been faked in Yugoslavia.

Then I asked him why he was stooping. Was he in pain? Yes, he said, ceaseless backache blighted his life. I dowsed again and found a muscle was pulling his spine out of line. This was easily corrected and he disappeared into his back room, returning to present me with a scarab found in a Pharoah's tomb, the real thing and a 'souvenir' which I naturally cherish.

Outside the city limits, in the desert area where the Sphinx and the Pyramids – perhaps the world's ultimate resting places for the dead – stand in such majestic silence (if you can close your ears to the chatter and clatter of tourists and trinket vendors), I learned much. I dowsed and picked up some very negative vibrations coming in from the desert, where so many slaves had died, as these old energies hit each carved corner of the Sphinx. It was as if ley lines had been redirected, for the adverse energy was deflected directly into the heart of the Pyramids themselves, shrines of ancient Egypt's most distinguished. But remember that the mummified remains there also contain the DNA of ruling families weakened and damaged by incest, as well as by diseases caused by those biblically famous Seven Plagues

I couldn't possibly go into detail here about every finding I made there but one example may suffice. I realised that anyone entering the Pyramids is in danger of absorbing a tendency towards liver disorder because of a reduced ability to utilise iron. Curiously my taxi driver, who'd become quite a friend after several days, enabled me to find an antidote for this at least, by taking me to a park in the town centre where I found in the leaves of a fig tree there the power to cure this iron curse.

Unlike most tourists, I travelled around the Pyramids on a hired horse, mentally mapping out the very powerful negative ley lines there. Subsequent dowsing revealed that these lines were cleverly and diabolically aligned to the crucial chambers inside the Pyramids. My young driver was, of course, fascinated by these old man's antics and when I haltingly explained to him how dangerous it could be to remain for long on these lines a look of revelation crossed his face and he explained that all camels and horses who regularly needed to traverse these lines were regularly substituted with others, as they became sick.

After my ride I was invited back to the boss's shop and was asked whether I could help a camel boy – in such abdominal pain that he was virtually a stretcher-case. After dowsing I saw that he was suffering from some severe iron deficiency and, taking out the pestle and mortar and pure alcohol I always keep in my travel bag, I was able to pound the fig leaves I had collected earlier into a homeopathic solution. A single drop cured the boy's pain at once. Everyone working in the shop was silenced and I was offered enough trinkets, in thanks, to fill a lorry. I accepted one small item which I still cherish.

After that my taxi driver/minder asked me if I could take a look at his mother. She had, he told me, endured awful pains in her legs for several months. We drove to some outer suburb of the city and by the time we arrived it was almost dark. The streets seemed deserted. He lead me up into a smallish room, about the size of an average spare-bedroom in Britain and there we were greeted by the eight of his relatives who lived and slept in this constricted space. The mother was resting in a makeshift bed – allowed by other members of the family, I supposed, to remain there on account of her age and decrepitude.

Upon dowsing I was able to locate severe kidney and urethra blockages, which cleared with a mere touch of a finger. Almost at once this woman – classed as elderly by her own society, but philosophical and almost relaxed about her disorder – was on her feet again and walking for the first time in months. It was curious, almost as if she exemplified my belief that recovery from illness usually requires a trusting receptiveness verging upon blind faith and a two-way confidence between healer and patient. As we drove away, that previously darkened street seemed to have lightened somehow. There were certainly more people about and I got a huge cheer and lots of waves as I returned back to my hotel. Bit of a mystery there, but I like mysteries: they keep life interesting.

This story is a nice example of the quick – some might say 'miracle' – cure. A bit like the laying on of hands which so impressed New Testament believers. I wish resolution could always be achieved so fast and so easily. I'm afraid that, despite some spectacular examples like this, it's more common for relief to take time. If a person has spent a lifetime developing some serious disorder it should not be too much to ask of them to have the patience to allow two or three years for things to be corrected. That way they may have a whole new lifetime ahead of them.

I'd love to promise instant results as part of some easy package. But it would be irresponsible of me to do so. It's a complex thing, this relationship between patient and healer, and it is seldom articulated by either. Some of my patients, indeed, comment on my apparently lofty silences or lack, at any rate, of chatty concern. Actually I'm quite conversational with some patients and may sometimes offer more explanations than they really want to take in. In this aspect of my work I try to judge, as any healer might, whether I offer the equivalent of the trusted GP's 'hmm' or the careful detailing he or she may offer to a more questing patient. In either extreme I am concentrating and listening hard to what the pendulum is telling me – often dozens of facts within a single swing. And I have little doubt that if a patient is prepared to take me on trust and accept that whilst some disorders can be fixed quickly others need time, we will work together more effectively.

I'll often need to rebuild the health of a body step by step, bone by bone, organ by organ so that I can restore the patient's ideal and optimum homeostasis. Perhaps my patient that day, having the inner tranquillity that allowed her to endure such uncomfortable living conditions, had also some great spiritual strength as well, a strength that allowed her to be receptive to my simple dowsing treatment. Another patient may be frustrated, even enraged, by their poor health and that patient might well want more verbal explanation.

There is not always any point in attempting to effect a complete recovery if only one or two of the bodily systems have been corrected. The other systems cannot, somehow, deal with this renewed strength if they are still out of line. That's the sum of it. And that may be something of an answer to people who challenge me about why I can't always offer instant remedial results.

※ ※ ※

When I see, for instance, that a patient is deficient in vitamins A, B, D and K, I will look to seek star energy from my labyrinth for answers. The planets and stars of the heavens can take light years to dispense their healing energy. I feel privileged to have found a way of capturing them, but I respect them too much to assume that that long journey through the cosmos is going to yield me a fast response every time. Sometimes it's enough to use that energy, once I've tapped into a tincture, to help with one or other immediate problem. Somehow I could link-up the liver, for instance, which may be lacking in the vitamins mentioned, to star energy which will supply the healing force, along with the Crypto Power of the Hebrew Word. But the stars take their time, so can I and, I trust, so can some of my patients. Star energy and Crypto Power does already seem to yield some spectacular results.

I have found that many people suffering from heart defects have a problem in absorbing vitamin E. For this problem there is the simplest of remedies: when a small glass of water containing a tiny amount of vitamin E granules is placed over the correct verse of the Hebrew Word and is drunk, measurable healing begins at once and the heart regains strength.

Developments here will probably only be subjected to laboratory tests in years, perhaps many years, to come. In the meantime and the relatively short term I'm happy to report that I do my simple best to harness that energy anyway.

A patient whose daughter had difficulty in walking had heard about my work. I dowsed and found that there was a blockage in the triple warmer meridian near the base of her skull which was affecting her physical and motor movement and my pendulum dictated that I should go to Guernsey in exactly three weeks. I sent my patients home and waited. At the appropriate moment I flew to the Channel Islands in search of the help the young girl needed. Having dowsed I was taken by cab to a long stretch of beach and I sat on the sea wall, with a gloomy housing estate behind me – very different from the 'millionaires' row' villas you may associate with that tax haven – and looked out on a bleak open sea beyond a wide stretch of sands. The tide was out and soon, too, was my pendulum as I walked across the strand until I knew exactly where to dowse. I dug deep into a little pit of sand (a spot which would have been covered or at least lapped by tides at any other time within the previous three weeks, I discovered) and heaved up handfuls of the sand I found there.

Earlier I've mentioned those healing channels which arise from the heart of the earth – only inches wide and invisible to the naked eye but not to the intelligent pendulum. Here was just such an example: I was guided to the charged channel within the mud. A quick test with the baffled but willing young taxi driver waiting for me to finish my experiment confirmed things. I called across the beach and asked for his help. Even I was startled to see how the energy in those handfuls of sand increased his strength to the extent that I could not shake his grasp when he obligingly fisted up some

handfuls. To make sure that the test was valid we performed
the same experiment with mud taken only a few inches away
from the place which my pendulum had identified as
containing healing sand. This time his grip became slack
under pressure – behaving in a 'normal' way.

So I took a little of the sand charged with healing energy
and flew back home with it. Then I made some tablets from it
and called her father to say I was ready to offer treatment.

After the tablets were applied, the girl walked with more
energy for the first time in years.

So, whether you are simply travelling on holiday, or hoping
to have a successful business trip or seeking some souvenir
more healing than a postcard or trashy replica – travel
hopefully, with eyes, ears and mind open. I've seldom been let
down.

CHAPTER ELEVEN

The Bridge

I've been called a healer but I like to think that I'm a teacher, too. Nothing pleases me more than the thought that my ideas can spread, take hold and form a life-enhancing or even life-saving raft for the thousands of people, who for one reason or another cannot get to my clinic. I'm thrilled to think that I may have helped to train others to heal and that they – in their turn – will also teach potential new healers.

I've seen a lifetime of suppressive and invasive attempts at healing and I don't doubt that most of it was well meant. But I'm heartened to realise that invasive and suppressive methods are now under broad scrutiny and it's marvellous to be able to train younger healers, educate them in my methods, even as I continue to practise and learn.

The courses I hold at the clinic may seem superficially informal, with students seated in a circle in my airy reception area, as visiting tutors speak and demonstrate, but they are rigorous and intensive over ten one-day seminars each year. That level of concentration must be supplemented with homework which involves each student providing evidence that they have offered dowser-healing for twenty case histories before I'm prepared to 'sign them off' with a blessing, confident that they can practise independently. They are monitored as the course progresses and most feel reassured by this level of discipline although the courses themselves are structured informally.

Many students choose to go on to complete my advanced course. Both courses are run with a combination of trusted colleagues, such as Derek Talbot, Gillian Lim, Vincent Winter and Paul Stiffle, lecturing, demonstrating and offering the students every opportunity to air opinions and ask questions, giving a thorough orientation and grounding. My own lectures tend to concentrate on more recent developments in the field, which might seem baffling if the students hadn't already had an ongoing training in the basics. Each class has a mix of men and women with a broad age range. Many but not all of them already have some qualification in the wide and diverse field of complementary medicine and those who have no previous qualifications are required to show evidence of the basic studies of anatomy and physiology: no one can attempt to heal another with much credence if they are ignorant of the fundamental, almost architectural structures of the human body. Some students will want to set up clinics of their own, others simply wish to become informal healers with the confidence that completing a course such as mine can bring.

All devisers of such courses can expect a drop-out rate. That's human nature. But despite the fact that I have students coming from as far away as Aberdeen in the north east of Scotland and from Ireland, I'm delighted to say that the drop-out rate on my courses has been as low as 15 per cent. This despite the fact that the students pay for themselves. There are about fifteen of them at a time and I think this sort of number enables them to bond as friends as well as students, chatting as they take their lunch and – for all I know – conferring between sessions. It really heartens me to see these dedicated groups being trained to become healers all over the country. Some, but by no means all of the students, first came to me as patients – and that's some kind of recommendation, I guess.

Derek Talbot used to be a badminton international, playing for his country all over the world. Before that he trained as a metallurgist. He's also a natural, charismatic teacher. I first met him about seven years ago.

In my day as a sportsman we didn't travel with a team doctor, physio and all the rest. If you fell ill abroad you went to the local place and since quite often I found myself competing in the Far East, the natural thing was to consult a doctor nearby. That was how I came to respect the treatments, usually herbal and homeopathic, offered by such healers. Years ago in China, for example, I was with a group who were shown an appendectomy without anaesthetic. Maybe it was kind of set-up as a bit of a propaganda exhibition, but there wasn't any doubt that the patient was undergoing the surgery, with only a few acupuncture needles in place, that he was in no pain and that he was able to eat fruit and chat throughout. Naturally I was impressed.

My interest in the field of dowsing deepened when I learned that the human body loses a few ounces of weight at the point of death. This has nothing to do with the loss of bodily fluids. It's a simple fact, well-documented. I came to believe that this might be accounted for by the individual's spirit force departing. It's not provable, but I'm a scientist by training and I like explanations and answers. Having said that, I do accept that there are some things which defy logic and figures and we must sometimes rely on faith and judgement.

Even scientific truths aren't set in stone. Even aspects of the pioneering work of Louis Pasteur in the nineteenth century, for instance, are now widely challenged and doubted. That's the nature of research and science: it builds upon what has gone before but doesn't absolutely rely upon it if new findings seem to call for a re-think.

Something as simple and observable as seeing how tablets such as Jack's are steeped in toxins which have been extracted from a human body after a couple of hours of having been taped there, is remarkable. Those tablets, when placed in a jar with some known bacterium culture, simply cause the poisoned culture to die. It's as plain as that.

It was seeing experiments like that which convinced me. In Ibiza I'm surrounded by flowers, herbs, fossils and stones which bear the imprint, or DNA, of the past. The ecology of a small island is also going to be influenced, obviously, by the sea and I find a tremendous source of remedies locally. Having said that I'm a great believer in the ways in which conventional orthodox medicine can align with the kind of work we do and this is one of the strengths of the course Jack runs, since we're all anxious to see how the orthodox can be in tune with the alternative. The more co-operation the better... Like Jack I have learned to offer 'absent healing' whereby so long as I have a clipping of hair and nail I can advise patients thousands of miles away and send remedies to them

When I 'retired' I first had a sports shop business. But after a while I sold it and decided to give myself a year off – not to lounge around but to investigate other ways of spending my time. And so it was that I established my own clinic in Ibiza about five years ago. I now treat a combination of patients – local Spanish people, ex-pats, holiday-makers and people from elsewhere. Like Jack I travel a lot and I have numerous patients in North America whom I heal by

*sending remedies in the post and via the web and I
come over every month to teach at Jack's academy.*

*In these courses the students don't just takes notes
and absorb theory – they see measurable, observable
differences before their eyes.*

Like Derek, I've always wanted to see as many bridges as
possible built between alternative and conventional
medicines, so that people who are ill can, quite simply, have
the best of both worlds, I'm hugely pleased to be working now
with Gillian Lim, Senior Lecturer in Applied Biological
Sciences at Kingston University. Her academic and clinical
background should convince anyone that there is a strong
bridge between orthodox medicine and my own work. I would
like to hope that this collaboration has resulted in a mutually
beneficial learning curve – that I gain immeasurably from
what she can teach me about the latest developments in many
aspects of theory and practice of the biological sciences as
taught today and I, in turn, think that my ways of healing can
be shown to be useful and relevant to some of her work. The
bridges we are building could have so many positive
ramifications.

So far it's been a brilliant piece of teamwork – stimulating,
enjoyable and productive. Gillian, who teaches at my
advanced classes, notes:

*When Jack approached the Faculty of Healthcare
Science seeking someone to teach anatomy and
physiology to dowsers about four years ago I
volunteered even though I did not know what to expect
and had never heard of healer dowsing. I would say
that I made a slow start as I learned to assess the
needs of dowsers and to establish the link between
knowledge and practice so far as dowsing is
concerned. But where any aspect of health is concerned*

a steady learning curve is usually preferable to a hasty blaze of enthusiasm with no measurable confirmation of the effects.

The practice of dowser healing is firmly underpinned by a knowledge of homeopathy, energy and the meridians and also of nutrition, the metabolism and basic anatomy and physiology. I felt that there was certainly a way that my work in these fields could enhance the skills of healer dowsers. Jack has always maintained that this is not about curing a disease state or illness but about getting the body back to its maximum functioning state so that it can heal itself. Jack calls the body a 'temple' which one must respect and take care of. If the body is constantly under assault and neglect it will eventually run out of energy and resources to repair and heal.

The human body was designed to work in equilibrium and harmony. Cells are grouped together to form different tissues. For instance muscle, connective and nervous tissue forms an organ and a group of organs becomes responsible for an aspect of a functioning system. This is often the basic theme that students at my university begin with and at Jack's courses, it's much the same, but my teaching with Jack varies in that a more complex understanding of physiology seems less significant for the healer dowsers.

I am particularly interested in application of knowledge to practice and thus teaching of the importance of homeostasis. (Please refer to Chapter Four for a full explanation of homeostasis.)

When teaching at Jack's clinic I prefer an interactive approach wherein students are encouraged to participate in discussion. Such apparent informality, however, does not denote any lack of rigour on all sides. It's very important that every training

*dowser healer is able to articulate their ideas with
clarity and conviction because when they come to
practise they will inevitably be asked scores of baffled
questions by people who are troubled, unwell and
maybe just plain cynical. Furthermore, interactive
teaching encourages the autonomy which will be
needed when these students set up in independent
practice.*

*I think its important for the trainees to see how
well Jack and I interface. That trust and mutual
respect will help to show the trainees what a strong
bridge we are building. Together we address specific
illness and disorder and show, in discussion, how
conventional methods and Jack's methods merge over
concrete application to a problem.*

*Jack's work has spanned many years and I know
of scores of people who have been helped by it. I
wanted to design a course which would provide focus
and perspective – a foundation for all who seriously
want to become healer dowsers. For those students who
wish to learn even more after the initial course, I am
designing a more advanced one for people who are
really serious about helping other people.*

*As an educationalist I obviously hope that this is a
learning process for me, too, and that this cross-
fertilisation of complementary ideas will be not only
mutually stretching but something that I can bring
back to some courses at the university. As I said, I took
my time, concentrating hard, before I was prepared to
become involved with Jack and his work and perhaps
to begin with I was the 'senior partner' in some
respects, purely because I'd had a more conventional
scientific and academic training in things like
anatomy and physiology.*

*Four years on, I know how well we work together
and can envisage truly exciting results as this
collaboration comes to inform both my teaching and
Jack's healing work.*

So a new generation of dowser healers is experiencing, I
might humbly add, the very best of both worlds as they train:
all the orthodox learning of a scientifically trained
professional – but one with an open mind – and all my perhaps
more intuitive knowledge and depth of experience. Gillian will
explain how she sees this alternative route as being useful
when mainstream 'cures' have proved inadequate. She is now
able to discern which disorders are likely to respond best to
dowser healing whilst in no way dismissing the disciplines of
her traditional field. The dowser lecturers are thus addressing
students who have been given a clear knowledge of anatomy
and physiology and of the kind of illnesses they are most likely
to be able to help with. If that isn't homeopathic teaching
personified I don't know what is. Dowsing can step in to heal
and *regenerate* where earlier orthodox methods have failed or
resorted to replacement. But what good is a transplant or an
artificial limb if the body can only deal with it with massive
doses of drugs to prevent rejection?

Not all the students aspire to professional status. Mary
Ellis is a young woman who describes herself as having the
potential abilities of a 'barefoot doctor' – a reference to some of
the remarkable healers in China who went from remote
village to village bringing relief from suffering without
claiming to have conventional qualifications. Mary describes
herself as an intuitive person and can cite several examples of
her natural ability to sense when something is amiss – or
about to go wrong.

*I think we all have intuitive energies – it's a question
of having the confidence to know how and when to use
them. Anyone can dowse, but like all skills it takes*

practice, confidence, faith and belief. It also requires
the good health of the dowser: if I'm feeling under par
for any reason I can't expect my dowsing to be up to
scratch. The pendulum, after all, is just an extension of
the human who is using it.

Mary intends to work informally. She seems to me to be such a natural, instinctive healer that humanity will benefit. She even coin dowses – a simple version of the yes or no questioning but using pennies to head or tail her towards decisions, whether complex ones or everyday dilemmas. She's a great example of how the habit of dowsing can be brought into day-to-day life, as well as healing.

Another student is Vivian Cripps, a trained homeopath. She encountered some extraordinary surprises from homeopathic colleagues before she embarked on the course: inexplicably they failed to see how dowsing methods could happily co-exist with the ones she had been trained in. Undeterred she plans to go further with my courses and tackle the advanced one.

I agree with Mary – faith, trusting yourself, has so
much to do with it. I hope that soon my abilities will
become second-nature as I tune into my subconscious
when I'm trying to help someone else. In this respect
it's vital that my own health is good. We know that
Jack measures his energy every day before seeing his
first patient and that makes sense. The same must
apply to any healer who offers massage: the
practitioner needs to be in tune with all their most
subtle responses before they can advise others.

How different, sadly, this is from all those stories we've all heard about family GPs who smoke and maybe drink a little bit too much, or even of NHS nurses who also drink and smoke heavily and don't follow a sensible diet: could this all be somehow related to the discouragement, perhaps even depression, which these dedicated professionals feel when they observe that the methods of healing most easily available for them to prescribe are so seldom effective? For a health professional there can surely be little so depressing as reaching for the pad to scrawl out a repeat prescription.

As Vincent Winter, an independent healer and my fellow-teacher has astutely remarked:

> *Dowser healers need confidence. The irony is that sometimes when we've helped a patient reach a certain stage of recovery, they see that state as being normal. Maybe six months ago they couldn't get out of their wheelchair but now they can walk effortlessly to the car outside. In another six months they'll be able to drive again and that will be their normality. They won't necessarily remember how restricted they were a year ago.*

This sort of situation, actually, is what we all hope for and aspire to. We're not in the business of clocking up points or getting gushing praise, although it's nice that sometimes people acknowledge us. We all, really, want people to be able to recover the best of themselves and lead cheerful, normal, healthy lives again. That's just as much our job as delivering milk or the post is for other dedicated professionals...

As you know, I expect to live and work for a good few decades, until the age of 146 to be precise, and thus to have plenty of time left to learn and to help as many people as possible. But I don't want to be a 'sole trader' and that is why I have been running these courses and training people – many of whom came to me as patients in the first place – to become healers themselves if they choose to. I'm happy to say that the spread of my students, about twenty as I write, is pretty much nation-wide. They come down once a month for a seminar and only when I am happy with their progress and results will I deem them ready to work as healers on their own, although I will always be there for my 'graduates' if they need support or advice. But I don't sign the students on the advance course off, so to speak, until they have a portfolio of at least twenty cases relating to people they've treated as students. And I like some of those patients to have paid return visits because that – above almost all else – is the proof that initial consultation has inspired confidence.

Teaching people how to dowse isn't as simple and basic as it might seem, as Gillian has indicated. Derek, Vincent and Paul would agree. There's much more to it than getting hold of a nice silver pendulum and hoping it will obligingly swing. It has to be asked the right questions and the answers must be interpreted correctly if the dowsing is to be of any use. Naturally I also show my students how they can make their own remedies – normally the tablets which are microtaped to the patient. This stage of healing requires an exact knowledge of human anatomy, so that the healing pads are placed along correct meridian lines.

You may imagine how all the ideas simplified in this book must be amplified and understood to the point where confidence in ability to heal must become almost instinctive. This is why I want my students – as an act of faith almost – to successfully treat a good portfolio of patients as they train. It would do the reputation of dowsers and their way of healing no favours at all if I allowed them to 'graduate' before they are ready. It is still all too easy for some to jeer and sneer and there's no point in giving the mockers unnecessary ammunition.

One of my students, Pam Brooks, who lives in the Wrekin near Wales, first came to me as a patient nearly twenty-five years ago. She had suffered awful headaches after the birth of her second daughter in her mid-thirties and was also enduring an early menopause. A very forward-thinking GP suggested she came to see me, even though my practice was still in its infancy then. Apart from anything else, Pam's pharmacist husband was uneasy about the number of drugs another doctor had prescribed for her problems.

> *Now I'm gradually learning to do as Jack wishes – to offer his kind of healing in another part of the country. As soon as I have my twenty cases to prove that I'm qualified to heal in his way I hope to open my own clinic. In the meantime I heal informally. Actually what I already do professionally – matching the needs of children with learning difficulties to the skills of particular teachers – fits in very well with this. I've dowsed to help me find the right relationship, successfully, I think.*
>
> *I dowse all the time now, sometimes with a special pendulum which Jack made for me and sometimes with other instruments, even with my little finger if I don't want to seem obtrusive. My entire garden is now organic and with some of my crops I can make the tablets I need for healing work.*
>
> *I know I've got a bit of a way to go yet, but my successes include that of a chap whose backache was so bad that he could barely function professionally or socially. He said that after seeing me he was able to spring, energised out of bed and was ready for anything the day threw at him for the first time in two years. Another great pleasure was to see how a three-year-old who had been given the MMR vaccine twice and who behaved – if this is not a contradiction – like an angry vegetable was able to sleep calmly and recover social skills which have enabled him to attend normal nursery school. This would have been unthinkable before I was able to extract a double-dose of vaccine poison, thanks to Jack.*

Another of my trainees is Donna Swann, who comes to my seminars from her home in Kent. Donna and her husband came to see me to de-tox before starting their family. So pleased were they by the vaccine-free health of little Eleanor and Samuel that Donna decided to train to become a dowser healer too. A former actress, she was particularly sensitive to human emotional responses and in recent years she had also worked as a masseuse, offering simple muscular healing. But she wanted to learn more.

I have been very struck by how scientific Jack's work is compared to that of some healers. There's nothing vague or overly mystic about it. He doesn't just talk about energy realignment as some healers do: it's hard and technical as well, which I find reassuring. If I hadn't already had some sort of training in anatomy and physiology I would have had to work very hard with books and homework, as if I was preparing for exams at school. As it is I've had to learn a great deal about cells and genetics and although I've already seen more than the twenty patients that Jack specifies I feel I need to learn more before opening my own clinic, although that is my ambition, and I'd like to specialise in helping children.

I want to learn how to become as good at extracting specific poisons as he is. I already make the tablets myself – that's the easy bit. Knowing how to dowse is also superficially easy: but you have to know what questions to ask and I'm learning all the time. Knowing that my studies will continue with Jack and Gillian in brilliant collaboration, showing us how the two fields of medicine can interact, is very exciting. I feel that I'm learning the healing of the future. This must be the way that medicine has to go forward.

Another aspect of the teamwork is exemplified by Paul Stiffle who now has his own clinic near West Wickham. Paul trained as an osteopath and was well versed in many aspects of complementary medicine before he came to know about me. Now he teaches with me at my weekend seminars, helping to train new dowser-healers.

Jack's always got something new to enthuse about and explain. I tend to prepare the students for the exciting developments he always has to describe by keeping them well grounded in the basics of dowsing and physiology. When I first started working with Jack I was already a healer and herbalist and becoming concerned about how chemicals contributed to peoples' back and neck pains. I also felt there was much more to be understood about how the emotions contribute to our physical health. My way of working at my own clinic has certainly altered since I began this association with Jack and I hope it's a mutual thing – that I've had something to teach him, too. Anyway, I think we have a kind of partnership which suits us both and which ultimately benefits the trainees.

I met Vincent Winter, who works for a homeopathic pharmacy and is a homeopathic chemist, when I was thinking of asking his firm to become a supplier. Vincent, already a qualified cranio-sacral therapist, was interested in my work at the clinic and is considering opening a clinic of his own in Kent. Not everyone can reach my clinic easily and others find it hard to learn from even the best 'how to' books, so I'm delighted that people like Vincent are going to provide a practical service all over the country. He attends my monthly 'academy' and runs the preliminary teaching forum there.

*In the Dark Ages there often used to be some old
woman who lived on the fringes of the village and she
healed people with herbs. People were both grateful
and frightened and she got to be called a witch and we
all know what sort of 'justice' was metered out to them.
They got dunked in the nearest river. If they drowned
they were innocent of witchcraft but if they survived
they were guilty and burnt. In a way I think that the
fear – sometimes hostility – shown towards healers like
Jack even today relates to this ancient fear and
ignorance. He's not about to be criminalised, thank
heavens, but the old unease persists when people can't
see a written explanation in some orthodox medical
textbook. His work, his healing, remains a mystery. To
some people that mystery is exciting but to others it's
somehow a threat. We can't always expect to
understand why some treatments work – although one
always tries. It is in observing Jack's results that my
trust in his methods is rooted. Who can say why sitting
for a while within a stone circle can be so beneficial?
Sometimes the patients don't even need to have
homeopathic tablets taped on them to feel better.*

*So I'm very pleased to be involved in the teaching
of Jack's foundation course, the programme which
reassures us and de-mystifies things, as well as
educates potential future dowser healers. I really
would say that I've been inspired by Jack. I first
attended the academy as a student – and I am still
one, as I learn something at each monthly seminar –
but I now also help with the foundation students who
need to have some grounding in the basics of his
methods and the disciplines involved there before
graduating onto the more complex ideas that seem to
explode all the time. It's important that the basics are
understood and I'm happy to help in this respect. I*

started off as a believer – that always helps – but now
I dowse with sufficient confidence to teach new
students and hope to open my own clinic.

We may be out of what Vincent terms the 'Dark Ages' but we have a way to go yet before enlightenment is as widespread as I would like.

Derek Talbot, who works from his own clinic in Ibiza, is, of course, but one of many who feels exactly the same.

My friend and occasional colleague Sylvia Caplin, already so distinguished in the field of holistic health, has cogent comments about the way we complementary healers can collaborate with practitioners in other fields of medicine. Sometimes she will see someone whom she feels could benefit from my type of healing.and feels strongly that our different, yet mutually supporting banks and pools of knowledge could and should be shared.

Most healers have closed minds, locked in their dogma
and unwilling to share their knowledge and
discoveries, if any. Jack is different – keen to see how
his ideas can be spread and taught. There's a constant
flow of renewal and this, of course, requires faith on
the part of the patient as they try to understand and
participate in their own healing. For many people this
sense of partnership is a real help as they try to get
better. Most people are able to grasp that some
inherited problem can influence their health today, but
I know this is only one aspect of his work.

I have personal reasons to understand the
importance of the bridges that may be built between
orthodox medicine and complementary healing. I
recently accepted that I needed some surgery – only the
latest operation in a dismal recent series. Jack took a
look and saw that there was a weakness in my thymus

and a good deal of inherited anxiety. I was consulting another healer at the time and came to realise that this surgery could be avoided.

Interestingly, I now believe that the influences which enabled me to cancel this operation came from three sources – 30 per cent from Jack, 30 per cent from the other healer and 40 per cent from my own will. In any case, I feel very much better now and am told I look a lot better, too, and I feel stronger in a different way.

This is a good example of what I mean by 'the bridge': I'm involved in another teaching centre, at Steyning, near Worthing in Sussex, run by May Estler and her daughter Elizabeth. May is a hugely respected professional in the field of caring for the elderly. These regular seminars tend to attract people who are already highly skilled in various fields of medicine and who have kept open minds about the potential of dowsing to supplement and compliment their work. Far from being in charge here, I'm a visiting lecturer and I learn, as we all do, from the stimulating exchange of ideas.

Between us we can make the bridge such a long and strong one – linking the best of brains and hearts, scholars and scientists, dowsers and dreamers all over the world.

CHAPTER TWELVE

Last Notes

Like most of us, I hate goodbyes. Hovering from foot to foot on that station platform, not quite knowing what to say, even if the departing person is one's very dearest, half- hoping the whistle will blow and the train begin its slow departure, half-hoping it's not happening after all and that things will swing along as usual...

Well, this isn't a real goodbye. How could it be when I've got another sixty years of work and discovery ahead of me? It's just a pause in the journey – yours and mine. It's more of a 'So long, see you soon. Take care of yourself in the meantime.'

It's late spring as I write and the bluebells are out. We've had a hard winter in Britain, especially the farmers here and their animals, but even after scores of springtimes I find it hard not to sniff a little breath of optimism in the air when the branches of trees are somehow lifted rather than weighted with the feathery gauze of new leaf, when the daffs give way to tulips, when the first Jersey Royals appear in the shops, when we can turn down the central heating and see brave souls in the street in their shirtsleeves instead of being bundled up against wind and rain.

Sentimental tosh? I don't think so. Our hearts are almost genetically primed to lift at the first signs of spring. By the time this book is published another season or more will have come and gone and I think that we in Britain are rather lucky to have observably different ones: it makes us somehow more aware of the pleasure of a sunny day in winter, the welcome warm rain after a dry spell in July, the smoky, woody smells of autumn that somehow manage to reach the dingiest corners of our cities. For every dark and dismal winter's day there is at least the hope of a bright light indoors and a hot meal in a soft chair... No I don't always envy our friends in the South who gaze at clear blue skies every single day. In lands where the climate is predictably fine there can seldom be that special, sometimes miraculous feeling when the weather springs a nice surprise.

And whilst I can't deny the still pleasurable, cheerful sight of a strawberry in January, I really do prefer the ones which arrive in May or June, properly, organically raised and bursting with natural flavour. Don't let us forget that however artificially we may farm and foster our foods, nature will always have the last word and this is expressed in how our taste-buds respond.

I find it rather heartening to know that if all the motorways and trunk roads of Britain were shut down, all the bypasses blocked, there would be no visible evidence of their existence after a couple of years. Grasses, shoots, herbs and bushes would have pushed their triumphant way through and turned those roads into pasture again. Without actually wishing for such an eventuality – for like it or not, most of us need those roads and even the most fervently reclusive amongst us would be displeased if their tea could not come in from China or their oatmeal from some distant part of Britain – I retain the greatest confidence in the forces of nature and their powers to adapt, providing what is needed – when and where it is needed.

Good farmers and food producers understand this and play what in chess is called the 'long game'. Tortoises and hares also spring to mind, as does that old adage about more haste, less speed. It was back in the nineteenth century that Britain led the world, during the Agricultural Revolution, with classic tracts such as Adam Smith's *Horse Hoeing Husbandry,* which startled farmers and the landowners of the day by advocating that every few years a field should be allowed to rest for a while, thus replenishing the soil as it took 'time off' as a meadow. How the wild flowers flourished! An influential institute still bears Smith's name. Wouldn't it be a shame if that wise old message was forgotten in an age of pesticides and fungicides which promote the idea of land in constant full-on production? How would *you* feel, I'm tempted to ask the offenders, if you barely had a decent night's sleep, let alone a holiday?

By the time I embark upon my next book you may be sure that some aspects of this one will be overtaken by new developments – not out of date exactly, but standing now as building blocks for further advances in all the fields of health. It has already happened here: I use my first book, *The Healer,* constantly for reference and to remind myself what was pivotal to my work a few years ago and I see that many ideas remain steady and rock solid. But I have progressed since then and I hope to progress further.

Every month there seems to be some new hope, some challenge, some exciting result. It thrills me to think that this upward curve will continue until we meet again. I sometimes venture down what seems to be a blind alley and begin to wonder if I've wasted my time, but more often than not my dowser has proved to send me in the right direction even if the results aren't always instantaneous, overnight or immediately obvious.

The distinguished Australian psychologist Dorothy Rowe has pointed out in her book, *The Real Meaning of Money* (HarperCollins, 1997), that despite our modern contempt for their tiny brains, the dinosaurs survived on earth for millions of years and our Neanderthal ancestors managed about 250,000 years. Homosapiens has lasted around 100,000 years so far. The implication here is that man and his planet don't coexist as well as they might, but surely experience and intelligence can be harnessed to improve chances of survival – for the planet and for ourselves? We still have time to mend our ways.

Who knows what secrets will be released by the stones in my circles, the 'newer' ones and the old? I don't yet, but I'm looking forward to discovering them. Who knows what new messages the stars will deign to send down? A thousand years is but a blink on the time-scale of a distant planet and I must remember that messages received today could have beamed down long, long ago: wisdom from outer space, even sent at the speed of light, takes time to reach us.

In the meantime I wish all of my readers, my patients, my students, my friends and even my critics a happy and healthy future. The certainty of this is there, all around us, in the stones, the soil, the stars, in the Crypto Power of the Hebrew Word – even if you have no religious inclinations whatsoever – and in a simple glass of water, steeped and charged with a healing power like nothing on earth.

I raise my glass to your good health and merely wish you *au revoir* because I hope we'll meet again.

Addresses

Suppliers

Helios Homoeopathy Pharmacy
Telephone: 01892 537254
24 hours: 01892 536393
Fax: 01892 546850
Email: pharmacy@helios.co.uk
Website: www.helios.co.uk

Biopathy Natural Nutritional Centre
Bioceutical Limited
Nutri House
26 Zennor Road
London SW12 0PS
Tel/Fax: 020 8675 5664

Courses

Jack Temple Dowsing Academy
Vincent Winter, Secretary
4 Norfolk House
Walshes Road
Crowborough
East Sussex TN6 3RE
Telephone: 01892 662499

The British Society of Dowsers
Sycamore Barn
Hastingleigh
Ashford
Kent TN25 5HW
Tel/Fax: 01233 750253

May Estler
Nash
Horsham Road
Steyning
West Sussex BN44 3AA